Tucker Grizzwell's

Worst Week Ever

For Aidan, Cooper, Finnlee, Addison, and Eleecia.

Tucker Grizzwell's
Worst Week Ever

Bill Schorr and Ralph Smith

Andrews McMeel
Publishing®

a division of Andrews McMeel Universal

Contents

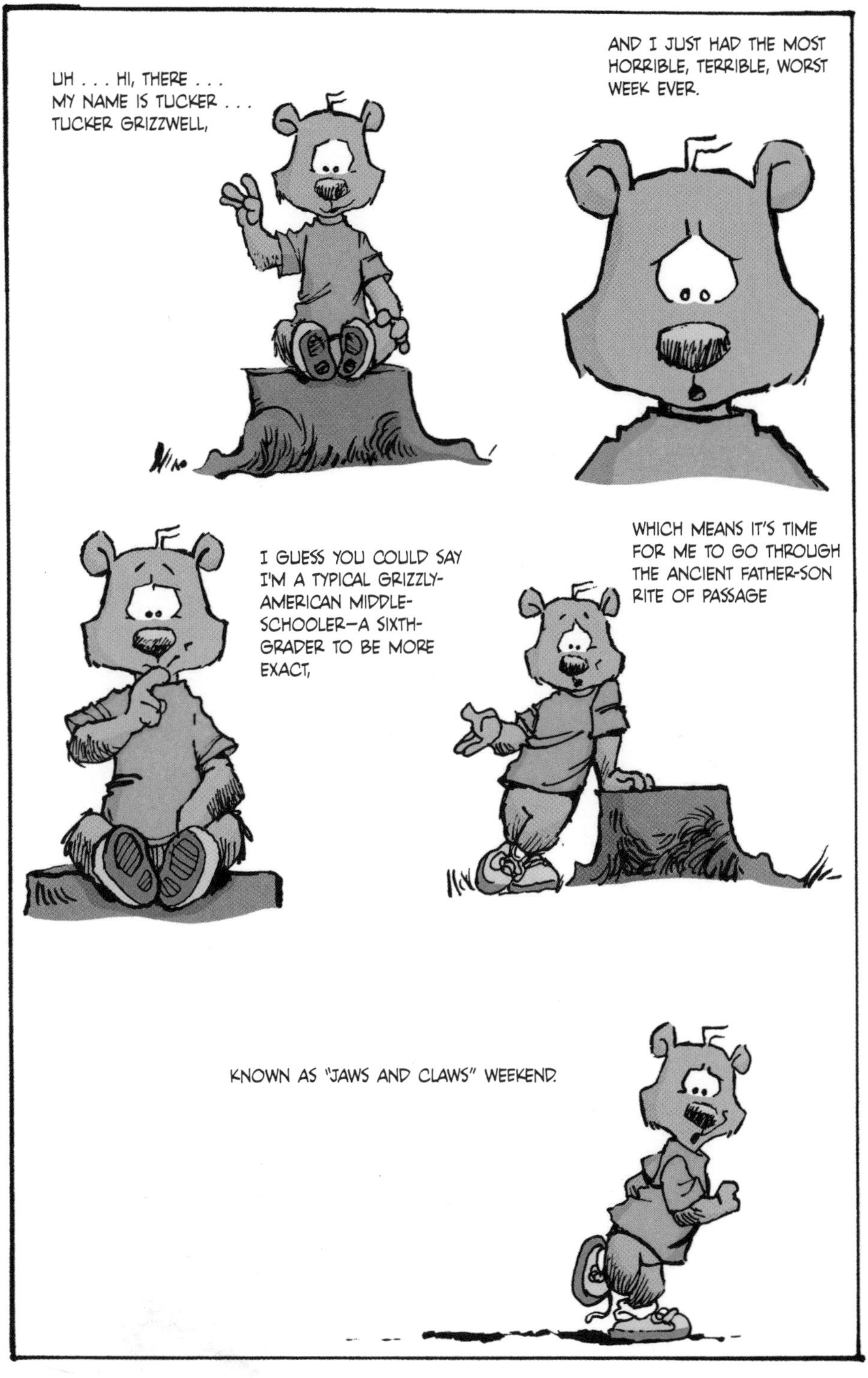
UH . . . HI, THERE . . . MY NAME IS TUCKER . . . TUCKER GRIZZWELL,
AND I JUST HAD THE MOST HORRIBLE, TERRIBLE, WORST WEEK EVER.
I GUESS YOU COULD SAY I'M A TYPICAL GRIZZLY-AMERICAN MIDDLE-SCHOOLER—A SIXTH-GRADER TO BE MORE EXACT,
WHICH MEANS IT'S TIME FOR ME TO GO THROUGH THE ANCIENT FATHER-SON RITE OF PASSAGE
KNOWN AS "JAWS AND CLAWS" WEEKEND.

MONDAY

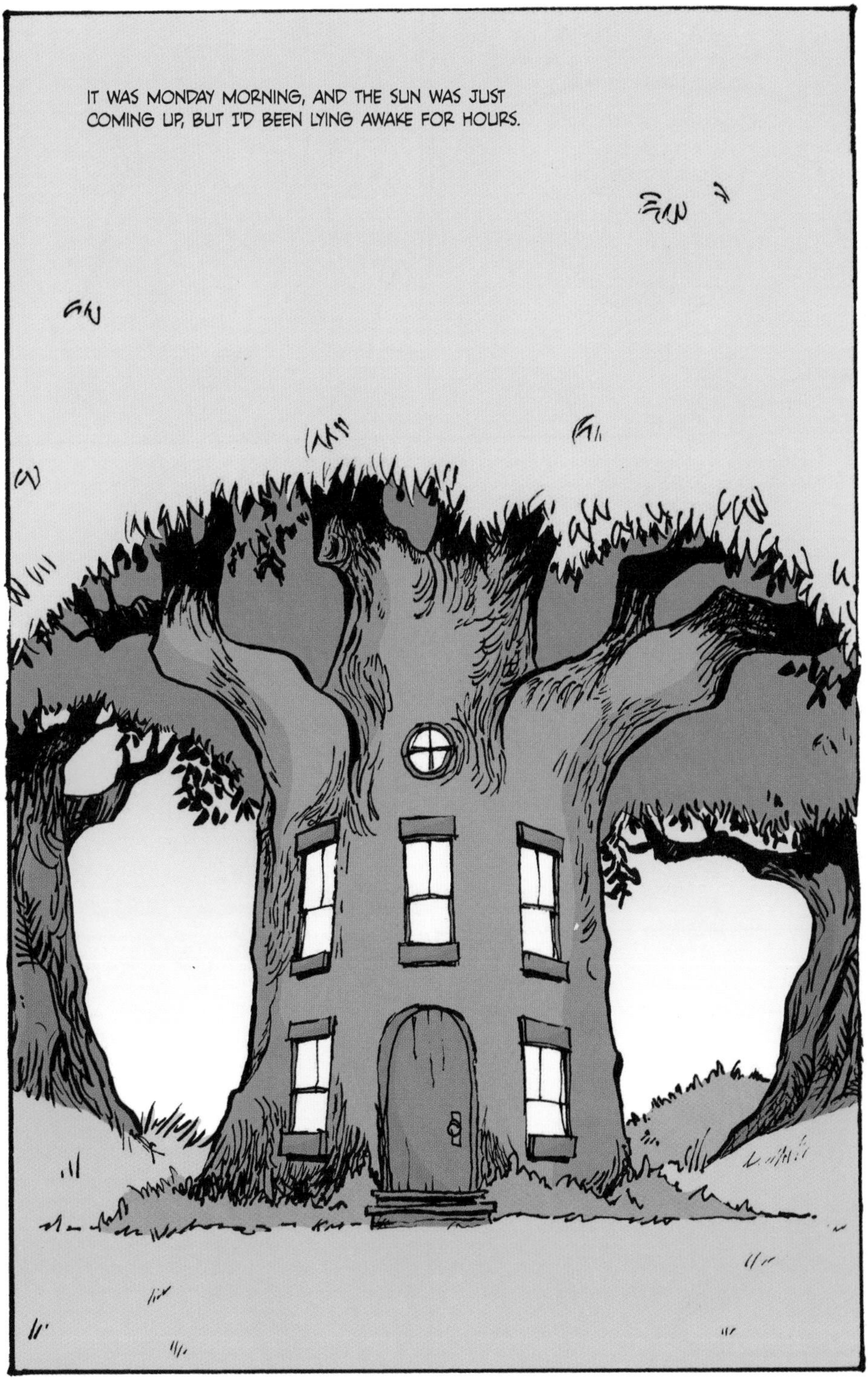
IT WAS MONDAY MORNING, AND THE SUN WAS JUST COMING UP, BUT I'D BEEN LYING AWAKE FOR HOURS.

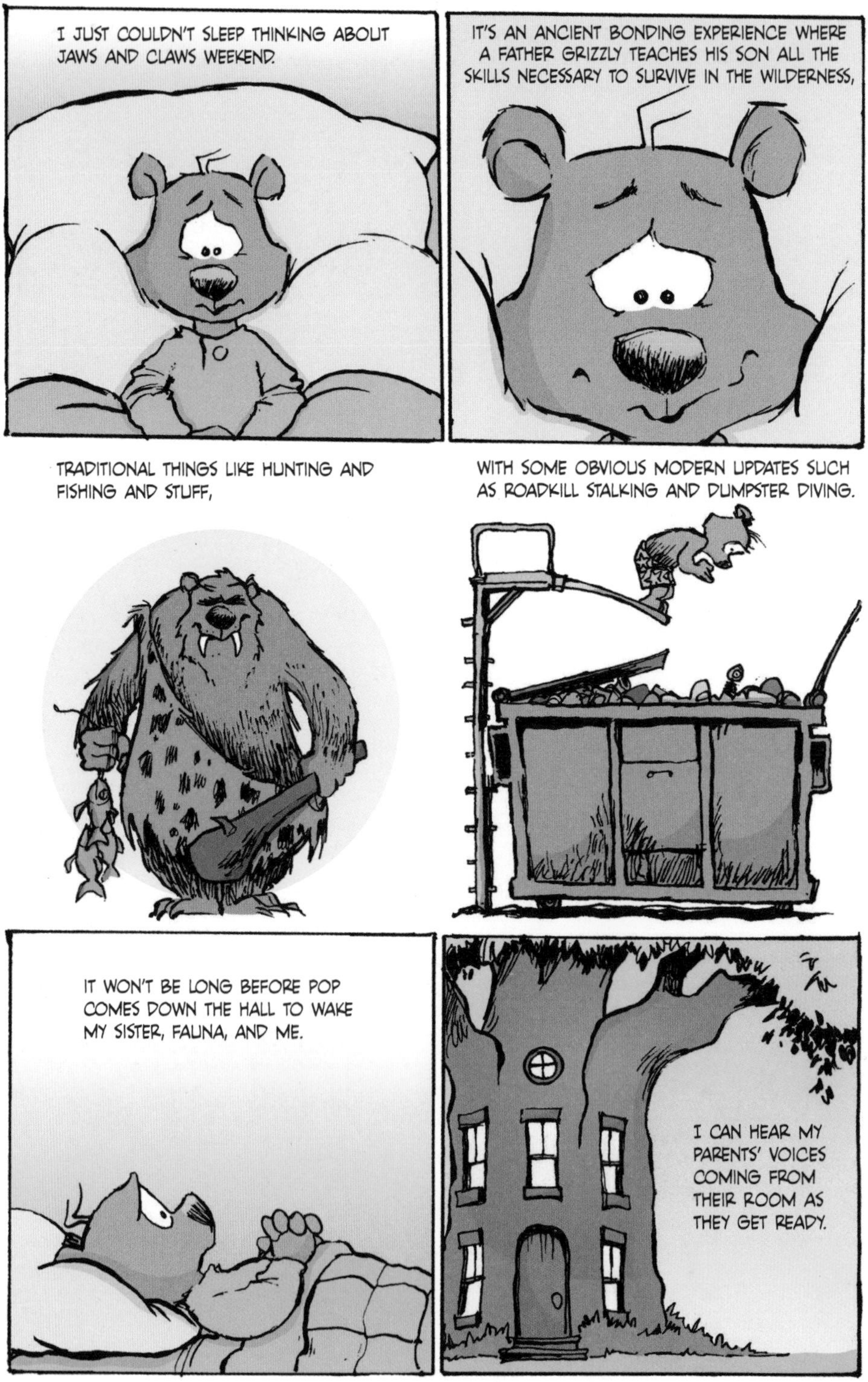
I JUST COULDN'T SLEEP THINKING ABOUT JAWS AND CLAWS WEEKEND.
IT'S AN ANCIENT BONDING EXPERIENCE WHERE A FATHER GRIZZLY TEACHES HIS SON ALL THE SKILLS NECESSARY TO SURVIVE IN THE WILDERNESS,
TRADITIONAL THINGS LIKE HUNTING AND FISHING AND STUFF,
WITH SOME OBVIOUS MODERN UPDATES SUCH AS ROADKILL STALKING AND DUMPSTER DIVING.
IT WON'T BE LONG BEFORE POP COMES DOWN THE HALL TO WAKE MY SISTER, FAUNA, AND ME.
I CAN HEAR MY PARENTS' VOICES COMING FROM THEIR ROOM AS THEY GET READY.

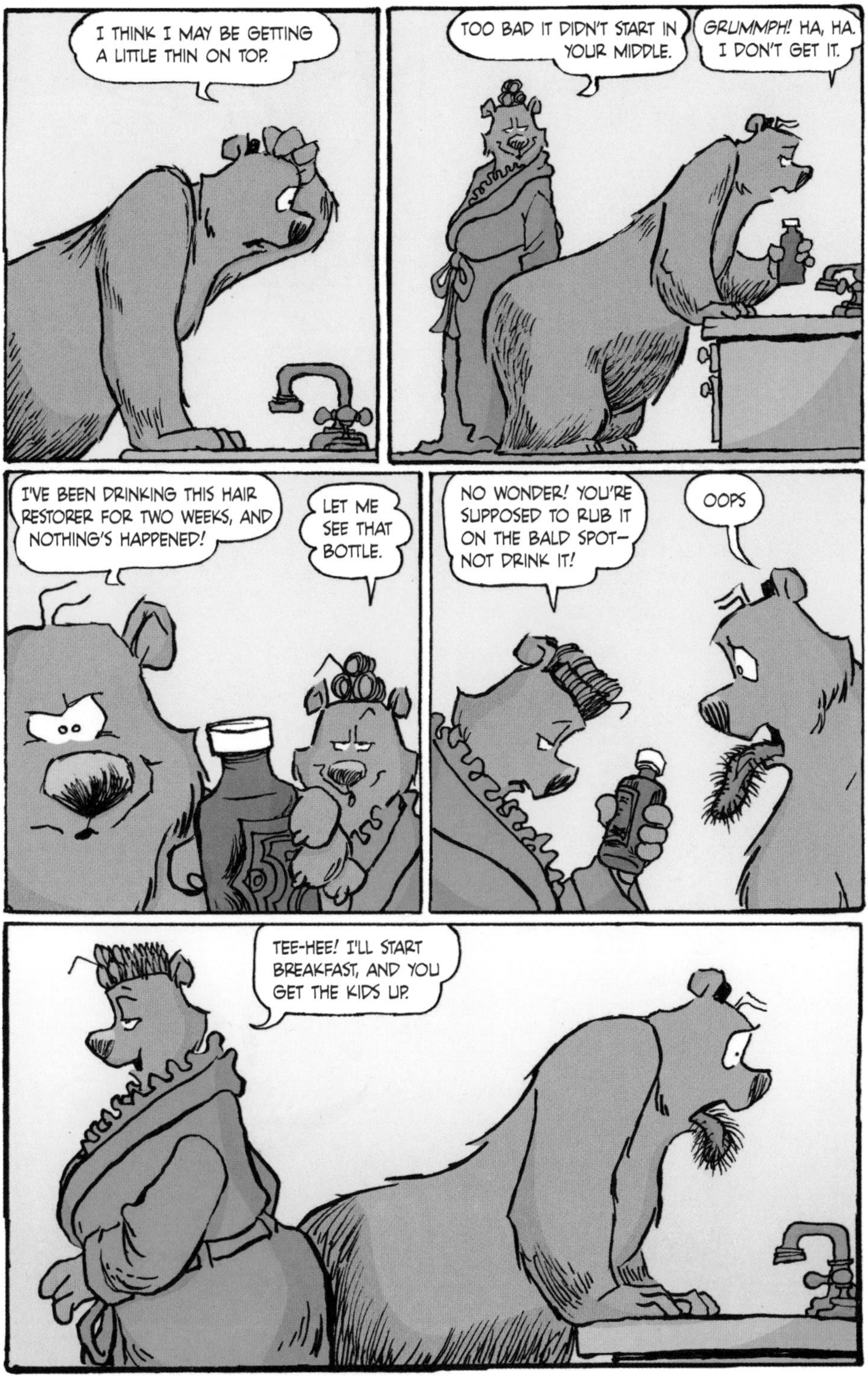
I THINK I MAY BE GETTING A LITTLE THIN ON TOP.
TOO BAD IT DIDN'T START IN YOUR MIDDLE.
GRUMMPH! HA, HA. I DON'T GET IT.
I'VE BEEN DRINKING THIS HAIR RESTORER FOR TWO WEEKS, AND NOTHING'S HAPPENED!
LET ME SEE THAT BOTTLE.
NO WONDER! YOU'RE SUPPOSED TO RUB IT ON THE BALD SPOT—NOT DRINK IT!
OOPS
TEE-HEE! I'LL START BREAKFAST, AND YOU GET THE KIDS UP.

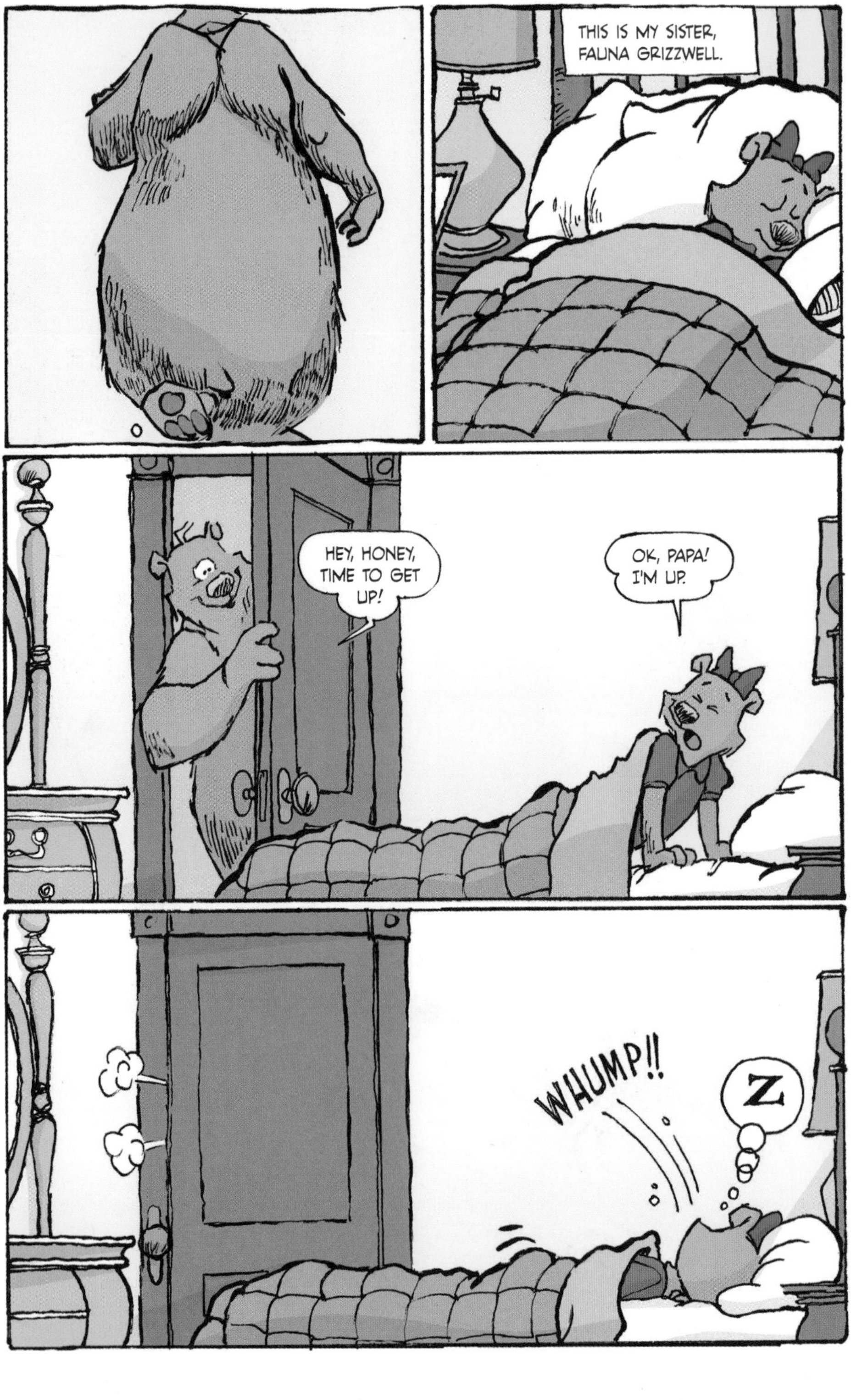
THIS IS MY SISTER, FAUNA GRIZZWELL.
HEY, HONEY, TIME TO GET UP!
OK, PAPA! I'M UP.
WHUMP!!
Z

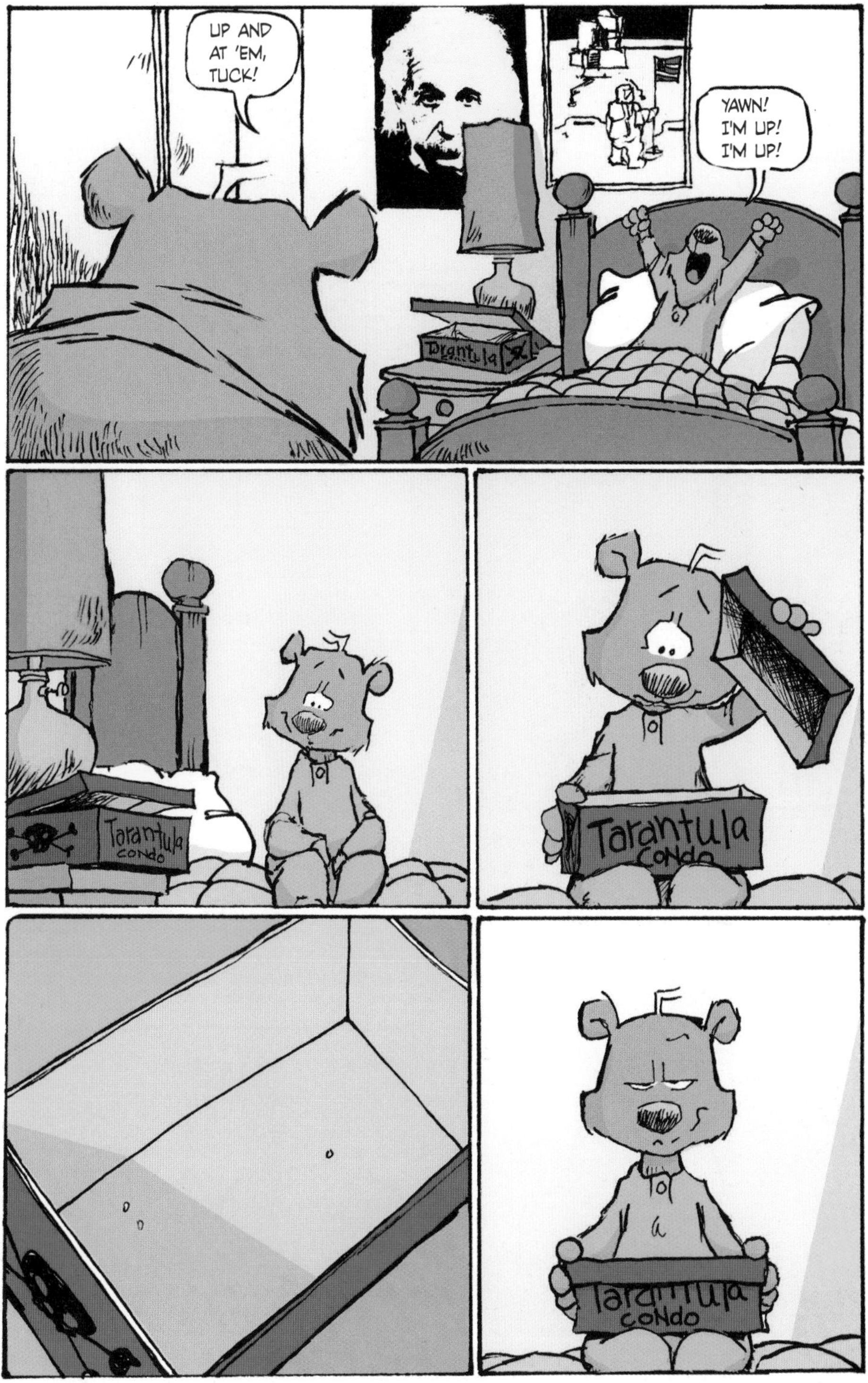
UP AND AT 'EM, TUCK!
YAWN! I'M UP! I'M UP!
Tarantula
Tarantula CONDO
Tarantula CONDO
Tarantula CONDO

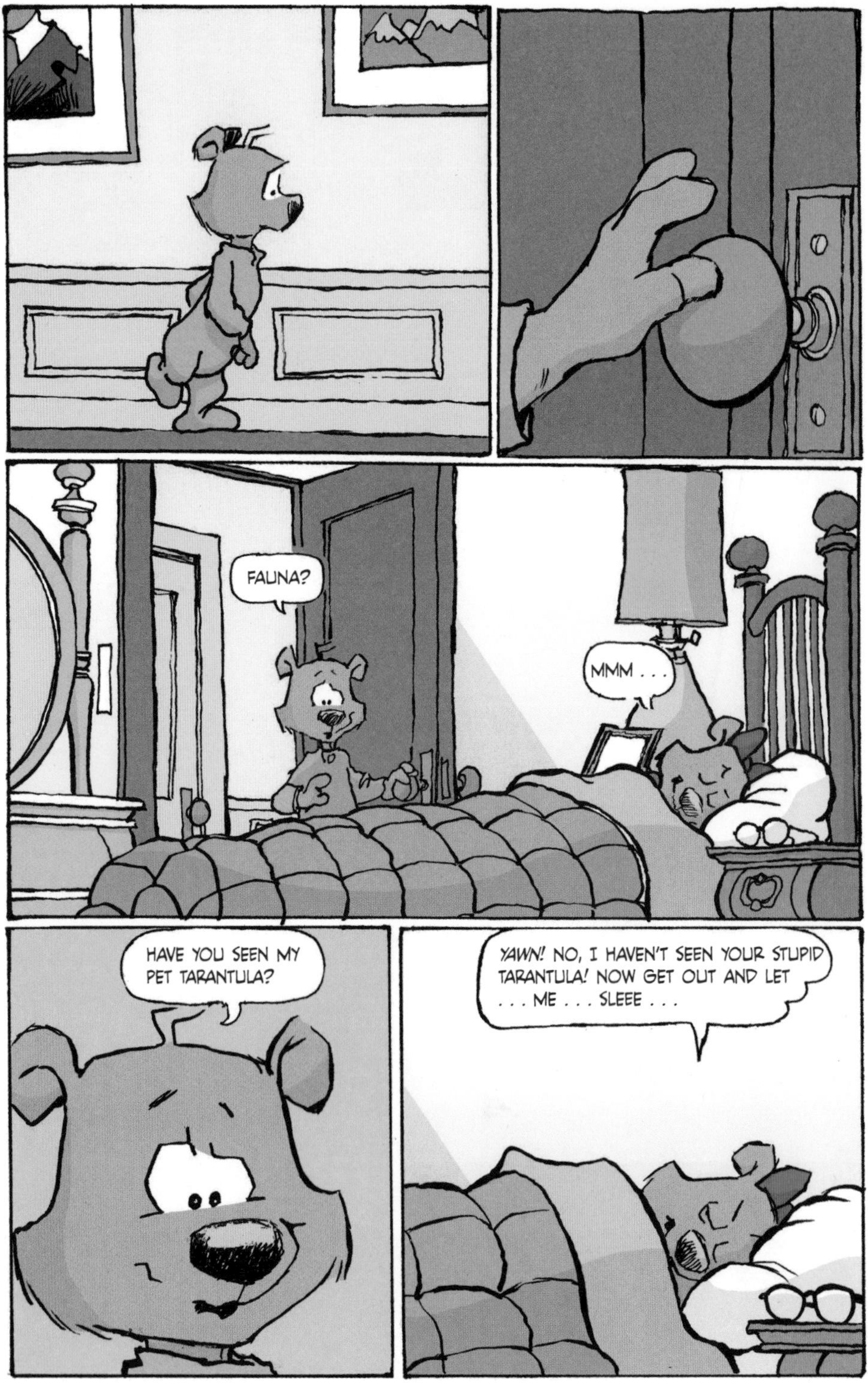
FAUNA?
MMM . . .
HAVE YOU SEEN MY PET TARANTULA?
YAWN! NO, I HAVEN'T SEEN YOUR STUPID TARANTULA! NOW GET OUT AND LET . . . ME . . . SLEEE . . .

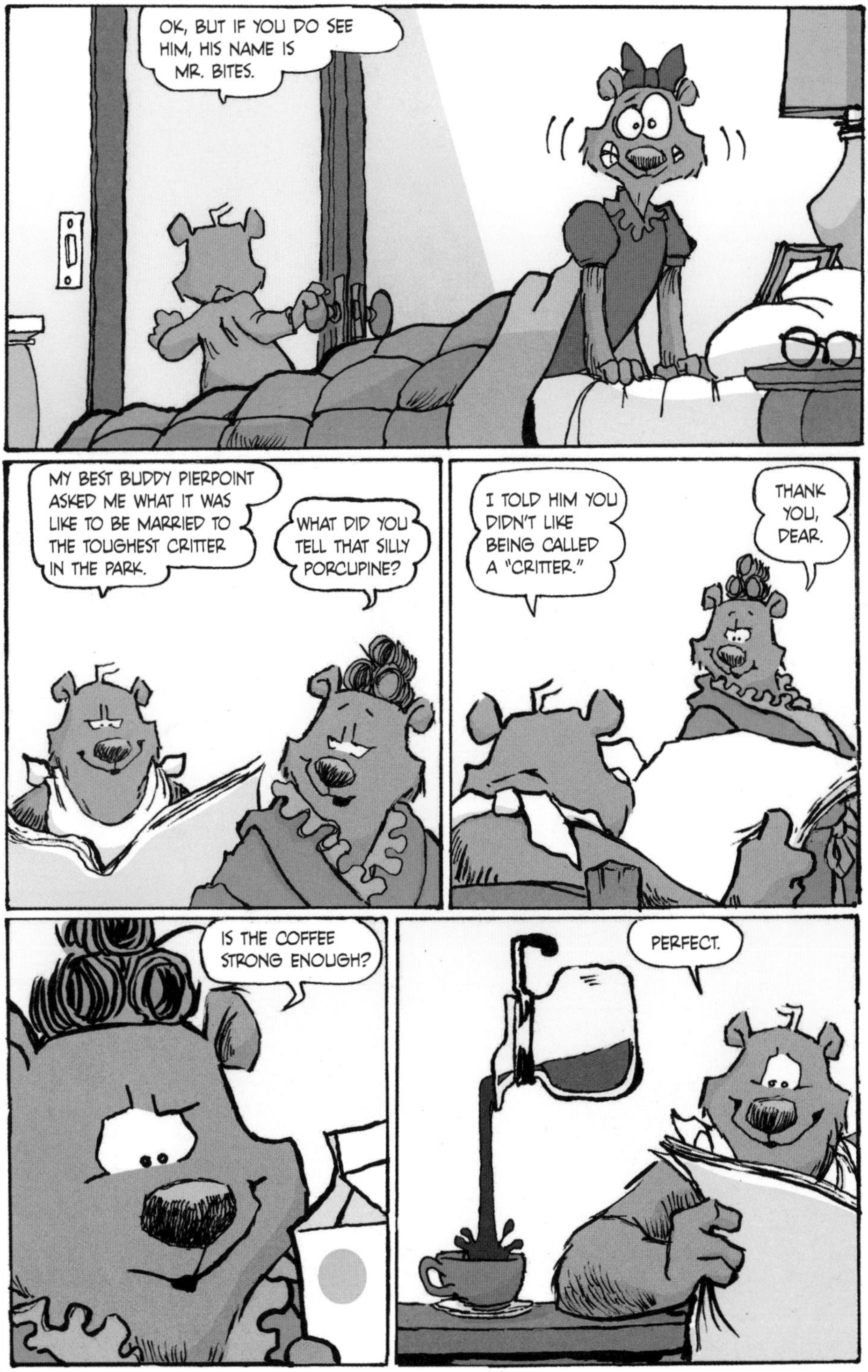
OK, BUT IF YOU DO SEE HIM, HIS NAME IS MR. BITES.
MY BEST BUDDY PIERPOINT ASKED ME WHAT IT WAS LIKE TO BE MARRIED TO THE TOUGHEST CRITTER IN THE PARK.
WHAT DID YOU TELL THAT SILLY PORCUPINE?
I TOLD HIM YOU DIDN'T LIKE BEING CALLED A "CRITTER."
THANK YOU, DEAR.
IS THE COFFEE STRONG ENOUGH?
PERFECT.

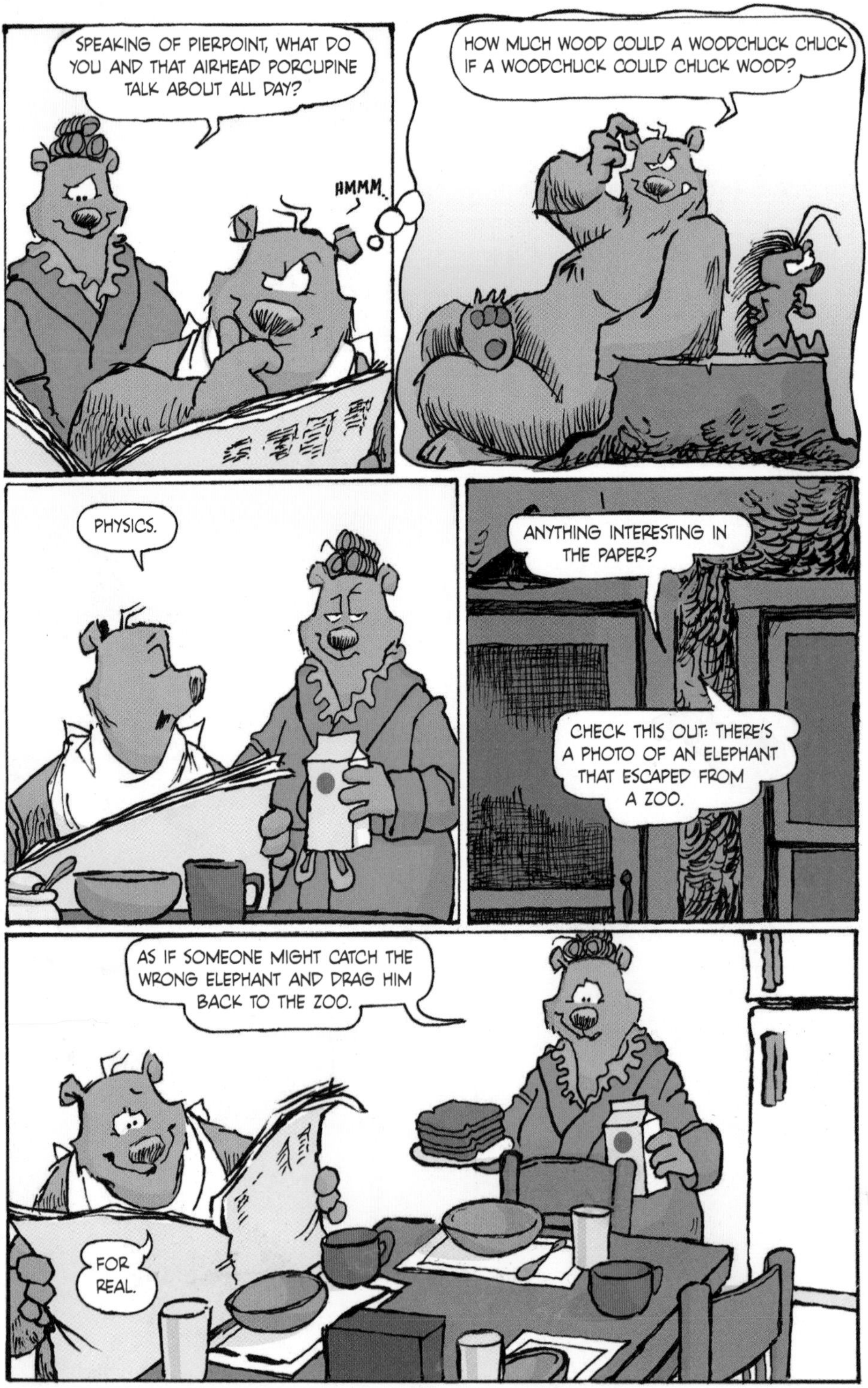
SPEAKING OF PIERPOINT, WHAT DO YOU AND THAT AIRHEAD PORCUPINE TALK ABOUT ALL DAY?
HMMM..
HOW MUCH WOOD COULD A WOODCHUCK CHUCK IF A WOODCHUCK COULD CHUCK WOOD?
PHYSICS.
ANYTHING INTERESTING IN THE PAPER?
CHECK THIS OUT: THERE'S A PHOTO OF AN ELEPHANT THAT ESCAPED FROM A ZOO.
AS IF SOMEONE MIGHT CATCH THE WRONG ELEPHANT AND DRAG HIM BACK TO THE ZOO.
FOR REAL.

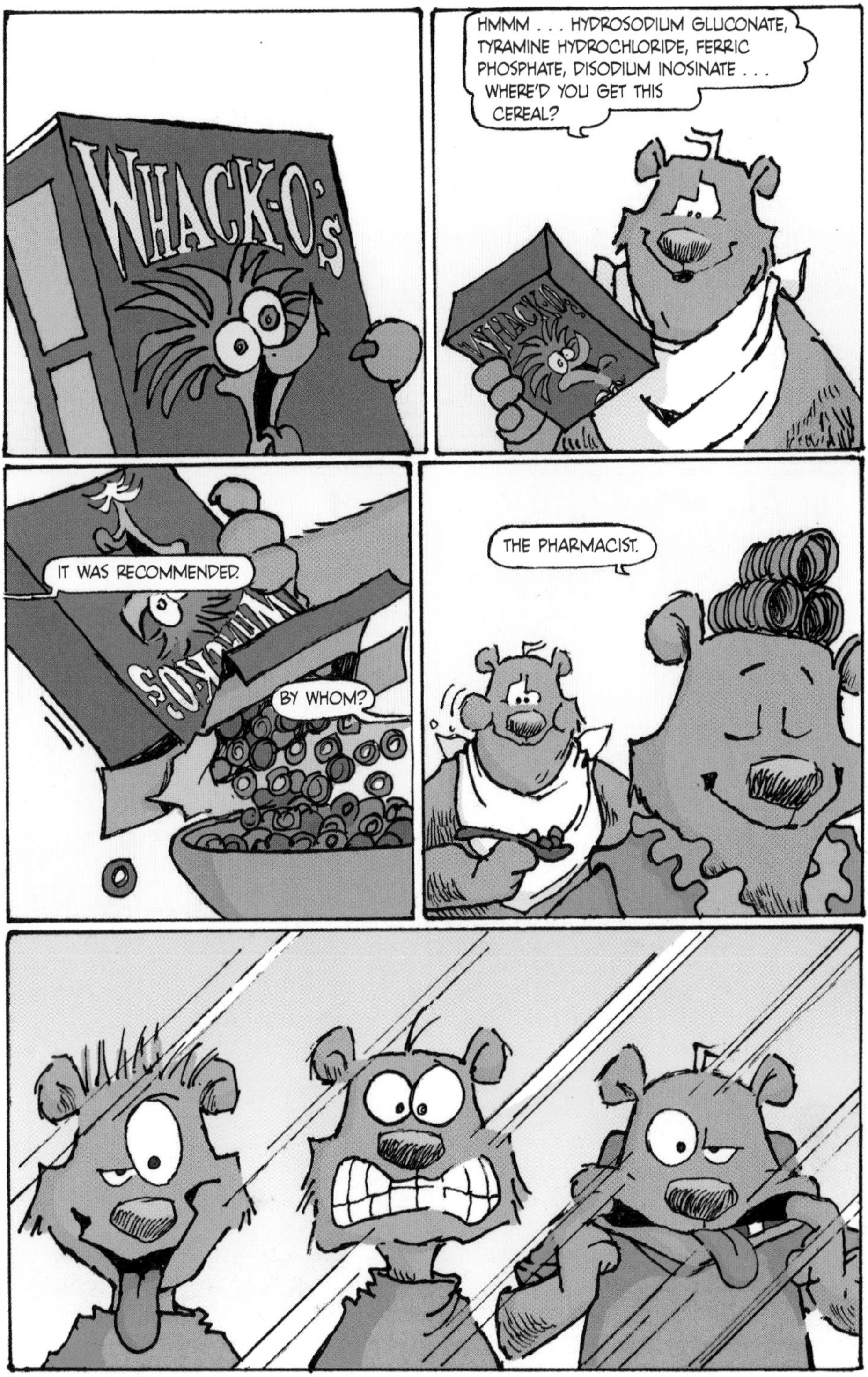
WHACK-O'S
HMMM . . . HYDROSODIUM GLUCONATE, TYRAMINE HYDROCHLORIDE, FERRIC PHOSPHATE, DISODIUM INOSINATE . . . WHERE'D YOU GET THIS CEREAL?
WHACK-O'S
IT WAS RECOMMENDED.
BY WHOM?
THE PHARMACIST.

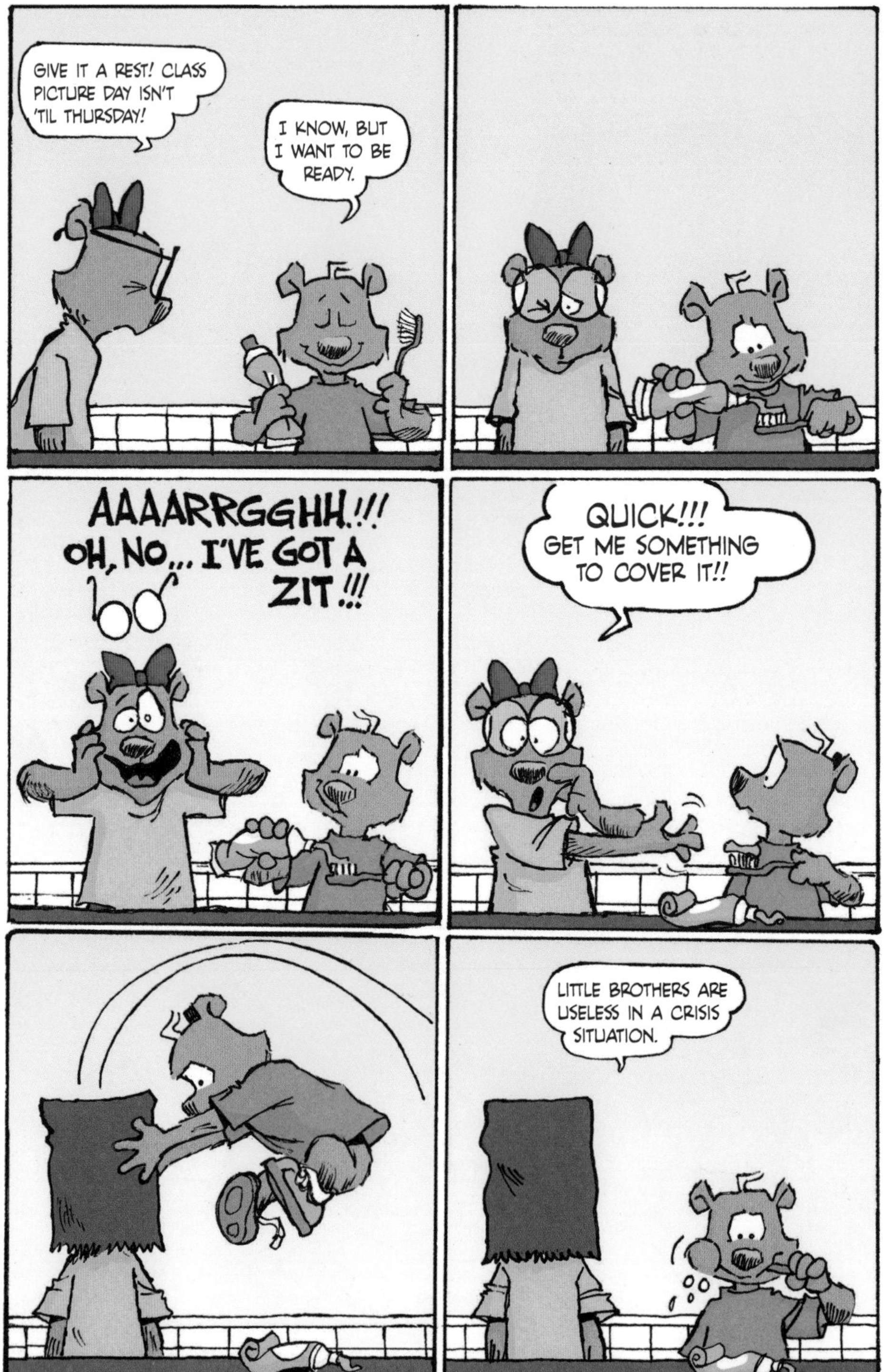
GIVE IT A REST! CLASS PICTURE DAY ISN'T 'TIL THURSDAY!
I KNOW, BUT I WANT TO BE READY.
AAAARRGGHH!!!
OH, NO... I'VE GOT A ZIT!!!
QUICK!!! GET ME SOMETHING TO COVER IT!!
LITTLE BROTHERS ARE USELESS IN A CRISIS SITUATION.

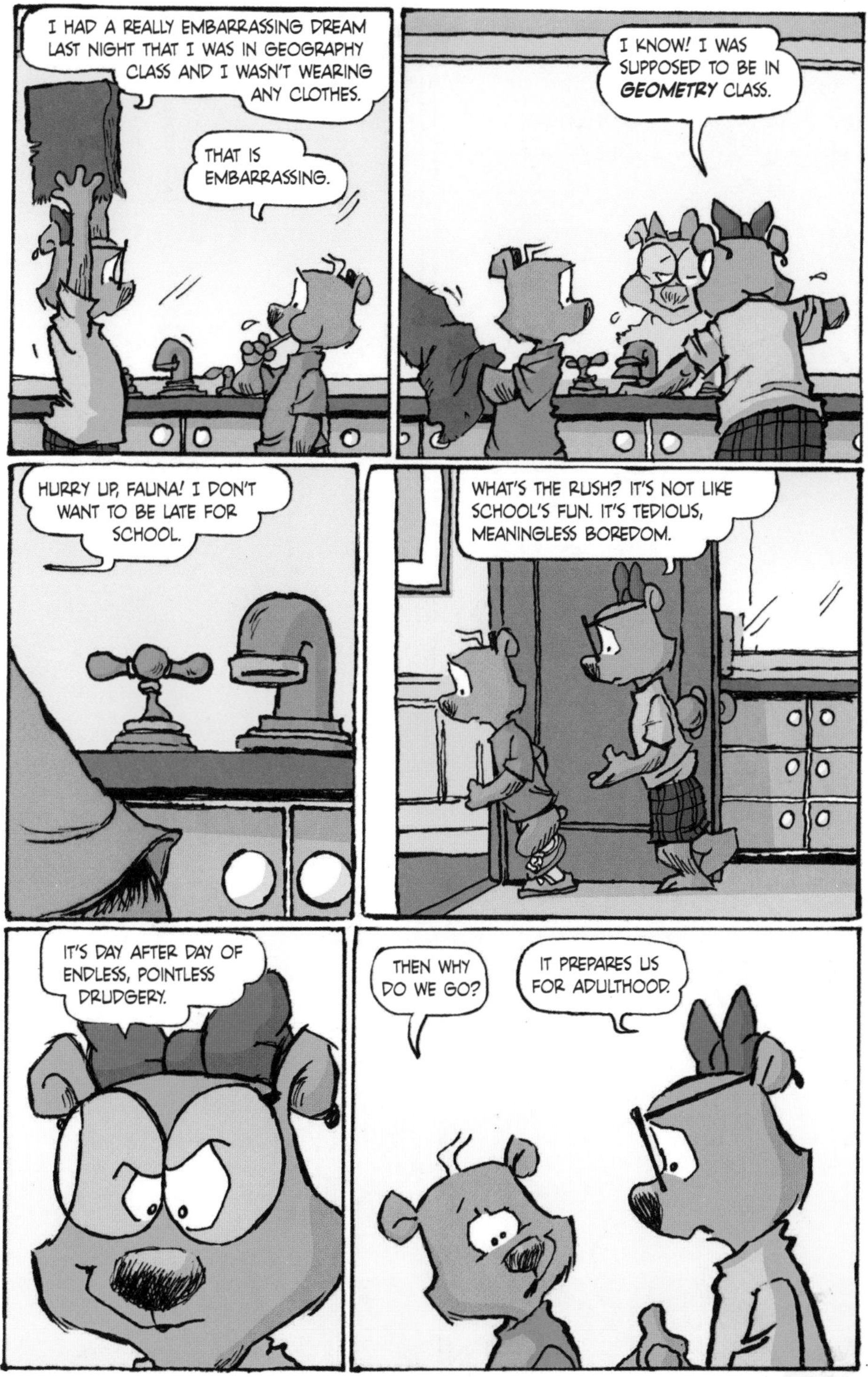
I HAD A REALLY EMBARRASSING DREAM LAST NIGHT THAT I WAS IN GEOGRAPHY CLASS AND I WASN'T WEARING ANY CLOTHES.
THAT IS EMBARRASSING.
I KNOW! I WAS SUPPOSED TO BE IN GEOMETRY CLASS.
HURRY UP, FAUNA! I DON'T WANT TO BE LATE FOR SCHOOL.
WHAT'S THE RUSH? IT'S NOT LIKE SCHOOL'S FUN. IT'S TEDIOUS, MEANINGLESS BOREDOM.
IT'S DAY AFTER DAY OF ENDLESS, POINTLESS DRUDGERY.
THEN WHY DO WE GO?
IT PREPARES US FOR ADULTHOOD.

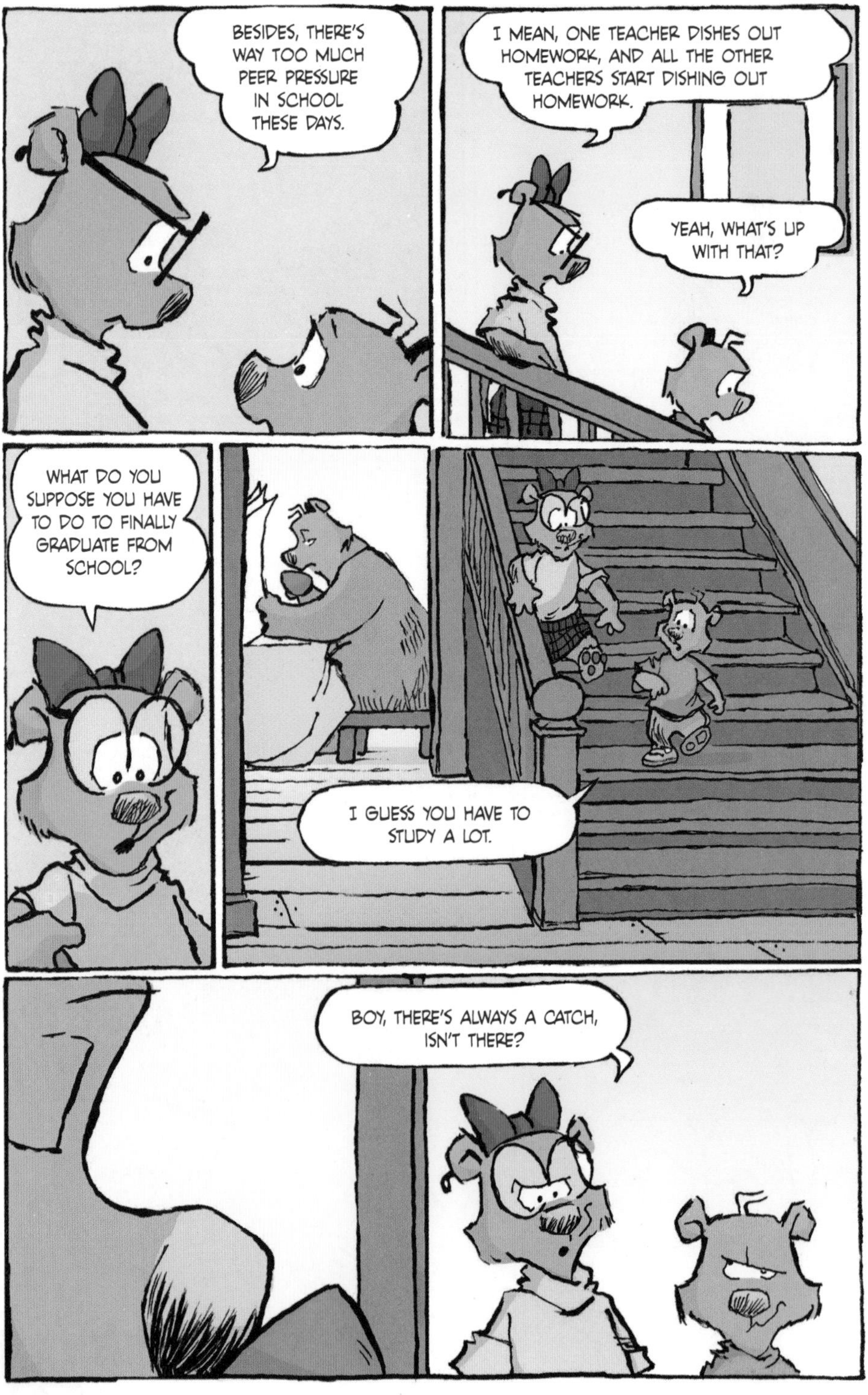
BESIDES, THERE'S WAY TOO MUCH PEER PRESSURE IN SCHOOL THESE DAYS.
I MEAN, ONE TEACHER DISHES OUT HOMEWORK, AND ALL THE OTHER TEACHERS START DISHING OUT HOMEWORK.
YEAH, WHAT'S UP WITH THAT?
WHAT DO YOU SUPPOSE YOU HAVE TO DO TO FINALLY GRADUATE FROM SCHOOL?
I GUESS YOU HAVE TO STUDY A LOT.
BOY, THERE'S ALWAYS A CATCH, ISN'T THERE?

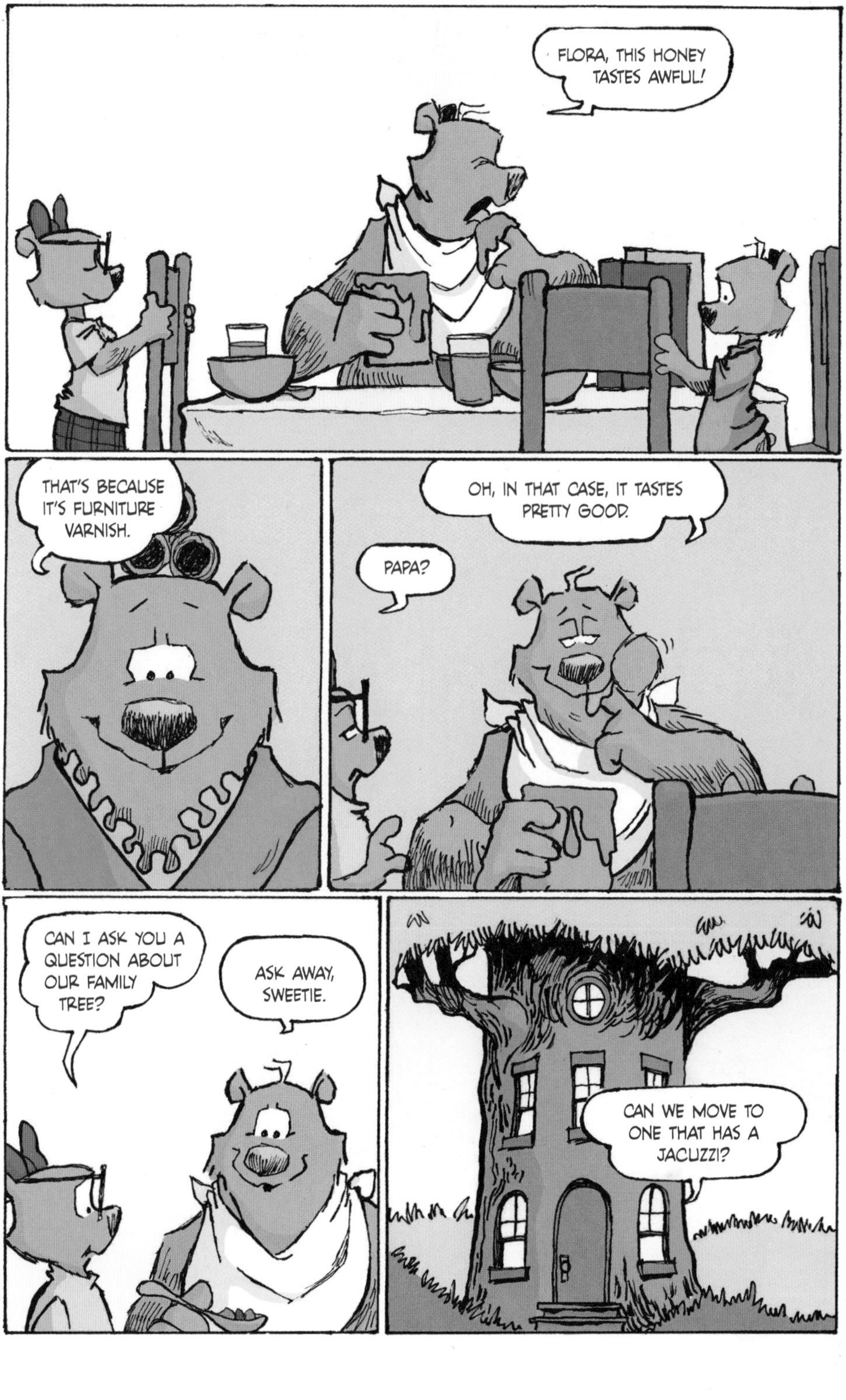
FLORA, THIS HONEY TASTES AWFUL!
THAT'S BECAUSE IT'S FURNITURE VARNISH.
OH, IN THAT CASE, IT TASTES PRETTY GOOD.
PAPA?
CAN I ASK YOU A QUESTION ABOUT OUR FAMILY TREE?
ASK AWAY, SWEETIE.
CAN WE MOVE TO ONE THAT HAS A JACUZZI?

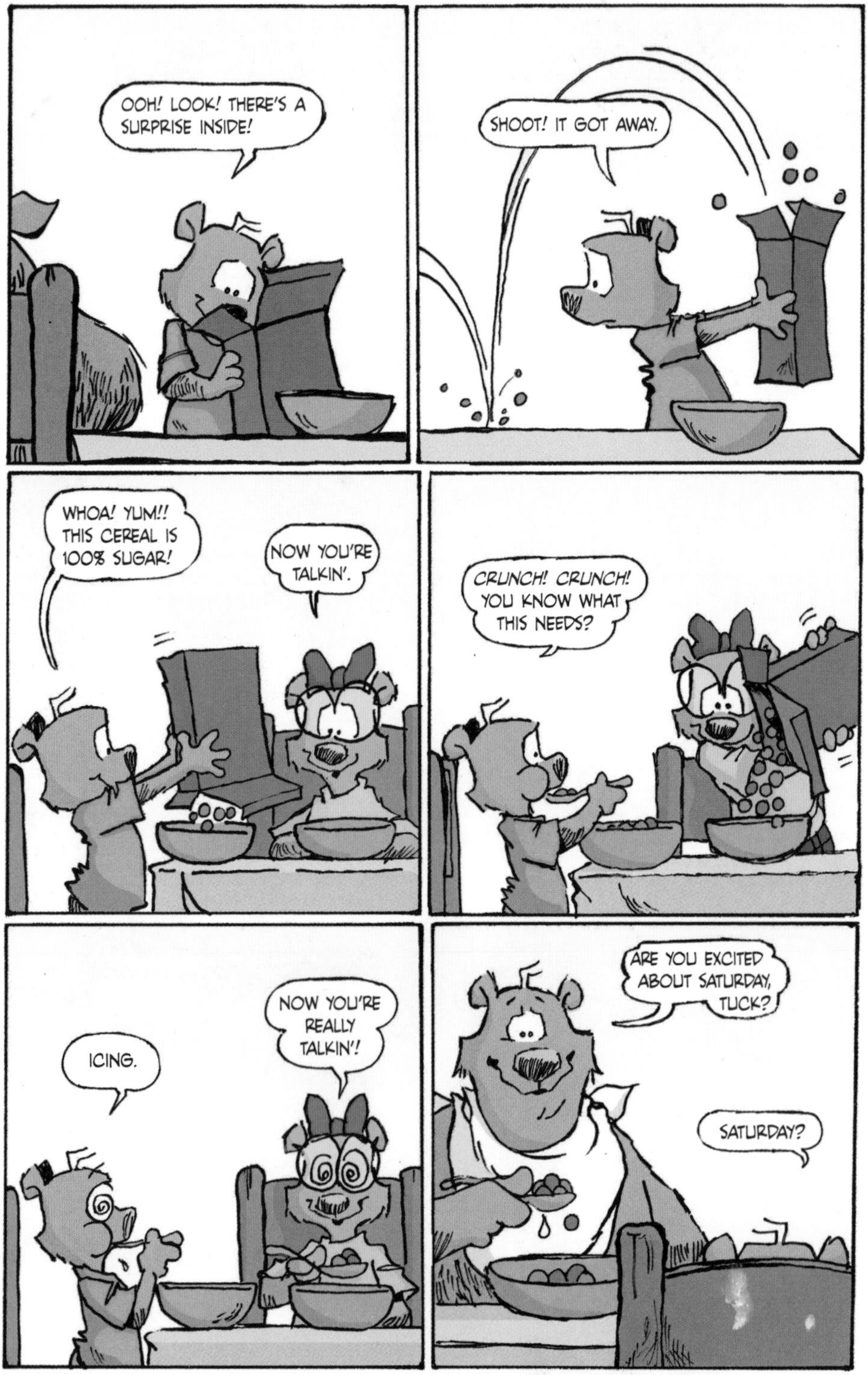
OOH! LOOK! THERE'S A SURPRISE INSIDE!
SHOOT! IT GOT AWAY.
WHOA! YUM!! THIS CEREAL IS 100% SUGAR!
NOW YOU'RE TALKIN'.
CRUNCH! CRUNCH! YOU KNOW WHAT THIS NEEDS?
ICING.
NOW YOU'RE REALLY TALKIN'!
ARE YOU EXCITED ABOUT SATURDAY, TUCK?
SATURDAY?

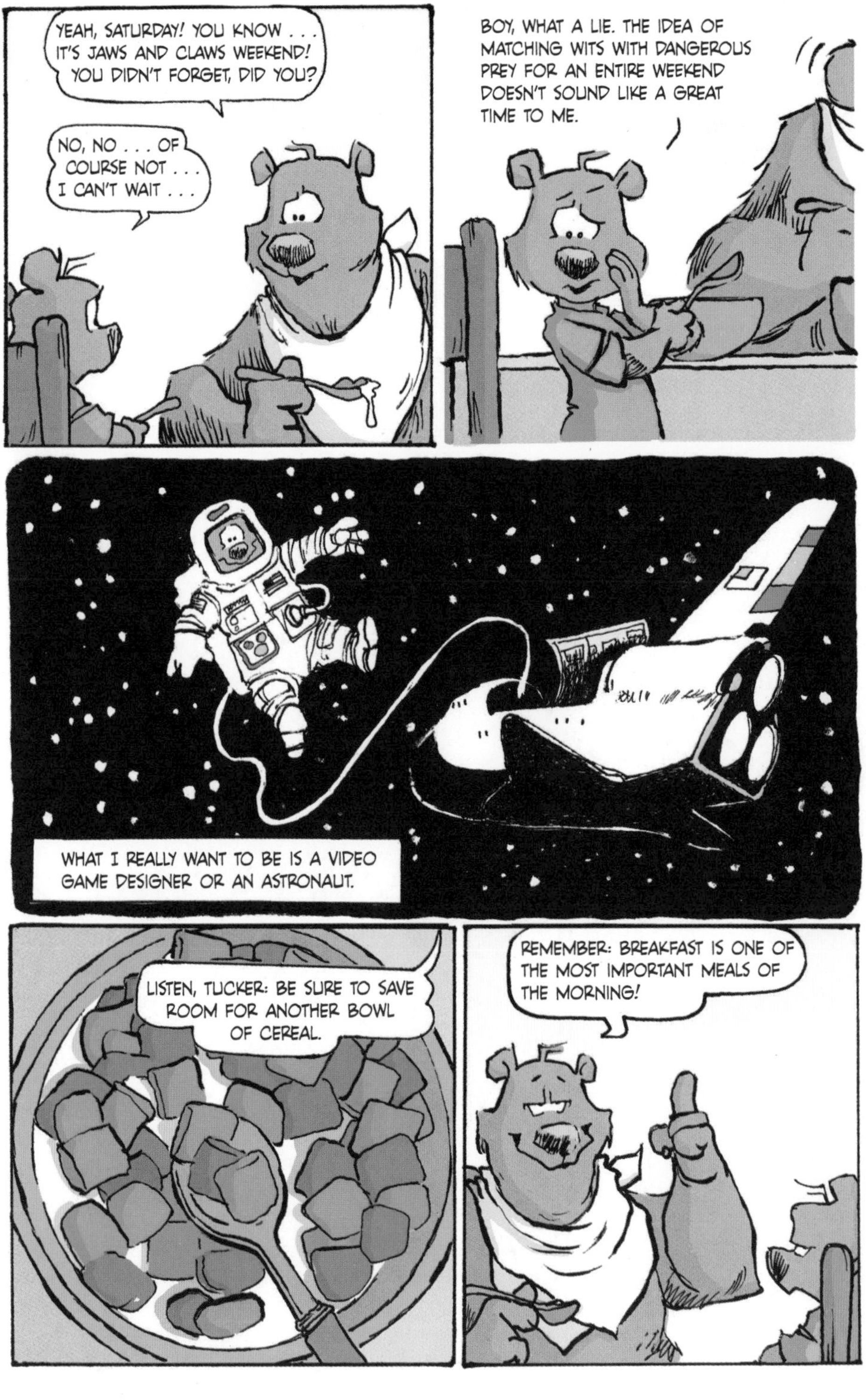
YEAH, SATURDAY! YOU KNOW . . . IT'S JAWS AND CLAWS WEEKEND! YOU DIDN'T FORGET, DID YOU?
NO, NO . . . OF COURSE NOT . . . I CAN'T WAIT . . .
BOY, WHAT A LIE. THE IDEA OF MATCHING WITS WITH DANGEROUS PREY FOR AN ENTIRE WEEKEND DOESN'T SOUND LIKE A GREAT TIME TO ME.
WHAT I REALLY WANT TO BE IS A VIDEO GAME DESIGNER OR AN ASTRONAUT.
LISTEN, TUCKER: BE SURE TO SAVE ROOM FOR ANOTHER BOWL OF CEREAL.
REMEMBER: BREAKFAST IS ONE OF THE MOST IMPORTANT MEALS OF THE MORNING!

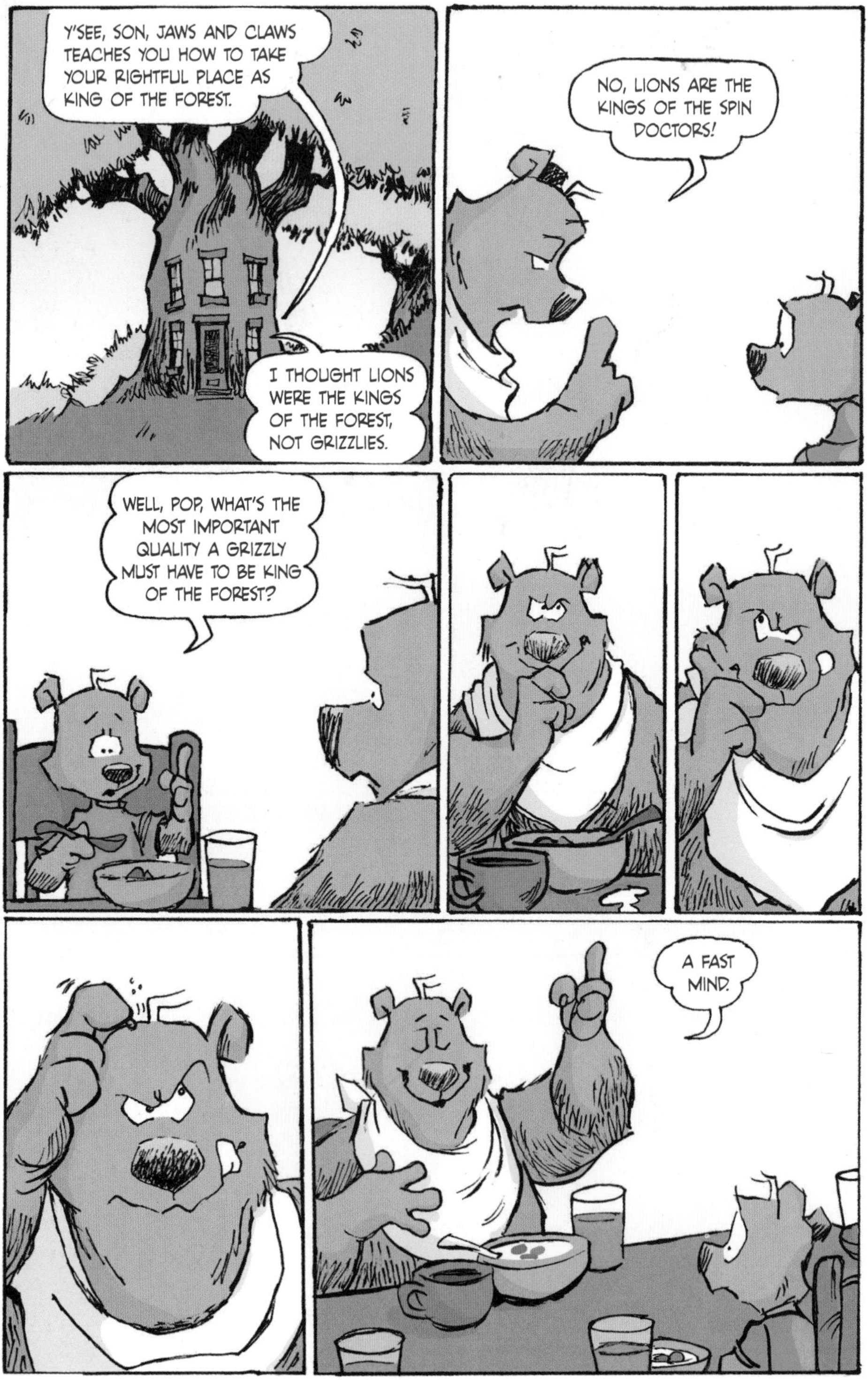

Y'SEE, SON, JAWS AND CLAWS TEACHES YOU HOW TO TAKE YOUR RIGHTFUL PLACE AS KING OF THE FOREST.
I THOUGHT LIONS WERE THE KINGS OF THE FOREST, NOT GRIZZLIES.
NO, LIONS ARE THE KINGS OF THE SPIN DOCTORS!
WELL, POP, WHAT'S THE MOST IMPORTANT QUALITY A GRIZZLY MUST HAVE TO BE KING OF THE FOREST?
A FAST MIND.

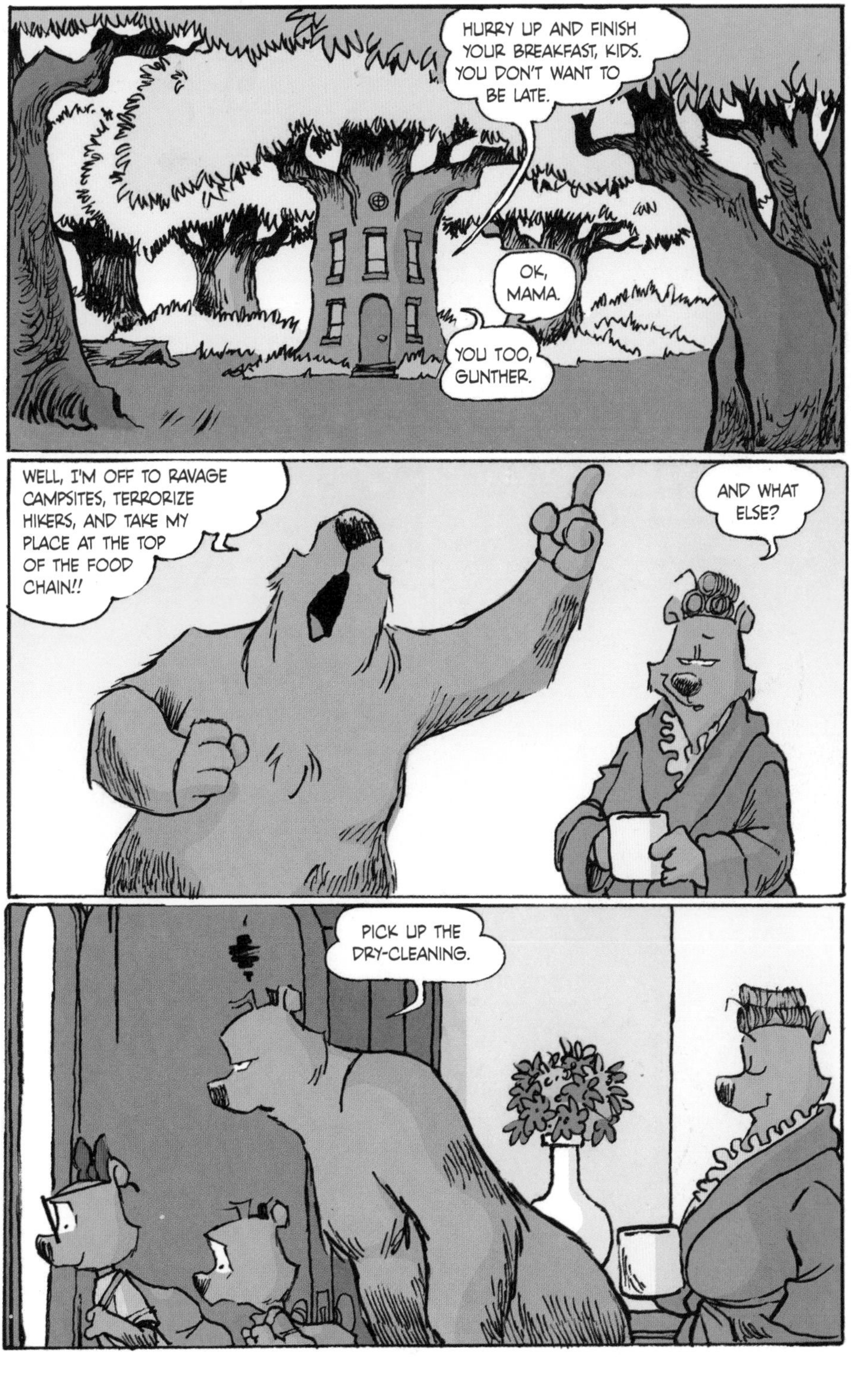
HURRY UP AND FINISH YOUR BREAKFAST, KIDS. YOU DON'T WANT TO BE LATE.
OK, MAMA.
YOU TOO, GUNTHER.
WELL, I'M OFF TO RAVAGE CAMPSITES, TERRORIZE HIKERS, AND TAKE MY PLACE AT THE TOP OF THE FOOD CHAIN!!
AND WHAT ELSE?
PICK UP THE DRY-CLEANING.

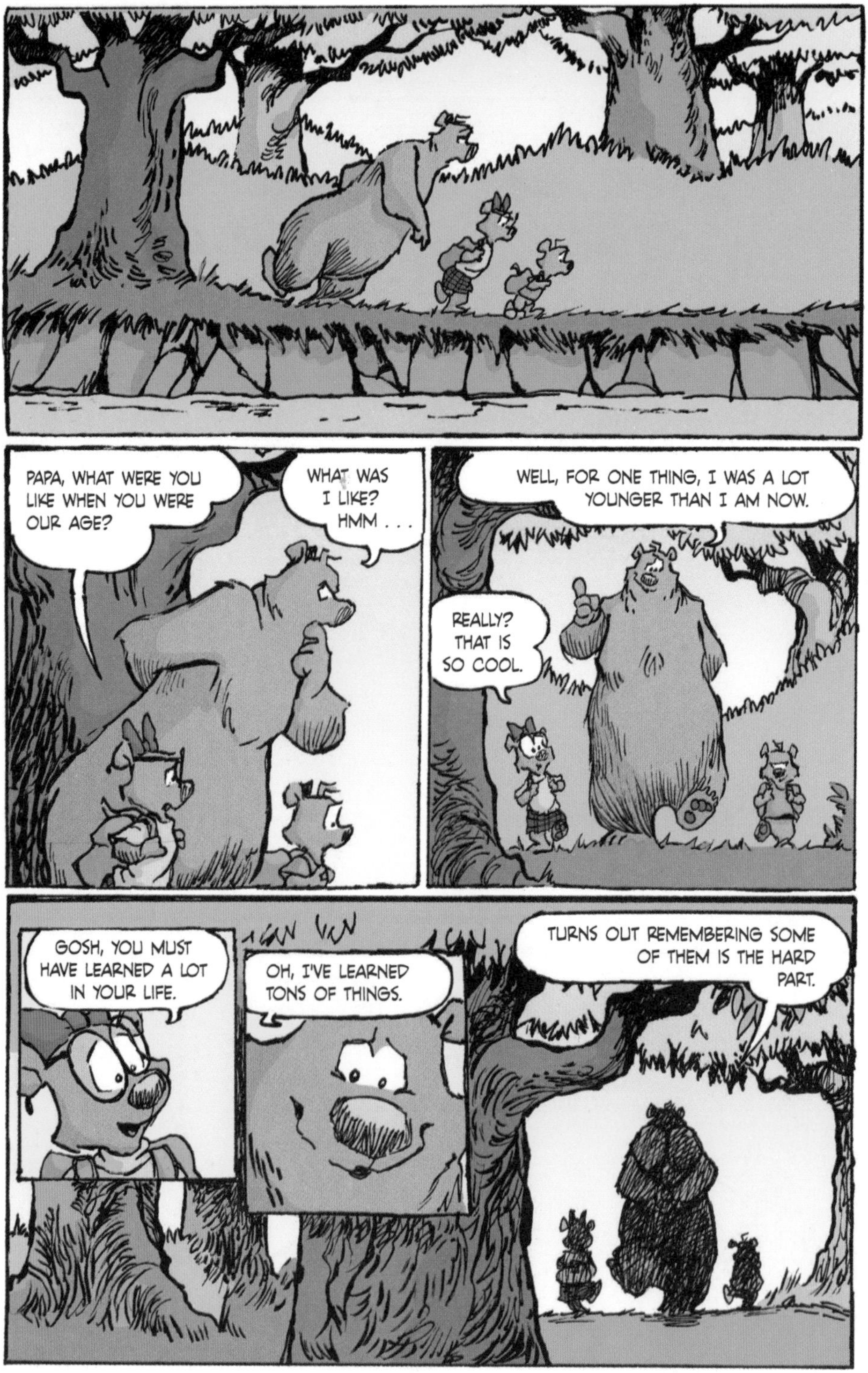
PAPA, WHAT WERE YOU LIKE WHEN YOU WERE OUR AGE?
WHAT WAS I LIKE? HMM . . .
WELL, FOR ONE THING, I WAS A LOT YOUNGER THAN I AM NOW.
REALLY? THAT IS SO COOL.
GOSH, YOU MUST HAVE LEARNED A LOT IN YOUR LIFE.
OH, I'VE LEARNED TONS OF THINGS.
TURNS OUT REMEMBERING SOME OF THEM IS THE HARD PART.

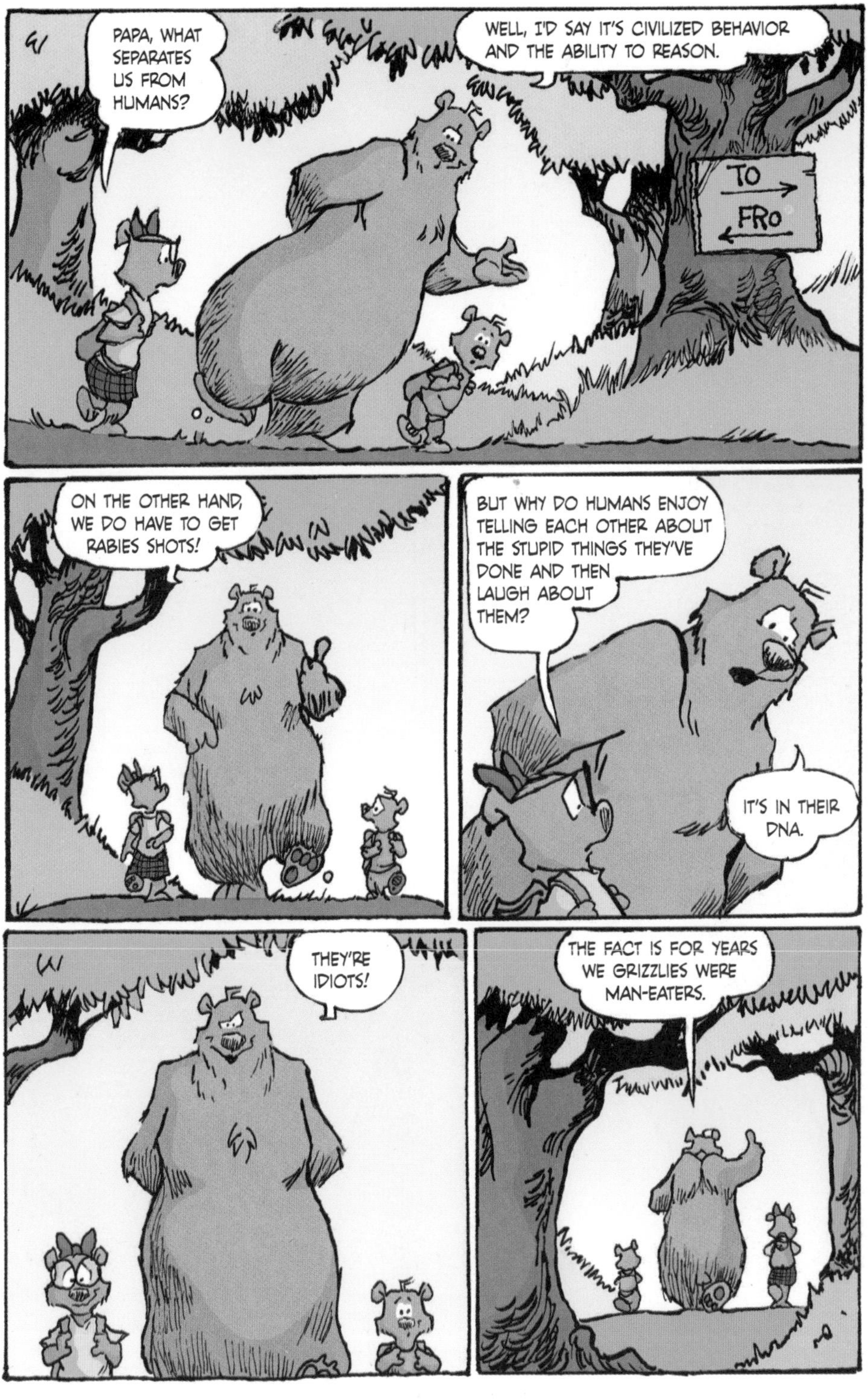
PAPA, WHAT SEPARATES US FROM HUMANS?
WELL, I'D SAY IT'S CIVILIZED BEHAVIOR AND THE ABILITY TO REASON.
TO
FRo
ON THE OTHER HAND, WE DO HAVE TO GET RABIES SHOTS!
BUT WHY DO HUMANS ENJOY TELLING EACH OTHER ABOUT THE STUPID THINGS THEY'VE DONE AND THEN LAUGH ABOUT THEM?
IT'S IN THEIR DNA.
THEY'RE IDIOTS!
THE FACT IS FOR YEARS WE GRIZZLIES WERE MAN-EATERS.

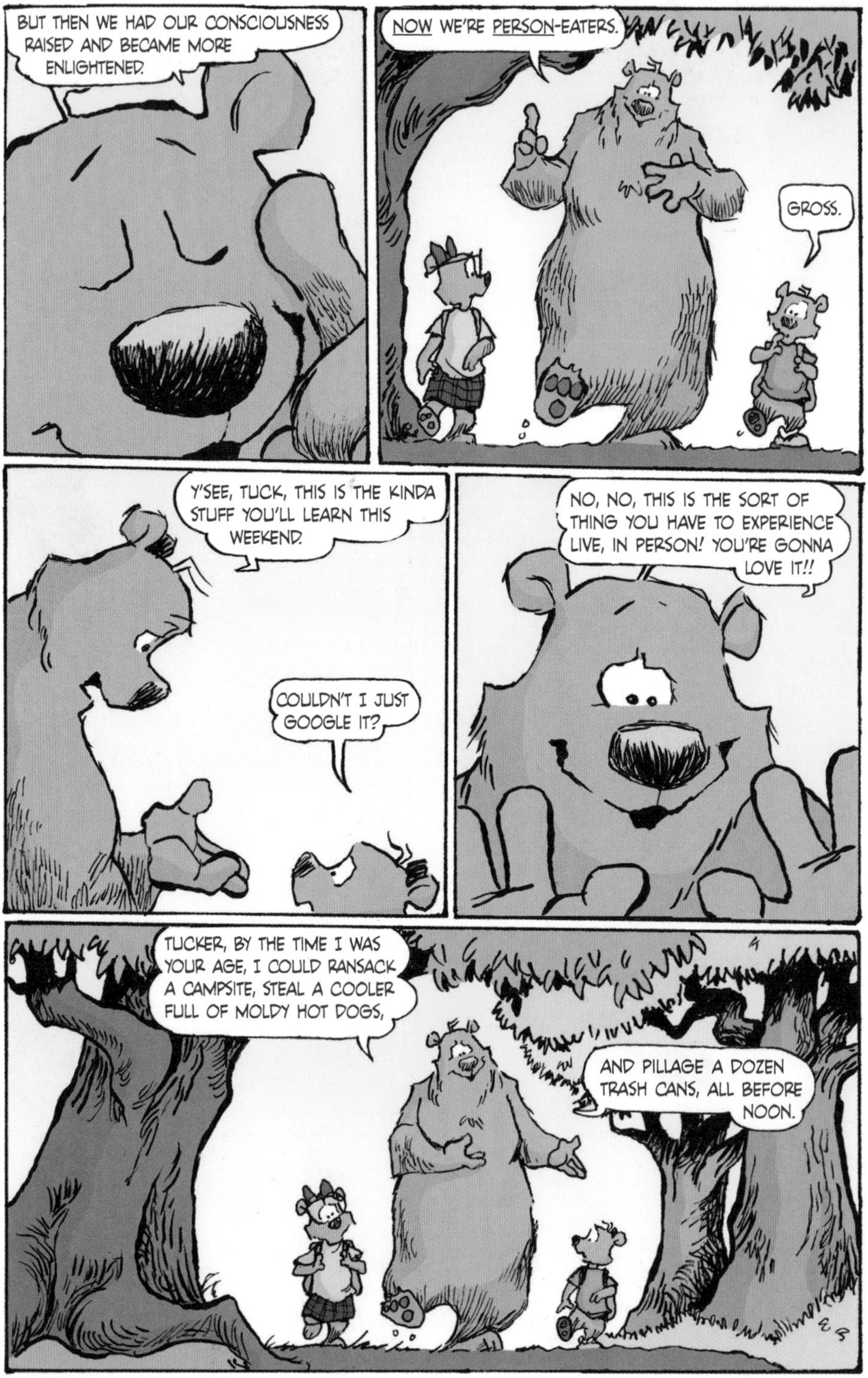

BUT THEN WE HAD OUR CONSCIOUSNESS RAISED AND BECAME MORE ENLIGHTENED.
NOW WE'RE PERSON-EATERS.
GROSS.
Y'SEE, TUCK, THIS IS THE KINDA STUFF YOU'LL LEARN THIS WEEKEND.
COULDN'T I JUST GOOGLE IT?
NO, NO, THIS IS THE SORT OF THING YOU HAVE TO EXPERIENCE LIVE, IN PERSON! YOU'RE GONNA LOVE IT!!
TUCKER, BY THE TIME I WAS YOUR AGE, I COULD RANSACK A CAMPSITE, STEAL A COOLER FULL OF MOLDY HOT DOGS,
AND PILLAGE A DOZEN TRASH CANS, ALL BEFORE NOON.

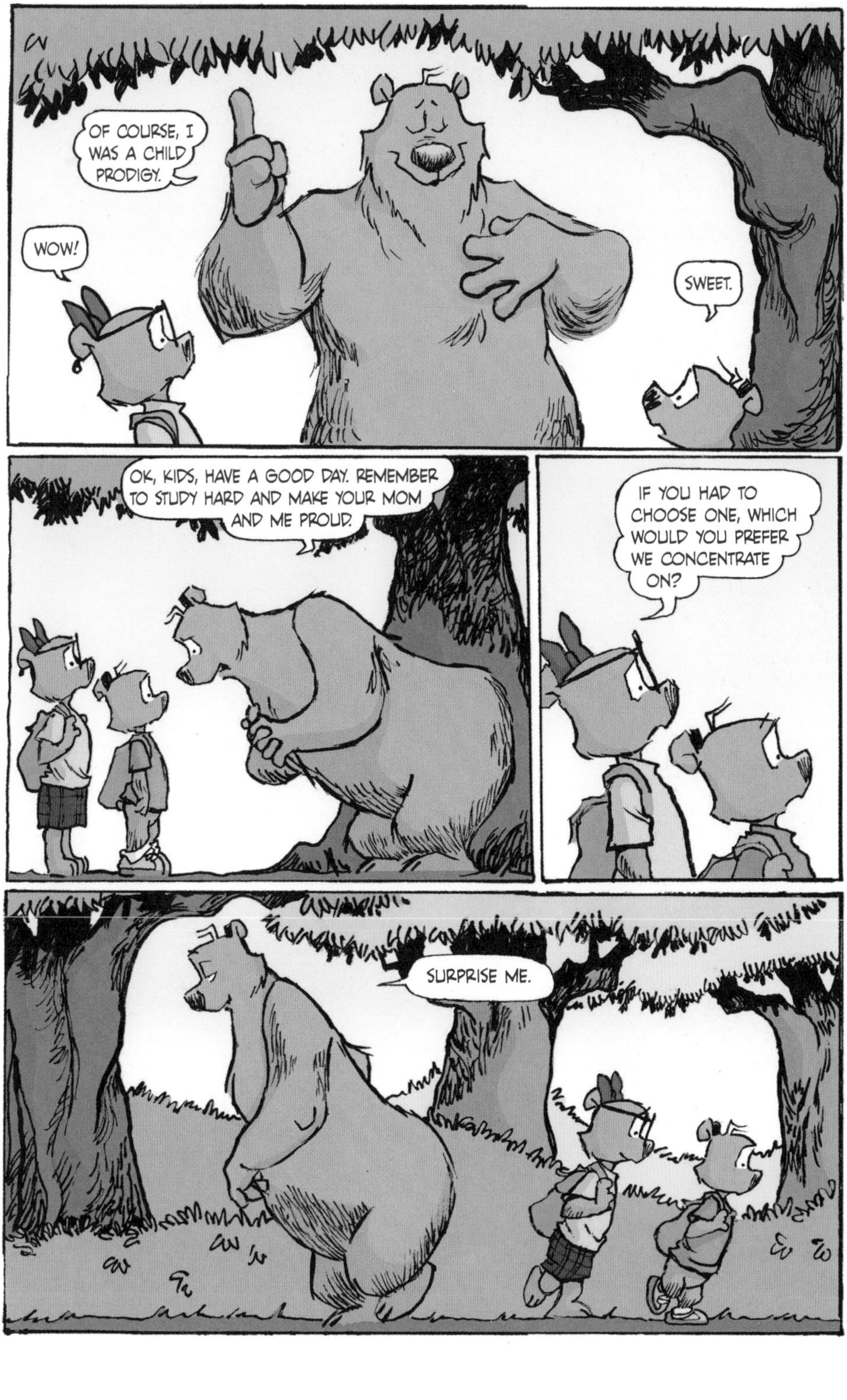
OF COURSE, I WAS A CHILD PRODIGY.
WOW!
SWEET.
OK, KIDS, HAVE A GOOD DAY. REMEMBER TO STUDY HARD AND MAKE YOUR MOM AND ME PROUD.
IF YOU HAD TO CHOOSE ONE, WHICH WOULD YOU PREFER WE CONCENTRATE ON?
SURPRISE ME.

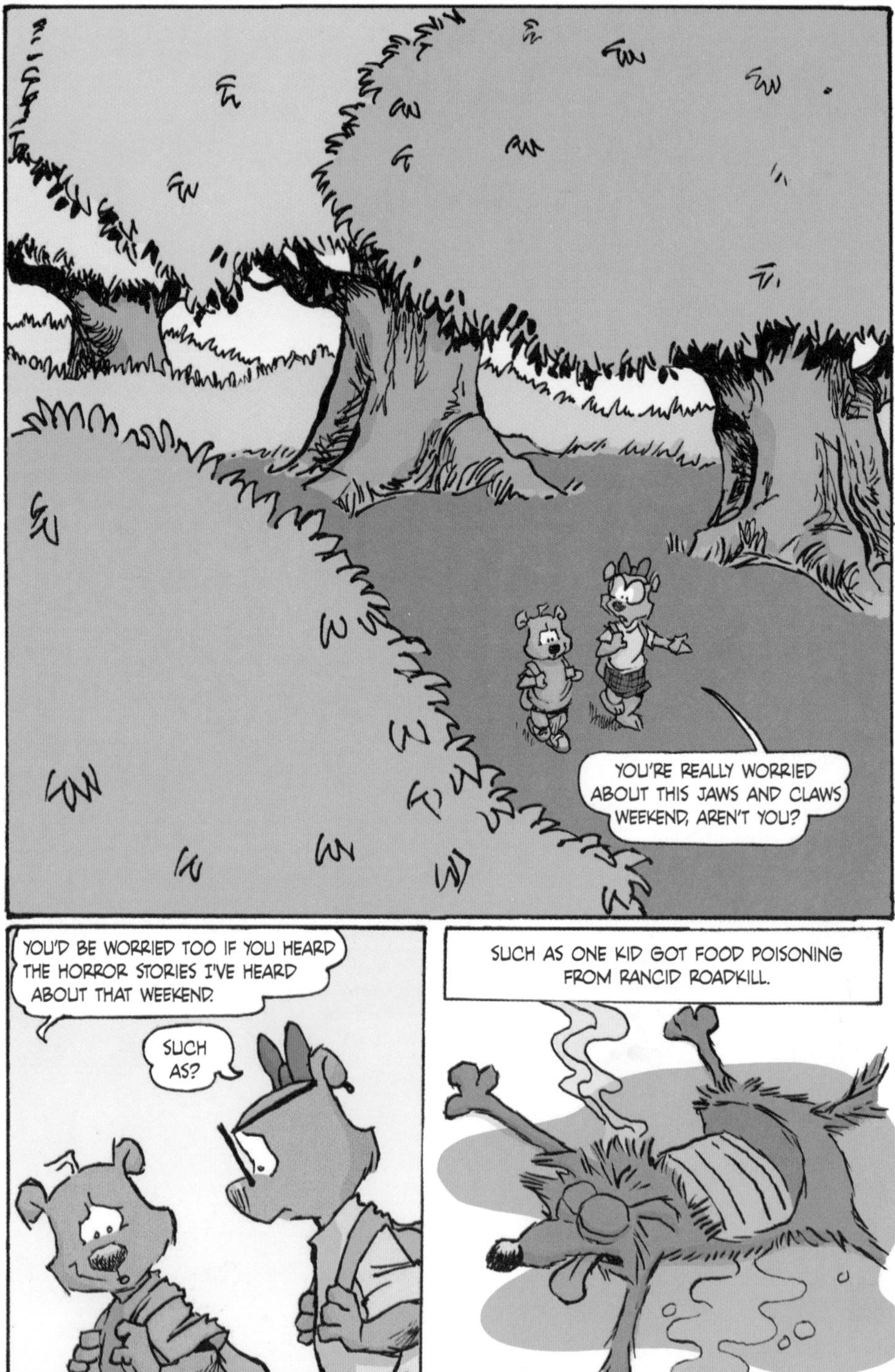
YOU'RE REALLY WORRIED ABOUT THIS JAWS AND CLAWS WEEKEND, AREN'T YOU?
YOU'D BE WORRIED TOO IF YOU HEARD THE HORROR STORIES I'VE HEARD ABOUT THAT WEEKEND.
SUCH AS?
SUCH AS ONE KID GOT FOOD POISONING FROM RANCID ROADKILL.

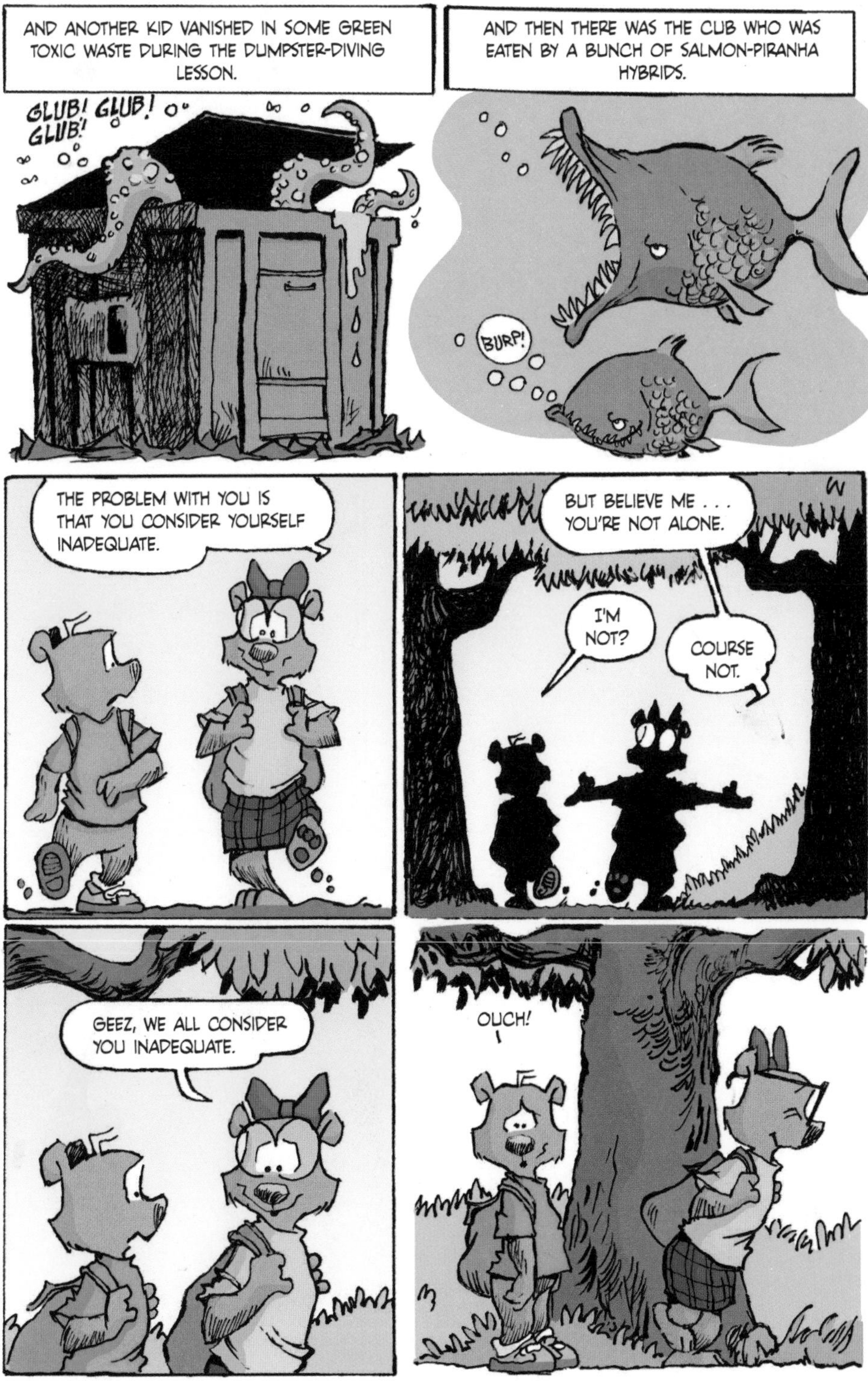
AND ANOTHER KID VANISHED IN SOME GREEN TOXIC WASTE DURING THE DUMPSTER-DIVING LESSON.
GLUB! GLUB! GLUB!
AND THEN THERE WAS THE CUB WHO WAS EATEN BY A BUNCH OF SALMON-PIRANHA HYBRIDS.
BURP!
THE PROBLEM WITH YOU IS THAT YOU CONSIDER YOURSELF INADEQUATE.
BUT BELIEVE ME . . . YOU'RE NOT ALONE.
I'M NOT?
COURSE NOT.
GEEZ, WE ALL CONSIDER YOU INADEQUATE.
OUCH!

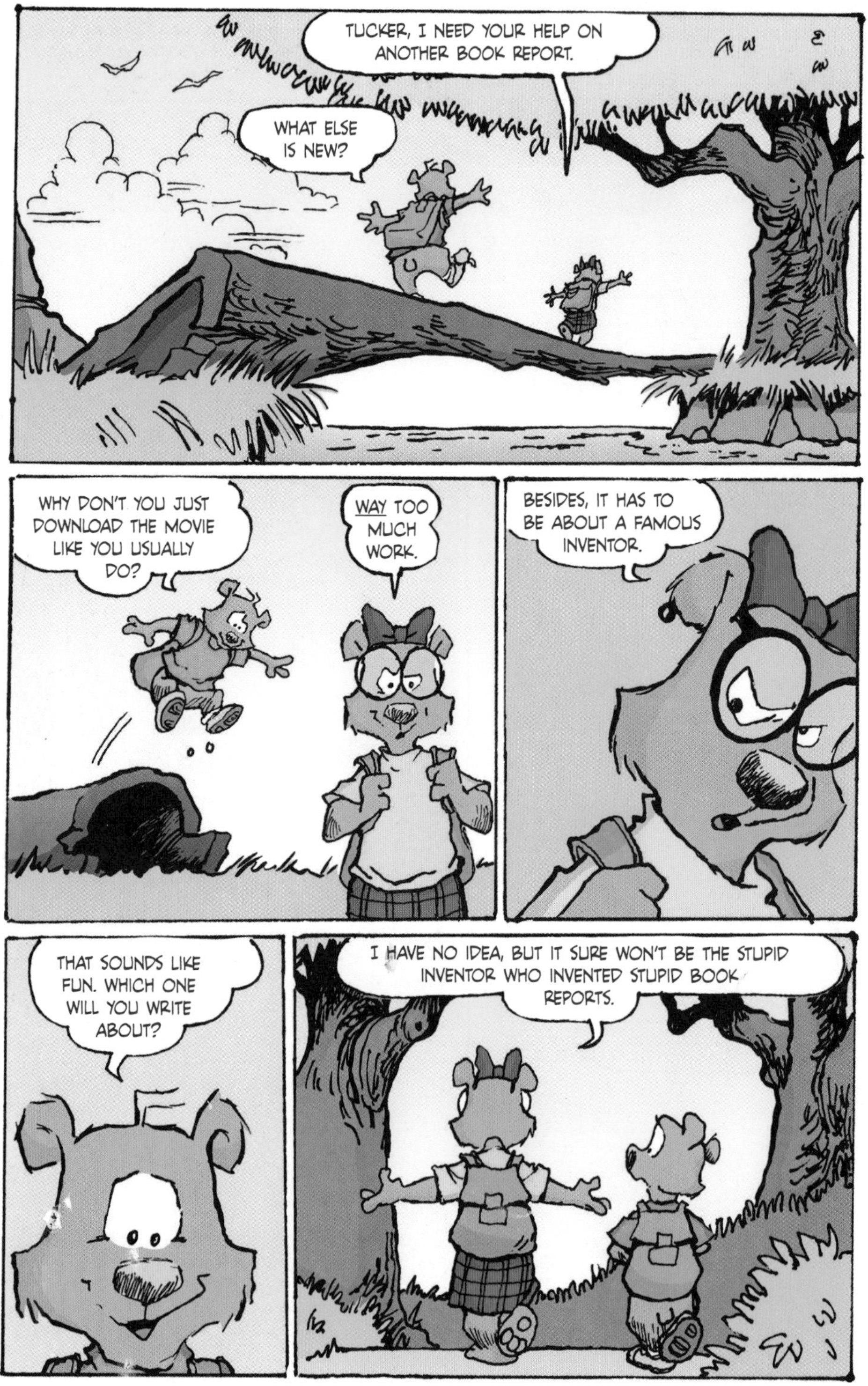
TUCKER, I NEED YOUR HELP ON ANOTHER BOOK REPORT.
WHAT ELSE IS NEW?
WHY DON'T YOU JUST DOWNLOAD THE MOVIE LIKE YOU USUALLY DO?
WAY TOO MUCH WORK.
BESIDES, IT HAS TO BE ABOUT A FAMOUS INVENTOR.
THAT SOUNDS LIKE FUN. WHICH ONE WILL YOU WRITE ABOUT?
I HAVE NO IDEA, BUT IT SURE WON'T BE THE STUPID INVENTOR WHO INVENTED STUPID BOOK REPORTS.

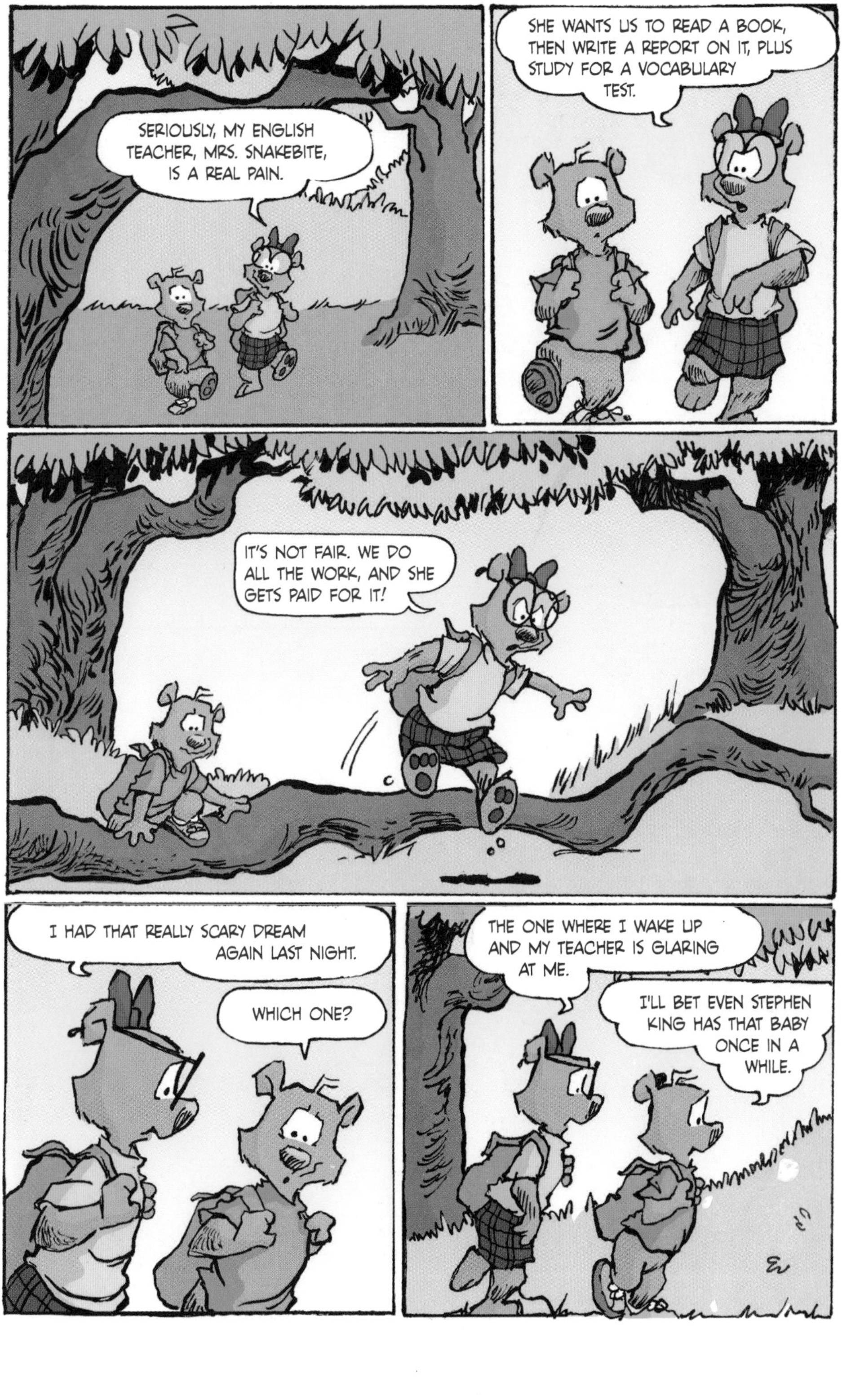
SERIOUSLY, MY ENGLISH TEACHER, MRS. SNAKEBITE, IS A REAL PAIN.
SHE WANTS US TO READ A BOOK, THEN WRITE A REPORT ON IT, PLUS STUDY FOR A VOCABULARY TEST.
IT'S NOT FAIR. WE DO ALL THE WORK, AND SHE GETS PAID FOR IT!
I HAD THAT REALLY SCARY DREAM AGAIN LAST NIGHT.
WHICH ONE?
THE ONE WHERE I WAKE UP AND MY TEACHER IS GLARING AT ME.
I'LL BET EVEN STEPHEN KING HAS THAT BABY ONCE IN A WHILE.

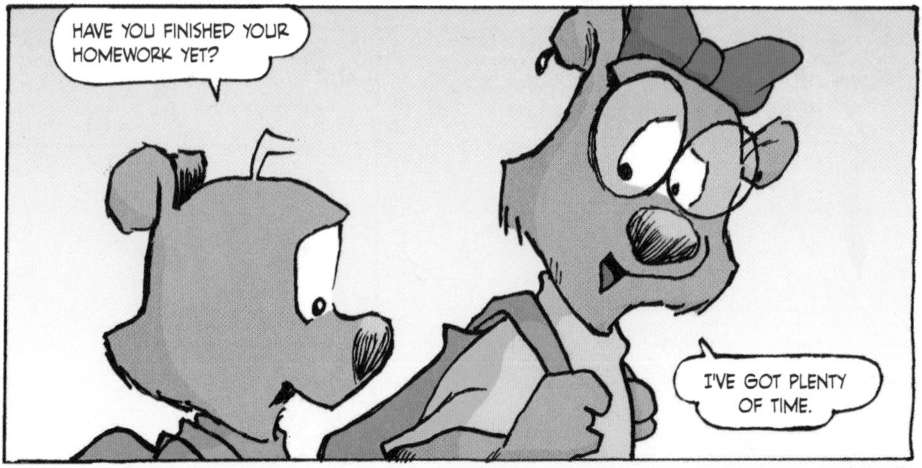
HAVE YOU FINISHED YOUR HOMEWORK YET?
I'VE GOT PLENTY OF TIME.

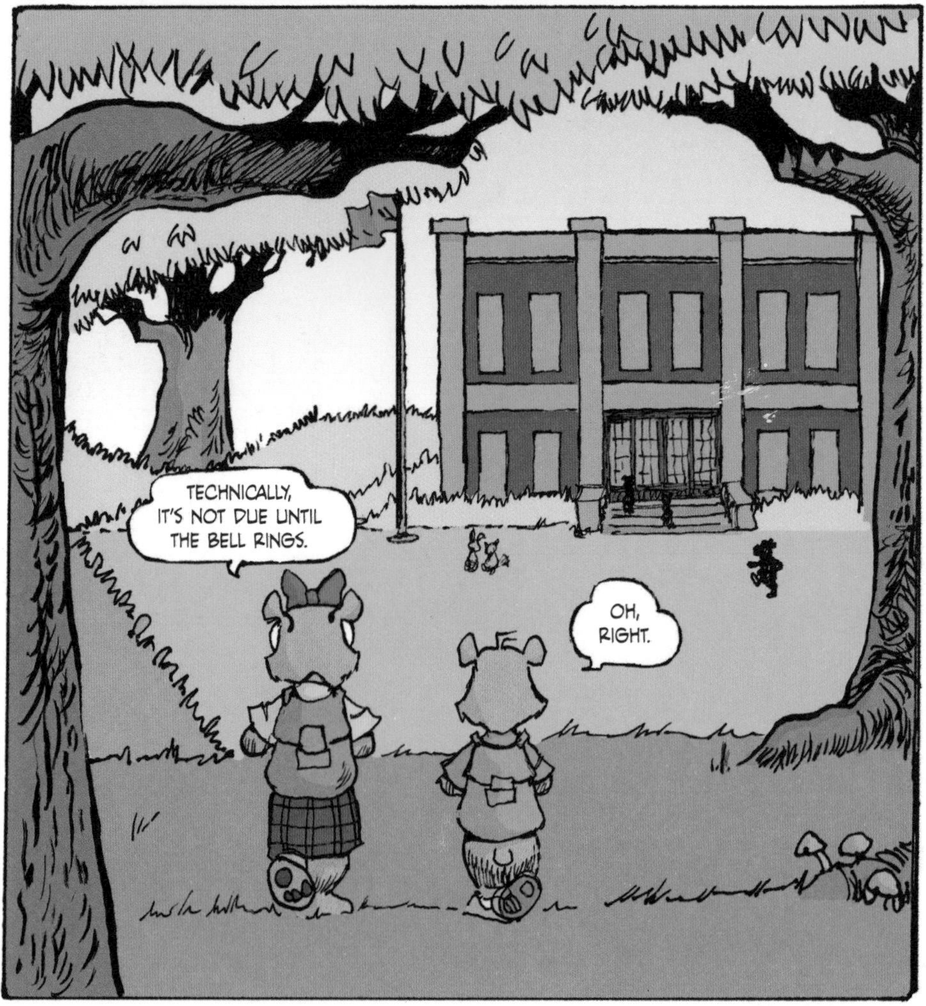
TECHNICALLY, IT'S NOT DUE UNTIL THE BELL RINGS.
OH, RIGHT.

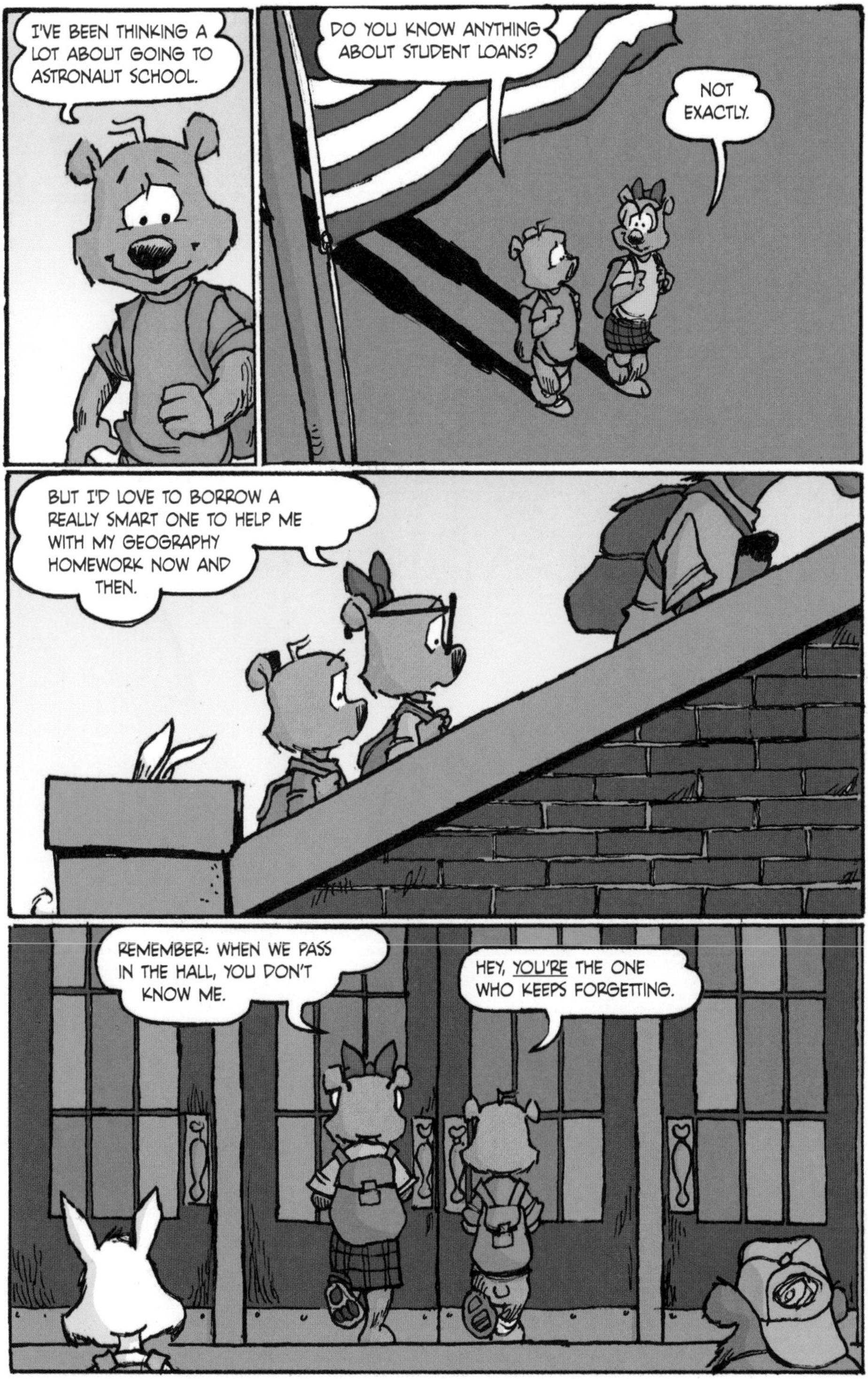
I'VE BEEN THINKING A LOT ABOUT GOING TO ASTRONAUT SCHOOL.
DO YOU KNOW ANYTHING ABOUT STUDENT LOANS?
NOT EXACTLY.
BUT I'D LOVE TO BORROW A REALLY SMART ONE TO HELP ME WITH MY GEOGRAPHY HOMEWORK NOW AND THEN.
REMEMBER: WHEN WE PASS IN THE HALL, YOU DON'T KNOW ME.
HEY, YOU'RE THE ONE WHO KEEPS FORGETTING.

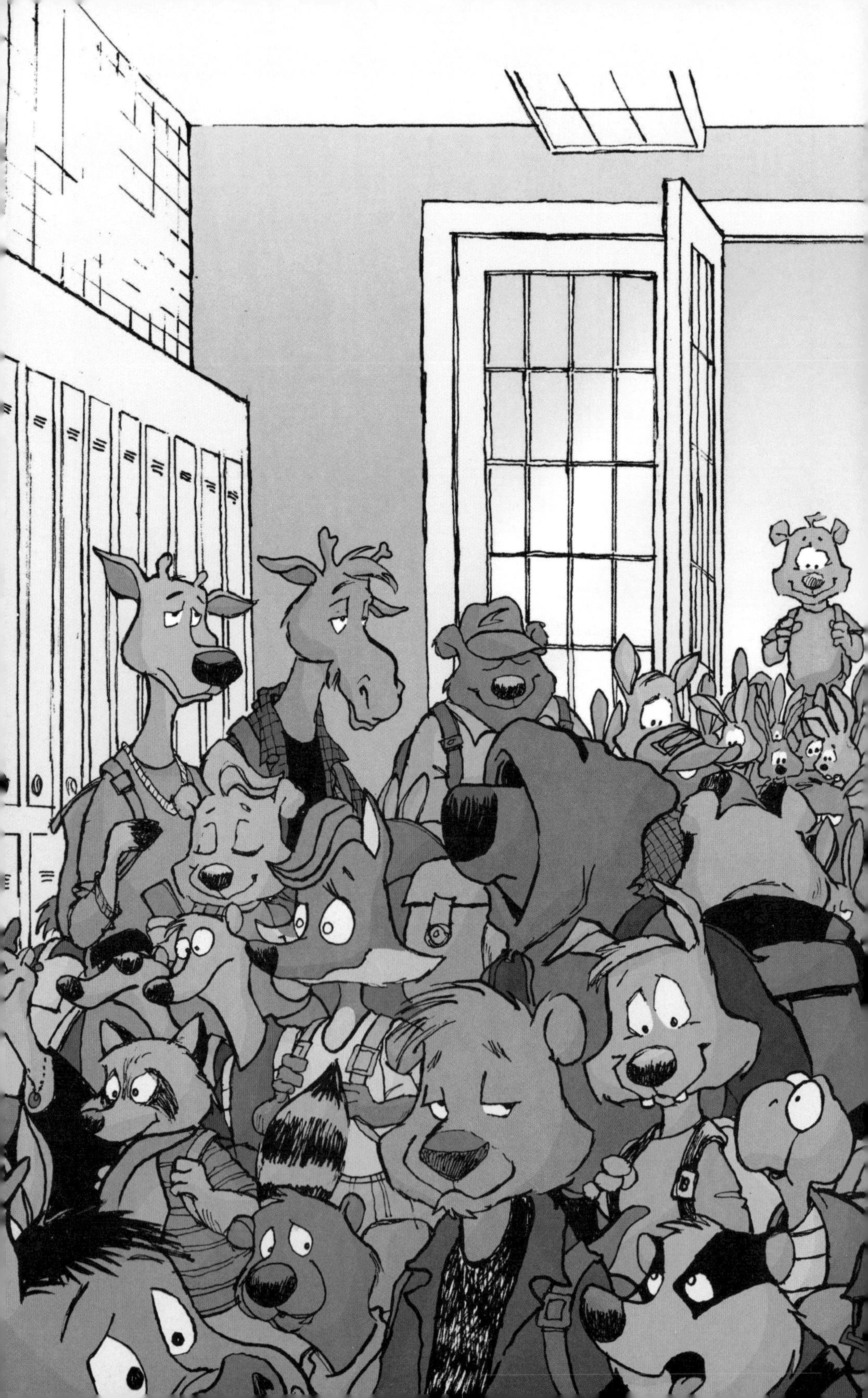

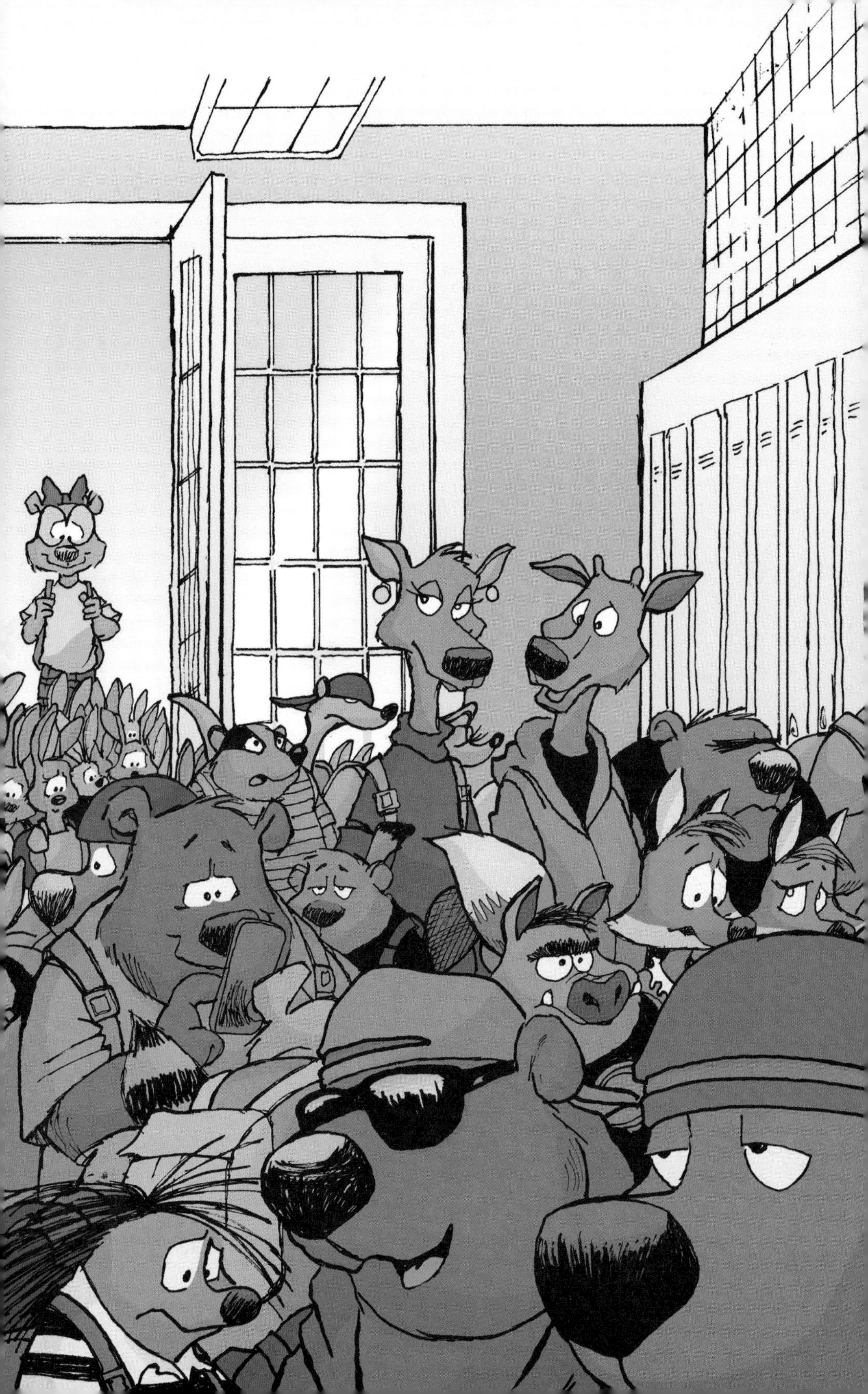

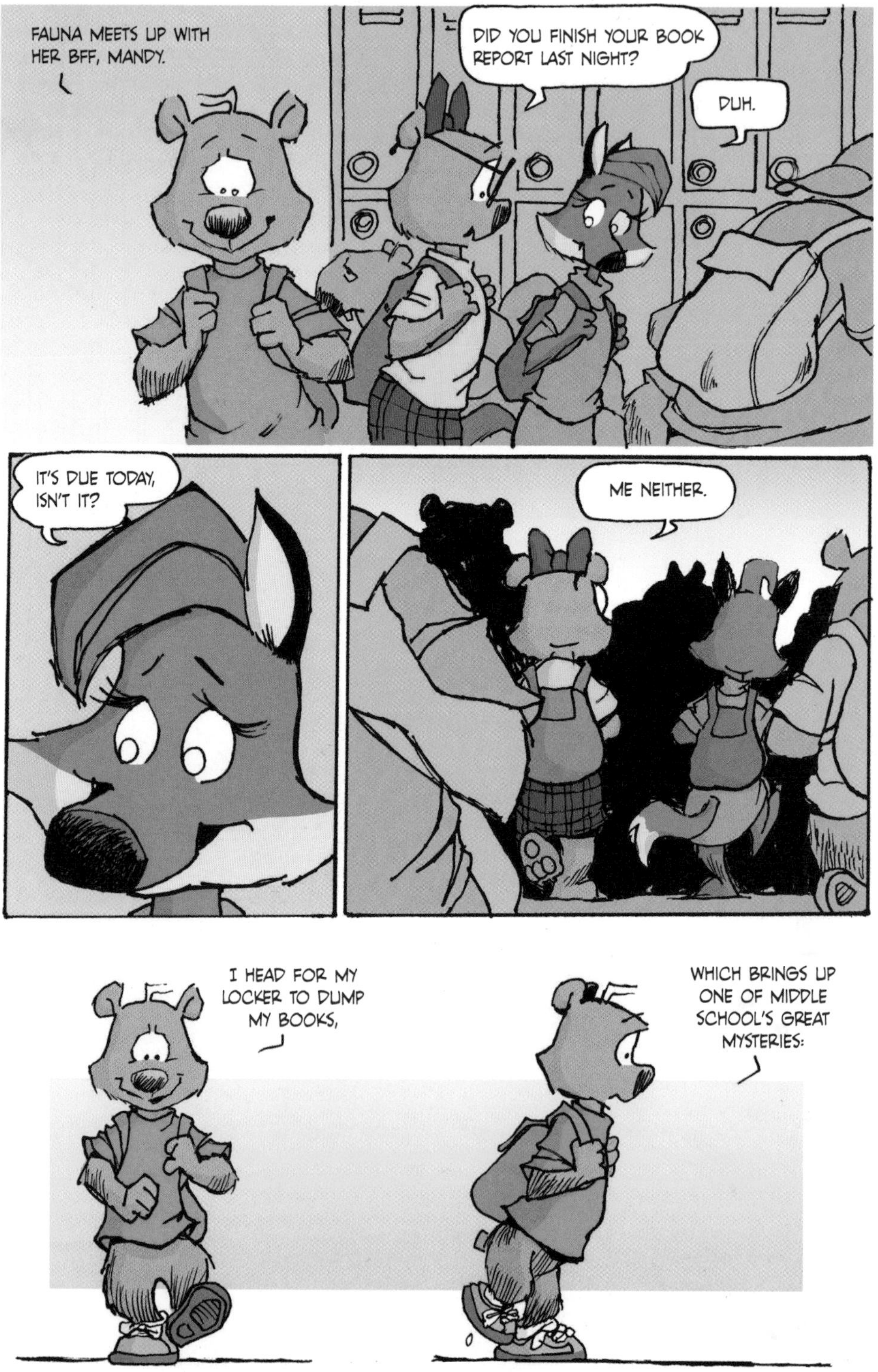
FAUNA MEETS UP WITH HER BFF, MANDY.
DID YOU FINISH YOUR BOOK REPORT LAST NIGHT?
DUH.
IT'S DUE TODAY, ISN'T IT?
ME NEITHER.
I HEAD FOR MY LOCKER TO DUMP MY BOOKS,
WHICH BRINGS UP ONE OF MIDDLE SCHOOL'S GREAT MYSTERIES:

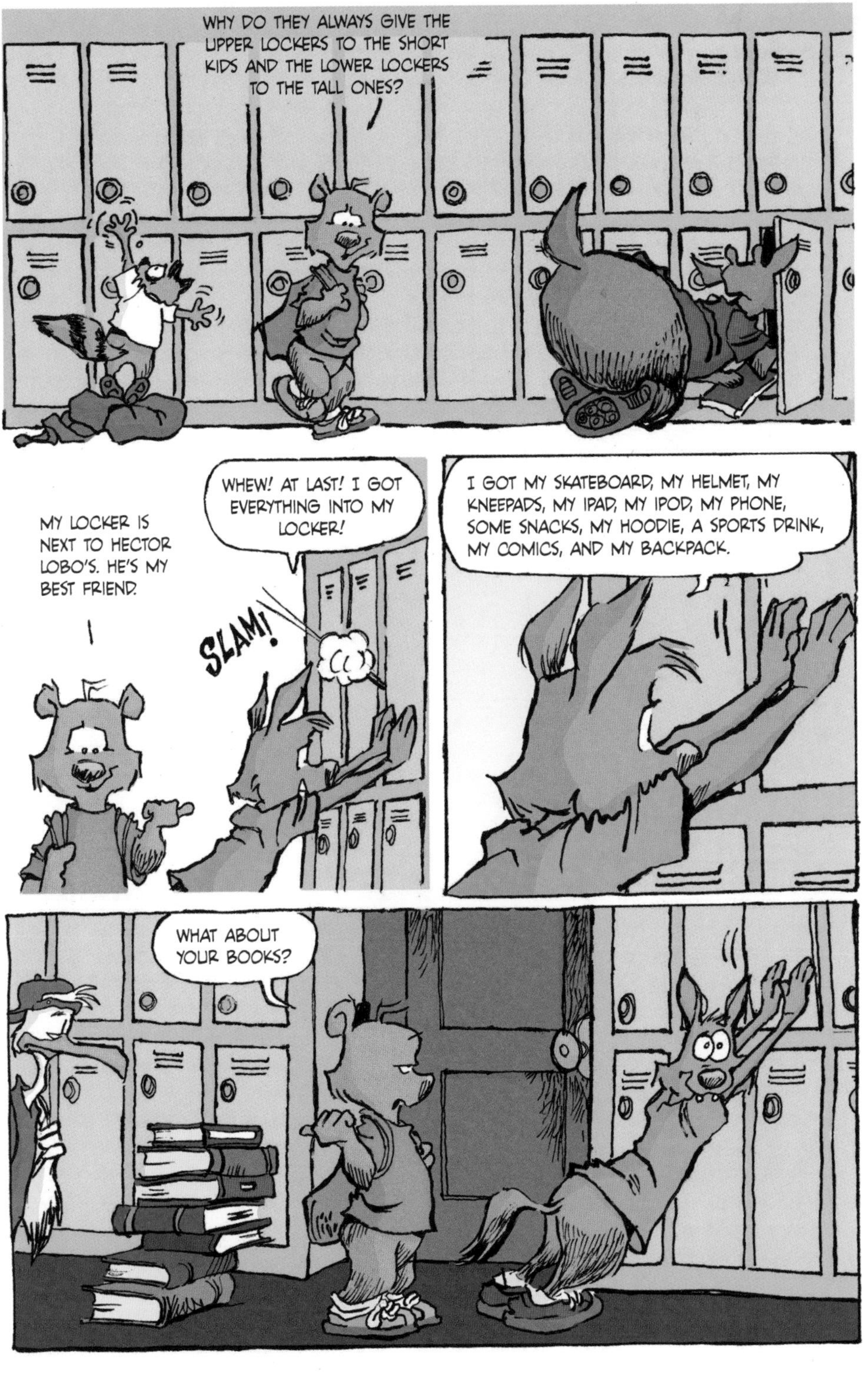
WHY DO THEY ALWAYS GIVE THE UPPER LOCKERS TO THE SHORT KIDS AND THE LOWER LOCKERS TO THE TALL ONES?
MY LOCKER IS NEXT TO HECTOR LOBO'S. HE'S MY BEST FRIEND.
WHEW! AT LAST! I GOT EVERYTHING INTO MY LOCKER!
SLAM!
I GOT MY SKATEBOARD, MY HELMET, MY KNEEPADS, MY IPAD, MY IPOD, MY PHONE, SOME SNACKS, MY HOODIE, A SPORTS DRINK, MY COMICS, AND MY BACKPACK.
WHAT ABOUT YOUR BOOKS?

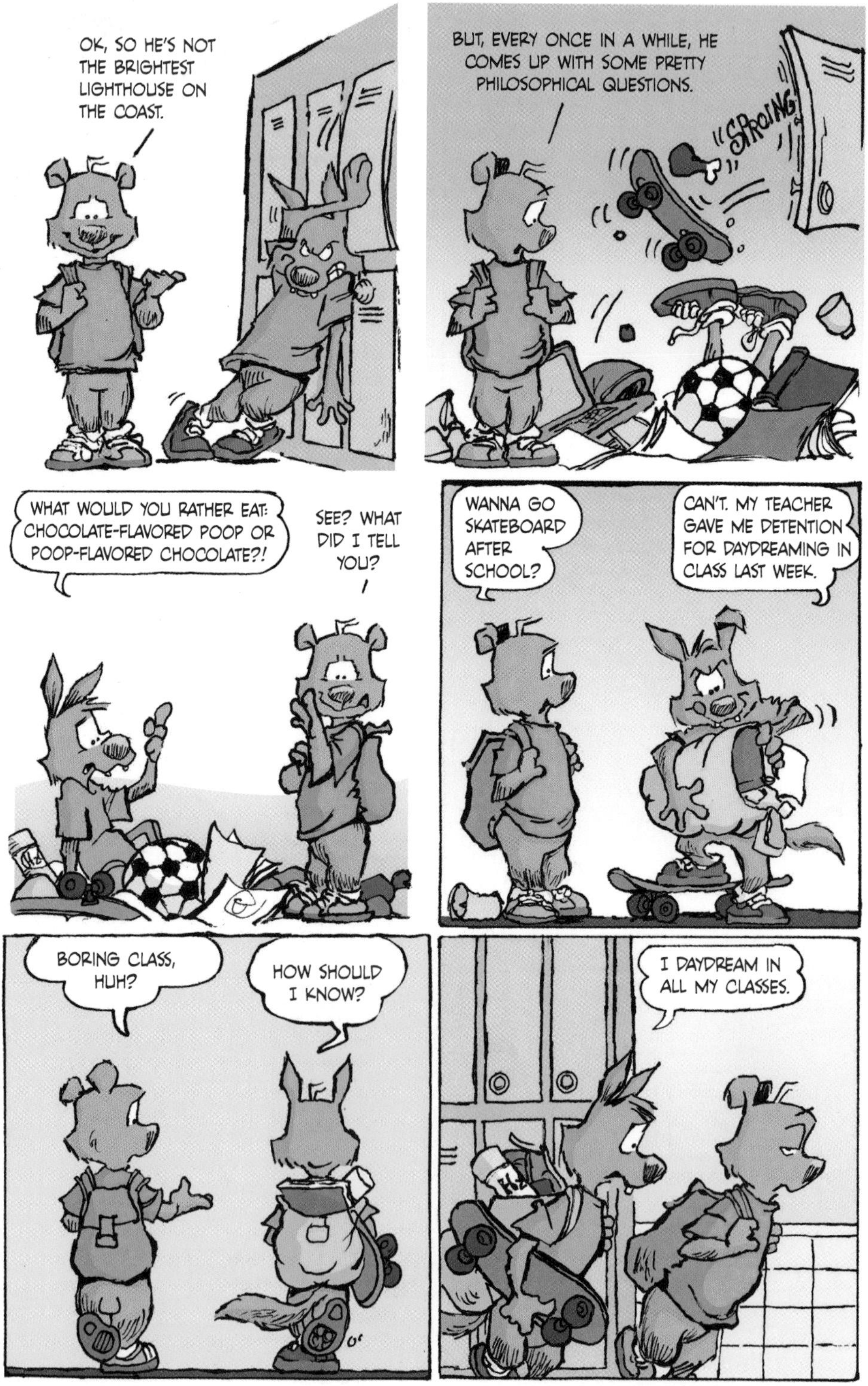

OK, SO HE'S NOT THE BRIGHTEST LIGHTHOUSE ON THE COAST.
BUT, EVERY ONCE IN A WHILE, HE COMES UP WITH SOME PRETTY PHILOSOPHICAL QUESTIONS.
SPROING
WHAT WOULD YOU RATHER EAT: CHOCOLATE-FLAVORED POOP OR POOP-FLAVORED CHOCOLATE?!
SEE? WHAT DID I TELL YOU?
WANNA GO SKATEBOARD AFTER SCHOOL?
CAN'T. MY TEACHER GAVE ME DETENTION FOR DAYDREAMING IN CLASS LAST WEEK.
BORING CLASS, HUH?
HOW SHOULD I KNOW?
I DAYDREAM IN ALL MY CLASSES.

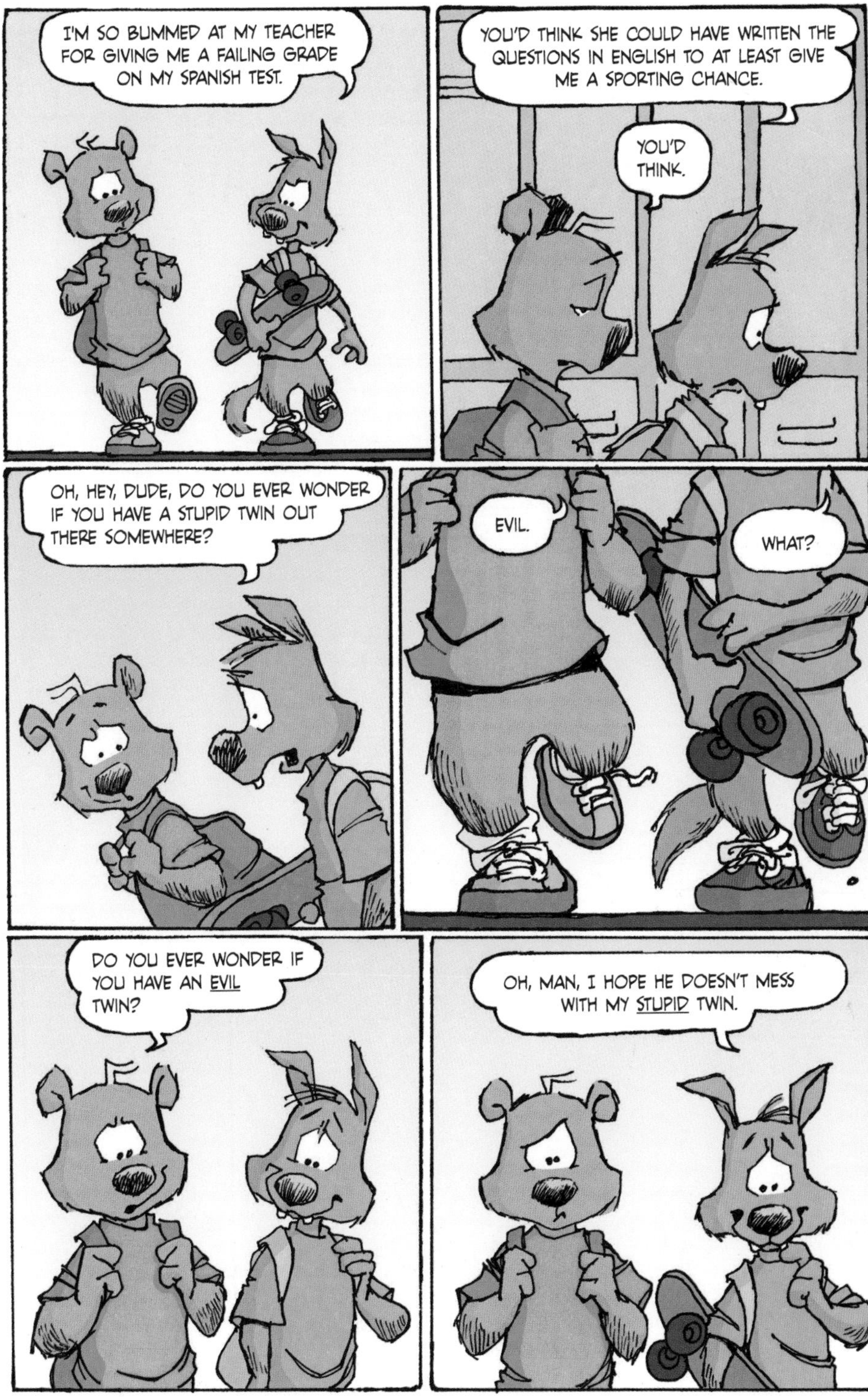
I'M SO BUMMED AT MY TEACHER FOR GIVING ME A FAILING GRADE ON MY SPANISH TEST.
YOU'D THINK SHE COULD HAVE WRITTEN THE QUESTIONS IN ENGLISH TO AT LEAST GIVE ME A SPORTING CHANCE.
YOU'D THINK.
OH, HEY, DUDE, DO YOU EVER WONDER IF YOU HAVE A STUPID TWIN OUT THERE SOMEWHERE?
EVIL.
WHAT?
DO YOU EVER WONDER IF YOU HAVE AN EVIL TWIN?
OH, MAN, I HOPE HE DOESN'T MESS WITH MY STUPID TWIN.

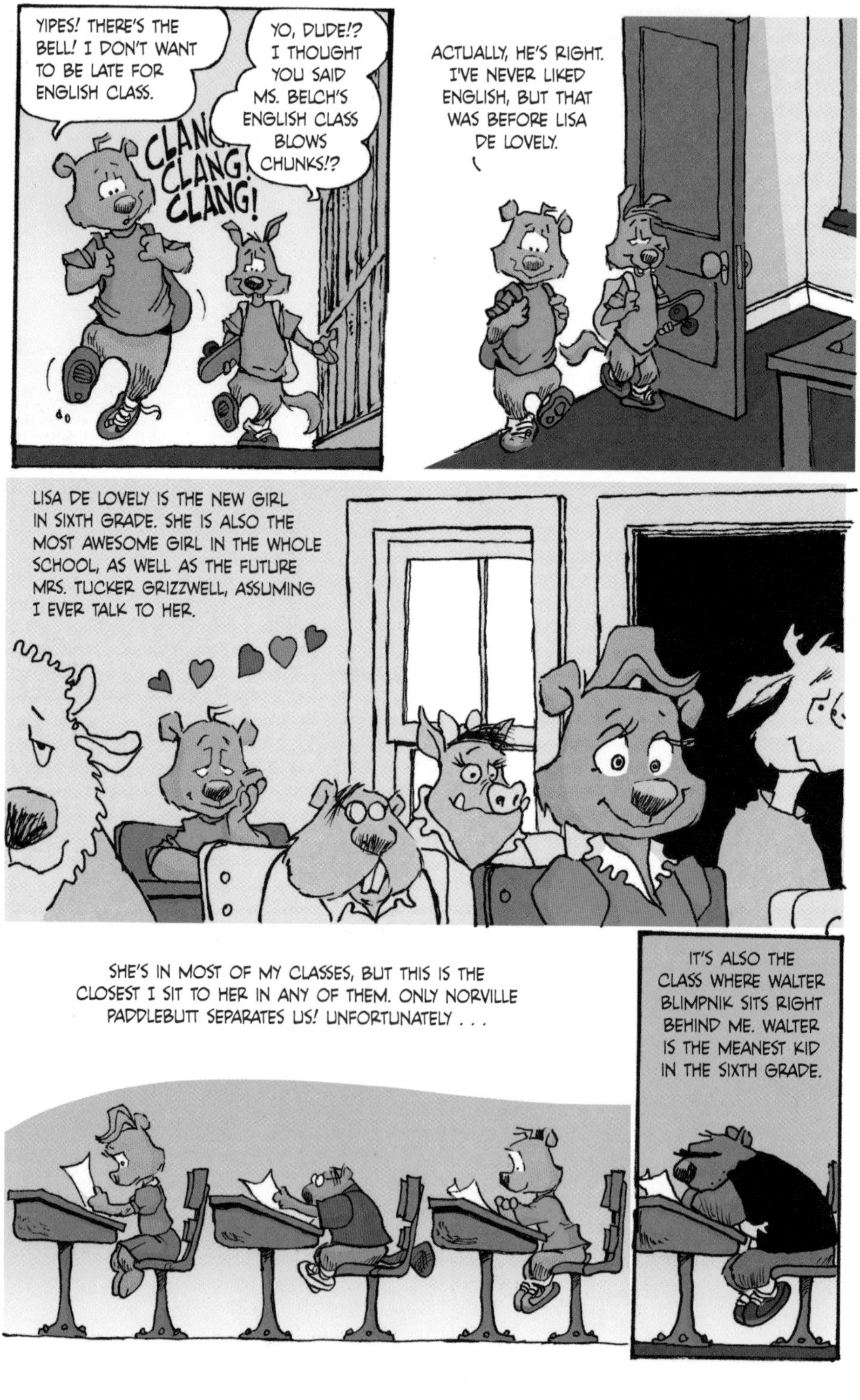
YIPES! THERE'S THE BELL! I DON'T WANT TO BE LATE FOR ENGLISH CLASS.
CLANG! CLANG! CLANG!
YO, DUDE!? I THOUGHT YOU SAID MS. BELCH'S ENGLISH CLASS BLOWS CHUNKS!?
ACTUALLY, HE'S RIGHT. I'VE NEVER LIKED ENGLISH, BUT THAT WAS BEFORE LISA DE LOVELY.
LISA DE LOVELY IS THE NEW GIRL IN SIXTH GRADE. SHE IS ALSO THE MOST AWESOME GIRL IN THE WHOLE SCHOOL, AS WELL AS THE FUTURE MRS. TUCKER GRIZZWELL, ASSUMING I EVER TALK TO HER.
SHE'S IN MOST OF MY CLASSES, BUT THIS IS THE CLOSEST I SIT TO HER IN ANY OF THEM. ONLY NORVILLE PADDLEBUTT SEPARATES US! UNFORTUNATELY . . .
IT'S ALSO THE CLASS WHERE WALTER BLIMPNIK SITS RIGHT BEHIND ME. WALTER IS THE MEANEST KID IN THE SIXTH GRADE.

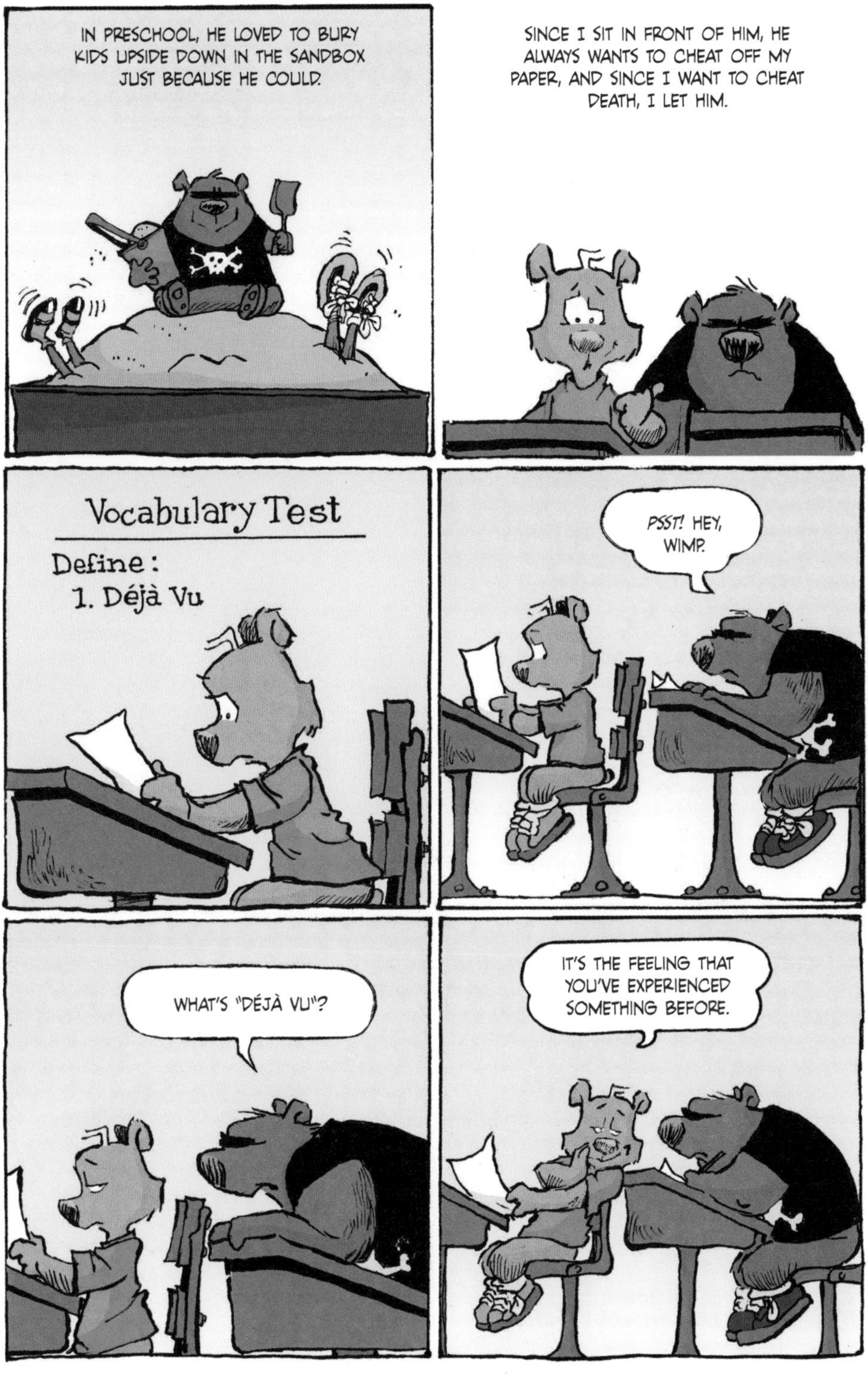
IN PRESCHOOL, HE LOVED TO BURY KIDS UPSIDE DOWN IN THE SANDBOX JUST BECAUSE HE COULD.
SINCE I SIT IN FRONT OF HIM, HE ALWAYS WANTS TO CHEAT OFF MY PAPER, AND SINCE I WANT TO CHEAT DEATH, I LET HIM.
Vocabulary Test
Define:
1. Déjà Vu
PSST! HEY, WIMP.
WHAT'S "DÉJÀ VU"?
IT'S THE FEELING THAT YOU'VE EXPERIENCED SOMETHING BEFORE.

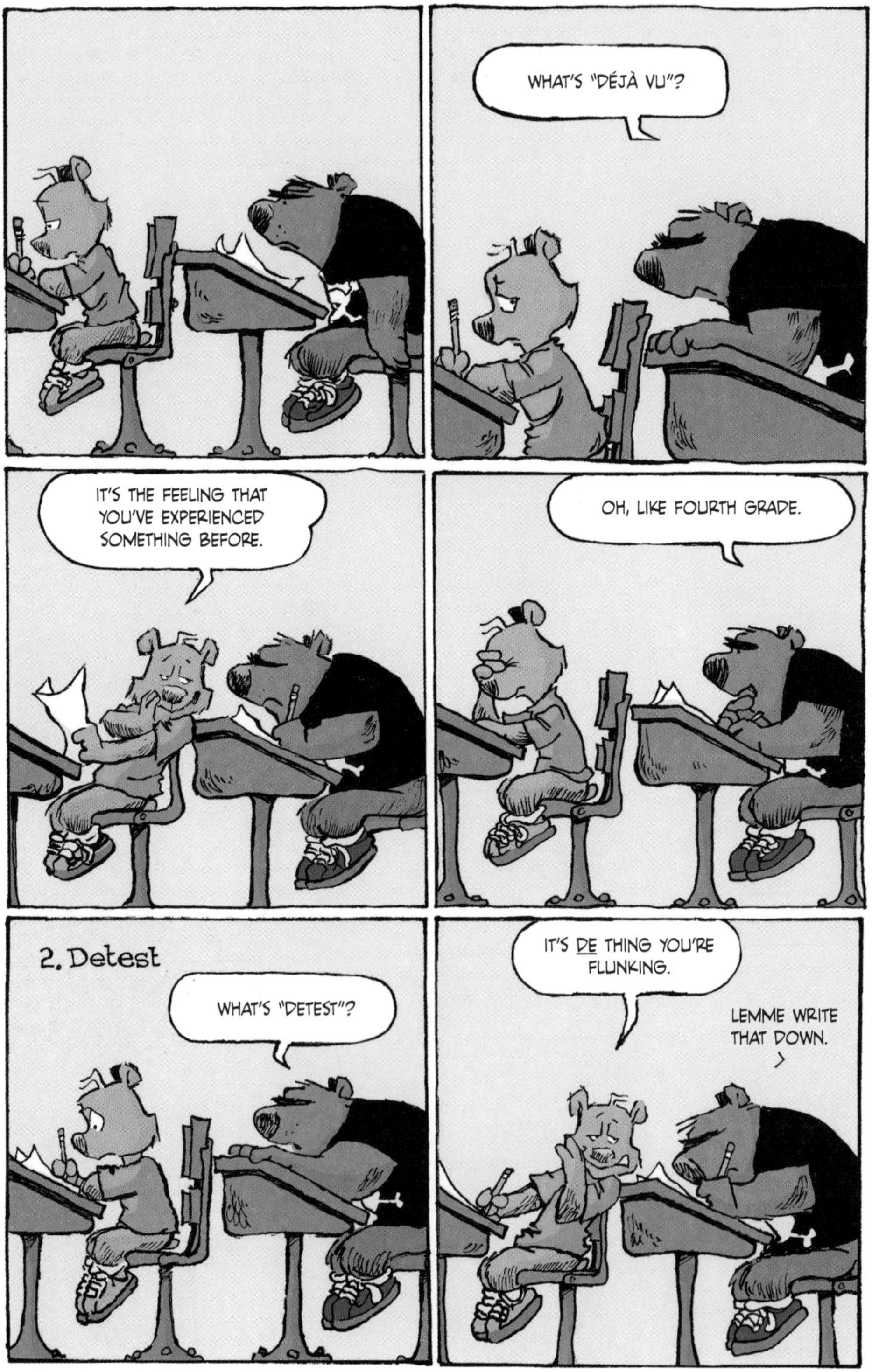
WHAT'S "DÉJÀ VU"?
IT'S THE FEELING THAT YOU'VE EXPERIENCED SOMETHING BEFORE.
OH, LIKE FOURTH GRADE.
2. Detest
WHAT'S "DETEST"?
IT'S DE THING YOU'RE FLUNKING.
LEMME WRITE THAT DOWN.

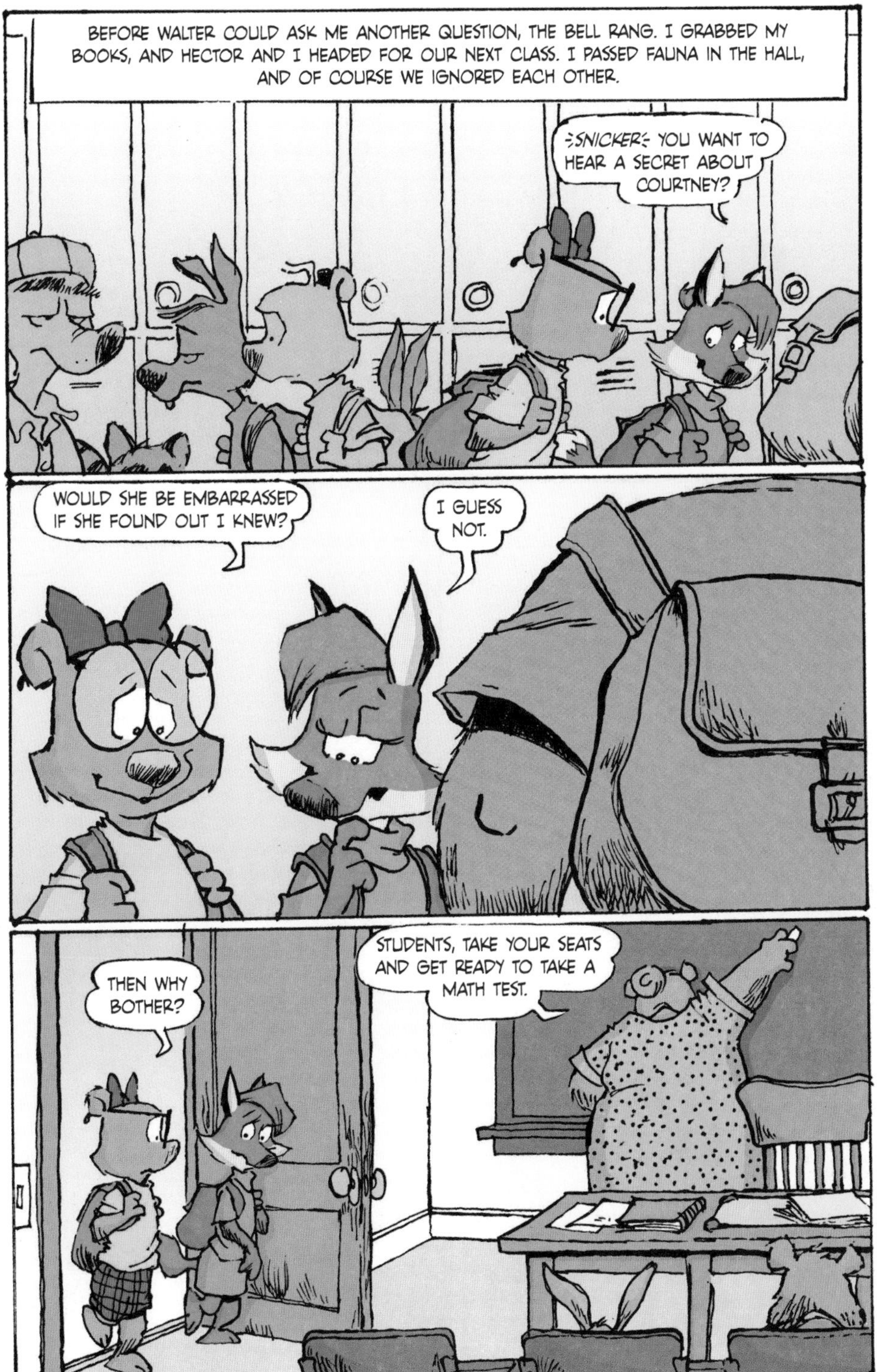
BEFORE WALTER COULD ASK ME ANOTHER QUESTION, THE BELL RANG. I GRABBED MY BOOKS, AND HECTOR AND I HEADED FOR OUR NEXT CLASS. I PASSED FAUNA IN THE HALL, AND OF COURSE WE IGNORED EACH OTHER.
SNICKER YOU WANT TO HEAR A SECRET ABOUT COURTNEY?
WOULD SHE BE EMBARRASSED IF SHE FOUND OUT I KNEW?
I GUESS NOT.
THEN WHY BOTHER?
STUDENTS, TAKE YOUR SEATS AND GET READY TO TAKE A MATH TEST.

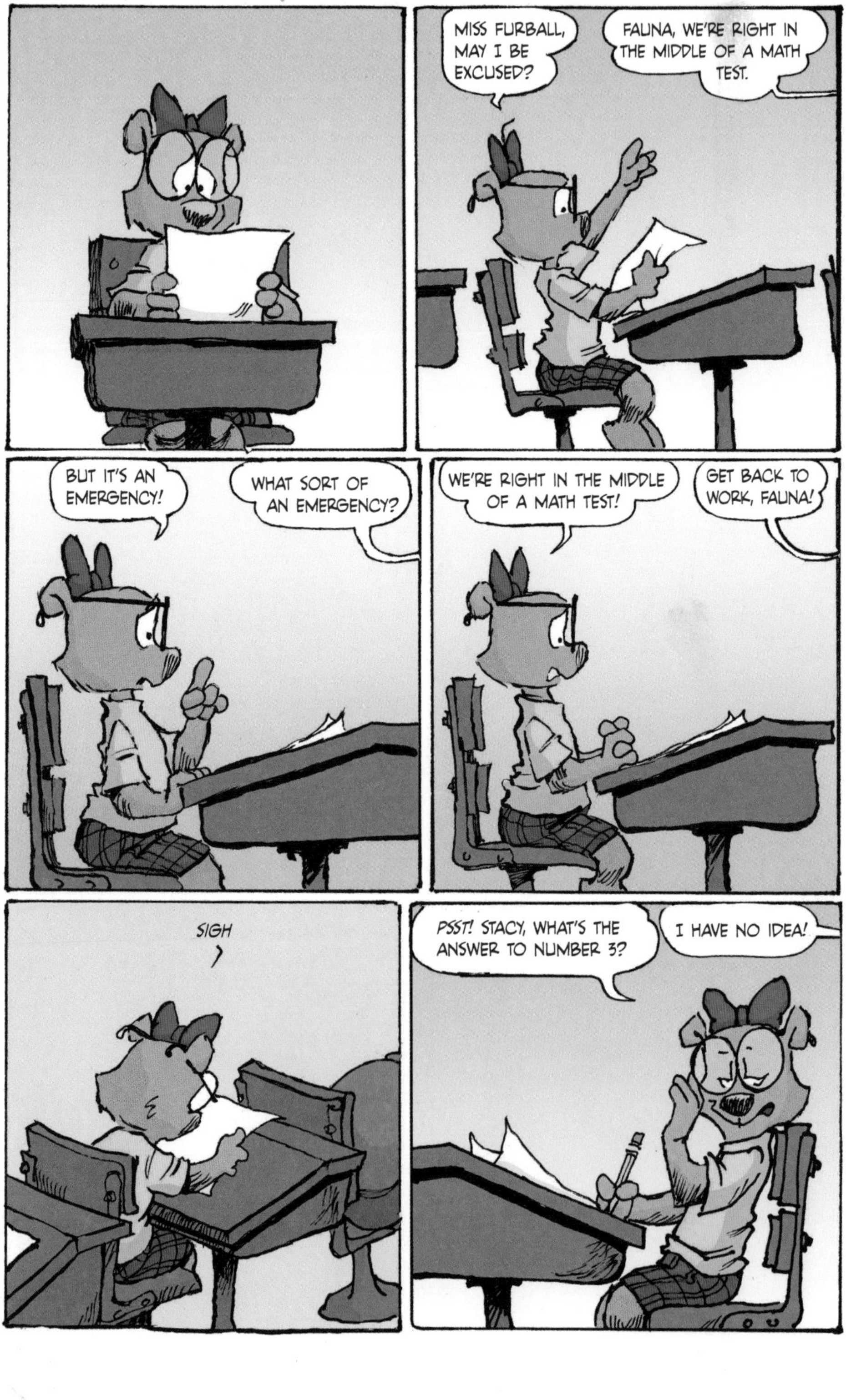
MISS FURBALL, MAY I BE EXCUSED?
FAUNA, WE'RE RIGHT IN THE MIDDLE OF A MATH TEST.
BUT IT'S AN EMERGENCY!
WHAT SORT OF AN EMERGENCY?
WE'RE RIGHT IN THE MIDDLE OF A MATH TEST!
GET BACK TO WORK, FAUNA!
SIGH
PSST! STACY, WHAT'S THE ANSWER TO NUMBER 3?
I HAVE NO IDEA!

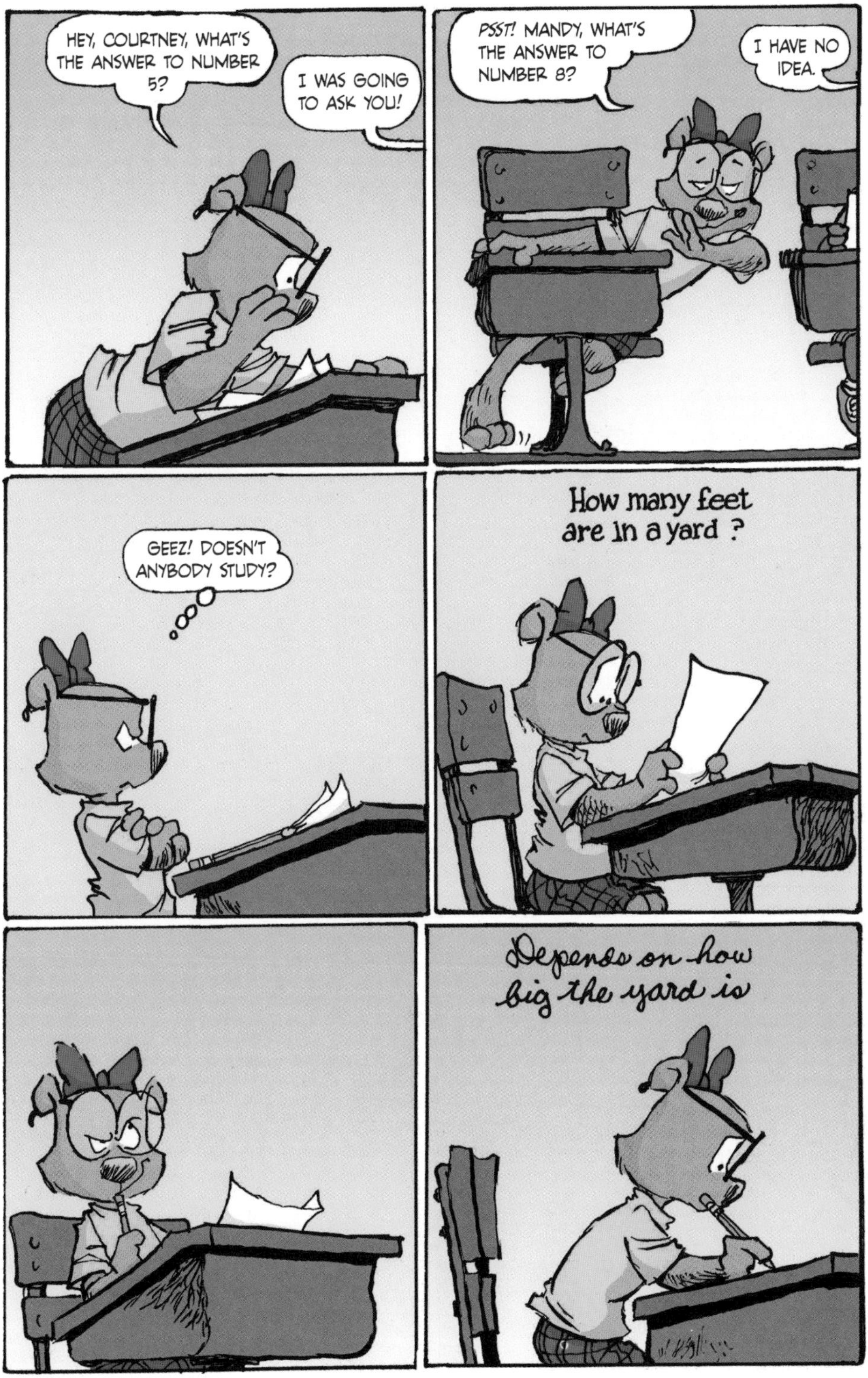
HEY, COURTNEY, WHAT'S THE ANSWER TO NUMBER 5?
I WAS GOING TO ASK YOU!
PSST! MANDY, WHAT'S THE ANSWER TO NUMBER 8?
I HAVE NO IDEA.
GEEZ! DOESN'T ANYBODY STUDY?
How many feet are in a yard ?
Depends on how big the yard is

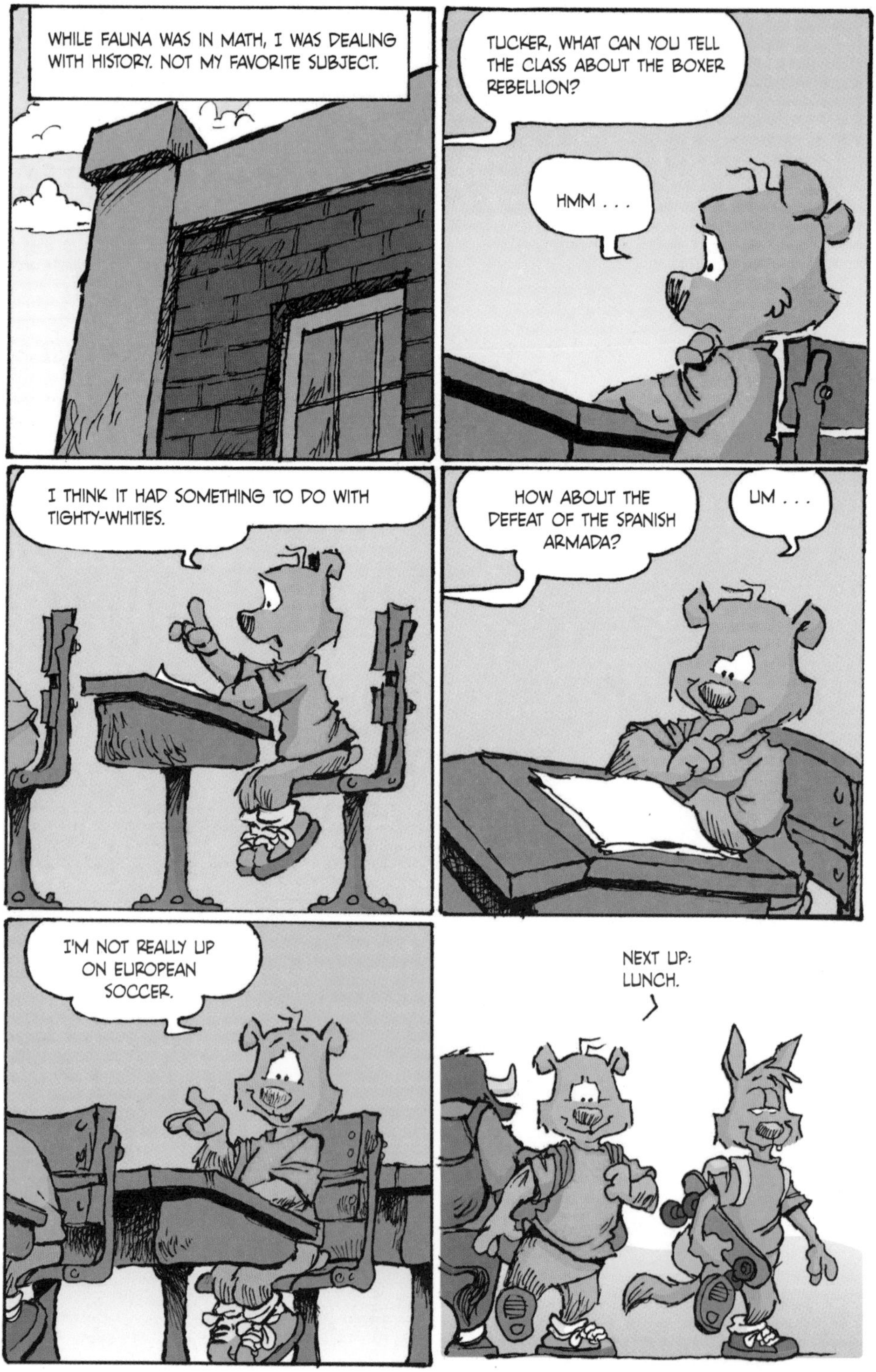
WHILE FAUNA WAS IN MATH, I WAS DEALING WITH HISTORY. NOT MY FAVORITE SUBJECT.
TUCKER, WHAT CAN YOU TELL THE CLASS ABOUT THE BOXER REBELLION?
HMM . . .
I THINK IT HAD SOMETHING TO DO WITH TIGHTY-WHITIES.
HOW ABOUT THE DEFEAT OF THE SPANISH ARMADA?
UM . . .
I'M NOT REALLY UP ON EUROPEAN SOCCER.
NEXT UP: LUNCH.

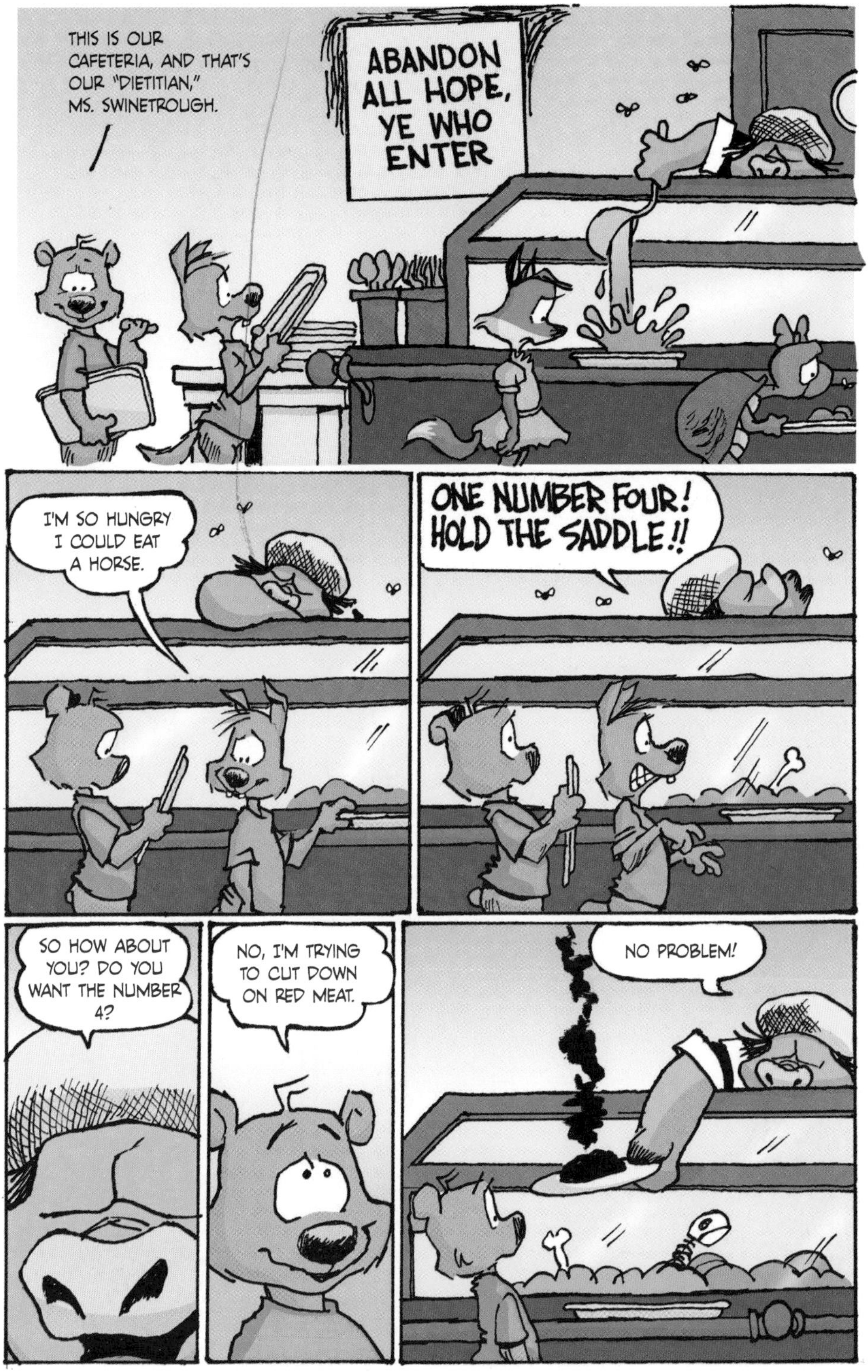
THIS IS OUR CAFETERIA, AND THAT'S OUR "DIETITIAN," MS. SWINETROUGH.
ABANDON ALL HOPE, YE WHO ENTER
I'M SO HUNGRY I COULD EAT A HORSE.
ONE NUMBER FOUR! HOLD THE SADDLE!!
SO HOW ABOUT YOU? DO YOU WANT THE NUMBER 4?
NO, I'M TRYING TO CUT DOWN ON RED MEAT.
NO PROBLEM!

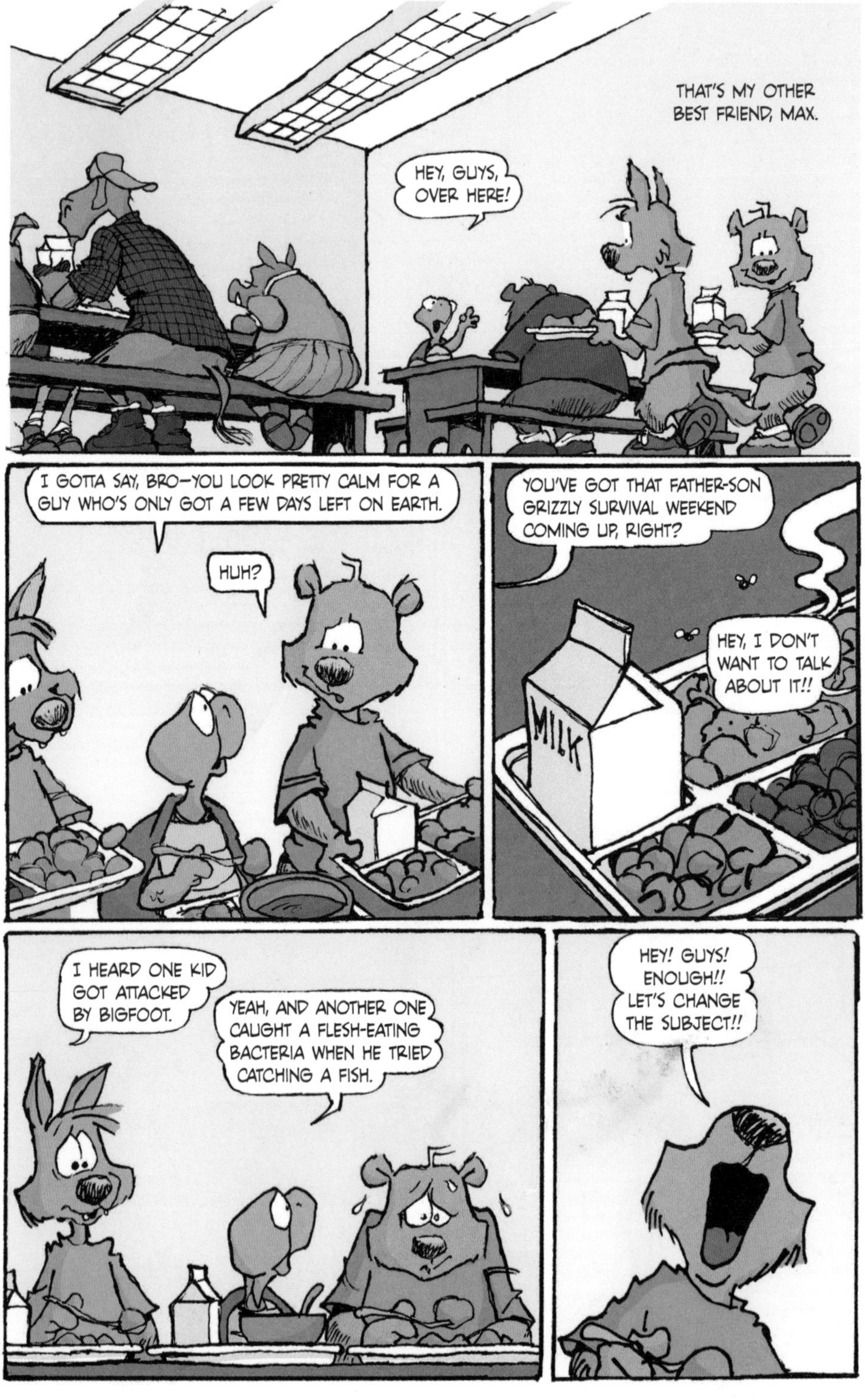
THAT'S MY OTHER BEST FRIEND, MAX.
HEY, GUYS, OVER HERE!
I GOTTA SAY, BRO—YOU LOOK PRETTY CALM FOR A GUY WHO'S ONLY GOT A FEW DAYS LEFT ON EARTH.
HUH?
YOU'VE GOT THAT FATHER-SON GRIZZLY SURVIVAL WEEKEND COMING UP, RIGHT?
MILK
HEY, I DON'T WANT TO TALK ABOUT IT!!
I HEARD ONE KID GOT ATTACKED BY BIGFOOT.
YEAH, AND ANOTHER ONE CAUGHT A FLESH-EATING BACTERIA WHEN HE TRIED CATCHING A FISH.
HEY! GUYS! ENOUGH!! LET'S CHANGE THE SUBJECT!!

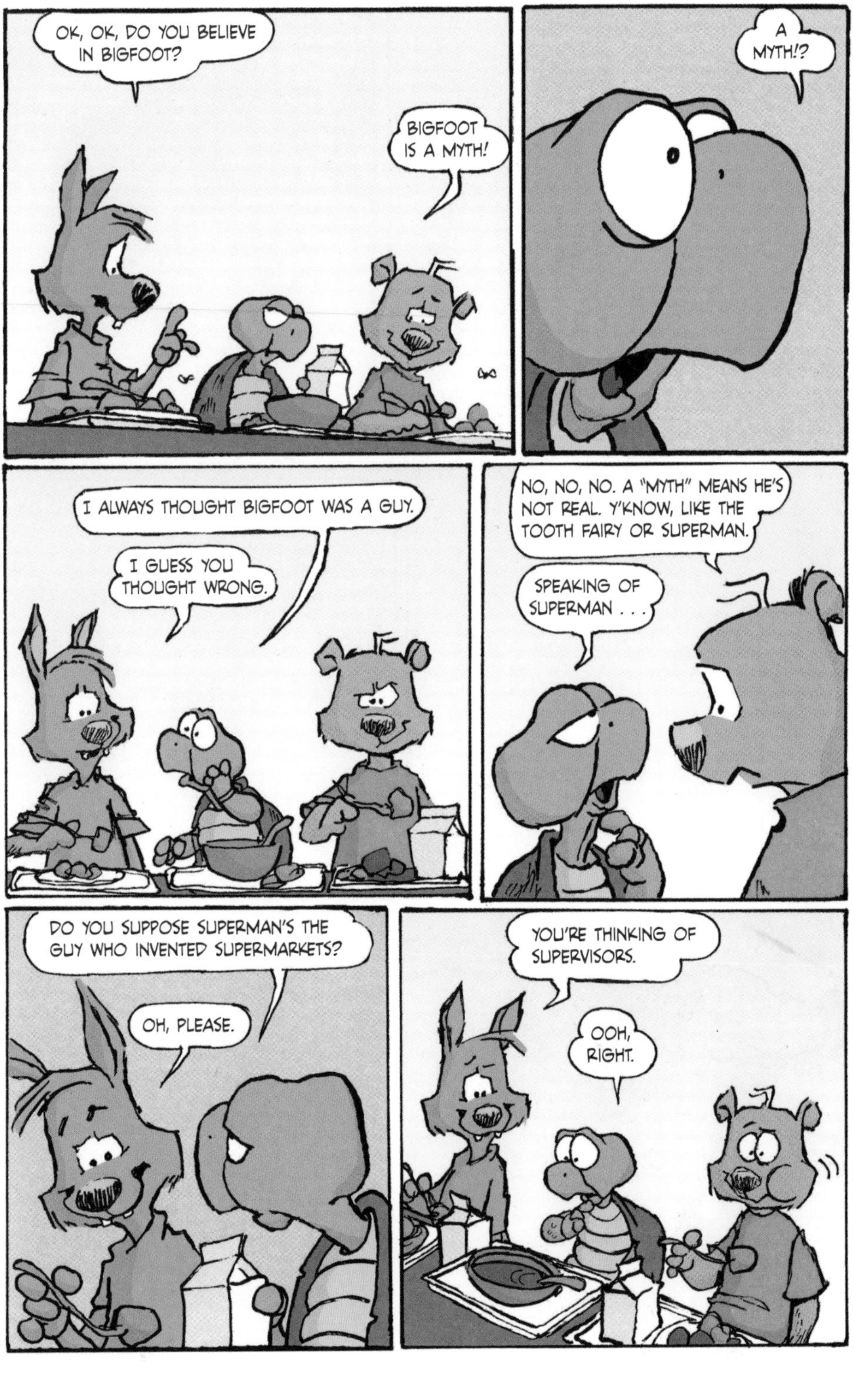
OK, OK, DO YOU BELIEVE IN BIGFOOT?
BIGFOOT IS A MYTH!
A MYTH!?
I ALWAYS THOUGHT BIGFOOT WAS A GUY.
I GUESS YOU THOUGHT WRONG.
NO, NO, NO. A "MYTH" MEANS HE'S NOT REAL. Y'KNOW, LIKE THE TOOTH FAIRY OR SUPERMAN.
SPEAKING OF SUPERMAN . . .
DO YOU SUPPOSE SUPERMAN'S THE GUY WHO INVENTED SUPERMARKETS?
OH, PLEASE.
YOU'RE THINKING OF SUPERVISORS.
OOH, RIGHT.

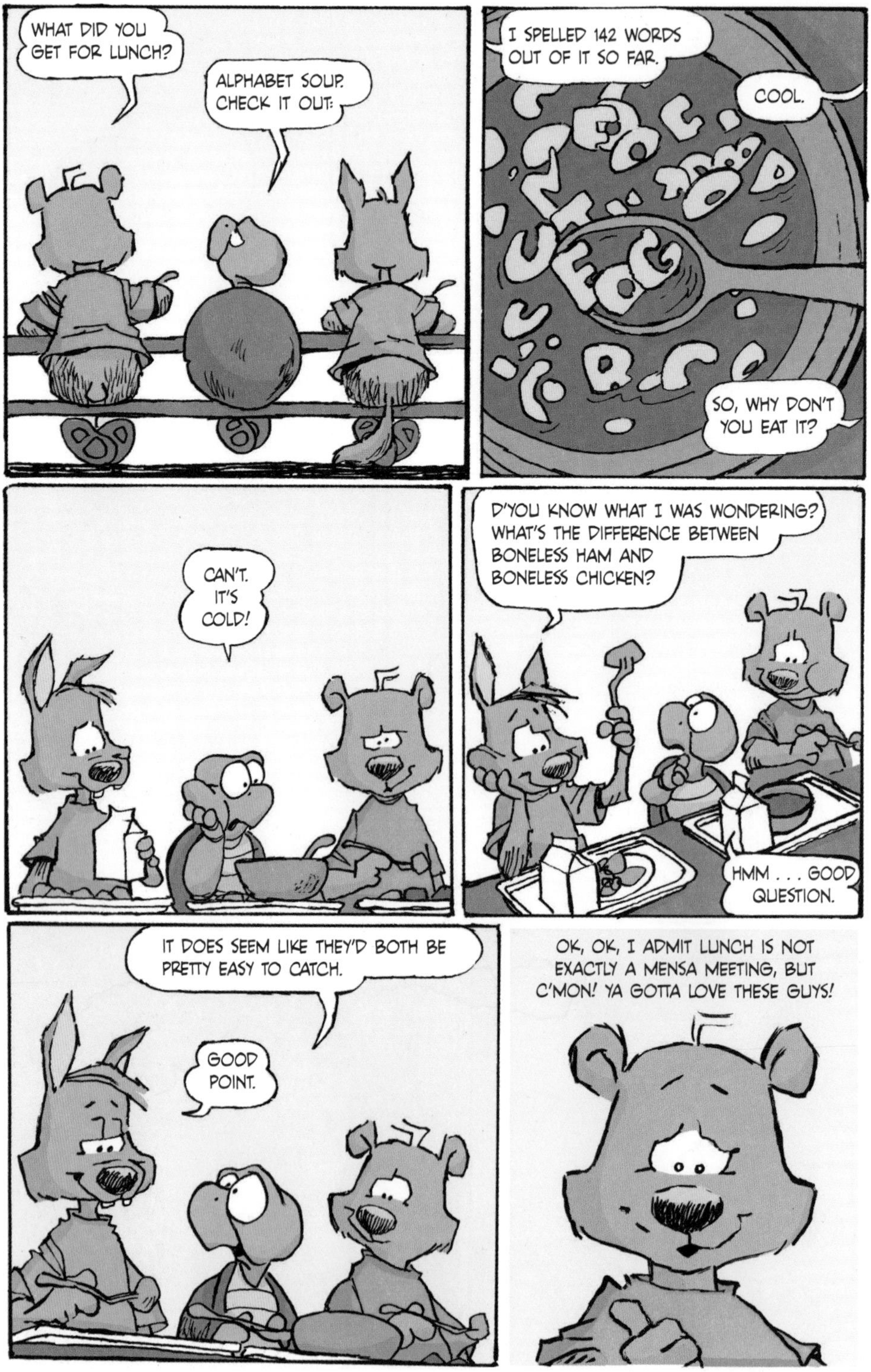
WHAT DID YOU GET FOR LUNCH?
ALPHABET SOUP. CHECK IT OUT:
I SPELLED 142 WORDS OUT OF IT SO FAR.
COOL.
SO, WHY DON'T YOU EAT IT?
CAN'T. IT'S COLD!
D'YOU KNOW WHAT I WAS WONDERING? WHAT'S THE DIFFERENCE BETWEEN BONELESS HAM AND BONELESS CHICKEN?
HMM . . . GOOD QUESTION.
IT DOES SEEM LIKE THEY'D BOTH BE PRETTY EASY TO CATCH.
GOOD POINT.
OK, OK, I ADMIT LUNCH IS NOT EXACTLY A MENSA MEETING, BUT C'MON! YA GOTTA LOVE THESE GUYS!

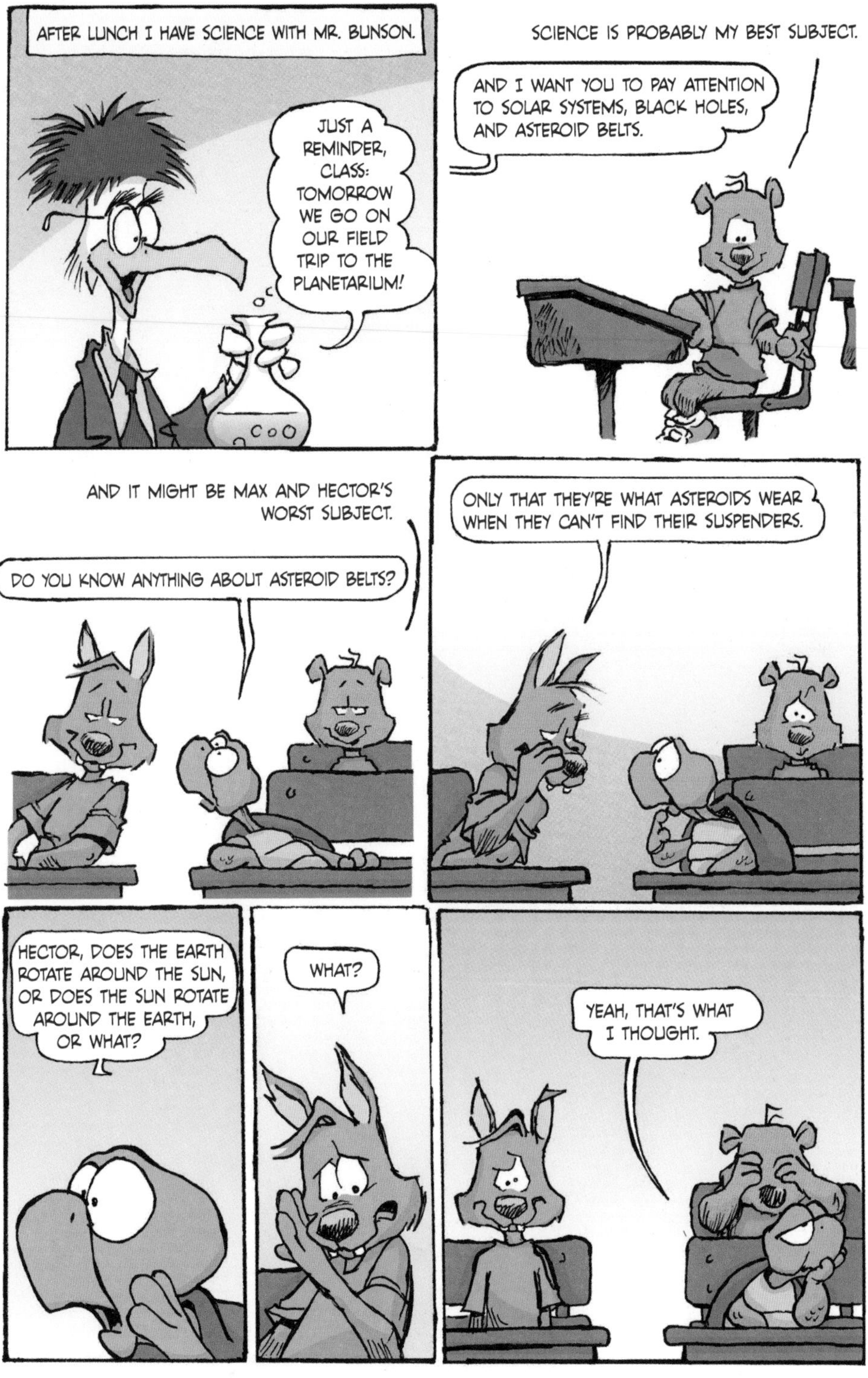

AFTER LUNCH I HAVE SCIENCE WITH MR. BUNSON.
JUST A REMINDER, CLASS: TOMORROW WE GO ON OUR FIELD TRIP TO THE PLANETARIUM!
SCIENCE IS PROBABLY MY BEST SUBJECT.
AND I WANT YOU TO PAY ATTENTION TO SOLAR SYSTEMS, BLACK HOLES, AND ASTEROID BELTS.
AND IT MIGHT BE MAX AND HECTOR'S WORST SUBJECT.
DO YOU KNOW ANYTHING ABOUT ASTEROID BELTS?
ONLY THAT THEY'RE WHAT ASTEROIDS WEAR WHEN THEY CAN'T FIND THEIR SUSPENDERS.
HECTOR, DOES THE EARTH ROTATE AROUND THE SUN, OR DOES THE SUN ROTATE AROUND THE EARTH, OR WHAT?
WHAT?
YEAH, THAT'S WHAT I THOUGHT.

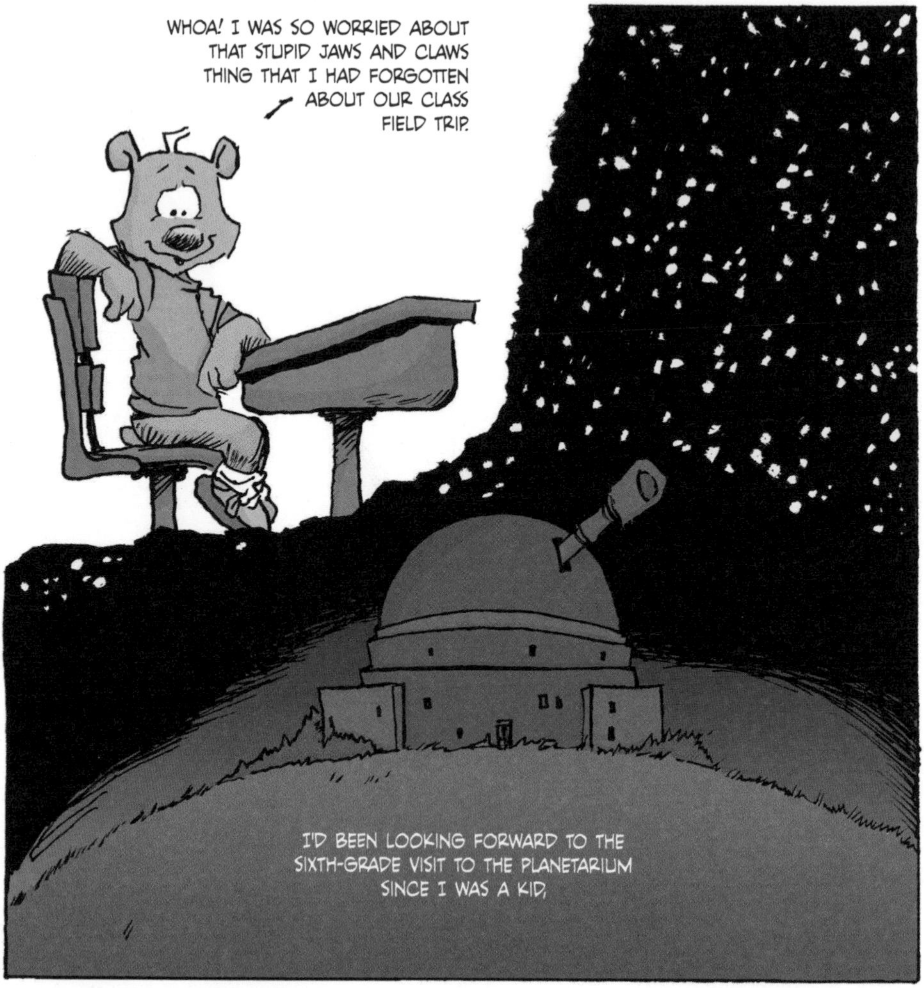
WHOA! I WAS SO WORRIED ABOUT THAT STUPID JAWS AND CLAWS THING THAT I HAD FORGOTTEN ABOUT OUR CLASS FIELD TRIP.
I'D BEEN LOOKING FORWARD TO THE SIXTH-GRADE VISIT TO THE PLANETARIUM SINCE I WAS A KID,

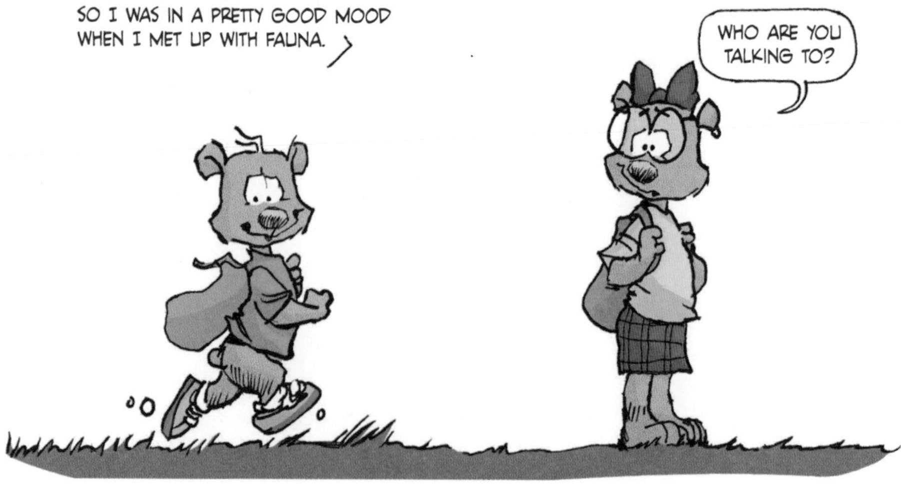
SO I WAS IN A PRETTY GOOD MOOD WHEN I MET UP WITH FAUNA.
WHO ARE YOU TALKING TO?

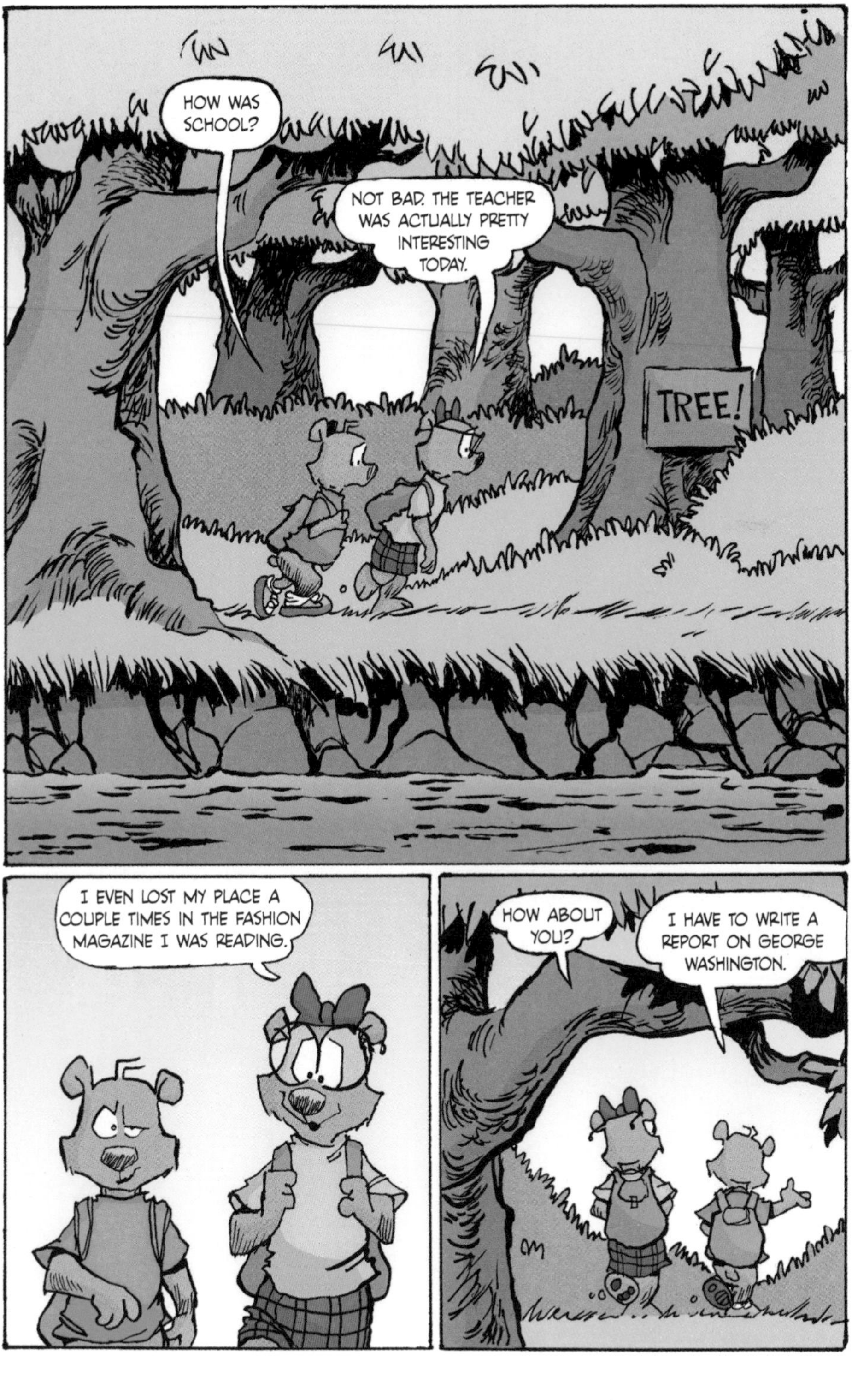
HOW WAS SCHOOL?
NOT BAD. THE TEACHER WAS ACTUALLY PRETTY INTERESTING TODAY.
TREE!
I EVEN LOST MY PLACE A COUPLE TIMES IN THE FASHION MAGAZINE I WAS READING.
HOW ABOUT YOU?
I HAVE TO WRITE A REPORT ON GEORGE WASHINGTON.

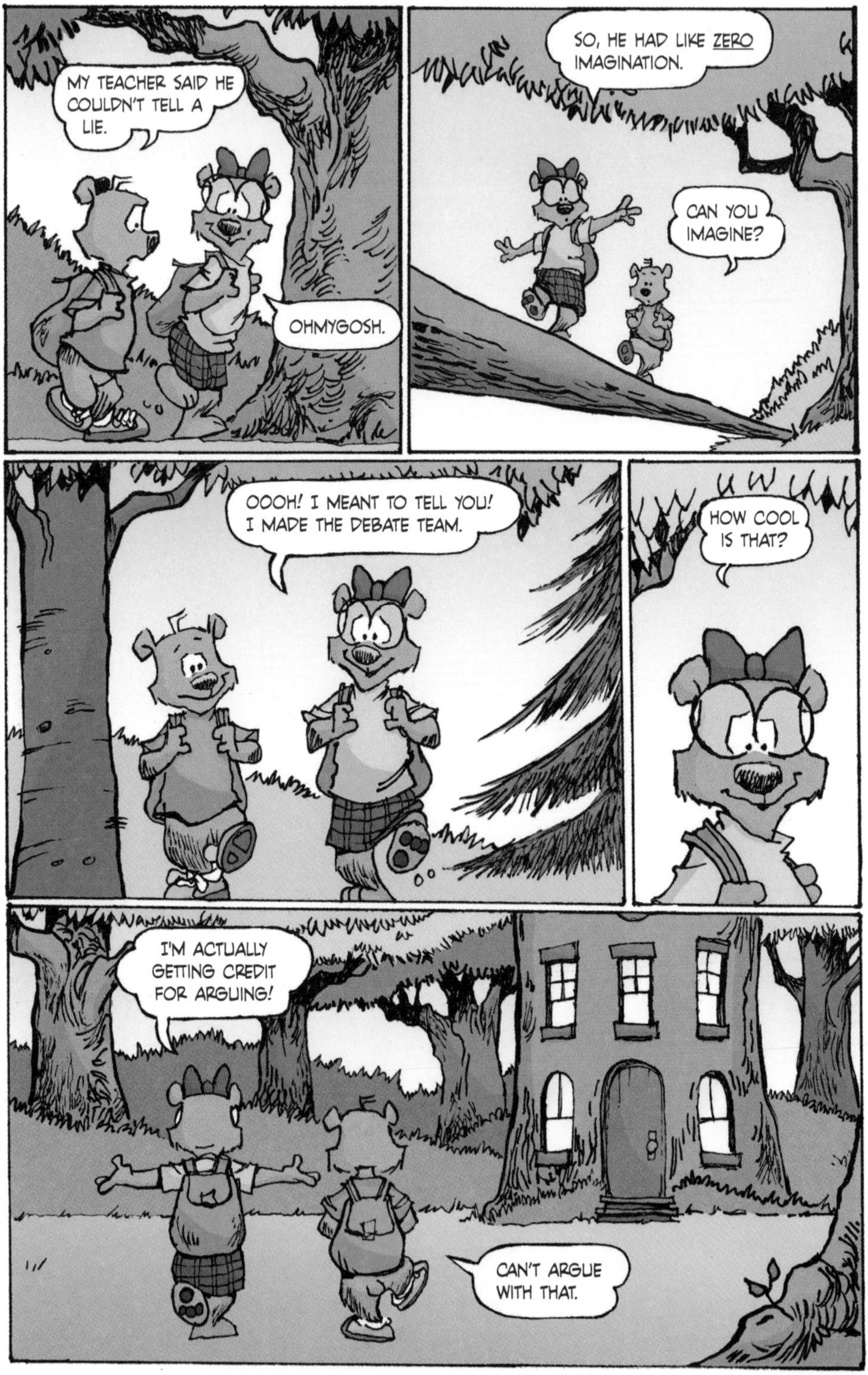
MY TEACHER SAID HE COULDN'T TELL A LIE.
OHMYGOSH.
SO, HE HAD LIKE ZERO IMAGINATION.
CAN YOU IMAGINE?
OOOH! I MEANT TO TELL YOU! I MADE THE DEBATE TEAM.
HOW COOL IS THAT?
I'M ACTUALLY GETTING CREDIT FOR ARGUING!
CAN'T ARGUE WITH THAT.

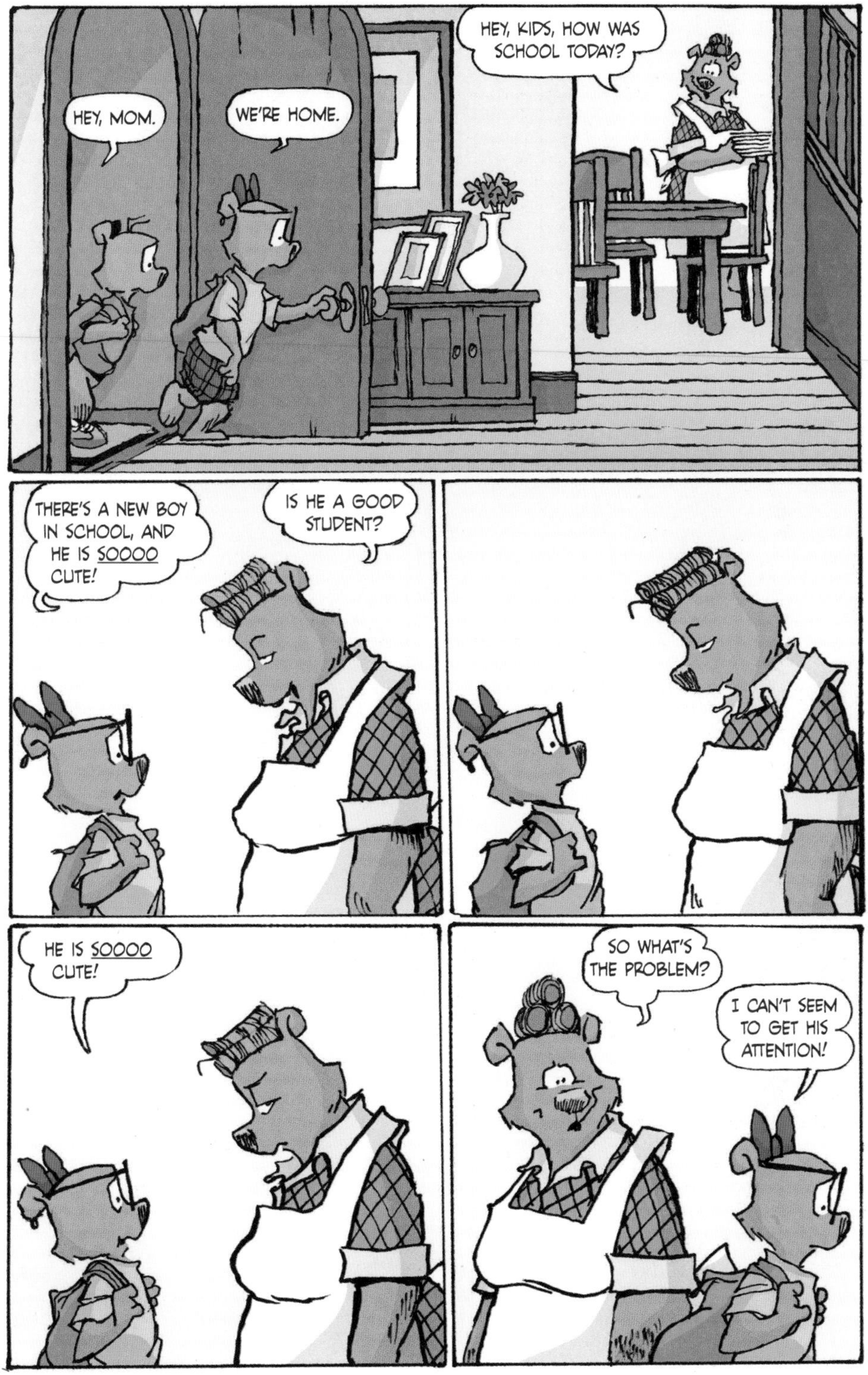
HEY, MOM.
WE'RE HOME.
HEY, KIDS, HOW WAS SCHOOL TODAY?
THERE'S A NEW BOY IN SCHOOL, AND HE IS SOOOO CUTE!
IS HE A GOOD STUDENT?
HE IS SOOOO CUTE!
SO WHAT'S THE PROBLEM?
I CAN'T SEEM TO GET HIS ATTENTION!

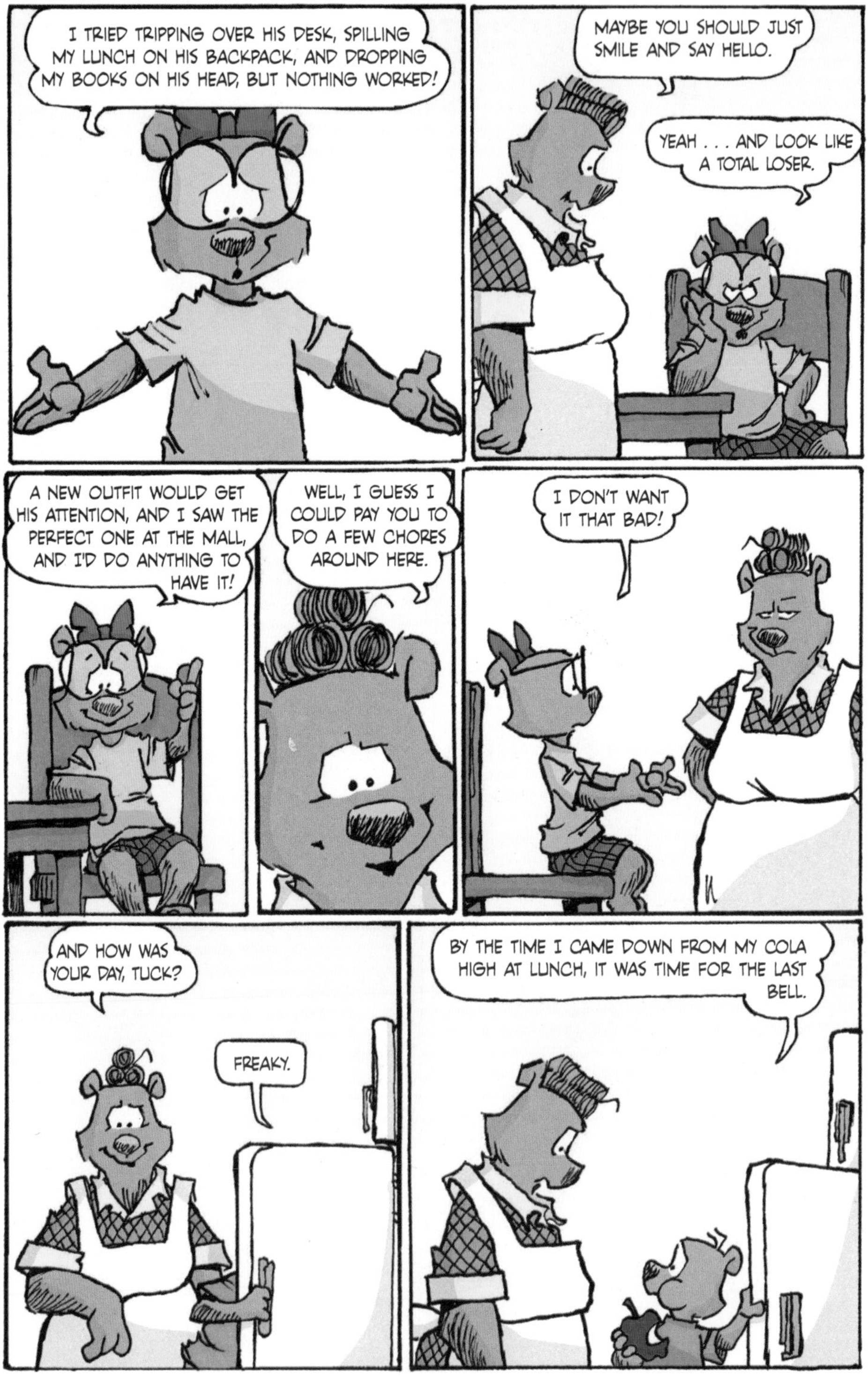
I TRIED TRIPPING OVER HIS DESK, SPILLING MY LUNCH ON HIS BACKPACK, AND DROPPING MY BOOKS ON HIS HEAD, BUT NOTHING WORKED!
MAYBE YOU SHOULD JUST SMILE AND SAY HELLO.
YEAH . . . AND LOOK LIKE A TOTAL LOSER.
A NEW OUTFIT WOULD GET HIS ATTENTION, AND I SAW THE PERFECT ONE AT THE MALL, AND I'D DO ANYTHING TO HAVE IT!
WELL, I GUESS I COULD PAY YOU TO DO A FEW CHORES AROUND HERE.
I DON'T WANT IT THAT BAD!
AND HOW WAS YOUR DAY, TUCK?
FREAKY.
BY THE TIME I CAME DOWN FROM MY COLA HIGH AT LUNCH, IT WAS TIME FOR THE LAST BELL.

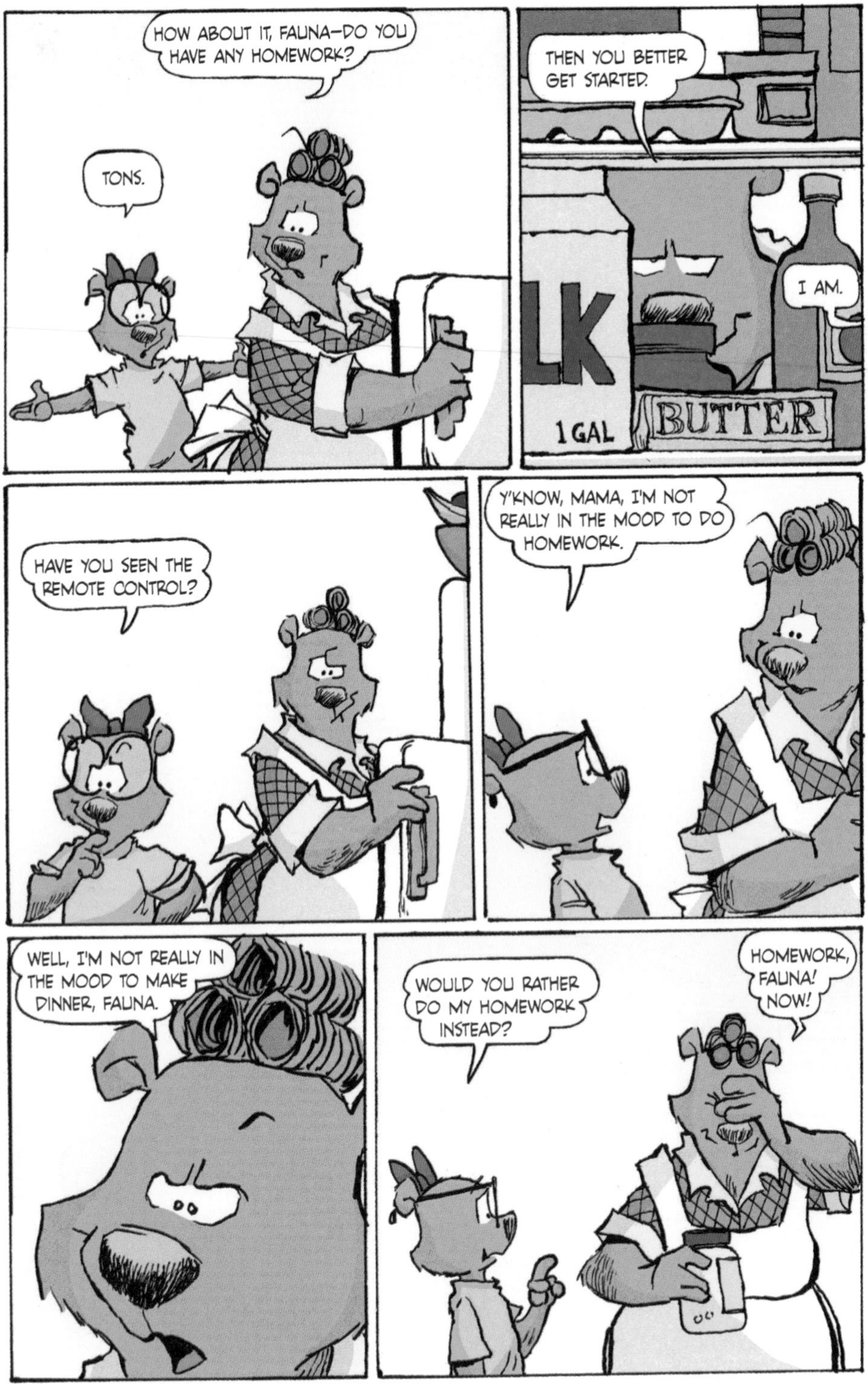

HOW ABOUT IT, FAUNA—DO YOU HAVE ANY HOMEWORK?
TONS.
THEN YOU BETTER GET STARTED.
I AM.
LK
1 GAL
BUTTER
HAVE YOU SEEN THE REMOTE CONTROL?
Y'KNOW, MAMA, I'M NOT REALLY IN THE MOOD TO DO HOMEWORK.
WELL, I'M NOT REALLY IN THE MOOD TO MAKE DINNER, FAUNA.
WOULD YOU RATHER DO MY HOMEWORK INSTEAD?
HOMEWORK, FAUNA! NOW!

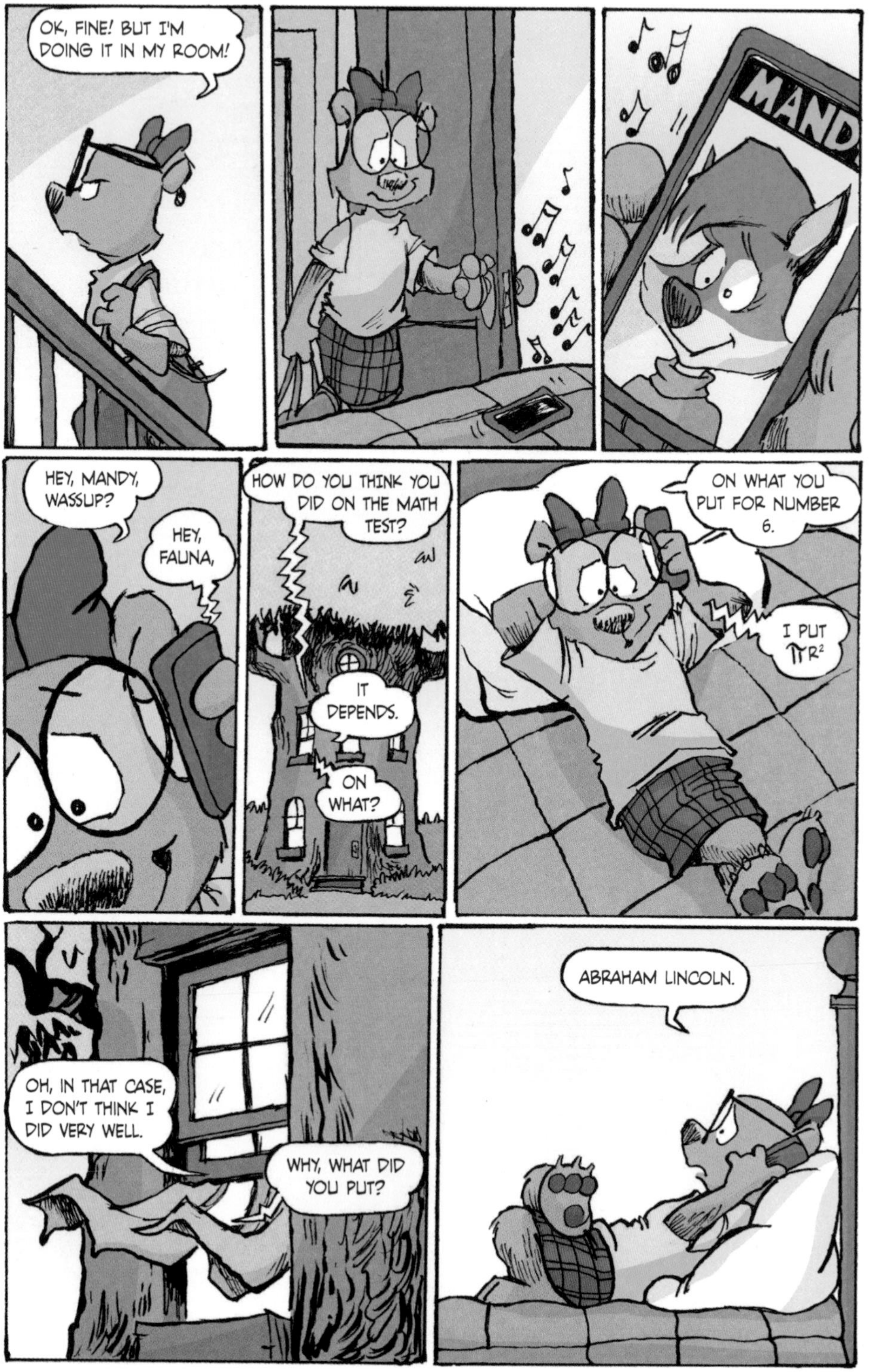
OK, FINE! BUT I'M DOING IT IN MY ROOM!
MANDY
HEY, MANDY, WASSUP?
HEY, FAUNA,
HOW DO YOU THINK YOU DID ON THE MATH TEST?
IT DEPENDS.
ON WHAT?
ON WHAT YOU PUT FOR NUMBER 6.
I PUT πR^2
OH, IN THAT CASE, I DON'T THINK I DID VERY WELL.
WHY, WHAT DID YOU PUT?
ABRAHAM LINCOLN.

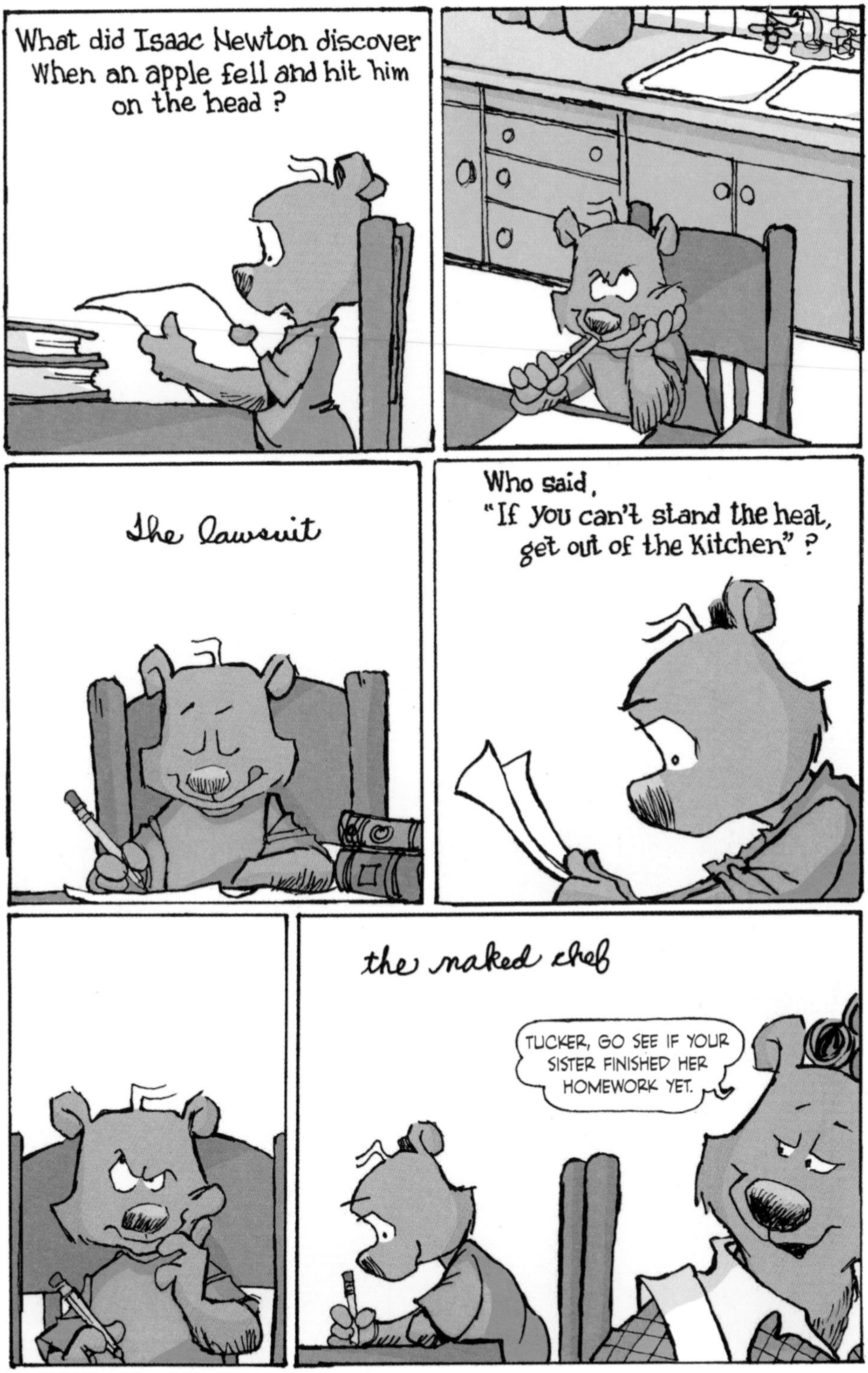
What did Isaac Newton discover when an apple fell and hit him on the head ?
The lawsuit
Who said, "If you can't stand the heat, get out of the Kitchen" ?
the naked chef
TUCKER, GO SEE IF YOUR SISTER FINISHED HER HOMEWORK YET.

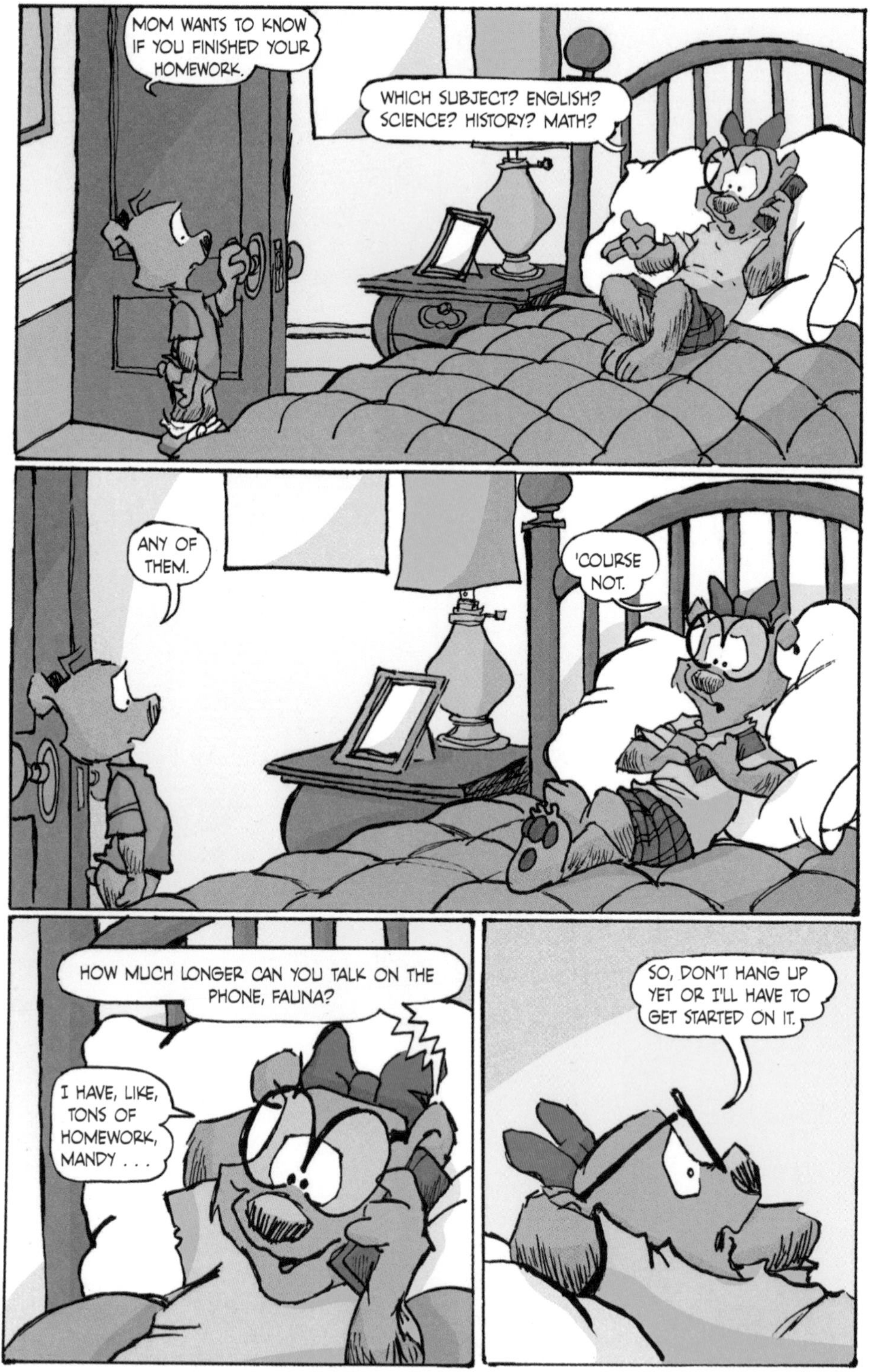
MOM WANTS TO KNOW IF YOU FINISHED YOUR HOMEWORK.
WHICH SUBJECT? ENGLISH? SCIENCE? HISTORY? MATH?
ANY OF THEM.
'COURSE NOT.
HOW MUCH LONGER CAN YOU TALK ON THE PHONE, FAUNA?
I HAVE, LIKE, TONS OF HOMEWORK, MANDY . . .
SO, DON'T HANG UP YET OR I'LL HAVE TO GET STARTED ON IT.

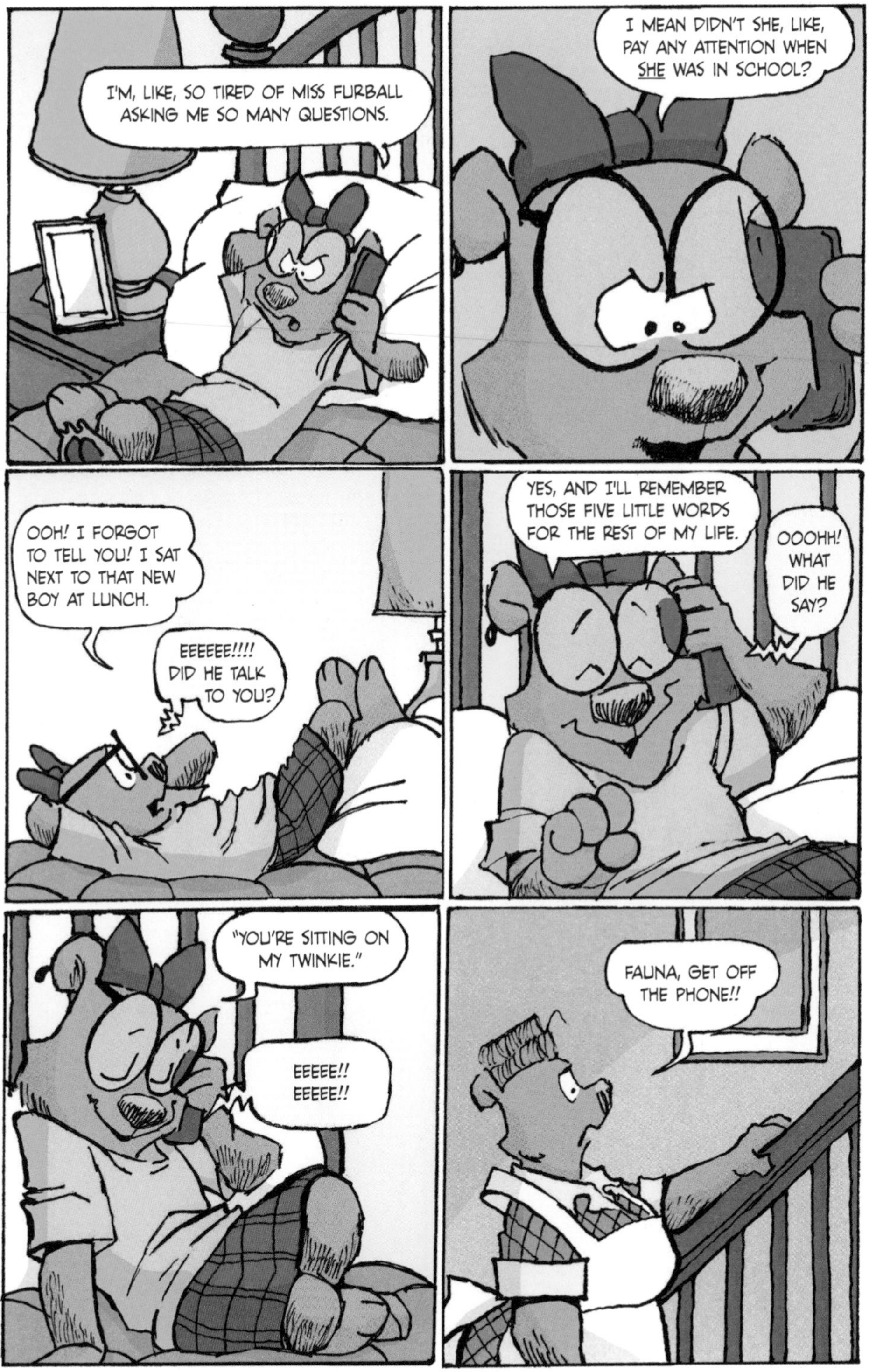
I'M, LIKE, SO TIRED OF MISS FURBALL ASKING ME SO MANY QUESTIONS.
I MEAN DIDN'T SHE, LIKE, PAY ANY ATTENTION WHEN SHE WAS IN SCHOOL?
OOH! I FORGOT TO TELL YOU! I SAT NEXT TO THAT NEW BOY AT LUNCH.
EEEEEE!!!! DID HE TALK TO YOU?
YES, AND I'LL REMEMBER THOSE FIVE LITTLE WORDS FOR THE REST OF MY LIFE.
OOOHH! WHAT DID HE SAY?
"YOU'RE SITTING ON MY TWINKIE."
EEEEE!! EEEEE!!
FAUNA, GET OFF THE PHONE!!

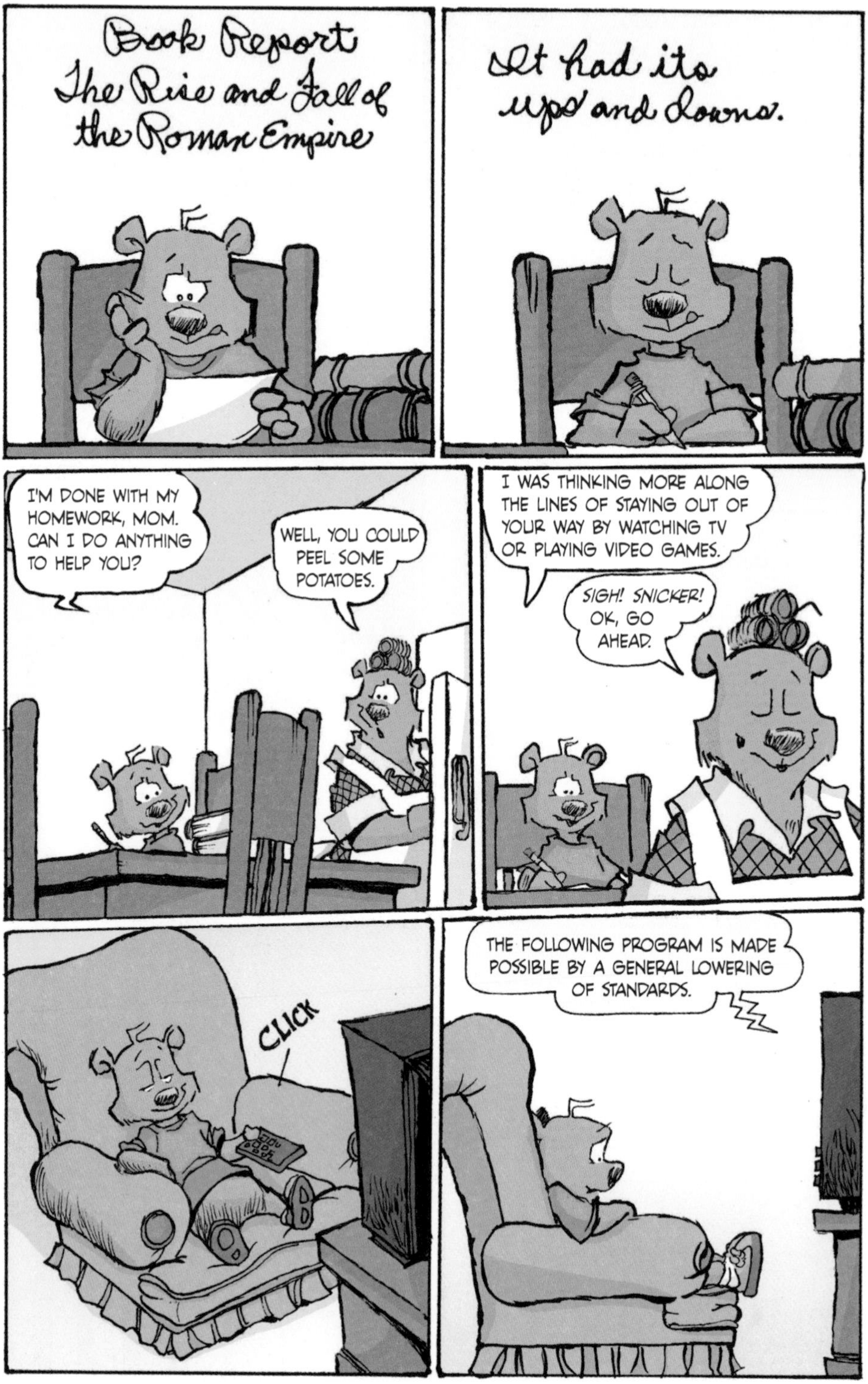
Book Report
The Rise and Fall of the Roman Empire
It had its ups and downs.
I'M DONE WITH MY HOMEWORK, MOM. CAN I DO ANYTHING TO HELP YOU?
WELL, YOU COULD PEEL SOME POTATOES.
I WAS THINKING MORE ALONG THE LINES OF STAYING OUT OF YOUR WAY BY WATCHING TV OR PLAYING VIDEO GAMES.
SIGH! SNICKER! OK, GO AHEAD.
CLICK
THE FOLLOWING PROGRAM IS MADE POSSIBLE BY A GENERAL LOWERING OF STANDARDS.

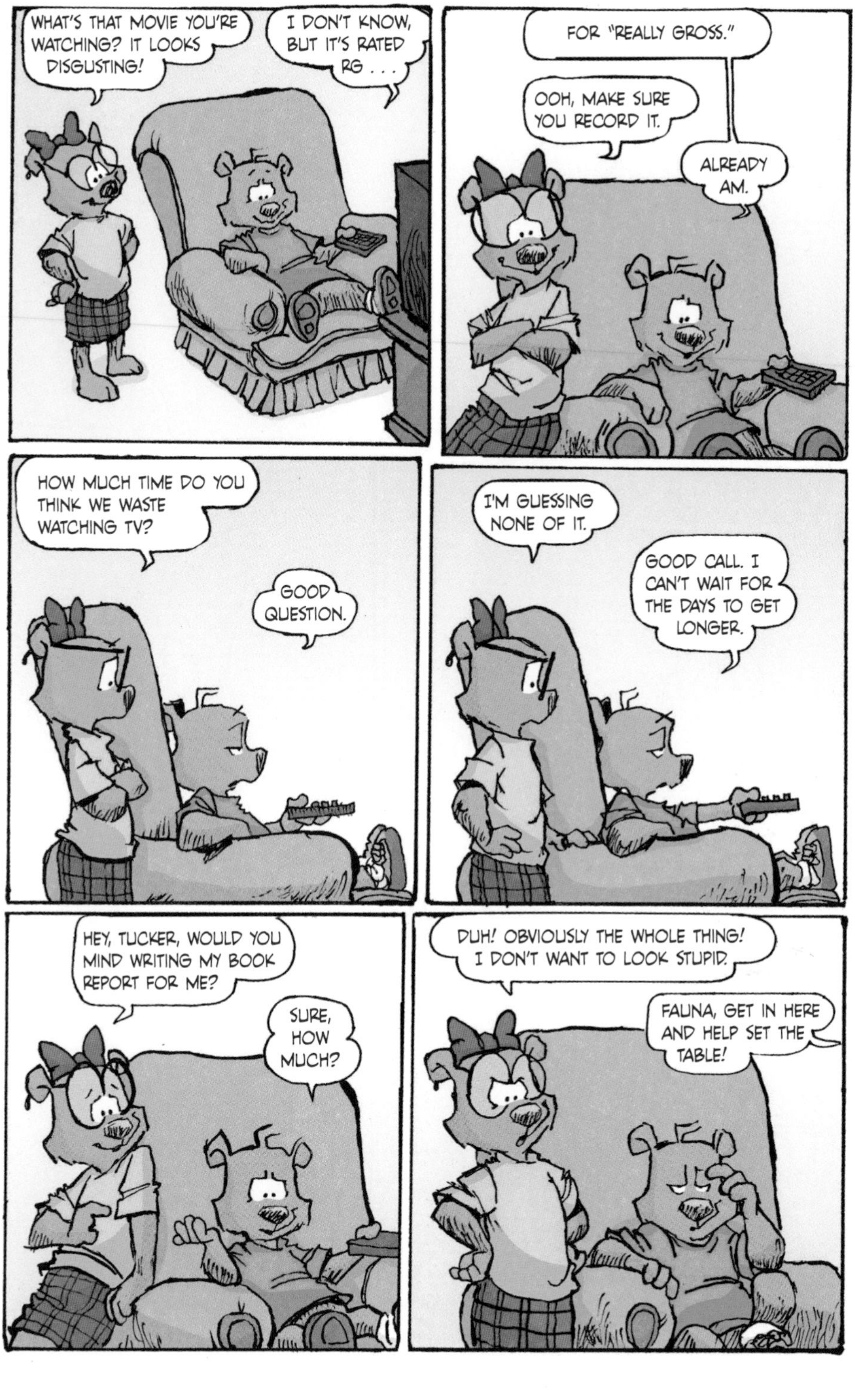
WHAT'S THAT MOVIE YOU'RE WATCHING? IT LOOKS DISGUSTING!
I DON'T KNOW, BUT IT'S RATED RG . . .
FOR "REALLY GROSS."
OOH, MAKE SURE YOU RECORD IT.
ALREADY AM.
HOW MUCH TIME DO YOU THINK WE WASTE WATCHING TV?
GOOD QUESTION.
I'M GUESSING NONE OF IT.
GOOD CALL. I CAN'T WAIT FOR THE DAYS TO GET LONGER.
HEY, TUCKER, WOULD YOU MIND WRITING MY BOOK REPORT FOR ME?
SURE, HOW MUCH?
DUH! OBVIOUSLY THE WHOLE THING! I DON'T WANT TO LOOK STUPID.
FAUNA, GET IN HERE AND HELP SET THE TABLE!

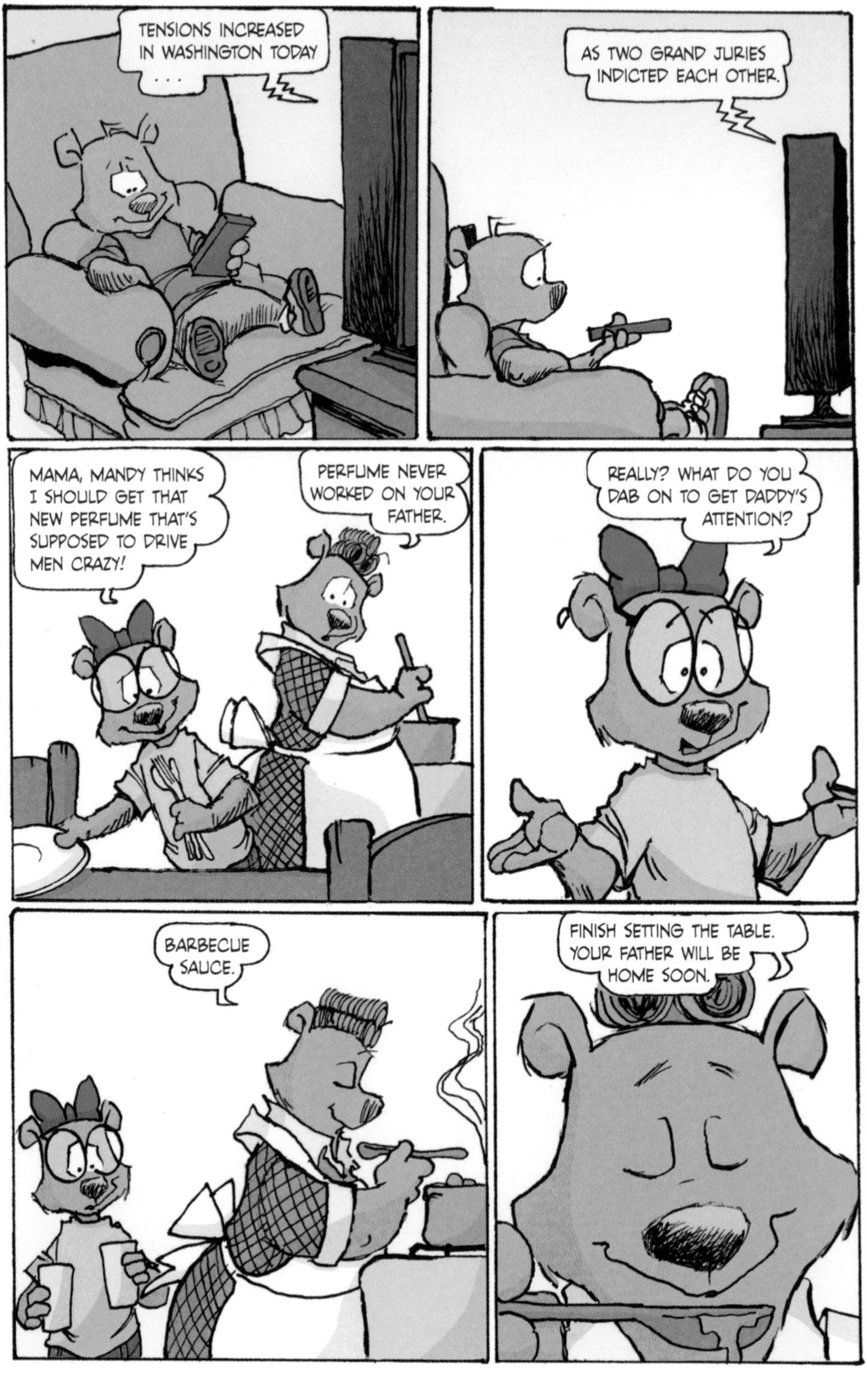
TENSIONS INCREASED IN WASHINGTON TODAY . . .
AS TWO GRAND JURIES INDICTED EACH OTHER.
MAMA, MANDY THINKS I SHOULD GET THAT NEW PERFUME THAT'S SUPPOSED TO DRIVE MEN CRAZY!
PERFUME NEVER WORKED ON YOUR FATHER.
REALLY? WHAT DO YOU DAB ON TO GET DADDY'S ATTENTION?
BARBECUE SAUCE.
FINISH SETTING THE TABLE. YOUR FATHER WILL BE HOME SOON.

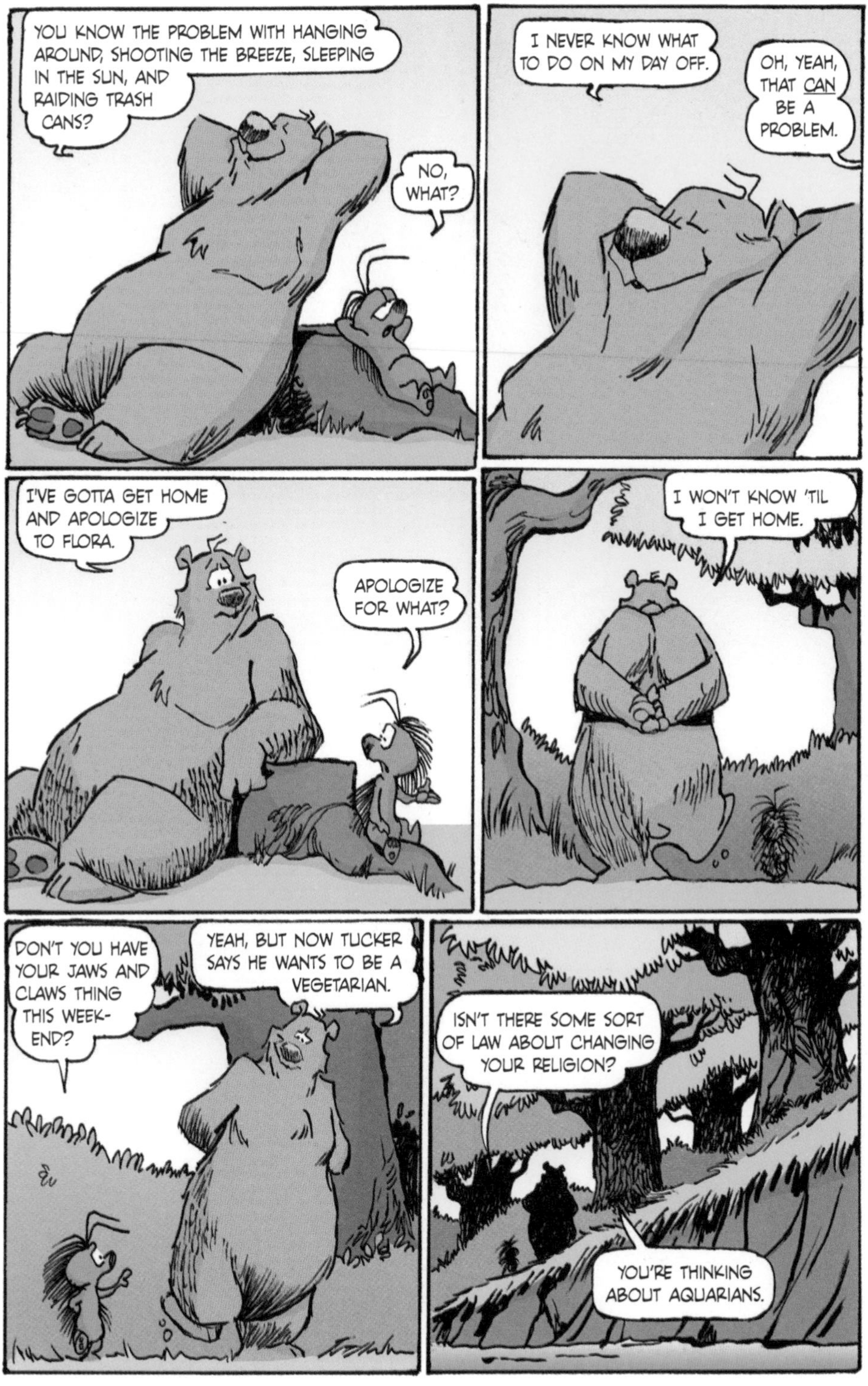
YOU KNOW THE PROBLEM WITH HANGING AROUND, SHOOTING THE BREEZE, SLEEPING IN THE SUN, AND RAIDING TRASH CANS?
NO, WHAT?
I NEVER KNOW WHAT TO DO ON MY DAY OFF.
OH, YEAH, THAT CAN BE A PROBLEM.
I'VE GOTTA GET HOME AND APOLOGIZE TO FLORA.
APOLOGIZE FOR WHAT?
I WON'T KNOW 'TIL I GET HOME.
DON'T YOU HAVE YOUR JAWS AND CLAWS THING THIS WEEK-END?
YEAH, BUT NOW TUCKER SAYS HE WANTS TO BE A VEGETARIAN.
ISN'T THERE SOME SORT OF LAW ABOUT CHANGING YOUR RELIGION?
YOU'RE THINKING ABOUT AQUARIANS.

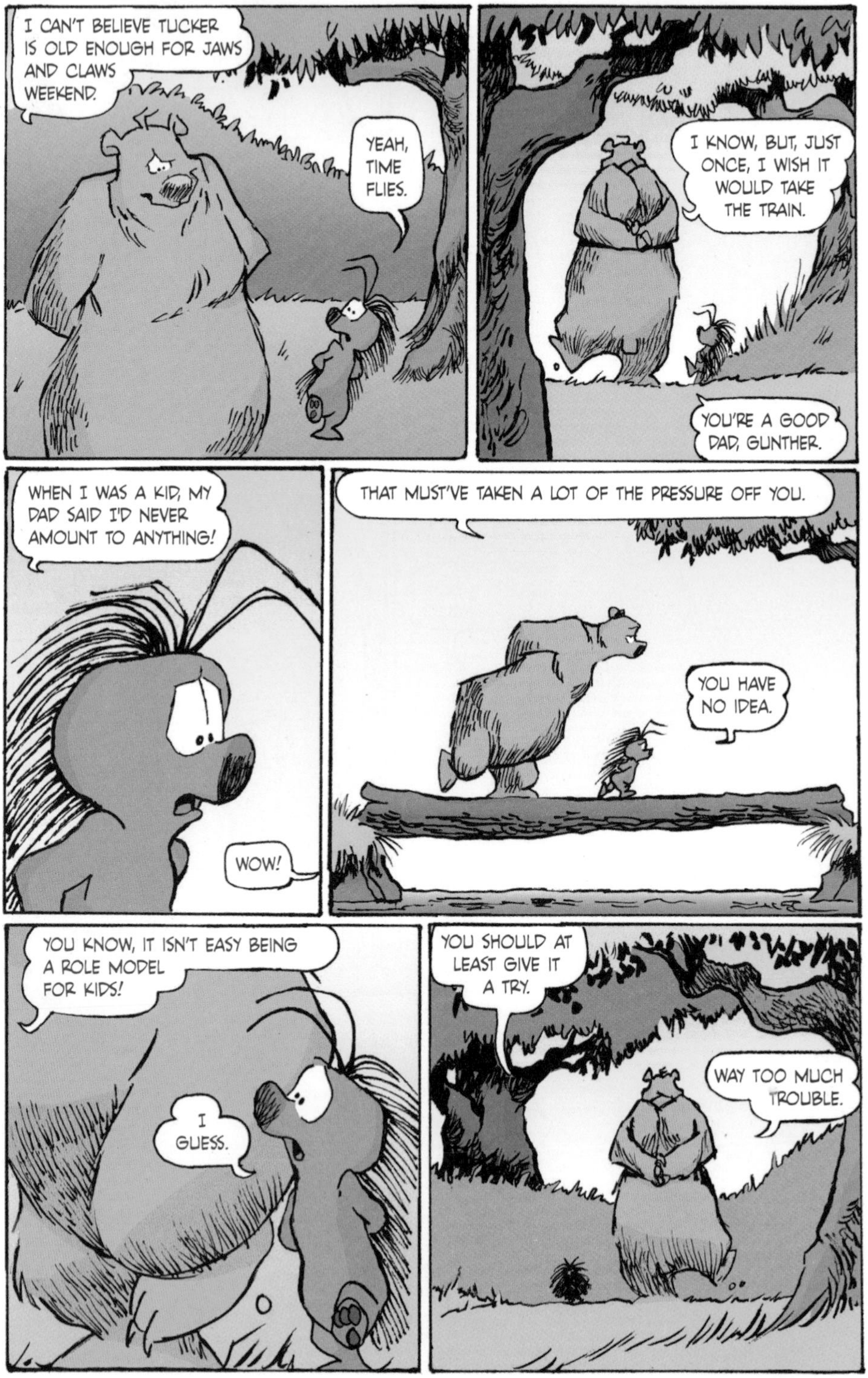
I CAN'T BELIEVE TUCKER IS OLD ENOUGH FOR JAWS AND CLAWS WEEKEND.
YEAH, TIME FLIES.
I KNOW, BUT, JUST ONCE, I WISH IT WOULD TAKE THE TRAIN.
YOU'RE A GOOD DAD, GUNTHER.
WHEN I WAS A KID, MY DAD SAID I'D NEVER AMOUNT TO ANYTHING!
WOW!
THAT MUST'VE TAKEN A LOT OF THE PRESSURE OFF YOU.
YOU HAVE NO IDEA.
YOU KNOW, IT ISN'T EASY BEING A ROLE MODEL FOR KIDS!
I GUESS.
YOU SHOULD AT LEAST GIVE IT A TRY.
WAY TOO MUCH TROUBLE.

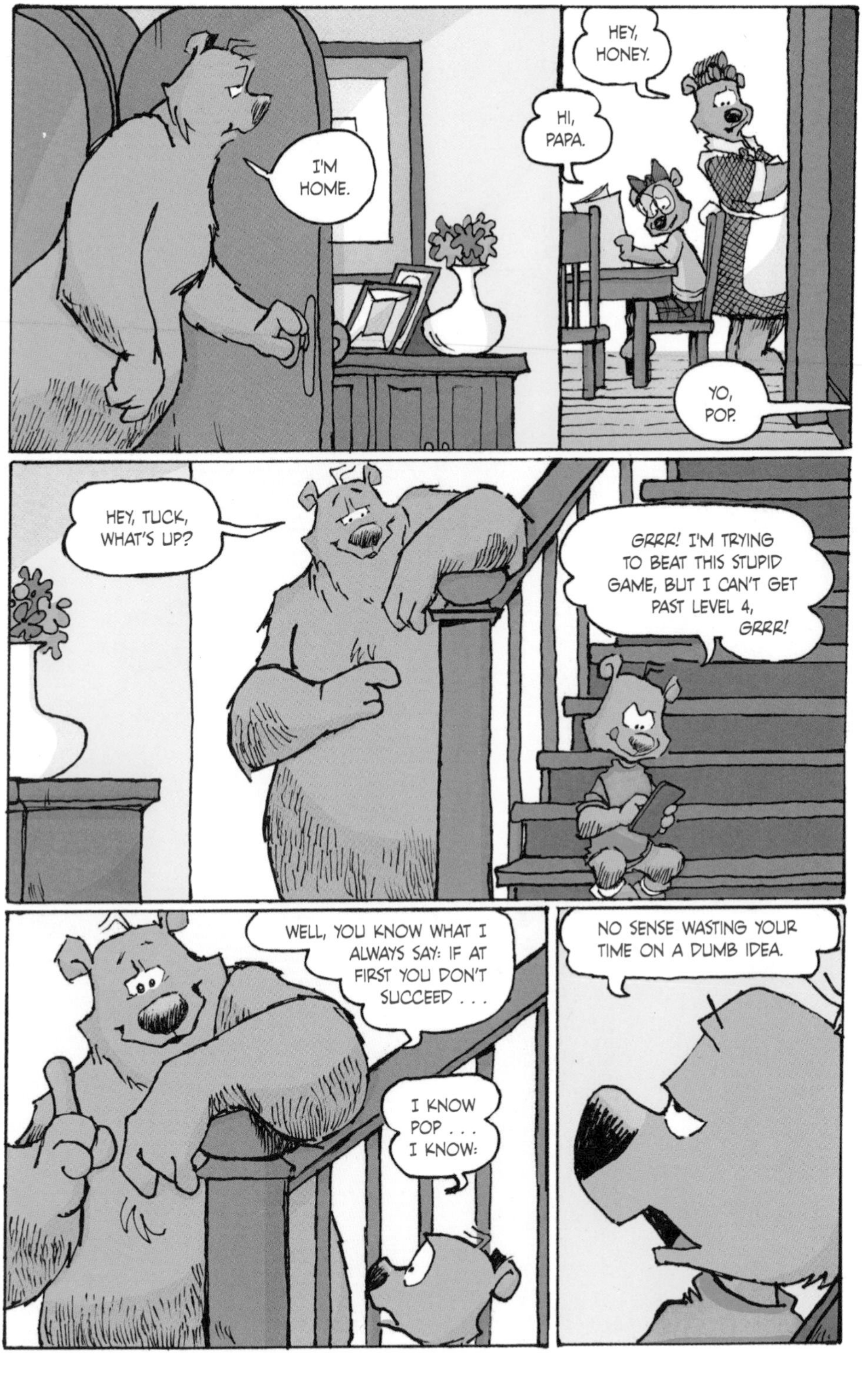
I'M HOME.
HEY, HONEY.
HI, PAPA.
YO, POP.
HEY, TUCK, WHAT'S UP?
GRRR! I'M TRYING TO BEAT THIS STUPID GAME, BUT I CAN'T GET PAST LEVEL 4, GRRR!
WELL, YOU KNOW WHAT I ALWAYS SAY: IF AT FIRST YOU DON'T SUCCEED . . .
I KNOW POP . . . I KNOW:
NO SENSE WASTING YOUR TIME ON A DUMB IDEA.

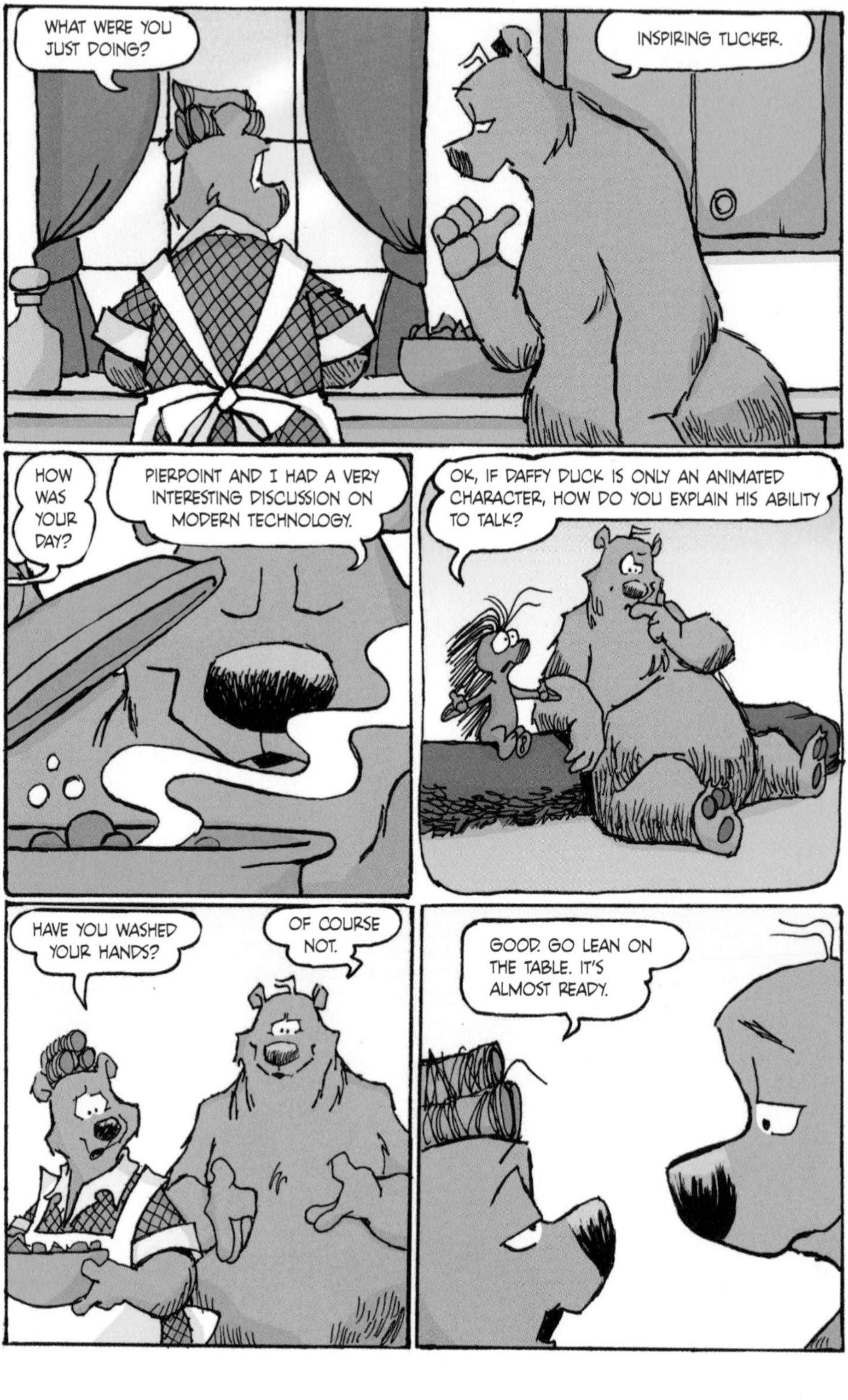
WHAT WERE YOU JUST DOING?
INSPIRING TUCKER.
HOW WAS YOUR DAY?
PIERPOINT AND I HAD A VERY INTERESTING DISCUSSION ON MODERN TECHNOLOGY.
OK, IF DAFFY DUCK IS ONLY AN ANIMATED CHARACTER, HOW DO YOU EXPLAIN HIS ABILITY TO TALK?
HAVE YOU WASHED YOUR HANDS?
OF COURSE NOT.
GOOD. GO LEAN ON THE TABLE. IT'S ALMOST READY.

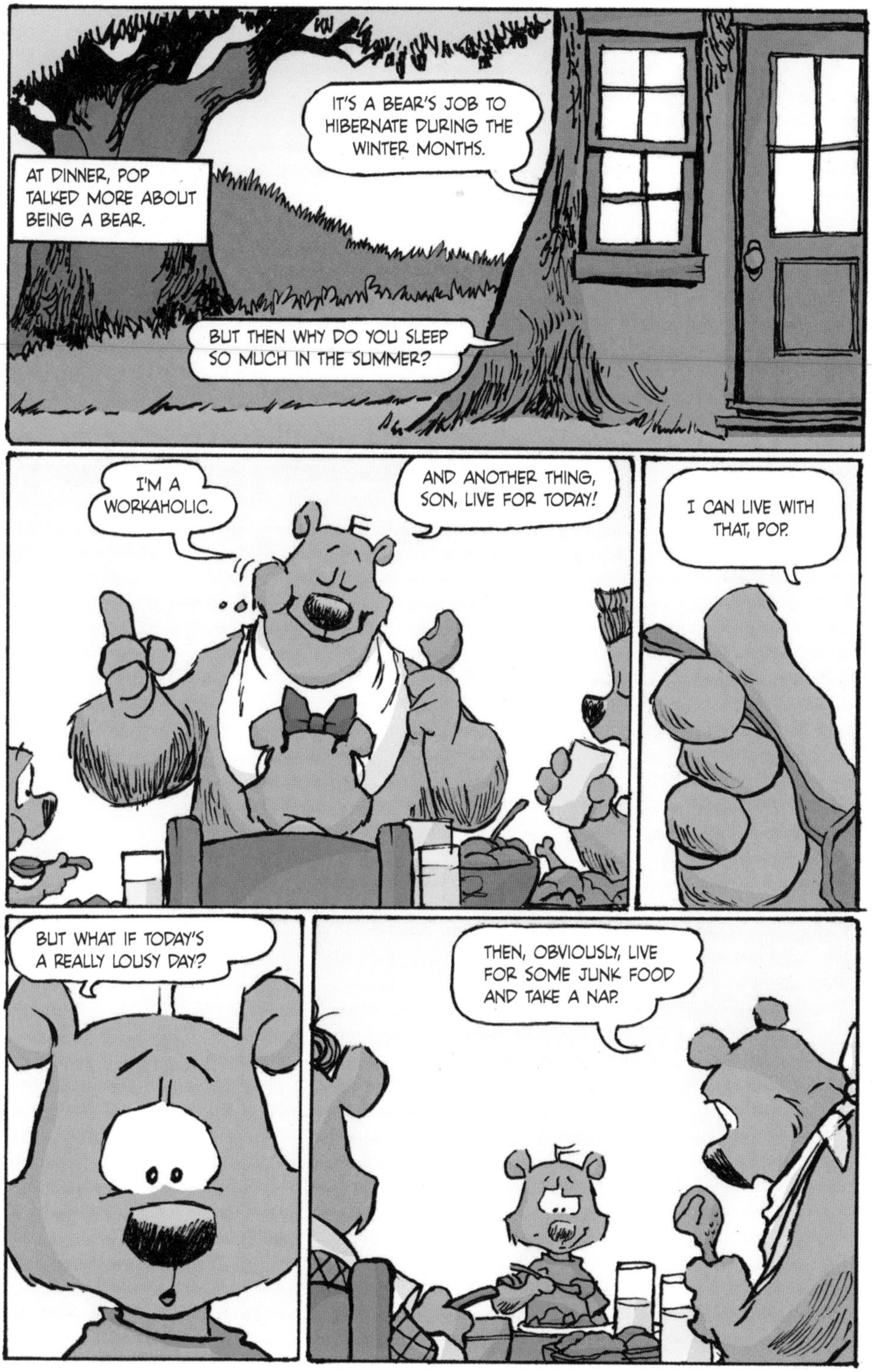
AT DINNER, POP TALKED MORE ABOUT BEING A BEAR.
IT'S A BEAR'S JOB TO HIBERNATE DURING THE WINTER MONTHS.
BUT THEN WHY DO YOU SLEEP SO MUCH IN THE SUMMER?
I'M A WORKAHOLIC.
AND ANOTHER THING, SON, LIVE FOR TODAY!
I CAN LIVE WITH THAT, POP.
BUT WHAT IF TODAY'S A REALLY LOUSY DAY?
THEN, OBVIOUSLY, LIVE FOR SOME JUNK FOOD AND TAKE A NAP.

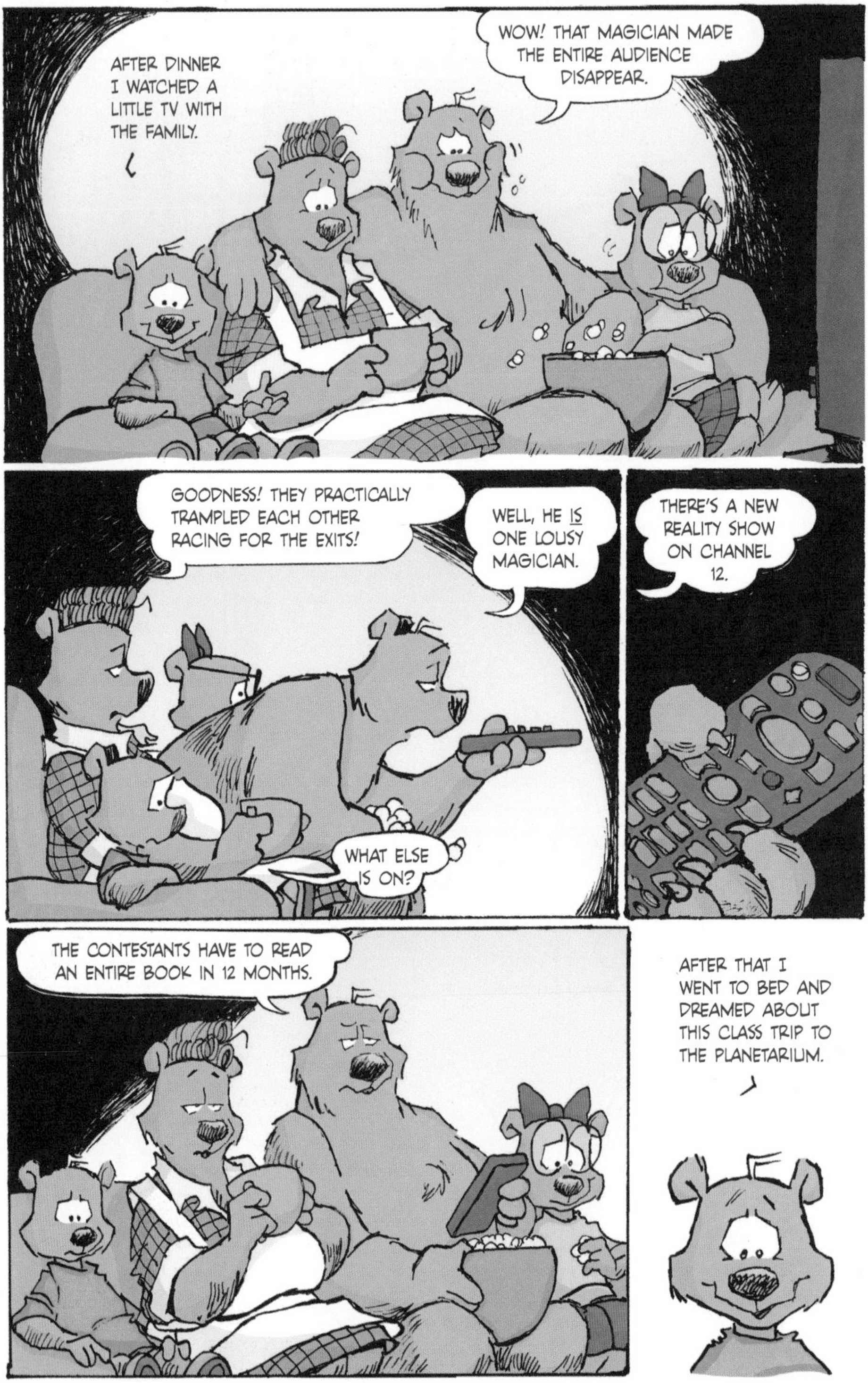
AFTER DINNER I WATCHED A LITTLE TV WITH THE FAMILY.
WOW! THAT MAGICIAN MADE THE ENTIRE AUDIENCE DISAPPEAR.
GOODNESS! THEY PRACTICALLY TRAMPLED EACH OTHER RACING FOR THE EXITS!
WELL, HE IS ONE LOUSY MAGICIAN.
WHAT ELSE IS ON?
THERE'S A NEW REALITY SHOW ON CHANNEL 12.
THE CONTESTANTS HAVE TO READ AN ENTIRE BOOK IN 12 MONTHS.
AFTER THAT I WENT TO BED AND DREAMED ABOUT THIS CLASS TRIP TO THE PLANETARIUM.

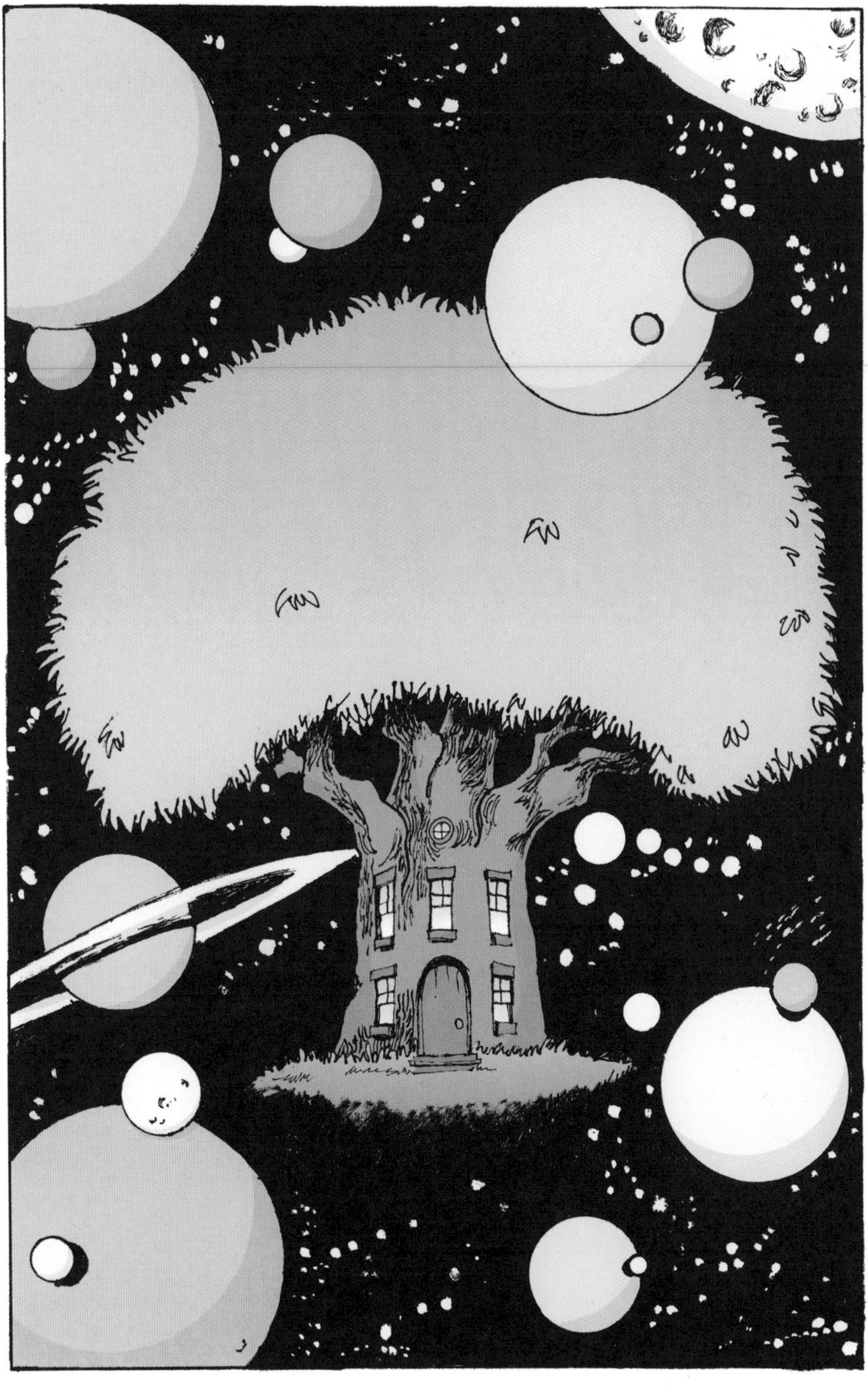

TUESDAY

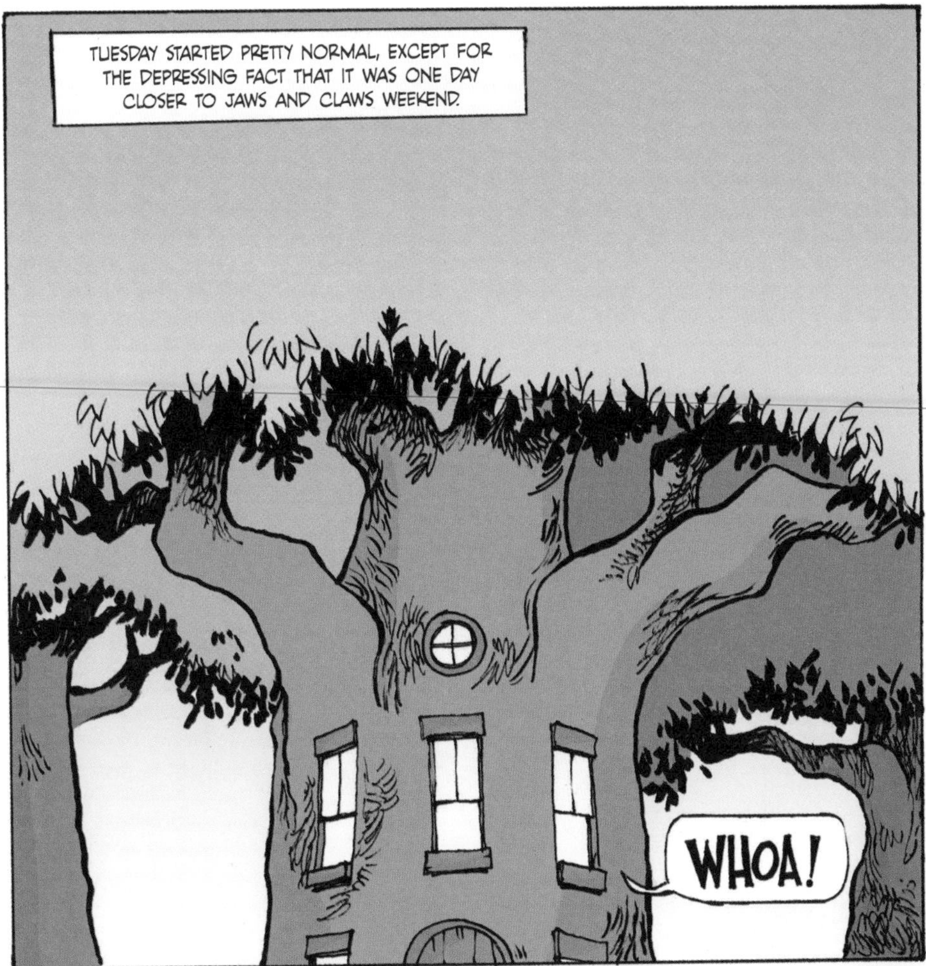
TUESDAY STARTED PRETTY NORMAL, EXCEPT FOR THE DEPRESSING FACT THAT IT WAS ONE DAY CLOSER TO JAWS AND CLAWS WEEKEND.
WHOA!

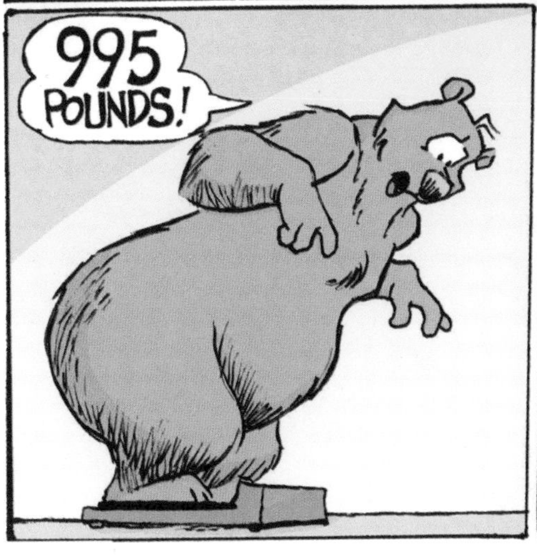
995 POUNDS!

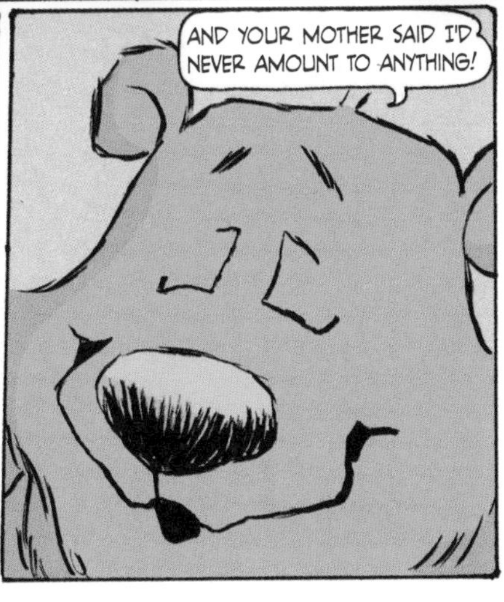
AND YOUR MOTHER SAID I'D NEVER AMOUNT TO ANYTHING!

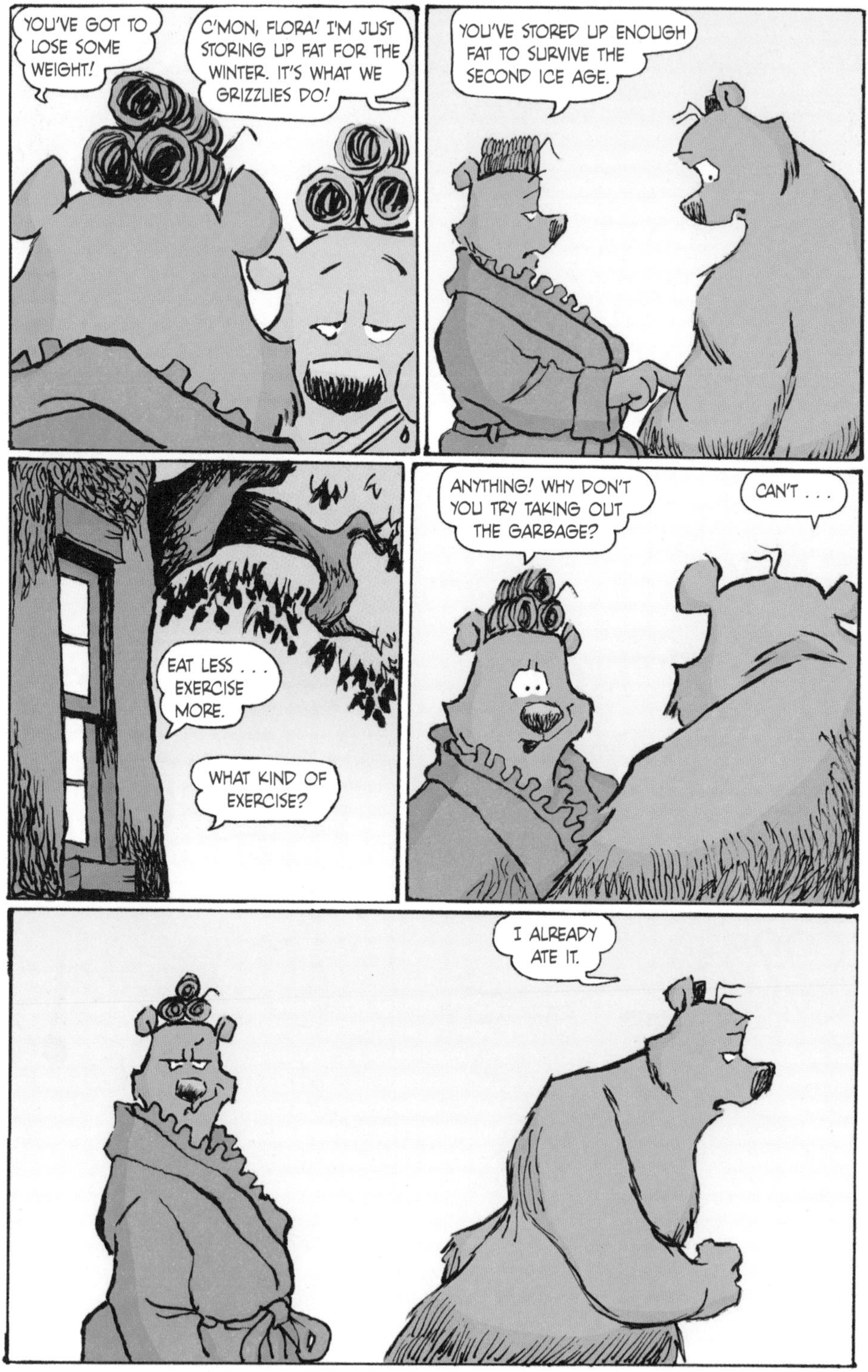
YOU'VE GOT TO LOSE SOME WEIGHT!
C'MON, FLORA! I'M JUST STORING UP FAT FOR THE WINTER. IT'S WHAT WE GRIZZLIES DO!
YOU'VE STORED UP ENOUGH FAT TO SURVIVE THE SECOND ICE AGE.
EAT LESS . . . EXERCISE MORE.
WHAT KIND OF EXERCISE?
ANYTHING! WHY DON'T YOU TRY TAKING OUT THE GARBAGE?
CAN'T . . .
I ALREADY ATE IT.

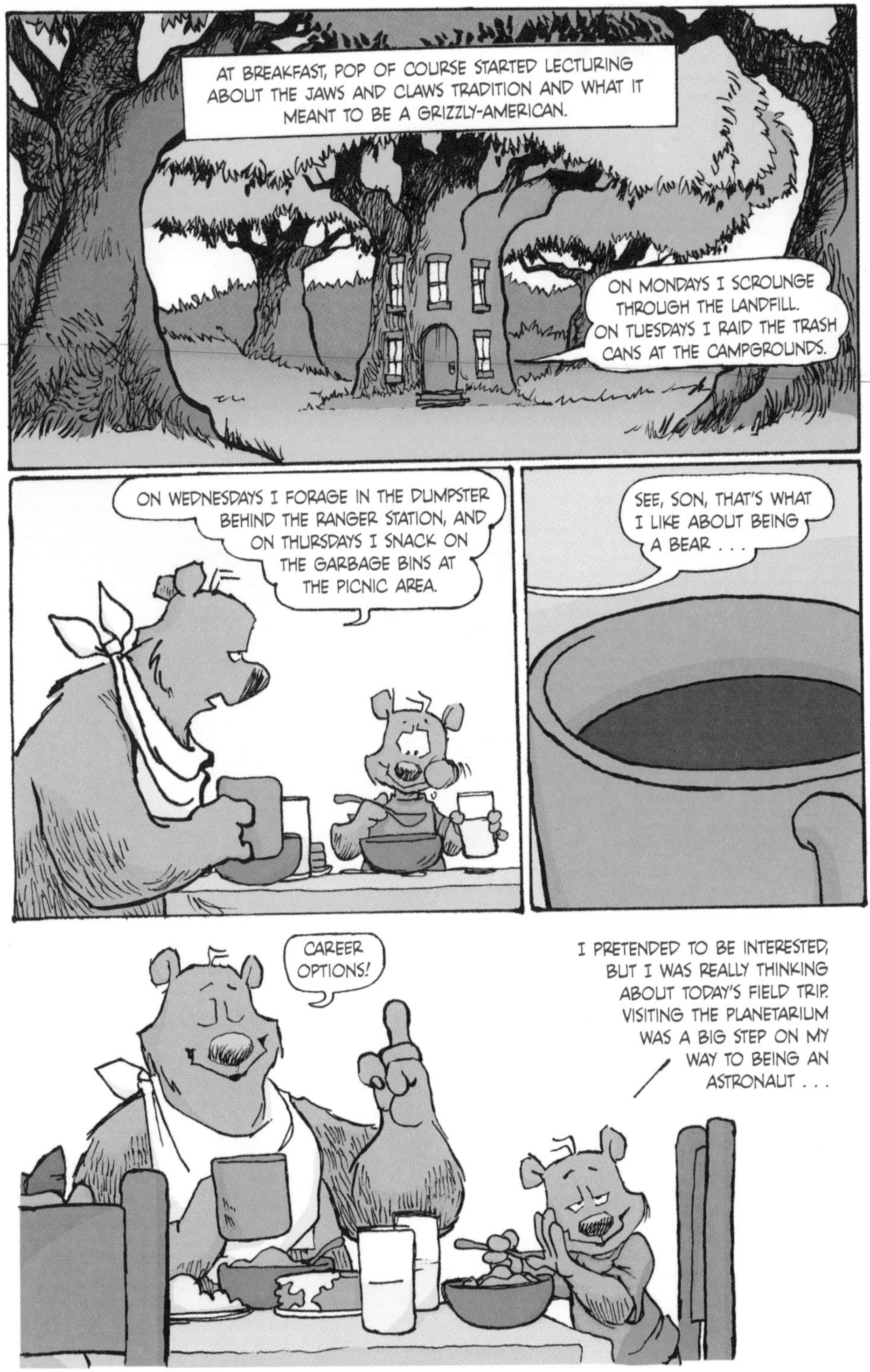
AT BREAKFAST, POP OF COURSE STARTED LECTURING ABOUT THE JAWS AND CLAWS TRADITION AND WHAT IT MEANT TO BE A GRIZZLY-AMERICAN.
ON MONDAYS I SCROUNGE THROUGH THE LANDFILL. ON TUESDAYS I RAID THE TRASH CANS AT THE CAMPGROUNDS.
ON WEDNESDAYS I FORAGE IN THE DUMPSTER BEHIND THE RANGER STATION, AND ON THURSDAYS I SNACK ON THE GARBAGE BINS AT THE PICNIC AREA.
SEE, SON, THAT'S WHAT I LIKE ABOUT BEING A BEAR . . .
CAREER OPTIONS!
I PRETENDED TO BE INTERESTED, BUT I WAS REALLY THINKING ABOUT TODAY'S FIELD TRIP. VISITING THE PLANETARIUM WAS A BIG STEP ON MY WAY TO BEING AN ASTRONAUT . . .

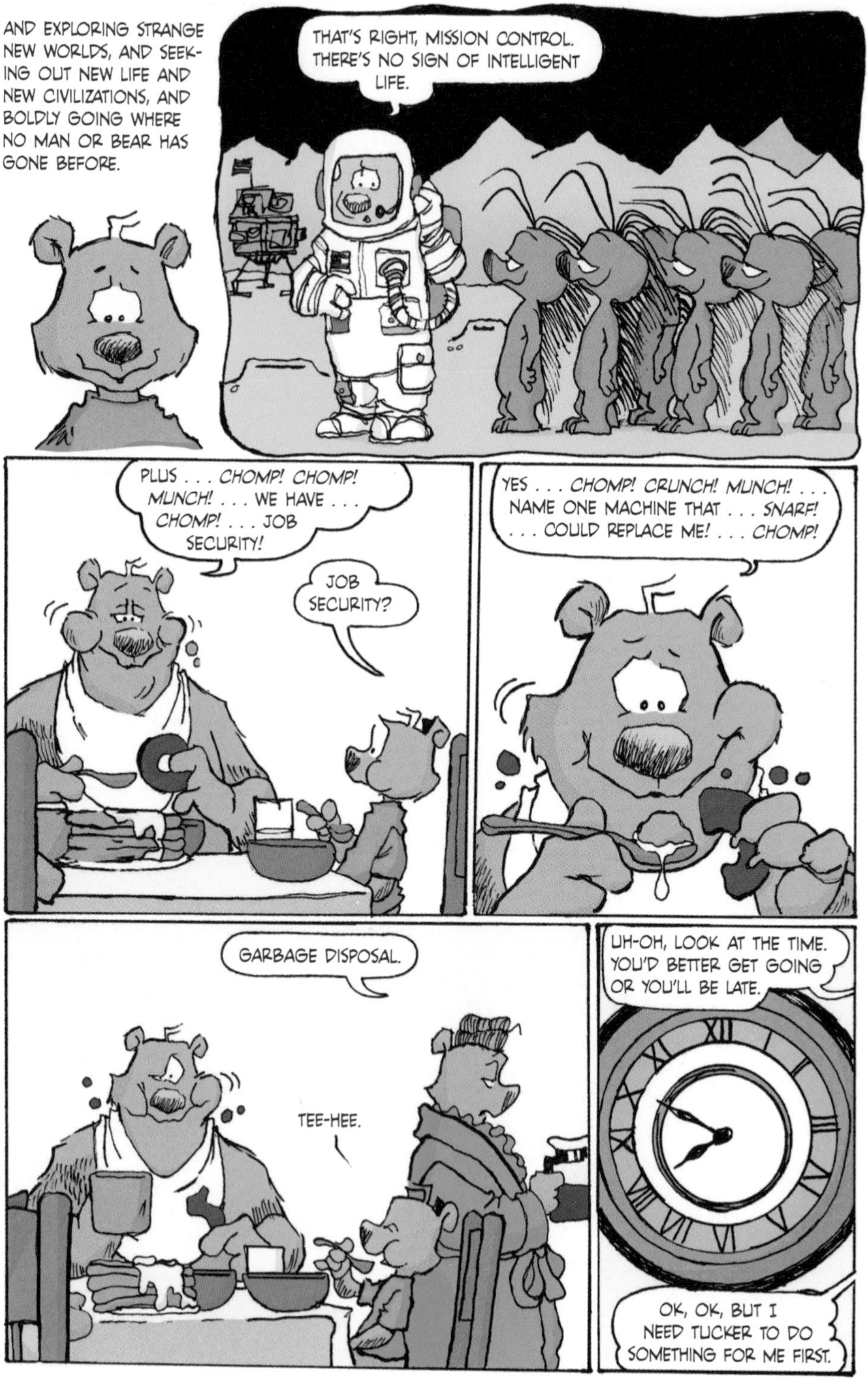
AND EXPLORING STRANGE NEW WORLDS, AND SEEK-ING OUT NEW LIFE AND NEW CIVILIZATIONS, AND BOLDLY GOING WHERE NO MAN OR BEAR HAS GONE BEFORE.
THAT'S RIGHT, MISSION CONTROL. THERE'S NO SIGN OF INTELLIGENT LIFE.
PLUS . . . CHOMP! CHOMP! MUNCH! . . . WE HAVE . . . CHOMP! . . . JOB SECURITY!
JOB SECURITY?
YES . . . CHOMP! CRUNCH! MUNCH! . . . NAME ONE MACHINE THAT . . . SNARF! . . . COULD REPLACE ME! . . . CHOMP!
GARBAGE DISPOSAL.
TEE-HEE.
UH-OH, LOOK AT THE TIME. YOU'D BETTER GET GOING OR YOU'LL BE LATE.
OK, OK, BUT I NEED TUCKER TO DO SOMETHING FOR ME FIRST.

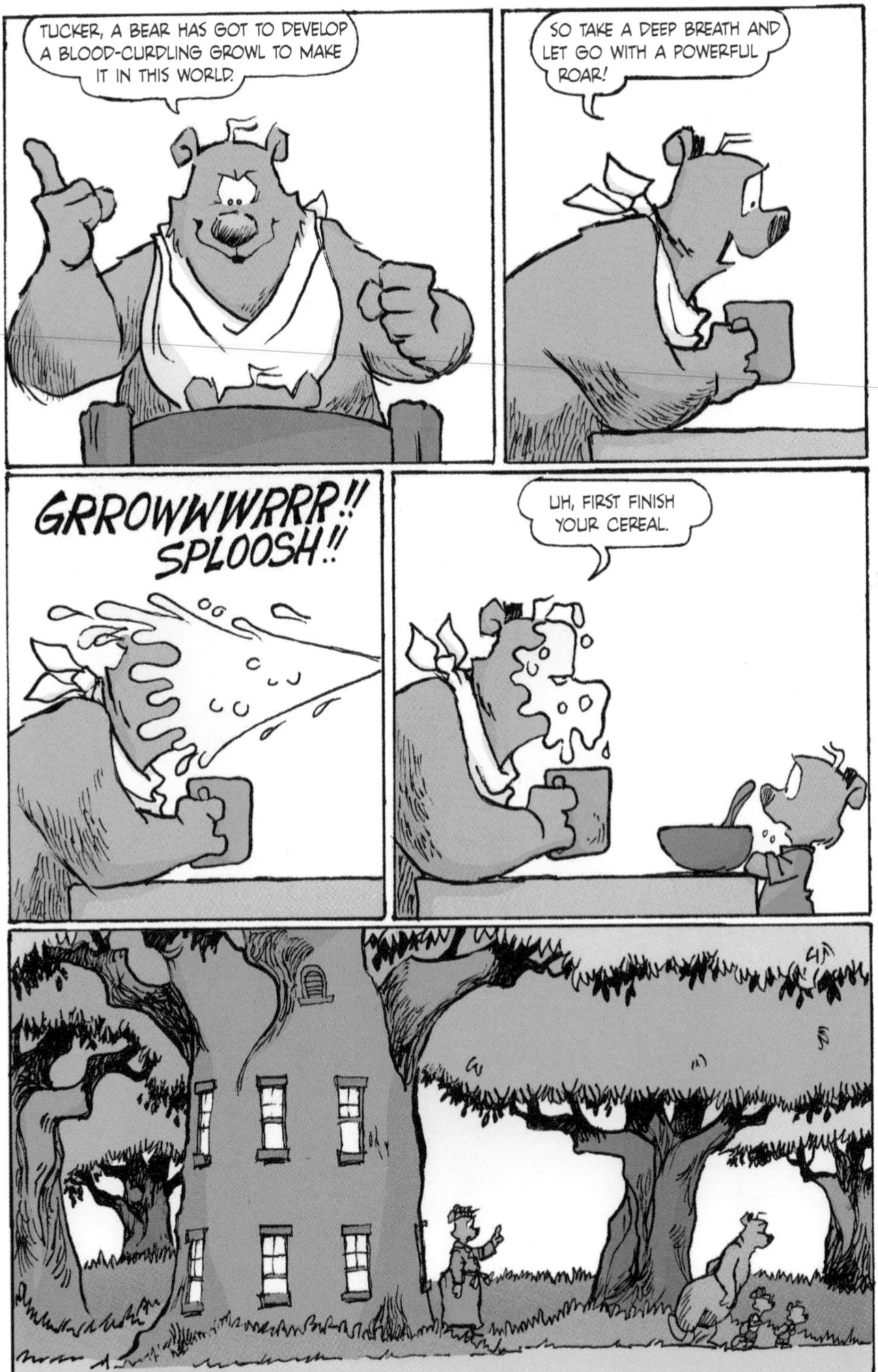
TUCKER, A BEAR HAS GOT TO DEVELOP A BLOOD-CURDLING GROWL TO MAKE IT IN THIS WORLD.
SO TAKE A DEEP BREATH AND LET GO WITH A POWERFUL ROAR!
GRROWWWRRR!!
SPLOOSH!!
UH, FIRST FINISH YOUR CEREAL.

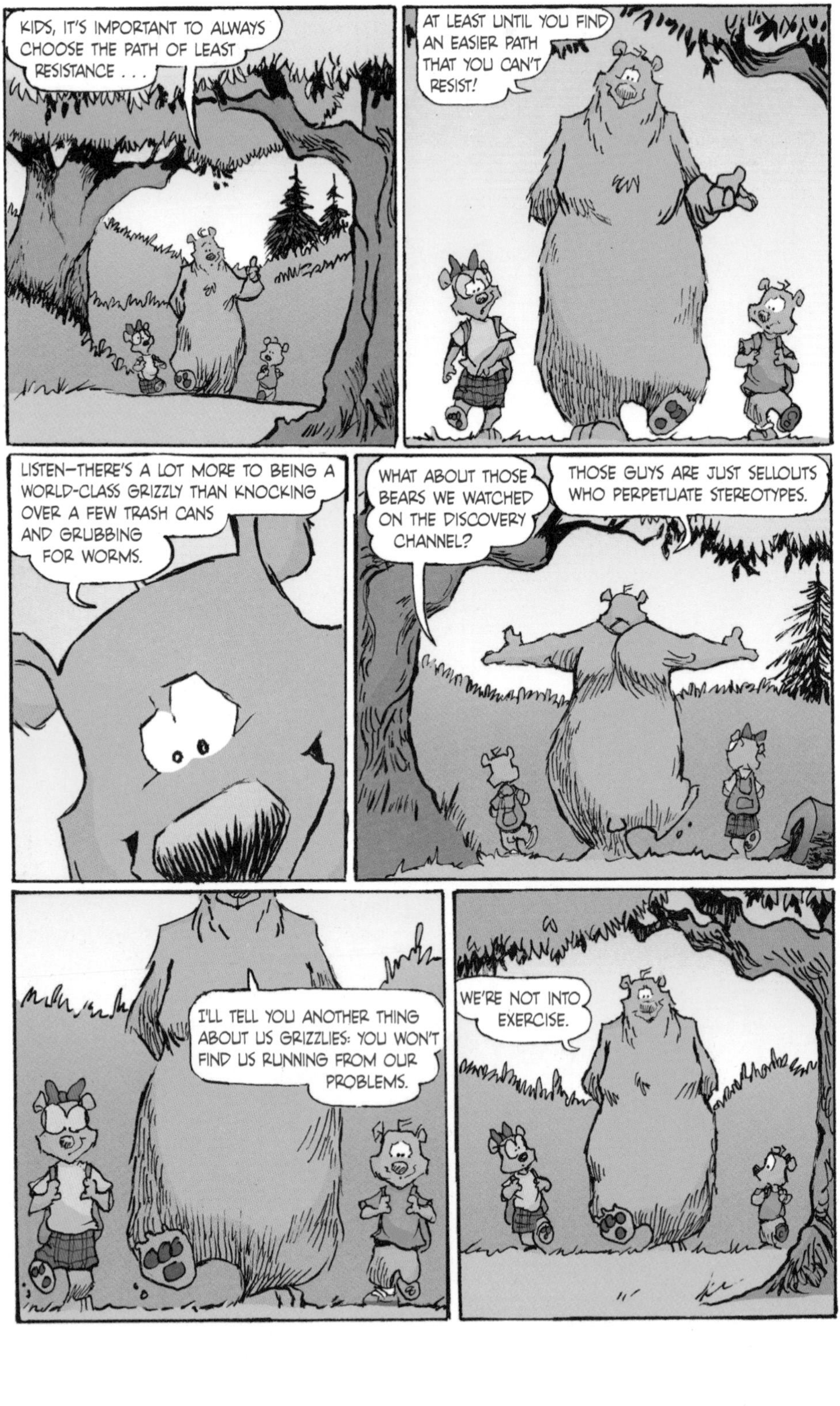
KIDS, IT'S IMPORTANT TO ALWAYS CHOOSE THE PATH OF LEAST RESISTANCE . . .
AT LEAST UNTIL YOU FIND AN EASIER PATH THAT YOU CAN'T RESIST!
LISTEN—THERE'S A LOT MORE TO BEING A WORLD-CLASS GRIZZLY THAN KNOCKING OVER A FEW TRASH CANS AND GRUBBING FOR WORMS.
WHAT ABOUT THOSE BEARS WE WATCHED ON THE DISCOVERY CHANNEL?
THOSE GUYS ARE JUST SELLOUTS WHO PERPETUATE STEREOTYPES.
I'LL TELL YOU ANOTHER THING ABOUT US GRIZZLIES: YOU WON'T FIND US RUNNING FROM OUR PROBLEMS.
WE'RE NOT INTO EXERCISE.

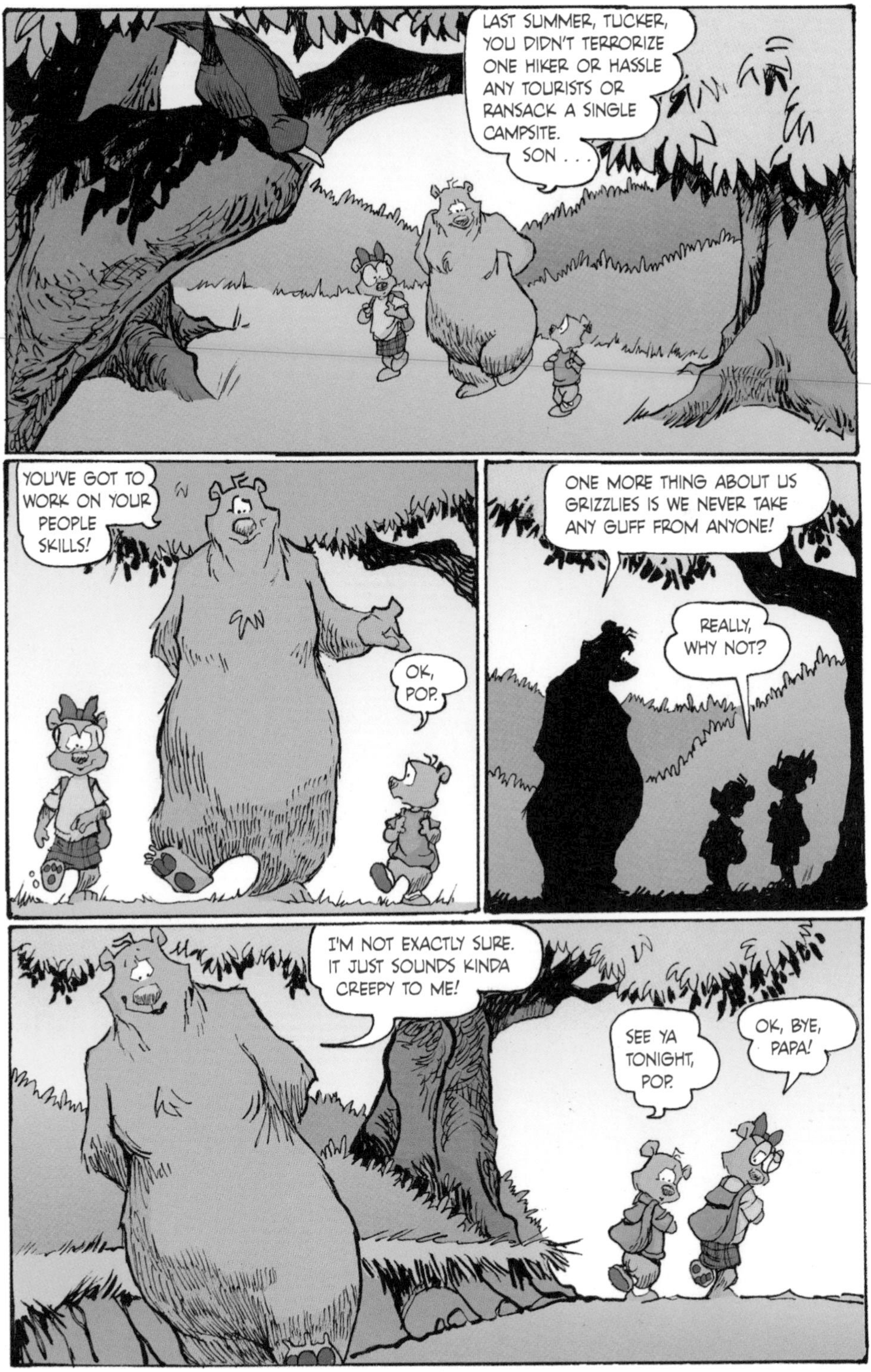
LAST SUMMER, TUCKER, YOU DIDN'T TERRORIZE ONE HIKER OR HASSLE ANY TOURISTS OR RANSACK A SINGLE CAMPSITE. SON . . .
YOU'VE GOT TO WORK ON YOUR PEOPLE SKILLS!
OK, POP.
ONE MORE THING ABOUT US GRIZZLIES IS WE NEVER TAKE ANY GUFF FROM ANYONE!
REALLY, WHY NOT?
I'M NOT EXACTLY SURE. IT JUST SOUNDS KINDA CREEPY TO ME!
SEE YA TONIGHT, POP.
OK, BYE, PAPA!

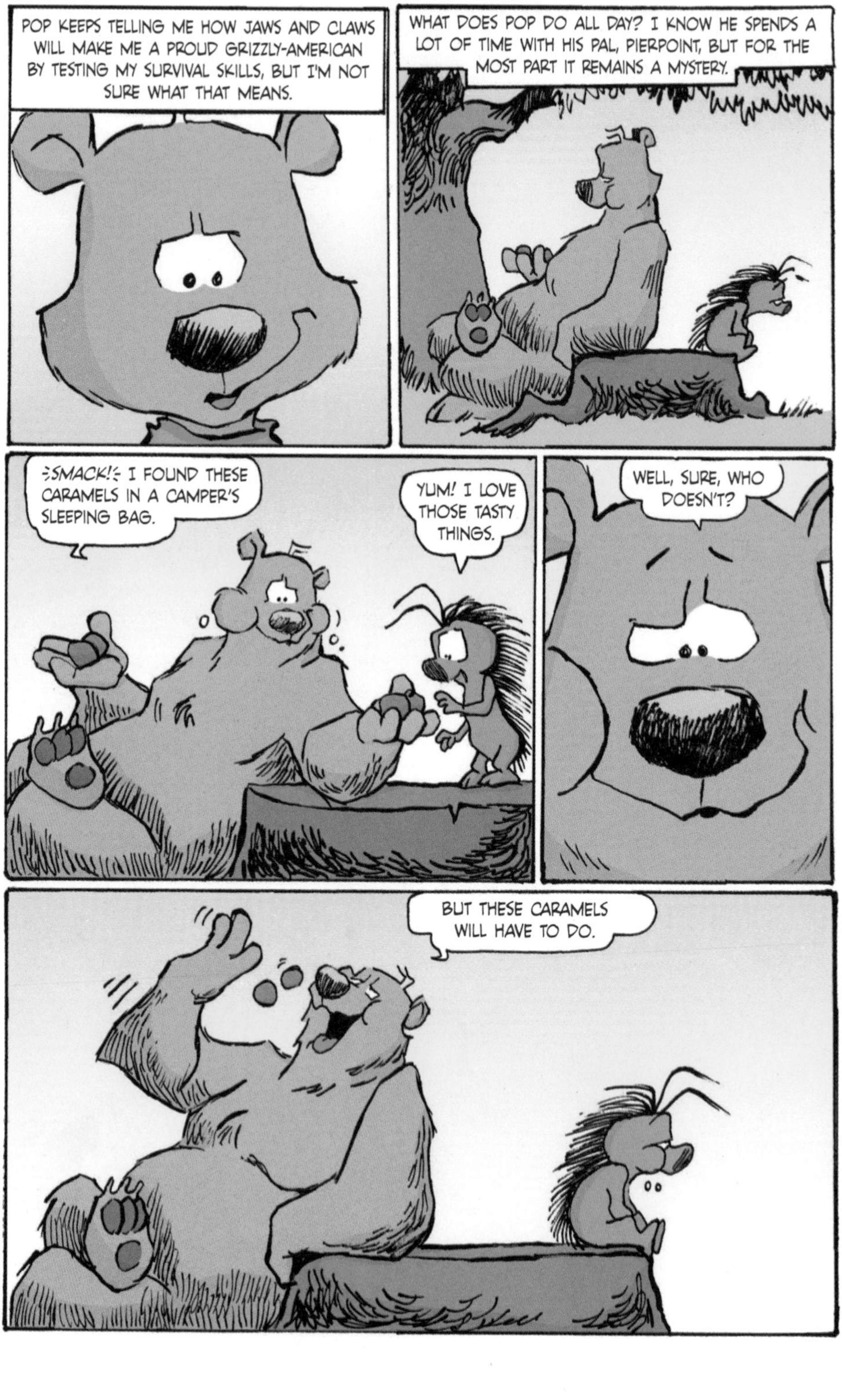
POP KEEPS TELLING ME HOW JAWS AND CLAWS WILL MAKE ME A PROUD GRIZZLY-AMERICAN BY TESTING MY SURVIVAL SKILLS, BUT I'M NOT SURE WHAT THAT MEANS.
WHAT DOES POP DO ALL DAY? I KNOW HE SPENDS A LOT OF TIME WITH HIS PAL, PIERPOINT, BUT FOR THE MOST PART IT REMAINS A MYSTERY.
SMACK! I FOUND THESE CARAMELS IN A CAMPER'S SLEEPING BAG.
YUM! I LOVE THOSE TASTY THINGS.
WELL, SURE, WHO DOESN'T?
BUT THESE CARAMELS WILL HAVE TO DO.

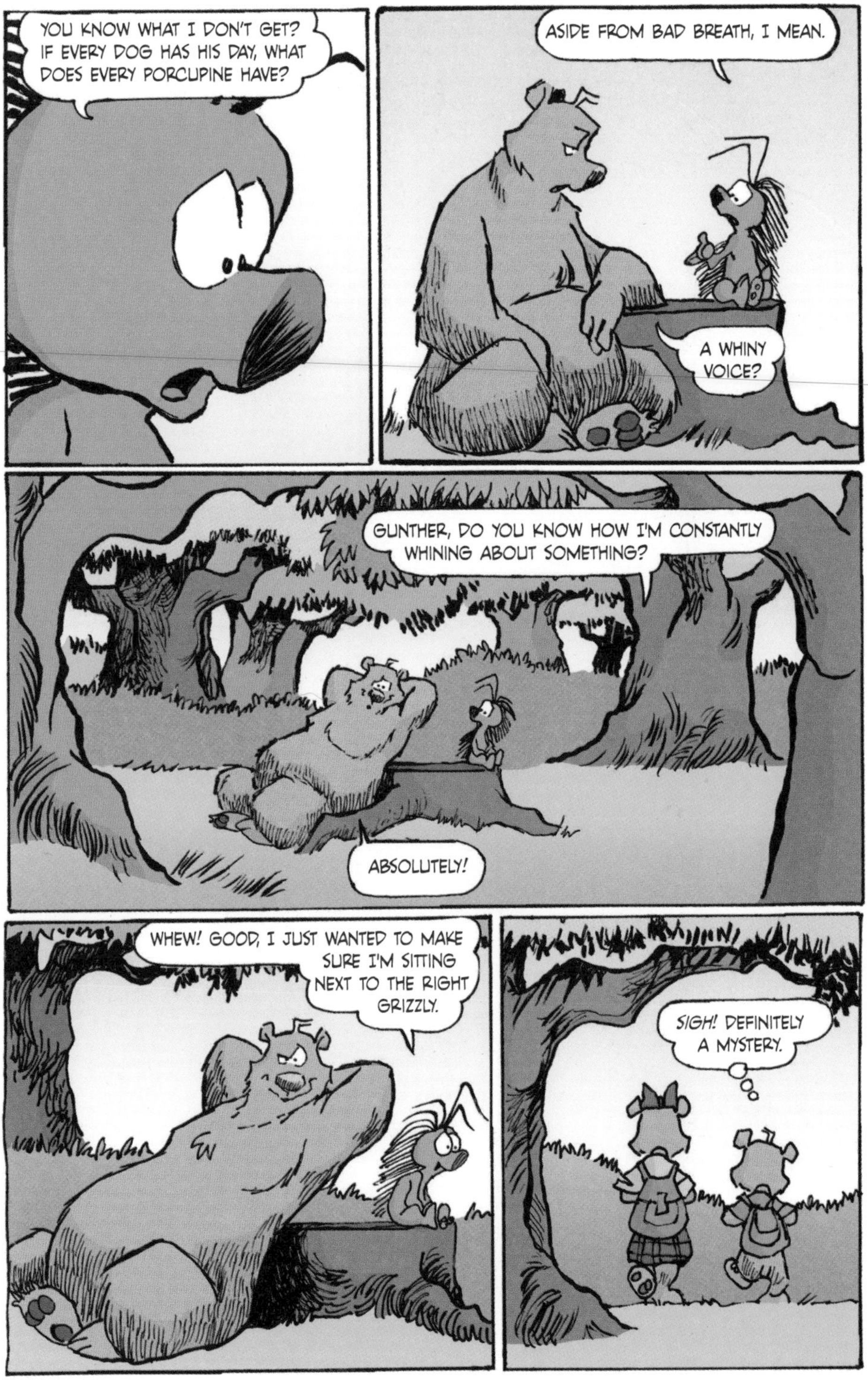
YOU KNOW WHAT I DON'T GET? IF EVERY DOG HAS HIS DAY, WHAT DOES EVERY PORCUPINE HAVE?
ASIDE FROM BAD BREATH, I MEAN.
A WHINY VOICE?
GUNTHER, DO YOU KNOW HOW I'M CONSTANTLY WHINING ABOUT SOMETHING?
ABSOLUTELY!
WHEW! GOOD, I JUST WANTED TO MAKE SURE I'M SITTING NEXT TO THE RIGHT GRIZZLY.
SIGH! DEFINITELY A MYSTERY.

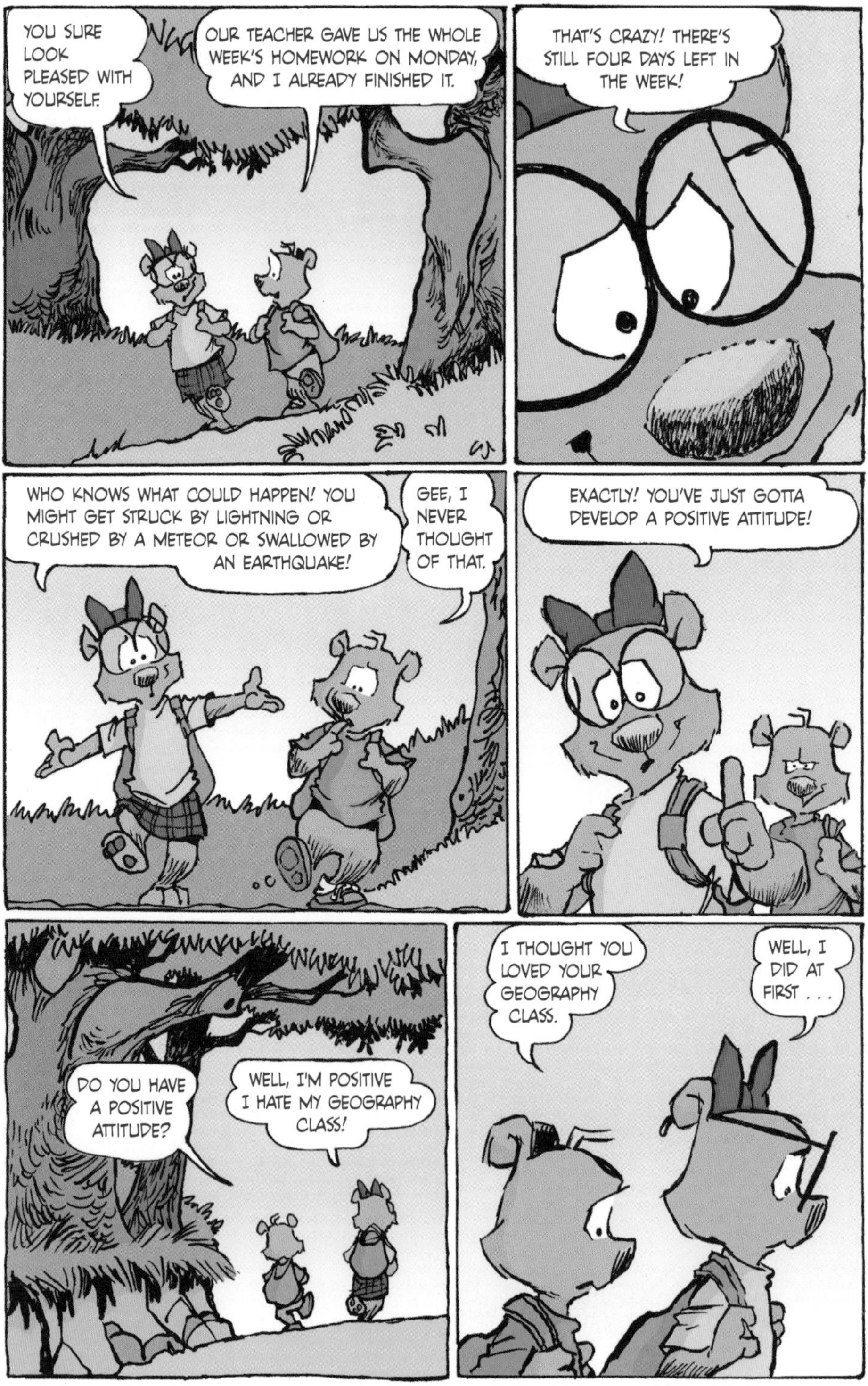
YOU SURE LOOK PLEASED WITH YOURSELF.
OUR TEACHER GAVE US THE WHOLE WEEK'S HOMEWORK ON MONDAY, AND I ALREADY FINISHED IT.
THAT'S CRAZY! THERE'S STILL FOUR DAYS LEFT IN THE WEEK!
WHO KNOWS WHAT COULD HAPPEN! YOU MIGHT GET STRUCK BY LIGHTNING OR CRUSHED BY A METEOR OR SWALLOWED BY AN EARTHQUAKE!
GEE, I NEVER THOUGHT OF THAT.
EXACTLY! YOU'VE JUST GOTTA DEVELOP A POSITIVE ATTITUDE!
DO YOU HAVE A POSITIVE ATTITUDE?
WELL, I'M POSITIVE I HATE MY GEOGRAPHY CLASS!
I THOUGHT YOU LOVED YOUR GEOGRAPHY CLASS.
WELL, I DID AT FIRST . . .

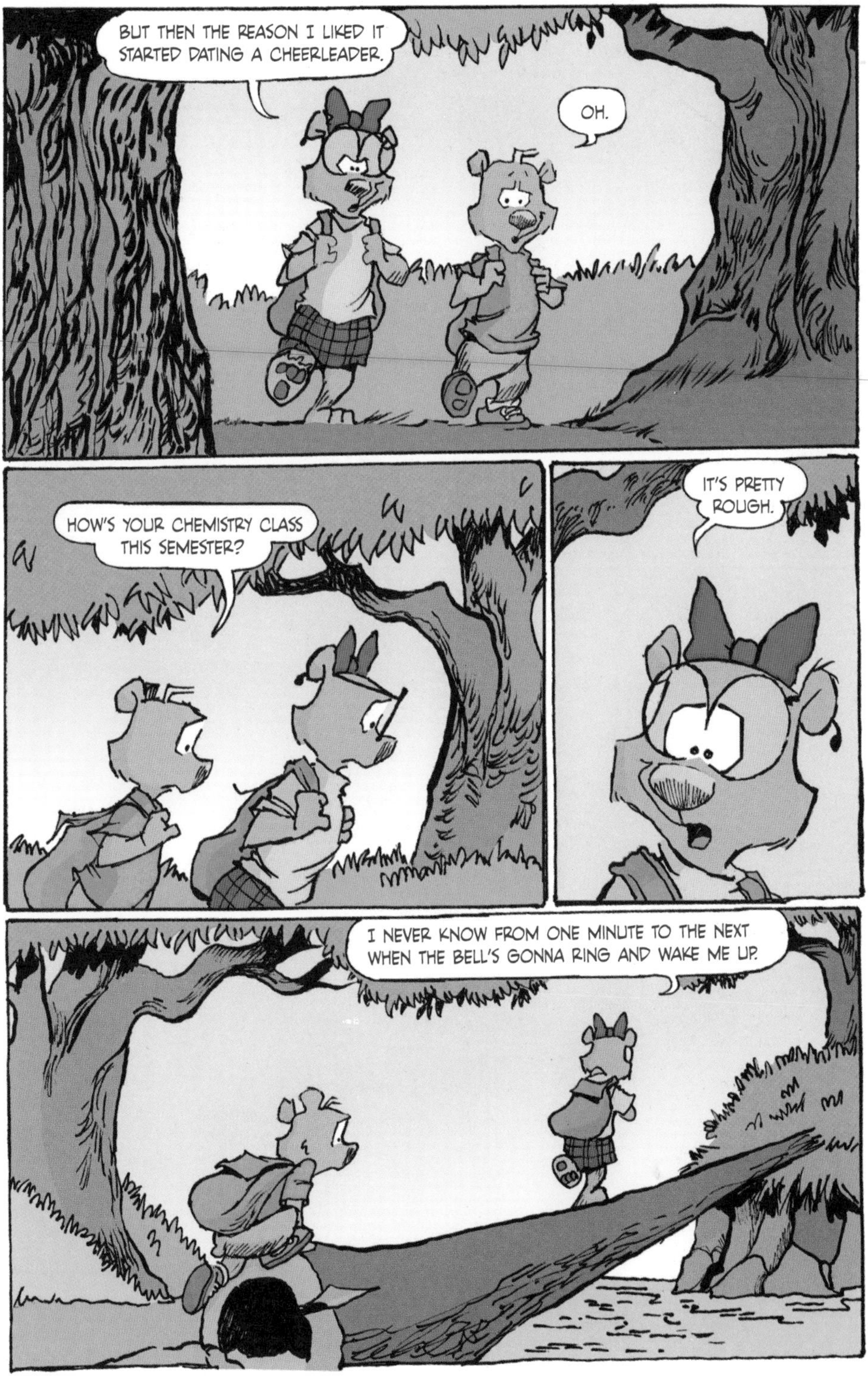
BUT THEN THE REASON I LIKED IT STARTED DATING A CHEERLEADER.
OH.
HOW'S YOUR CHEMISTRY CLASS THIS SEMESTER?
IT'S PRETTY ROUGH.
I NEVER KNOW FROM ONE MINUTE TO THE NEXT WHEN THE BELL'S GONNA RING AND WAKE ME UP.

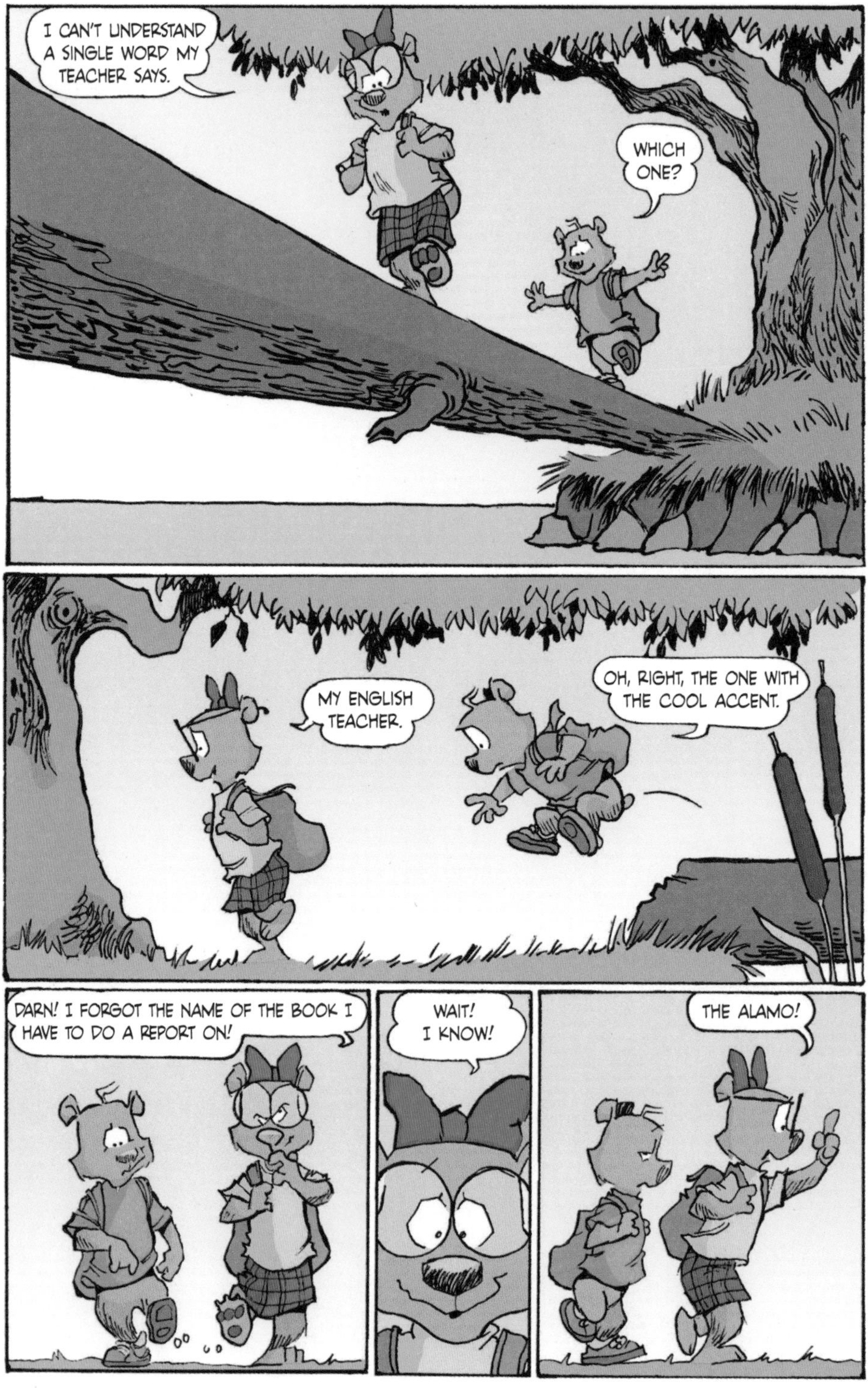
I CAN'T UNDERSTAND A SINGLE WORD MY TEACHER SAYS.
WHICH ONE?
MY ENGLISH TEACHER.
OH, RIGHT, THE ONE WITH THE COOL ACCENT.
DARN! I FORGOT THE NAME OF THE BOOK I HAVE TO DO A REPORT ON!
WAIT! I KNOW!
THE ALAMO!

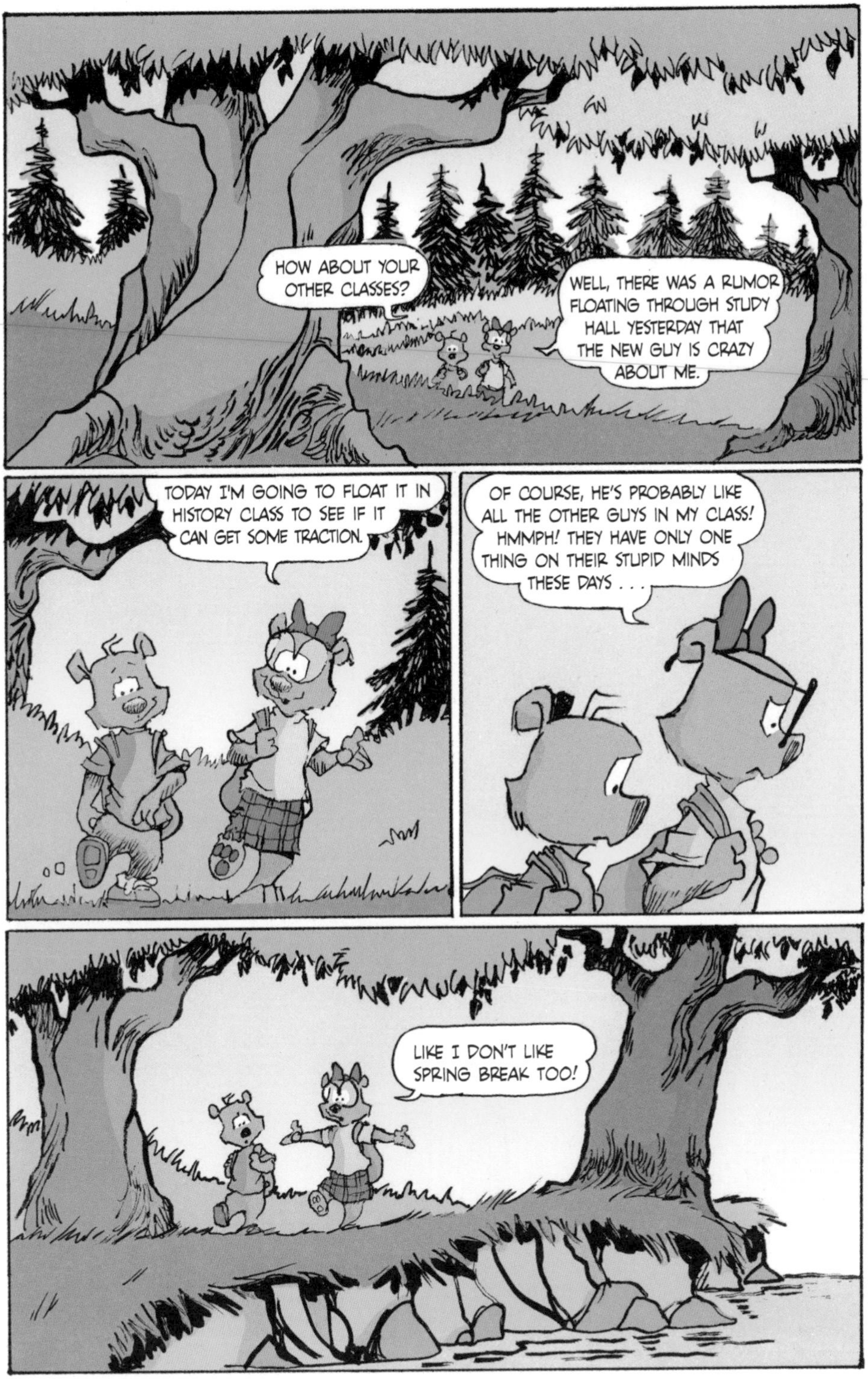

HOW ABOUT YOUR OTHER CLASSES?
WELL, THERE WAS A RUMOR FLOATING THROUGH STUDY HALL YESTERDAY THAT THE NEW GUY IS CRAZY ABOUT ME.
TODAY I'M GOING TO FLOAT IT IN HISTORY CLASS TO SEE IF IT CAN GET SOME TRACTION.
OF COURSE, HE'S PROBABLY LIKE ALL THE OTHER GUYS IN MY CLASS! HMMPH! THEY HAVE ONLY ONE THING ON THEIR STUPID MINDS THESE DAYS . . .
LIKE I DON'T LIKE SPRING BREAK TOO!

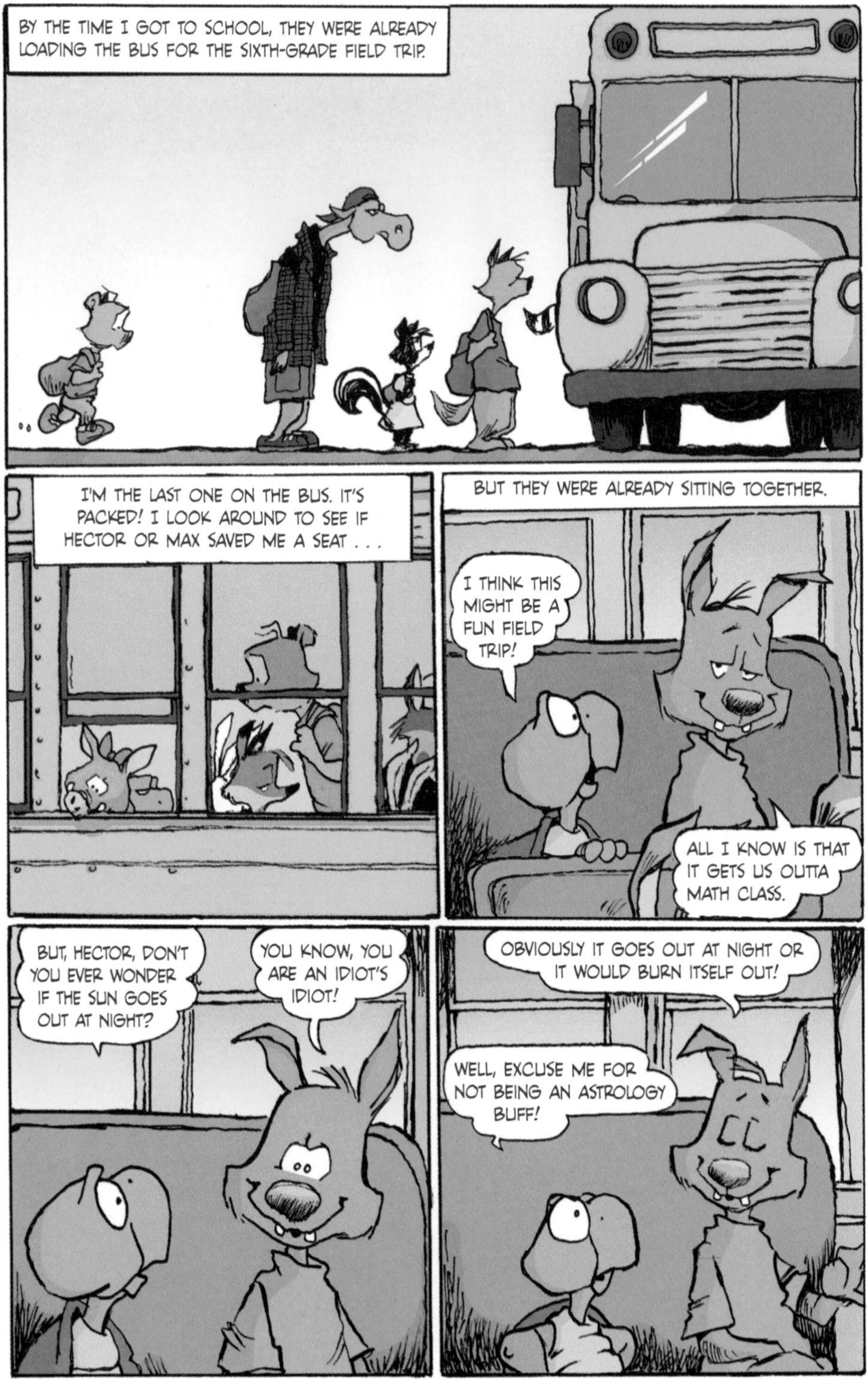
BY THE TIME I GOT TO SCHOOL, THEY WERE ALREADY LOADING THE BUS FOR THE SIXTH-GRADE FIELD TRIP.
I'M THE LAST ONE ON THE BUS. IT'S PACKED! I LOOK AROUND TO SEE IF HECTOR OR MAX SAVED ME A SEAT . . .
BUT THEY WERE ALREADY SITTING TOGETHER.
I THINK THIS MIGHT BE A FUN FIELD TRIP!
ALL I KNOW IS THAT IT GETS US OUTTA MATH CLASS.
BUT, HECTOR, DON'T YOU EVER WONDER IF THE SUN GOES OUT AT NIGHT?
YOU KNOW, YOU ARE AN IDIOT'S IDIOT!
OBVIOUSLY IT GOES OUT AT NIGHT OR IT WOULD BURN ITSELF OUT!
WELL, EXCUSE ME FOR NOT BEING AN ASTROLOGY BUFF!

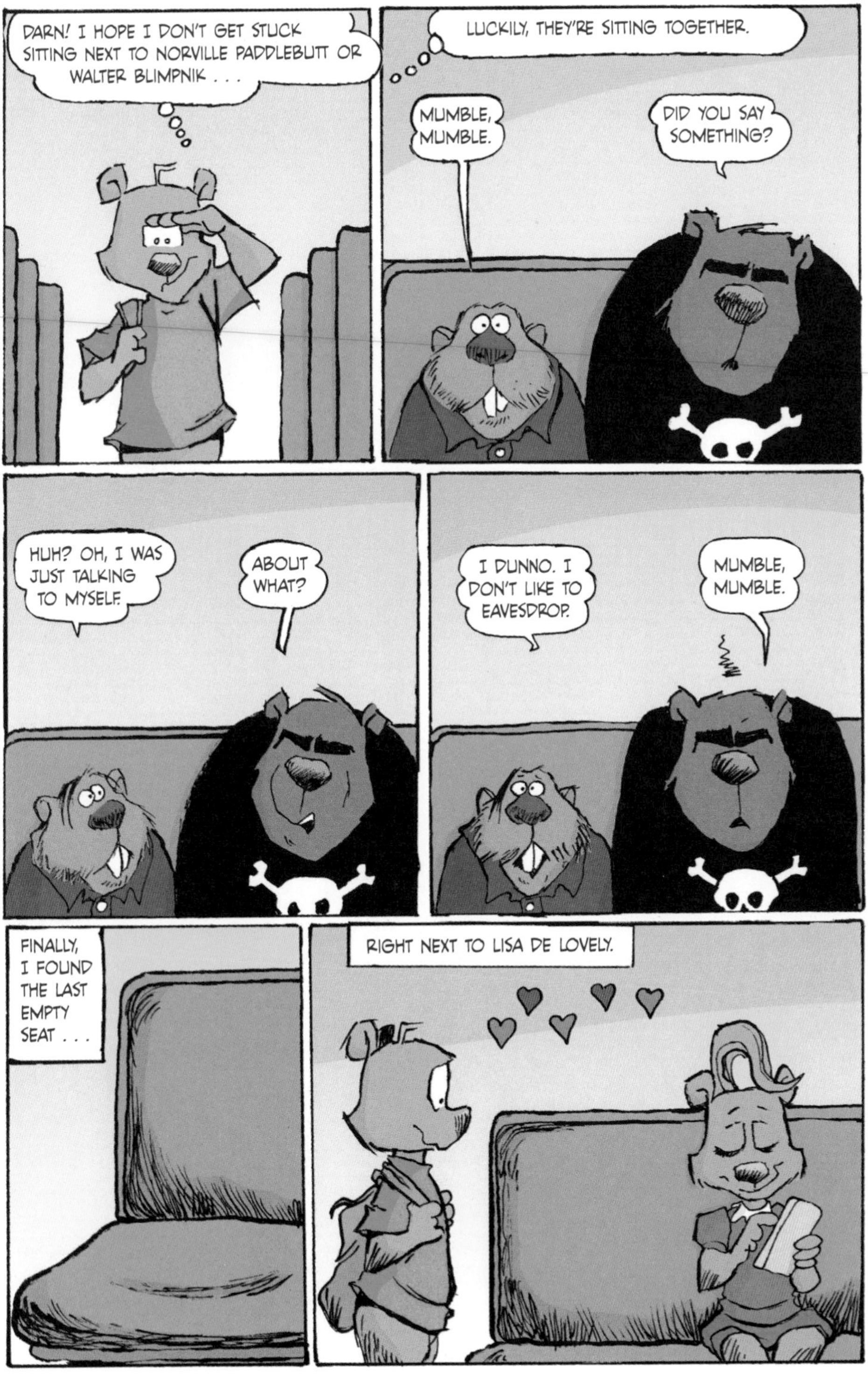
DARN! I HOPE I DON'T GET STUCK SITTING NEXT TO NORVILLE PADDLEBUTT OR WALTER BLIMPNIK . . .
LUCKILY, THEY'RE SITTING TOGETHER.
MUMBLE, MUMBLE.
DID YOU SAY SOMETHING?
HUH? OH, I WAS JUST TALKING TO MYSELF.
ABOUT WHAT?
I DUNNO. I DON'T LIKE TO EAVESDROP.
MUMBLE, MUMBLE.
FINALLY, I FOUND THE LAST EMPTY SEAT . . .
RIGHT NEXT TO LISA DE LOVELY.

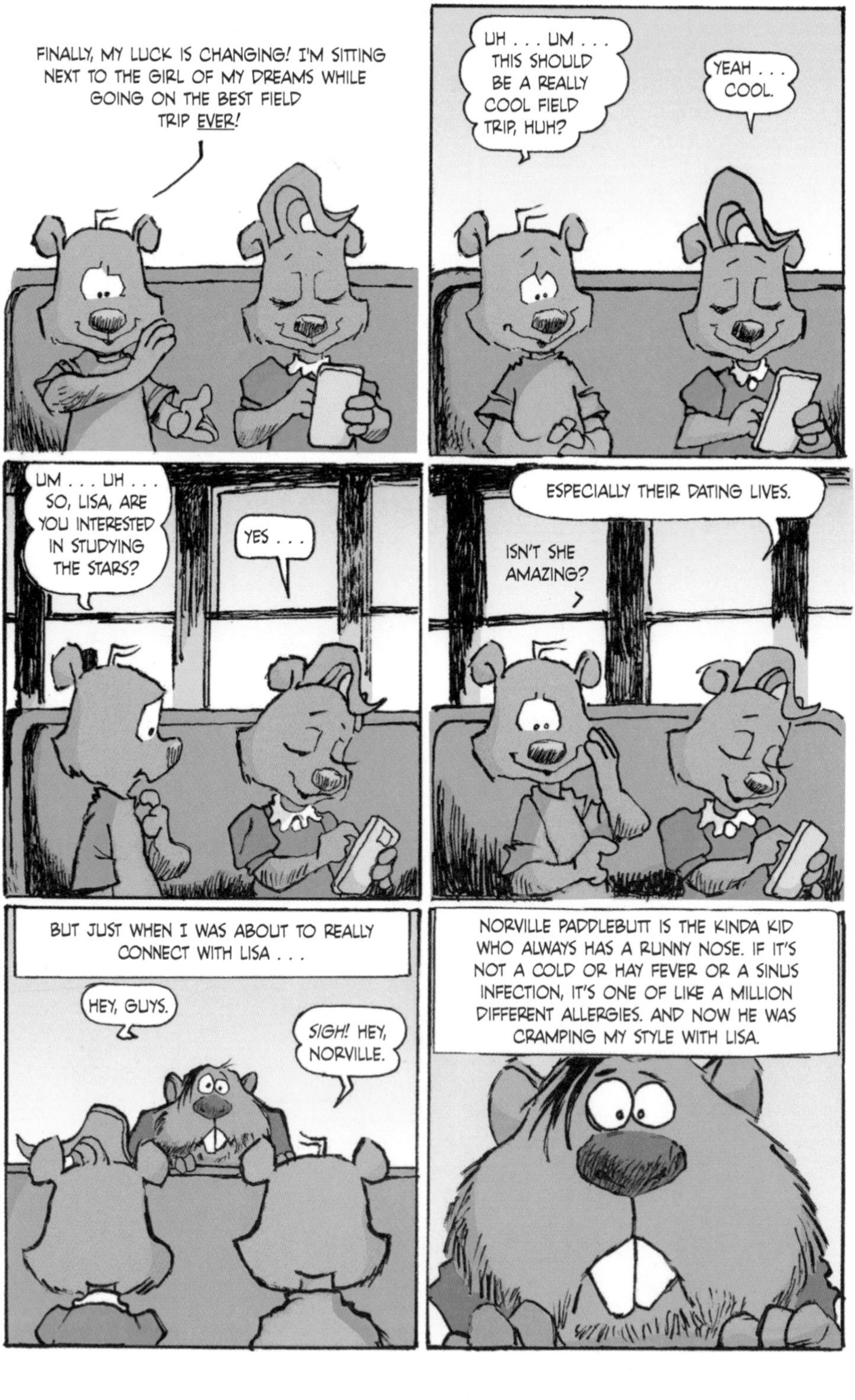
FINALLY, MY LUCK IS CHANGING! I'M SITTING NEXT TO THE GIRL OF MY DREAMS WHILE GOING ON THE BEST FIELD TRIP EVER!
UH . . . UM . . . THIS SHOULD BE A REALLY COOL FIELD TRIP, HUH?
YEAH . . . COOL.
UM . . . UH . . . SO, LISA, ARE YOU INTERESTED IN STUDYING THE STARS?
YES . . .
ESPECIALLY THEIR DATING LIVES.
ISN'T SHE AMAZING?
BUT JUST WHEN I WAS ABOUT TO REALLY CONNECT WITH LISA . . .
HEY, GUYS.
SIGH! HEY, NORVILLE.
NORVILLE PADDLEBUTT IS THE KINDA KID WHO ALWAYS HAS A RUNNY NOSE. IF IT'S NOT A COLD OR HAY FEVER OR A SINUS INFECTION, IT'S ONE OF LIKE A MILLION DIFFERENT ALLERGIES. AND NOW HE WAS CRAMPING MY STYLE WITH LISA.

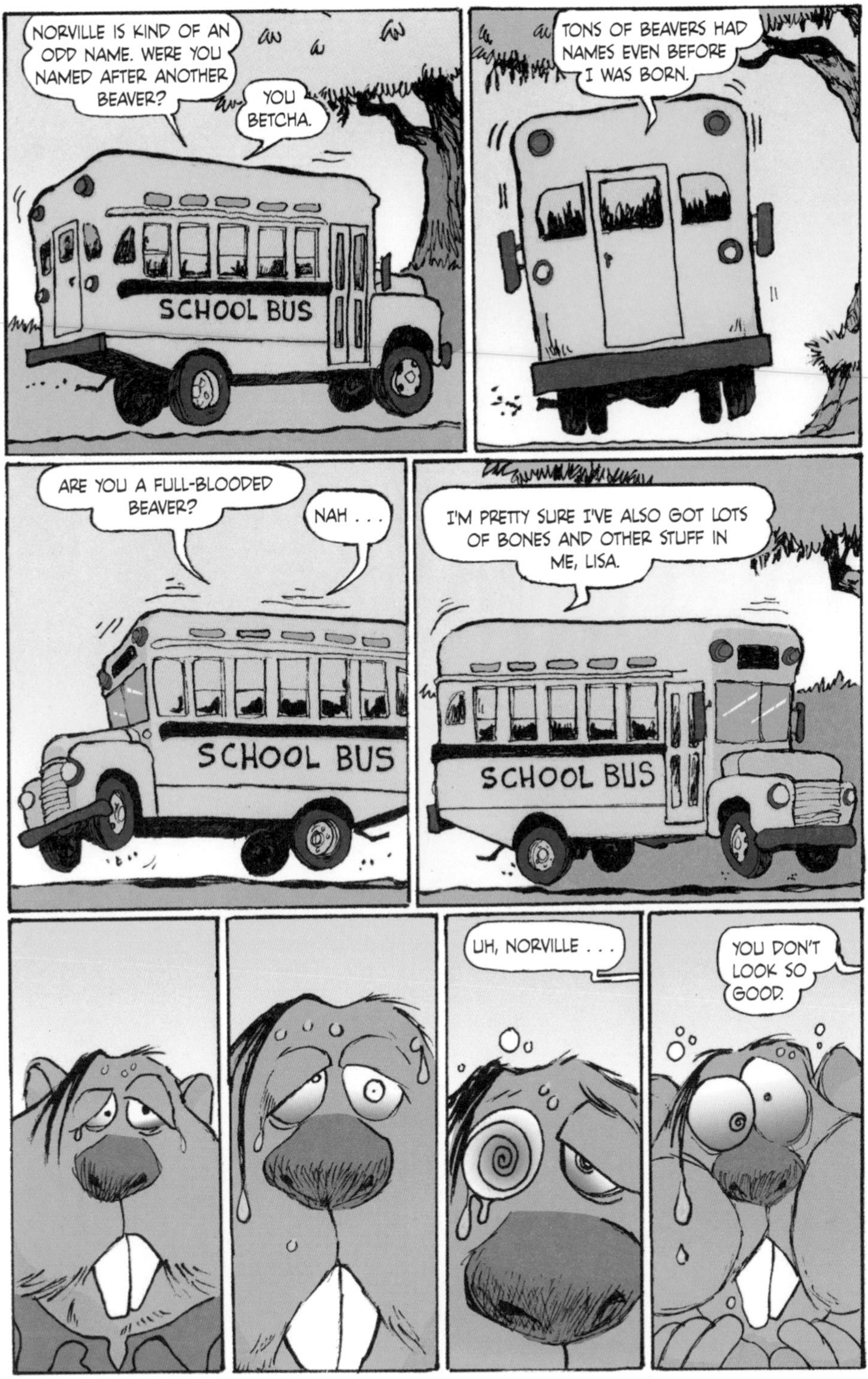
NORVILLE IS KIND OF AN ODD NAME. WERE YOU NAMED AFTER ANOTHER BEAVER?
YOU BETCHA.
TONS OF BEAVERS HAD NAMES EVEN BEFORE I WAS BORN.
SCHOOL BUS
ARE YOU A FULL-BLOODED BEAVER?
NAH . . .
I'M PRETTY SURE I'VE ALSO GOT LOTS OF BONES AND OTHER STUFF IN ME, LISA.
SCHOOL BUS
SCHOOL BUS
UH, NORVILLE . . .
YOU DON'T LOOK SO GOOD.

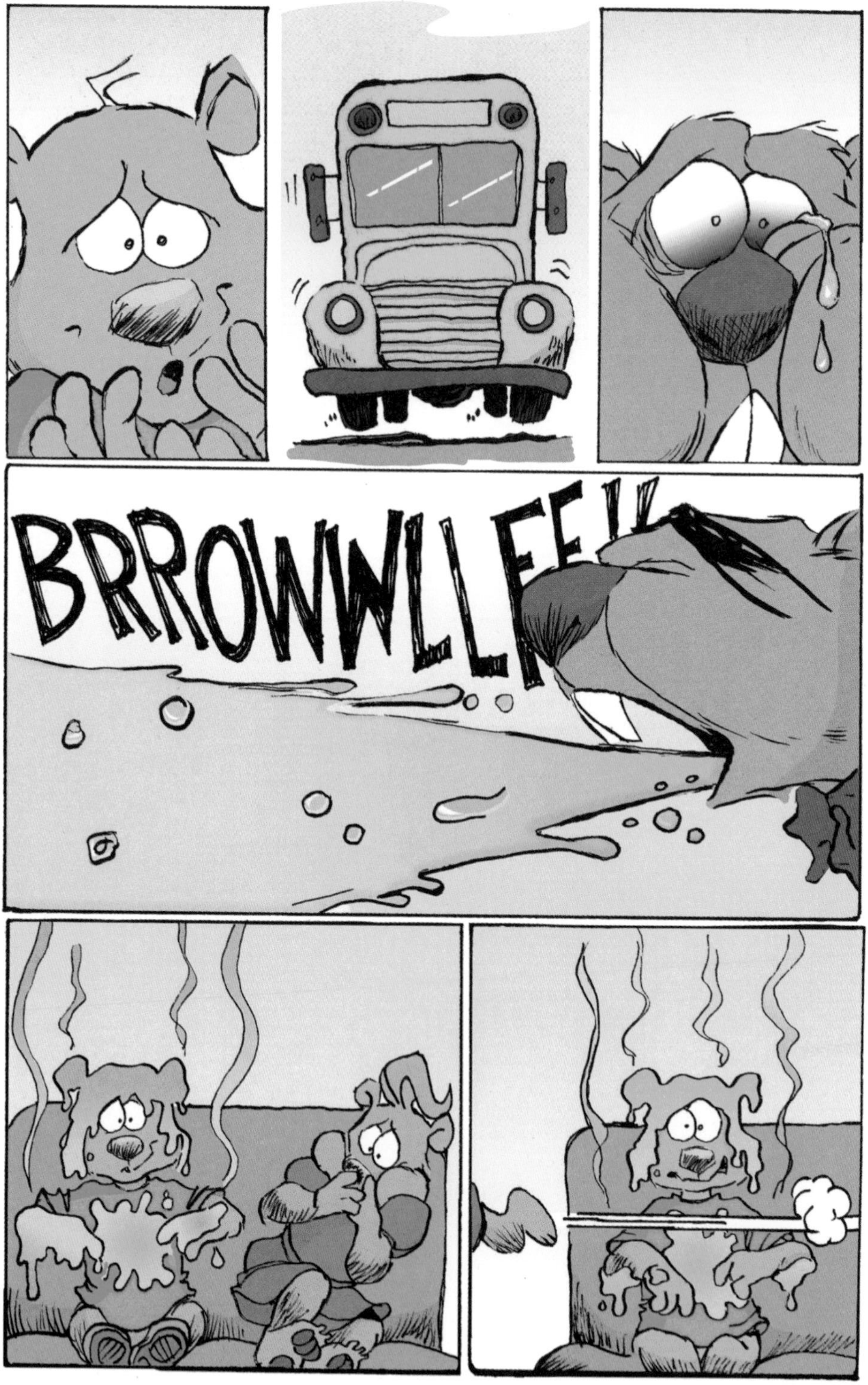
BRRROWWLLFF!!

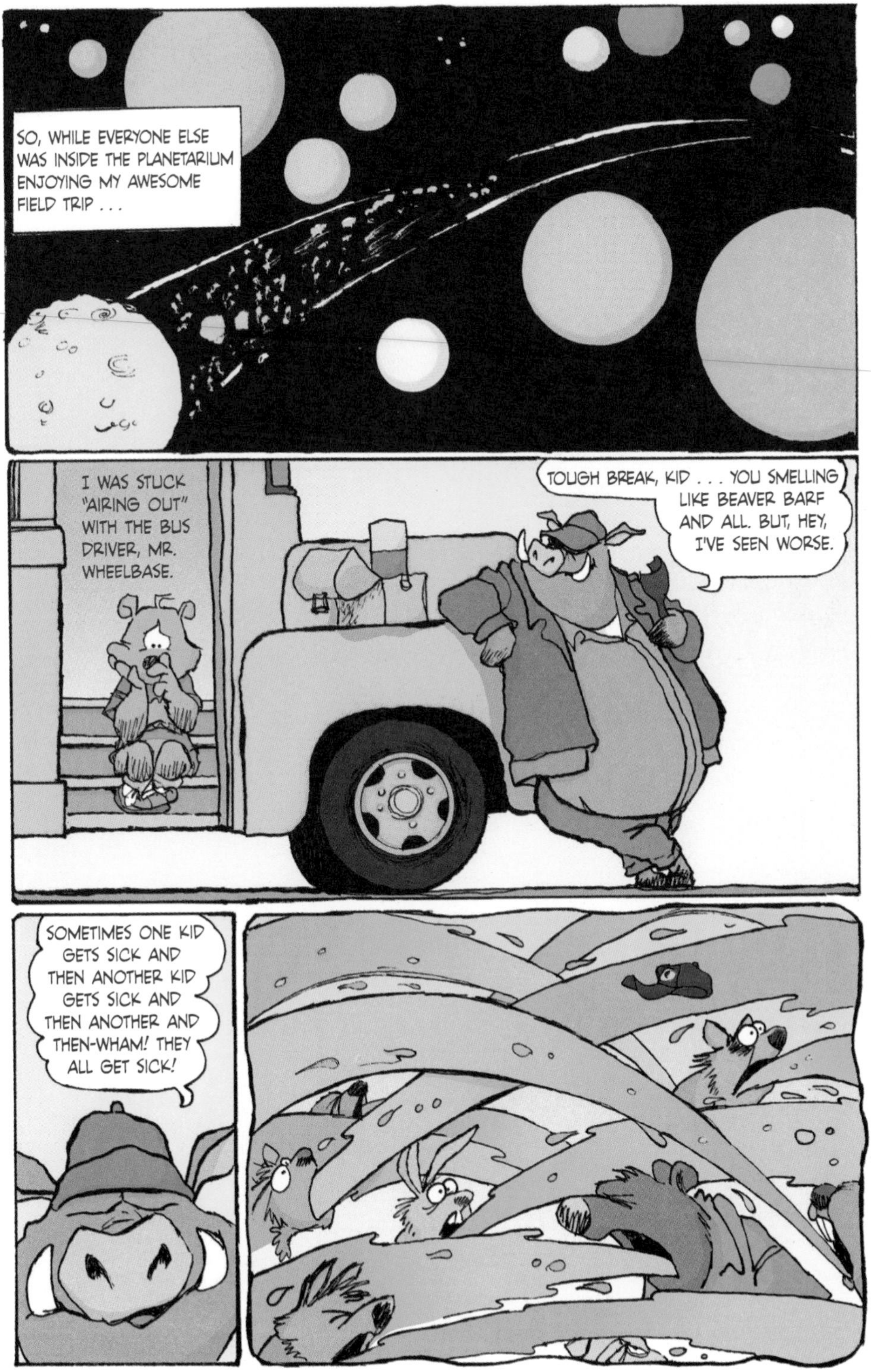
SO, WHILE EVERYONE ELSE WAS INSIDE THE PLANETARIUM ENJOYING MY AWESOME FIELD TRIP . . .
I WAS STUCK "AIRING OUT" WITH THE BUS DRIVER, MR. WHEELBASE.
TOUGH BREAK, KID . . . YOU SMELLING LIKE BEAVER BARF AND ALL. BUT, HEY, I'VE SEEN WORSE.
SOMETIMES ONE KID GETS SICK AND THEN ANOTHER KID GETS SICK AND THEN ANOTHER AND THEN-WHAM! THEY ALL GET SICK!

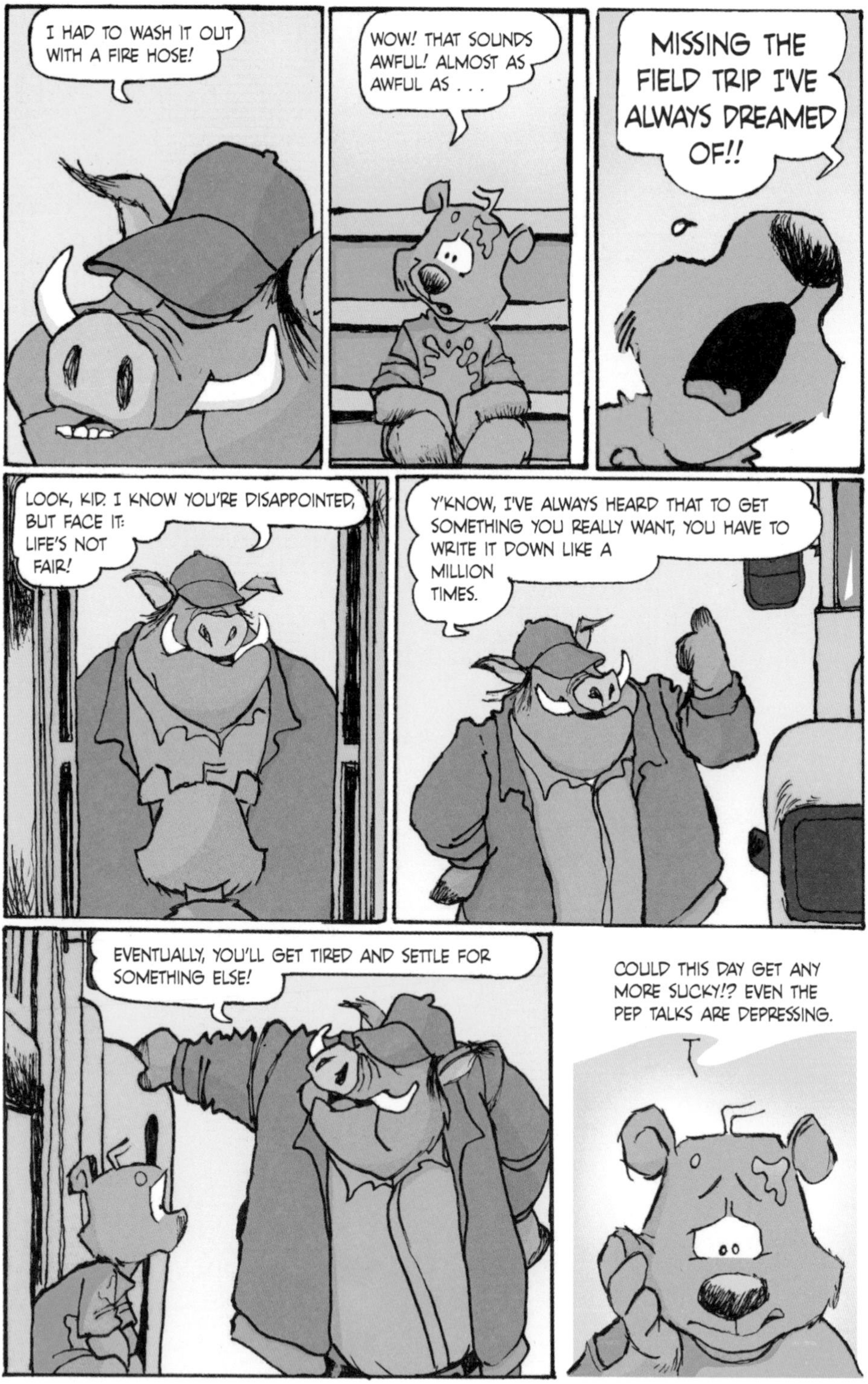
I HAD TO WASH IT OUT WITH A FIRE HOSE!
WOW! THAT SOUNDS AWFUL! ALMOST AS AWFUL AS . . .
MISSING THE FIELD TRIP I'VE ALWAYS DREAMED OF!!
LOOK, KID. I KNOW YOU'RE DISAPPOINTED, BUT FACE IT: LIFE'S NOT FAIR!
Y'KNOW, I'VE ALWAYS HEARD THAT TO GET SOMETHING YOU REALLY WANT, YOU HAVE TO WRITE IT DOWN LIKE A MILLION TIMES.
EVENTUALLY, YOU'LL GET TIRED AND SETTLE FOR SOMETHING ELSE!
COULD THIS DAY GET ANY MORE SUCKY!? EVEN THE PEP TALKS ARE DEPRESSING.

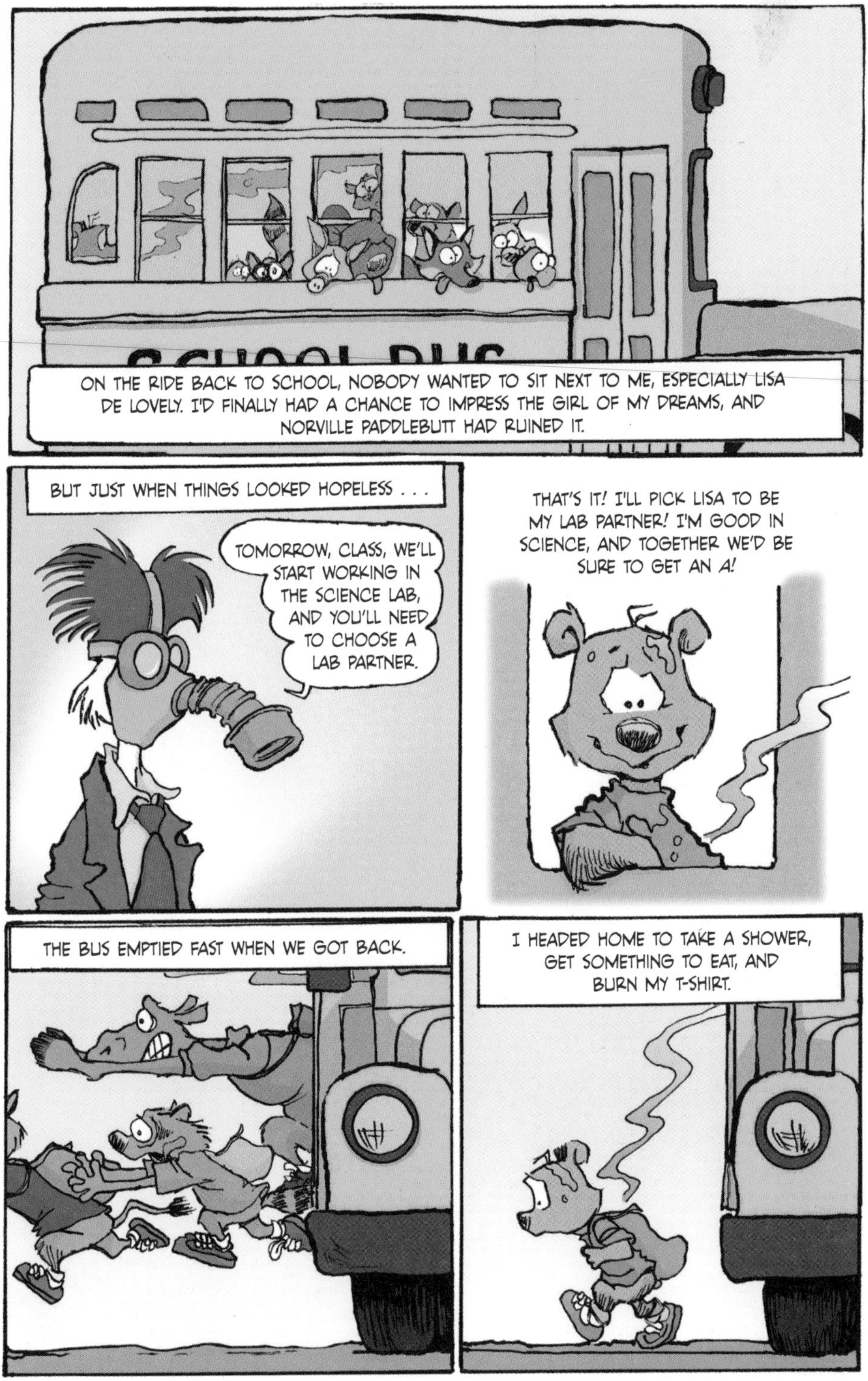
SCHOOL BUS
ON THE RIDE BACK TO SCHOOL, NOBODY WANTED TO SIT NEXT TO ME, ESPECIALLY LISA DE LOVELY. I'D FINALLY HAD A CHANCE TO IMPRESS THE GIRL OF MY DREAMS, AND NORVILLE PADDLEBUTT HAD RUINED IT.
BUT JUST WHEN THINGS LOOKED HOPELESS . . .
TOMORROW, CLASS, WE'LL START WORKING IN THE SCIENCE LAB, AND YOU'LL NEED TO CHOOSE A LAB PARTNER.
THAT'S IT! I'LL PICK LISA TO BE MY LAB PARTNER! I'M GOOD IN SCIENCE, AND TOGETHER WE'D BE SURE TO GET AN *A*!
THE BUS EMPTIED FAST WHEN WE GOT BACK.
I HEADED HOME TO TAKE A SHOWER, GET SOMETHING TO EAT, AND BURN MY T-SHIRT.

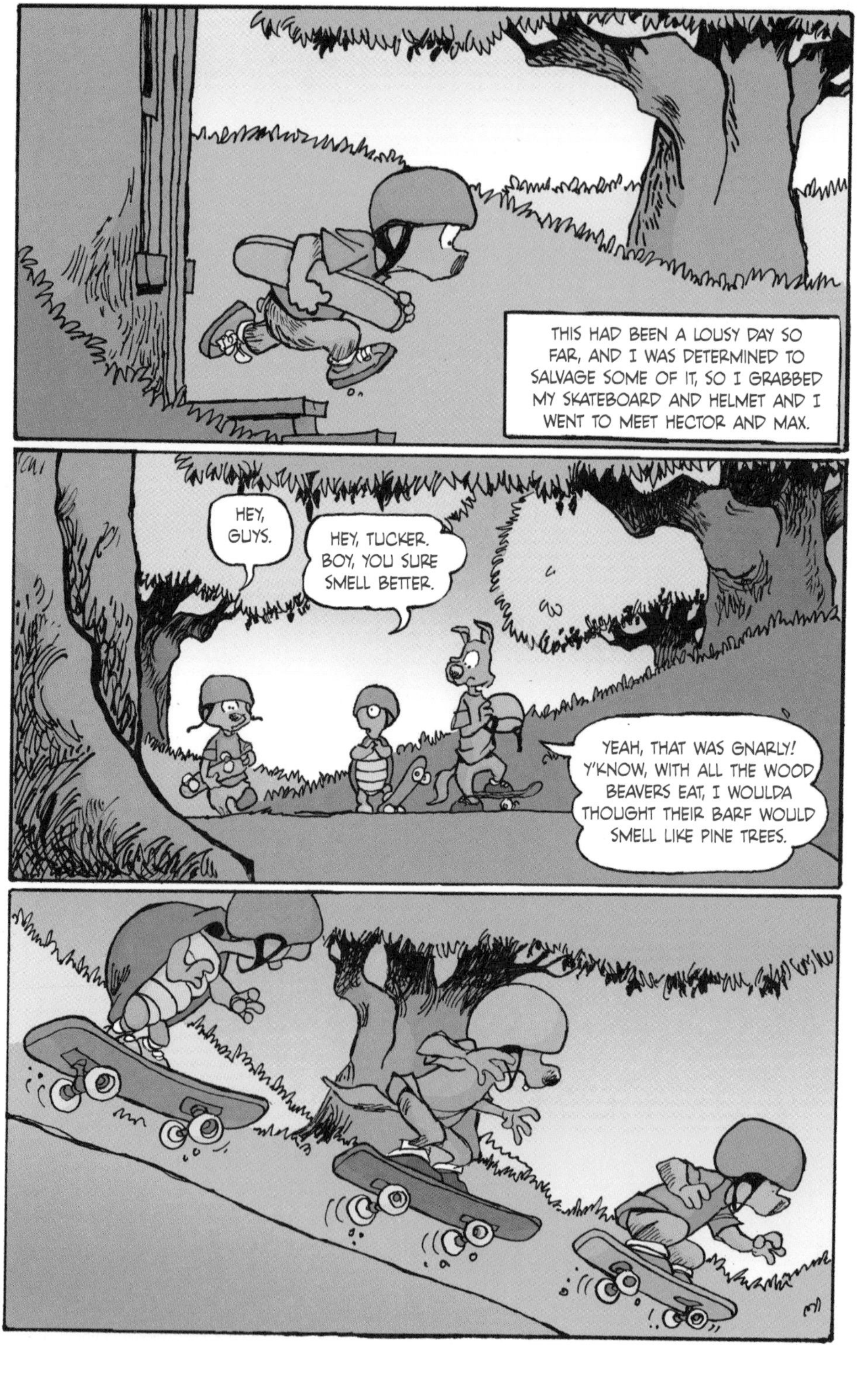
THIS HAD BEEN A LOUSY DAY SO FAR, AND I WAS DETERMINED TO SALVAGE SOME OF IT, SO I GRABBED MY SKATEBOARD AND HELMET AND I WENT TO MEET HECTOR AND MAX.
HEY, GUYS.
HEY, TUCKER. BOY, YOU SURE SMELL BETTER.
YEAH, THAT WAS GNARLY! Y'KNOW, WITH ALL THE WOOD BEAVERS EAT, I WOULDA THOUGHT THEIR BARF WOULD SMELL LIKE PINE TREES.

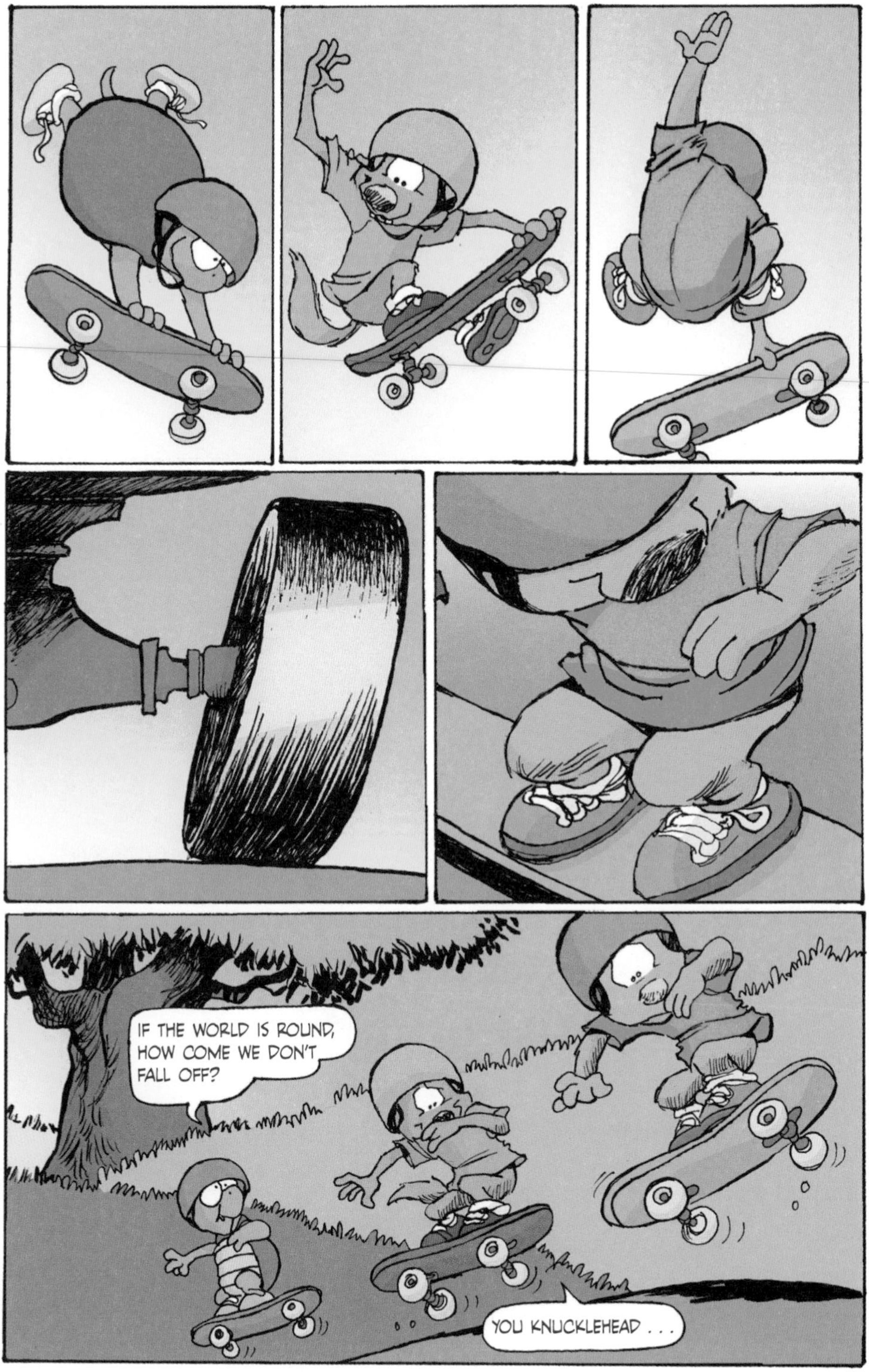
IF THE WORLD IS ROUND, HOW COME WE DON'T FALL OFF?
YOU KNUCKLEHEAD . . .

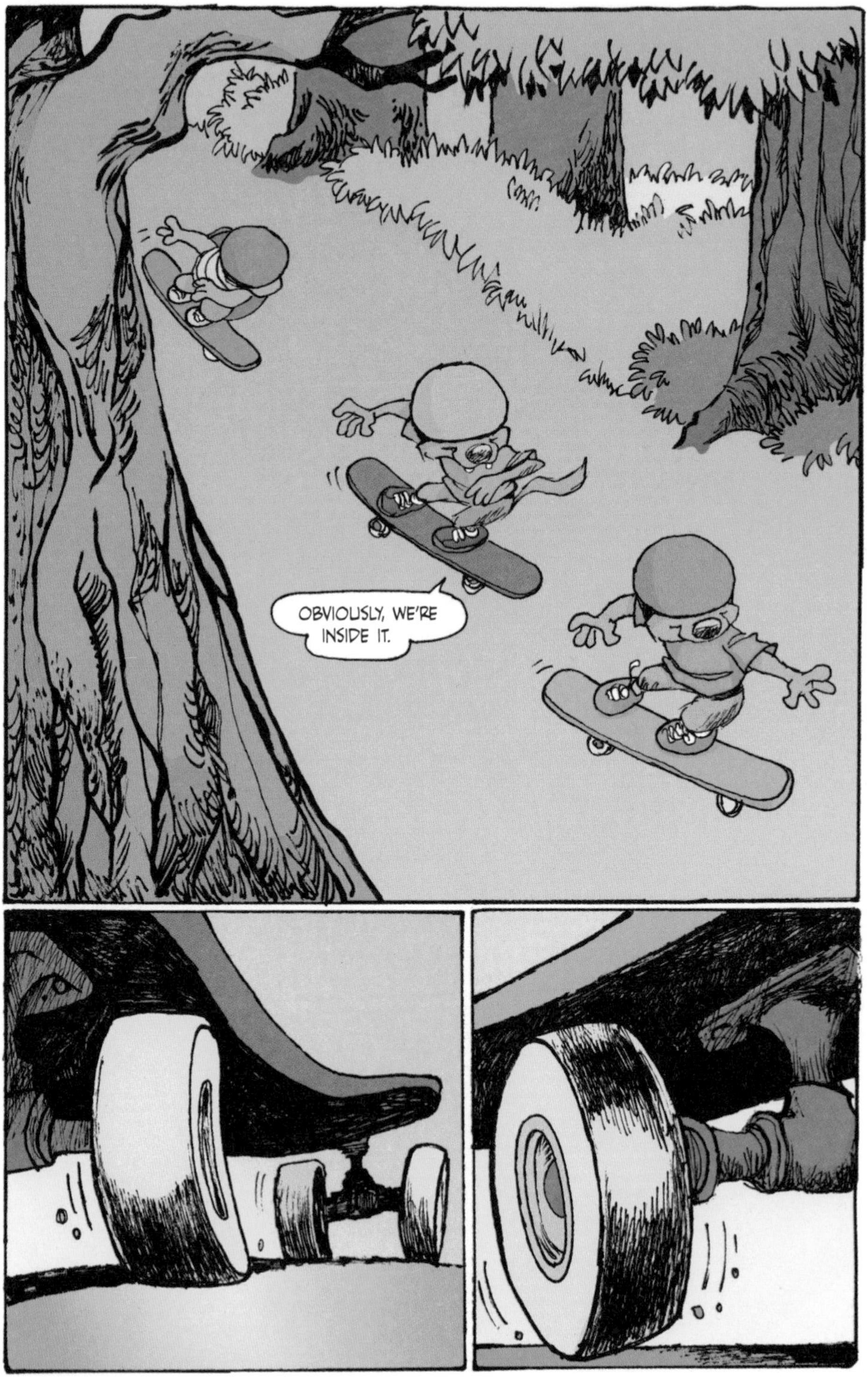
OBVIOUSLY, WE'RE INSIDE IT.

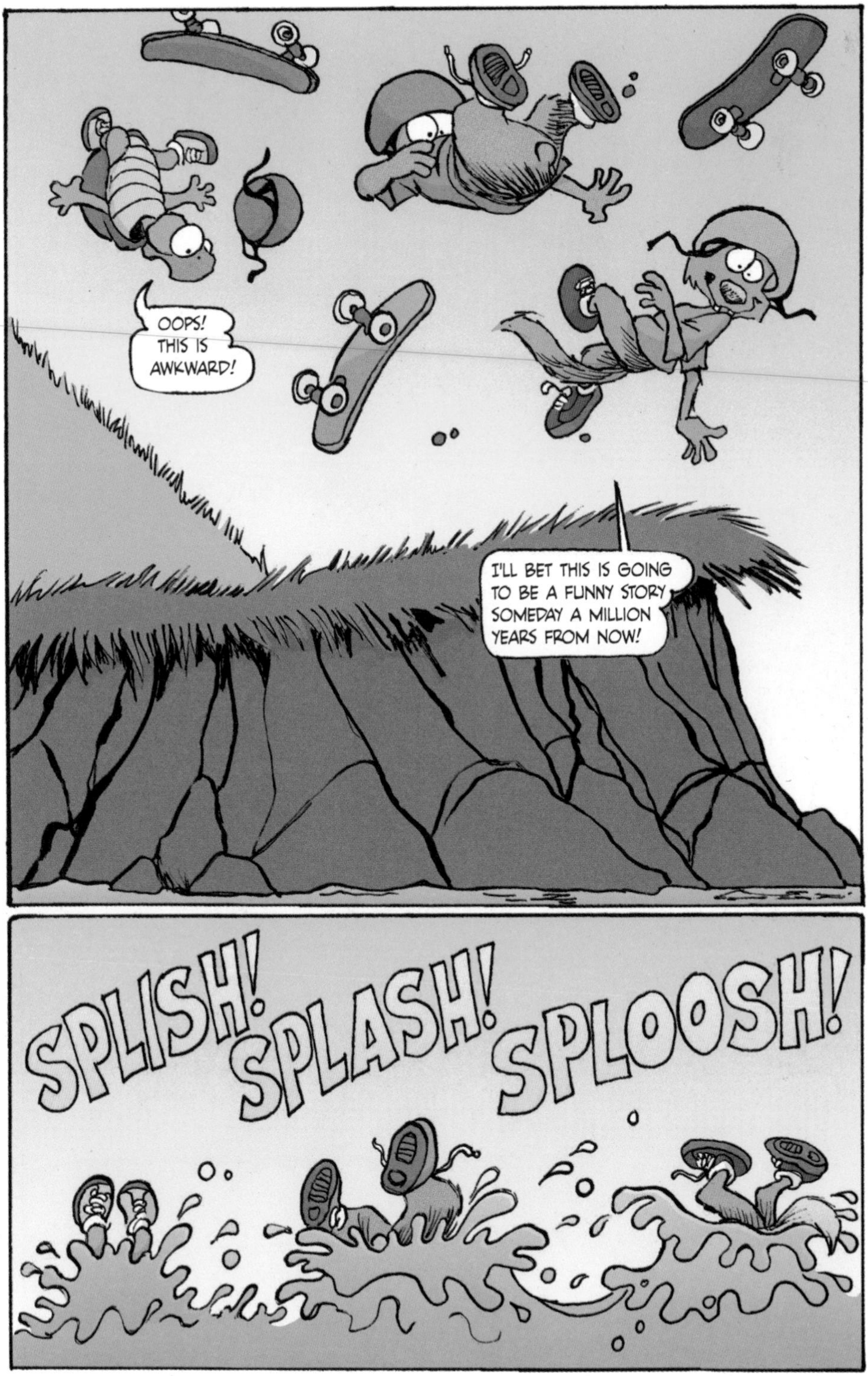
OOPS! THIS IS AWKWARD!
I'LL BET THIS IS GOING TO BE A FUNNY STORY SOMEDAY A MILLION YEARS FROM NOW!
SPLISH! SPLASH! SPLOOSH!

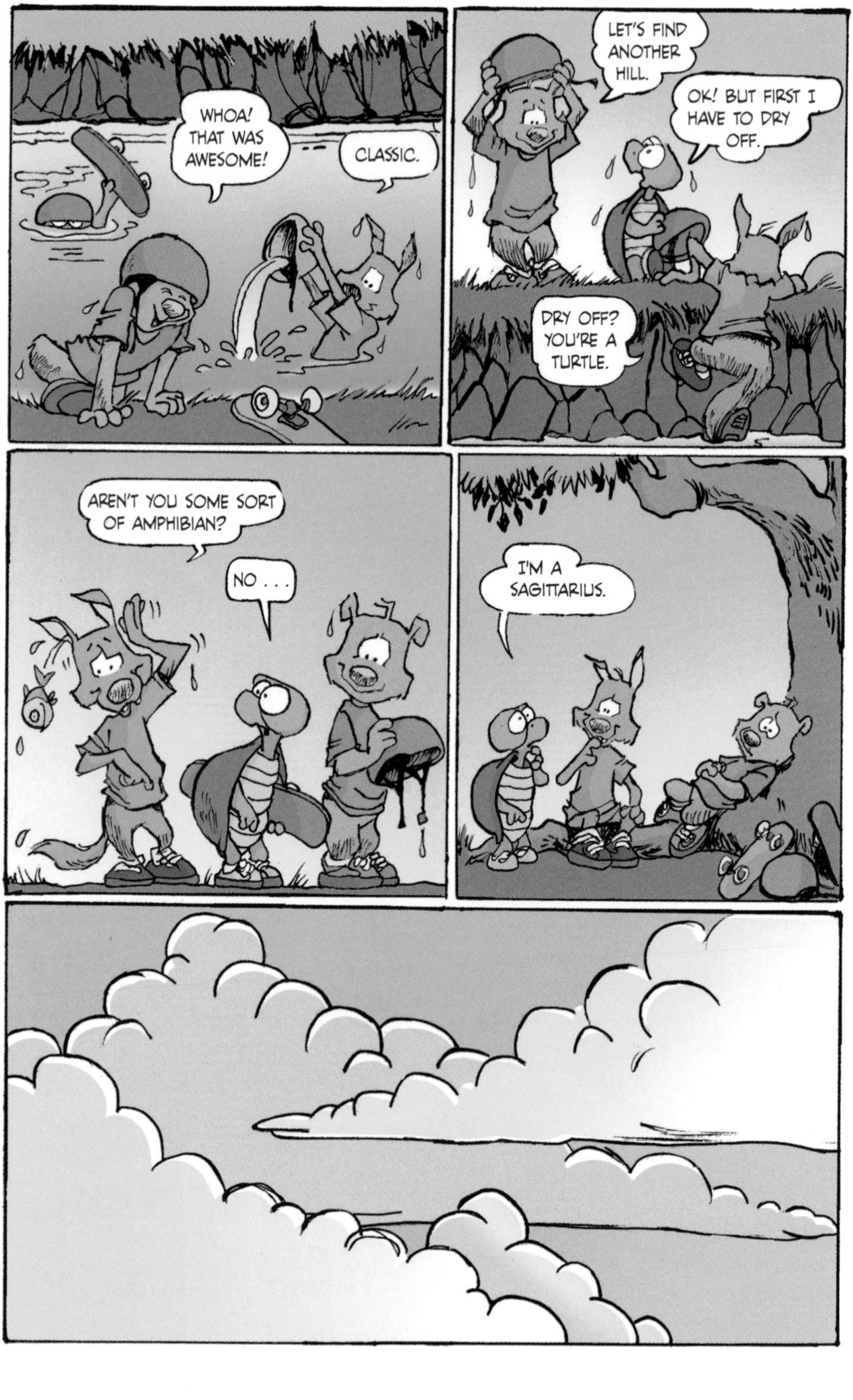
WHOA! THAT WAS AWESOME!
CLASSIC.
LET'S FIND ANOTHER HILL.
OK! BUT FIRST I HAVE TO DRY OFF.
DRY OFF? YOU'RE A TURTLE.
AREN'T YOU SOME SORT OF AMPHIBIAN?
NO . . .
I'M A SAGITTARIUS.

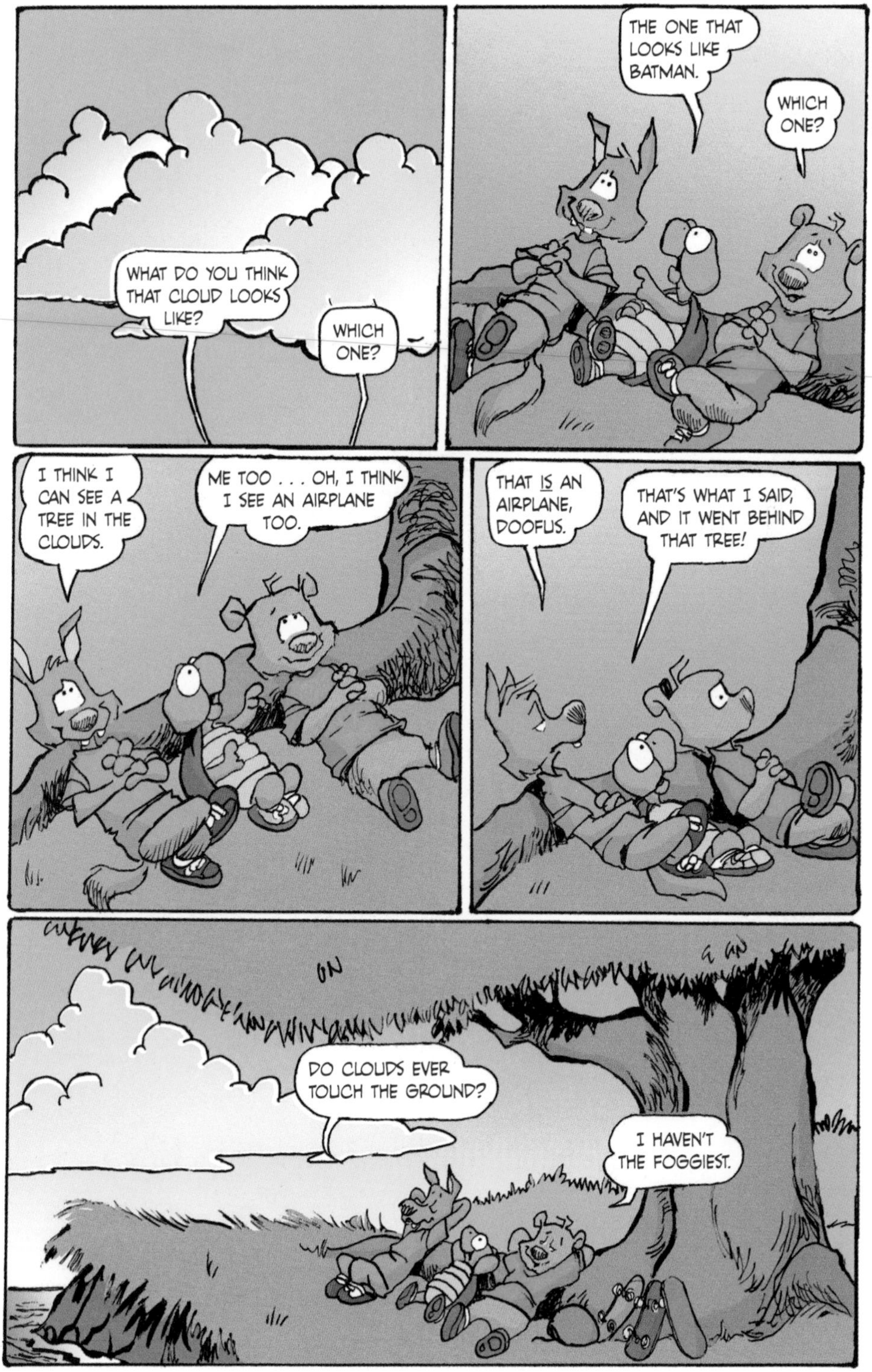
WHAT DO YOU THINK THAT CLOUD LOOKS LIKE?
WHICH ONE?
THE ONE THAT LOOKS LIKE BATMAN.
WHICH ONE?
I THINK I CAN SEE A TREE IN THE CLOUDS.
ME TOO . . . OH, I THINK I SEE AN AIRPLANE TOO.
THAT IS AN AIRPLANE, DOOFUS.
THAT'S WHAT I SAID, AND IT WENT BEHIND THAT TREE!
DO CLOUDS EVER TOUCH THE GROUND?
I HAVEN'T THE FOGGIEST.

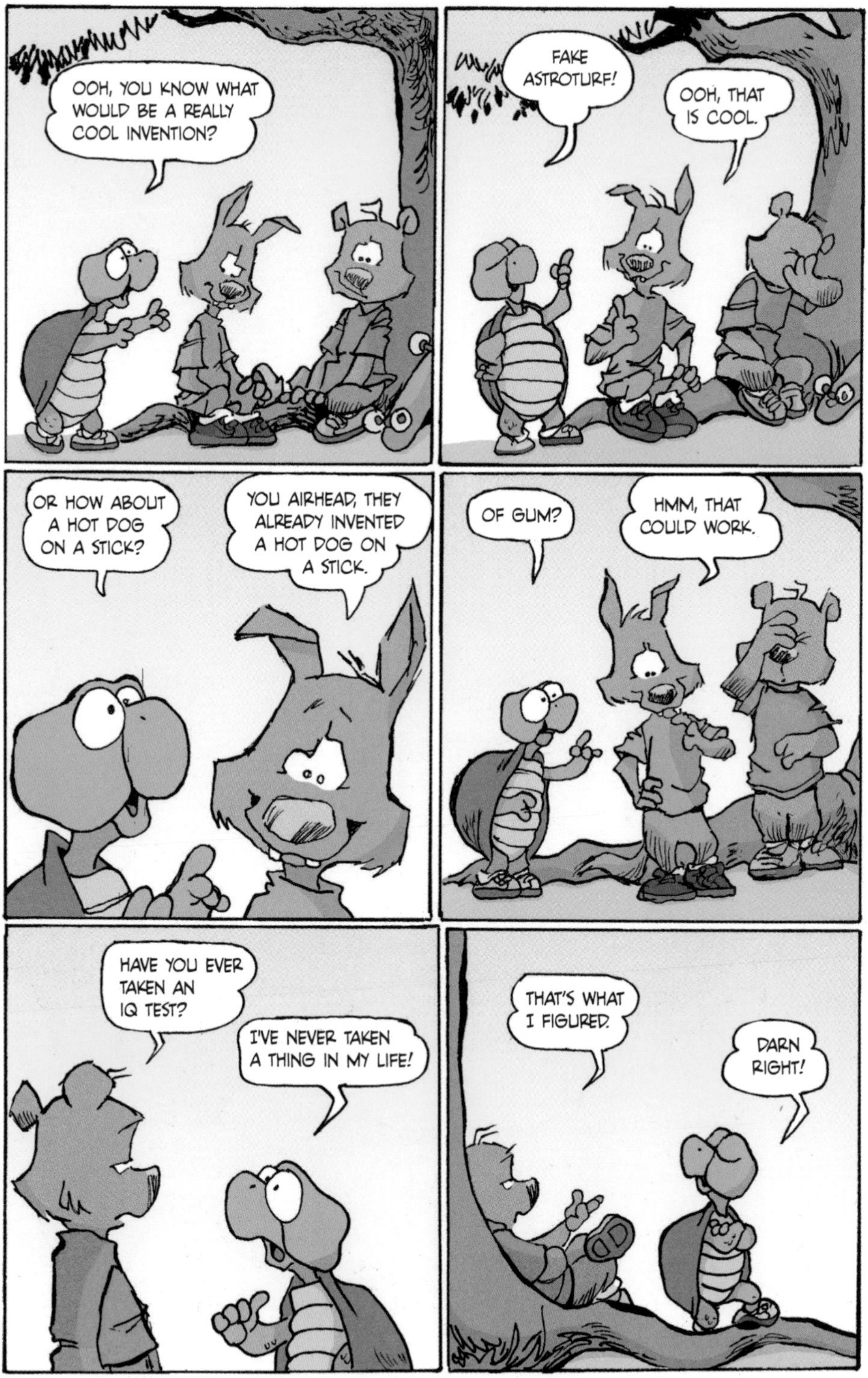
OOH, YOU KNOW WHAT WOULD BE A REALLY COOL INVENTION?
FAKE ASTROTURF!
OOH, THAT IS COOL.
OR HOW ABOUT A HOT DOG ON A STICK?
YOU AIRHEAD, THEY ALREADY INVENTED A HOT DOG ON A STICK.
OF GUM?
HMM, THAT COULD WORK.
HAVE YOU EVER TAKEN AN IQ TEST?
I'VE NEVER TAKEN A THING IN MY LIFE!
THAT'S WHAT I FIGURED.
DARN RIGHT!

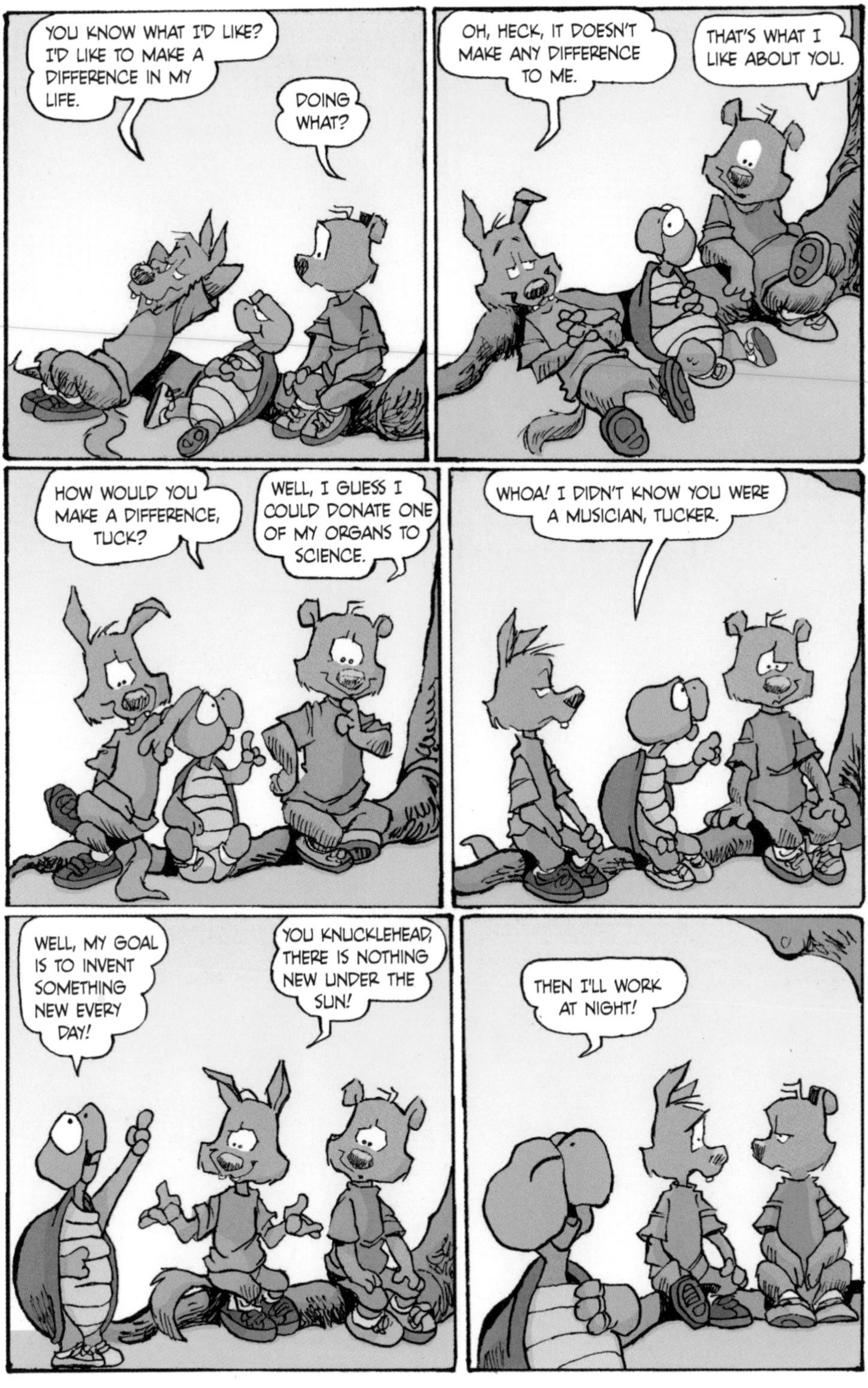
YOU KNOW WHAT I'D LIKE? I'D LIKE TO MAKE A DIFFERENCE IN MY LIFE.
DOING WHAT?
OH, HECK, IT DOESN'T MAKE ANY DIFFERENCE TO ME.
THAT'S WHAT I LIKE ABOUT YOU.
HOW WOULD YOU MAKE A DIFFERENCE, TUCK?
WELL, I GUESS I COULD DONATE ONE OF MY ORGANS TO SCIENCE.
WHOA! I DIDN'T KNOW YOU WERE A MUSICIAN, TUCKER.
WELL, MY GOAL IS TO INVENT SOMETHING NEW EVERY DAY!
YOU KNUCKLEHEAD, THERE IS NOTHING NEW UNDER THE SUN!
THEN I'LL WORK AT NIGHT!

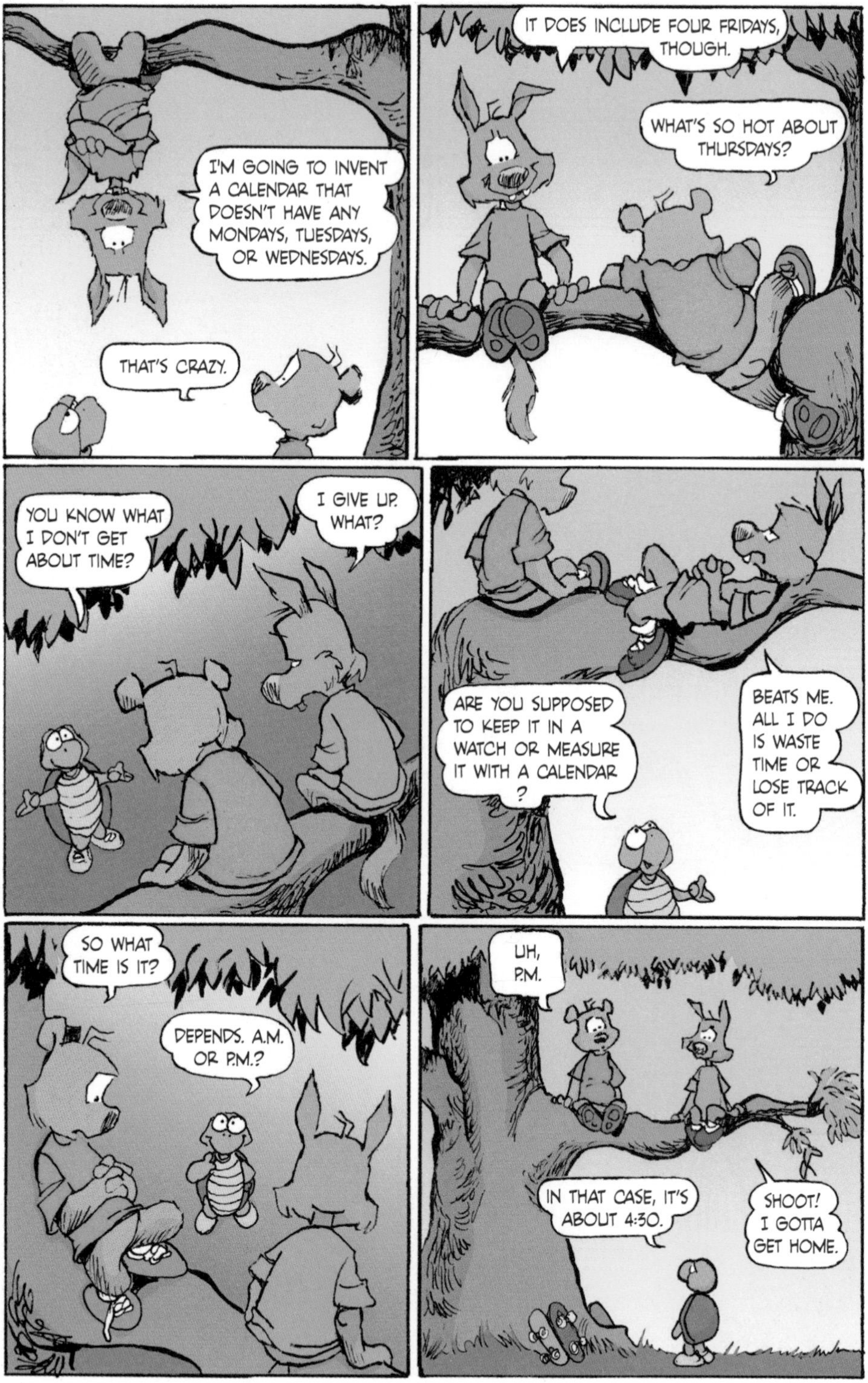
I'M GOING TO INVENT A CALENDAR THAT DOESN'T HAVE ANY MONDAYS, TUESDAYS, OR WEDNESDAYS.
THAT'S CRAZY.
IT DOES INCLUDE FOUR FRIDAYS, THOUGH.
WHAT'S SO HOT ABOUT THURSDAYS?
YOU KNOW WHAT I DON'T GET ABOUT TIME?
I GIVE UP. WHAT?
ARE YOU SUPPOSED TO KEEP IT IN A WATCH OR MEASURE IT WITH A CALENDAR?
BEATS ME. ALL I DO IS WASTE TIME OR LOSE TRACK OF IT.
SO WHAT TIME IS IT?
DEPENDS. A.M. OR P.M.?
UH, P.M.
IN THAT CASE, IT'S ABOUT 4:30.
SHOOT! I GOTTA GET HOME.

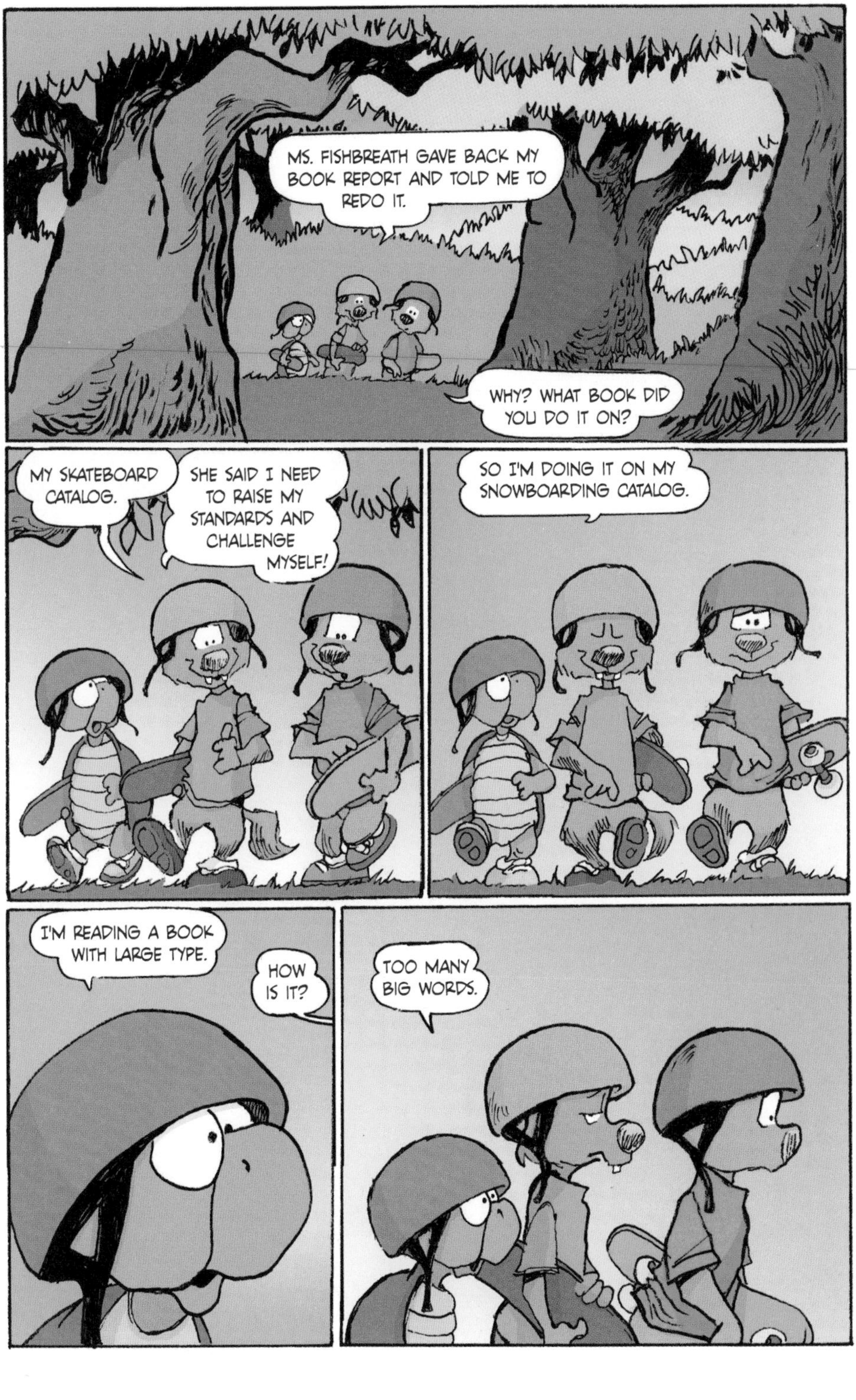
MS. FISHBREATH GAVE BACK MY BOOK REPORT AND TOLD ME TO REDO IT.
WHY? WHAT BOOK DID YOU DO IT ON?
MY SKATEBOARD CATALOG.
SHE SAID I NEED TO RAISE MY STANDARDS AND CHALLENGE MYSELF!
SO I'M DOING IT ON MY SNOWBOARDING CATALOG.
I'M READING A BOOK WITH LARGE TYPE.
HOW IS IT?
TOO MANY BIG WORDS.

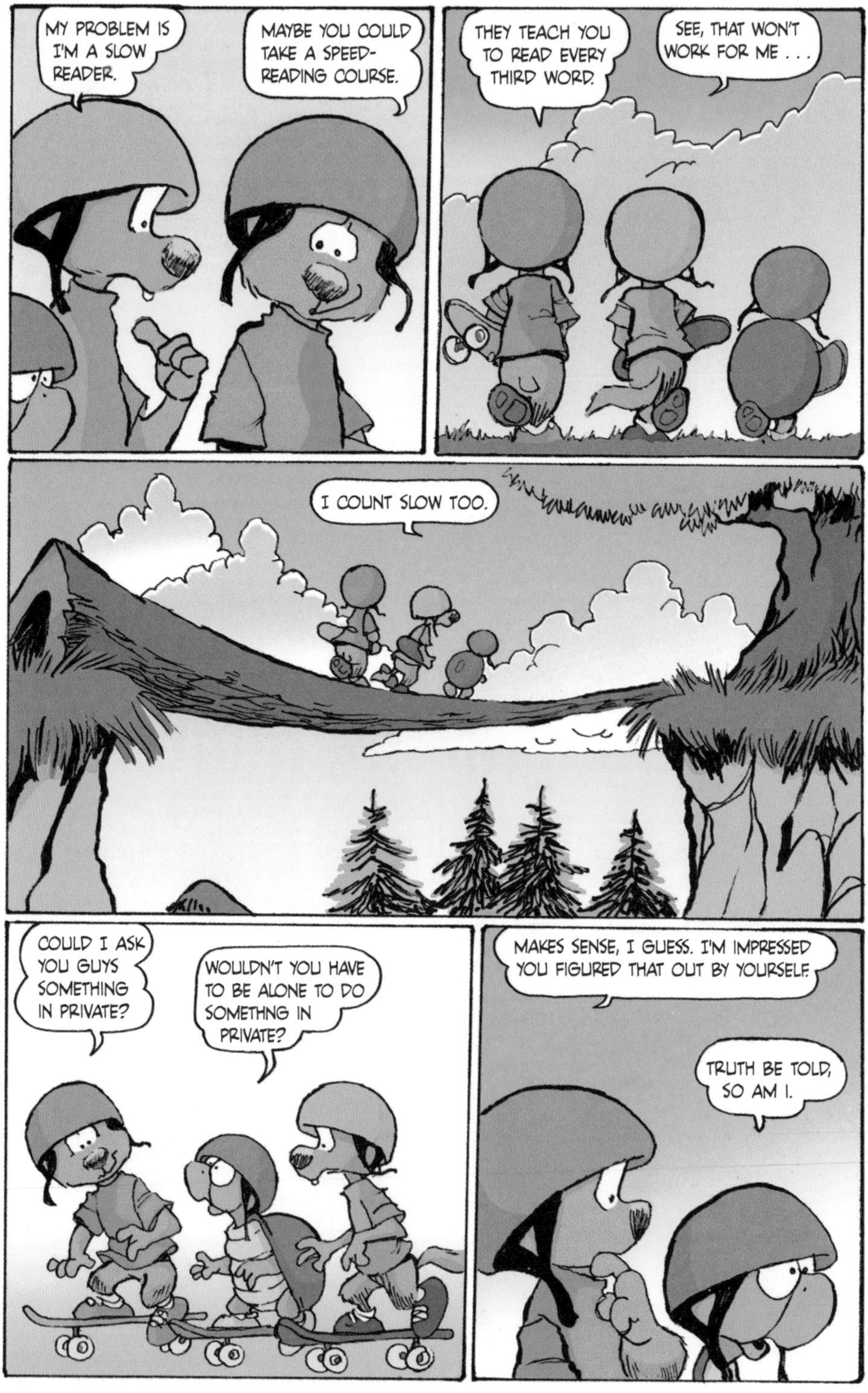
MY PROBLEM IS I'M A SLOW READER.
MAYBE YOU COULD TAKE A SPEED-READING COURSE.
THEY TEACH YOU TO READ EVERY THIRD WORD.
SEE, THAT WON'T WORK FOR ME . . .
I COUNT SLOW TOO.
COULD I ASK YOU GUYS SOMETHING IN PRIVATE?
WOULDN'T YOU HAVE TO BE ALONE TO DO SOMETHNG IN PRIVATE?
MAKES SENSE, I GUESS. I'M IMPRESSED YOU FIGURED THAT OUT BY YOURSELF.
TRUTH BE TOLD, SO AM I.

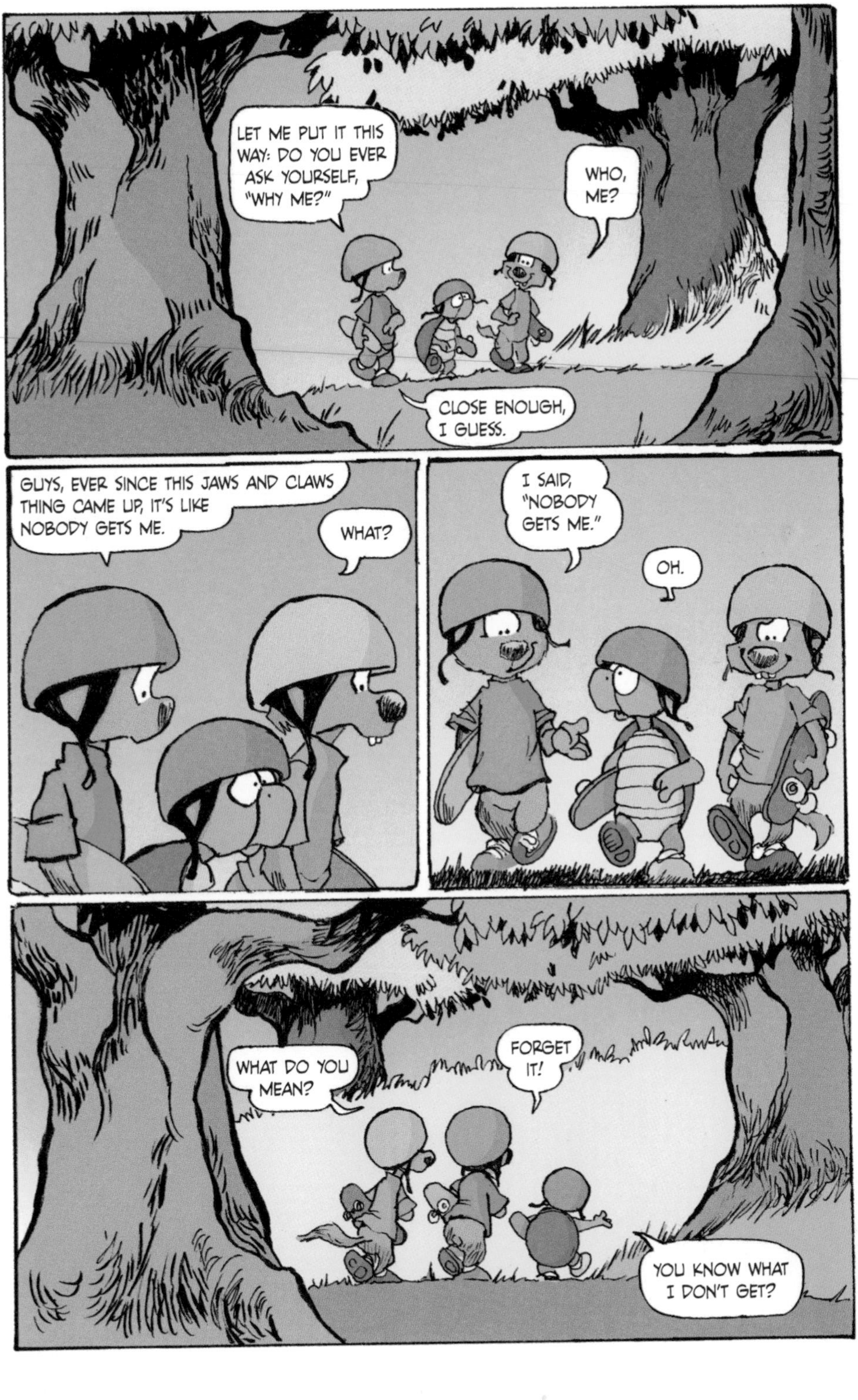
LET ME PUT IT THIS WAY: DO YOU EVER ASK YOURSELF, "WHY ME?"
WHO, ME?
CLOSE ENOUGH, I GUESS.
GUYS, EVER SINCE THIS JAWS AND CLAWS THING CAME UP, IT'S LIKE NOBODY GETS ME.
WHAT?
I SAID, "NOBODY GETS ME."
OH.
WHAT DO YOU MEAN?
FORGET IT!
YOU KNOW WHAT I DON'T GET?

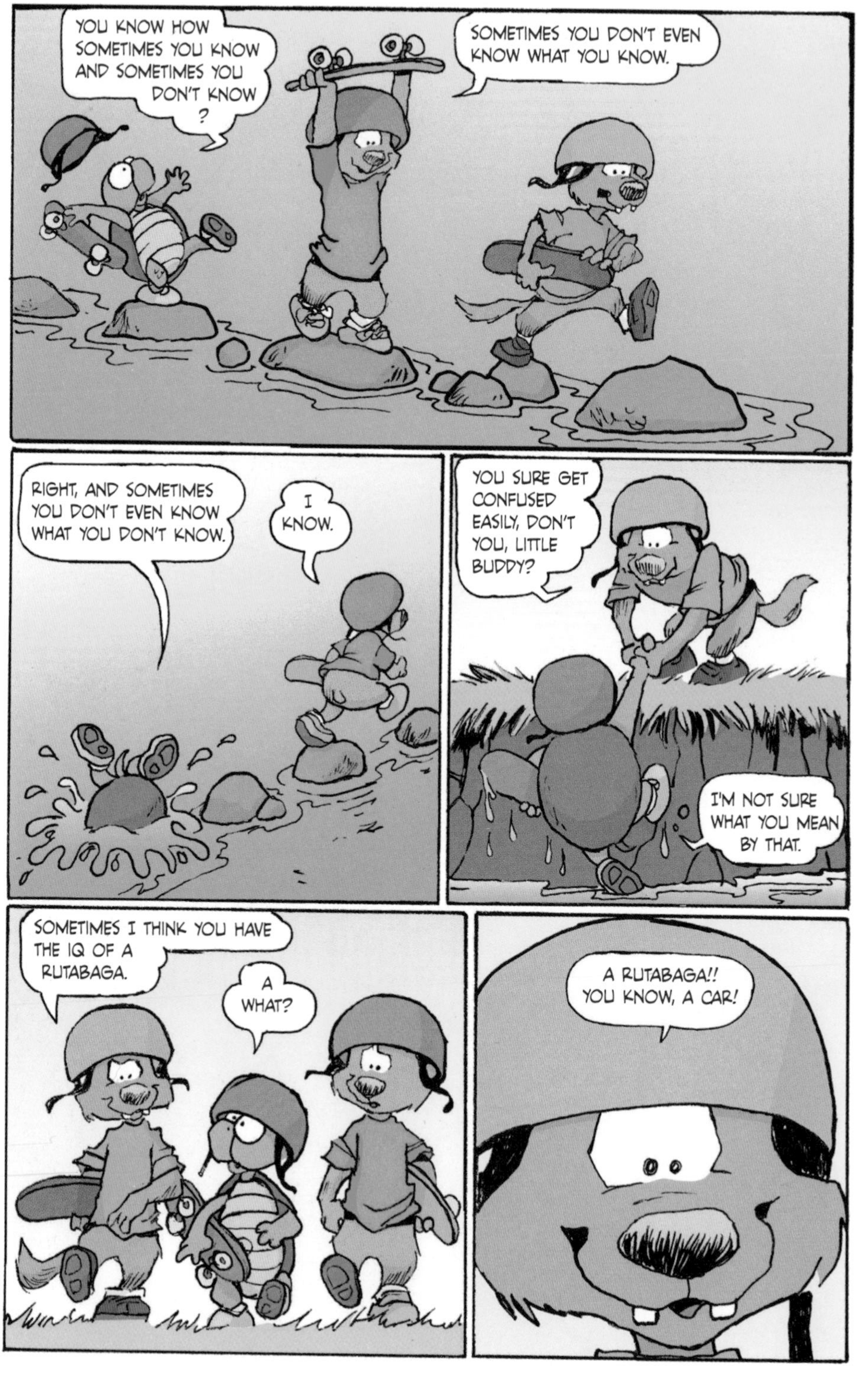
YOU KNOW HOW SOMETIMES YOU KNOW AND SOMETIMES YOU DON'T KNOW ?
SOMETIMES YOU DON'T EVEN KNOW WHAT YOU KNOW.
RIGHT, AND SOMETIMES YOU DON'T EVEN KNOW WHAT YOU DON'T KNOW.
I KNOW.
YOU SURE GET CONFUSED EASILY, DON'T YOU, LITTLE BUDDY?
I'M NOT SURE WHAT YOU MEAN BY THAT.
SOMETIMES I THINK YOU HAVE THE IQ OF A RUTABAGA.
A WHAT?
A RUTABAGA!! YOU KNOW, A CAR!

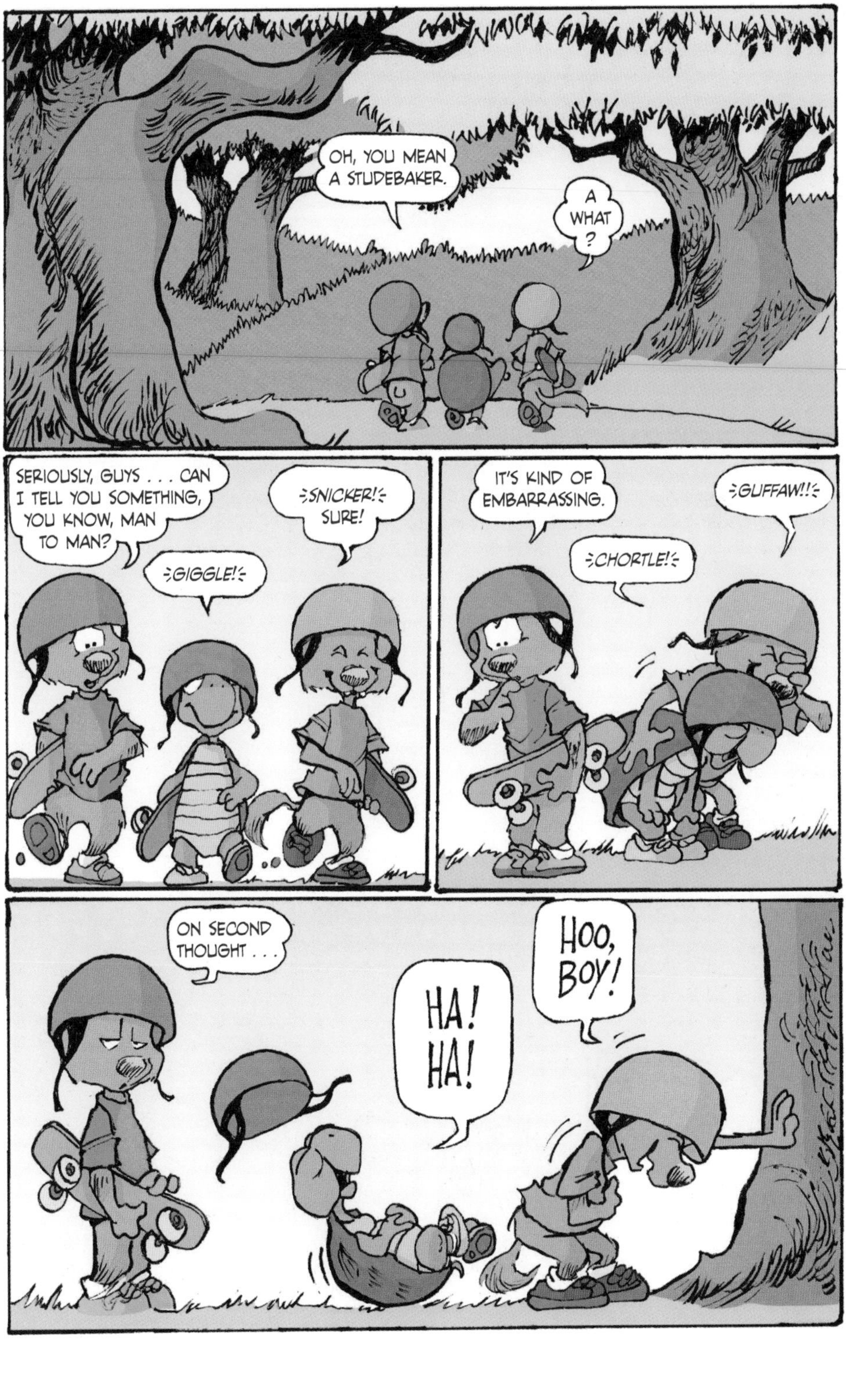
OH, YOU MEAN A STUDEBAKER.
A WHAT?
SERIOUSLY, GUYS . . . CAN I TELL YOU SOMETHING, YOU KNOW, MAN TO MAN?
GIGGLE!
SNICKER! SURE!
IT'S KIND OF EMBARRASSING.
CHORTLE!
GUFFAW!!
ON SECOND THOUGHT . . .
HA! HA!
HOO, BOY!

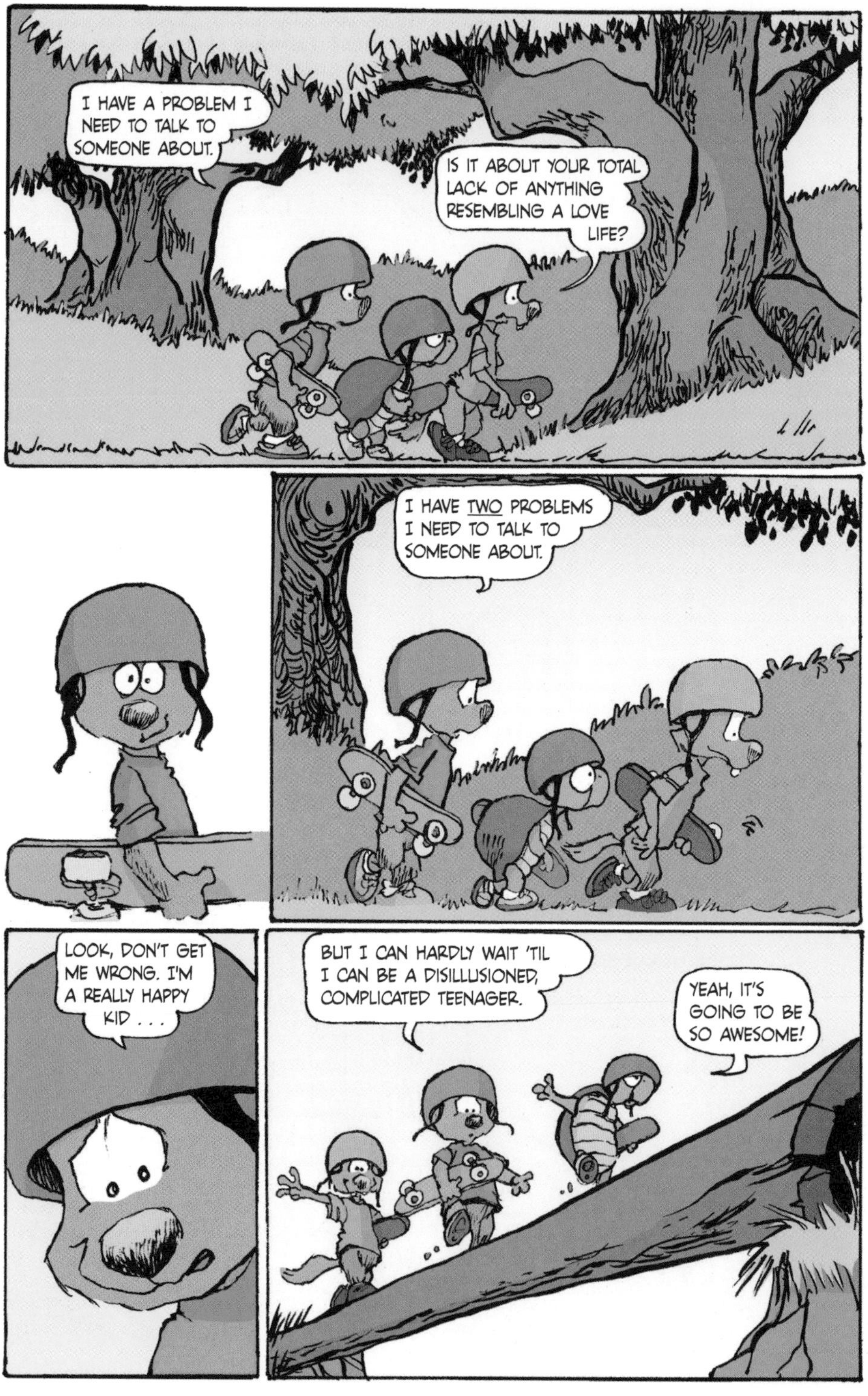
I HAVE A PROBLEM I NEED TO TALK TO SOMEONE ABOUT.
IS IT ABOUT YOUR TOTAL LACK OF ANYTHING RESEMBLING A LOVE LIFE?
I HAVE TWO PROBLEMS I NEED TO TALK TO SOMEONE ABOUT.
LOOK, DON'T GET ME WRONG. I'M A REALLY HAPPY KID . . .
BUT I CAN HARDLY WAIT 'TIL I CAN BE A DISILLUSIONED, COMPLICATED TEENAGER.
YEAH, IT'S GOING TO BE SO AWESOME!

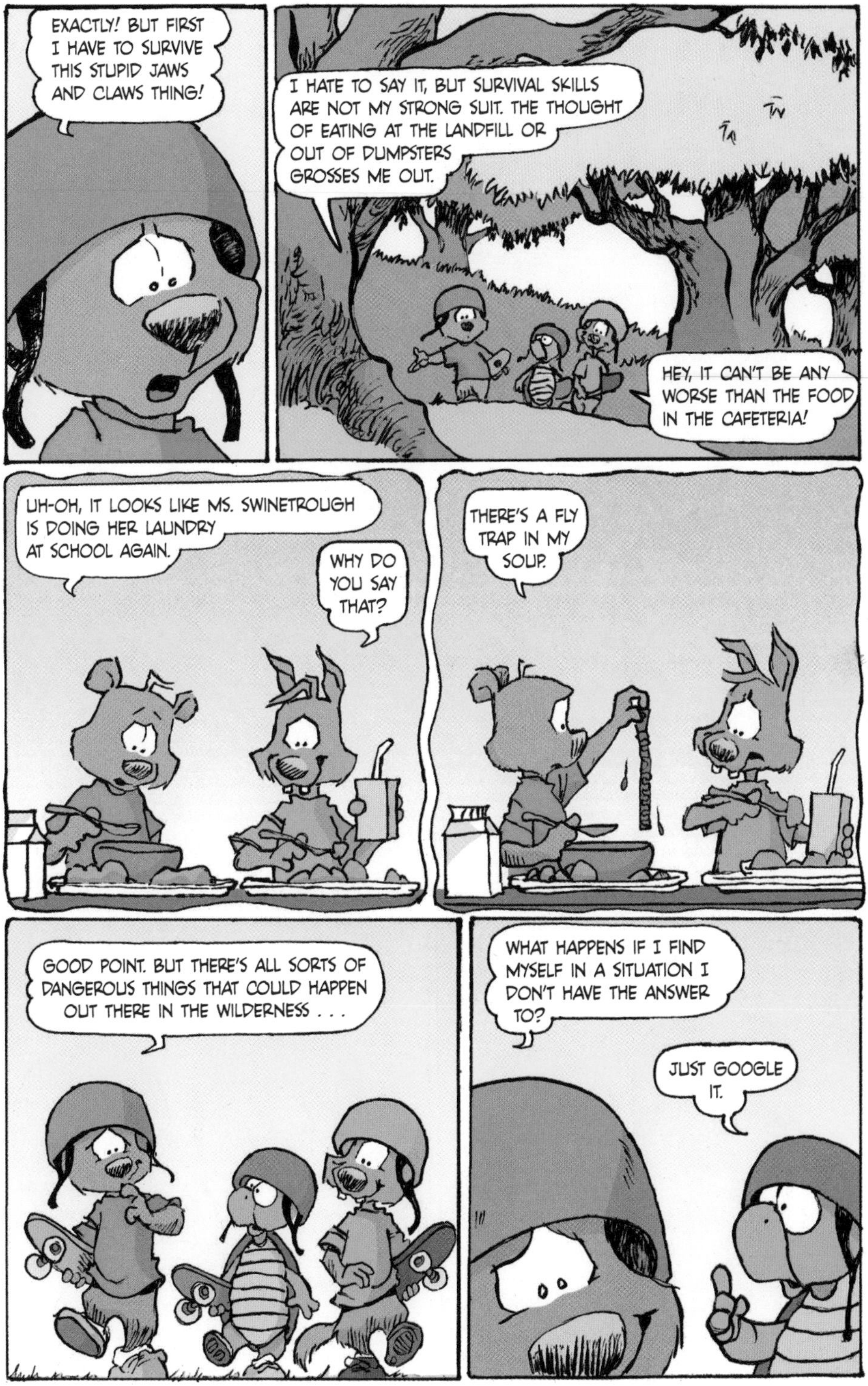
EXACTLY! BUT FIRST I HAVE TO SURVIVE THIS STUPID JAWS AND CLAWS THING!
I HATE TO SAY IT, BUT SURVIVAL SKILLS ARE NOT MY STRONG SUIT. THE THOUGHT OF EATING AT THE LANDFILL OR OUT OF DUMPSTERS GROSSES ME OUT.
HEY, IT CAN'T BE ANY WORSE THAN THE FOOD IN THE CAFETERIA!
UH-OH, IT LOOKS LIKE MS. SWINETROUGH IS DOING HER LAUNDRY AT SCHOOL AGAIN.
WHY DO YOU SAY THAT?
THERE'S A FLY TRAP IN MY SOUP.
GOOD POINT. BUT THERE'S ALL SORTS OF DANGEROUS THINGS THAT COULD HAPPEN OUT THERE IN THE WILDERNESS . . .
WHAT HAPPENS IF I FIND MYSELF IN A SITUATION I DON'T HAVE THE ANSWER TO?
JUST GOOGLE IT.

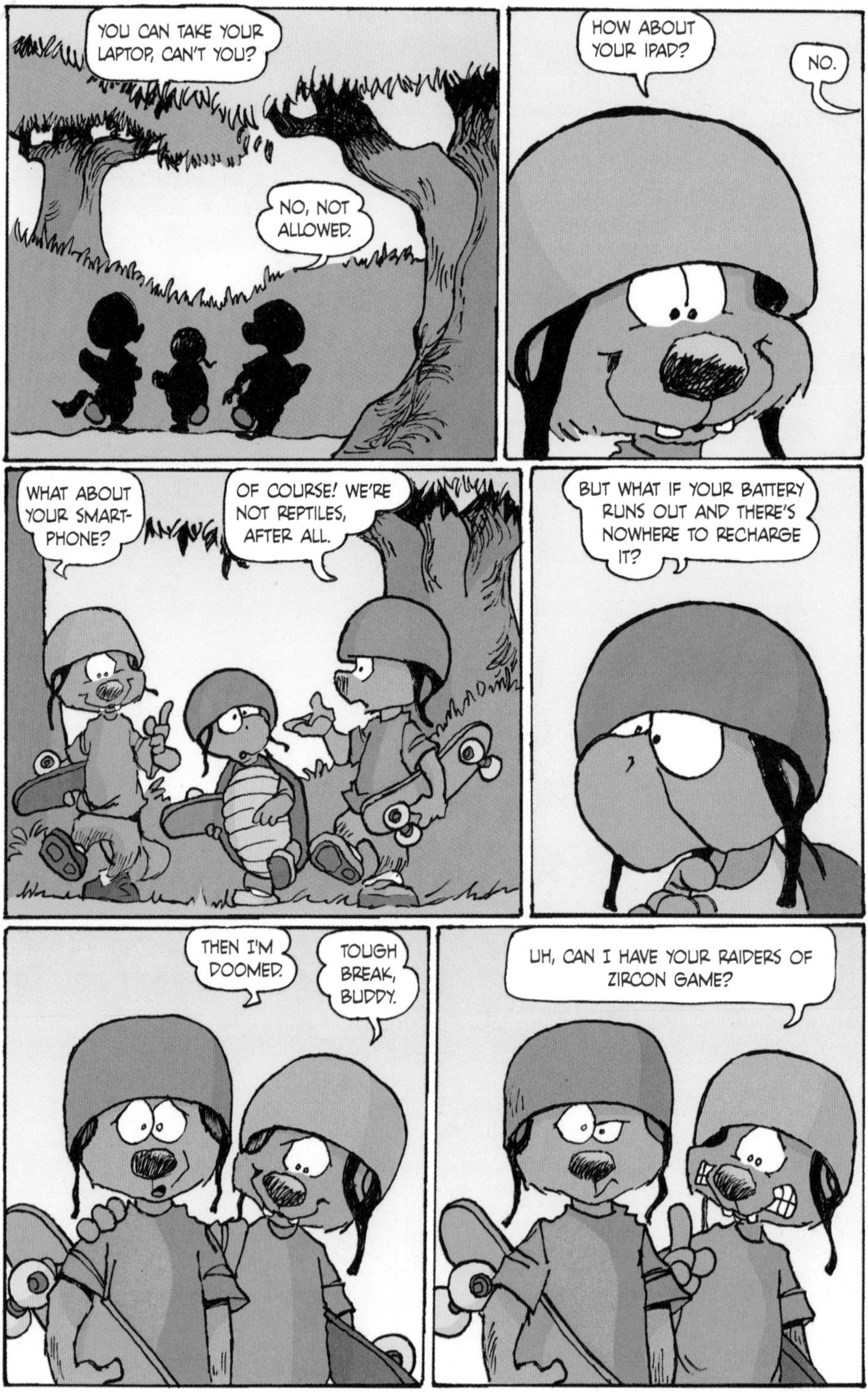

YOU CAN TAKE YOUR LAPTOP, CAN'T YOU?
NO, NOT ALLOWED.
HOW ABOUT YOUR IPAD?
NO.
WHAT ABOUT YOUR SMART-PHONE?
OF COURSE! WE'RE NOT REPTILES, AFTER ALL.
BUT WHAT IF YOUR BATTERY RUNS OUT AND THERE'S NOWHERE TO RECHARGE IT?
THEN I'M DOOMED.
TOUGH BREAK, BUDDY.
UH, CAN I HAVE YOUR RAIDERS OF ZIRCON GAME?

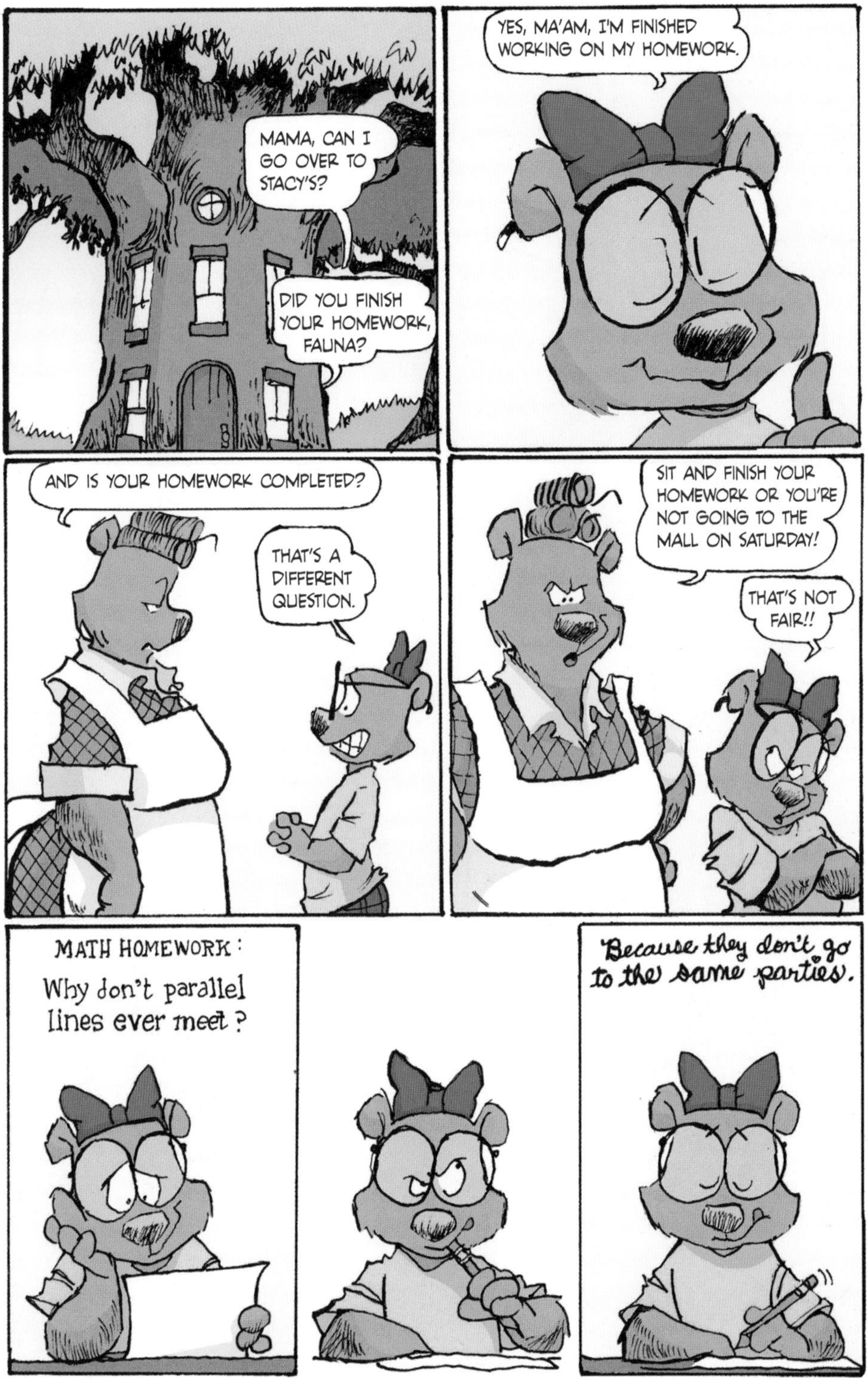
MAMA, CAN I GO OVER TO STACY'S?
DID YOU FINISH YOUR HOMEWORK, FAUNA?
YES, MA'AM, I'M FINISHED WORKING ON MY HOMEWORK.
AND IS YOUR HOMEWORK COMPLETED?
THAT'S A DIFFERENT QUESTION.
SIT AND FINISH YOUR HOMEWORK OR YOU'RE NOT GOING TO THE MALL ON SATURDAY!
THAT'S NOT FAIR!!
MATH HOMEWORK:
Why don't parallel lines ever meet?
Because they don't go to the same parties.

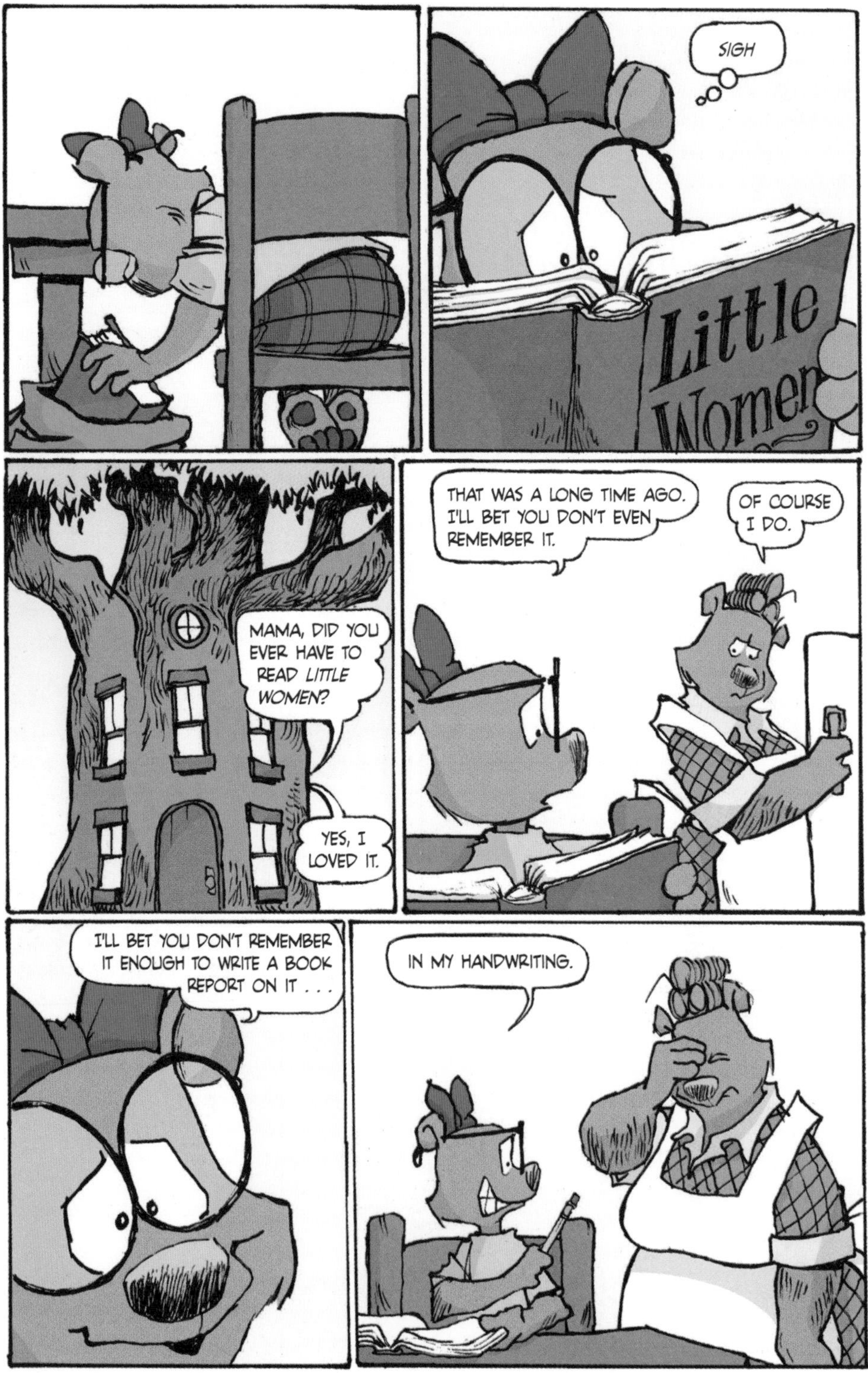
SIGH
Little Women
MAMA, DID YOU EVER HAVE TO READ LITTLE WOMEN?
YES, I LOVED IT.
THAT WAS A LONG TIME AGO. I'LL BET YOU DON'T EVEN REMEMBER IT.
OF COURSE I DO.
I'LL BET YOU DON'T REMEMBER IT ENOUGH TO WRITE A BOOK REPORT ON IT . . .
IN MY HANDWRITING.

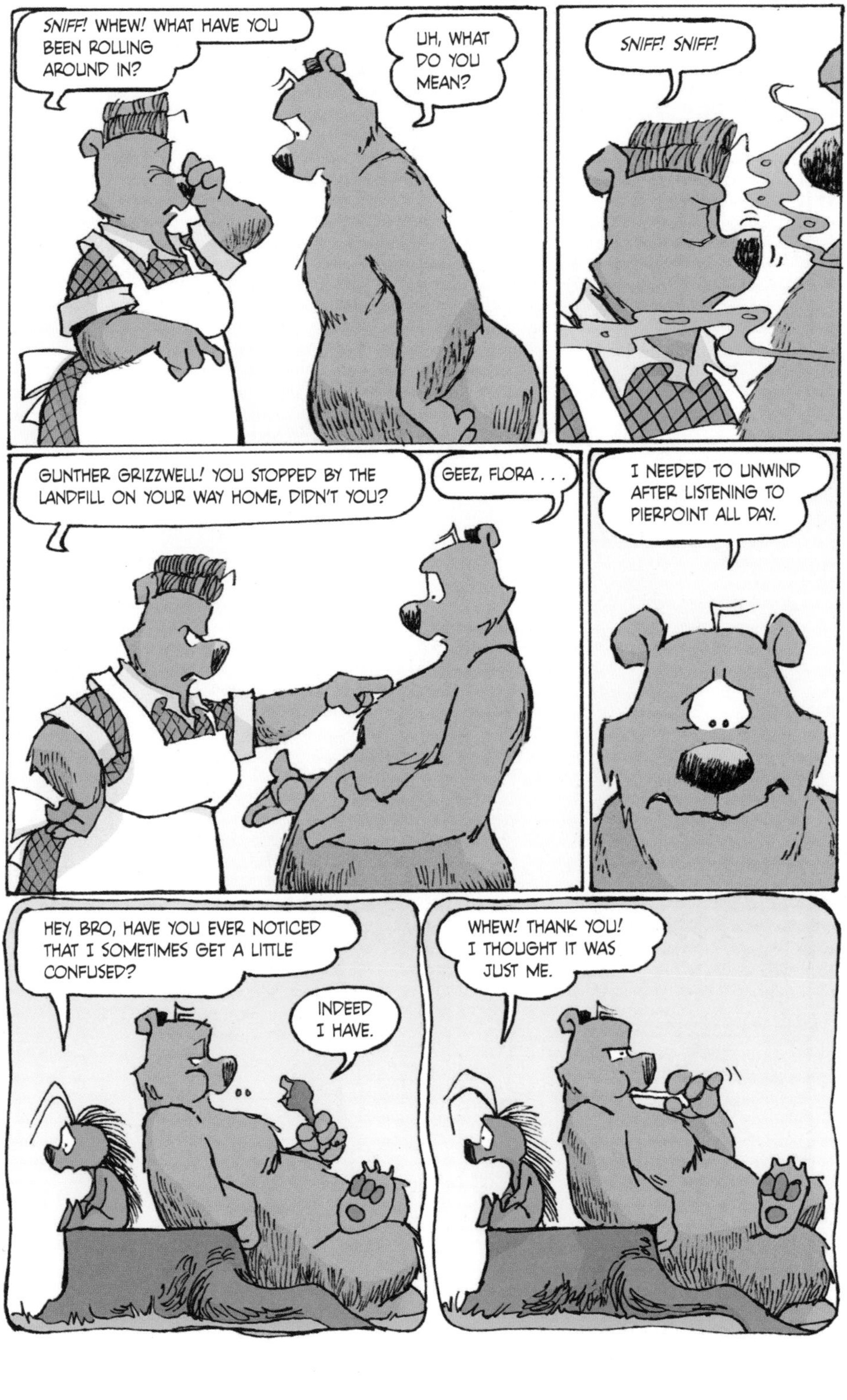
SNIFF! WHEW! WHAT HAVE YOU BEEN ROLLING AROUND IN?
UH, WHAT DO YOU MEAN?
SNIFF! SNIFF!
GUNTHER GRIZZWELL! YOU STOPPED BY THE LANDFILL ON YOUR WAY HOME, DIDN'T YOU?
GEEZ, FLORA . . .
I NEEDED TO UNWIND AFTER LISTENING TO PIERPOINT ALL DAY.
HEY, BRO, HAVE YOU EVER NOTICED THAT I SOMETIMES GET A LITTLE CONFUSED?
INDEED I HAVE.
WHEW! THANK YOU! I THOUGHT IT WAS JUST ME.

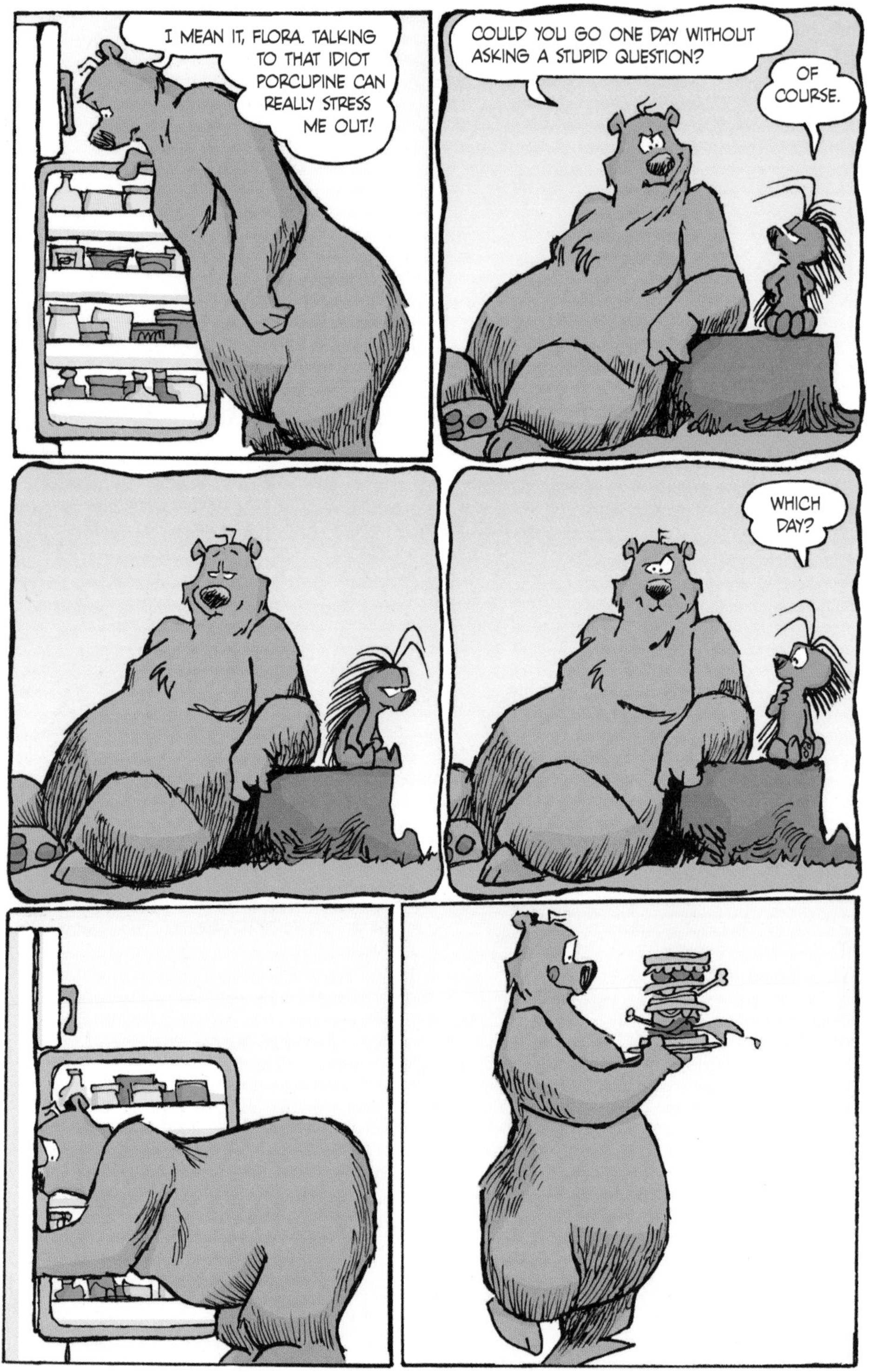
I MEAN IT, FLORA. TALKING TO THAT IDIOT PORCUPINE CAN REALLY STRESS ME OUT!
COULD YOU GO ONE DAY WITHOUT ASKING A STUPID QUESTION?
OF COURSE.
WHICH DAY?

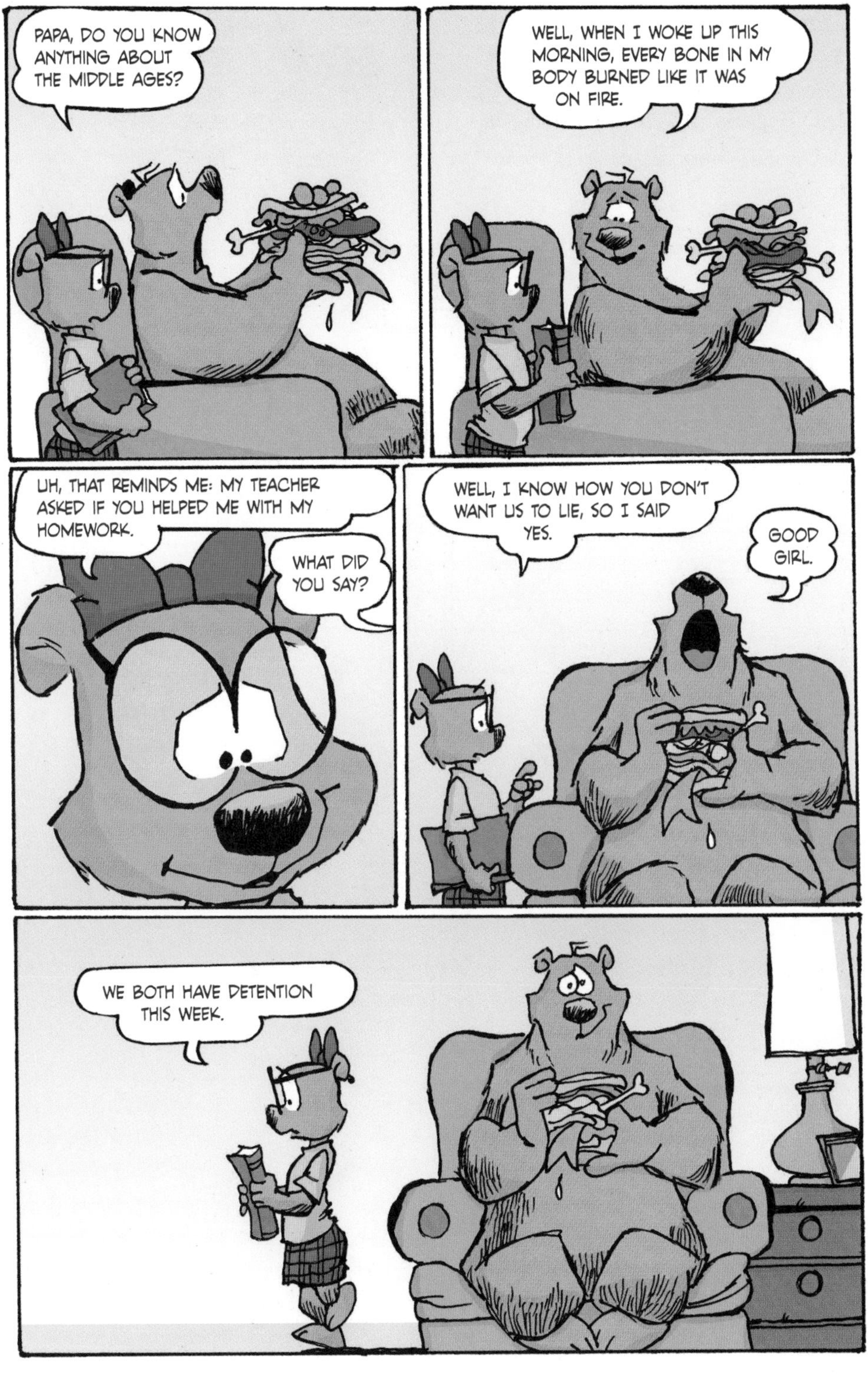
PAPA, DO YOU KNOW ANYTHING ABOUT THE MIDDLE AGES?
WELL, WHEN I WOKE UP THIS MORNING, EVERY BONE IN MY BODY BURNED LIKE IT WAS ON FIRE.
UH, THAT REMINDS ME: MY TEACHER ASKED IF YOU HELPED ME WITH MY HOMEWORK.
WHAT DID YOU SAY?
WELL, I KNOW HOW YOU DON'T WANT US TO LIE, SO I SAID YES.
GOOD GIRL.
WE BOTH HAVE DETENTION THIS WEEK.

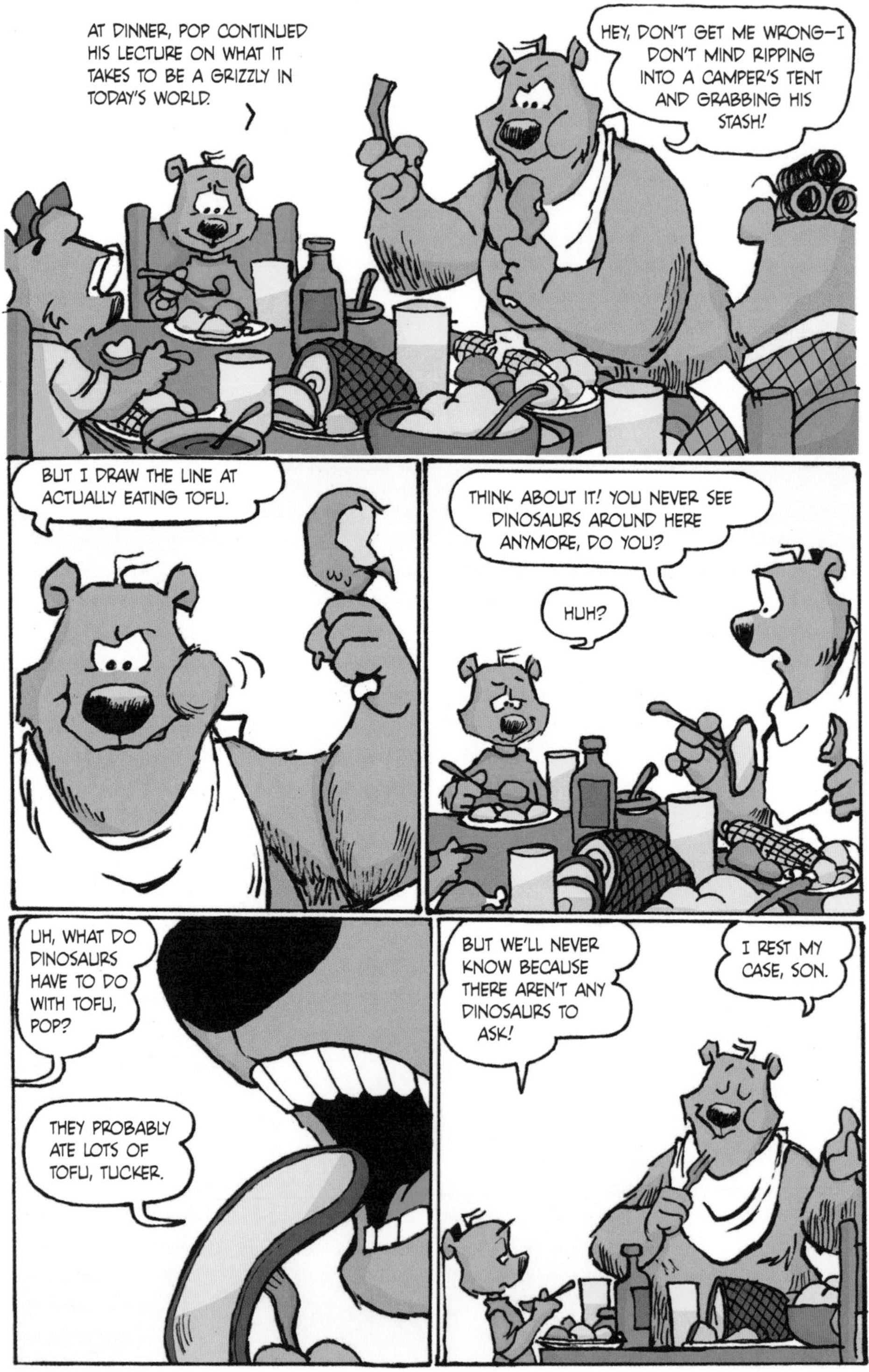
AT DINNER, POP CONTINUED HIS LECTURE ON WHAT IT TAKES TO BE A GRIZZLY IN TODAY'S WORLD.
HEY, DON'T GET ME WRONG—I DON'T MIND RIPPING INTO A CAMPER'S TENT AND GRABBING HIS STASH!
BUT I DRAW THE LINE AT ACTUALLY EATING TOFU.
THINK ABOUT IT! YOU NEVER SEE DINOSAURS AROUND HERE ANYMORE, DO YOU?
HUH?
UH, WHAT DO DINOSAURS HAVE TO DO WITH TOFU, POP?
THEY PROBABLY ATE LOTS OF TOFU, TUCKER.
BUT WE'LL NEVER KNOW BECAUSE THERE AREN'T ANY DINOSAURS TO ASK!
I REST MY CASE, SON.

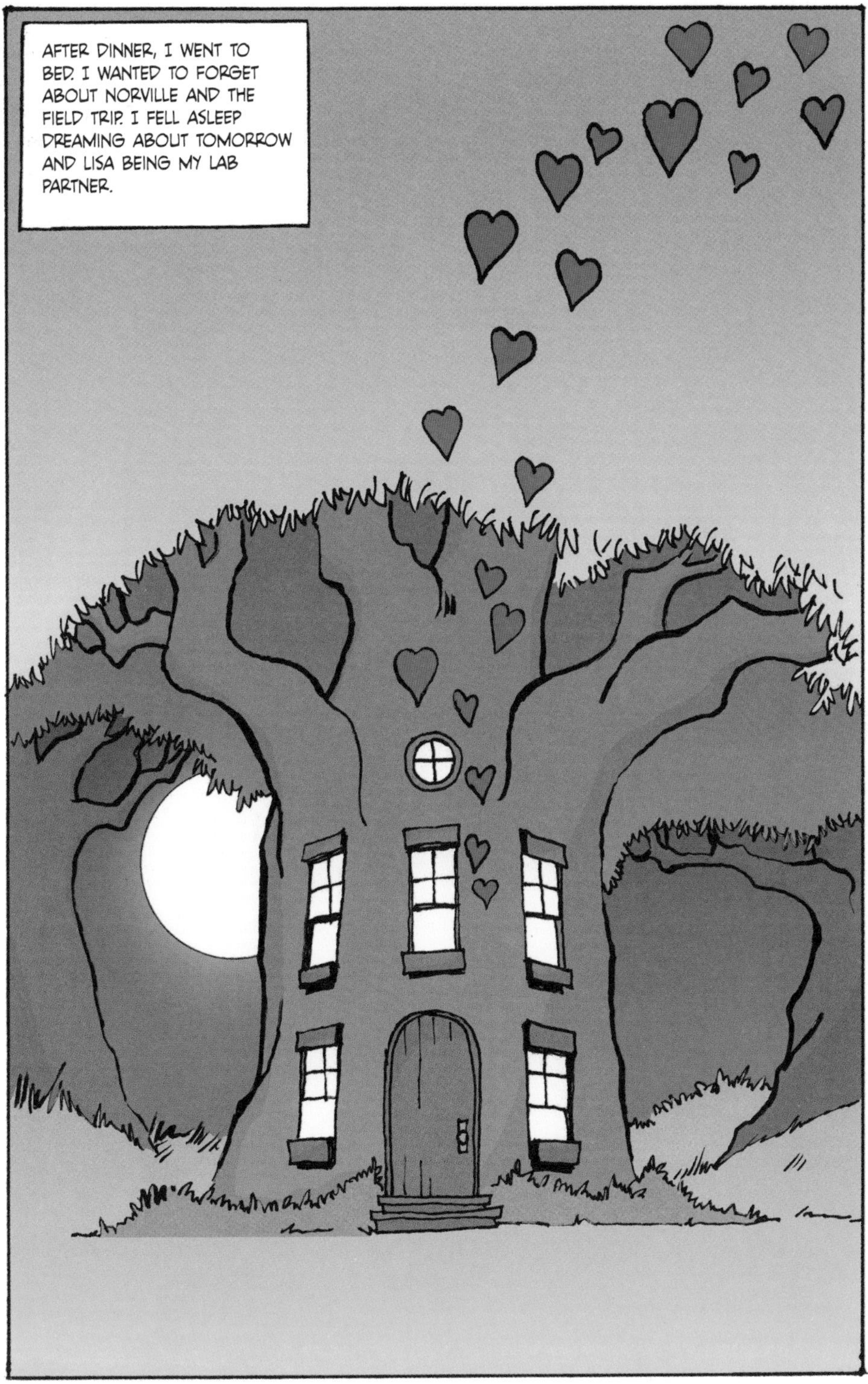
AFTER DINNER, I WENT TO BED. I WANTED TO FORGET ABOUT NORVILLE AND THE FIELD TRIP. I FELL ASLEEP DREAMING ABOUT TOMORROW AND LISA BEING MY LAB PARTNER.

WEDNESDAY

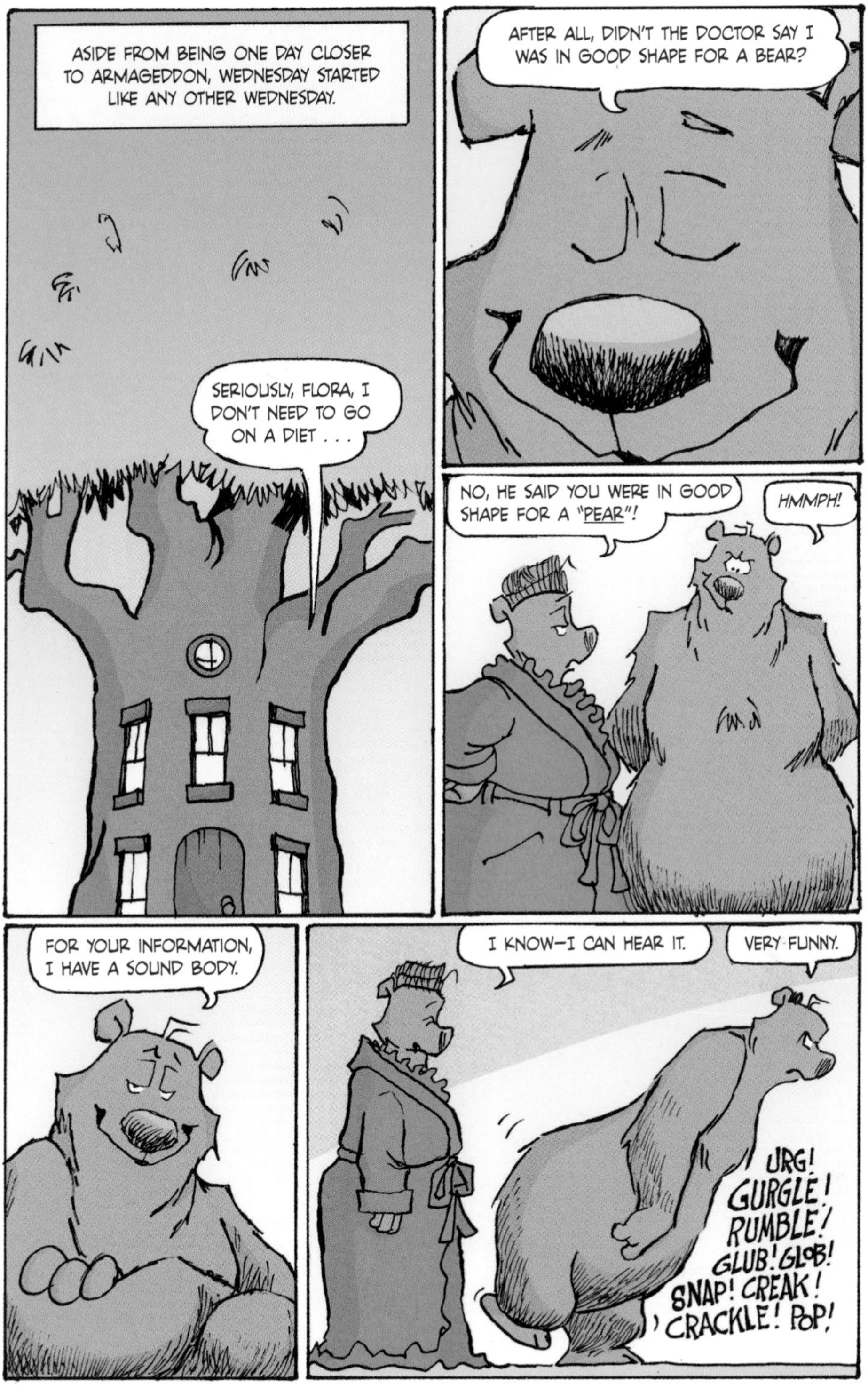
ASIDE FROM BEING ONE DAY CLOSER TO ARMAGEDDON, WEDNESDAY STARTED LIKE ANY OTHER WEDNESDAY.
SERIOUSLY, FLORA, I DON'T NEED TO GO ON A DIET . . .
AFTER ALL, DIDN'T THE DOCTOR SAY I WAS IN GOOD SHAPE FOR A BEAR?
NO, HE SAID YOU WERE IN GOOD SHAPE FOR A "PEAR"!
HMMPH!
FOR YOUR INFORMATION, I HAVE A SOUND BODY.
I KNOW—I CAN HEAR IT.
VERY FUNNY.
URG! GURGLE! RUMBLE! GLUB! GLOB! SNAP! CREAK! CRACKLE! POP!

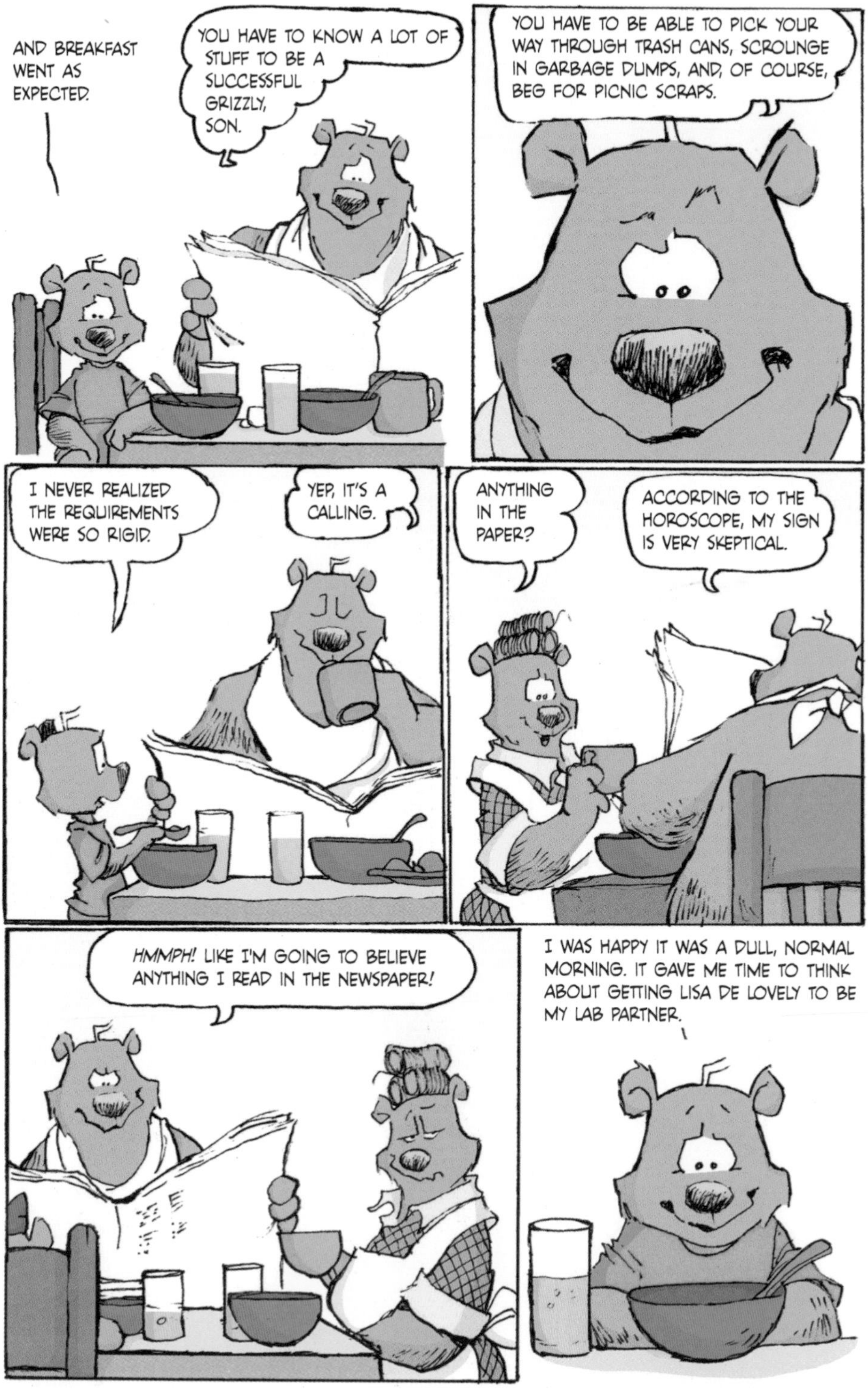
AND BREAKFAST WENT AS EXPECTED.
YOU HAVE TO KNOW A LOT OF STUFF TO BE A SUCCESSFUL GRIZZLY, SON.
YOU HAVE TO BE ABLE TO PICK YOUR WAY THROUGH TRASH CANS, SCROUNGE IN GARBAGE DUMPS, AND, OF COURSE, BEG FOR PICNIC SCRAPS.
I NEVER REALIZED THE REQUIREMENTS WERE SO RIGID.
YEP, IT'S A CALLING.
ANYTHING IN THE PAPER?
ACCORDING TO THE HOROSCOPE, MY SIGN IS VERY SKEPTICAL.
HMMPH! LIKE I'M GOING TO BELIEVE ANYTHING I READ IN THE NEWSPAPER!
I WAS HAPPY IT WAS A DULL, NORMAL MORNING. IT GAVE ME TIME TO THINK ABOUT GETTING LISA DE LOVELY TO BE MY LAB PARTNER.

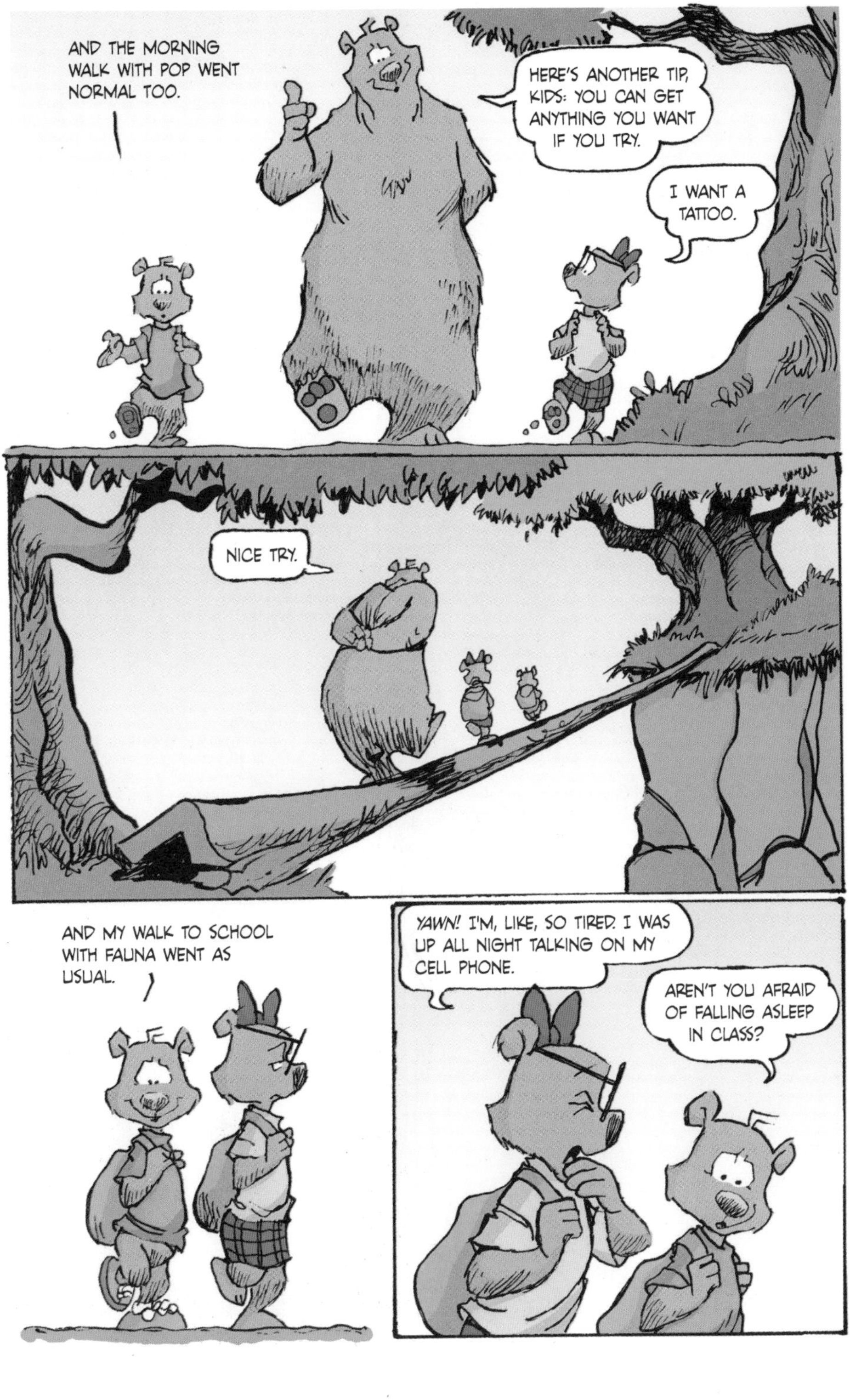
AND THE MORNING WALK WITH POP WENT NORMAL TOO.
HERE'S ANOTHER TIP, KIDS: YOU CAN GET ANYTHING YOU WANT IF YOU TRY.
I WANT A TATTOO.
NICE TRY.
AND MY WALK TO SCHOOL WITH FAUNA WENT AS USUAL.
YAWN! I'M, LIKE, SO TIRED. I WAS UP ALL NIGHT TALKING ON MY CELL PHONE.
AREN'T YOU AFRAID OF FALLING ASLEEP IN CLASS?

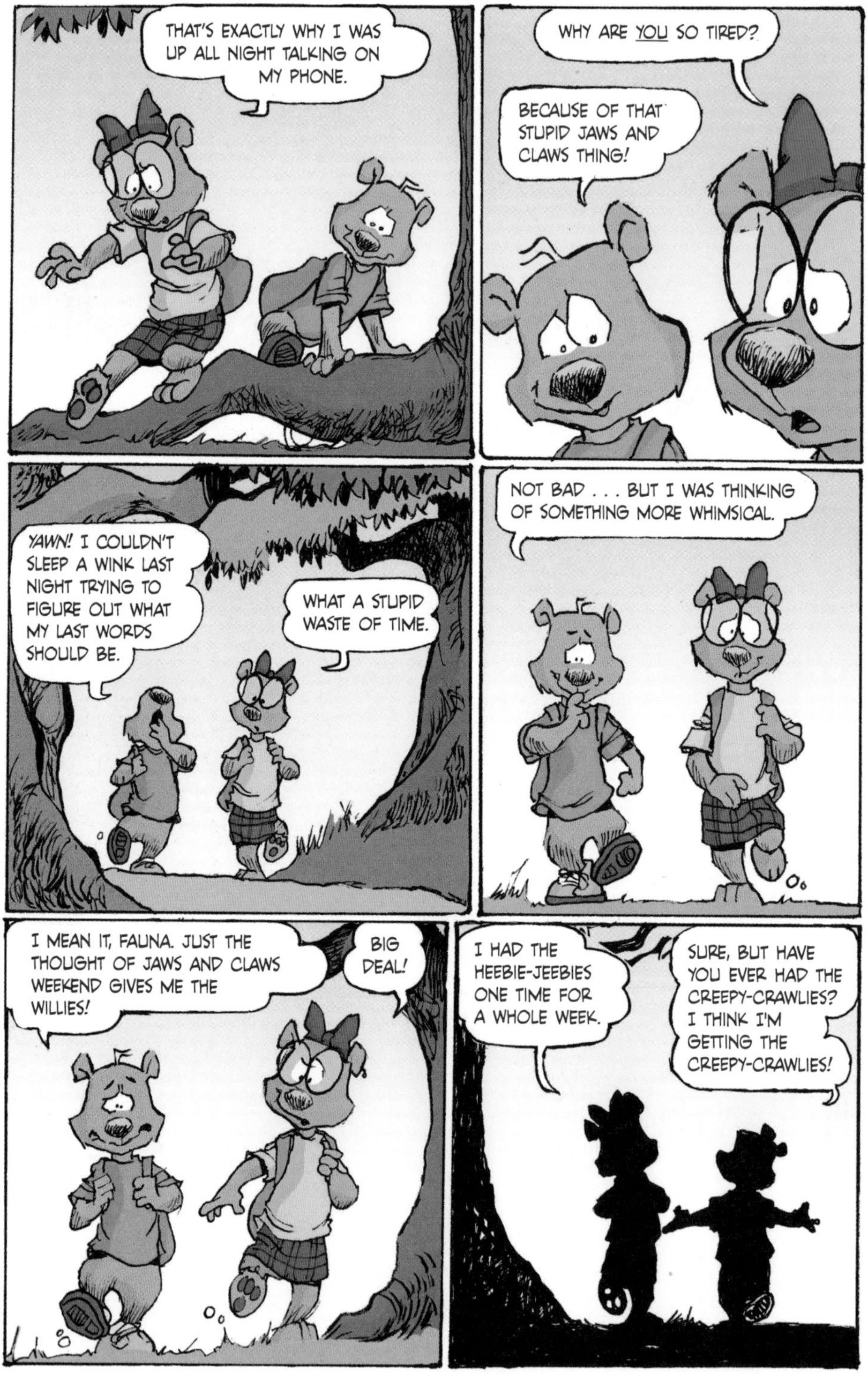
THAT'S EXACTLY WHY I WAS UP ALL NIGHT TALKING ON MY PHONE.
WHY ARE YOU SO TIRED?
BECAUSE OF THAT STUPID JAWS AND CLAWS THING!
YAWN! I COULDN'T SLEEP A WINK LAST NIGHT TRYING TO FIGURE OUT WHAT MY LAST WORDS SHOULD BE.
WHAT A STUPID WASTE OF TIME.
NOT BAD . . . BUT I WAS THINKING OF SOMETHING MORE WHIMSICAL.
I MEAN IT, FAUNA. JUST THE THOUGHT OF JAWS AND CLAWS WEEKEND GIVES ME THE WILLIES!
BIG DEAL!
I HAD THE HEEBIE-JEEBIES ONE TIME FOR A WHOLE WEEK.
SURE, BUT HAVE YOU EVER HAD THE CREEPY-CRAWLIES? I THINK I'M GETTING THE CREEPY-CRAWLIES!

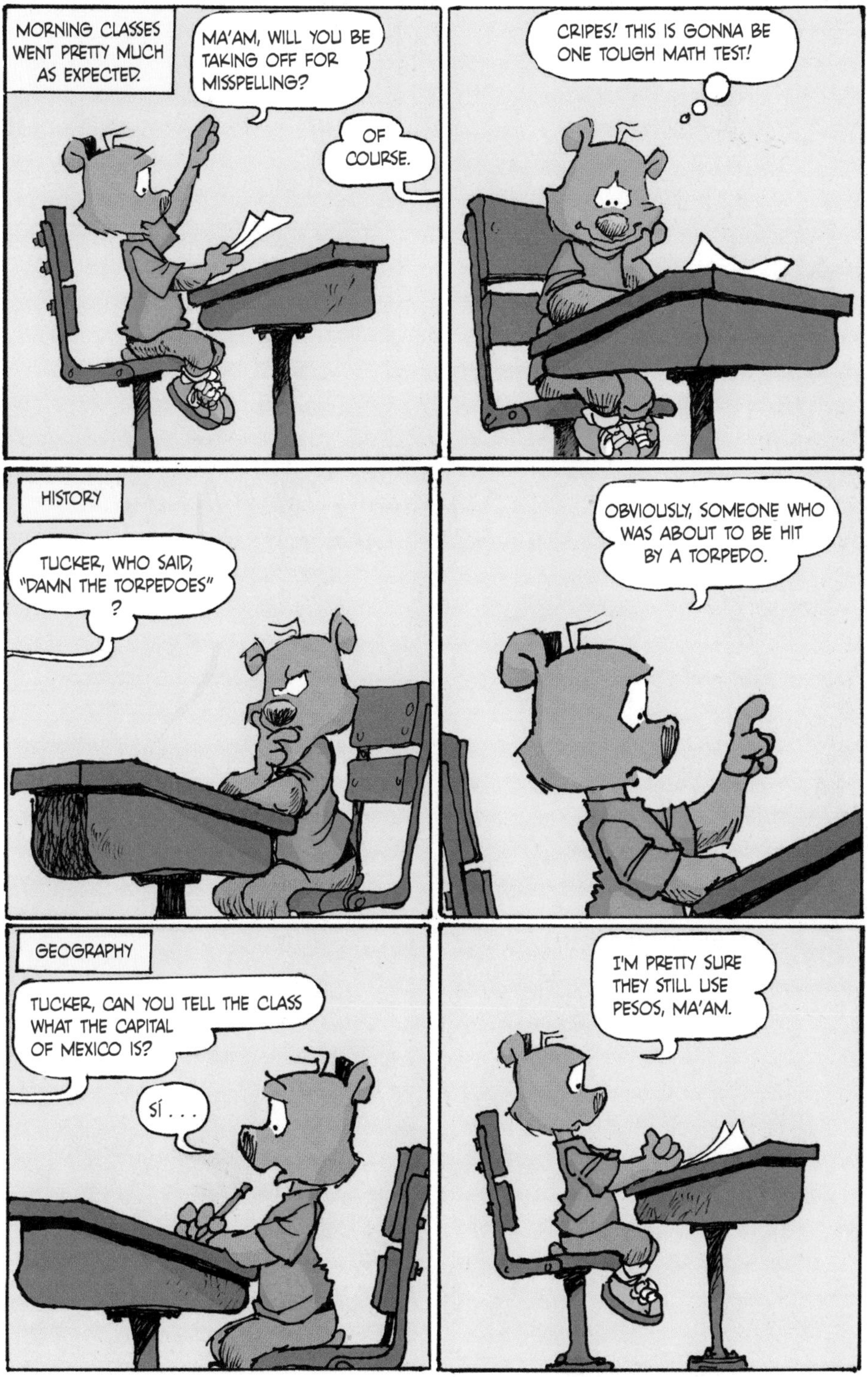
MORNING CLASSES WENT PRETTY MUCH AS EXPECTED.
MA'AM, WILL YOU BE TAKING OFF FOR MISSPELLING?
OF COURSE.
CRIPES! THIS IS GONNA BE ONE TOUGH MATH TEST!
HISTORY
TUCKER, WHO SAID, "DAMN THE TORPEDOES" ?
OBVIOUSLY, SOMEONE WHO WAS ABOUT TO BE HIT BY A TORPEDO.
GEOGRAPHY
TUCKER, CAN YOU TELL THE CLASS WHAT THE CAPITAL OF MEXICO IS?
SÍ . . .
I'M PRETTY SURE THEY STILL USE PESOS, MA'AM.

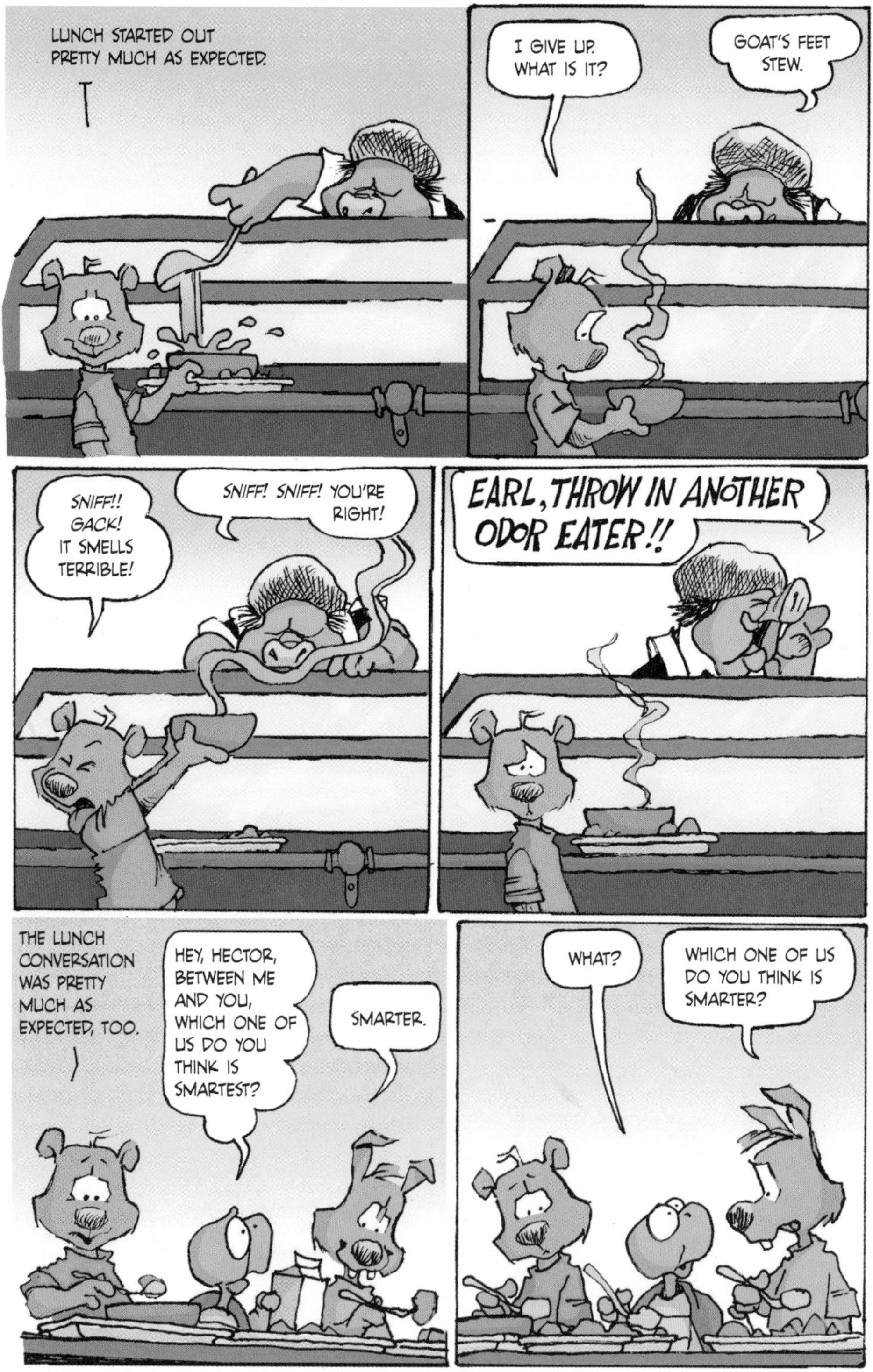
LUNCH STARTED OUT PRETTY MUCH AS EXPECTED.
I GIVE UP. WHAT IS IT?
GOAT'S FEET STEW.
SNIFF!! GACK! IT SMELLS TERRIBLE!
SNIFF! SNIFF! YOU'RE RIGHT!
EARL, THROW IN ANOTHER ODOR EATER!!
THE LUNCH CONVERSATION WAS PRETTY MUCH AS EXPECTED, TOO.
HEY, HECTOR, BETWEEN ME AND YOU, WHICH ONE OF US DO YOU THINK IS SMARTEST?
SMARTER.
WHAT?
WHICH ONE OF US DO YOU THINK IS SMARTER?

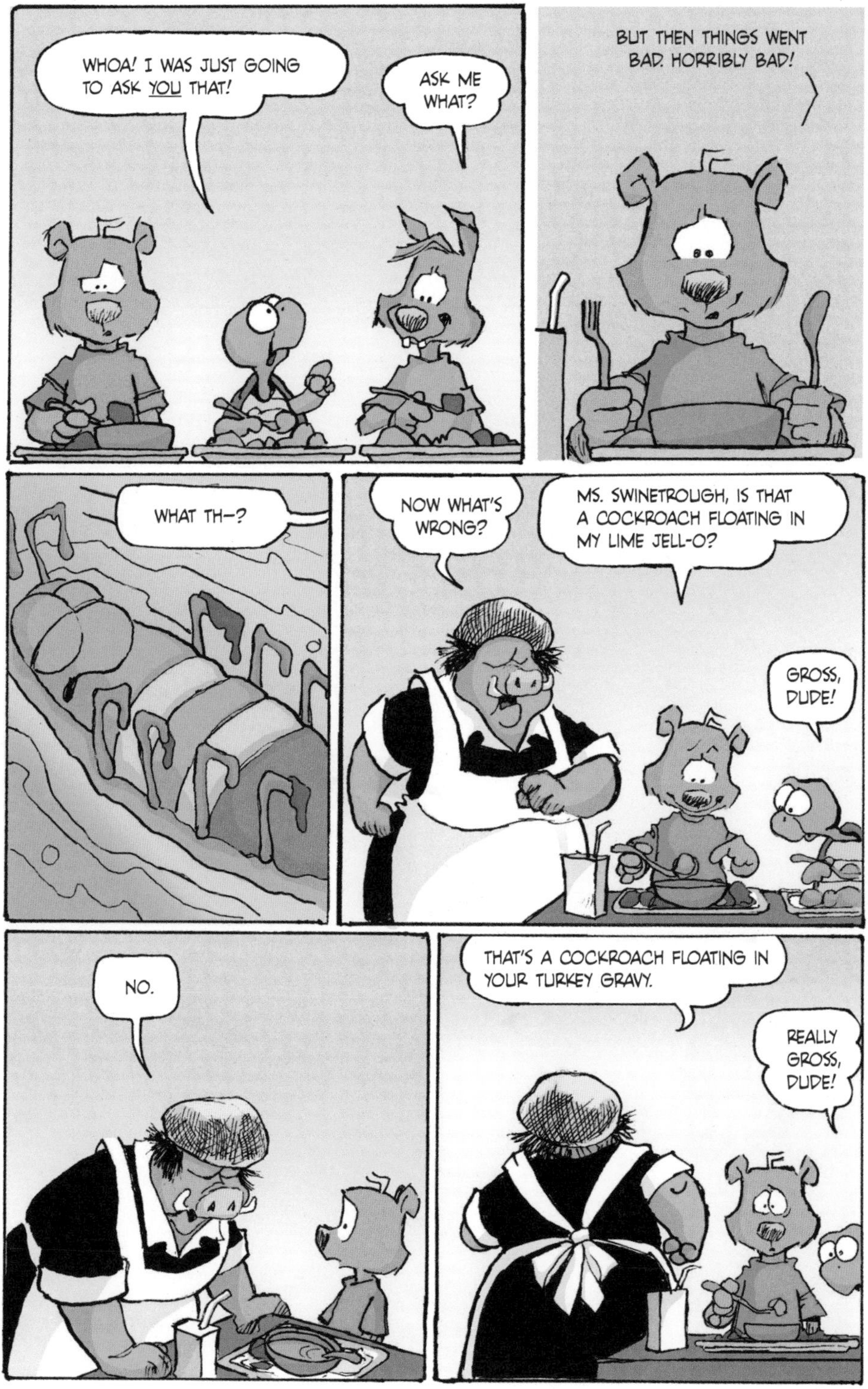
WHOA! I WAS JUST GOING TO ASK YOU THAT!
ASK ME WHAT?
BUT THEN THINGS WENT BAD. HORRIBLY BAD!
WHAT TH—?
NOW WHAT'S WRONG?
MS. SWINETROUGH, IS THAT A COCKROACH FLOATING IN MY LIME JELL-O?
GROSS, DUDE!
NO.
THAT'S A COCKROACH FLOATING IN YOUR TURKEY GRAVY.
REALLY GROSS, DUDE!

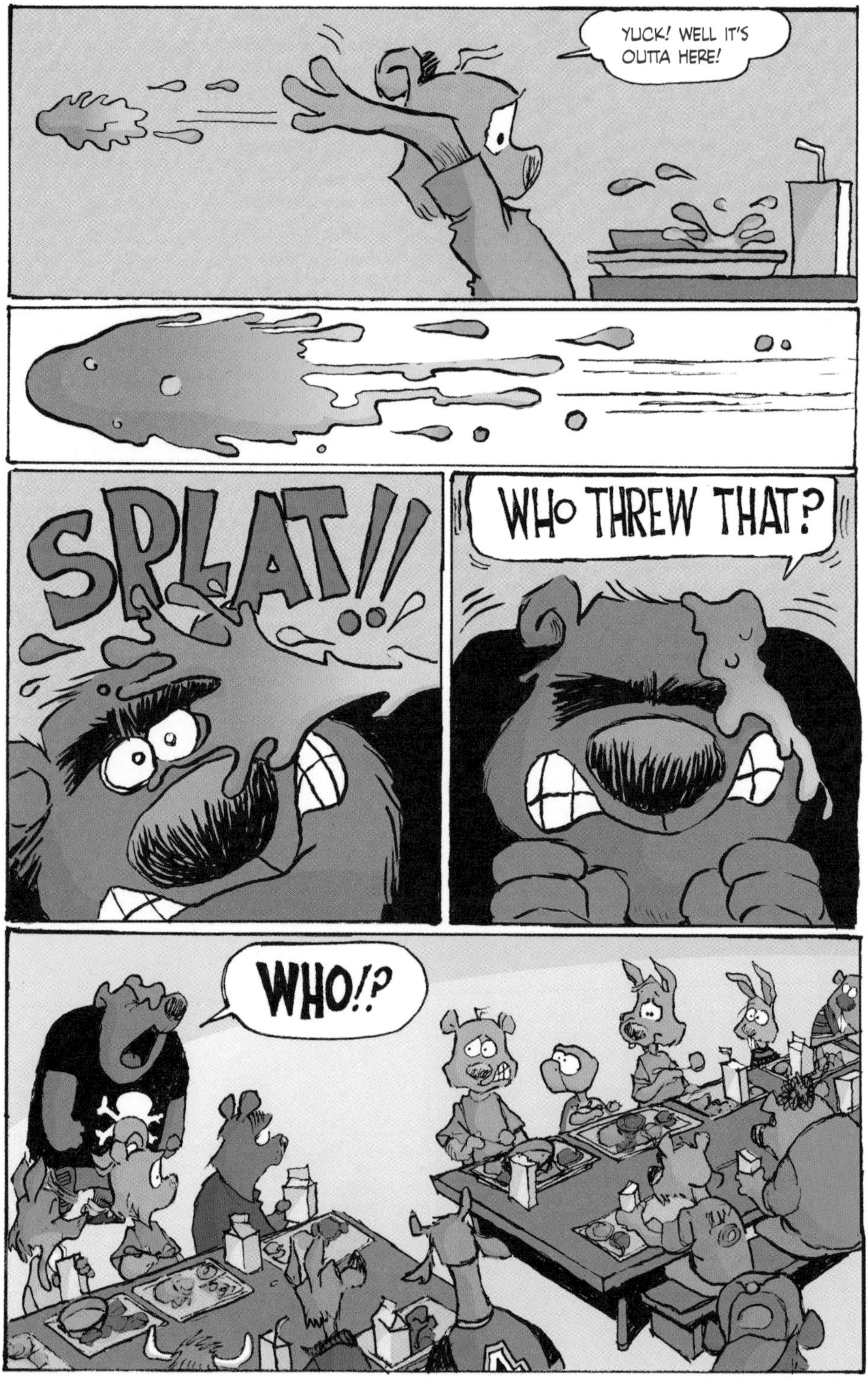
YUCK! WELL IT'S OUTTA HERE!
SPLAT!!
WHO THREW THAT?
WHO!?

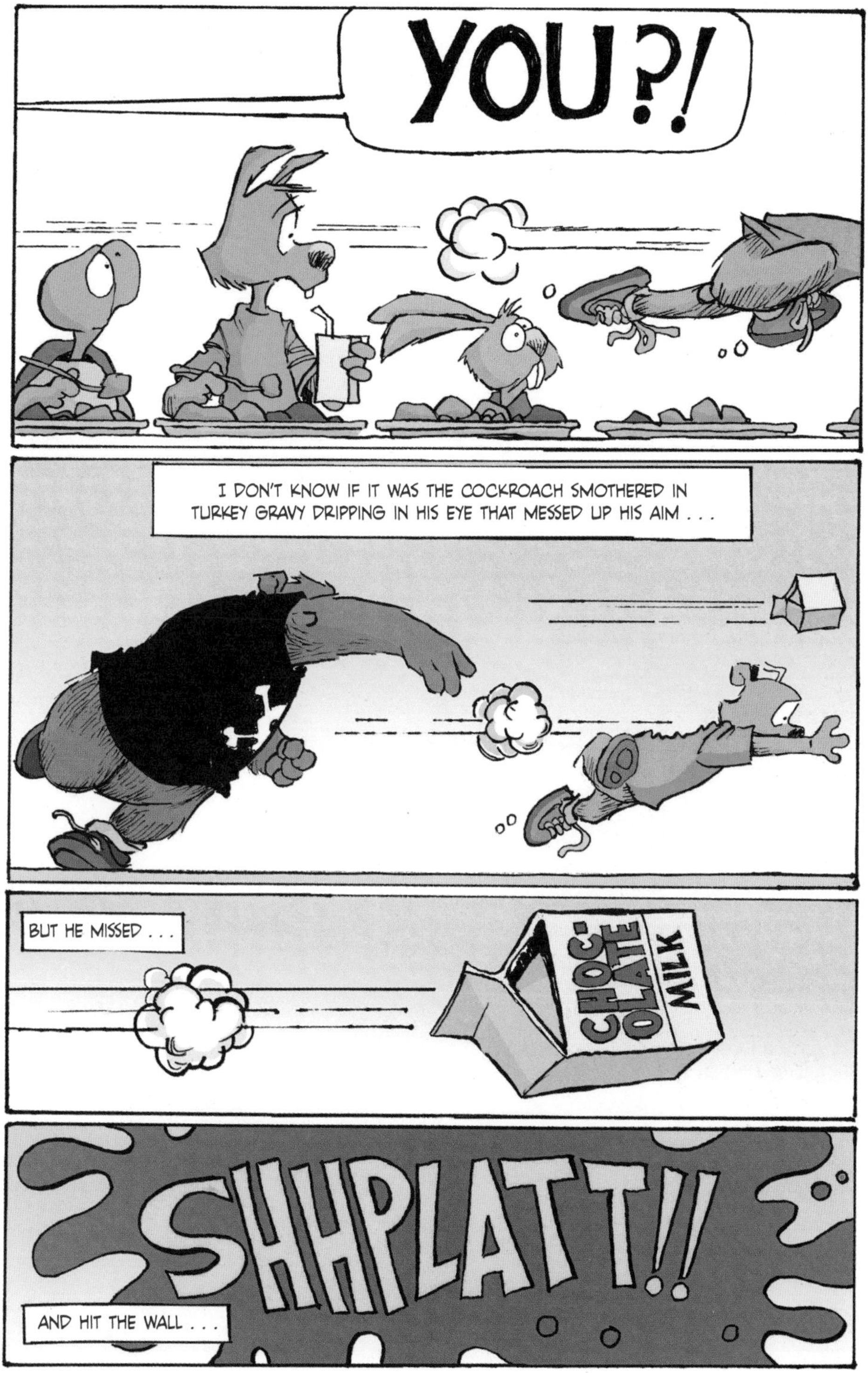
YOU?!
I DON'T KNOW IF IT WAS THE COCKROACH SMOTHERED IN TURKEY GRAVY DRIPPING IN HIS EYE THAT MESSED UP HIS AIM . . .
BUT HE MISSED . . .
CHOC-OLATE MILK
SHHPLATT!!
AND HIT THE WALL . . .

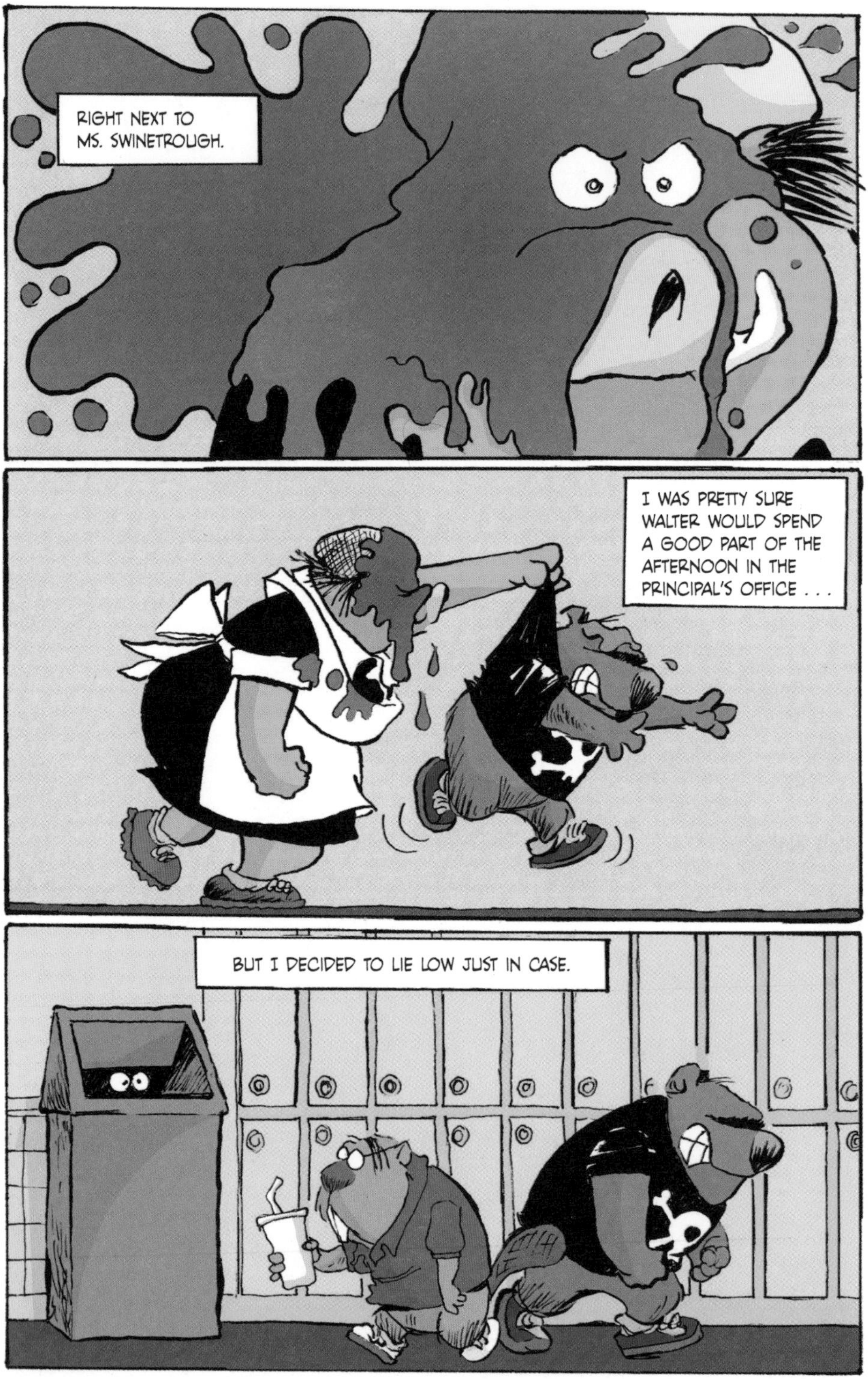
RIGHT NEXT TO
MS. SWINETROUGH.
I WAS PRETTY SURE WALTER WOULD SPEND A GOOD PART OF THE AFTERNOON IN THE PRINCIPAL'S OFFICE . . .
BUT I DECIDED TO LIE LOW JUST IN CASE.

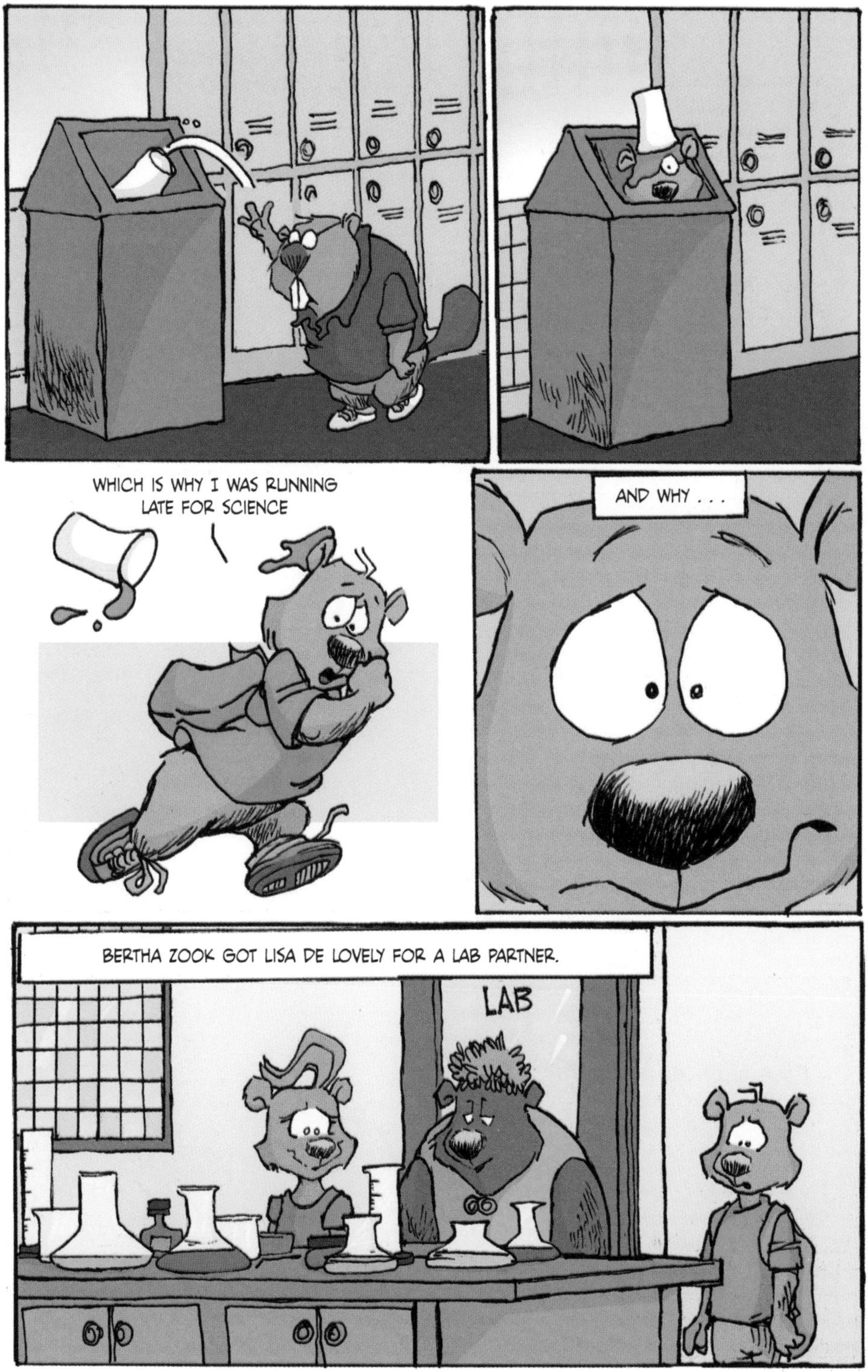
WHICH IS WHY I WAS RUNNING LATE FOR SCIENCE
AND WHY . . .
BERTHA ZOOK GOT LISA DE LOVELY FOR A LAB PARTNER.
LAB

AND I GOT STUCK WITH NORVILLE PADDLEBUTT.

BIRD DOGS, CATFISH, SPIDER MONKEYS . . .

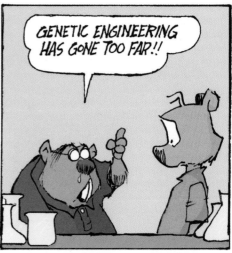

GENETIC ENGINEERING HAS GONE TOO FAR!!

BUT WHAT NORVILLE _HAD_ DONE RIGHT WAS GET THE LAB STATION CLOSEST TO LISA AND BERTHA.

AND WHAT ABOUT BATBOYS? WHAT'S WITH THOSE GUYS?

SO, WITH STEALTH PRECISION, I WAS ABLE TO SCOOT MY STOOL CLOSER TO LISA WITH NO ONE NOTICING.

SKREET! SKREET! SKREET! SKREET!

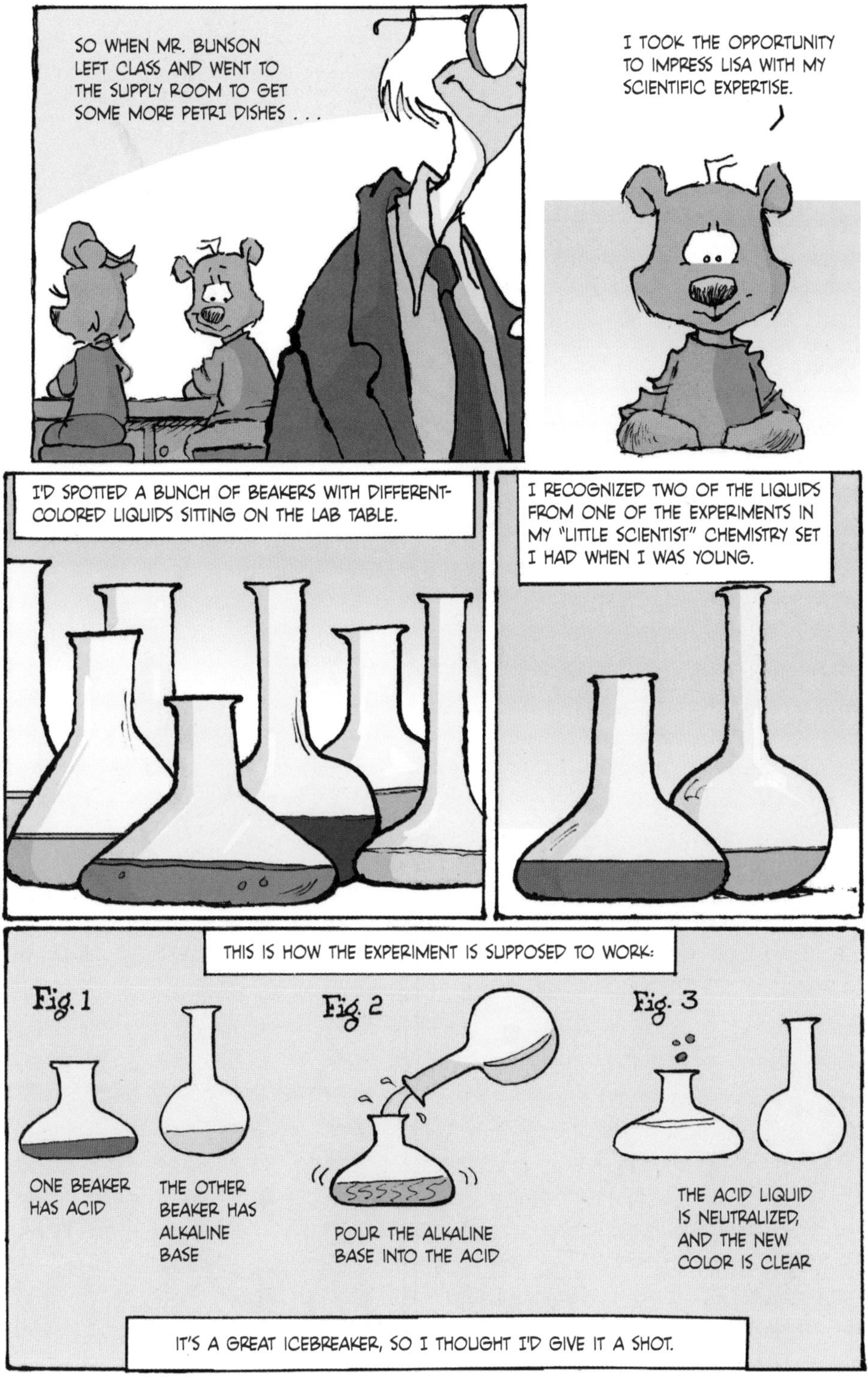
SO WHEN MR. BUNSON LEFT CLASS AND WENT TO THE SUPPLY ROOM TO GET SOME MORE PETRI DISHES . . .
I TOOK THE OPPORTUNITY TO IMPRESS LISA WITH MY SCIENTIFIC EXPERTISE.
I'D SPOTTED A BUNCH OF BEAKERS WITH DIFFERENT-COLORED LIQUIDS SITTING ON THE LAB TABLE.
I RECOGNIZED TWO OF THE LIQUIDS FROM ONE OF THE EXPERIMENTS IN MY "LITTLE SCIENTIST" CHEMISTRY SET I HAD WHEN I WAS YOUNG.
THIS IS HOW THE EXPERIMENT IS SUPPOSED TO WORK:
Fig. 1
ONE BEAKER HAS ACID
THE OTHER BEAKER HAS ALKALINE BASE
Fig. 2
POUR THE ALKALINE BASE INTO THE ACID
Fig. 3
THE ACID LIQUID IS NEUTRALIZED, AND THE NEW COLOR IS CLEAR
IT'S A GREAT ICEBREAKER, SO I THOUGHT I'D GIVE IT A SHOT.

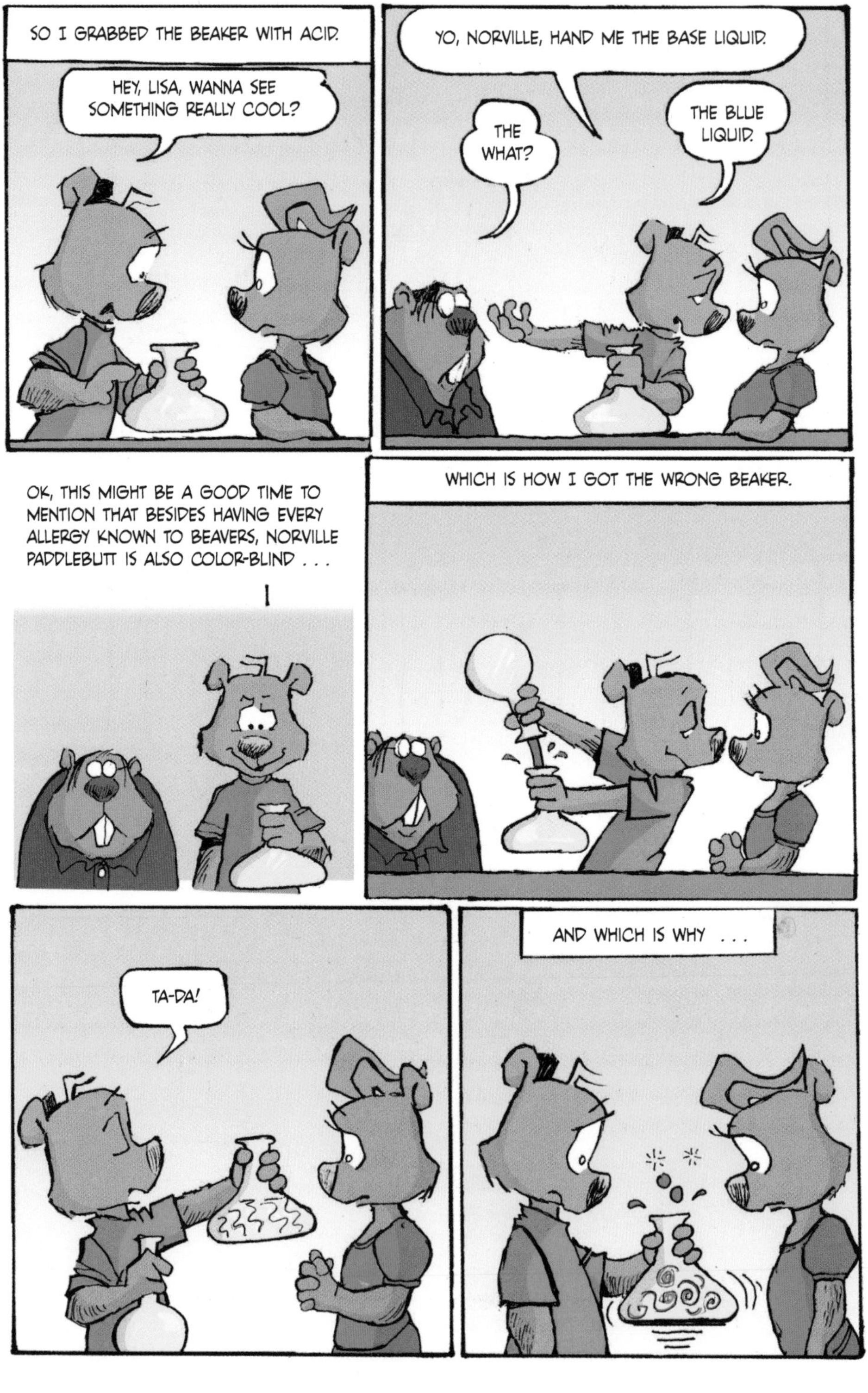
SO I GRABBED THE BEAKER WITH ACID.
HEY, LISA, WANNA SEE SOMETHING REALLY COOL?
YO, NORVILLE, HAND ME THE BASE LIQUID.
THE WHAT?
THE BLUE LIQUID.
OK, THIS MIGHT BE A GOOD TIME TO MENTION THAT BESIDES HAVING EVERY ALLERGY KNOWN TO BEAVERS, NORVILLE PADDLEBUTT IS ALSO COLOR-BLIND . . .
WHICH IS HOW I GOT THE WRONG BEAKER.
TA-DA!
AND WHICH IS WHY . . .

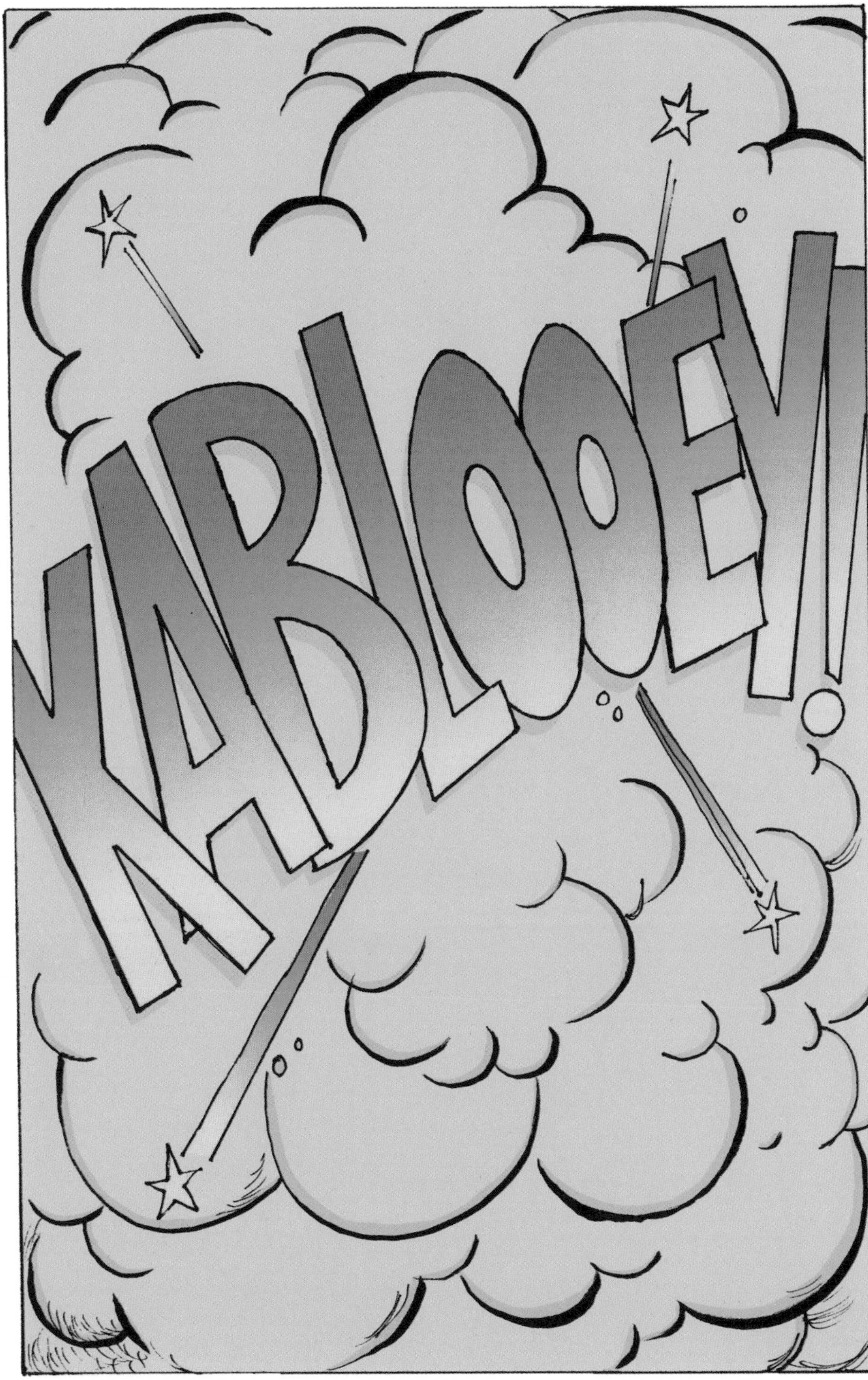
KABLOOEY!!

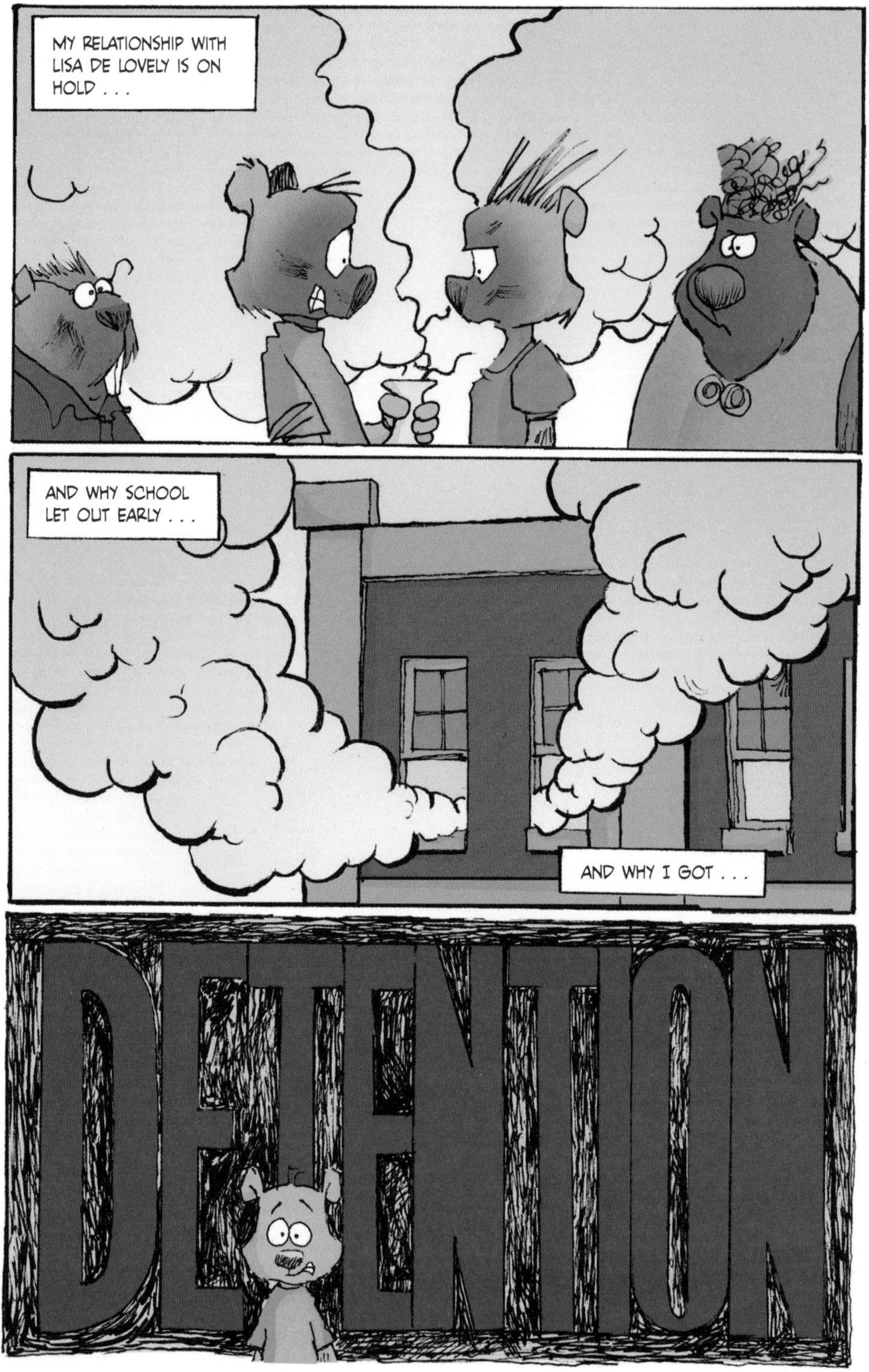
MY RELATIONSHIP WITH LISA DE LOVELY IS ON HOLD . . .
AND WHY SCHOOL LET OUT EARLY . . .
AND WHY I GOT . . .
DETENTION

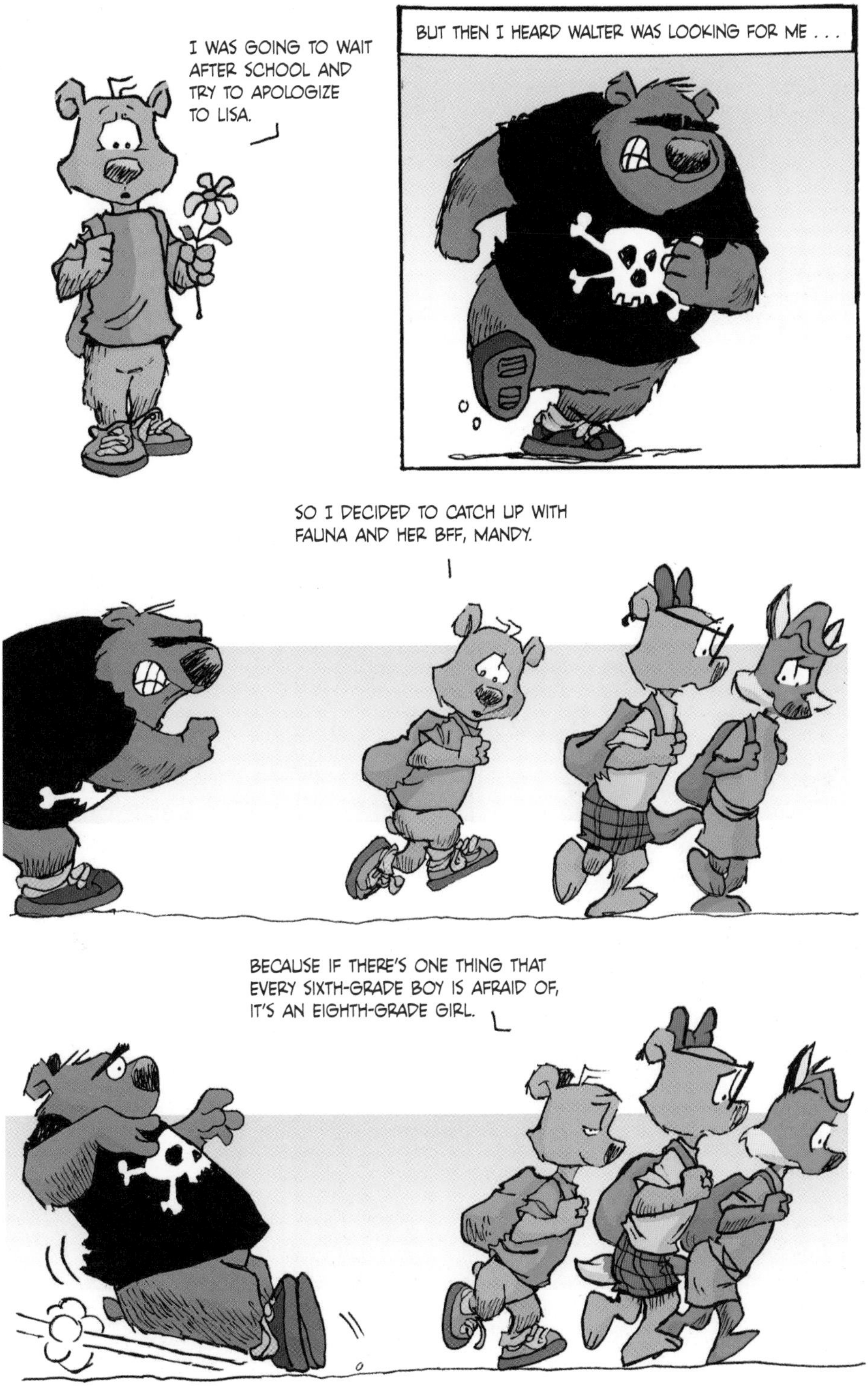
I WAS GOING TO WAIT AFTER SCHOOL AND TRY TO APOLOGIZE TO LISA.
BUT THEN I HEARD WALTER WAS LOOKING FOR ME . . .
SO I DECIDED TO CATCH UP WITH FAUNA AND HER BFF, MANDY.
BECAUSE IF THERE'S ONE THING THAT EVERY SIXTH-GRADE BOY IS AFRAID OF, IT'S AN EIGHTH-GRADE GIRL.

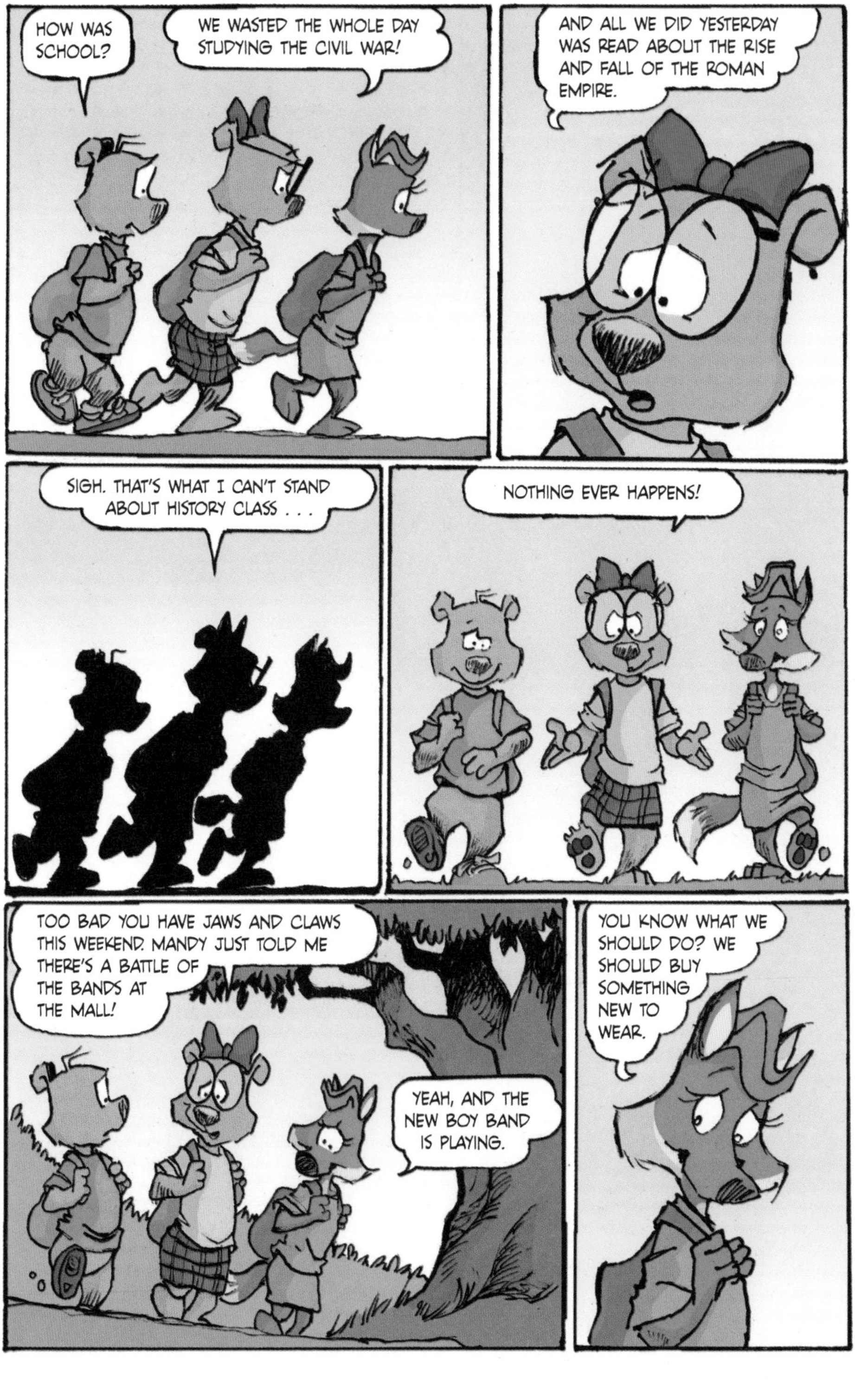
HOW WAS SCHOOL?
WE WASTED THE WHOLE DAY STUDYING THE CIVIL WAR!
AND ALL WE DID YESTERDAY WAS READ ABOUT THE RISE AND FALL OF THE ROMAN EMPIRE.
SIGH. THAT'S WHAT I CAN'T STAND ABOUT HISTORY CLASS . . .
NOTHING EVER HAPPENS!
TOO BAD YOU HAVE JAWS AND CLAWS THIS WEEKEND. MANDY JUST TOLD ME THERE'S A BATTLE OF THE BANDS AT THE MALL!
YEAH, AND THE NEW BOY BAND IS PLAYING.
YOU KNOW WHAT WE SHOULD DO? WE SHOULD BUY SOMETHING NEW TO WEAR.

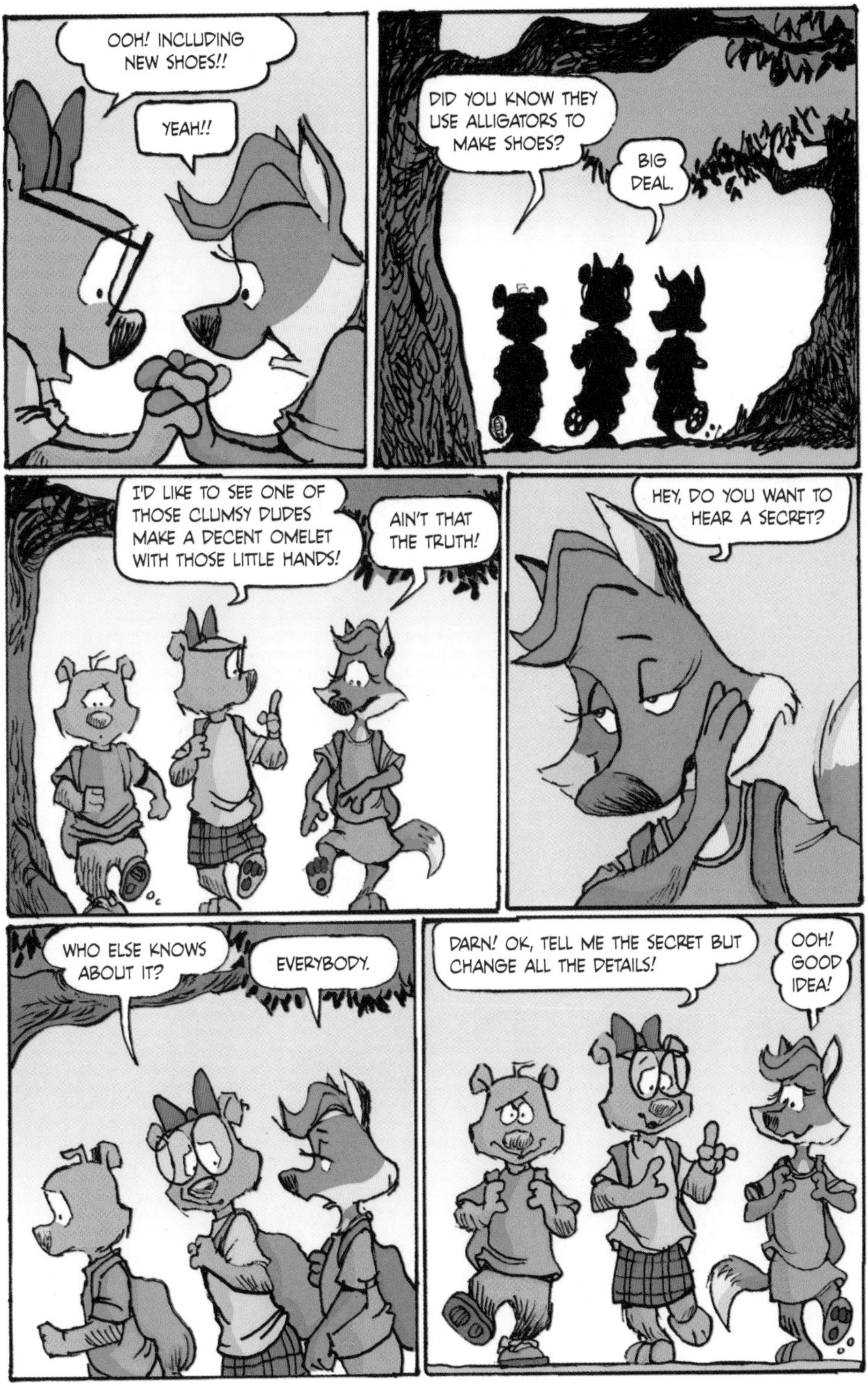
OOH! INCLUDING NEW SHOES!!
YEAH!!
DID YOU KNOW THEY USE ALLIGATORS TO MAKE SHOES?
BIG DEAL.
I'D LIKE TO SEE ONE OF THOSE CLUMSY DUDES MAKE A DECENT OMELET WITH THOSE LITTLE HANDS!
AIN'T THAT THE TRUTH!
HEY, DO YOU WANT TO HEAR A SECRET?
WHO ELSE KNOWS ABOUT IT?
EVERYBODY.
DARN! OK, TELL ME THE SECRET BUT CHANGE ALL THE DETAILS!
OOH! GOOD IDEA!

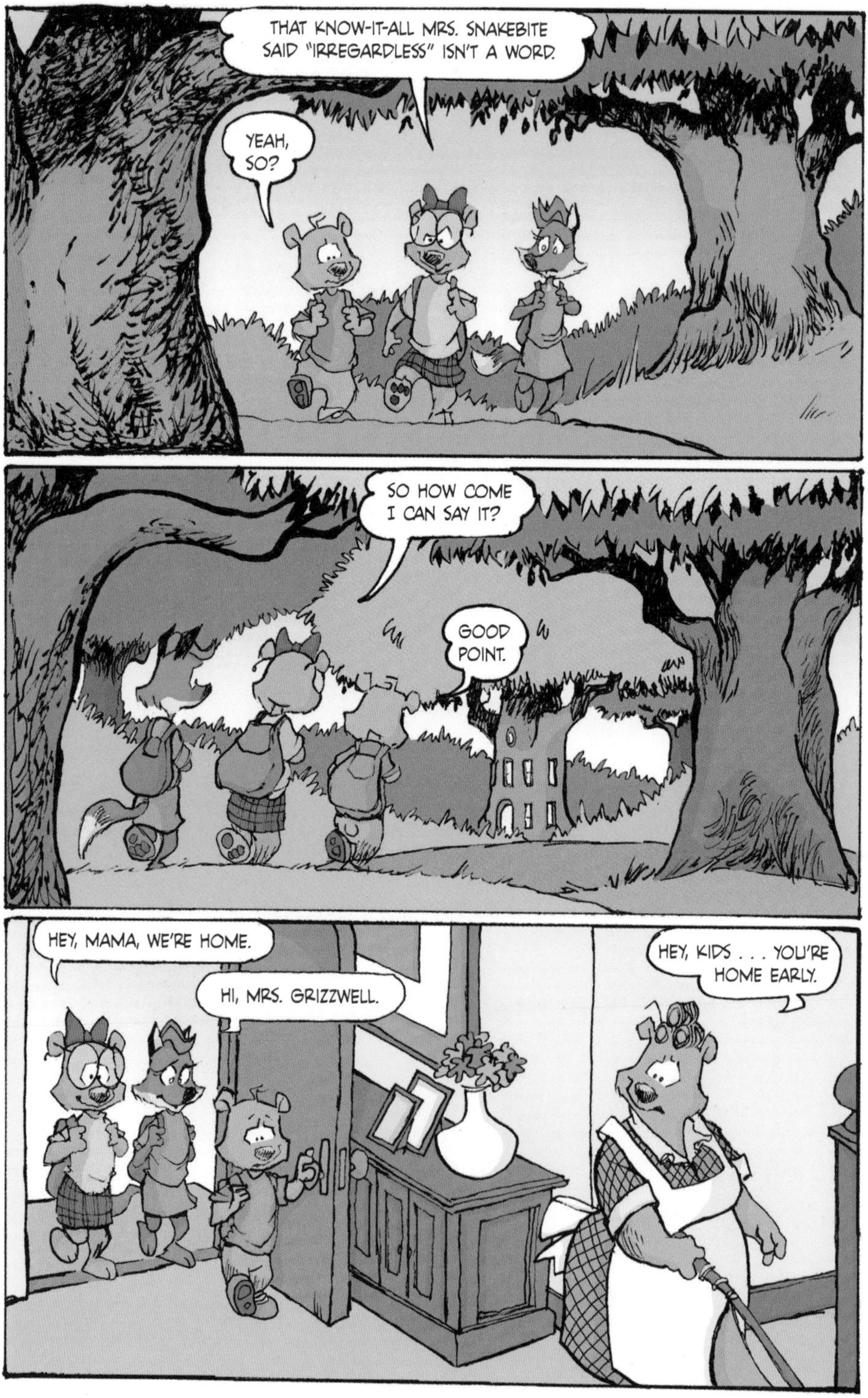
THAT KNOW-IT-ALL MRS. SNAKEBITE SAID "IRREGARDLESS" ISN'T A WORD.
YEAH, SO?
SO HOW COME I CAN SAY IT?
GOOD POINT.
HEY, MAMA, WE'RE HOME.
HI, MRS. GRIZZWELL.
HEY, KIDS . . . YOU'RE HOME EARLY.

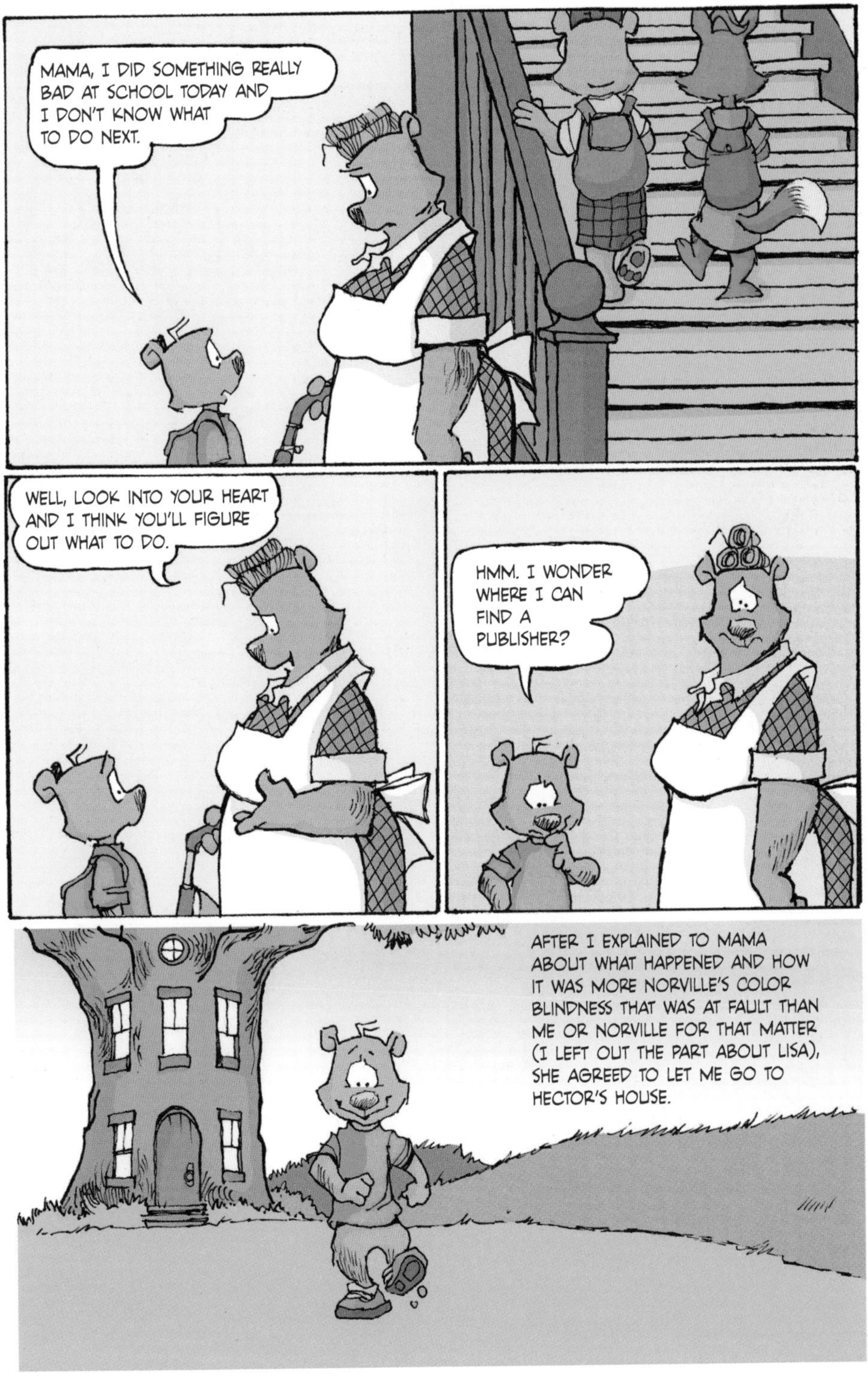
MAMA, I DID SOMETHING REALLY BAD AT SCHOOL TODAY AND I DON'T KNOW WHAT TO DO NEXT.
WELL, LOOK INTO YOUR HEART AND I THINK YOU'LL FIGURE OUT WHAT TO DO.
HMM. I WONDER WHERE I CAN FIND A PUBLISHER?
AFTER I EXPLAINED TO MAMA ABOUT WHAT HAPPENED AND HOW IT WAS MORE NORVILLE'S COLOR BLINDNESS THAT WAS AT FAULT THAN ME OR NORVILLE FOR THAT MATTER (I LEFT OUT THE PART ABOUT LISA), SHE AGREED TO LET ME GO TO HECTOR'S HOUSE.

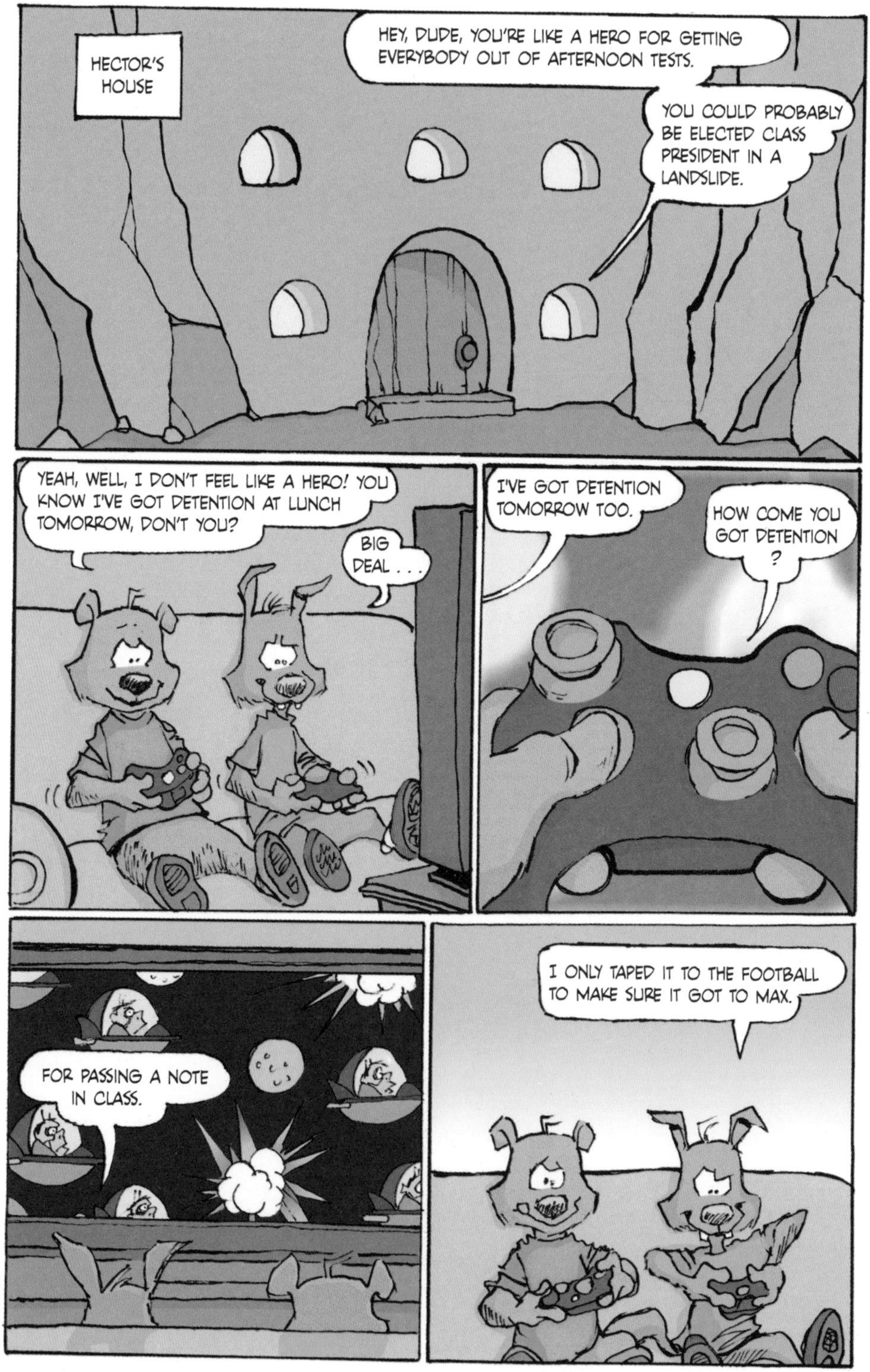
HECTOR'S HOUSE
HEY, DUDE, YOU'RE LIKE A HERO FOR GETTING EVERYBODY OUT OF AFTERNOON TESTS.
YOU COULD PROBABLY BE ELECTED CLASS PRESIDENT IN A LANDSLIDE.
YEAH, WELL, I DON'T FEEL LIKE A HERO! YOU KNOW I'VE GOT DETENTION AT LUNCH TOMORROW, DON'T YOU?
BIG DEAL . . .
I'VE GOT DETENTION TOMORROW TOO.
HOW COME YOU GOT DETENTION ?
FOR PASSING A NOTE IN CLASS.
I ONLY TAPED IT TO THE FOOTBALL TO MAKE SURE IT GOT TO MAX.

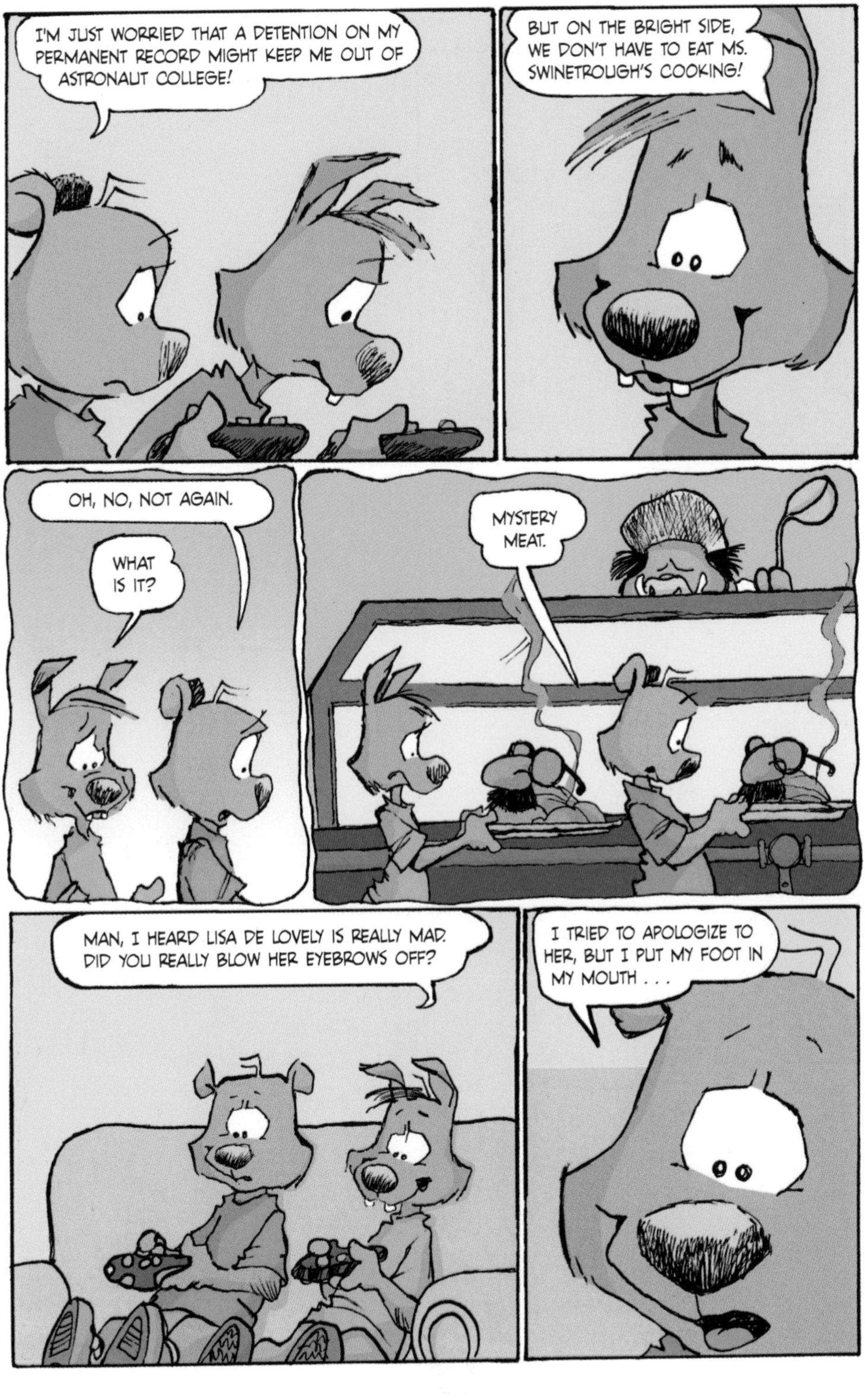
I'M JUST WORRIED THAT A DETENTION ON MY PERMANENT RECORD MIGHT KEEP ME OUT OF ASTRONAUT COLLEGE!
BUT ON THE BRIGHT SIDE, WE DON'T HAVE TO EAT MS. SWINETROUGH'S COOKING!
OH, NO, NOT AGAIN.
WHAT IS IT?
MYSTERY MEAT.
MAN, I HEARD LISA DE LOVELY IS REALLY MAD. DID YOU REALLY BLOW HER EYEBROWS OFF?
I TRIED TO APOLOGIZE TO HER, BUT I PUT MY FOOT IN MY MOUTH . . .

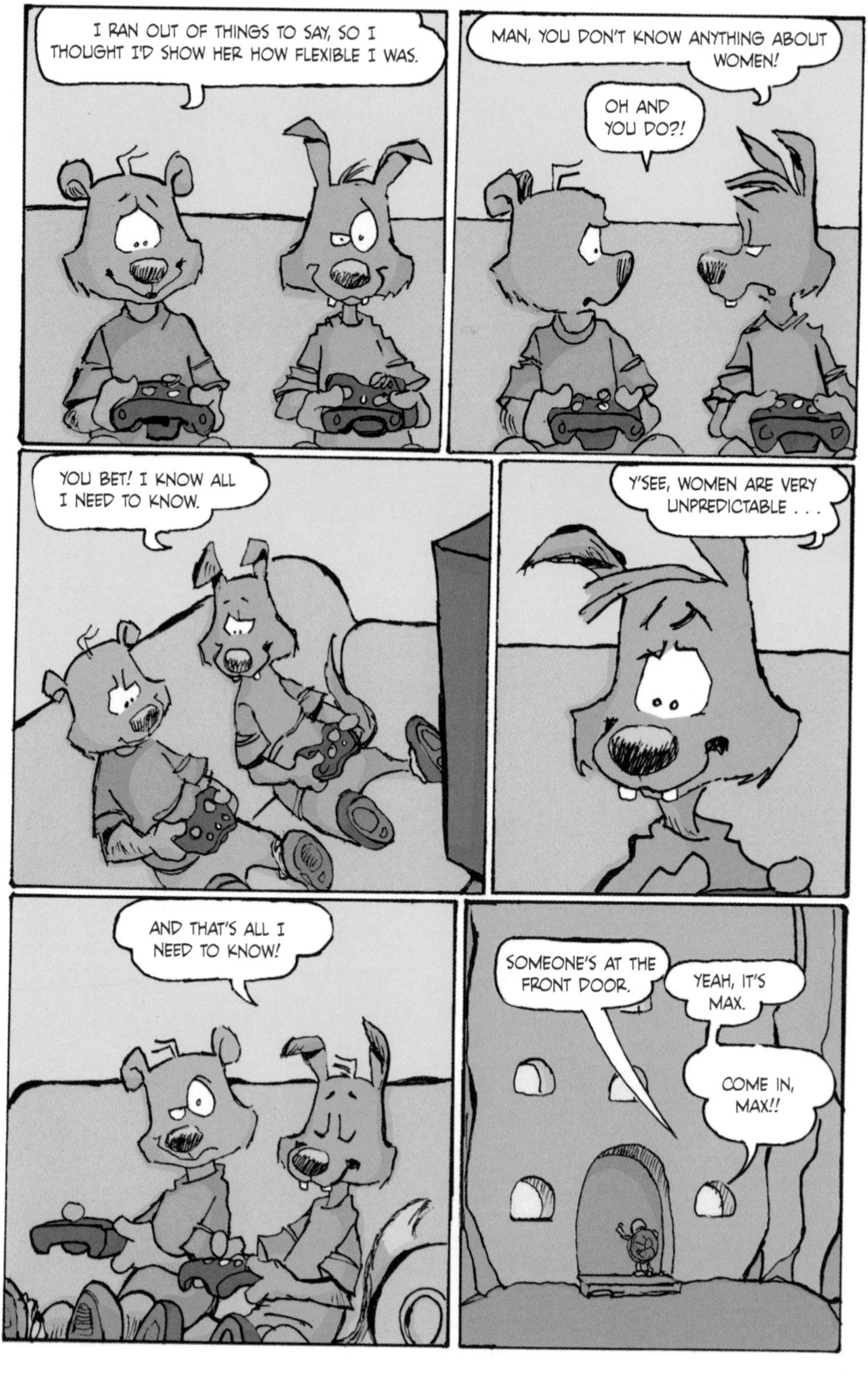
I RAN OUT OF THINGS TO SAY, SO I THOUGHT I'D SHOW HER HOW FLEXIBLE I WAS.
MAN, YOU DON'T KNOW ANYTHING ABOUT WOMEN!
OH AND YOU DO?!
YOU BET! I KNOW ALL I NEED TO KNOW.
Y'SEE, WOMEN ARE VERY UNPREDICTABLE . . .
AND THAT'S ALL I NEED TO KNOW!
SOMEONE'S AT THE FRONT DOOR.
YEAH, IT'S MAX.
COME IN, MAX!!

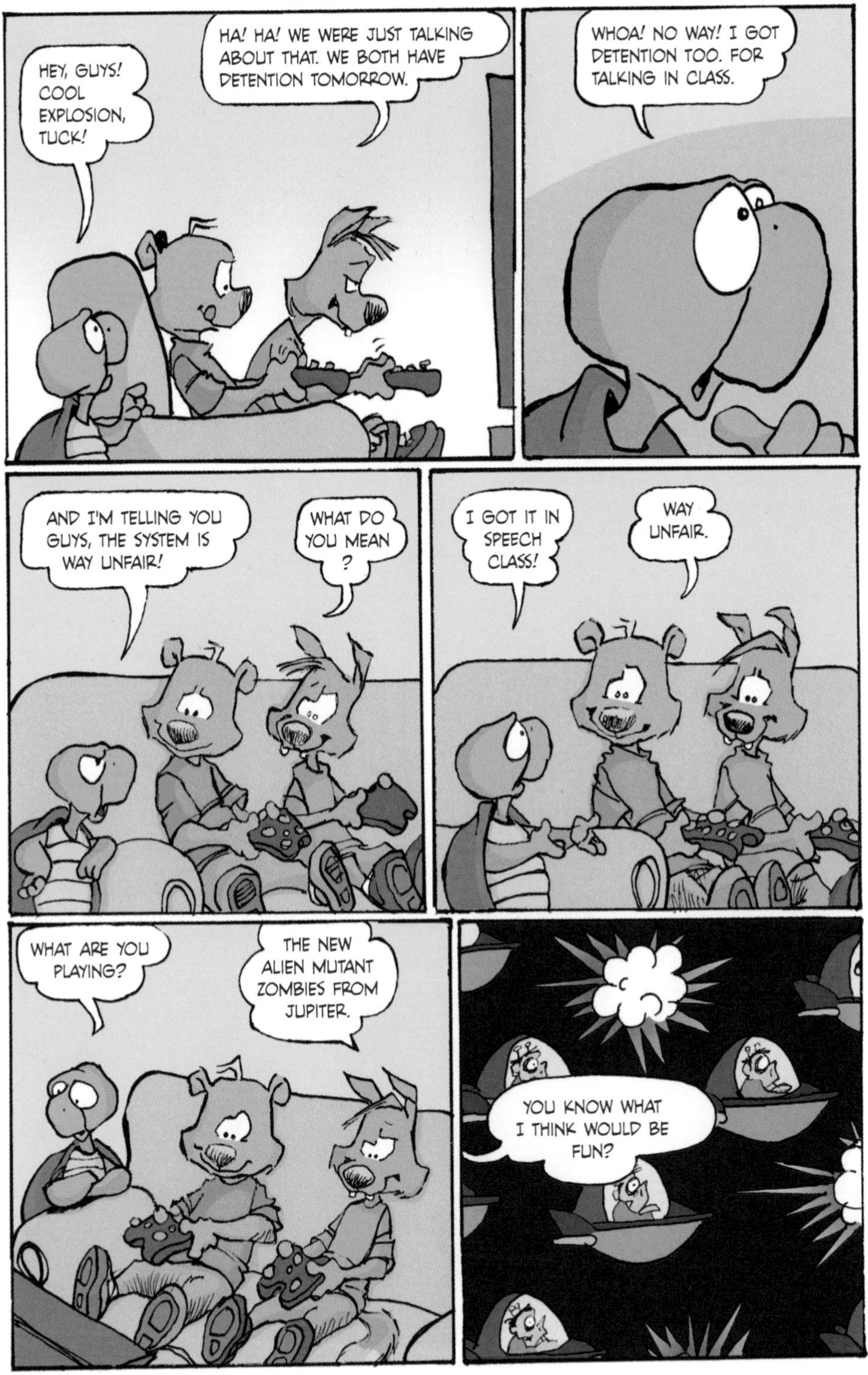
HEY, GUYS! COOL EXPLOSION, TUCK!
HA! HA! WE WERE JUST TALKING ABOUT THAT. WE BOTH HAVE DETENTION TOMORROW.
WHOA! NO WAY! I GOT DETENTION TOO. FOR TALKING IN CLASS.
AND I'M TELLING YOU GUYS, THE SYSTEM IS WAY UNFAIR!
WHAT DO YOU MEAN ?
I GOT IT IN SPEECH CLASS!
WAY UNFAIR.
WHAT ARE YOU PLAYING?
THE NEW ALIEN MUTANT ZOMBIES FROM JUPITER.
YOU KNOW WHAT I THINK WOULD BE FUN?

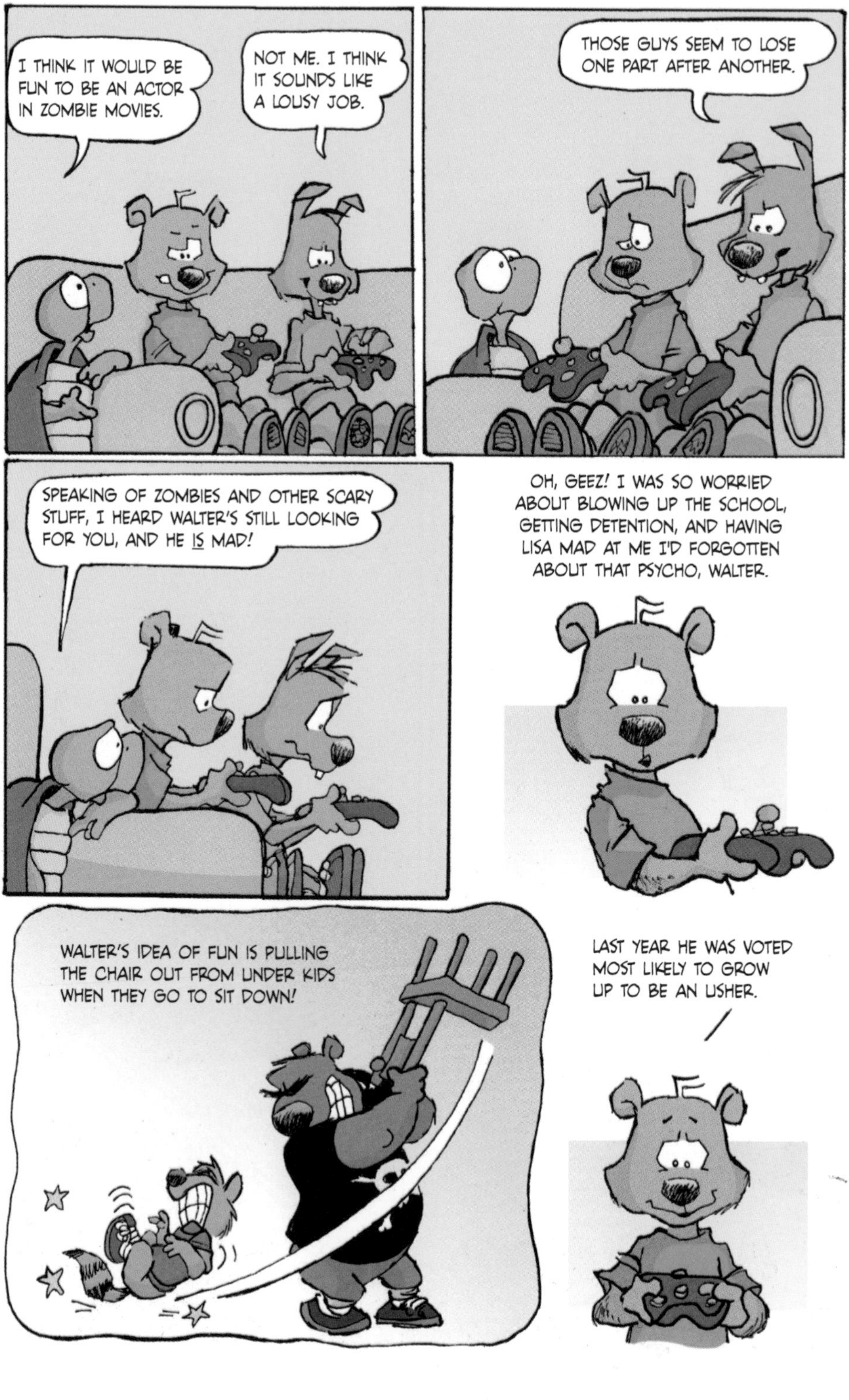
I THINK IT WOULD BE FUN TO BE AN ACTOR IN ZOMBIE MOVIES.
NOT ME. I THINK IT SOUNDS LIKE A LOUSY JOB.
THOSE GUYS SEEM TO LOSE ONE PART AFTER ANOTHER.
SPEAKING OF ZOMBIES AND OTHER SCARY STUFF, I HEARD WALTER'S STILL LOOKING FOR YOU, AND HE IS MAD!
OH, GEEZ! I WAS SO WORRIED ABOUT BLOWING UP THE SCHOOL, GETTING DETENTION, AND HAVING LISA MAD AT ME I'D FORGOTTEN ABOUT THAT PSYCHO, WALTER.
WALTER'S IDEA OF FUN IS PULLING THE CHAIR OUT FROM UNDER KIDS WHEN THEY GO TO SIT DOWN!
LAST YEAR HE WAS VOTED MOST LIKELY TO GROW UP TO BE AN USHER.

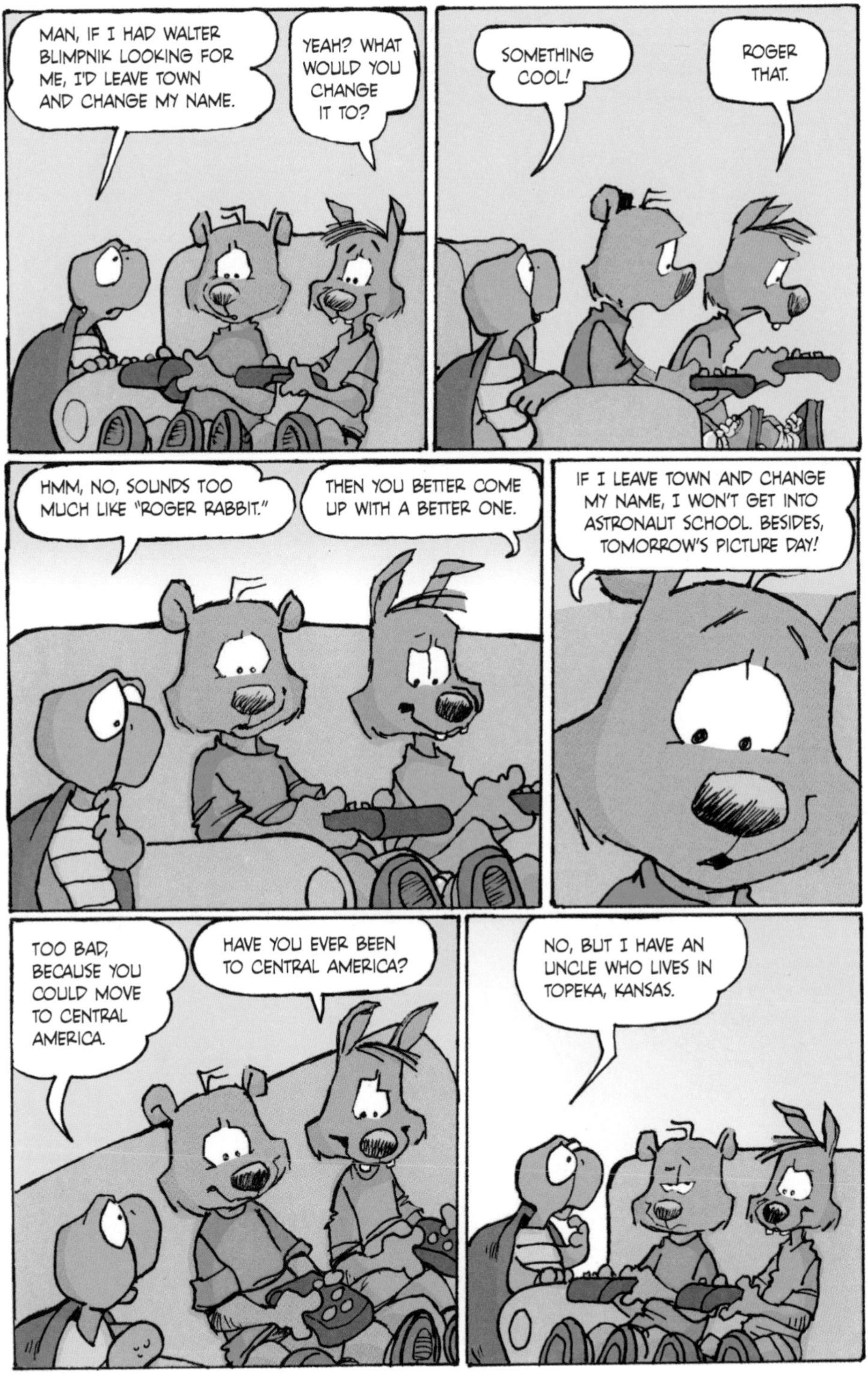
MAN, IF I HAD WALTER BLIMPNIK LOOKING FOR ME, I'D LEAVE TOWN AND CHANGE MY NAME.
YEAH? WHAT WOULD YOU CHANGE IT TO?
SOMETHING COOL!
ROGER THAT.
HMM, NO, SOUNDS TOO MUCH LIKE "ROGER RABBIT."
THEN YOU BETTER COME UP WITH A BETTER ONE.
IF I LEAVE TOWN AND CHANGE MY NAME, I WON'T GET INTO ASTRONAUT SCHOOL. BESIDES, TOMORROW'S PICTURE DAY!
TOO BAD, BECAUSE YOU COULD MOVE TO CENTRAL AMERICA.
HAVE YOU EVER BEEN TO CENTRAL AMERICA?
NO, BUT I HAVE AN UNCLE WHO LIVES IN TOPEKA, KANSAS.

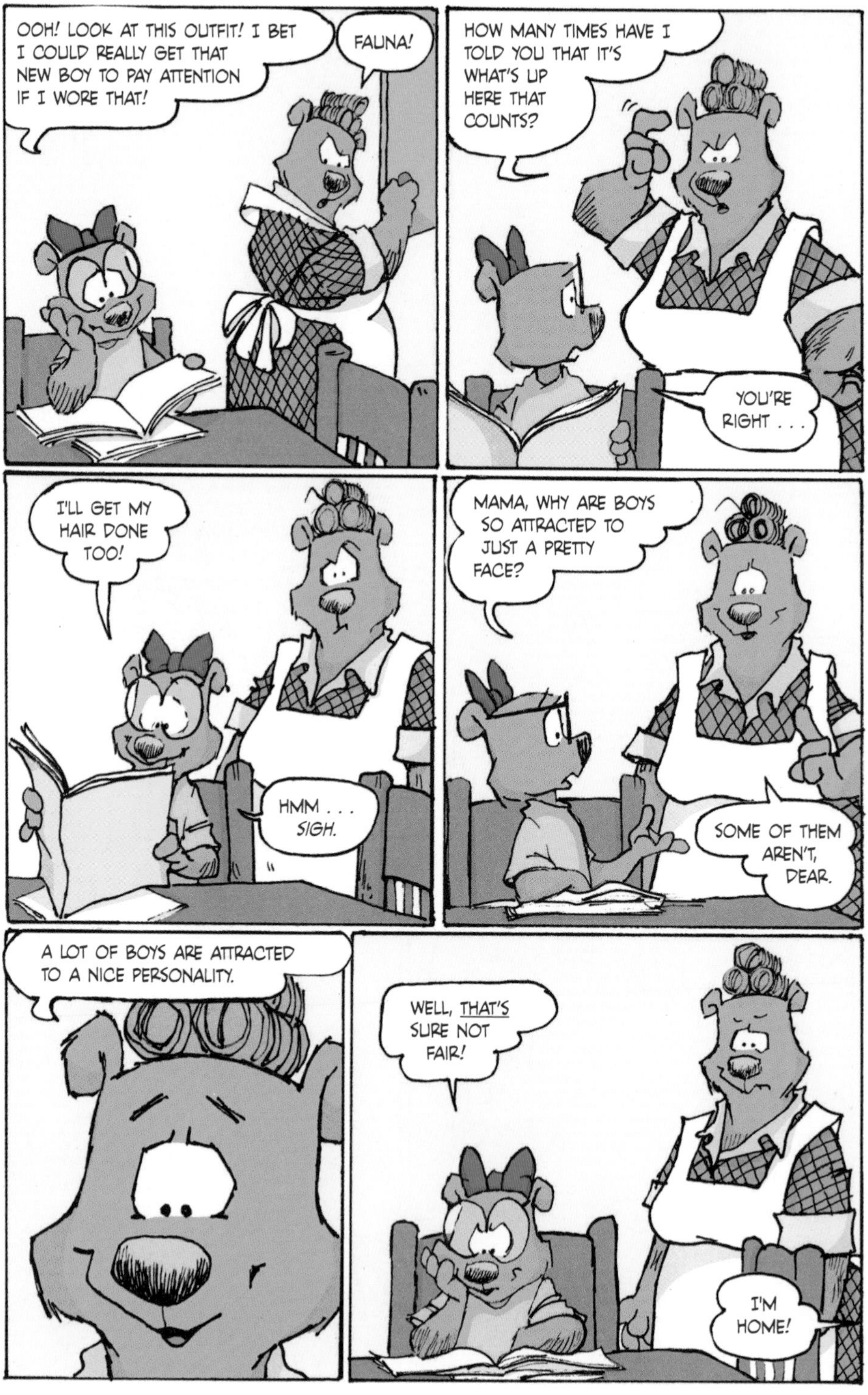
OOH! LOOK AT THIS OUTFIT! I BET I COULD REALLY GET THAT NEW BOY TO PAY ATTENTION IF I WORE THAT!
FAUNA!
HOW MANY TIMES HAVE I TOLD YOU THAT IT'S WHAT'S UP HERE THAT COUNTS?
YOU'RE RIGHT . . .
I'LL GET MY HAIR DONE TOO!
HMM . . . SIGH.
MAMA, WHY ARE BOYS SO ATTRACTED TO JUST A PRETTY FACE?
SOME OF THEM AREN'T, DEAR.
A LOT OF BOYS ARE ATTRACTED TO A NICE PERSONALITY.
WELL, THAT'S SURE NOT FAIR!
I'M HOME!

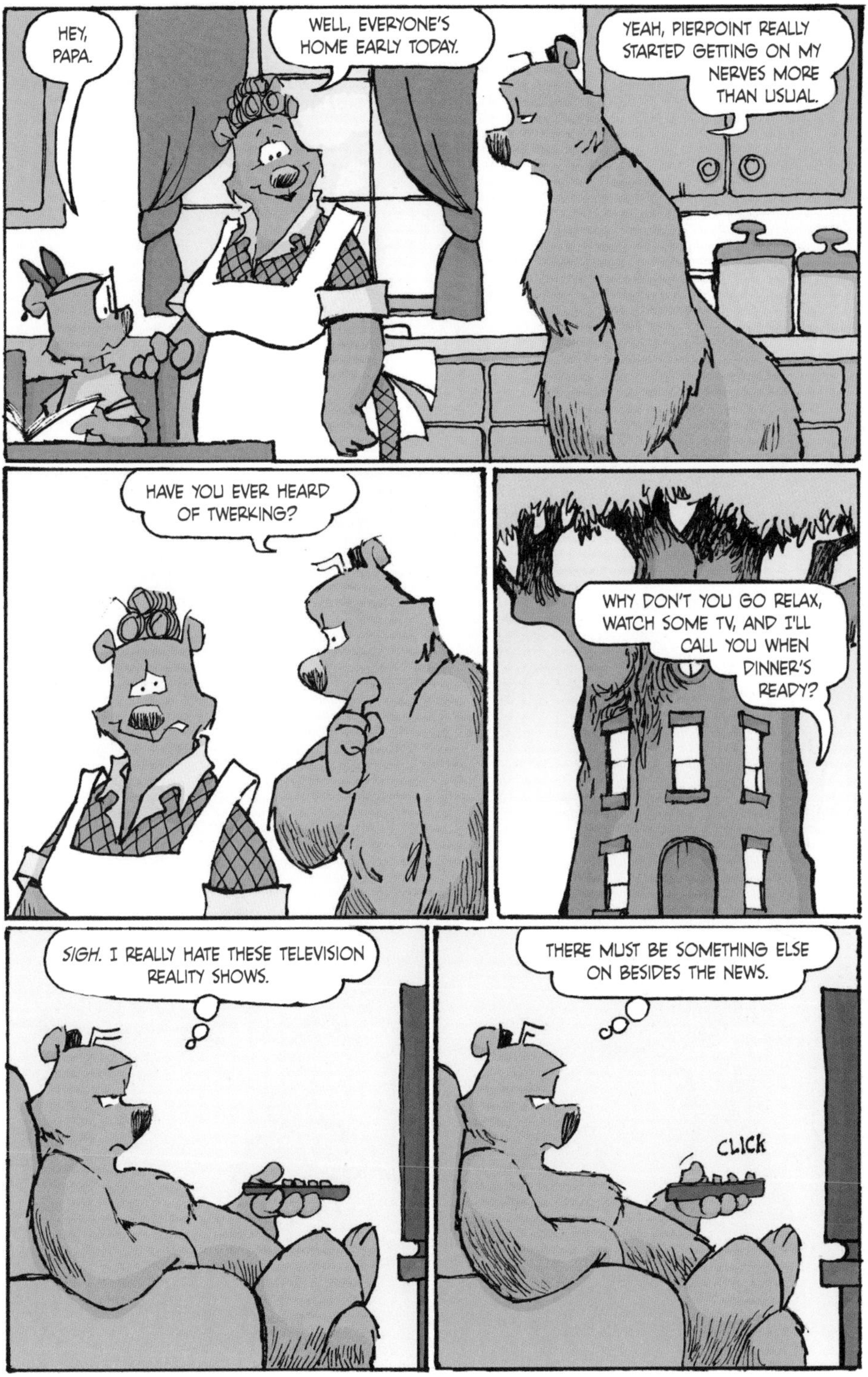
HEY, PAPA.
WELL, EVERYONE'S HOME EARLY TODAY.
YEAH, PIERPOINT REALLY STARTED GETTING ON MY NERVES MORE THAN USUAL.
HAVE YOU EVER HEARD OF TWERKING?
WHY DON'T YOU GO RELAX, WATCH SOME TV, AND I'LL CALL YOU WHEN DINNER'S READY?
SIGH. I REALLY HATE THESE TELEVISION REALITY SHOWS.
THERE MUST BE SOMETHING ELSE ON BESIDES THE NEWS.
CLICK

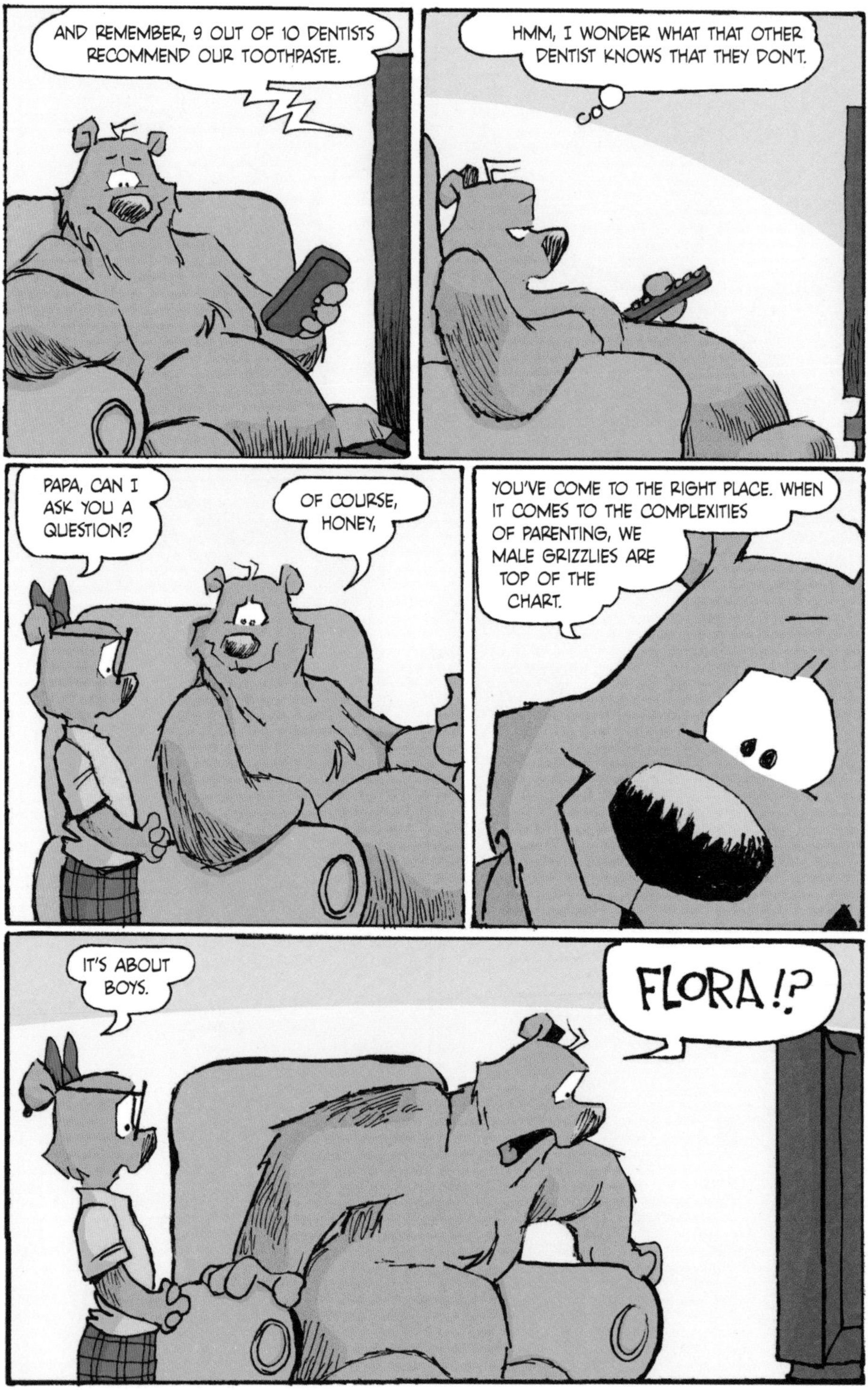
AND REMEMBER, 9 OUT OF 10 DENTISTS RECOMMEND OUR TOOTHPASTE.
HMM, I WONDER WHAT THAT OTHER DENTIST KNOWS THAT THEY DON'T.
PAPA, CAN I ASK YOU A QUESTION?
OF COURSE, HONEY,
YOU'VE COME TO THE RIGHT PLACE. WHEN IT COMES TO THE COMPLEXITIES OF PARENTING, WE MALE GRIZZLIES ARE TOP OF THE CHART.
IT'S ABOUT BOYS.
FLORA!?

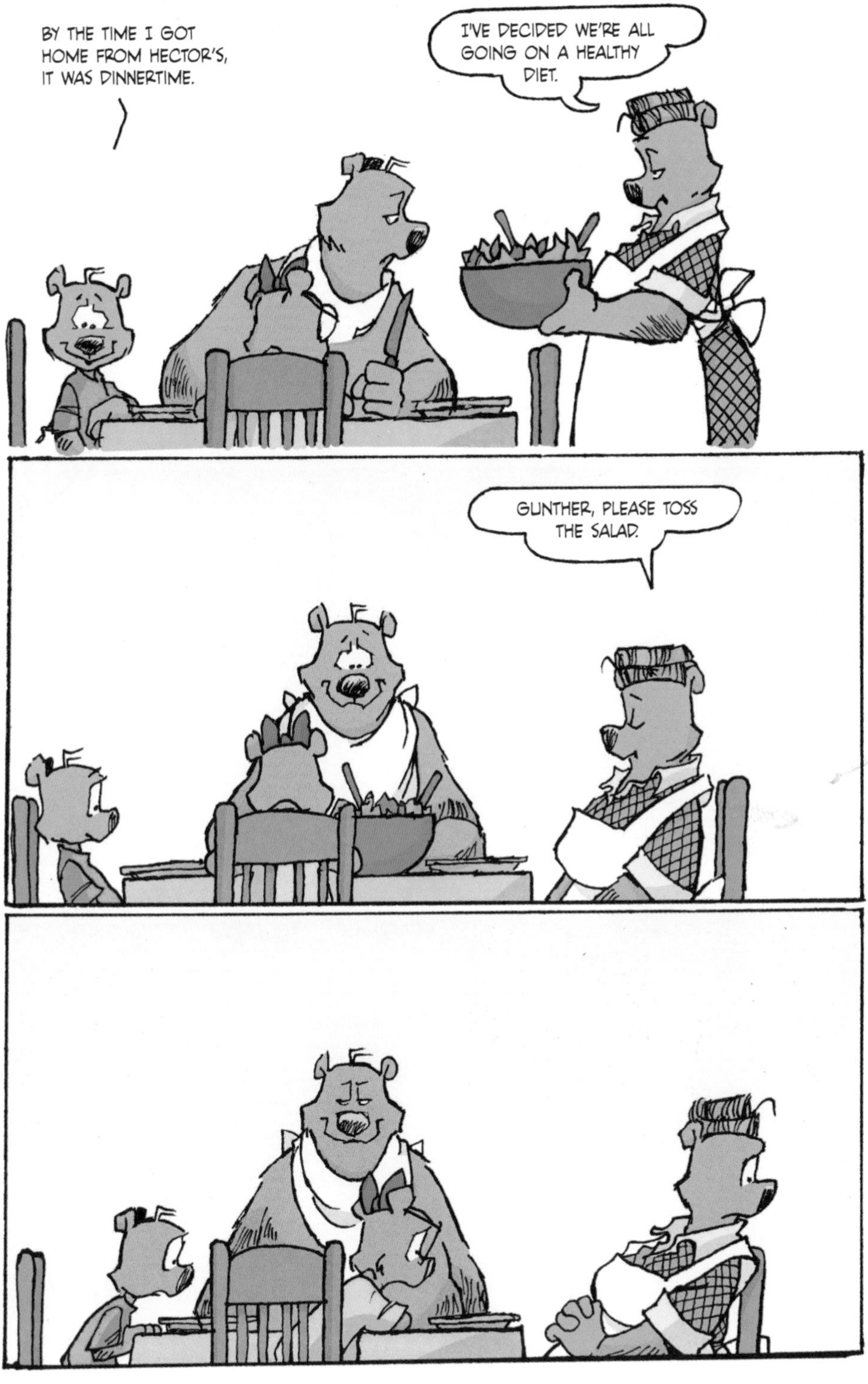
BY THE TIME I GOT HOME FROM HECTOR'S, IT WAS DINNERTIME.
I'VE DECIDED WE'RE ALL GOING ON A HEALTHY DIET.
GUNTHER, PLEASE TOSS THE SALAD.

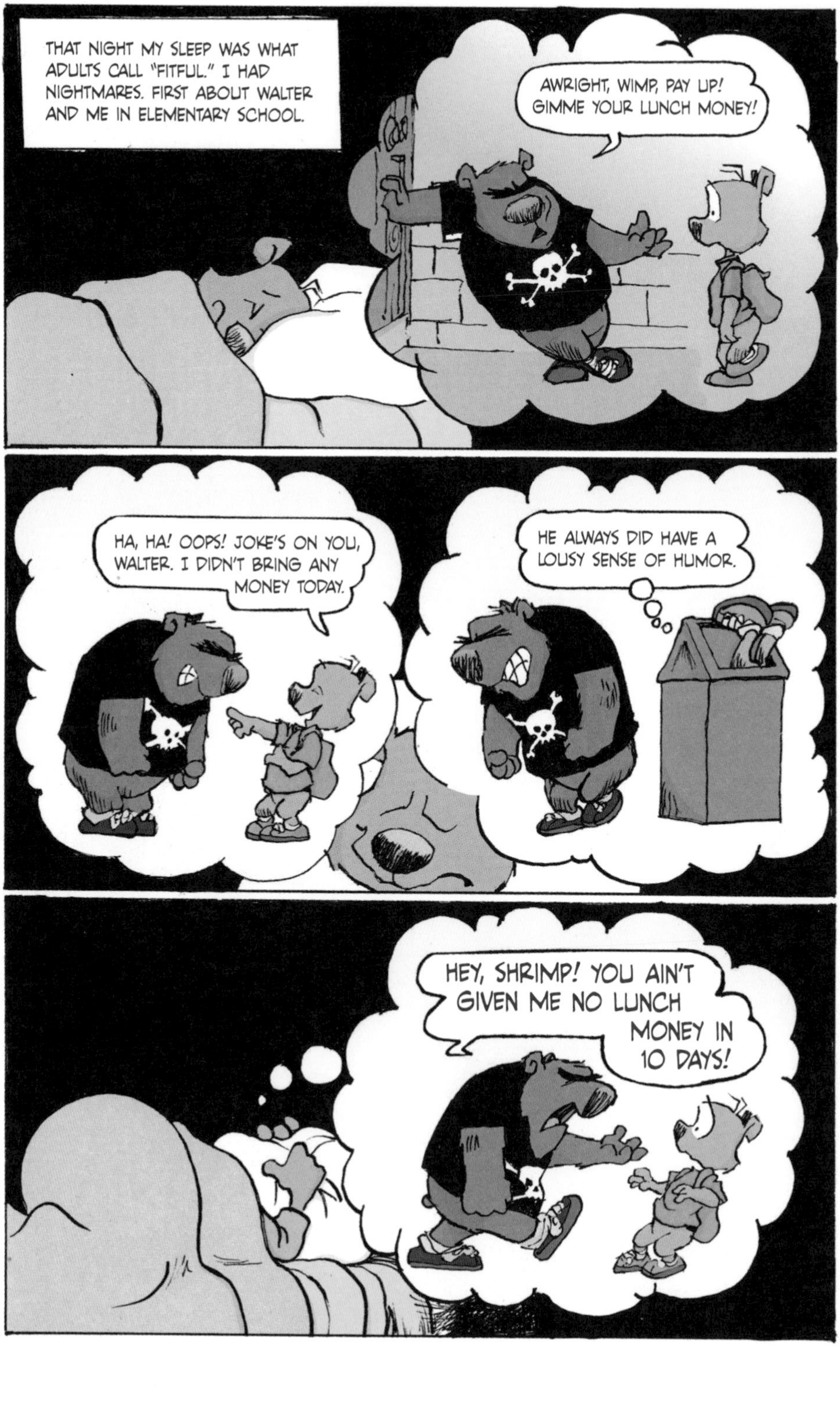
THAT NIGHT MY SLEEP WAS WHAT ADULTS CALL "FITFUL." I HAD NIGHTMARES. FIRST ABOUT WALTER AND ME IN ELEMENTARY SCHOOL.
AWRIGHT, WIMP, PAY UP! GIMME YOUR LUNCH MONEY!
HA, HA! OOPS! JOKE'S ON YOU, WALTER. I DIDN'T BRING ANY MONEY TODAY.
HE ALWAYS DID HAVE A LOUSY SENSE OF HUMOR.
HEY, SHRIMP! YOU AIN'T GIVEN ME NO LUNCH MONEY IN 10 DAYS!

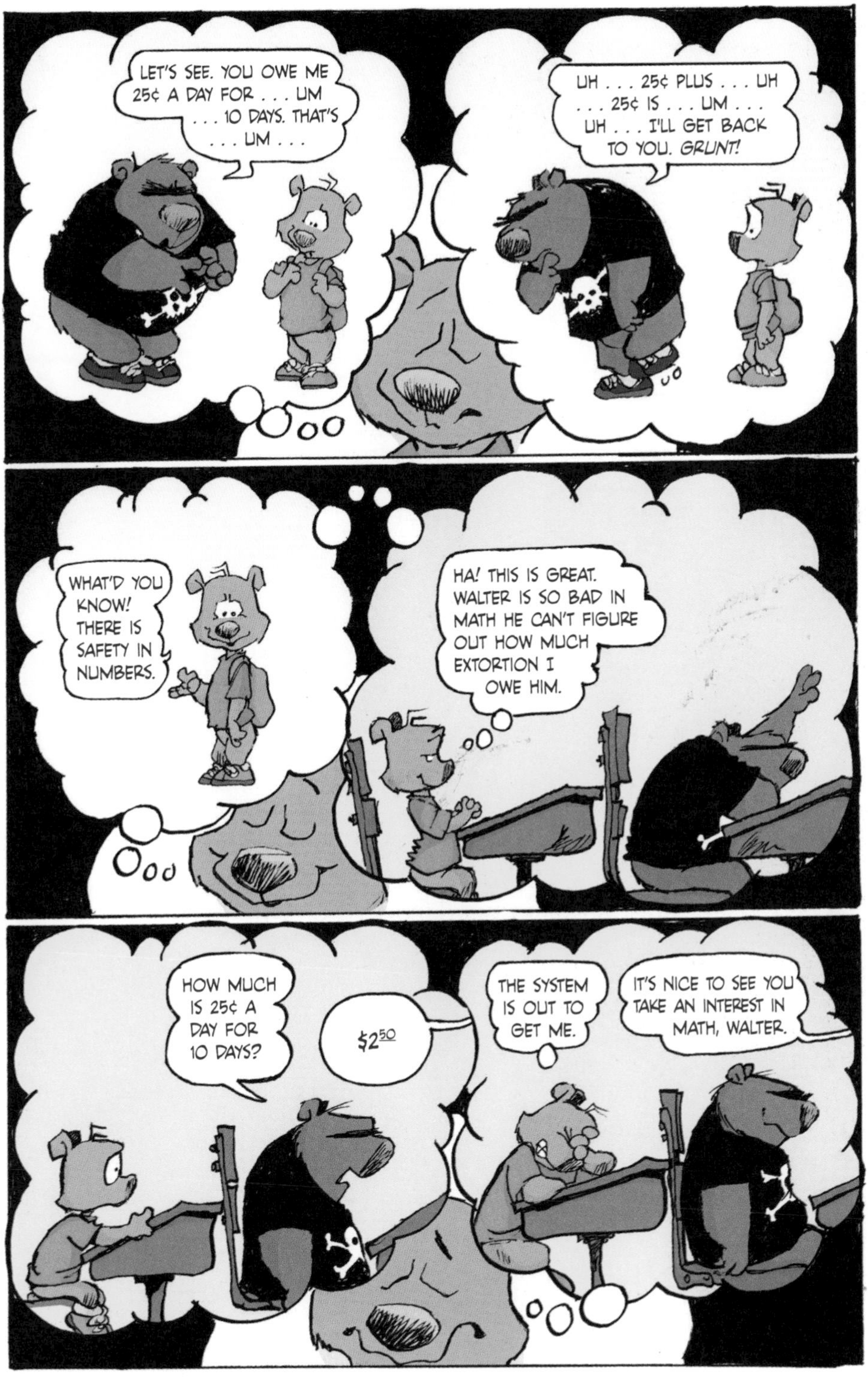

LET'S SEE. YOU OWE ME 25¢ A DAY FOR . . . UM . . . 10 DAYS. THAT'S . . . UM . . .
UH . . . 25¢ PLUS . . . UH . . . 25¢ IS . . . UM . . . UH . . . I'LL GET BACK TO YOU. *GRUNT!*
WHAT'D YOU KNOW! THERE IS SAFETY IN NUMBERS.
HA! THIS IS GREAT. WALTER IS SO BAD IN MATH HE CAN'T FIGURE OUT HOW MUCH EXTORTION I OWE HIM.
HOW MUCH IS 25¢ A DAY FOR 10 DAYS?
$2.50
THE SYSTEM IS OUT TO GET ME.
IT'S NICE TO SEE YOU TAKE AN INTEREST IN MATH, WALTER.

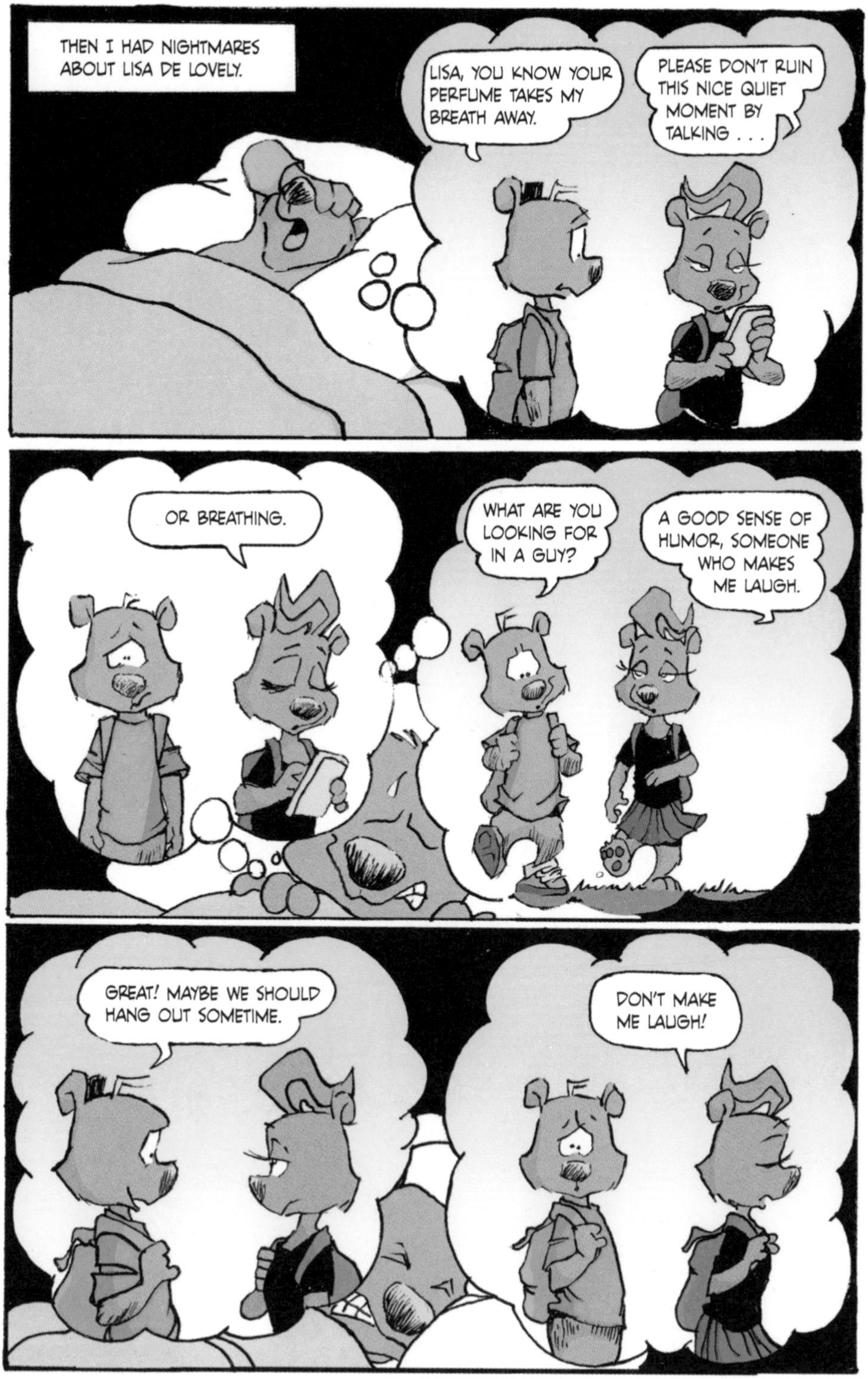
THEN I HAD NIGHTMARES ABOUT LISA DE LOVELY.
LISA, YOU KNOW YOUR PERFUME TAKES MY BREATH AWAY.
PLEASE DON'T RUIN THIS NICE QUIET MOMENT BY TALKING . . .
OR BREATHING.
WHAT ARE YOU LOOKING FOR IN A GUY?
A GOOD SENSE OF HUMOR, SOMEONE WHO MAKES ME LAUGH.
GREAT! MAYBE WE SHOULD HANG OUT SOMETIME.
DON'T MAKE ME LAUGH!

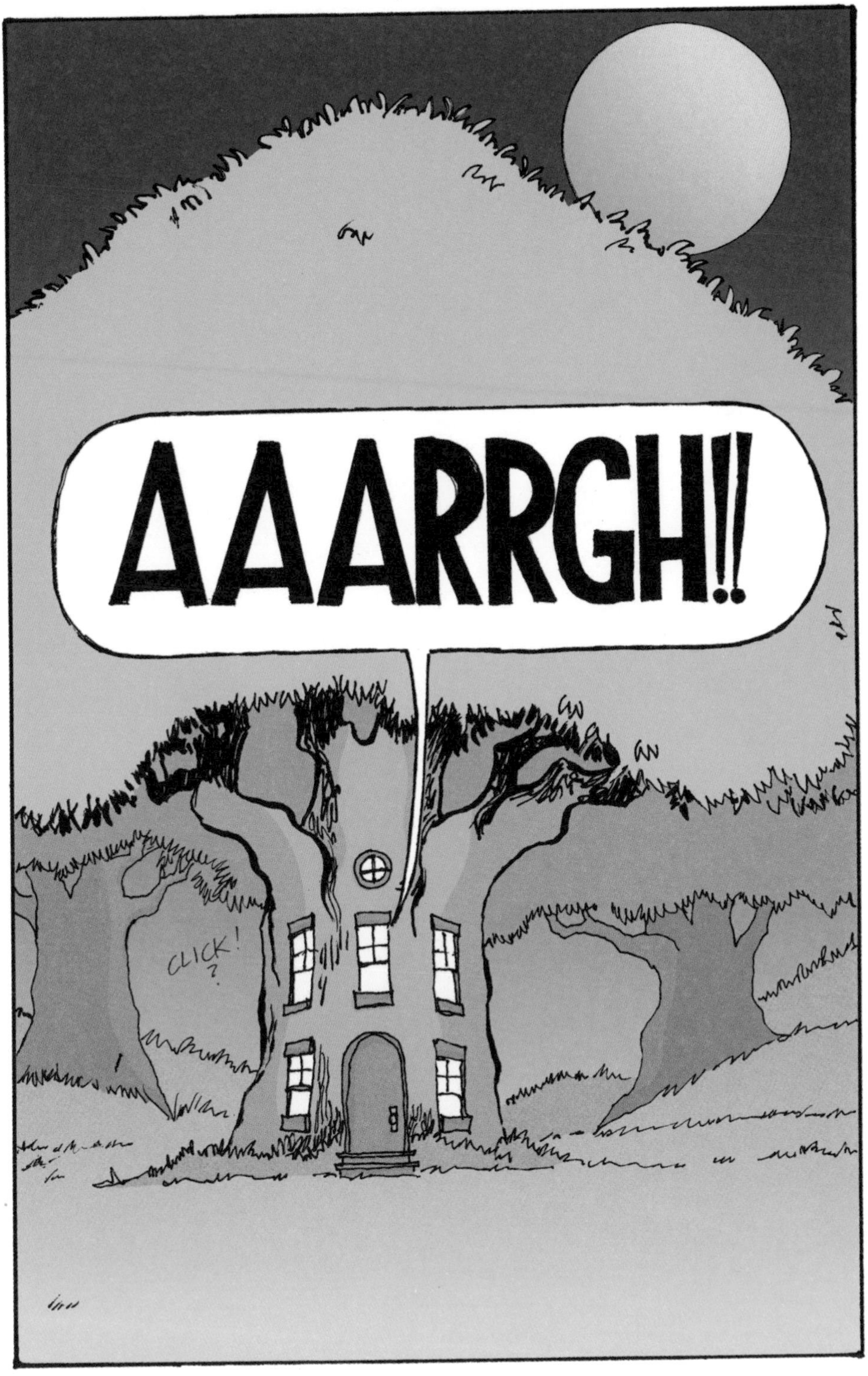
AAARRGH!!
CLICK!

THURSDAY

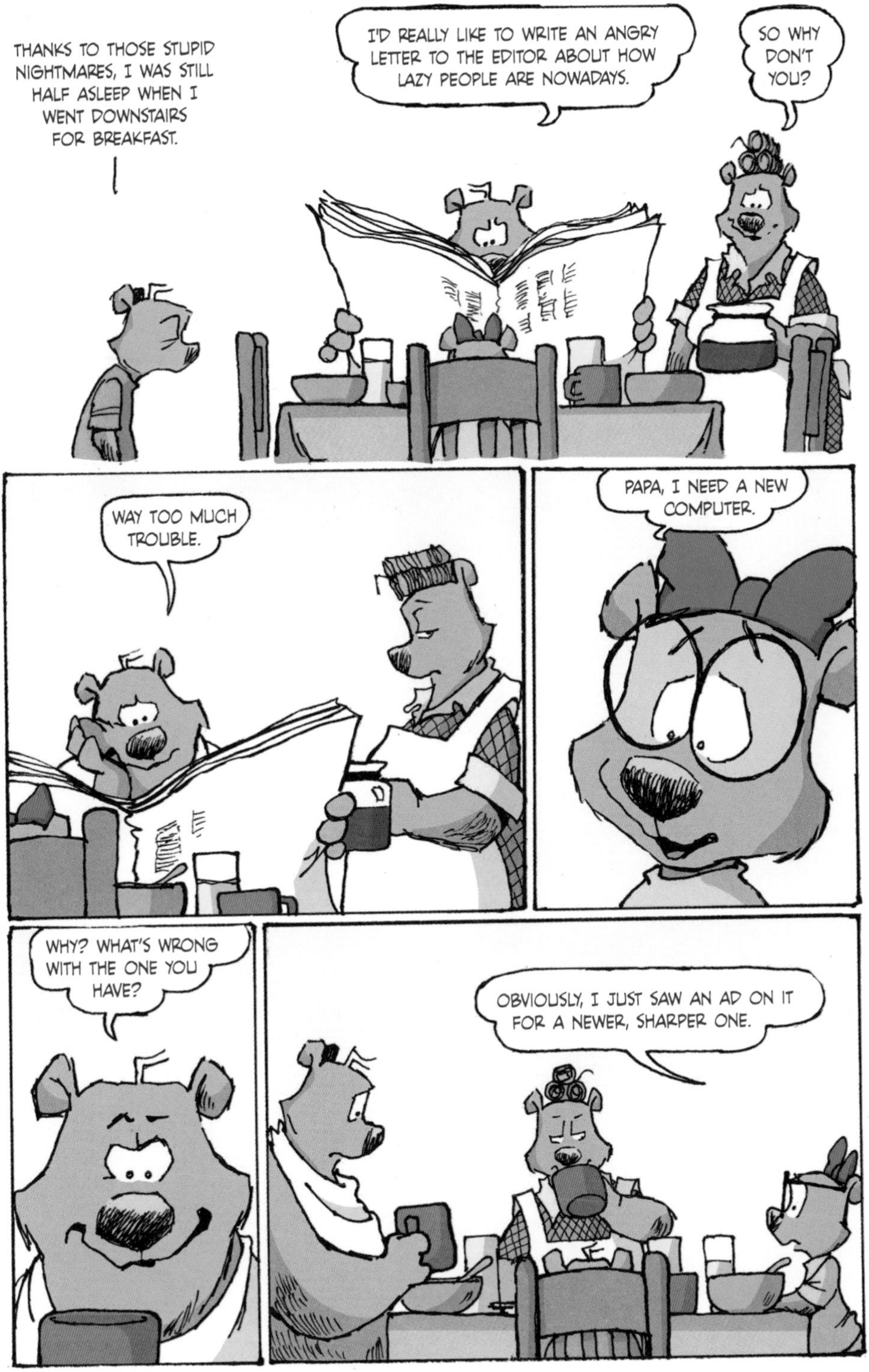

THANKS TO THOSE STUPID NIGHTMARES, I WAS STILL HALF ASLEEP WHEN I WENT DOWNSTAIRS FOR BREAKFAST.
I'D REALLY LIKE TO WRITE AN ANGRY LETTER TO THE EDITOR ABOUT HOW LAZY PEOPLE ARE NOWADAYS.
SO WHY DON'T YOU?
WAY TOO MUCH TROUBLE.
PAPA, I NEED A NEW COMPUTER.
WHY? WHAT'S WRONG WITH THE ONE YOU HAVE?
OBVIOUSLY, I JUST SAW AN AD ON IT FOR A NEWER, SHARPER ONE.

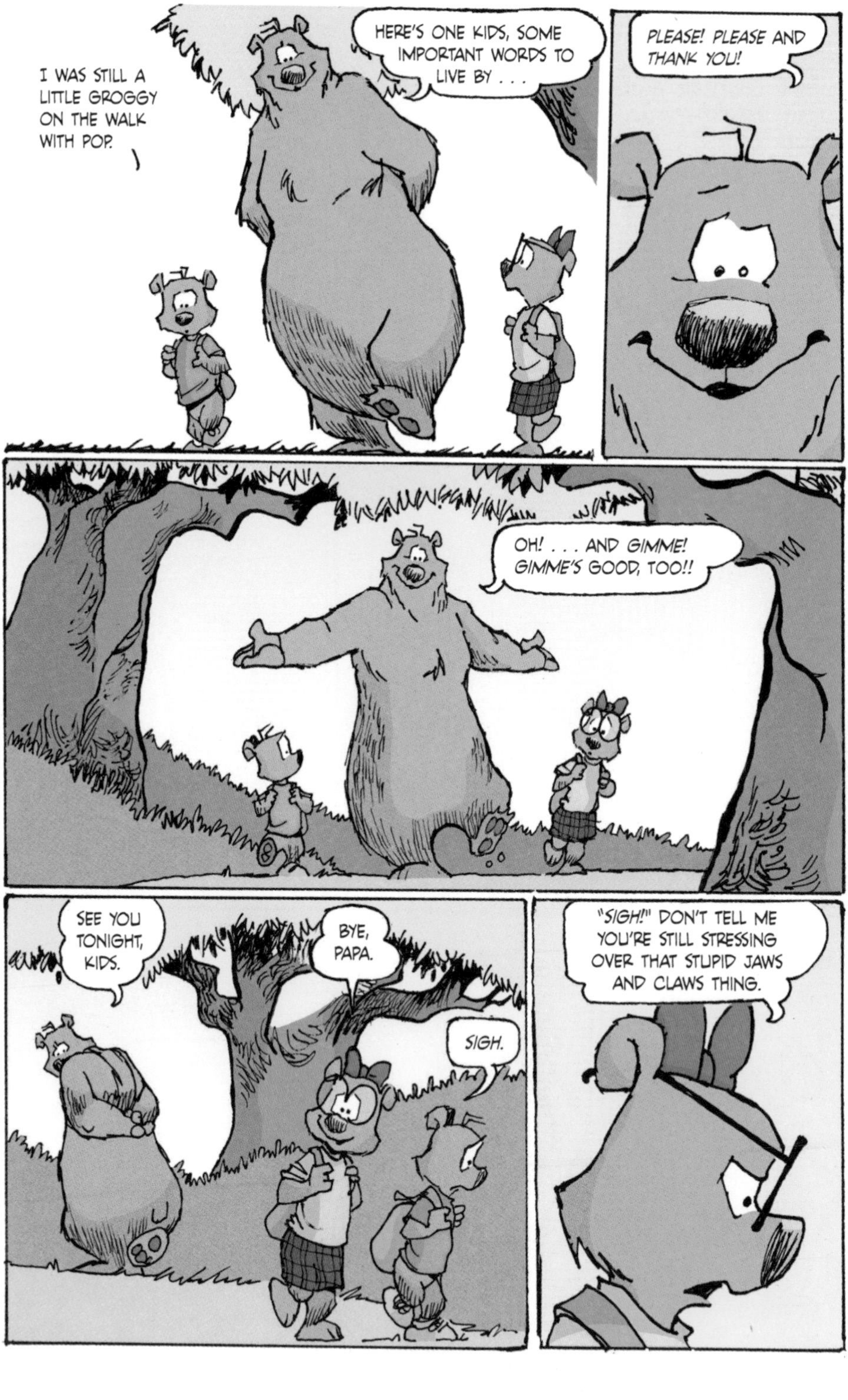
I WAS STILL A LITTLE GROGGY ON THE WALK WITH POP.
HERE'S ONE KIDS, SOME IMPORTANT WORDS TO LIVE BY . . .
PLEASE! PLEASE AND THANK YOU!
OH! . . . AND GIMME! GIMME'S GOOD, TOO!!
SEE YOU TONIGHT, KIDS.
BYE, PAPA.
SIGH.
"SIGH!" DON'T TELL ME YOU'RE STILL STRESSING OVER THAT STUPID JAWS AND CLAWS THING.

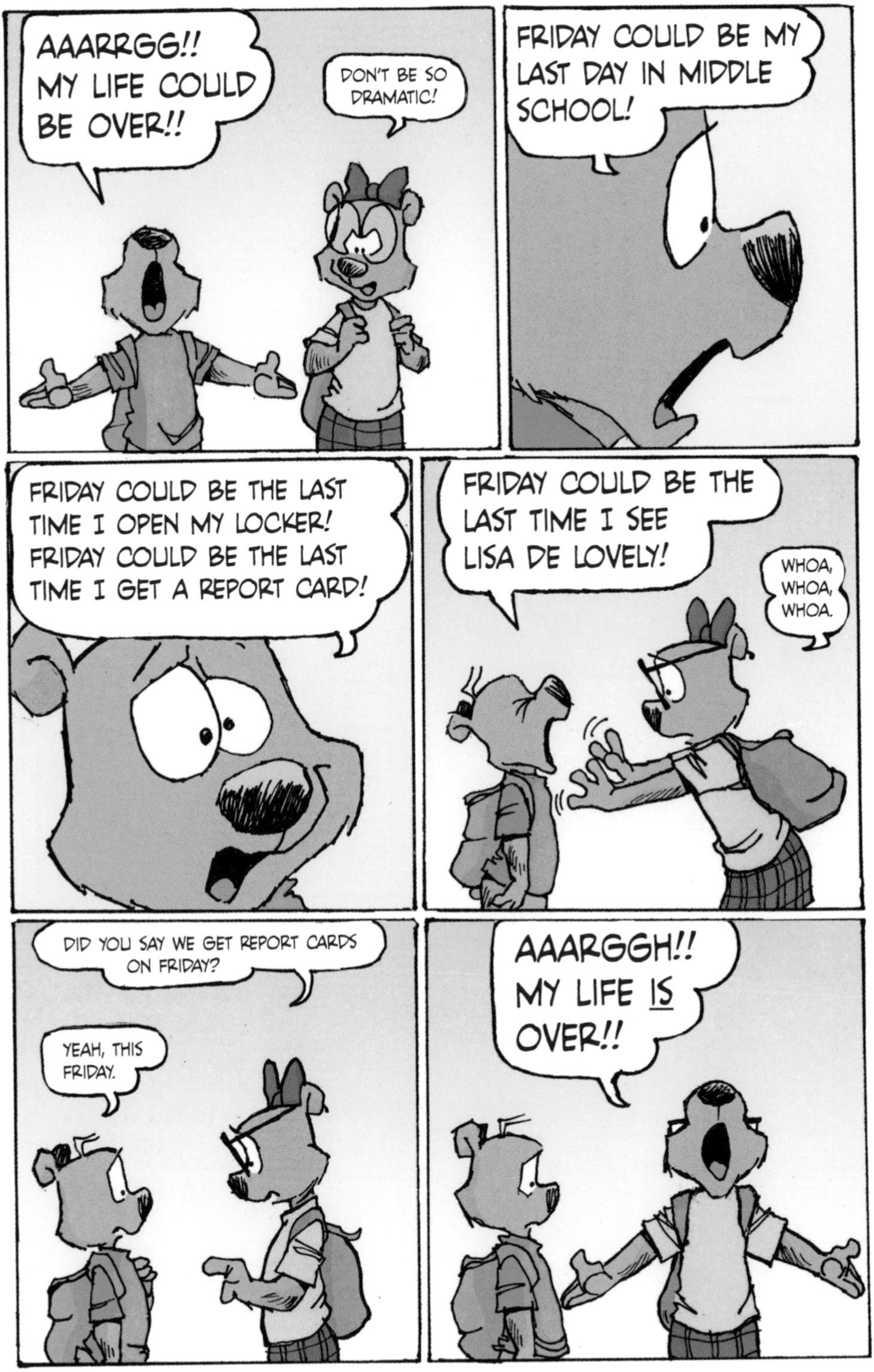
AAARRGG!! MY LIFE COULD BE OVER!!
DON'T BE SO DRAMATIC!
FRIDAY COULD BE MY LAST DAY IN MIDDLE SCHOOL!
FRIDAY COULD BE THE LAST TIME I OPEN MY LOCKER! FRIDAY COULD BE THE LAST TIME I GET A REPORT CARD!
FRIDAY COULD BE THE LAST TIME I SEE LISA DE LOVELY!
WHOA, WHOA, WHOA.
DID YOU SAY WE GET REPORT CARDS ON FRIDAY?
YEAH, THIS FRIDAY.
AAARGGH!! MY LIFE IS OVER!!

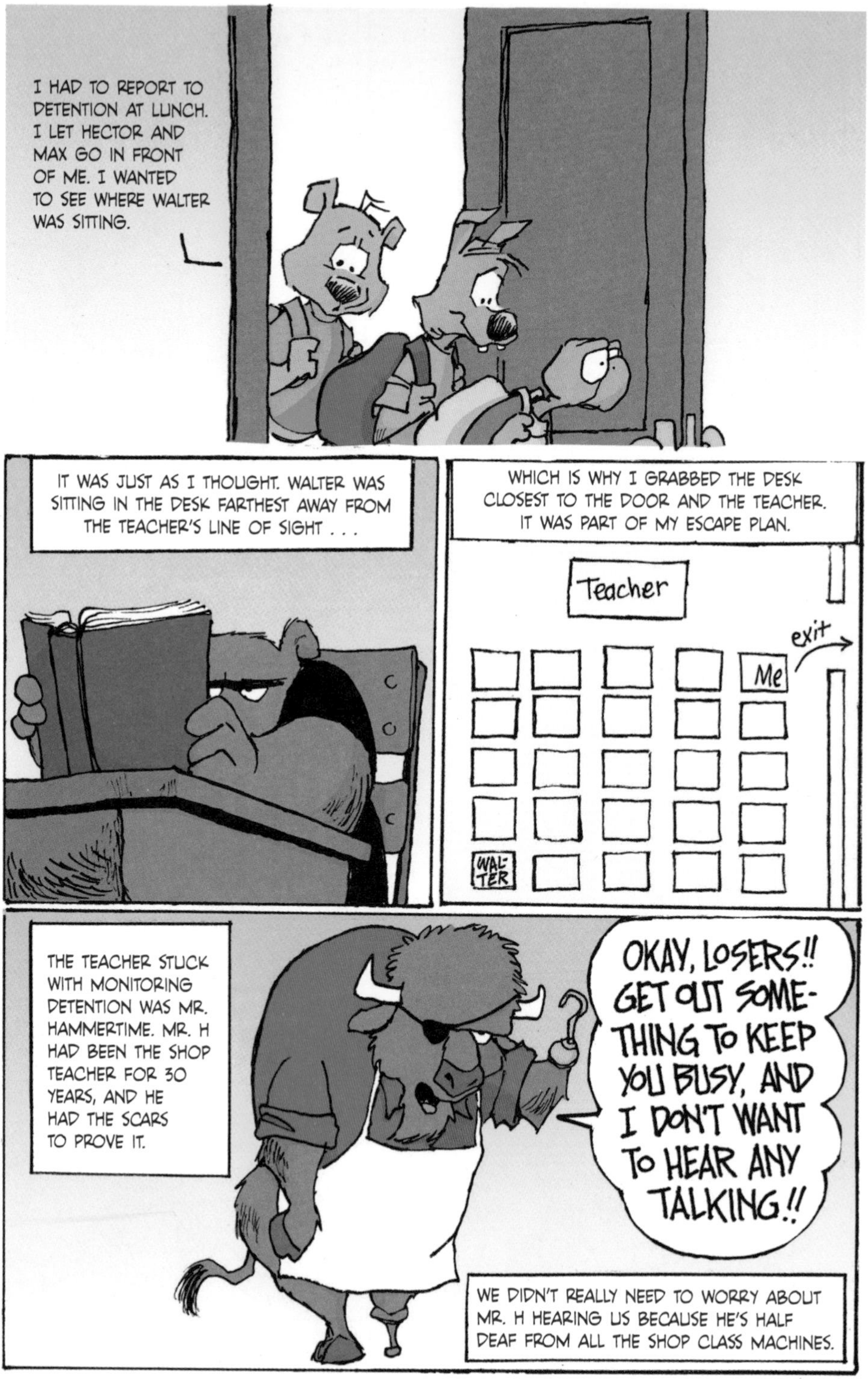
I HAD TO REPORT TO DETENTION AT LUNCH. I LET HECTOR AND MAX GO IN FRONT OF ME. I WANTED TO SEE WHERE WALTER WAS SITTING.
IT WAS JUST AS I THOUGHT. WALTER WAS SITTING IN THE DESK FARTHEST AWAY FROM THE TEACHER'S LINE OF SIGHT . . .
WHICH IS WHY I GRABBED THE DESK CLOSEST TO THE DOOR AND THE TEACHER. IT WAS PART OF MY ESCAPE PLAN.
Teacher
exit
Me
WALTER
THE TEACHER STUCK WITH MONITORING DETENTION WAS MR. HAMMERTIME. MR. H HAD BEEN THE SHOP TEACHER FOR 30 YEARS, AND HE HAD THE SCARS TO PROVE IT.
OKAY, LOSERS!! GET OUT SOMETHING TO KEEP YOU BUSY, AND I DON'T WANT TO HEAR ANY TALKING!!
WE DIDN'T REALLY NEED TO WORRY ABOUT MR. H HEARING US BECAUSE HE'S HALF DEAF FROM ALL THE SHOP CLASS MACHINES.

SO AS LONG AS WE KEPT A BOOK IN FRONT OF OUR FACES, WE COULD TALK IN A LOUD WHISPER.

IT SAYS HERE BABY KANGAROOS ARE ALL CALLED "JOEY."

NOT A BAD IDEA.

THAT ELIMINATES THE NEED FOR NAME TAGS AT REUNIONS.

NATURE'S AMAZING.

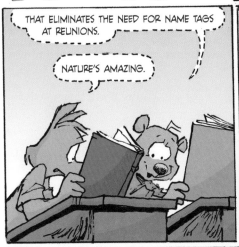

WHAT'S THAT YOU'RE READING?

THE LAST OF THE MOHICANS.

AND IF IT'S ANY GOOD, THEN I'LL READ ABOUT THE BEGINNING OF THE MOHICANS.

PSST! MAX, WHAT'RE YOU DOING?

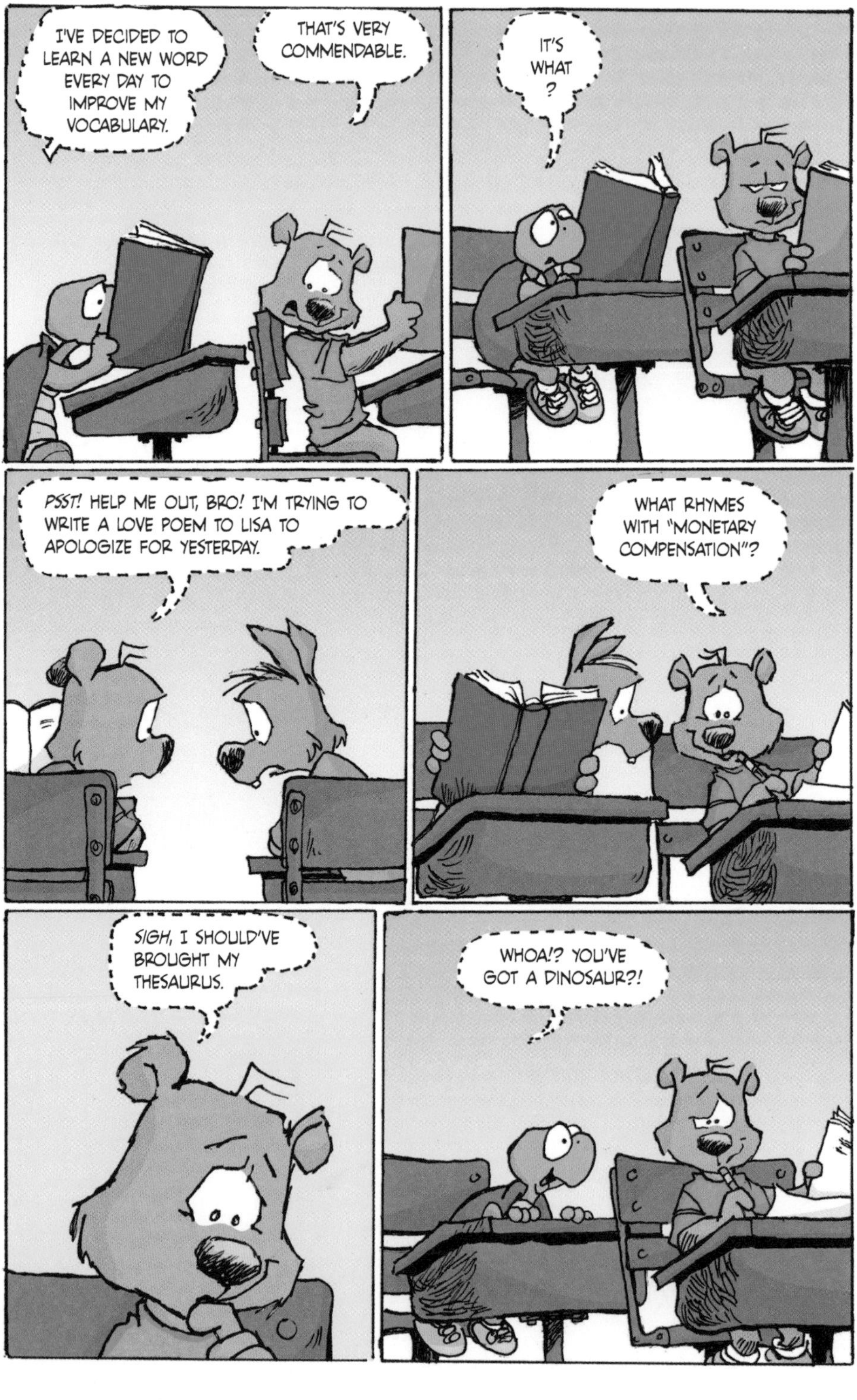
I'VE DECIDED TO LEARN A NEW WORD EVERY DAY TO IMPROVE MY VOCABULARY.
THAT'S VERY COMMENDABLE.
IT'S WHAT ?
PSST! HELP ME OUT, BRO! I'M TRYING TO WRITE A LOVE POEM TO LISA TO APOLOGIZE FOR YESTERDAY.
WHAT RHYMES WITH "MONETARY COMPENSATION"?
SIGH, I SHOULD'VE BROUGHT MY THESAURUS.
WHOA!? YOU'VE GOT A DINOSAUR?!

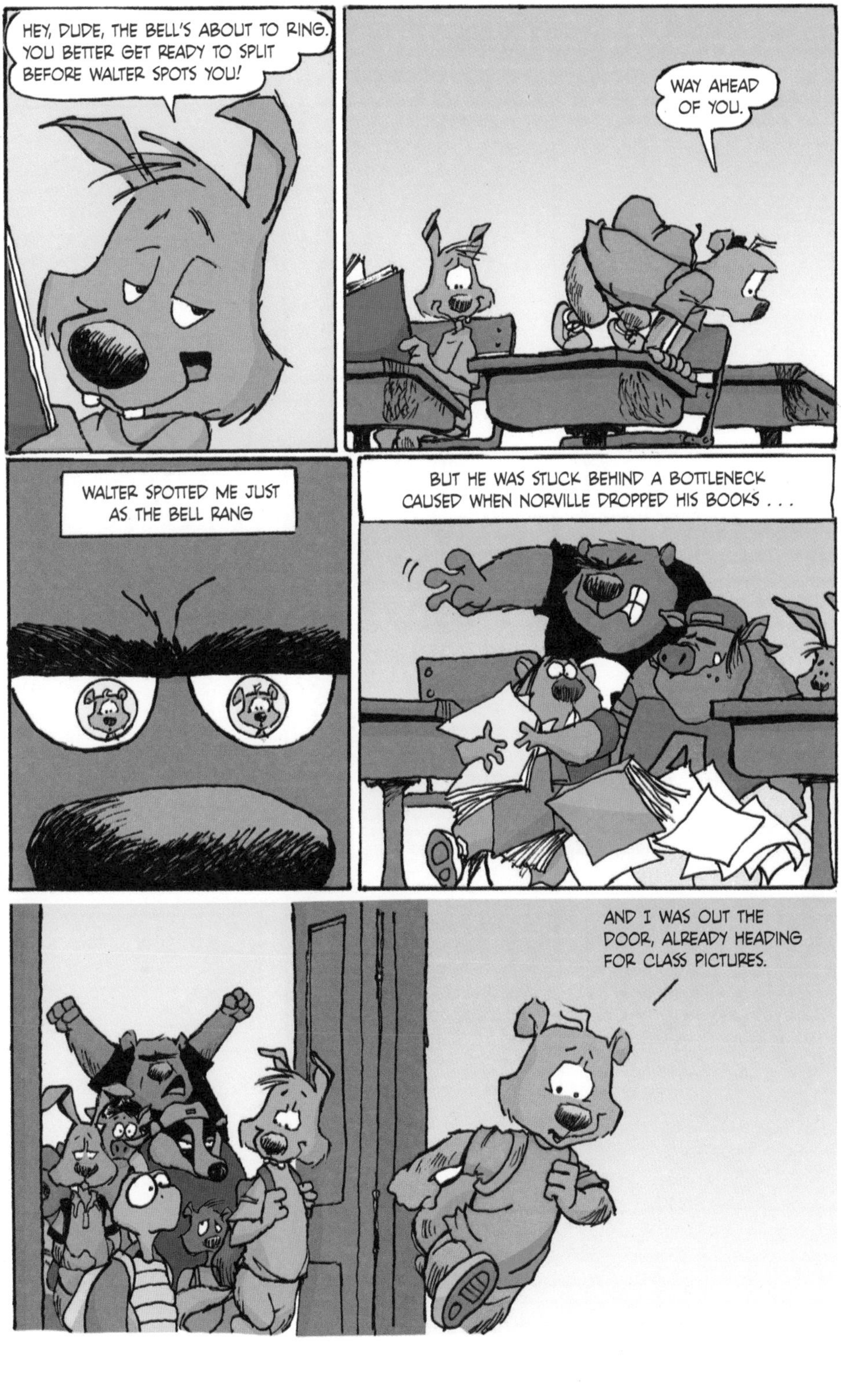
HEY, DUDE, THE BELL'S ABOUT TO RING. YOU BETTER GET READY TO SPLIT BEFORE WALTER SPOTS YOU!
WAY AHEAD OF YOU.
WALTER SPOTTED ME JUST AS THE BELL RANG
BUT HE WAS STUCK BEHIND A BOTTLENECK CAUSED WHEN NORVILLE DROPPED HIS BOOKS . . .
AND I WAS OUT THE DOOR, ALREADY HEADING FOR CLASS PICTURES.

I'VE BEEN TRYING TO TAKE A GOOD CLASS PICTURE SINCE FIRST GRADE, BUT SOMETHING ALWAYS SEEMS TO GO WRONG.

1ˢᵀ GRADE

2ᴺᴰ GRADE

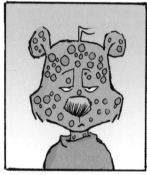

3ᴿᴰ GRADE

4ᵀᴴ GRADE

5ᵀᴴ GRADE

BUT THIS YEAR I WAS DETERMINED TO CHANGE THAT. I'D BEEN TAKING SELFIES FOR THE PAST FOUR MONTHS WORKING ON THE RIGHT POSE. I'D NARROWED IT DOWN TO THREE LOOKS:

GAME SHOW HOST

INTERNATIONAL MAN OF MYSTERY

BROODING ARTIST

UNFORTUNATELY, MY LACK OF SLEEP KICKED IN AND . . .

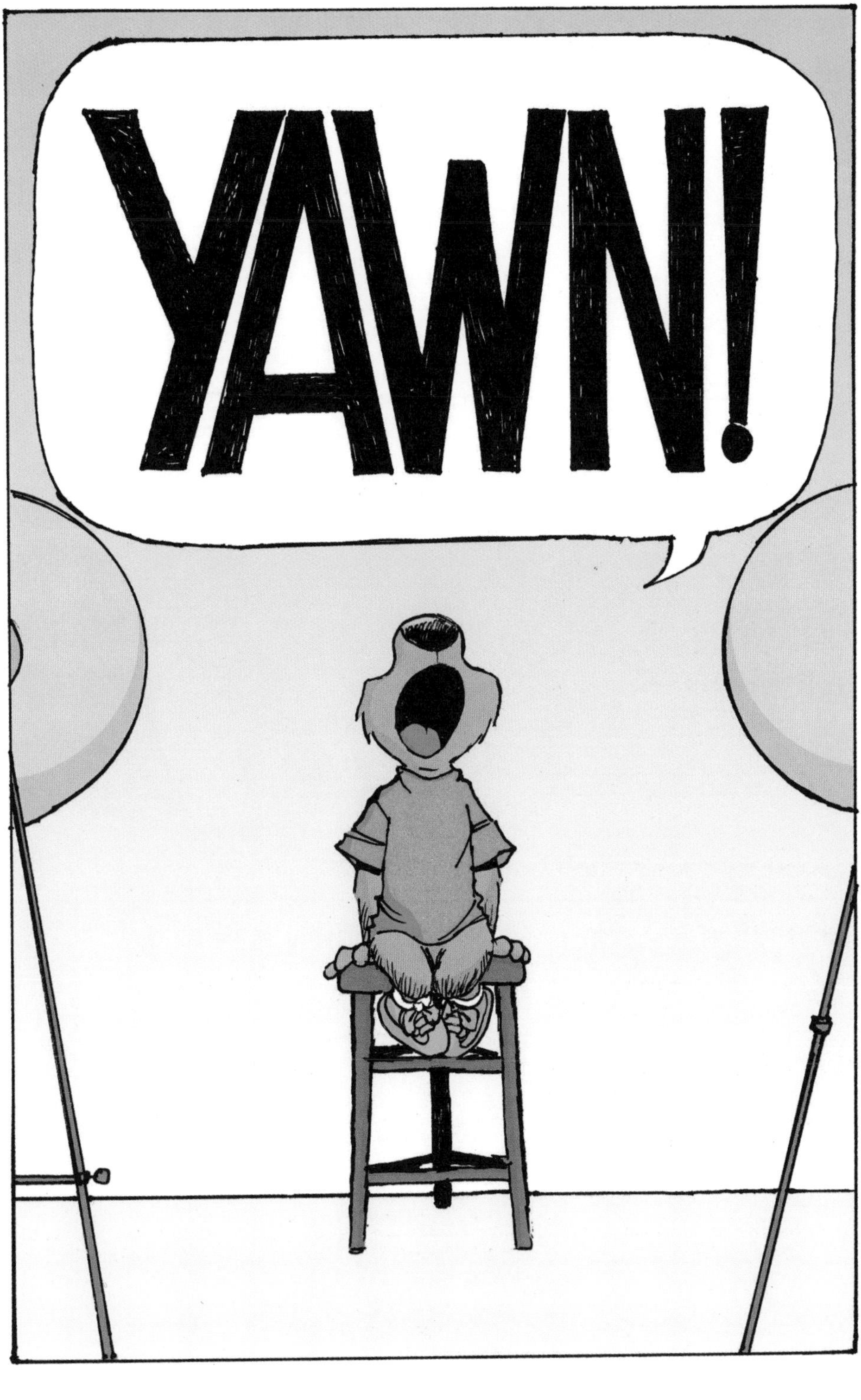
YAWN!

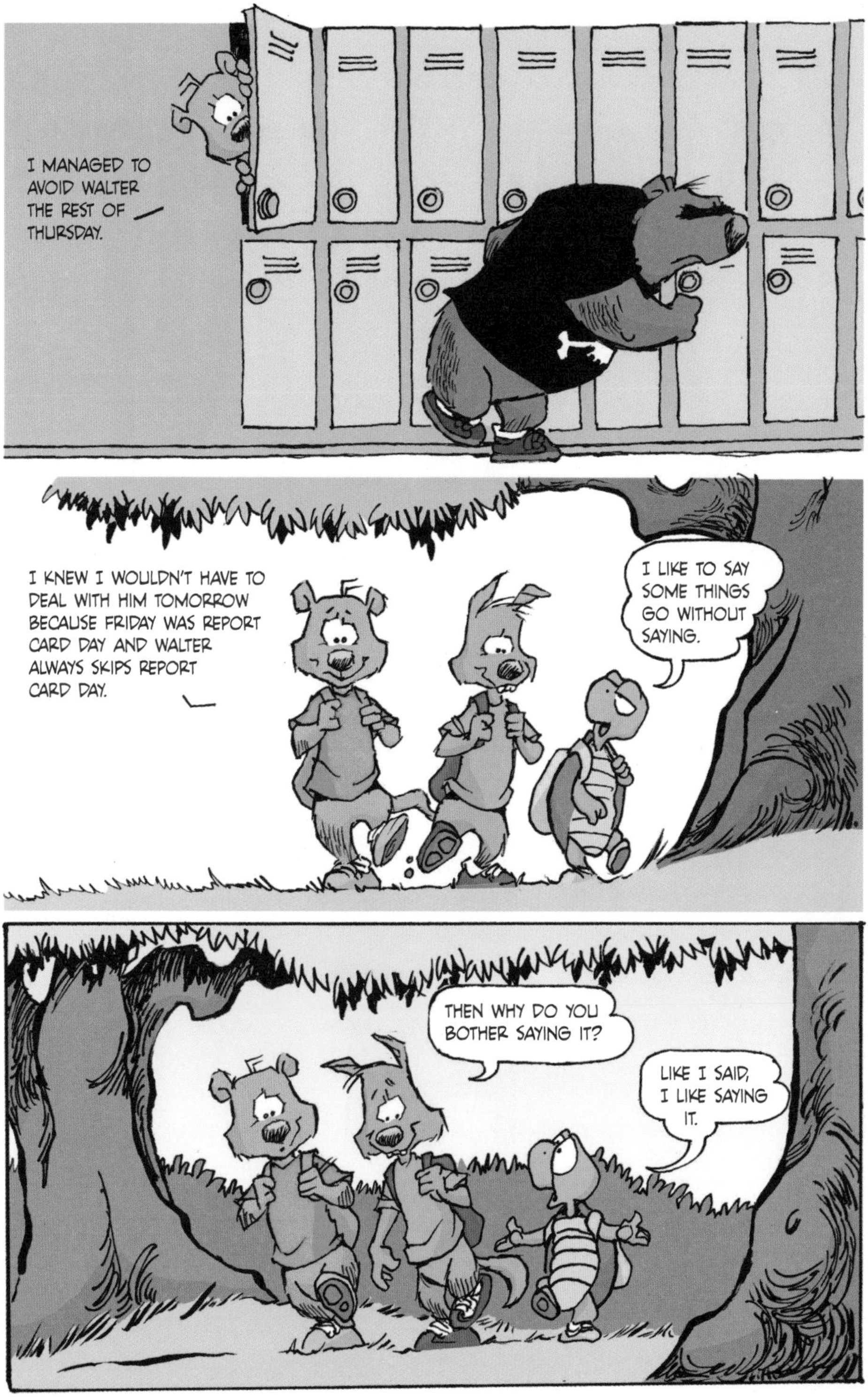
I MANAGED TO AVOID WALTER THE REST OF THURSDAY.
I KNEW I WOULDN'T HAVE TO DEAL WITH HIM TOMORROW BECAUSE FRIDAY WAS REPORT CARD DAY AND WALTER ALWAYS SKIPS REPORT CARD DAY.
I LIKE TO SAY SOME THINGS GO WITHOUT SAYING.
THEN WHY DO YOU BOTHER SAYING IT?
LIKE I SAID, I LIKE SAYING IT.

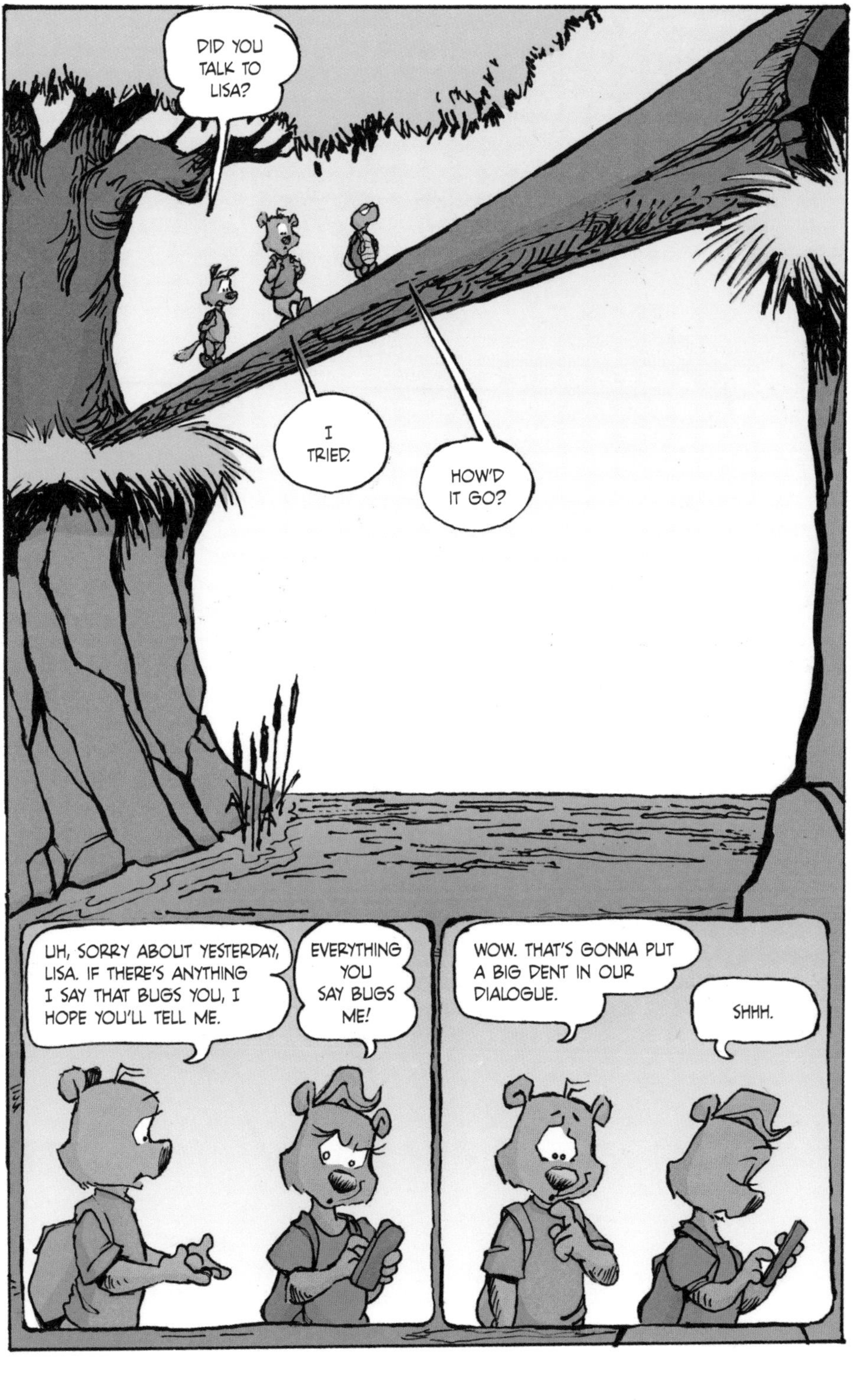
DID YOU TALK TO LISA?
I TRIED.
HOW'D IT GO?
UH, SORRY ABOUT YESTERDAY, LISA. IF THERE'S ANYTHING I SAY THAT BUGS YOU, I HOPE YOU'LL TELL ME.
EVERYTHING YOU SAY BUGS ME!
WOW. THAT'S GONNA PUT A BIG DENT IN OUR DIALOGUE.
SHHH.

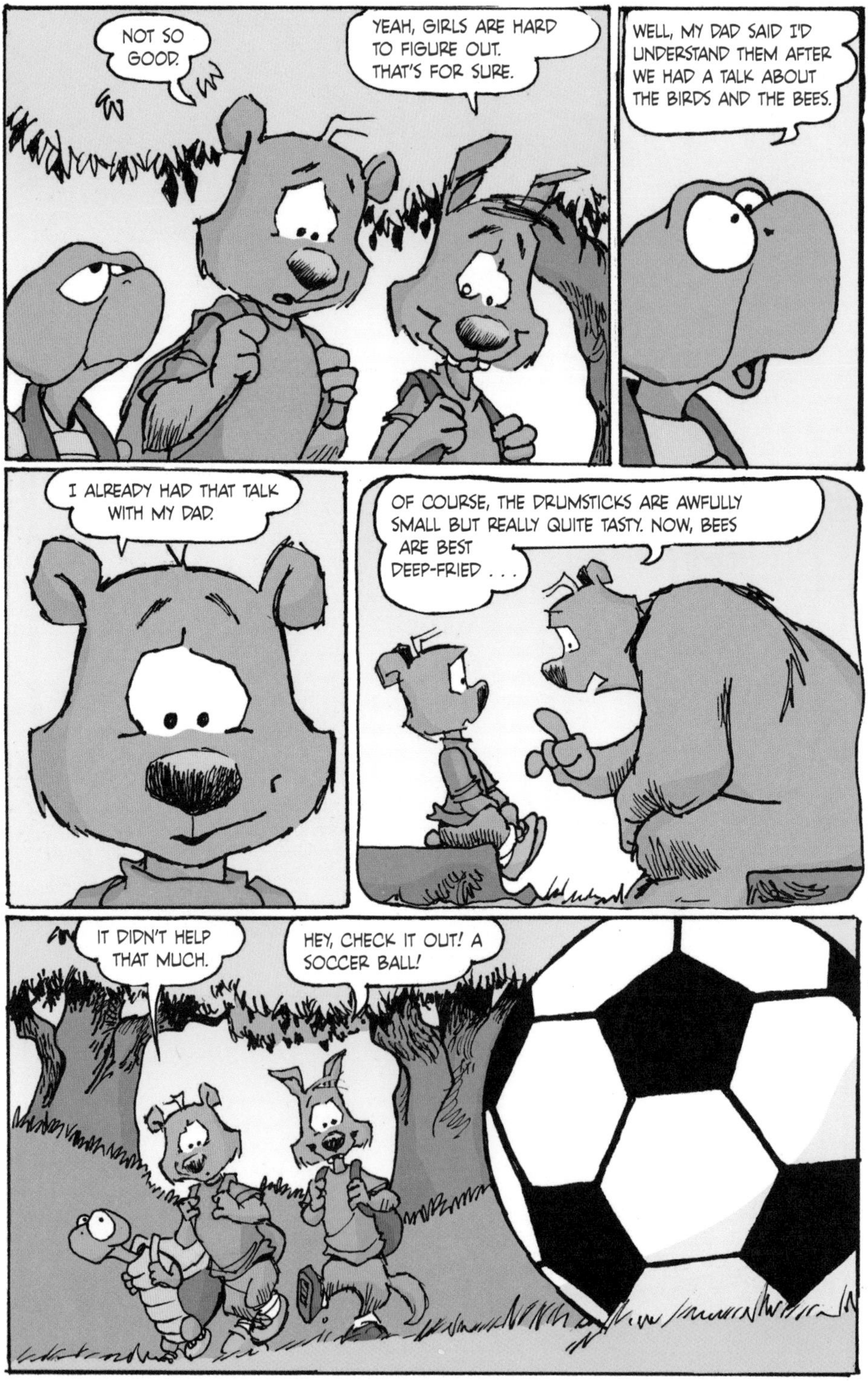
NOT SO GOOD.
YEAH, GIRLS ARE HARD TO FIGURE OUT. THAT'S FOR SURE.
WELL, MY DAD SAID I'D UNDERSTAND THEM AFTER WE HAD A TALK ABOUT THE BIRDS AND THE BEES.
I ALREADY HAD THAT TALK WITH MY DAD.
OF COURSE, THE DRUMSTICKS ARE AWFULLY SMALL BUT REALLY QUITE TASTY. NOW, BEES ARE BEST DEEP-FRIED . . .
IT DIDN'T HELP THAT MUCH.
HEY, CHECK IT OUT! A SOCCER BALL!

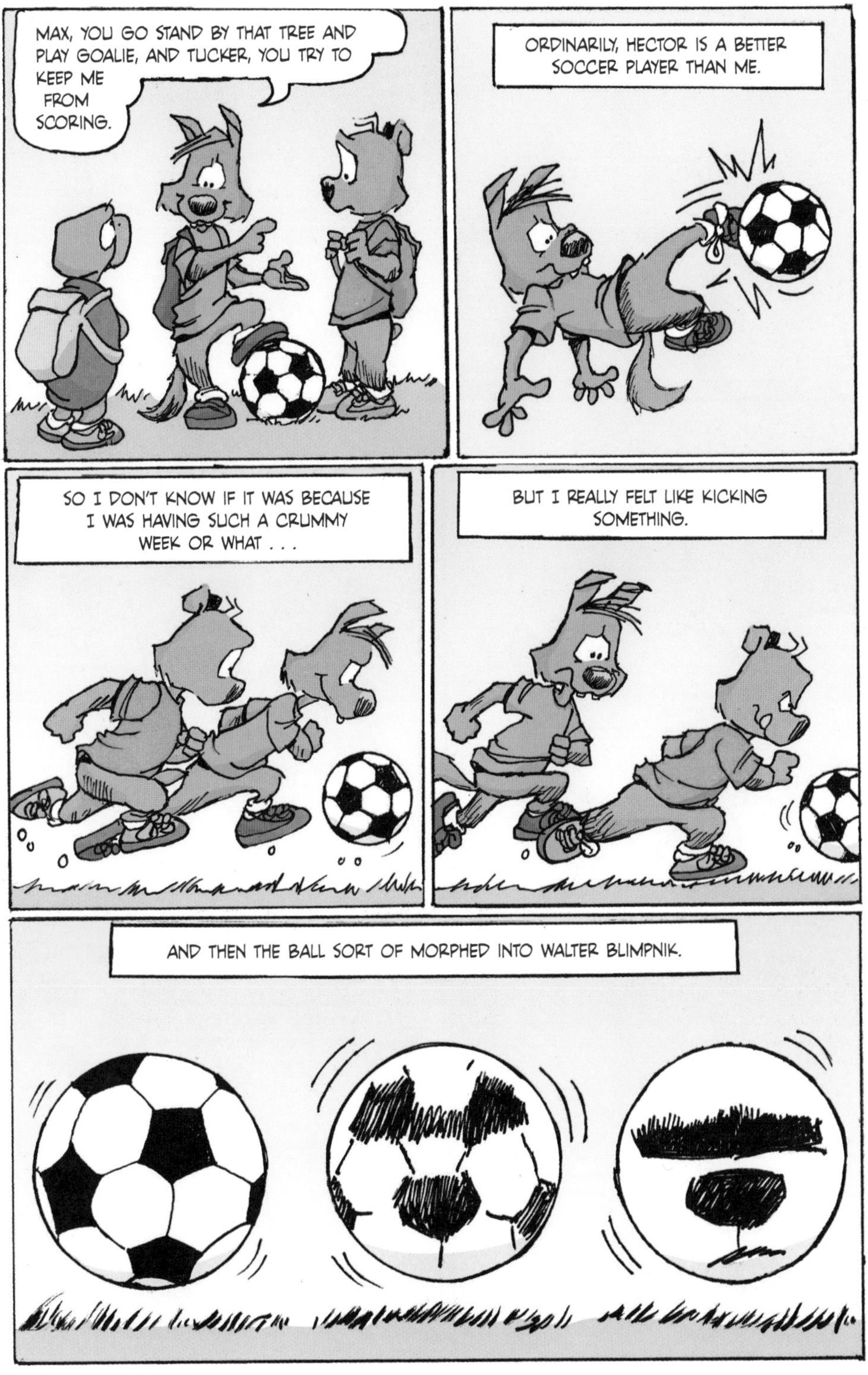
MAX, YOU GO STAND BY THAT TREE AND PLAY GOALIE, AND TUCKER, YOU TRY TO KEEP ME FROM SCORING.
ORDINARILY, HECTOR IS A BETTER SOCCER PLAYER THAN ME.
SO I DON'T KNOW IF IT WAS BECAUSE I WAS HAVING SUCH A CRUMMY WEEK OR WHAT . . .
BUT I REALLY FELT LIKE KICKING SOMETHING.
AND THEN THE BALL SORT OF MORPHED INTO WALTER BLIMPNIK.

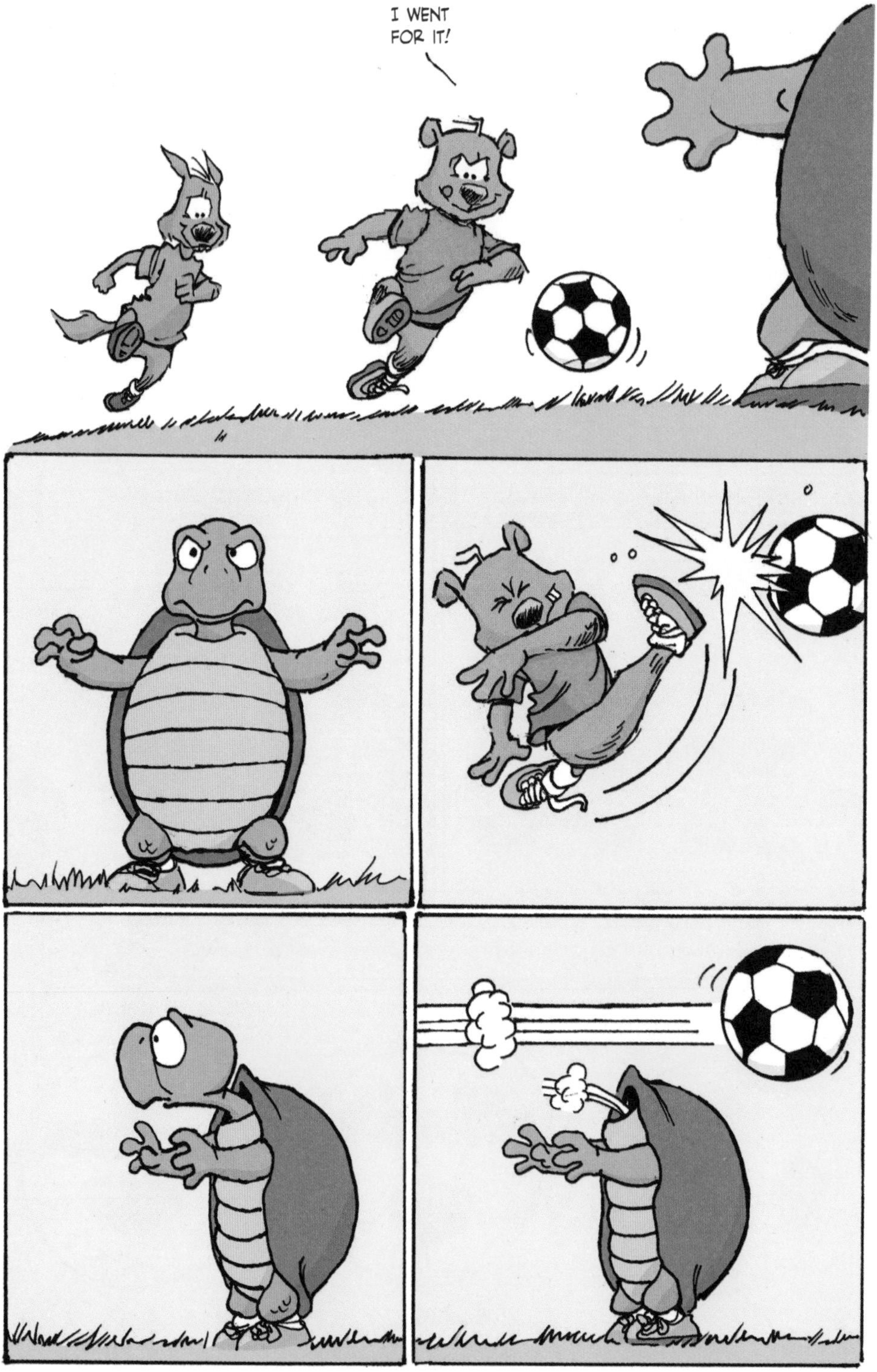
I WENT FOR IT!

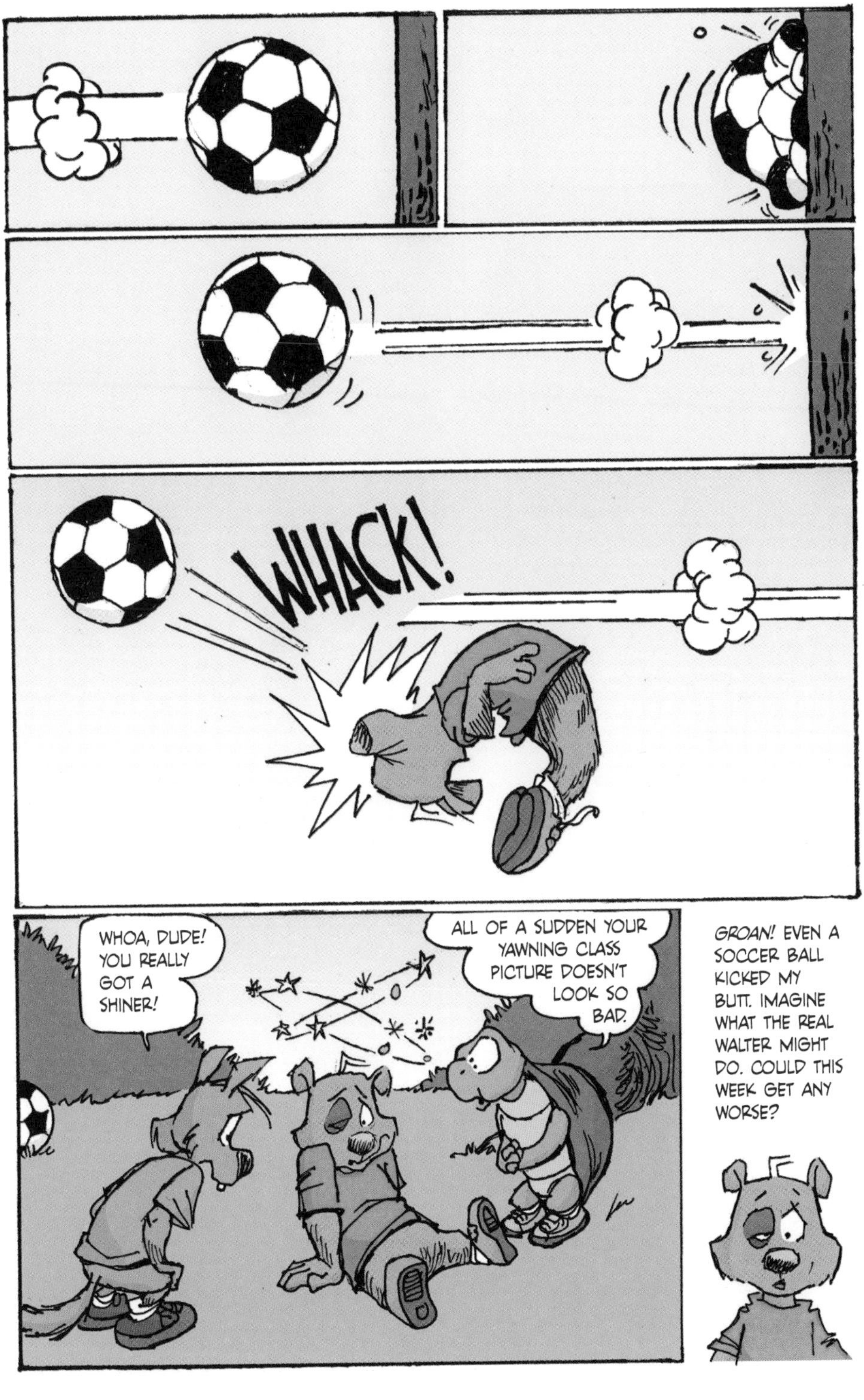
WHACK!
WHOA, DUDE! YOU REALLY GOT A SHINER!
ALL OF A SUDDEN YOUR YAWNING CLASS PICTURE DOESN'T LOOK SO BAD.
GROAN! EVEN A SOCCER BALL KICKED MY BUTT. IMAGINE WHAT THE REAL WALTER MIGHT DO. COULD THIS WEEK GET ANY WORSE?

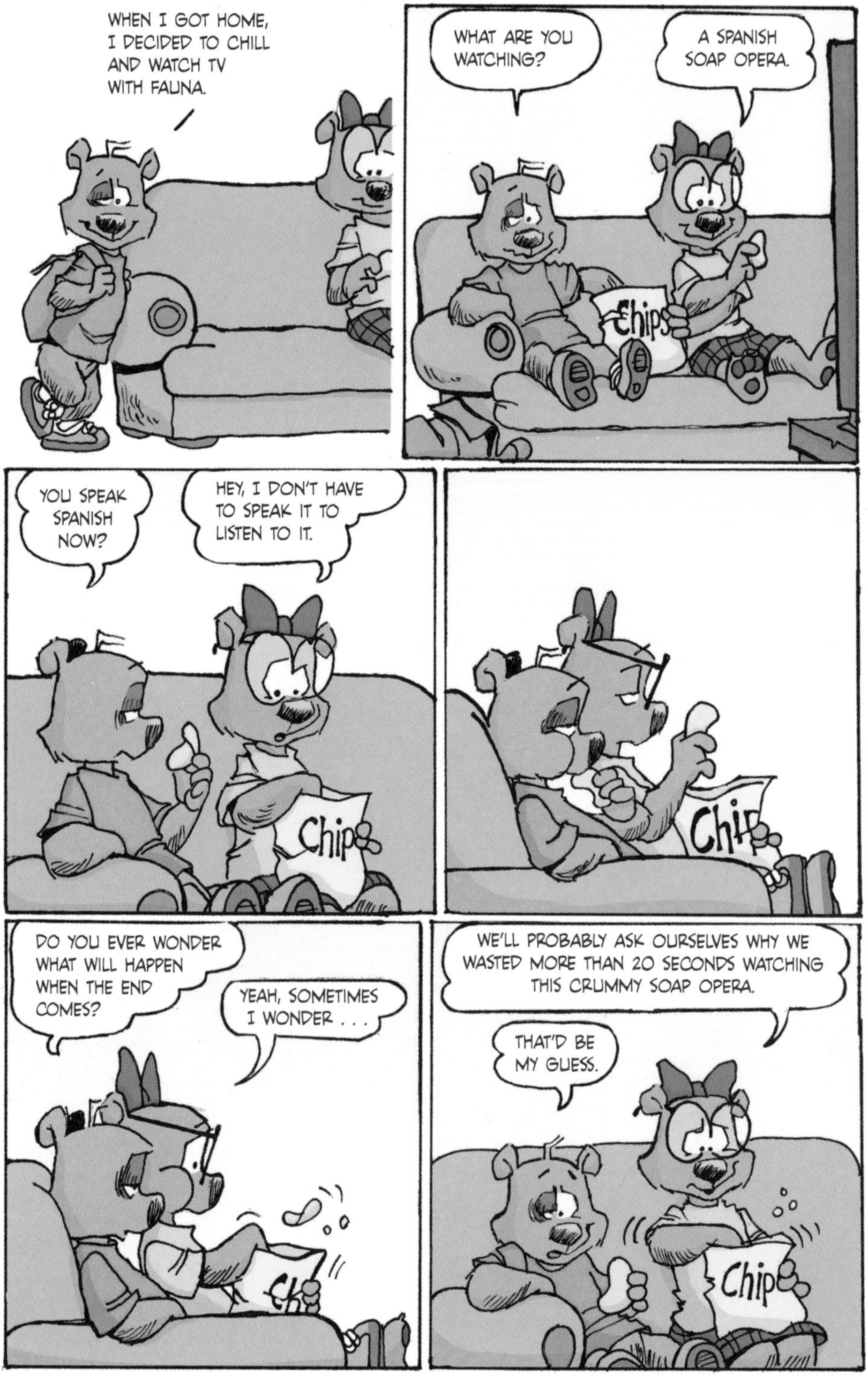
WHEN I GOT HOME, I DECIDED TO CHILL AND WATCH TV WITH FAUNA.
WHAT ARE YOU WATCHING?
A SPANISH SOAP OPERA.
Chips
YOU SPEAK SPANISH NOW?
HEY, I DON'T HAVE TO SPEAK IT TO LISTEN TO IT.
Chips
Chips
DO YOU EVER WONDER WHAT WILL HAPPEN WHEN THE END COMES?
YEAH, SOMETIMES I WONDER . . .
WE'LL PROBABLY ASK OURSELVES WHY WE WASTED MORE THAN 20 SECONDS WATCHING THIS CRUMMY SOAP OPERA.
THAT'D BE MY GUESS.
Chips

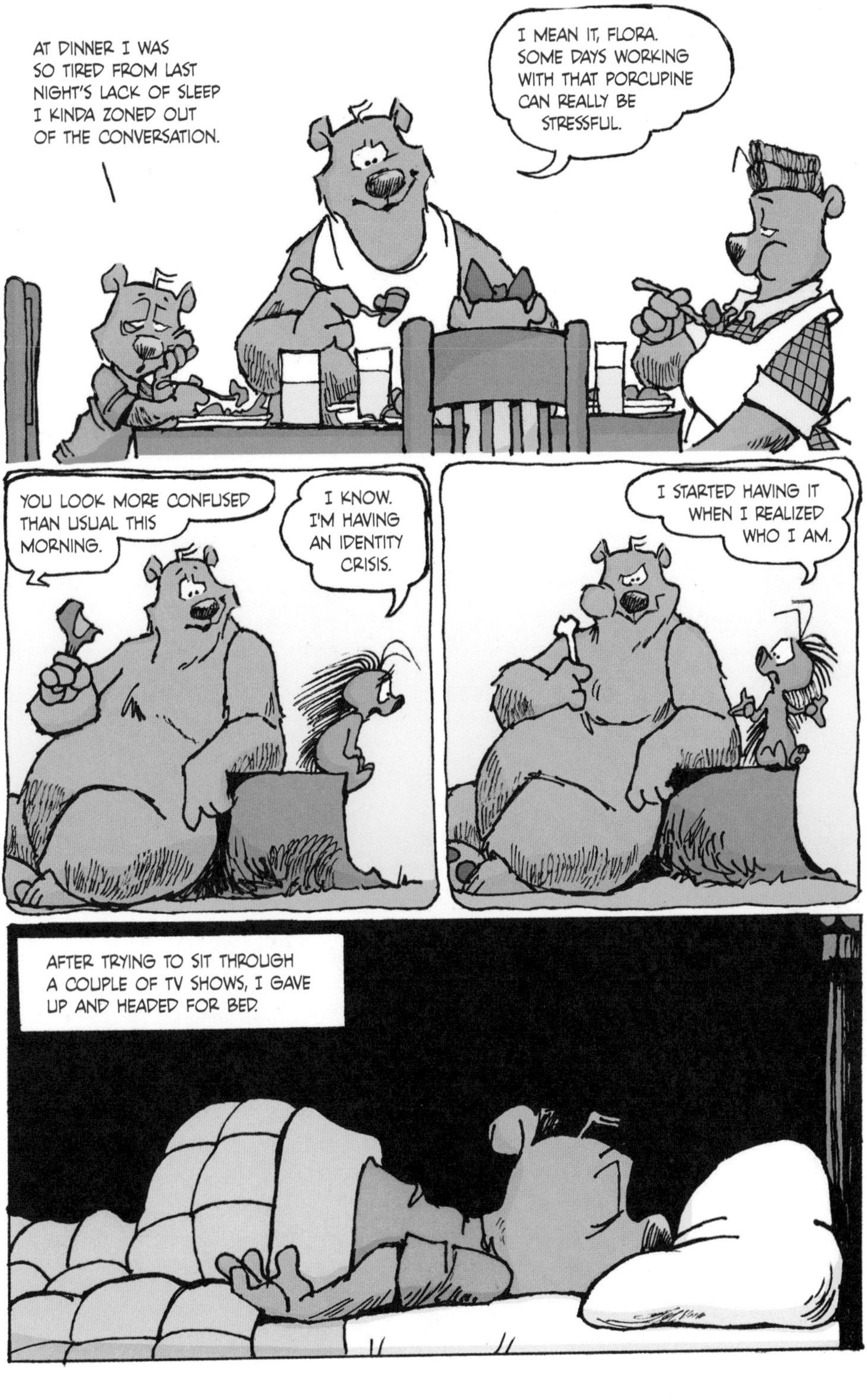
AT DINNER I WAS SO TIRED FROM LAST NIGHT'S LACK OF SLEEP I KINDA ZONED OUT OF THE CONVERSATION.
I MEAN IT, FLORA. SOME DAYS WORKING WITH THAT PORCUPINE CAN REALLY BE STRESSFUL.
YOU LOOK MORE CONFUSED THAN USUAL THIS MORNING.
I KNOW. I'M HAVING AN IDENTITY CRISIS.
I STARTED HAVING IT WHEN I REALIZED WHO I AM.
AFTER TRYING TO SIT THROUGH A COUPLE OF TV SHOWS, I GAVE UP AND HEADED FOR BED.

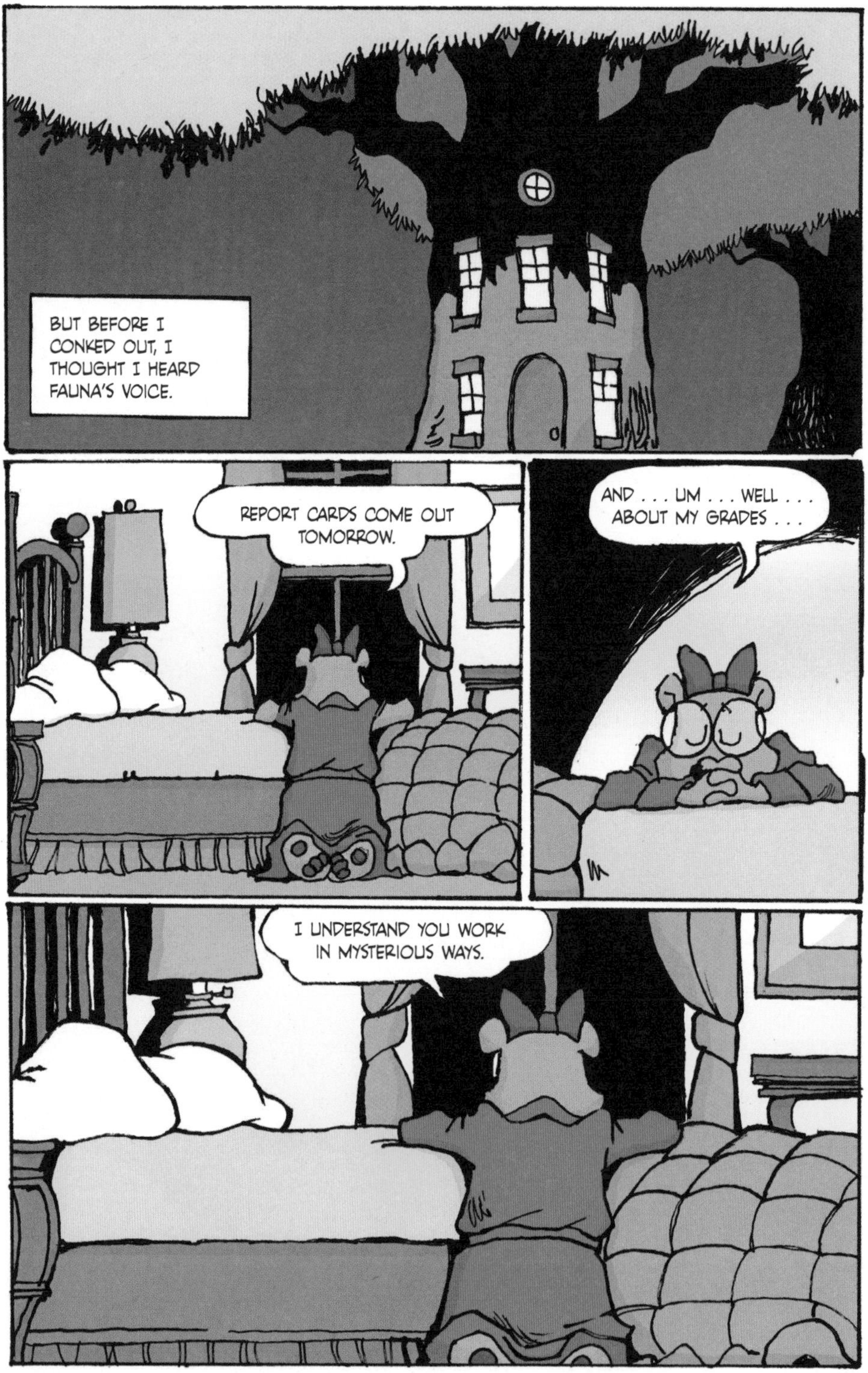
BUT BEFORE I CONKED OUT, I THOUGHT I HEARD FAUNA'S VOICE.
REPORT CARDS COME OUT TOMORROW.
AND . . . UM . . . WELL . . . ABOUT MY GRADES . . .
I UNDERSTAND YOU WORK IN MYSTERIOUS WAYS.

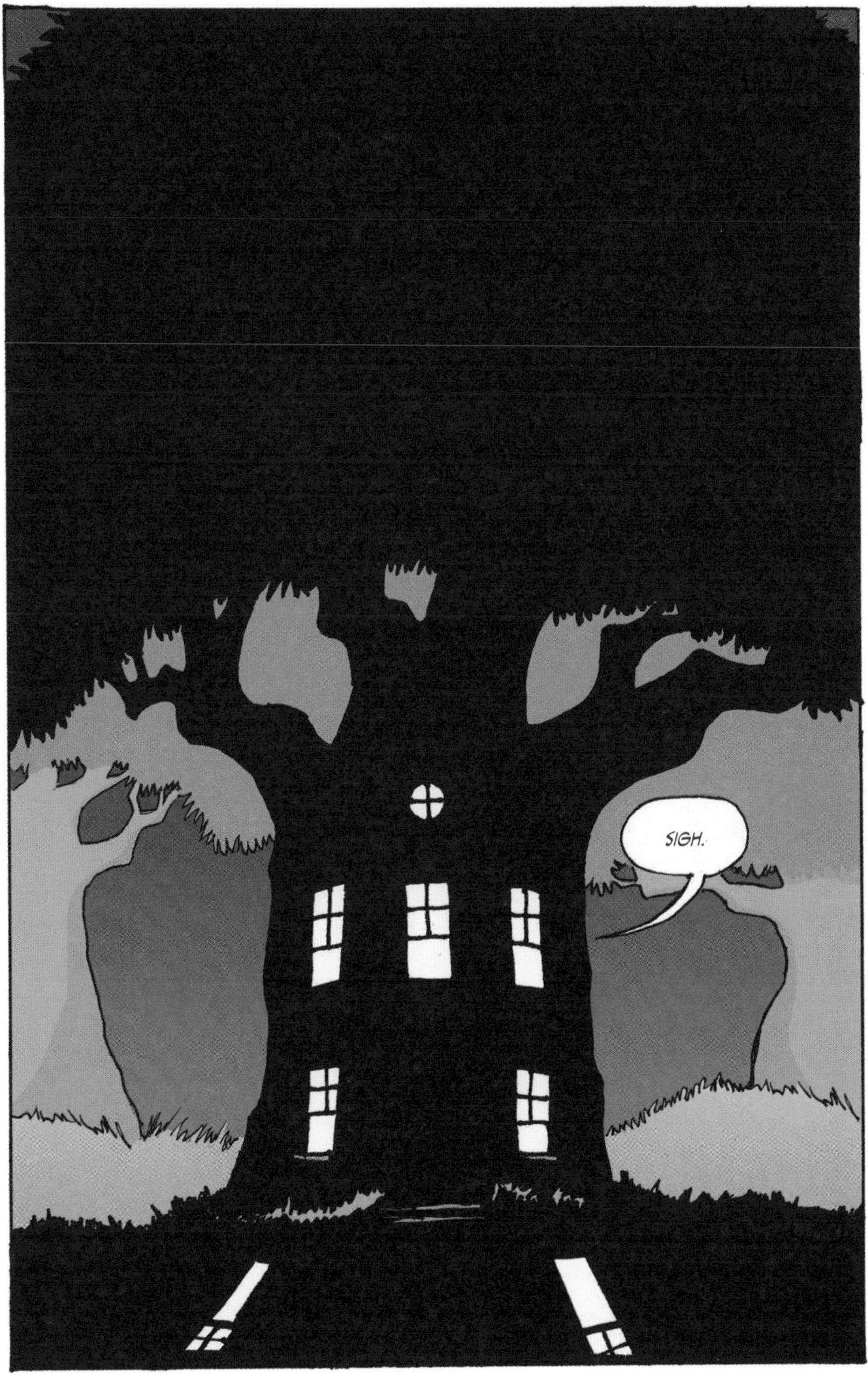
SIGH.

FRIDAY

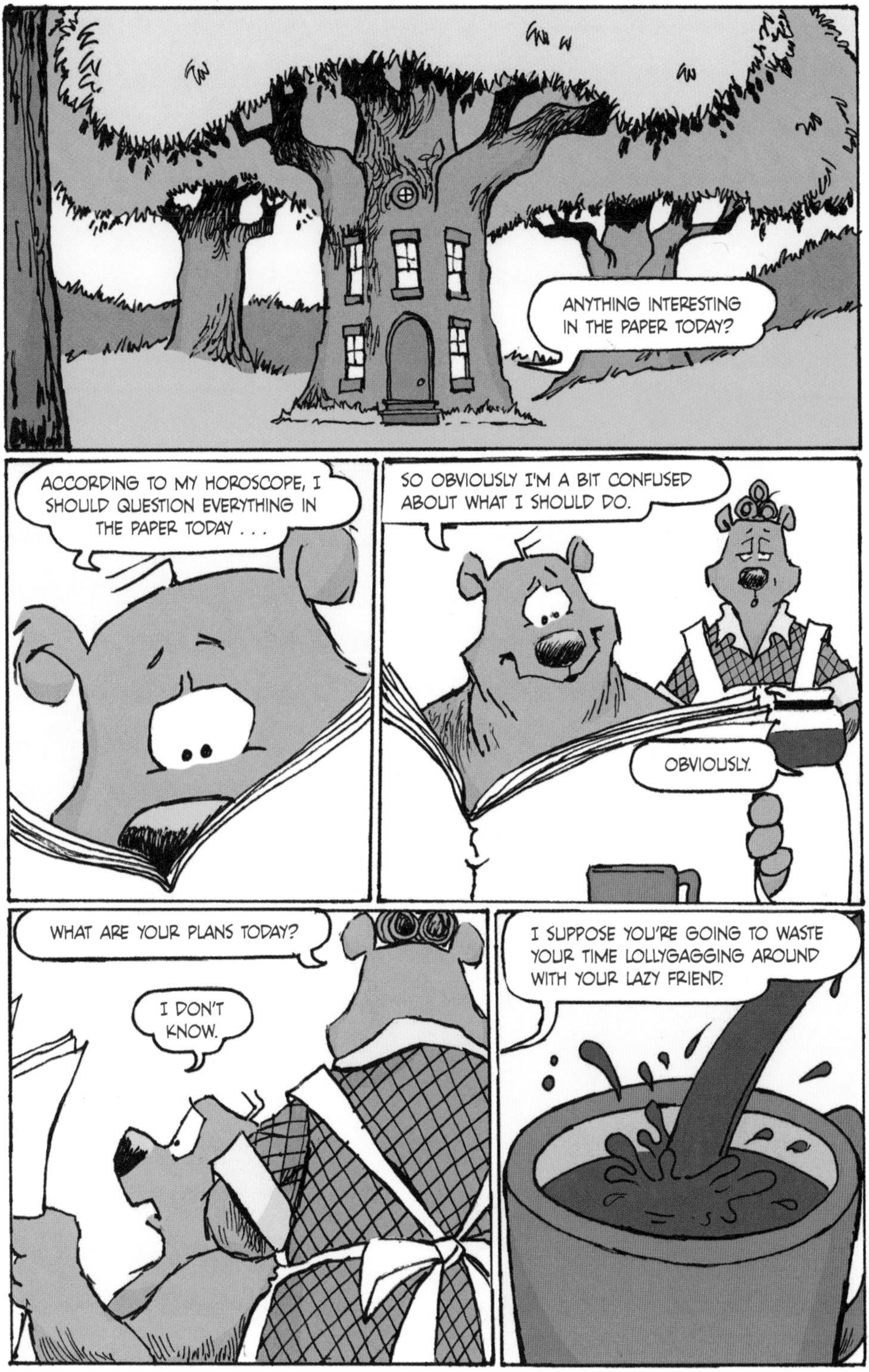
ANYTHING INTERESTING IN THE PAPER TODAY?
ACCORDING TO MY HOROSCOPE, I SHOULD QUESTION EVERYTHING IN THE PAPER TODAY . . .
SO OBVIOUSLY I'M A BIT CONFUSED ABOUT WHAT I SHOULD DO.
OBVIOUSLY.
WHAT ARE YOUR PLANS TODAY?
I DON'T KNOW.
I SUPPOSE YOU'RE GOING TO WASTE YOUR TIME LOLLYGAGGING AROUND WITH YOUR LAZY FRIEND.

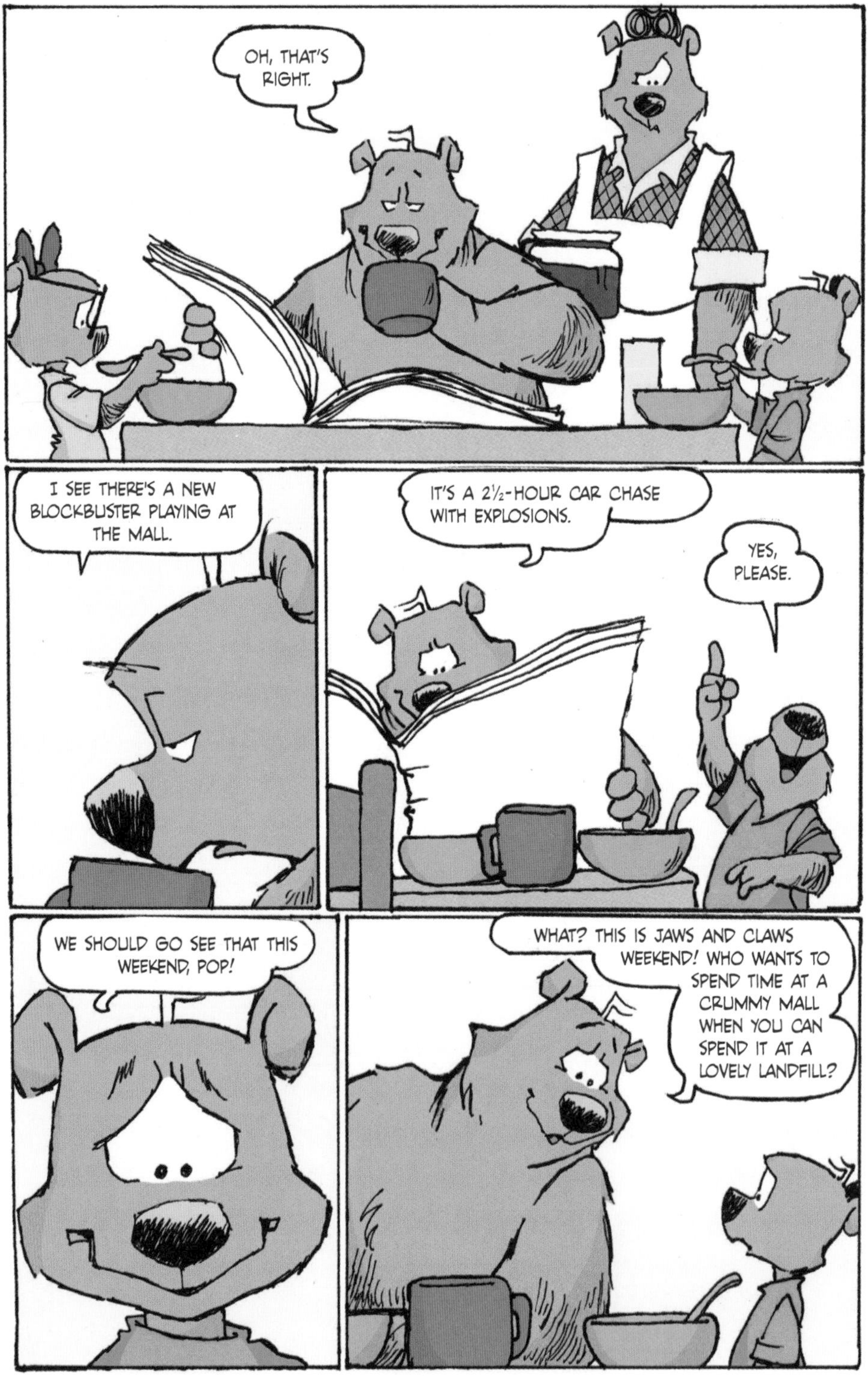
OH, THAT'S RIGHT.
I SEE THERE'S A NEW BLOCKBUSTER PLAYING AT THE MALL.
IT'S A 2½-HOUR CAR CHASE WITH EXPLOSIONS.
YES, PLEASE.
WE SHOULD GO SEE THAT THIS WEEKEND, POP!
WHAT? THIS IS JAWS AND CLAWS WEEKEND! WHO WANTS TO SPEND TIME AT A CRUMMY MALL WHEN YOU CAN SPEND IT AT A LOVELY LANDFILL?

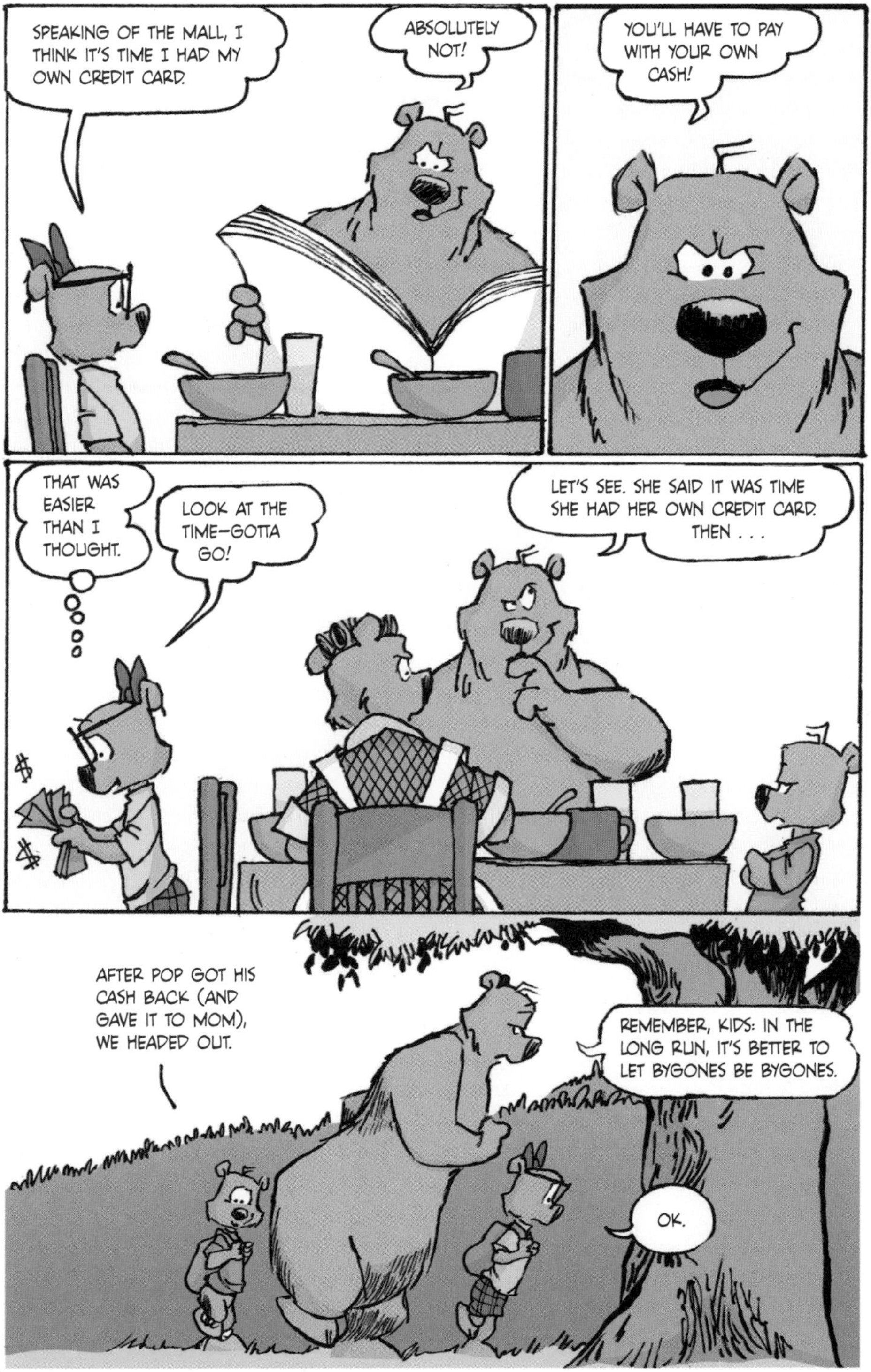
SPEAKING OF THE MALL, I THINK IT'S TIME I HAD MY OWN CREDIT CARD.
ABSOLUTELY NOT!
YOU'LL HAVE TO PAY WITH YOUR OWN CASH!
THAT WAS EASIER THAN I THOUGHT.
LOOK AT THE TIME—GOTTA GO!
LET'S SEE. SHE SAID IT WAS TIME SHE HAD HER OWN CREDIT CARD. THEN . . .
AFTER POP GOT HIS CASH BACK (AND GAVE IT TO MOM), WE HEADED OUT.
REMEMBER, KIDS: IN THE LONG RUN, IT'S BETTER TO LET BYGONES BE BYGONES.
OK.

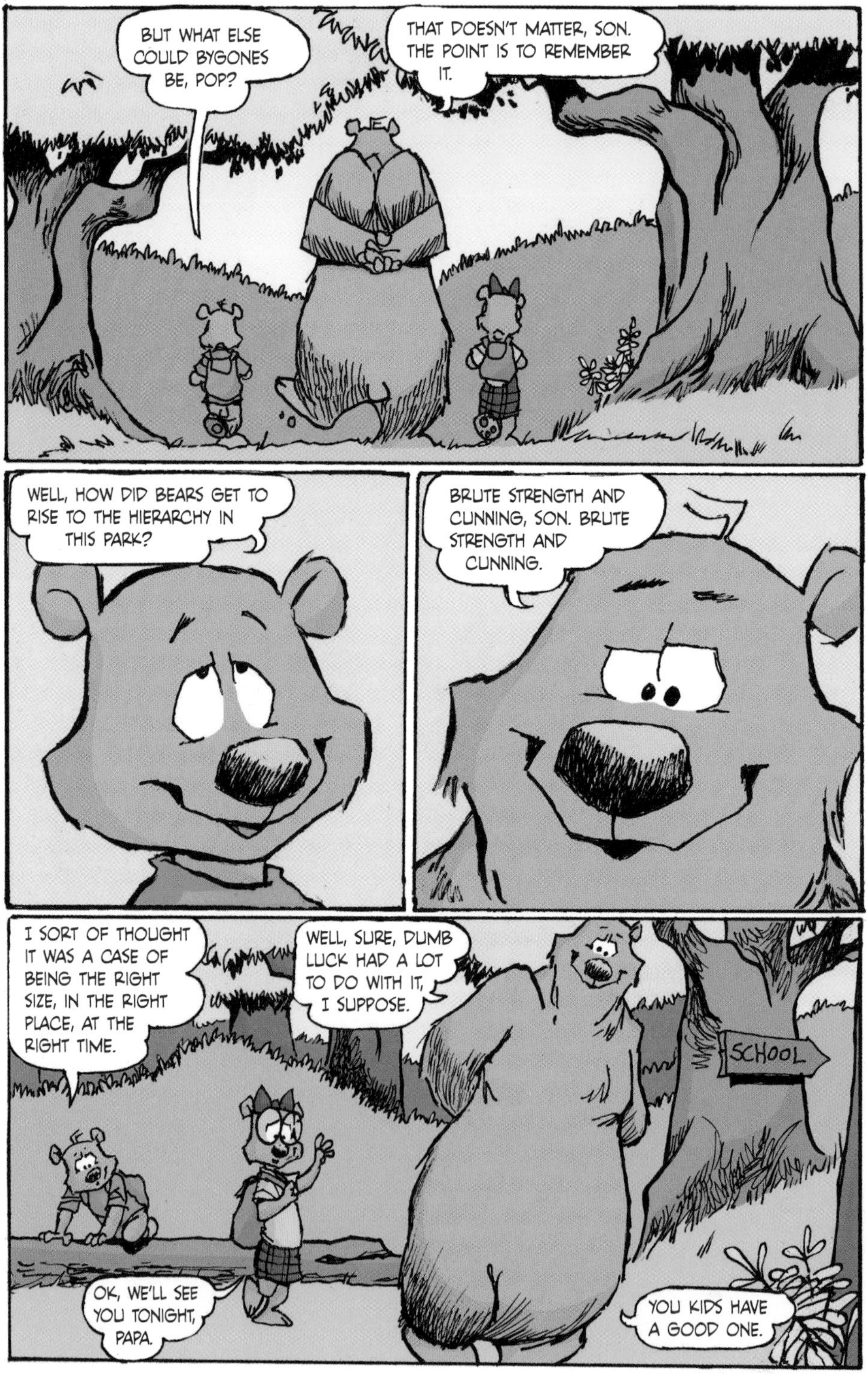
BUT WHAT ELSE COULD BYGONES BE, POP?
THAT DOESN'T MATTER, SON. THE POINT IS TO REMEMBER IT.
WELL, HOW DID BEARS GET TO RISE TO THE HIERARCHY IN THIS PARK?
BRUTE STRENGTH AND CUNNING, SON. BRUTE STRENGTH AND CUNNING.
I SORT OF THOUGHT IT WAS A CASE OF BEING THE RIGHT SIZE, IN THE RIGHT PLACE, AT THE RIGHT TIME.
WELL, SURE, DUMB LUCK HAD A LOT TO DO WITH IT, I SUPPOSE.
SCHOOL
OK, WE'LL SEE YOU TONIGHT, PAPA.
YOU KIDS HAVE A GOOD ONE.

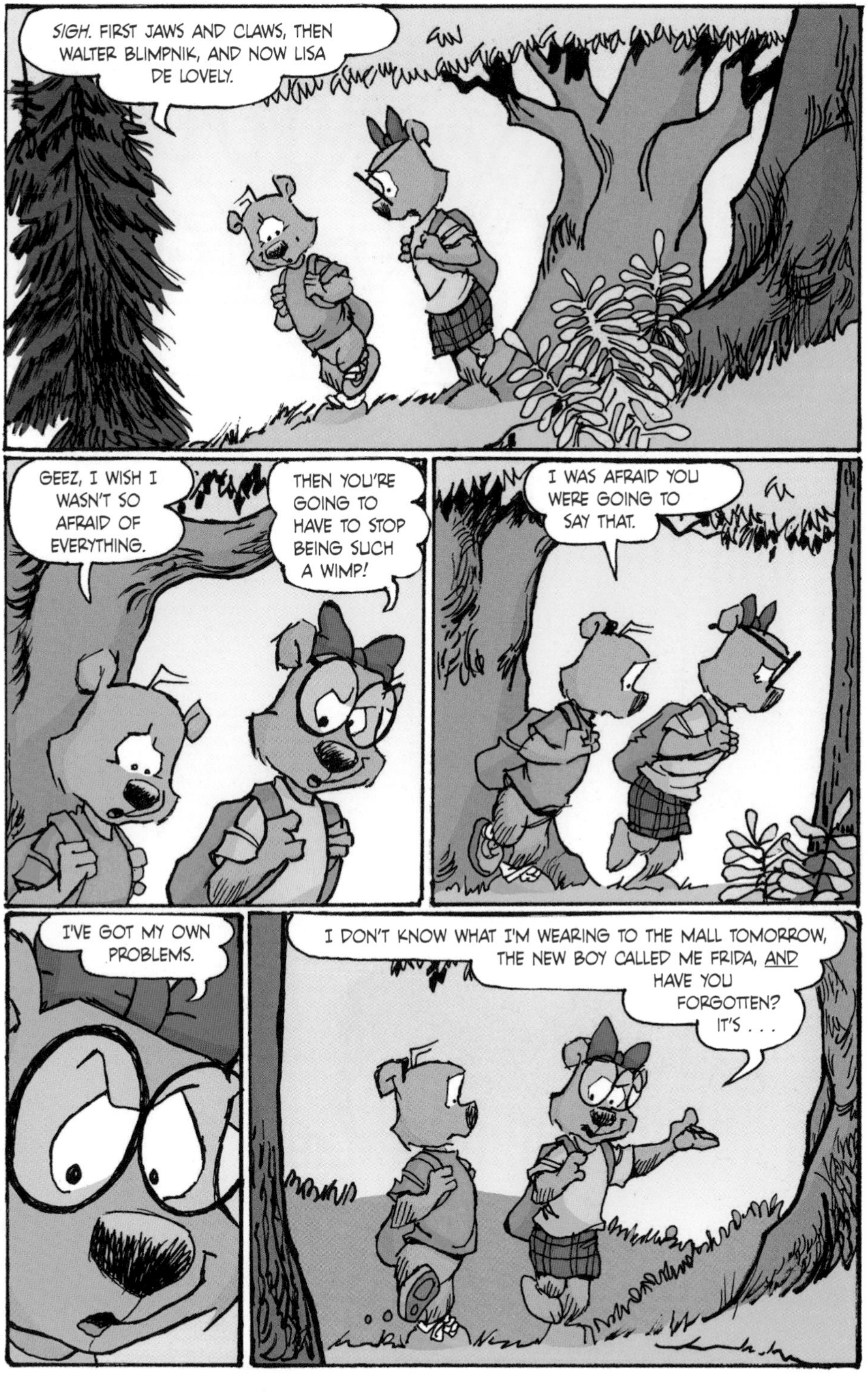
SIGH. FIRST JAWS AND CLAWS, THEN WALTER BLIMPNIK, AND NOW LISA DE LOVELY.
GEEZ, I WISH I WASN'T SO AFRAID OF EVERYTHING.
THEN YOU'RE GOING TO HAVE TO STOP BEING SUCH A WIMP!
I WAS AFRAID YOU WERE GOING TO SAY THAT.
I'VE GOT MY OWN PROBLEMS.
I DON'T KNOW WHAT I'M WEARING TO THE MALL TOMORROW, THE NEW BOY CALLED ME FRIDA, AND HAVE YOU FORGOTTEN? IT'S . . .

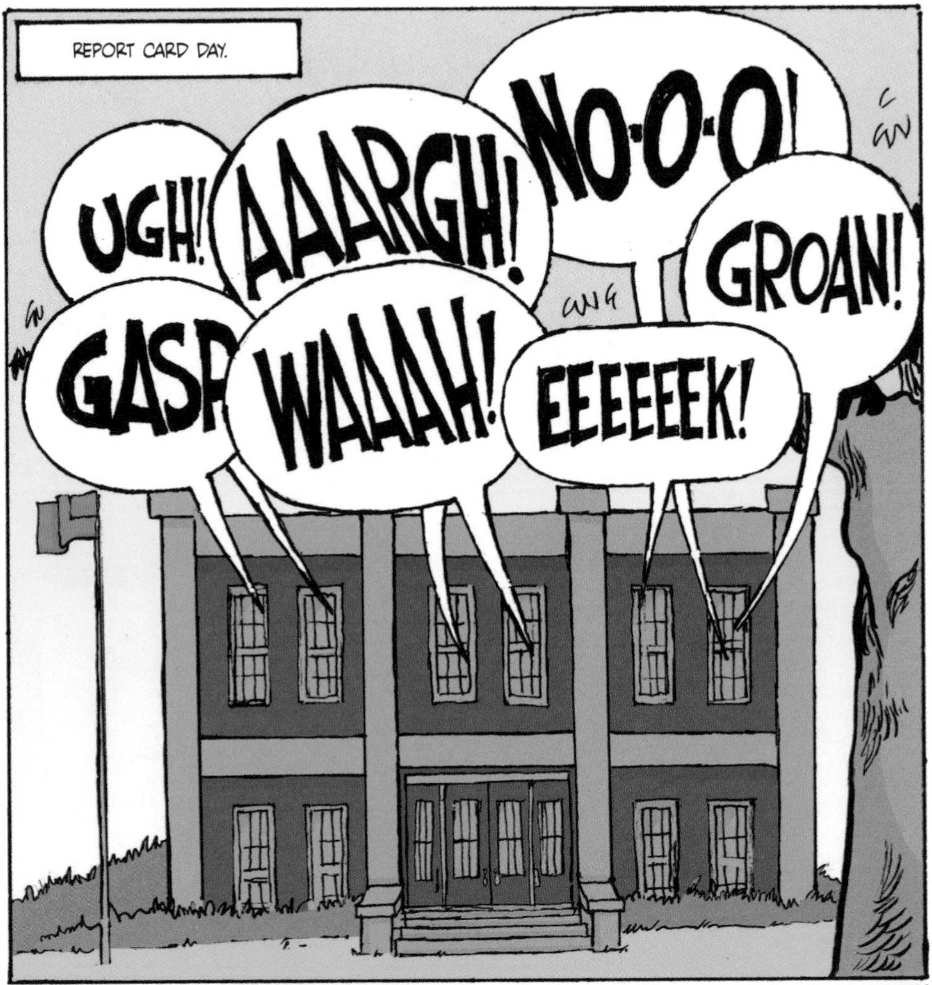
REPORT CARD DAY.
UGH!
AAARGH!
NO-O-O!
GROAN!
GASP
WAAAH!
EEEEEEK!

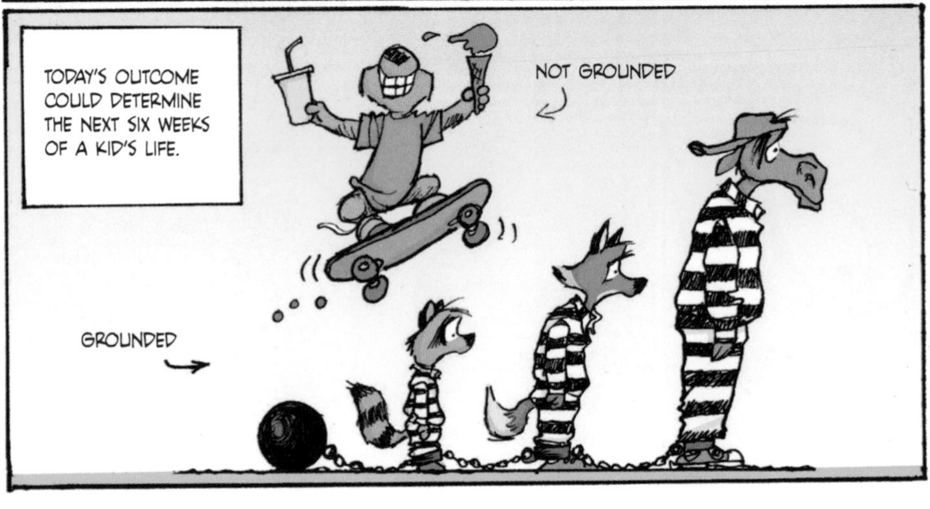
TODAY'S OUTCOME COULD DETERMINE THE NEXT SIX WEEKS OF A KID'S LIFE.
NOT GROUNDED
GROUNDED

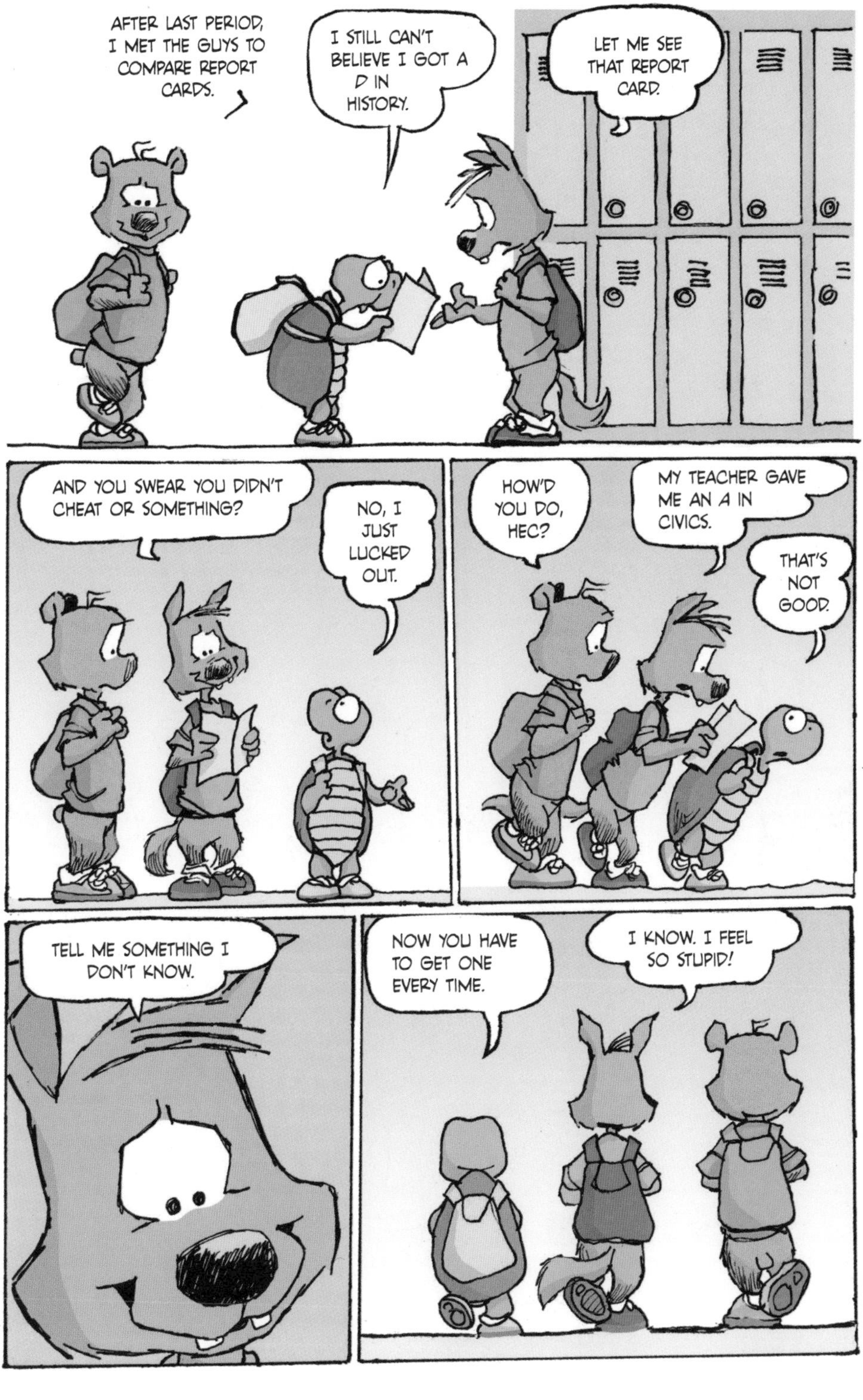
AFTER LAST PERIOD, I MET THE GUYS TO COMPARE REPORT CARDS.
I STILL CAN'T BELIEVE I GOT A D IN HISTORY.
LET ME SEE THAT REPORT CARD.
AND YOU SWEAR YOU DIDN'T CHEAT OR SOMETHING?
NO, I JUST LUCKED OUT.
HOW'D YOU DO, HEC?
MY TEACHER GAVE ME AN A IN CIVICS.
THAT'S NOT GOOD.
TELL ME SOMETHING I DON'T KNOW.
NOW YOU HAVE TO GET ONE EVERY TIME.
I KNOW. I FEEL SO STUPID!

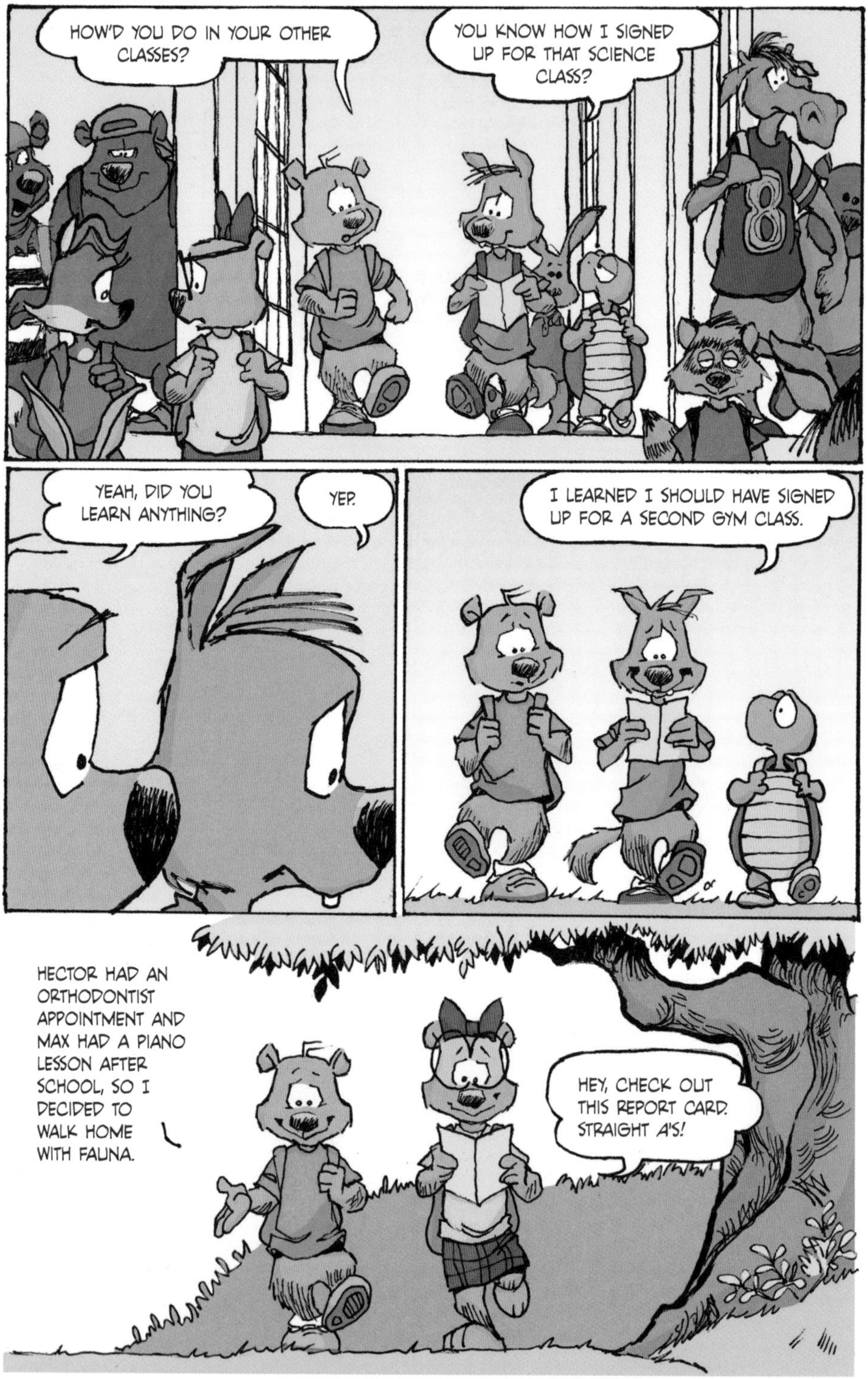
HOW'D YOU DO IN YOUR OTHER CLASSES?
YOU KNOW HOW I SIGNED UP FOR THAT SCIENCE CLASS?
8
YEAH, DID YOU LEARN ANYTHING?
YEP.
I LEARNED I SHOULD HAVE SIGNED UP FOR A SECOND GYM CLASS.
HECTOR HAD AN ORTHODONTIST APPOINTMENT AND MAX HAD A PIANO LESSON AFTER SCHOOL, SO I DECIDED TO WALK HOME WITH FAUNA.
HEY, CHECK OUT THIS REPORT CARD. STRAIGHT A'S!

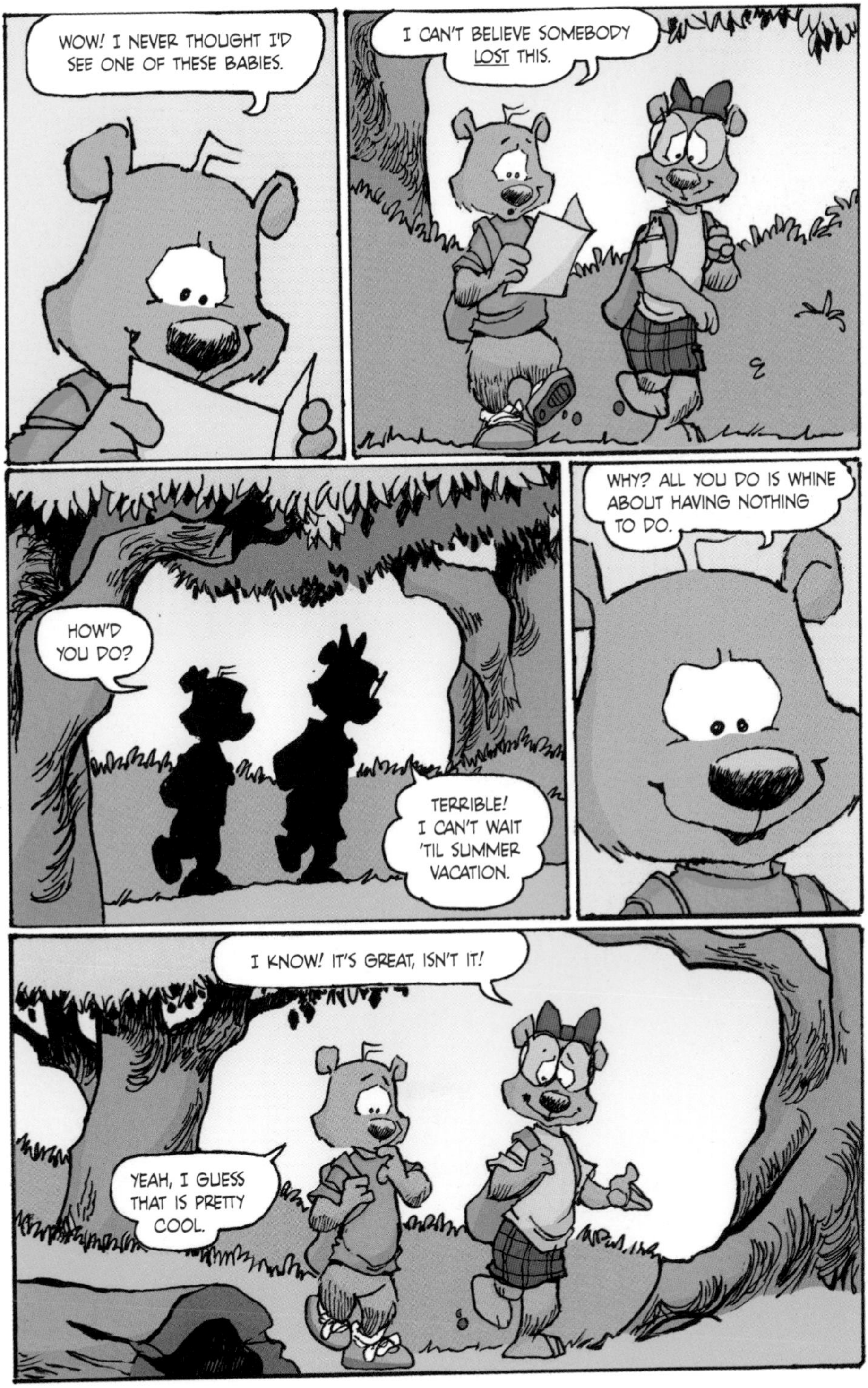
WOW! I NEVER THOUGHT I'D SEE ONE OF THESE BABIES.
I CAN'T BELIEVE SOMEBODY LOST THIS.
HOW'D YOU DO?
TERRIBLE! I CAN'T WAIT 'TIL SUMMER VACATION.
WHY? ALL YOU DO IS WHINE ABOUT HAVING NOTHING TO DO.
I KNOW! IT'S GREAT, ISN'T IT!
YEAH, I GUESS THAT IS PRETTY COOL.

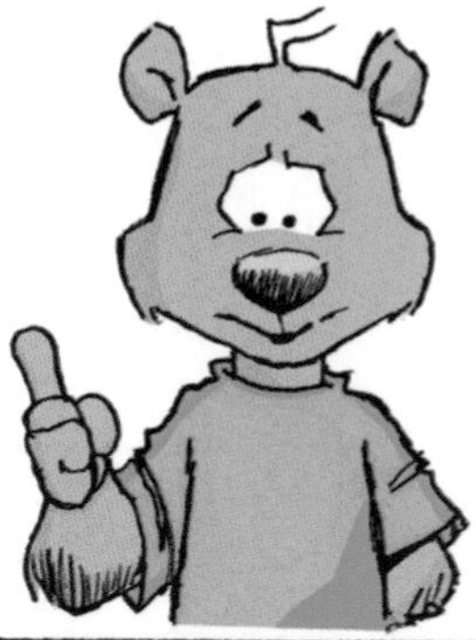
NOW I'LL SPARE YOU FOLKS THE GORY DETAILS, BUT LET'S JUST SAY MOM WAS NOT TOO HAPPY WITH FAUNA'S REPORT CARD.

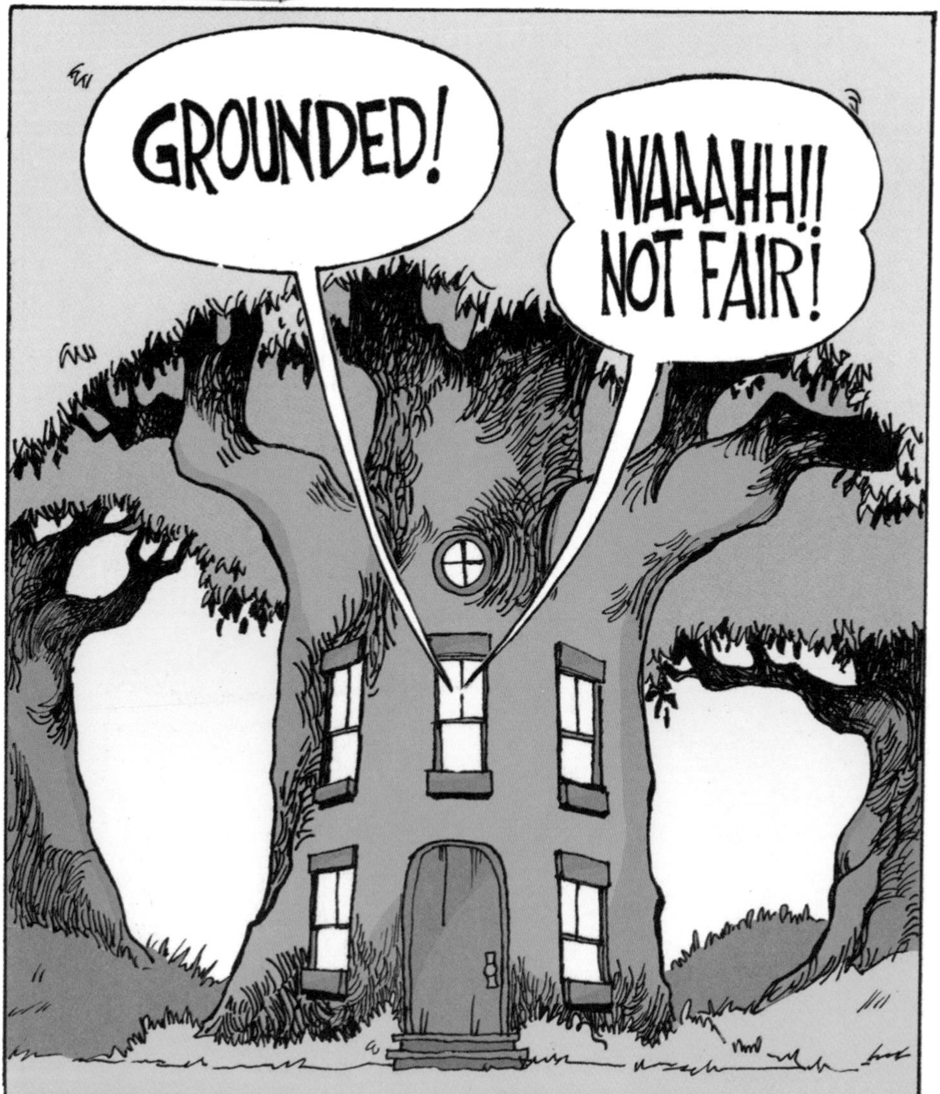
GROUNDED!
WAAAHH!! NOT FAIR!

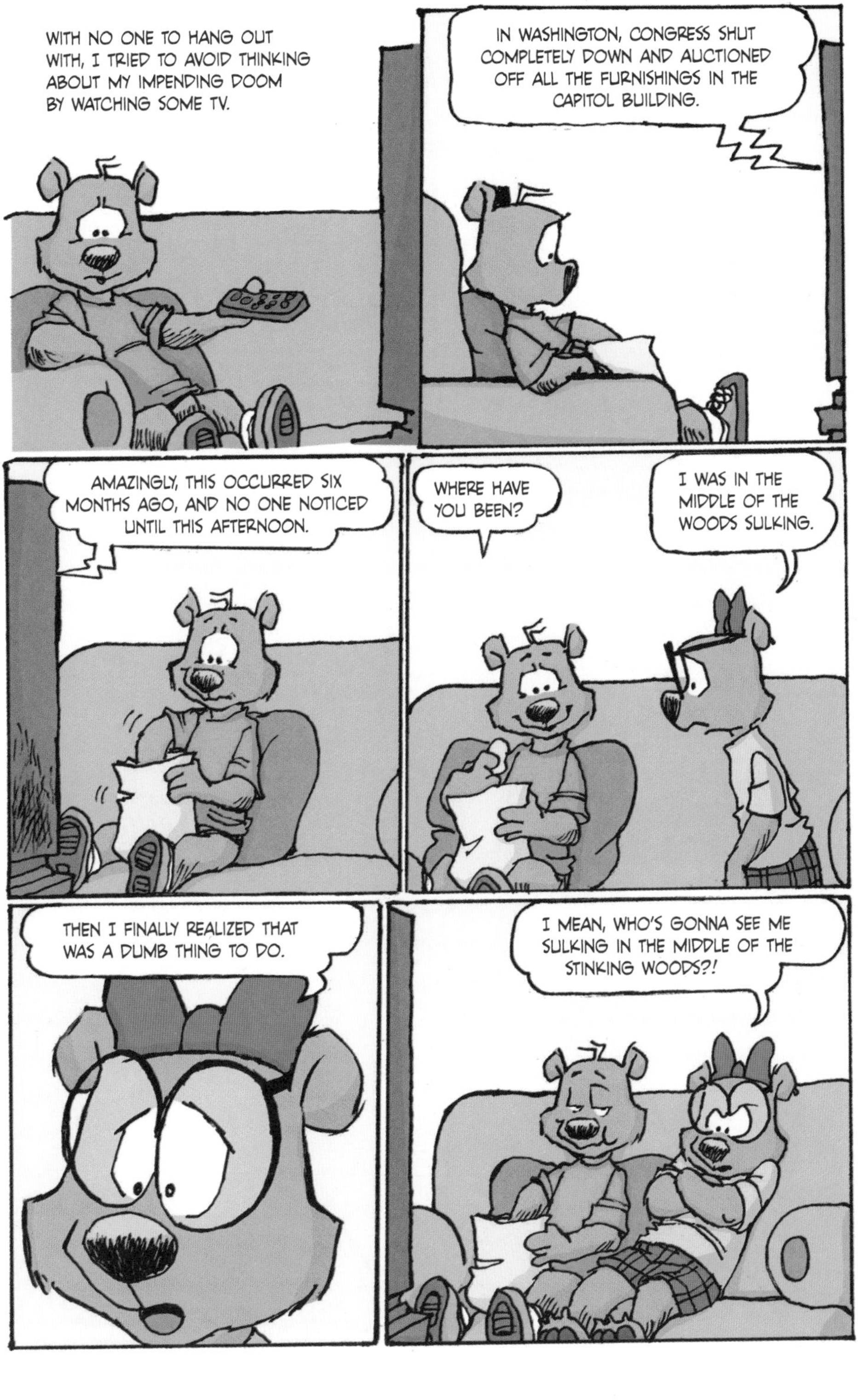
WITH NO ONE TO HANG OUT WITH, I TRIED TO AVOID THINKING ABOUT MY IMPENDING DOOM BY WATCHING SOME TV.
IN WASHINGTON, CONGRESS SHUT COMPLETELY DOWN AND AUCTIONED OFF ALL THE FURNISHINGS IN THE CAPITOL BUILDING.
AMAZINGLY, THIS OCCURRED SIX MONTHS AGO, AND NO ONE NOTICED UNTIL THIS AFTERNOON.
WHERE HAVE YOU BEEN?
I WAS IN THE MIDDLE OF THE WOODS SULKING.
THEN I FINALLY REALIZED THAT WAS A DUMB THING TO DO.
I MEAN, WHO'S GONNA SEE ME SULKING IN THE MIDDLE OF THE STINKING WOODS?!

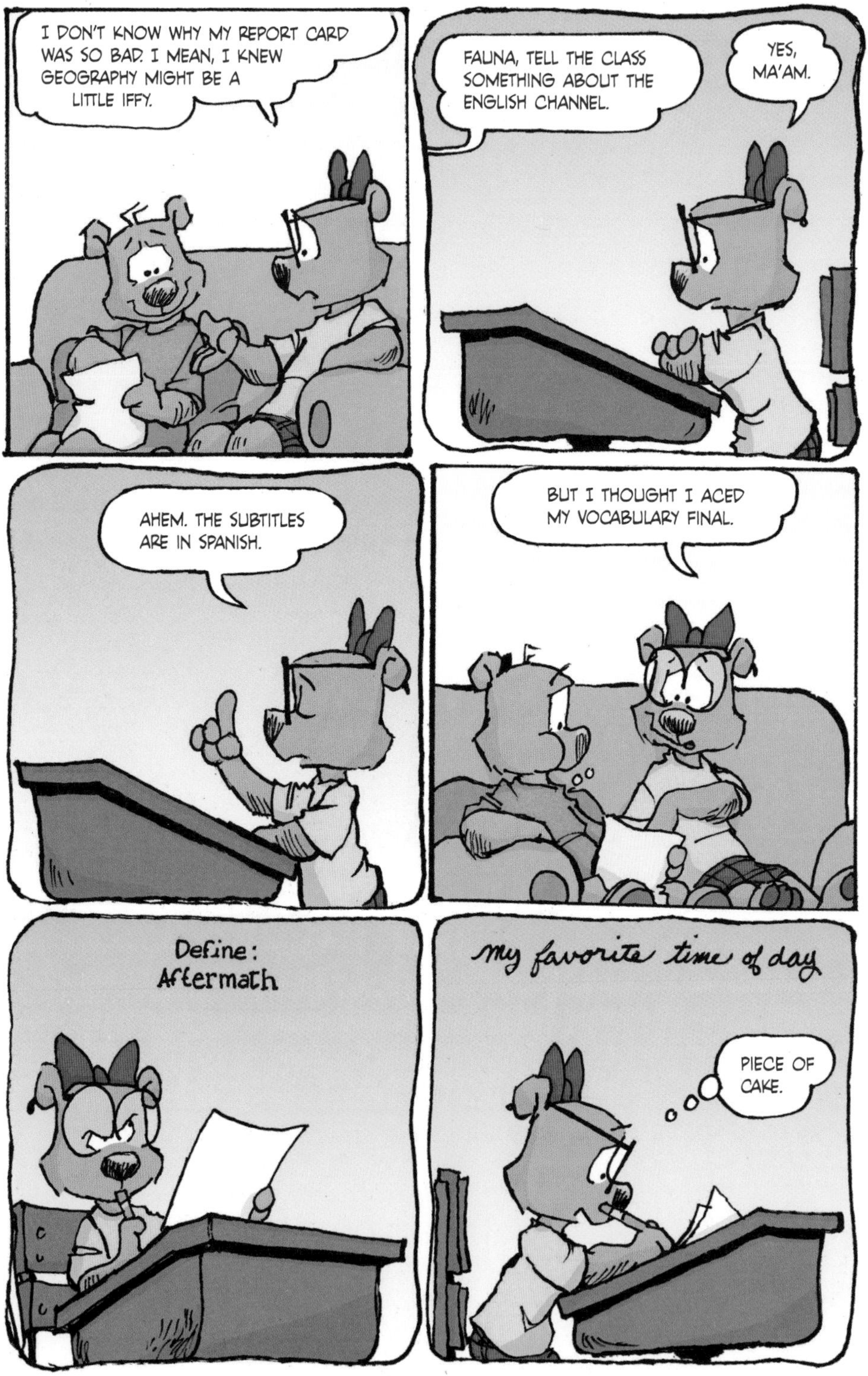
I DON'T KNOW WHY MY REPORT CARD WAS SO BAD. I MEAN, I KNEW GEOGRAPHY MIGHT BE A LITTLE IFFY.
FAUNA, TELL THE CLASS SOMETHING ABOUT THE ENGLISH CHANNEL.
YES, MA'AM.
AHEM. THE SUBTITLES ARE IN SPANISH.
BUT I THOUGHT I ACED MY VOCABULARY FINAL.
Define: Aftermath
my favorite time of day
PIECE OF CAKE.

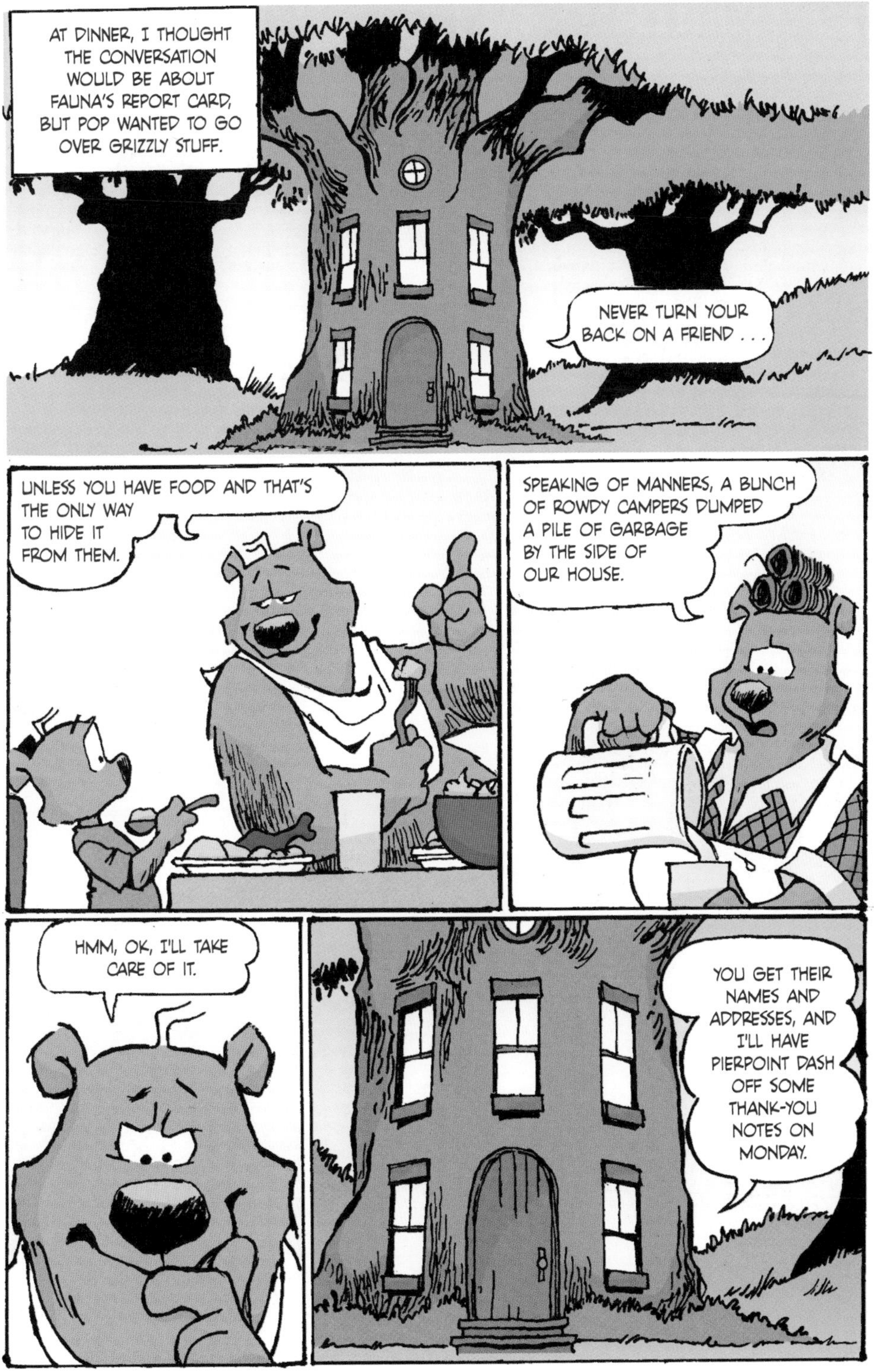
AT DINNER, I THOUGHT THE CONVERSATION WOULD BE ABOUT FAUNA'S REPORT CARD, BUT POP WANTED TO GO OVER GRIZZLY STUFF.
NEVER TURN YOUR BACK ON A FRIEND . . .
UNLESS YOU HAVE FOOD AND THAT'S THE ONLY WAY TO HIDE IT FROM THEM.
SPEAKING OF MANNERS, A BUNCH OF ROWDY CAMPERS DUMPED A PILE OF GARBAGE BY THE SIDE OF OUR HOUSE.
HMM, OK, I'LL TAKE CARE OF IT.
YOU GET THEIR NAMES AND ADDRESSES, AND I'LL HAVE PIERPOINT DASH OFF SOME THANK-YOU NOTES ON MONDAY.

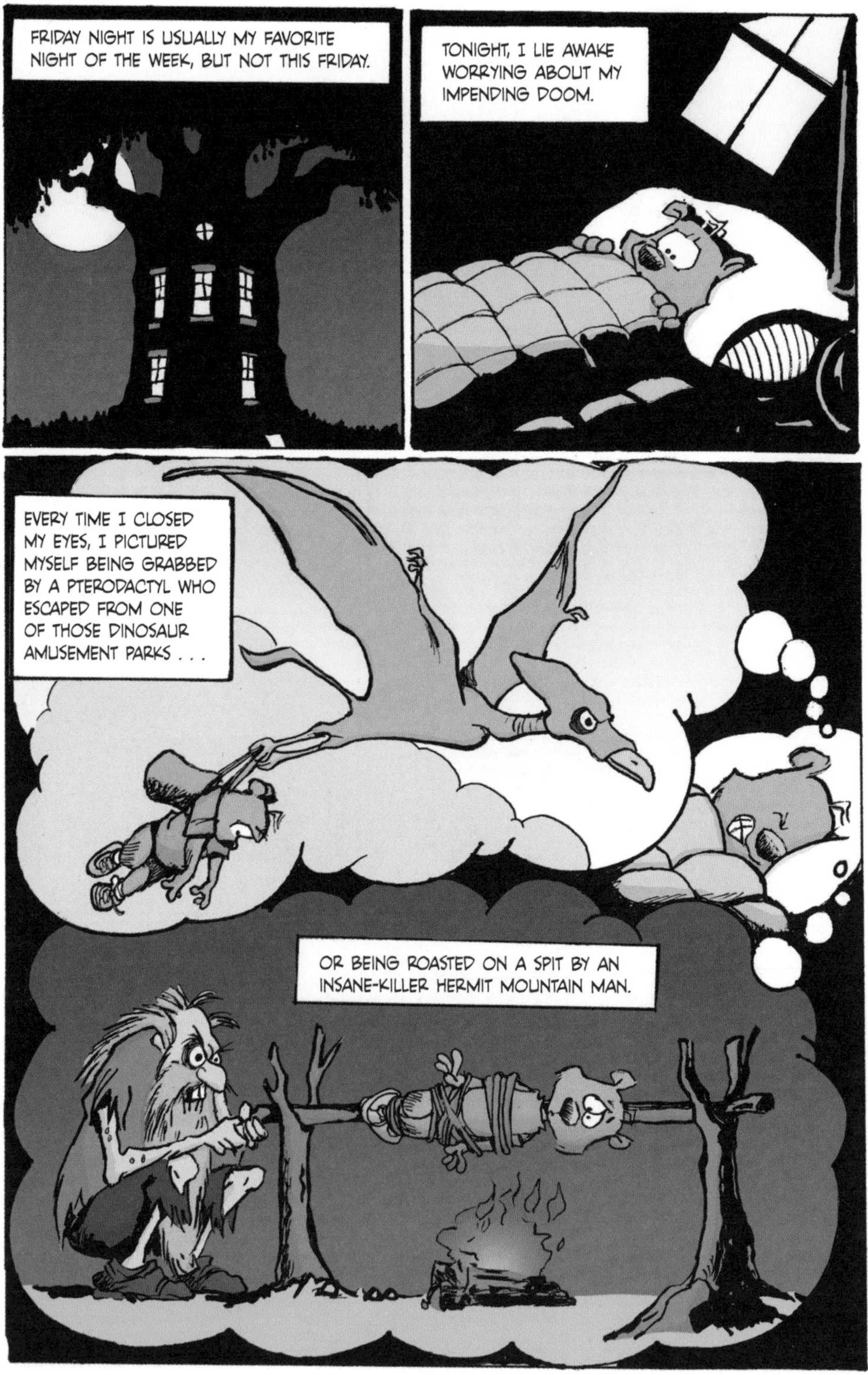
FRIDAY NIGHT IS USUALLY MY FAVORITE NIGHT OF THE WEEK, BUT NOT THIS FRIDAY.
TONIGHT, I LIE AWAKE WORRYING ABOUT MY IMPENDING DOOM.
EVERY TIME I CLOSED MY EYES, I PICTURED MYSELF BEING GRABBED BY A PTERODACTYL WHO ESCAPED FROM ONE OF THOSE DINOSAUR AMUSEMENT PARKS . . .
OR BEING ROASTED ON A SPIT BY AN INSANE-KILLER HERMIT MOUNTAIN MAN.

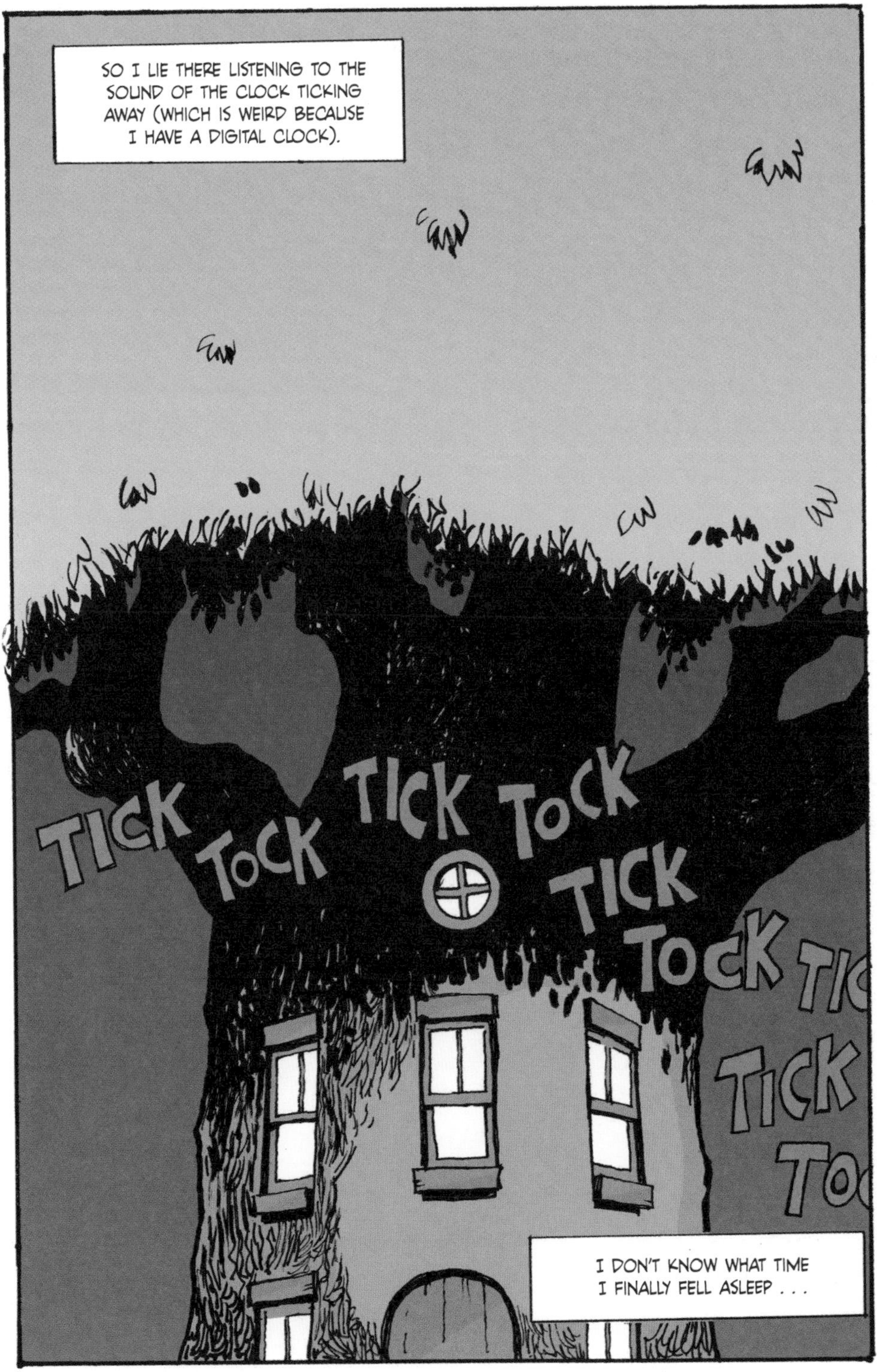
SO I LIE THERE LISTENING TO THE SOUND OF THE CLOCK TICKING AWAY (WHICH IS WEIRD BECAUSE I HAVE A DIGITAL CLOCK).
TICK
TOCK
TICK
TOCK
TICK
TOCK
TICK
I DON'T KNOW WHAT TIME I FINALLY FELL ASLEEP . . .

SATURDAY

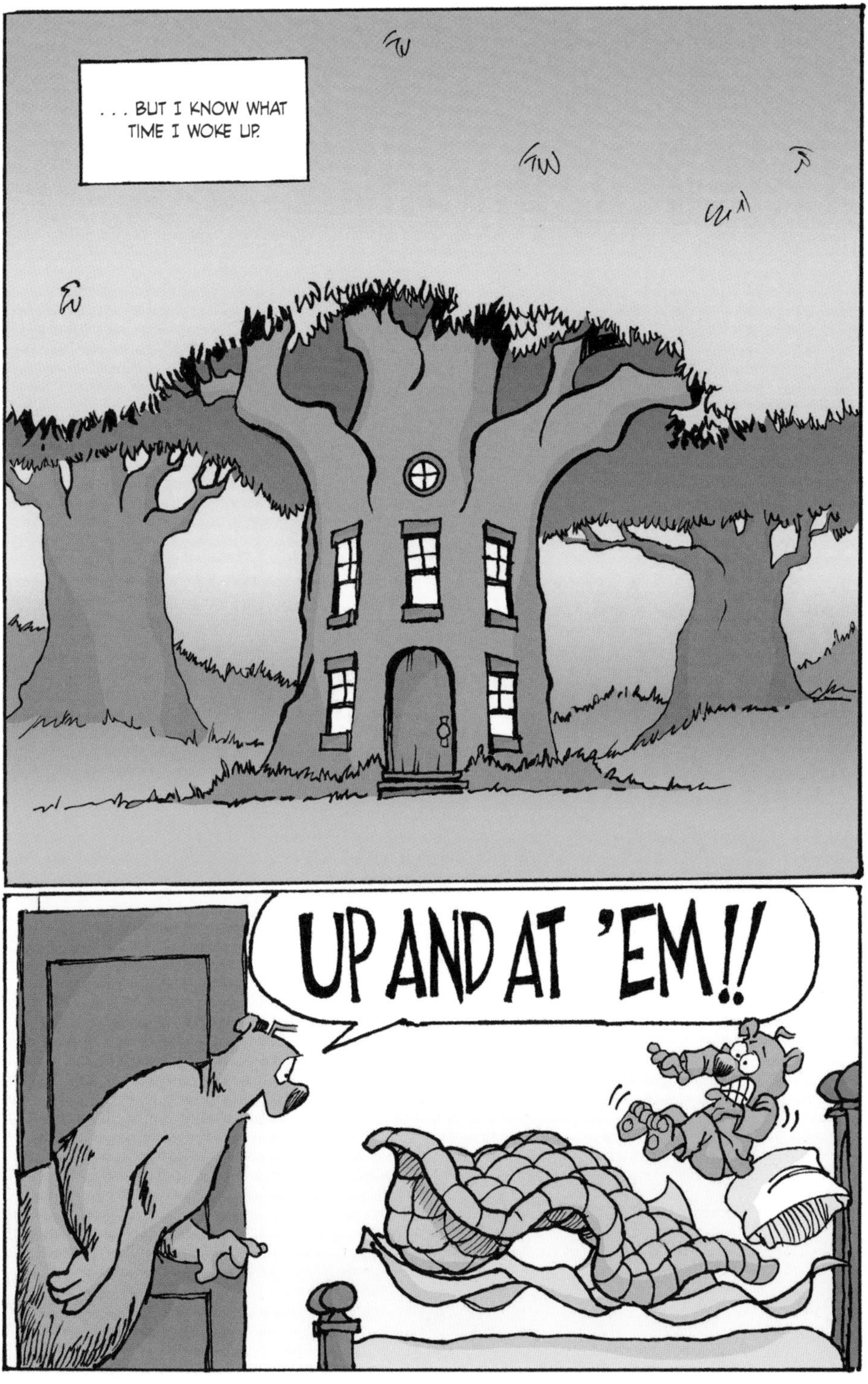
. . . BUT I KNOW WHAT TIME I WOKE UP.
UP AND AT 'EM!!

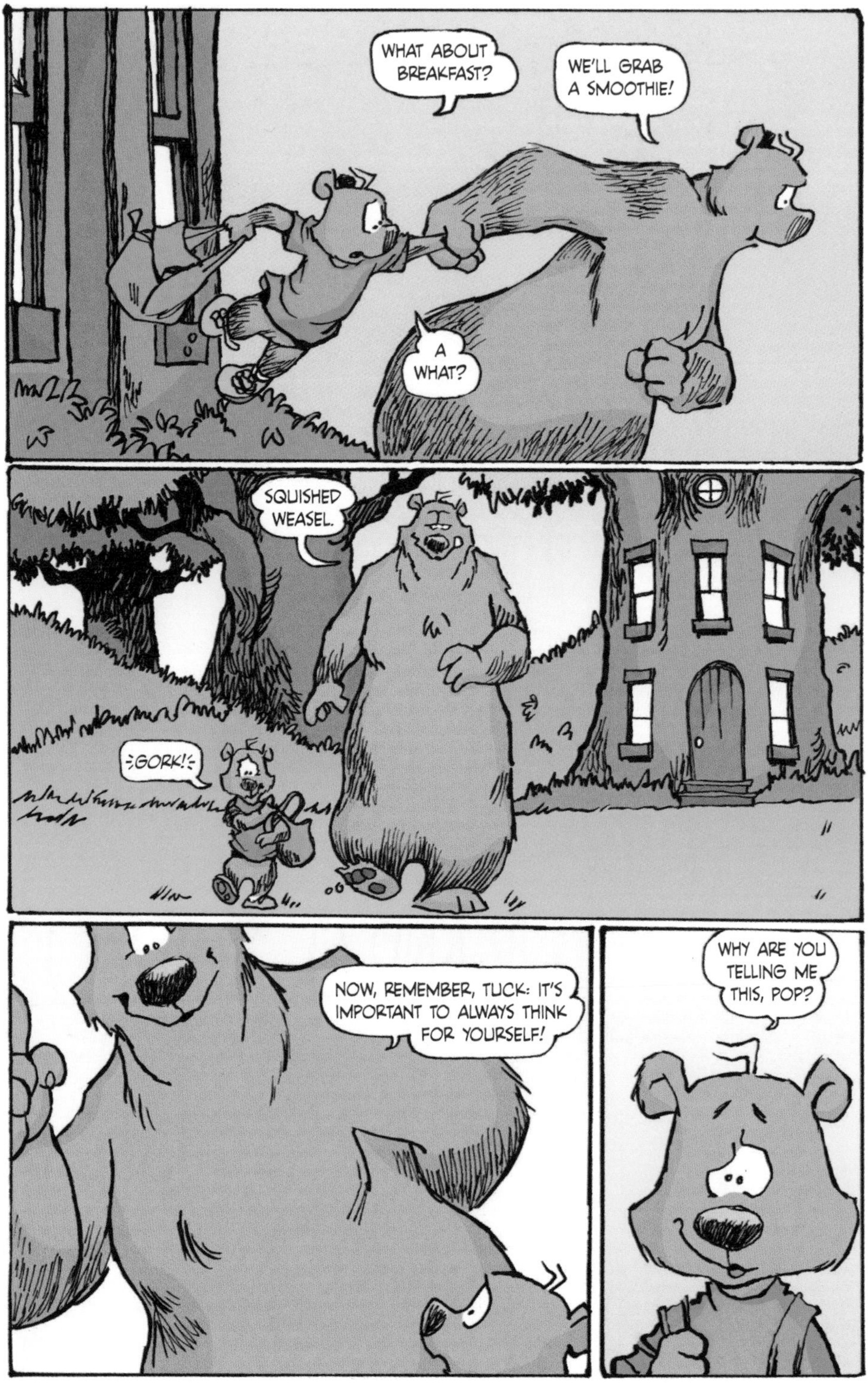
WHAT ABOUT BREAKFAST?
WE'LL GRAB A SMOOTHIE!
A WHAT?
SQUISHED WEASEL.
GORK!
NOW, REMEMBER, TUCK: IT'S IMPORTANT TO ALWAYS THINK FOR YOURSELF!
WHY ARE YOU TELLING ME THIS, POP?

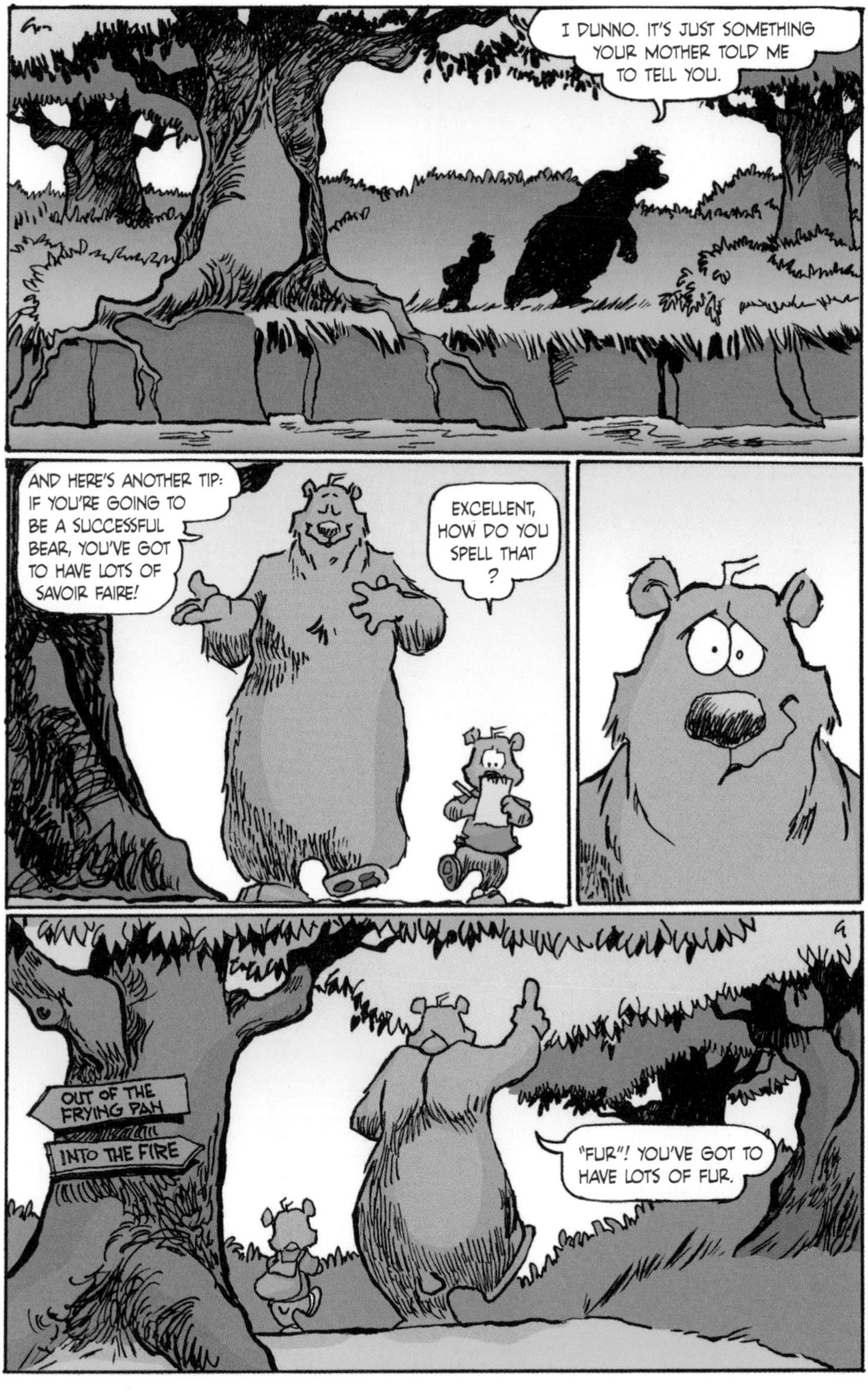
I DUNNO. IT'S JUST SOMETHING YOUR MOTHER TOLD ME TO TELL YOU.
AND HERE'S ANOTHER TIP: IF YOU'RE GOING TO BE A SUCCESSFUL BEAR, YOU'VE GOT TO HAVE LOTS OF SAVOIR FAIRE!
EXCELLENT, HOW DO YOU SPELL THAT ?
OUT OF THE FRYING PAN
INTO THE FIRE
"FUR"! YOU'VE GOT TO HAVE LOTS OF FUR.

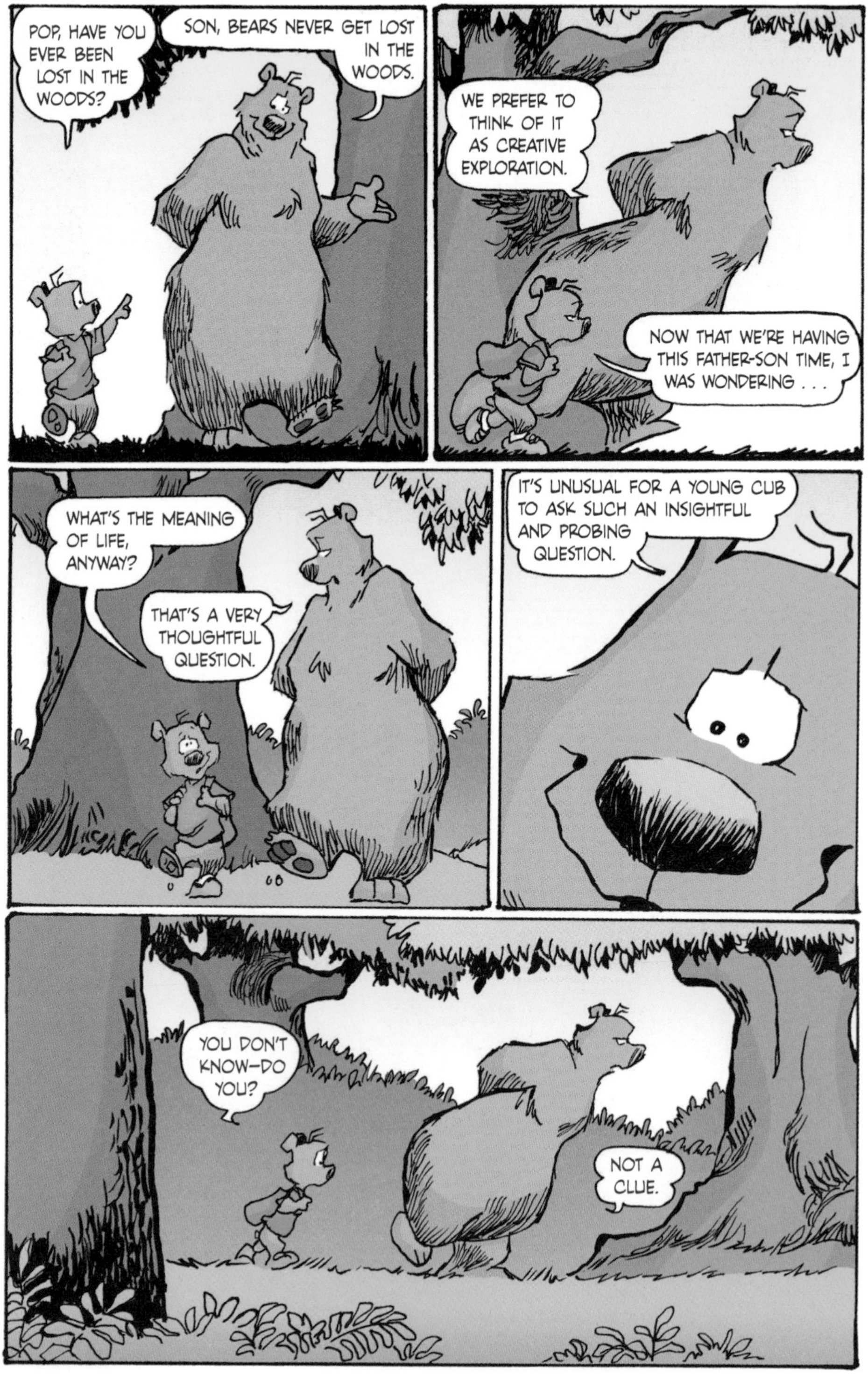
POP, HAVE YOU EVER BEEN LOST IN THE WOODS?
SON, BEARS NEVER GET LOST IN THE WOODS.
WE PREFER TO THINK OF IT AS CREATIVE EXPLORATION.
NOW THAT WE'RE HAVING THIS FATHER-SON TIME, I WAS WONDERING . . .
WHAT'S THE MEANING OF LIFE, ANYWAY?
THAT'S A VERY THOUGHTFUL QUESTION.
IT'S UNUSUAL FOR A YOUNG CUB TO ASK SUCH AN INSIGHTFUL AND PROBING QUESTION.
YOU DON'T KNOW—DO YOU?
NOT A CLUE.

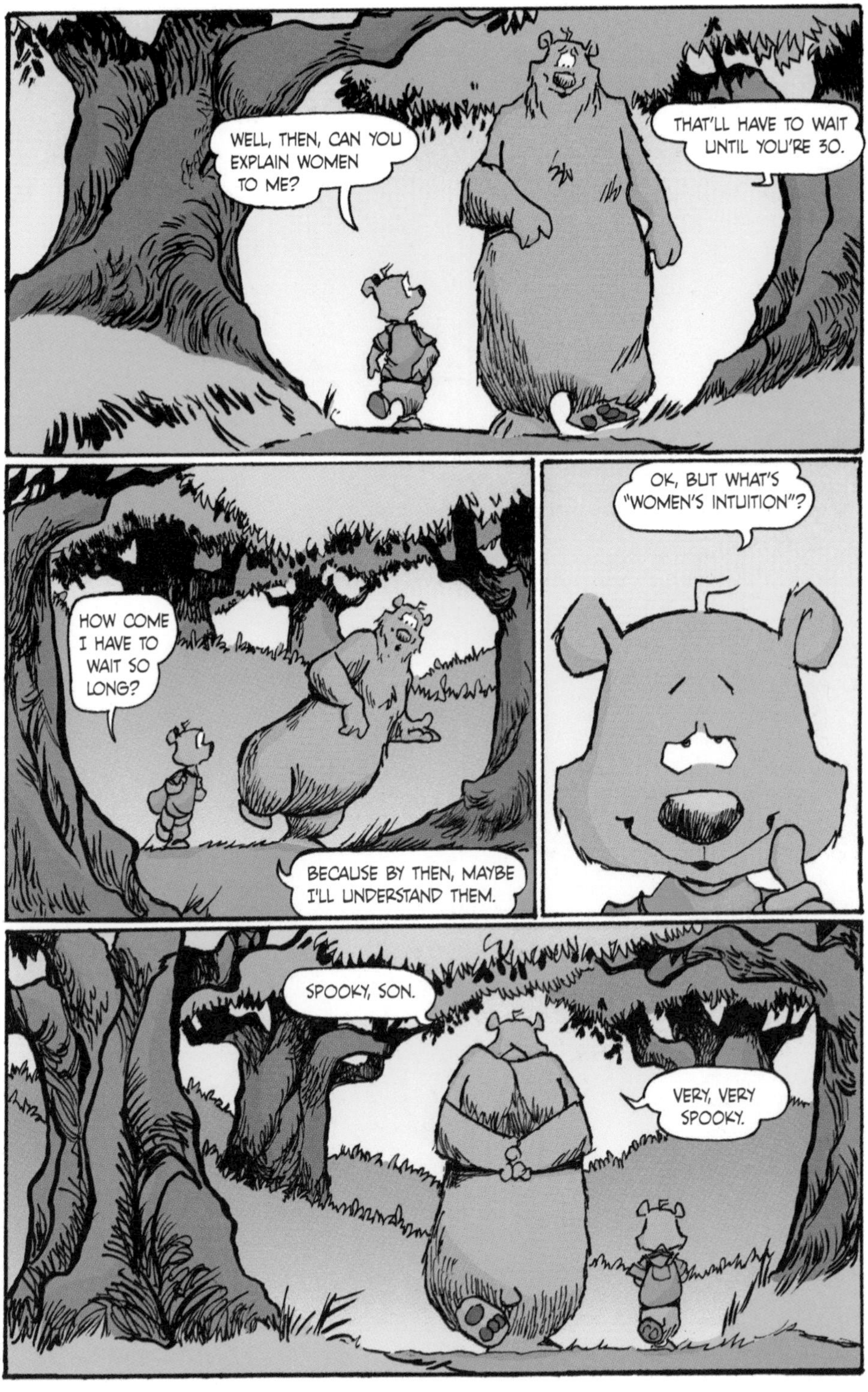
WELL, THEN, CAN YOU EXPLAIN WOMEN TO ME?
THAT'LL HAVE TO WAIT UNTIL YOU'RE 30.
HOW COME I HAVE TO WAIT SO LONG?
BECAUSE BY THEN, MAYBE I'LL UNDERSTAND THEM.
OK, BUT WHAT'S "WOMEN'S INTUITION"?
SPOOKY, SON.
VERY, VERY SPOOKY.

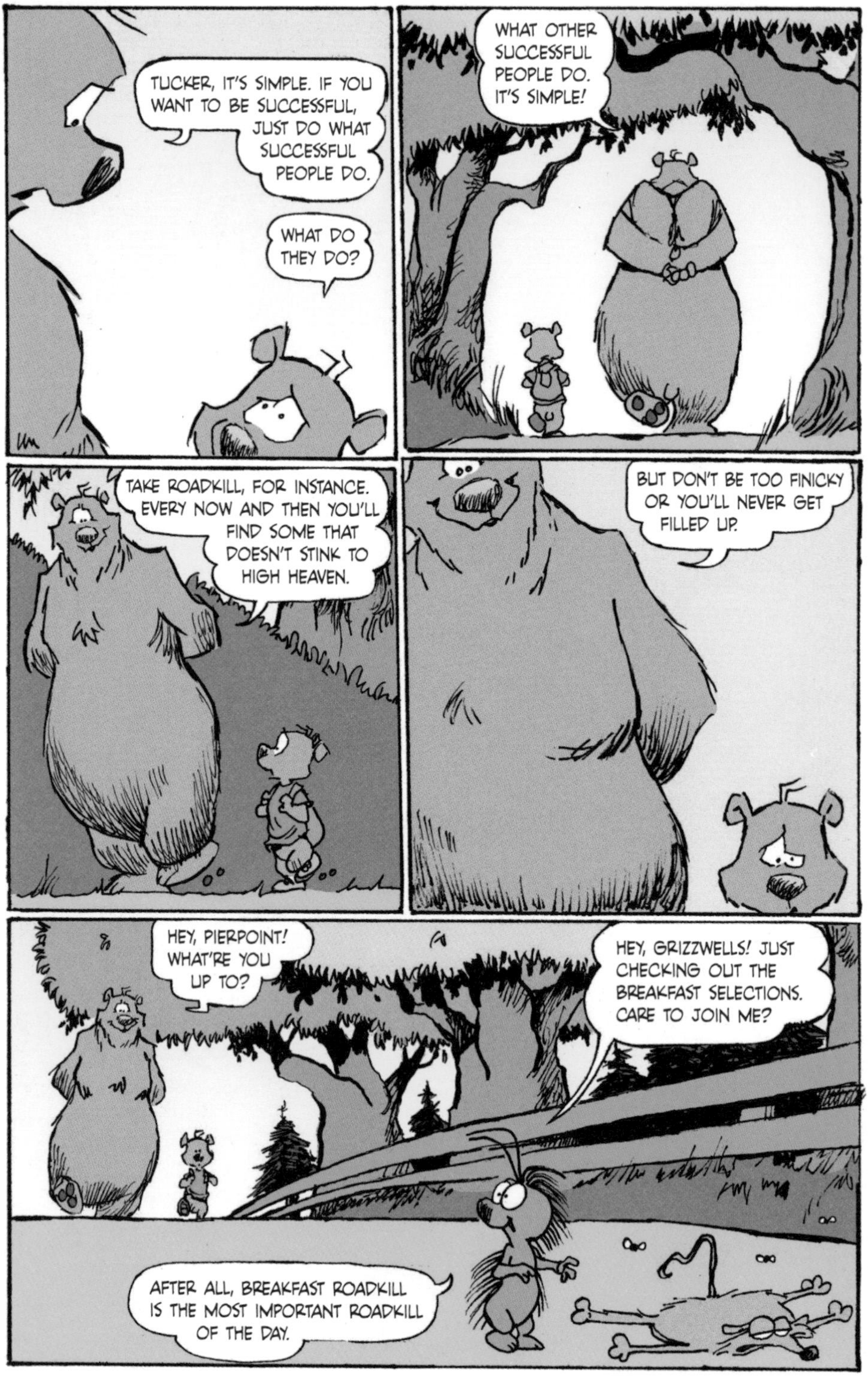
TUCKER, IT'S SIMPLE. IF YOU WANT TO BE SUCCESSFUL, JUST DO WHAT SUCCESSFUL PEOPLE DO.
WHAT DO THEY DO?
WHAT OTHER SUCCESSFUL PEOPLE DO. IT'S SIMPLE!
TAKE ROADKILL, FOR INSTANCE. EVERY NOW AND THEN YOU'LL FIND SOME THAT DOESN'T STINK TO HIGH HEAVEN.
BUT DON'T BE TOO FINICKY OR YOU'LL NEVER GET FILLED UP.
HEY, PIERPOINT! WHAT'RE YOU UP TO?
HEY, GRIZZWELLS! JUST CHECKING OUT THE BREAKFAST SELECTIONS. CARE TO JOIN ME?
AFTER ALL, BREAKFAST ROADKILL IS THE MOST IMPORTANT ROADKILL OF THE DAY.

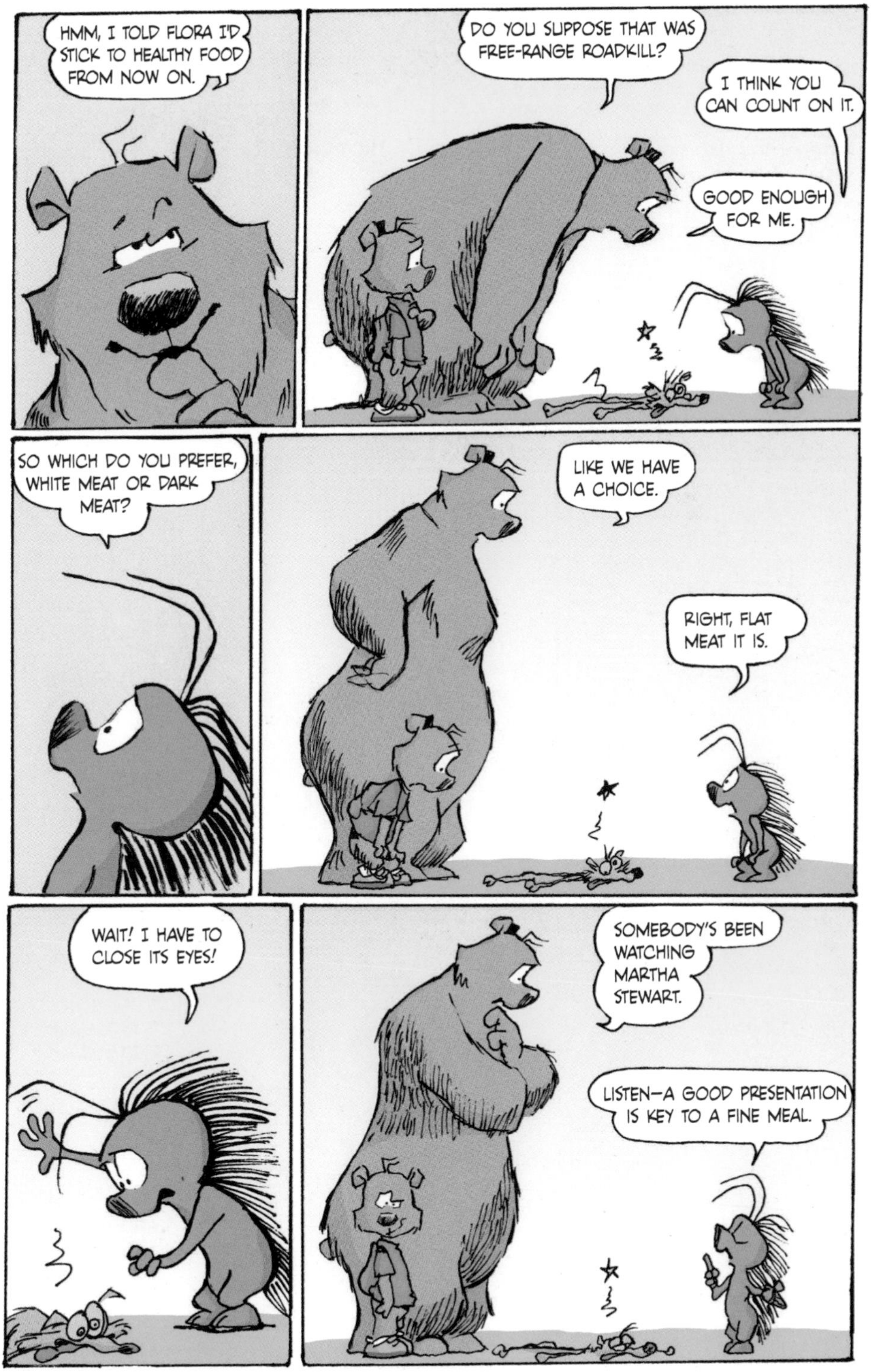
HMM, I TOLD FLORA I'D STICK TO HEALTHY FOOD FROM NOW ON.
DO YOU SUPPOSE THAT WAS FREE-RANGE ROADKILL?
I THINK YOU CAN COUNT ON IT.
GOOD ENOUGH FOR ME.
SO WHICH DO YOU PREFER, WHITE MEAT OR DARK MEAT?
LIKE WE HAVE A CHOICE.
RIGHT, FLAT MEAT IT IS.
WAIT! I HAVE TO CLOSE ITS EYES!
SOMEBODY'S BEEN WATCHING MARTHA STEWART.
LISTEN—A GOOD PRESENTATION IS KEY TO A FINE MEAL.

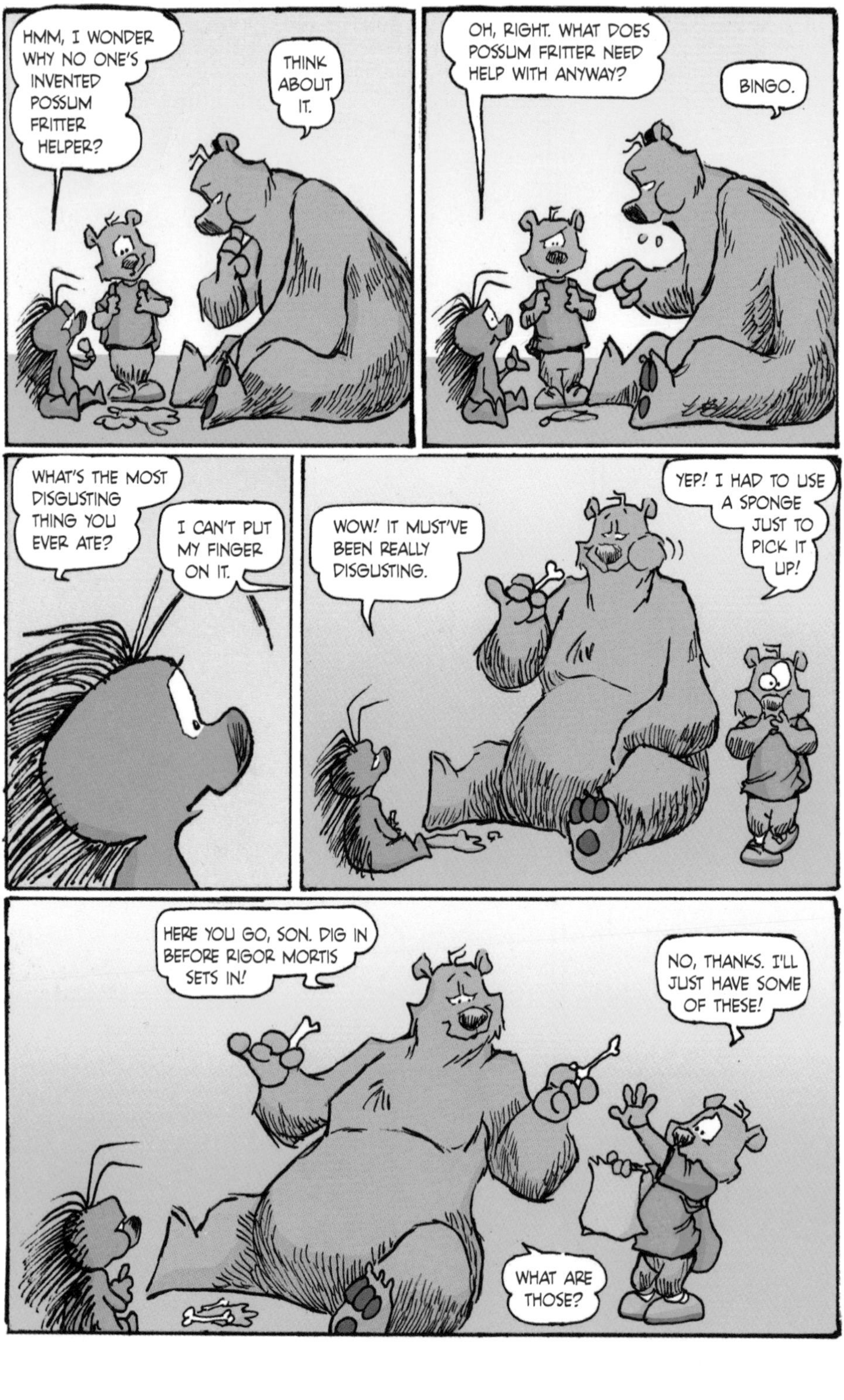
HMM, I WONDER WHY NO ONE'S INVENTED POSSUM FRITTER HELPER?
THINK ABOUT IT.
OH, RIGHT. WHAT DOES POSSUM FRITTER NEED HELP WITH ANYWAY?
BINGO.
WHAT'S THE MOST DISGUSTING THING YOU EVER ATE?
I CAN'T PUT MY FINGER ON IT.
WOW! IT MUST'VE BEEN REALLY DISGUSTING.
YEP! I HAD TO USE A SPONGE JUST TO PICK IT UP!
HERE YOU GO, SON. DIG IN BEFORE RIGOR MORTIS SETS IN!
NO, THANKS. I'LL JUST HAVE SOME OF THESE!
WHAT ARE THOSE?

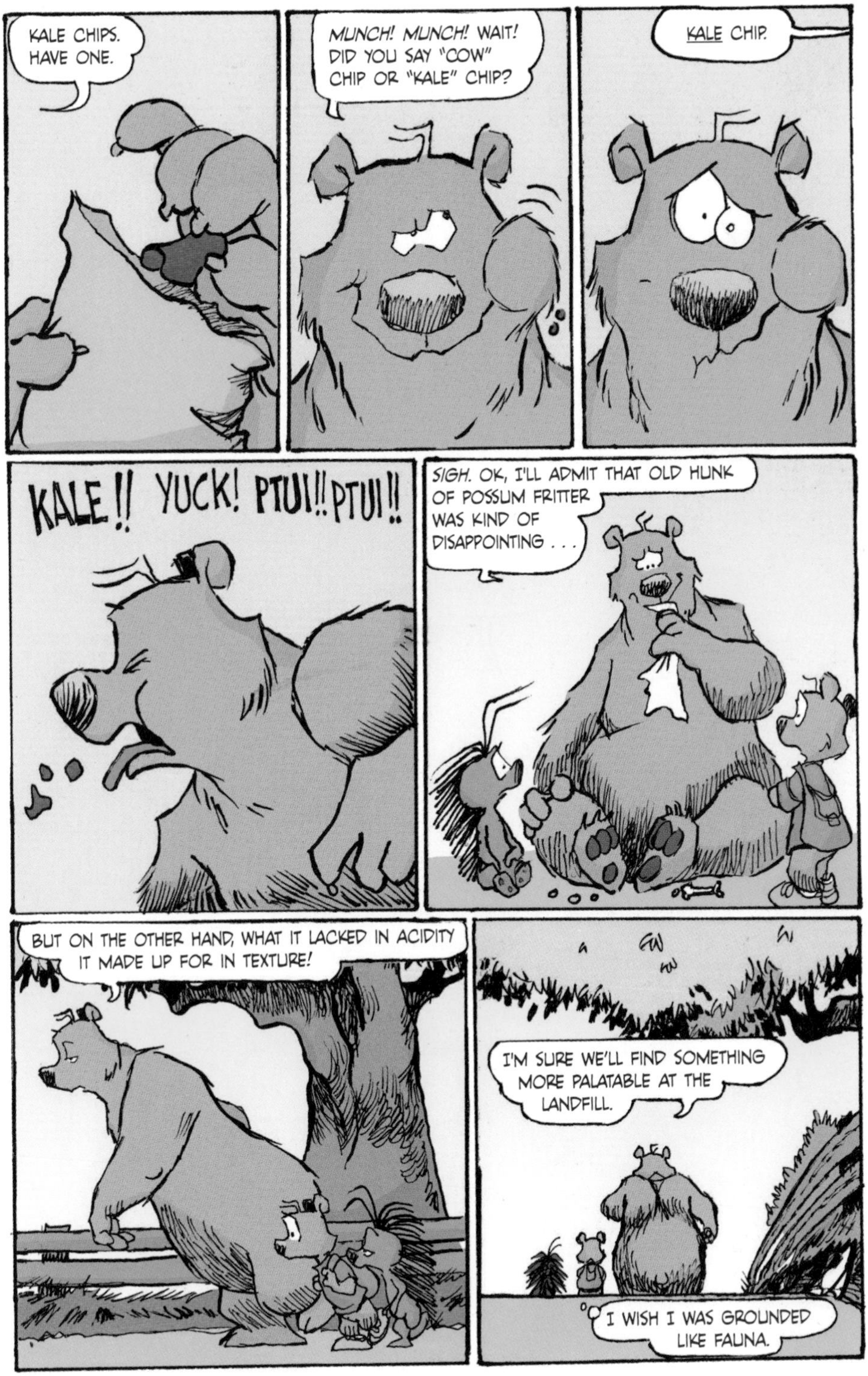
KALE CHIPS. HAVE ONE.
MUNCH! MUNCH! WAIT! DID YOU SAY "COW" CHIP OR "KALE" CHIP?
KALE CHIP.
KALE!! YUCK! PTUI!! PTUI!!
SIGH. OK, I'LL ADMIT THAT OLD HUNK OF POSSUM FRITTER WAS KIND OF DISAPPOINTING . . .
BUT ON THE OTHER HAND, WHAT IT LACKED IN ACIDITY IT MADE UP FOR IN TEXTURE!
I'M SURE WE'LL FIND SOMETHING MORE PALATABLE AT THE LANDFILL.
I WISH I WAS GROUNDED LIKE FAUNA.

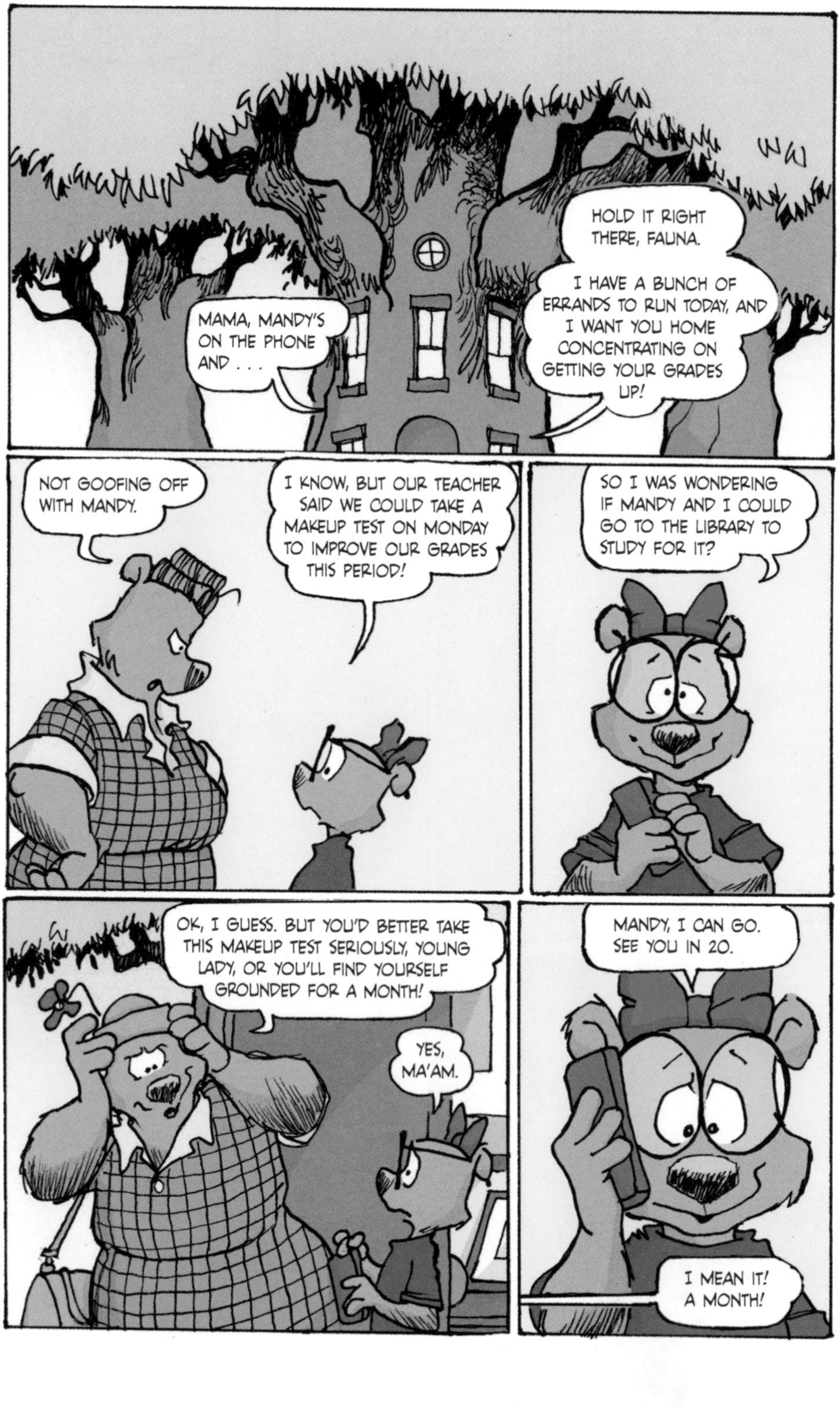
MAMA, MANDY'S ON THE PHONE AND . . .
HOLD IT RIGHT THERE, FAUNA.
I HAVE A BUNCH OF ERRANDS TO RUN TODAY, AND I WANT YOU HOME CONCENTRATING ON GETTING YOUR GRADES UP!
NOT GOOFING OFF WITH MANDY.
I KNOW, BUT OUR TEACHER SAID WE COULD TAKE A MAKEUP TEST ON MONDAY TO IMPROVE OUR GRADES THIS PERIOD!
SO I WAS WONDERING IF MANDY AND I COULD GO TO THE LIBRARY TO STUDY FOR IT?
OK, I GUESS. BUT YOU'D BETTER TAKE THIS MAKEUP TEST SERIOUSLY, YOUNG LADY, OR YOU'LL FIND YOURSELF GROUNDED FOR A MONTH!
YES, MA'AM.
MANDY, I CAN GO. SEE YOU IN 20.
I MEAN IT! A MONTH!

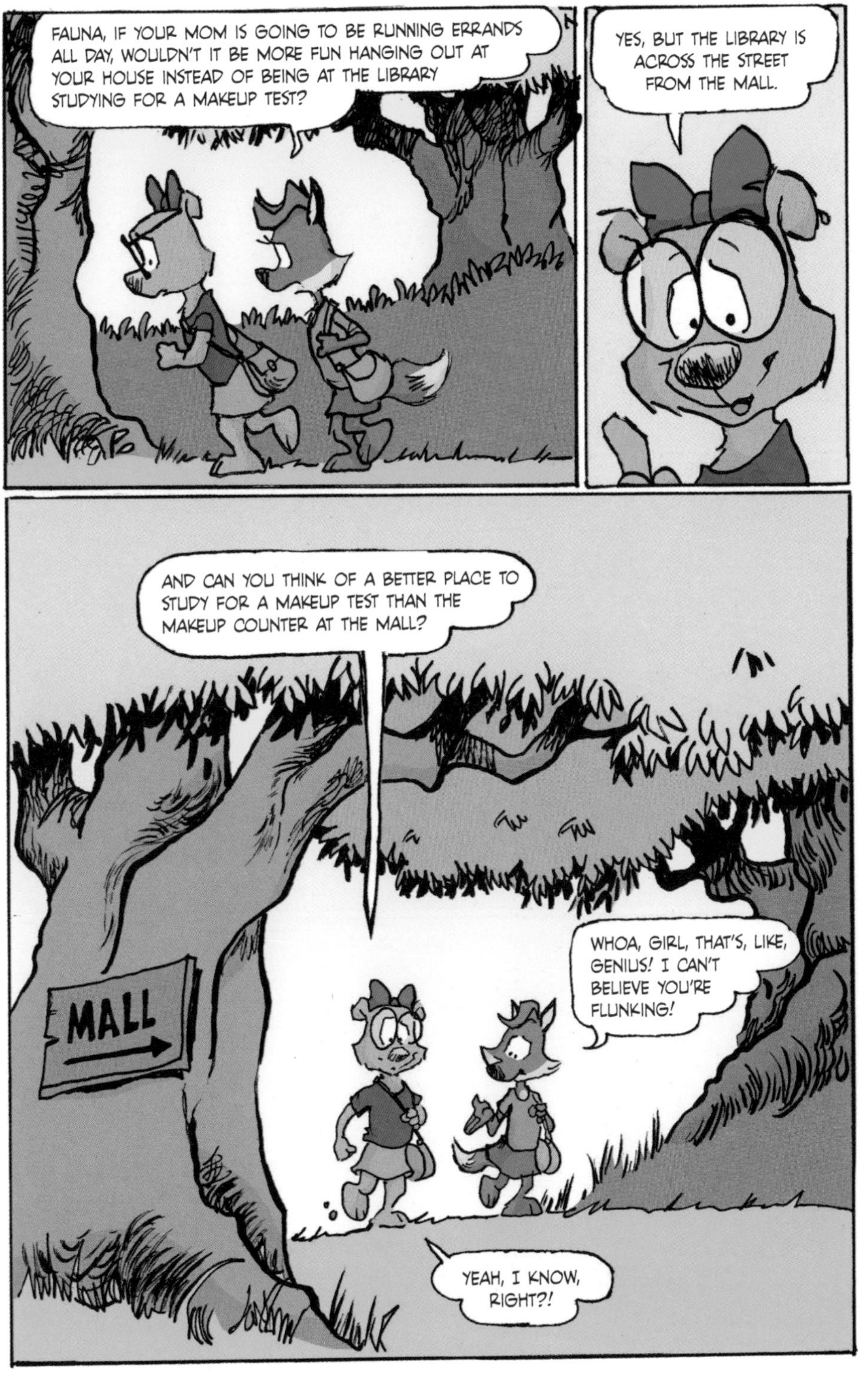
FAUNA, IF YOUR MOM IS GOING TO BE RUNNING ERRANDS ALL DAY, WOULDN'T IT BE MORE FUN HANGING OUT AT YOUR HOUSE INSTEAD OF BEING AT THE LIBRARY STUDYING FOR A MAKEUP TEST?
YES, BUT THE LIBRARY IS ACROSS THE STREET FROM THE MALL.
AND CAN YOU THINK OF A BETTER PLACE TO STUDY FOR A MAKEUP TEST THAN THE MAKEUP COUNTER AT THE MALL?
MALL
WHOA, GIRL, THAT'S, LIKE, GENIUS! I CAN'T BELIEVE YOU'RE FLUNKING!
YEAH, I KNOW, RIGHT?!

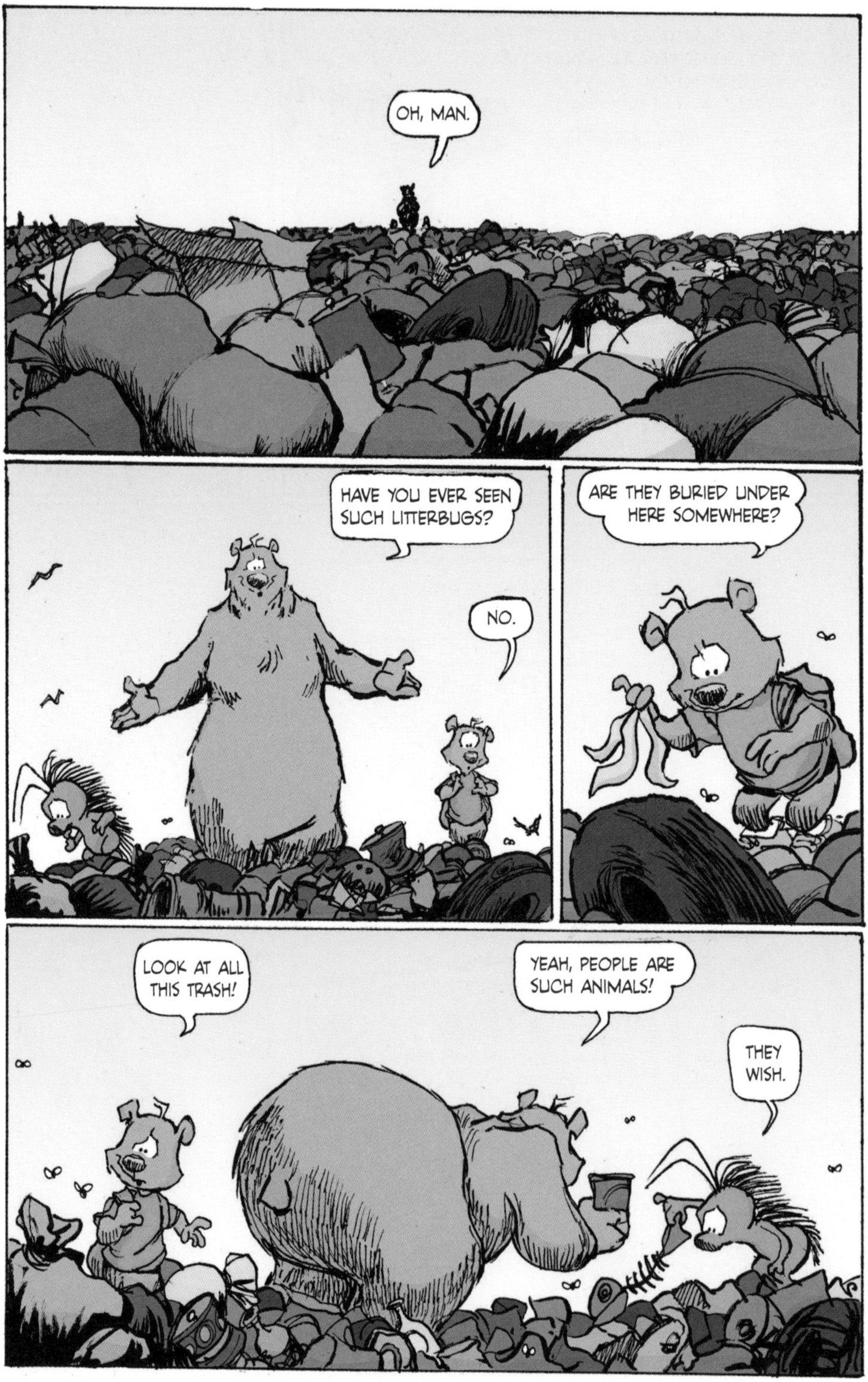
OH, MAN.
HAVE YOU EVER SEEN SUCH LITTERBUGS?
NO.
ARE THEY BURIED UNDER HERE SOMEWHERE?
LOOK AT ALL THIS TRASH!
YEAH, PEOPLE ARE SUCH ANIMALS!
THEY WISH.

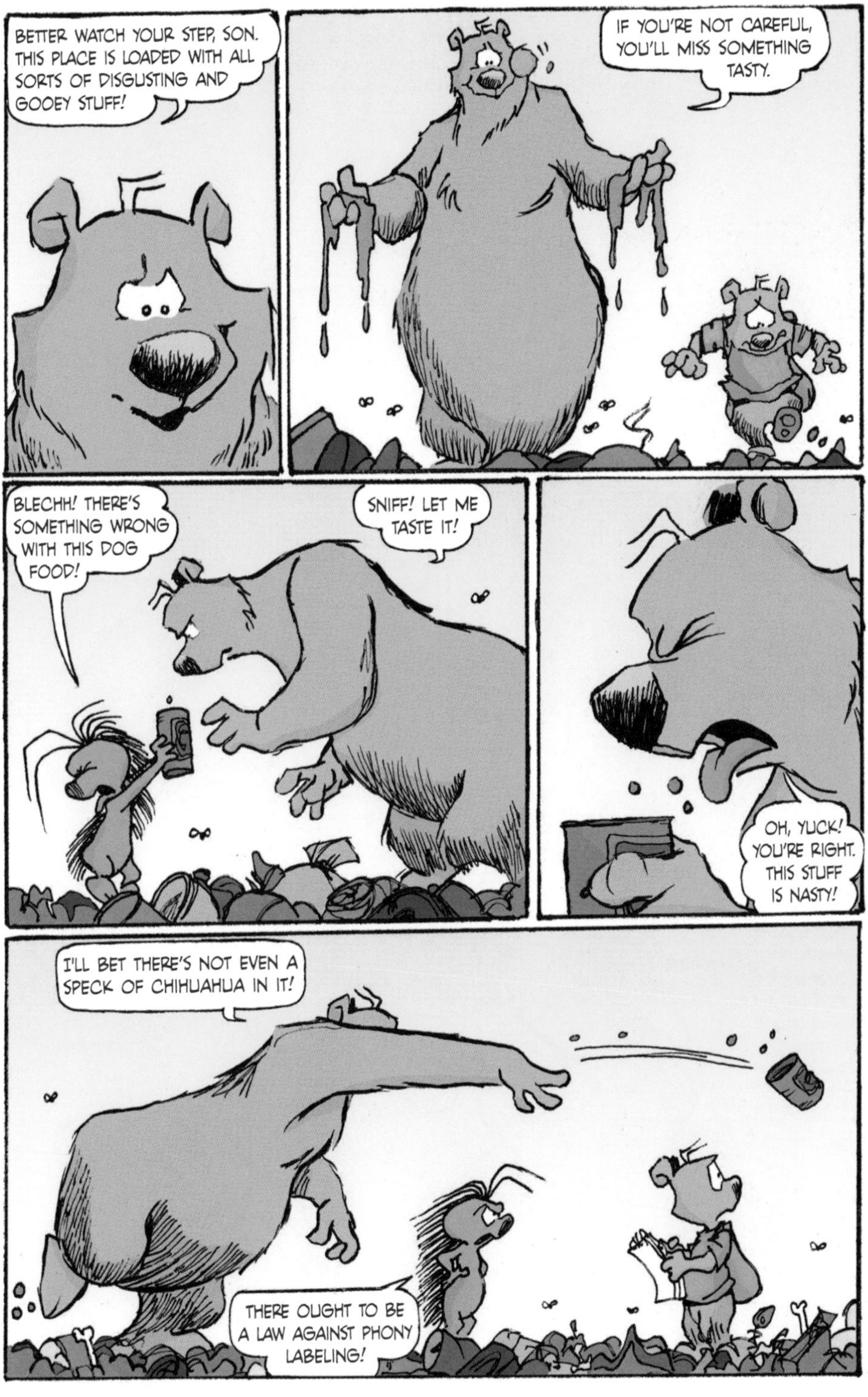
BETTER WATCH YOUR STEP, SON. THIS PLACE IS LOADED WITH ALL SORTS OF DISGUSTING AND GOOEY STUFF!
IF YOU'RE NOT CAREFUL, YOU'LL MISS SOMETHING TASTY.
BLECHH! THERE'S SOMETHING WRONG WITH THIS DOG FOOD!
SNIFF! LET ME TASTE IT!
OH, YUCK! YOU'RE RIGHT. THIS STUFF IS NASTY!
I'LL BET THERE'S NOT EVEN A SPECK OF CHIHUAHUA IN IT!
THERE OUGHT TO BE A LAW AGAINST PHONY LABELING!

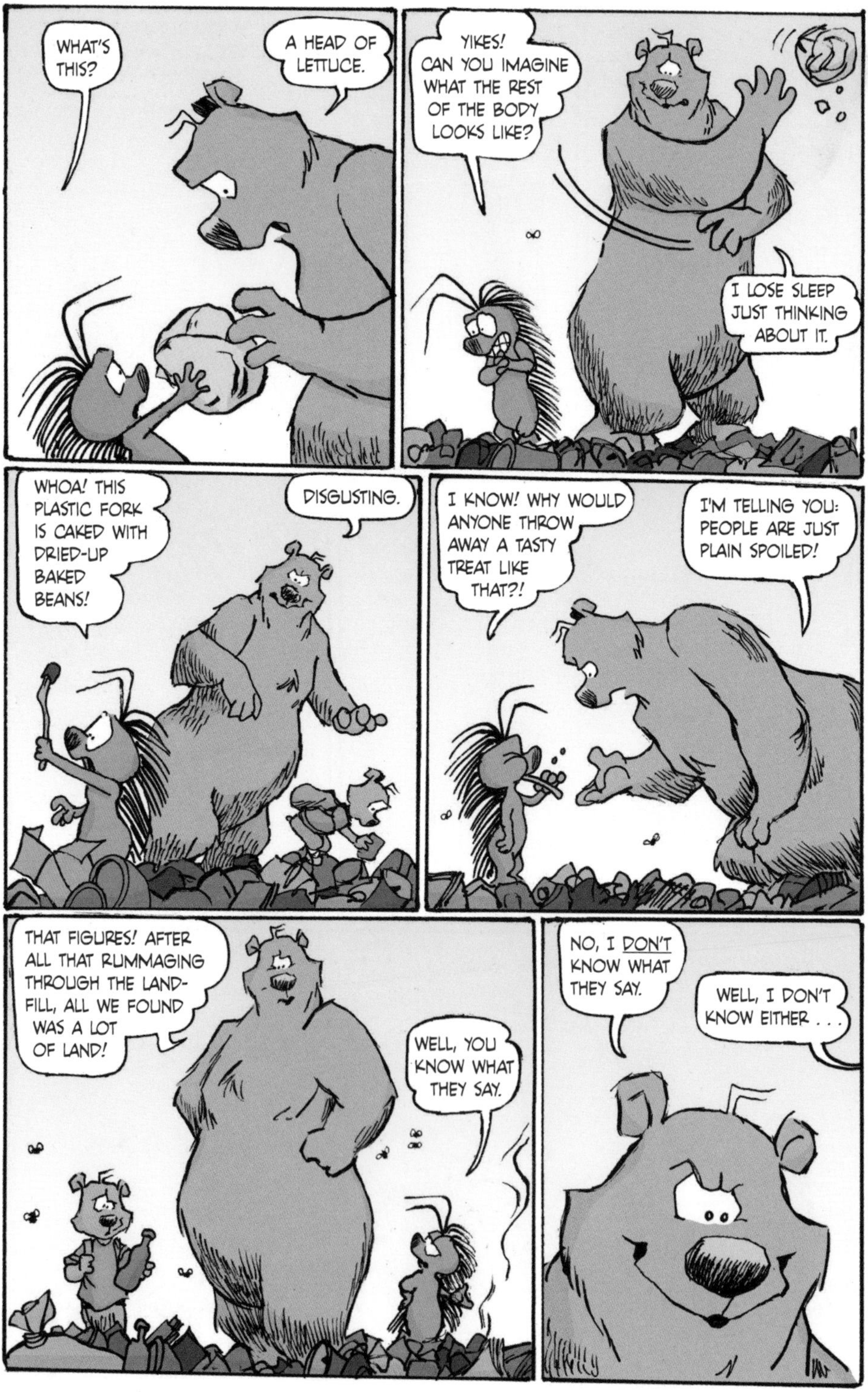
WHAT'S THIS?
A HEAD OF LETTUCE.
YIKES! CAN YOU IMAGINE WHAT THE REST OF THE BODY LOOKS LIKE?
I LOSE SLEEP JUST THINKING ABOUT IT.
WHOA! THIS PLASTIC FORK IS CAKED WITH DRIED-UP BAKED BEANS!
DISGUSTING.
I KNOW! WHY WOULD ANYONE THROW AWAY A TASTY TREAT LIKE THAT?!
I'M TELLING YOU: PEOPLE ARE JUST PLAIN SPOILED!
THAT FIGURES! AFTER ALL THAT RUMMAGING THROUGH THE LAND-FILL, ALL WE FOUND WAS A LOT OF LAND!
WELL, YOU KNOW WHAT THEY SAY.
NO, I DON'T KNOW WHAT THEY SAY.
WELL, I DON'T KNOW EITHER . . .

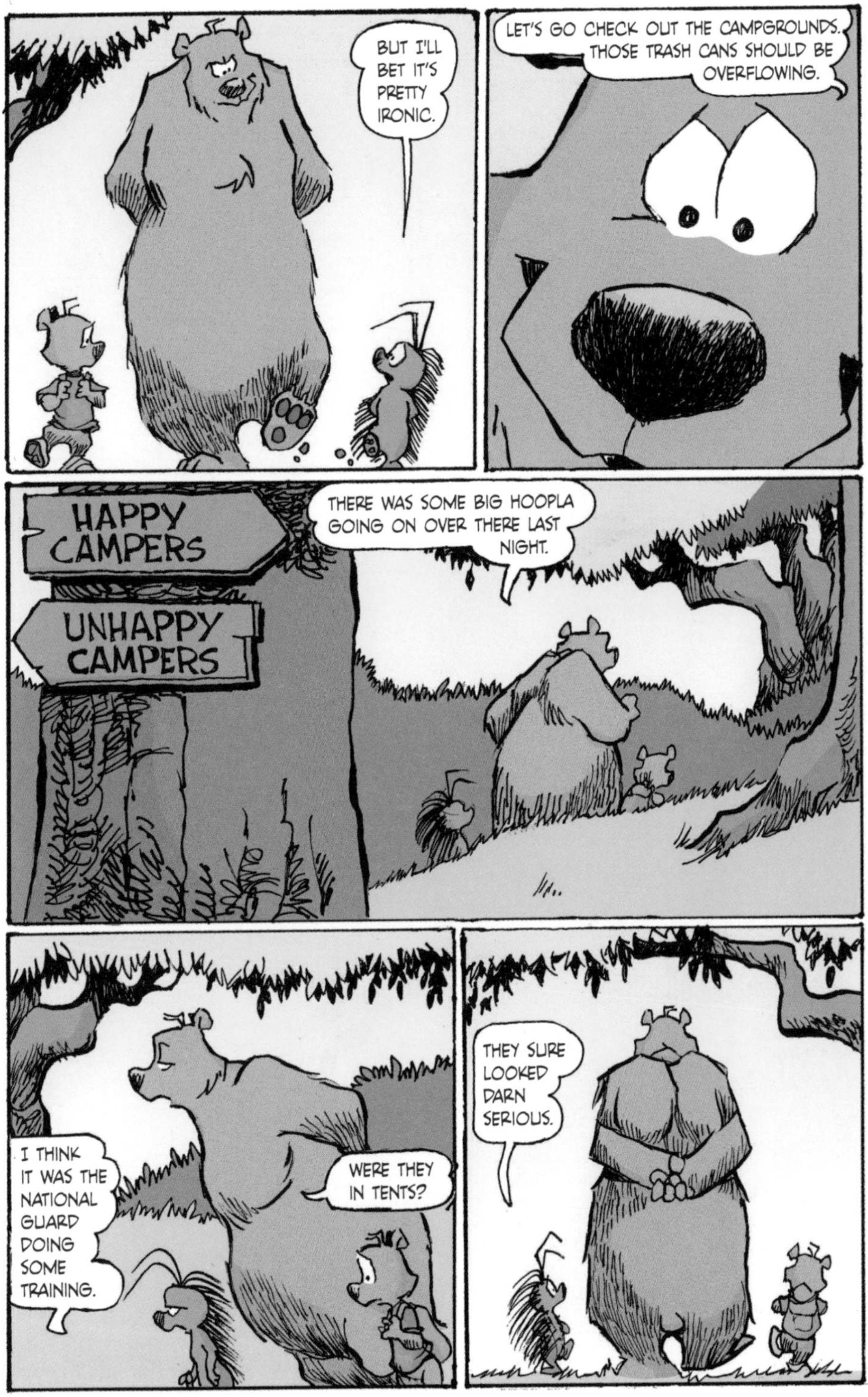

BUT I'LL BET IT'S PRETTY IRONIC.
LET'S GO CHECK OUT THE CAMPGROUNDS. THOSE TRASH CANS SHOULD BE OVERFLOWING.
HAPPY CAMPERS
UNHAPPY CAMPERS
THERE WAS SOME BIG HOOPLA GOING ON OVER THERE LAST NIGHT.
I THINK IT WAS THE NATIONAL GUARD DOING SOME TRAINING.
WERE THEY IN TENTS?
THEY SURE LOOKED DARN SERIOUS.

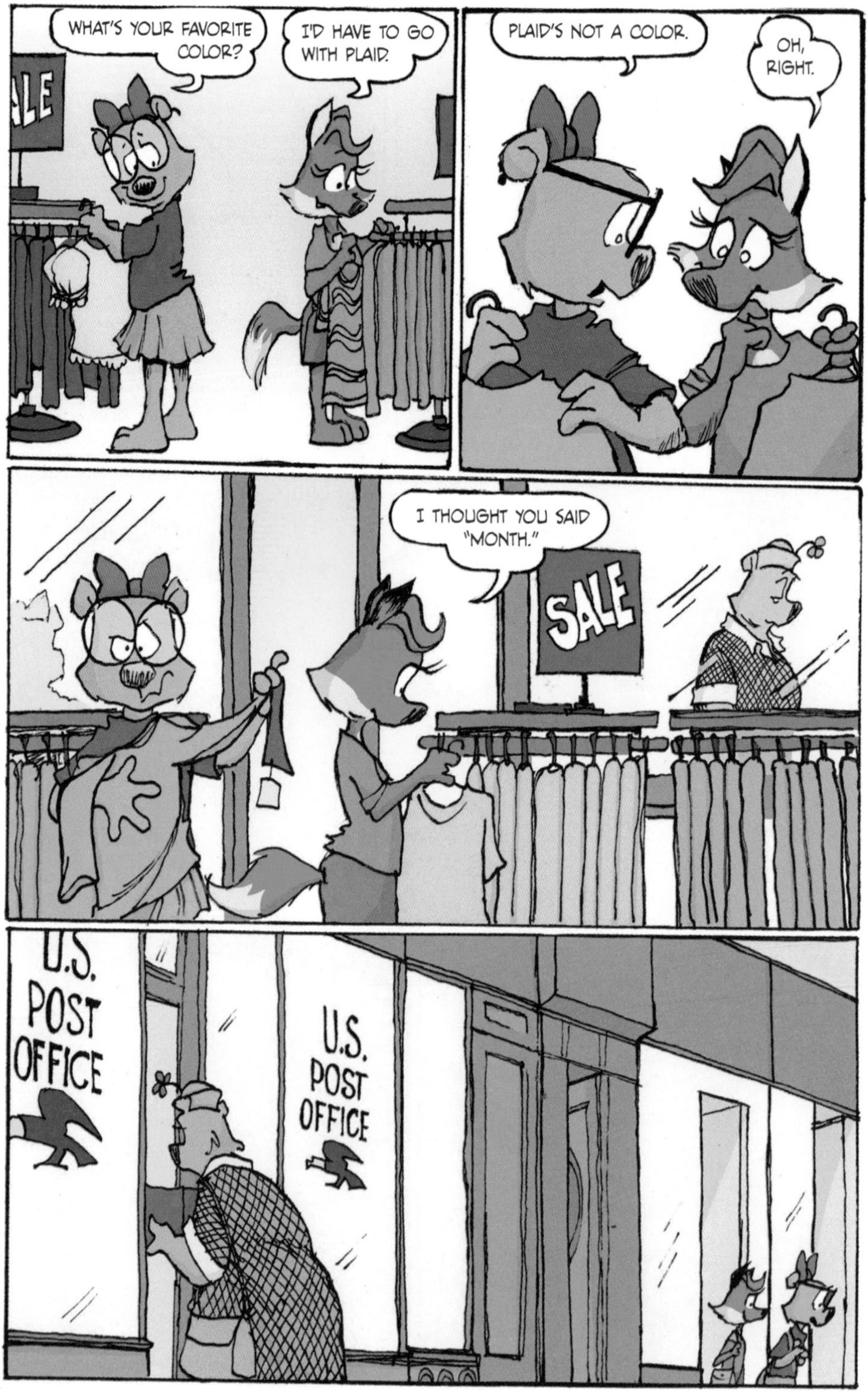
WHAT'S YOUR FAVORITE COLOR?
I'D HAVE TO GO WITH PLAID.
PLAID'S NOT A COLOR.
OH, RIGHT.
I THOUGHT YOU SAID "MONTH."
SALE
U.S. POST OFFICE
U.S. POST OFFICE

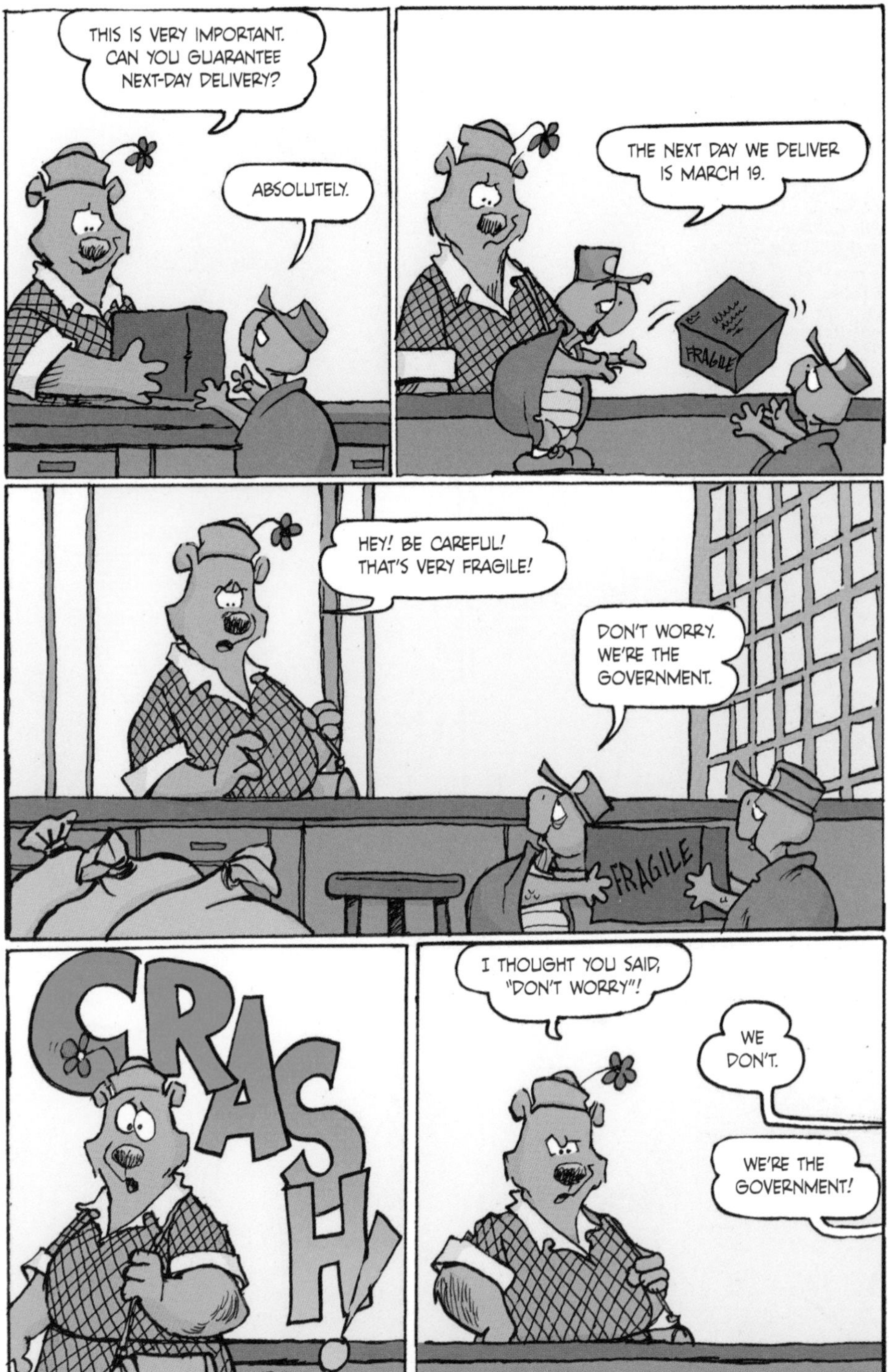
THIS IS VERY IMPORTANT. CAN YOU GUARANTEE NEXT-DAY DELIVERY?
ABSOLUTELY.
THE NEXT DAY WE DELIVER IS MARCH 19.
FRAGILE
HEY! BE CAREFUL! THAT'S VERY FRAGILE!
DON'T WORRY. WE'RE THE GOVERNMENT.
FRAGILE
CRASH!
I THOUGHT YOU SAID, "DON'T WORRY"!
WE DON'T.
WE'RE THE GOVERNMENT!

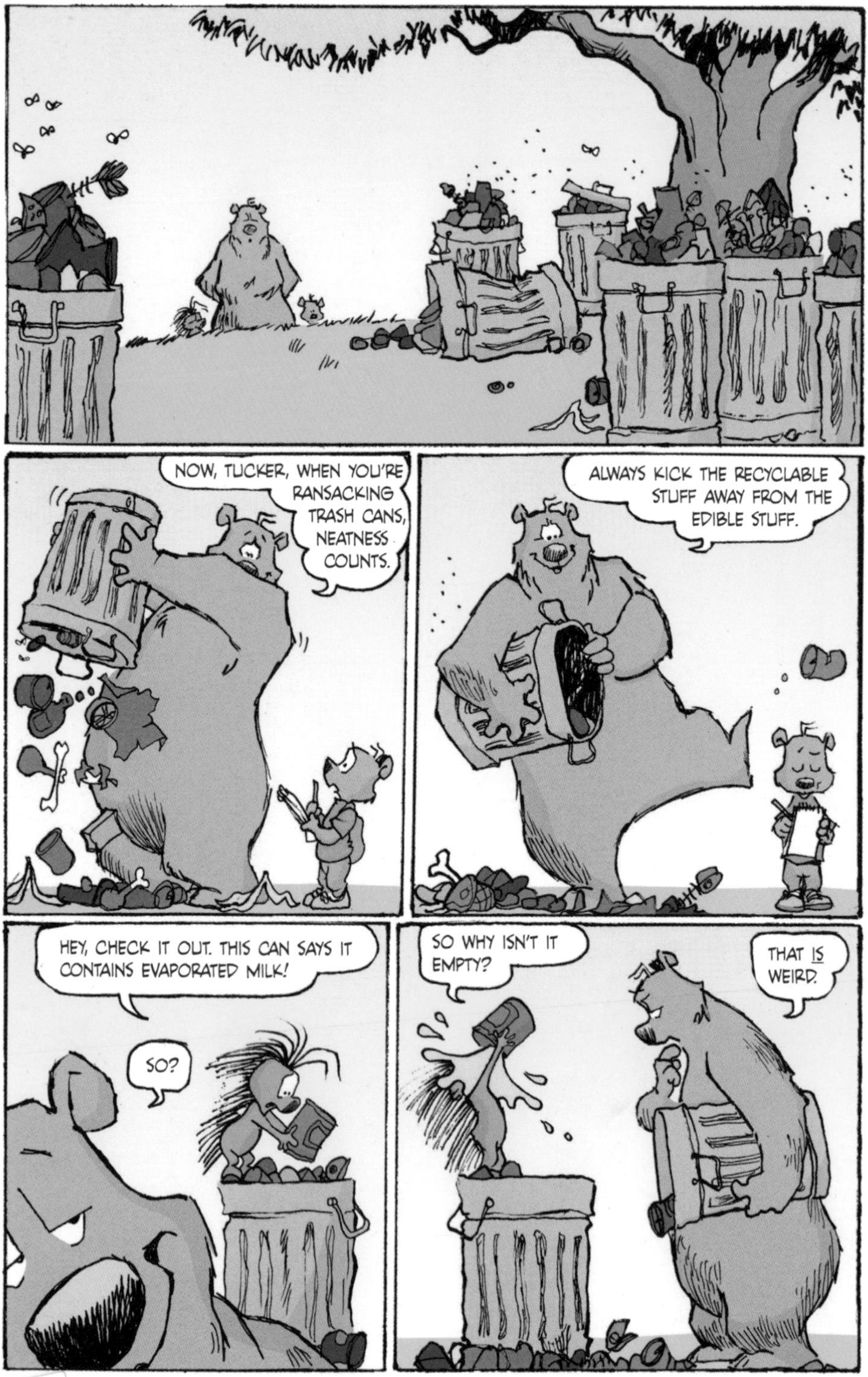
NOW, TUCKER, WHEN YOU'RE RANSACKING TRASH CANS, NEATNESS COUNTS.
ALWAYS KICK THE RECYCLABLE STUFF AWAY FROM THE EDIBLE STUFF.
HEY, CHECK IT OUT. THIS CAN SAYS IT CONTAINS EVAPORATED MILK!
SO?
SO WHY ISN'T IT EMPTY?
THAT IS WEIRD.

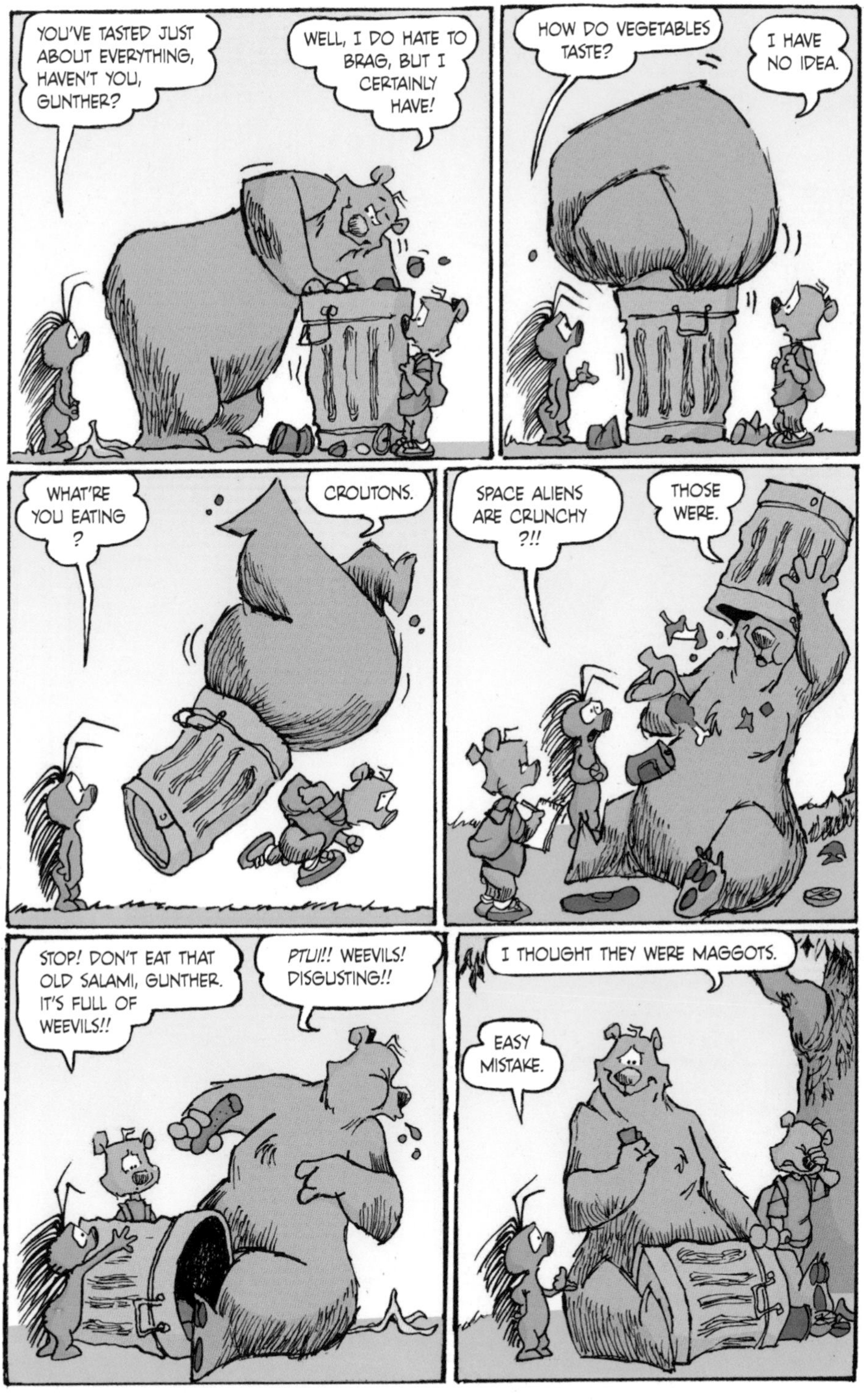
YOU'VE TASTED JUST ABOUT EVERYTHING, HAVEN'T YOU, GUNTHER?
WELL, I DO HATE TO BRAG, BUT I CERTAINLY HAVE!
HOW DO VEGETABLES TASTE?
I HAVE NO IDEA.
WHAT'RE YOU EATING?
CROUTONS.
SPACE ALIENS ARE CRUNCHY?!!
THOSE WERE.
STOP! DON'T EAT THAT OLD SALAMI, GUNTHER. IT'S FULL OF WEEVILS!!
PTUI!! WEEVILS! DISGUSTING!!
I THOUGHT THEY WERE MAGGOTS.
EASY MISTAKE.

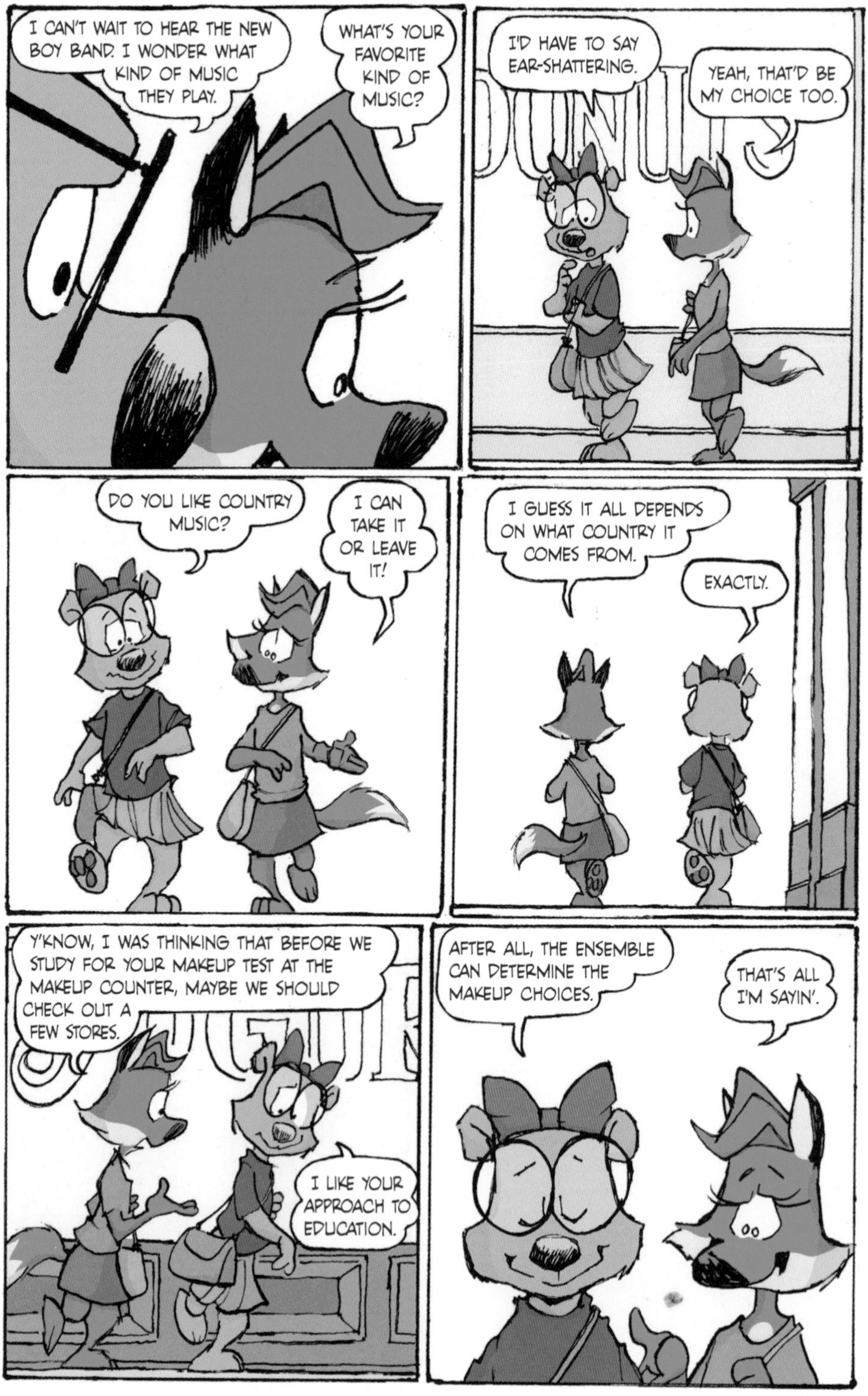
I CAN'T WAIT TO HEAR THE NEW BOY BAND. I WONDER WHAT KIND OF MUSIC THEY PLAY.
WHAT'S YOUR FAVORITE KIND OF MUSIC?
I'D HAVE TO SAY EAR-SHATTERING.
YEAH, THAT'D BE MY CHOICE TOO.
DO YOU LIKE COUNTRY MUSIC?
I CAN TAKE IT OR LEAVE IT!
I GUESS IT ALL DEPENDS ON WHAT COUNTRY IT COMES FROM.
EXACTLY.
Y'KNOW, I WAS THINKING THAT BEFORE WE STUDY FOR YOUR MAKEUP TEST AT THE MAKEUP COUNTER, MAYBE WE SHOULD CHECK OUT A FEW STORES.
I LIKE YOUR APPROACH TO EDUCATION.
AFTER ALL, THE ENSEMBLE CAN DETERMINE THE MAKEUP CHOICES.
THAT'S ALL I'M SAYIN'.

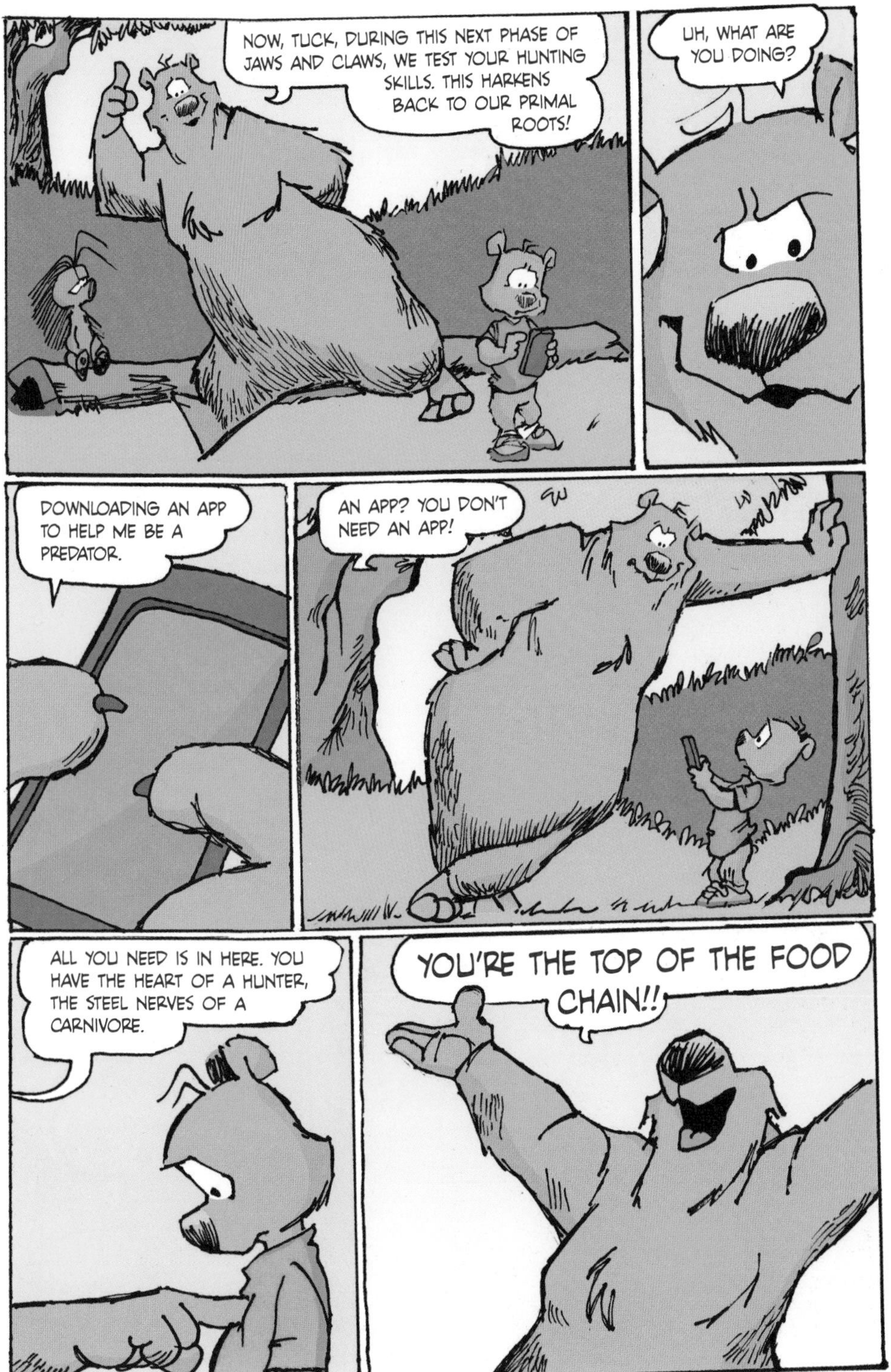
NOW, TUCK, DURING THIS NEXT PHASE OF JAWS AND CLAWS, WE TEST YOUR HUNTING SKILLS. THIS HARKENS BACK TO OUR PRIMAL ROOTS!
UH, WHAT ARE YOU DOING?
DOWNLOADING AN APP TO HELP ME BE A PREDATOR.
AN APP? YOU DON'T NEED AN APP!
ALL YOU NEED IS IN HERE. YOU HAVE THE HEART OF A HUNTER, THE STEEL NERVES OF A CARNIVORE.
YOU'RE THE TOP OF THE FOOD CHAIN!!

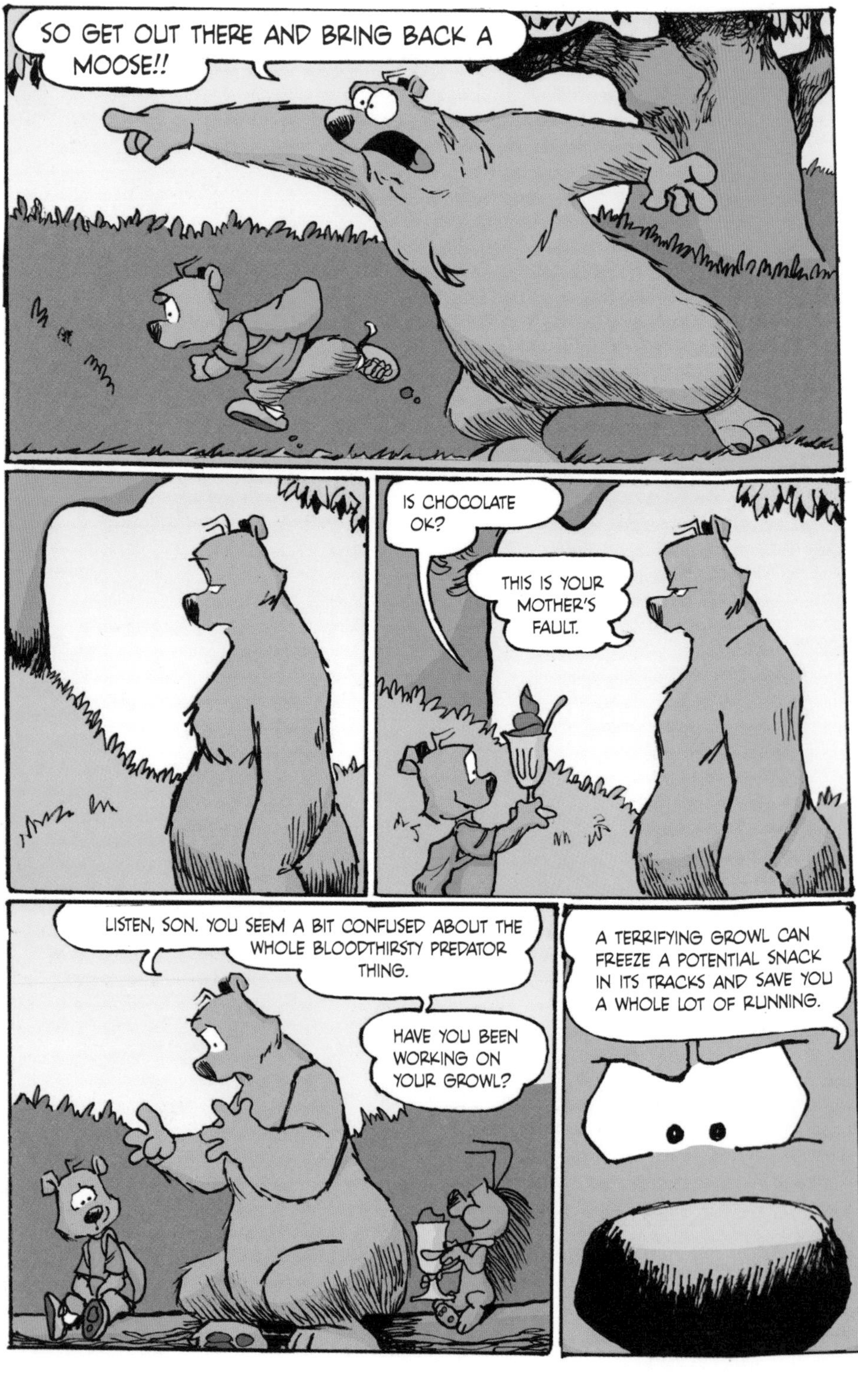
SO GET OUT THERE AND BRING BACK A MOOSE!!
IS CHOCOLATE OK?
THIS IS YOUR MOTHER'S FAULT.
LISTEN, SON. YOU SEEM A BIT CONFUSED ABOUT THE WHOLE BLOODTHIRSTY PREDATOR THING.
HAVE YOU BEEN WORKING ON YOUR GROWL?
A TERRIFYING GROWL CAN FREEZE A POTENTIAL SNACK IN ITS TRACKS AND SAVE YOU A WHOLE LOT OF RUNNING.

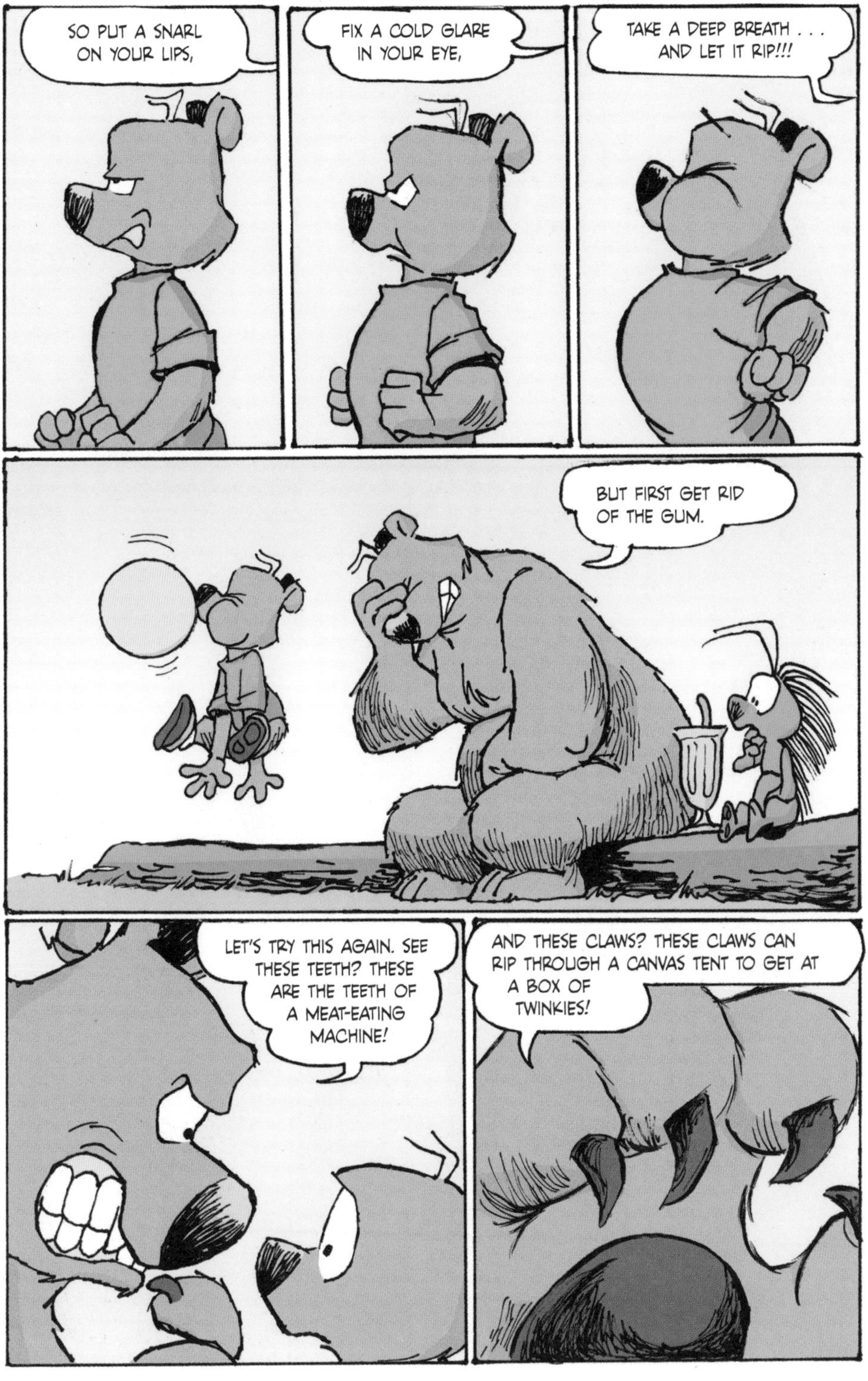
SO PUT A SNARL ON YOUR LIPS,
FIX A COLD GLARE IN YOUR EYE,
TAKE A DEEP BREATH . . . AND LET IT RIP!!!
BUT FIRST GET RID OF THE GUM.
LET'S TRY THIS AGAIN. SEE THESE TEETH? THESE ARE THE TEETH OF A MEAT-EATING MACHINE!
AND THESE CLAWS? THESE CLAWS CAN RIP THROUGH A CANVAS TENT TO GET AT A BOX OF TWINKIES!

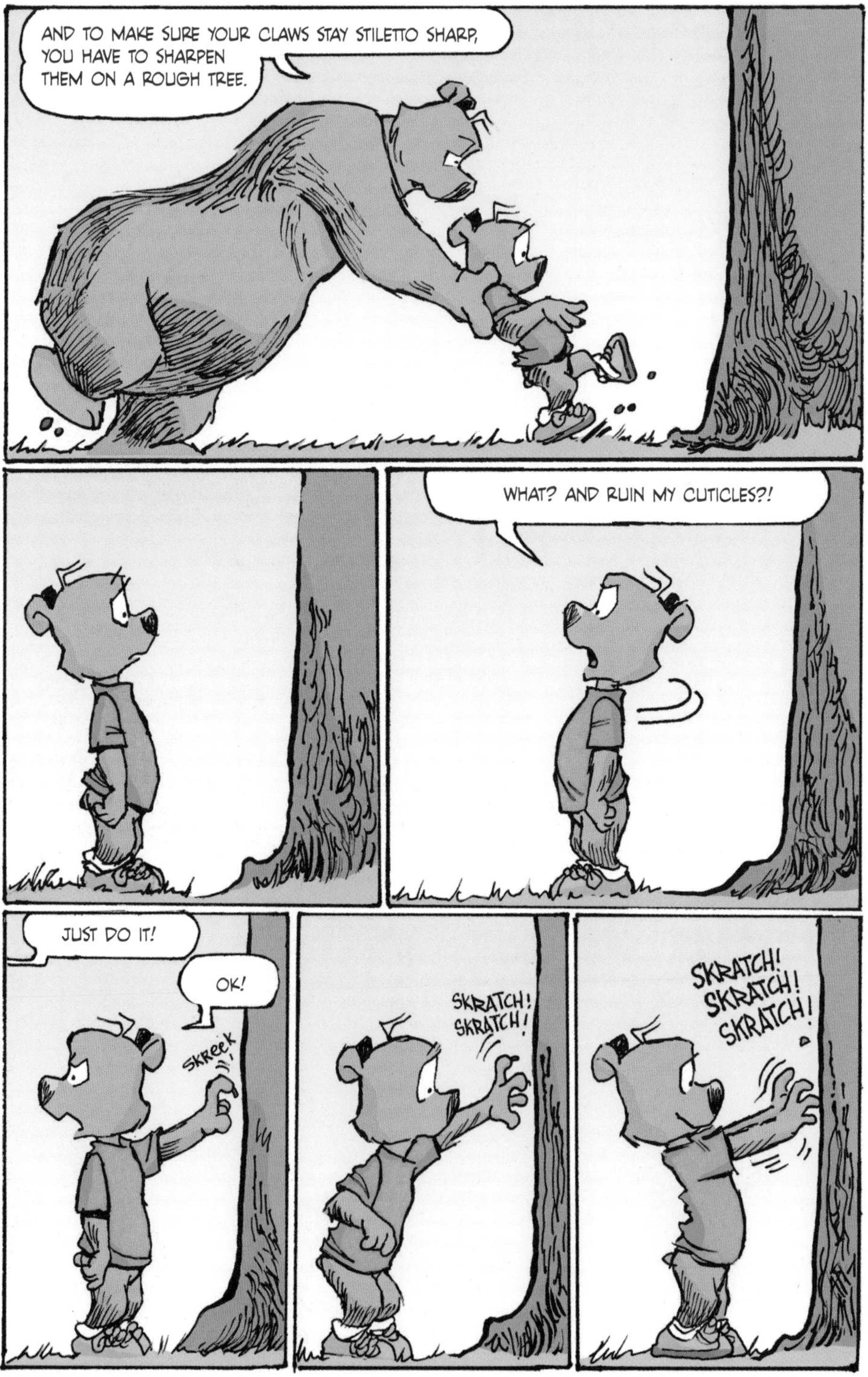
AND TO MAKE SURE YOUR CLAWS STAY STILETTO SHARP, YOU HAVE TO SHARPEN THEM ON A ROUGH TREE.
WHAT? AND RUIN MY CUTICLES?!
JUST DO IT!
OK!
SKREEK
SKRATCH! SKRATCH!
SKRATCH! SKRATCH! SKRATCH!

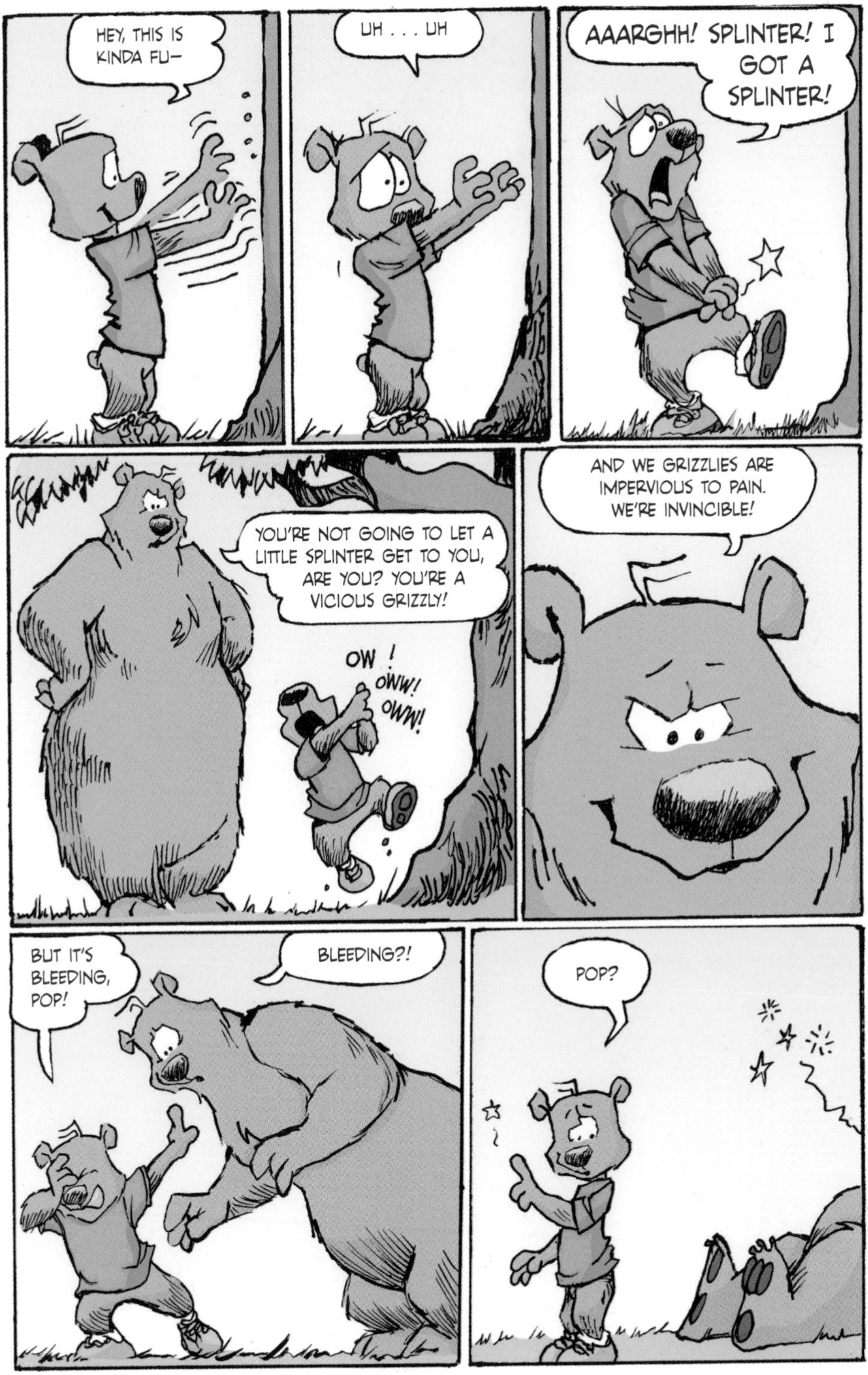
HEY, THIS IS KINDA FU—
UH . . . UH
AAARGHH! SPLINTER! I GOT A SPLINTER!
YOU'RE NOT GOING TO LET A LITTLE SPLINTER GET TO YOU, ARE YOU? YOU'RE A VICIOUS GRIZZLY!
OW! OWW! OWW!
AND WE GRIZZLIES ARE IMPERVIOUS TO PAIN. WE'RE INVINCIBLE!
BUT IT'S BLEEDING, POP!
BLEEDING?!
POP?

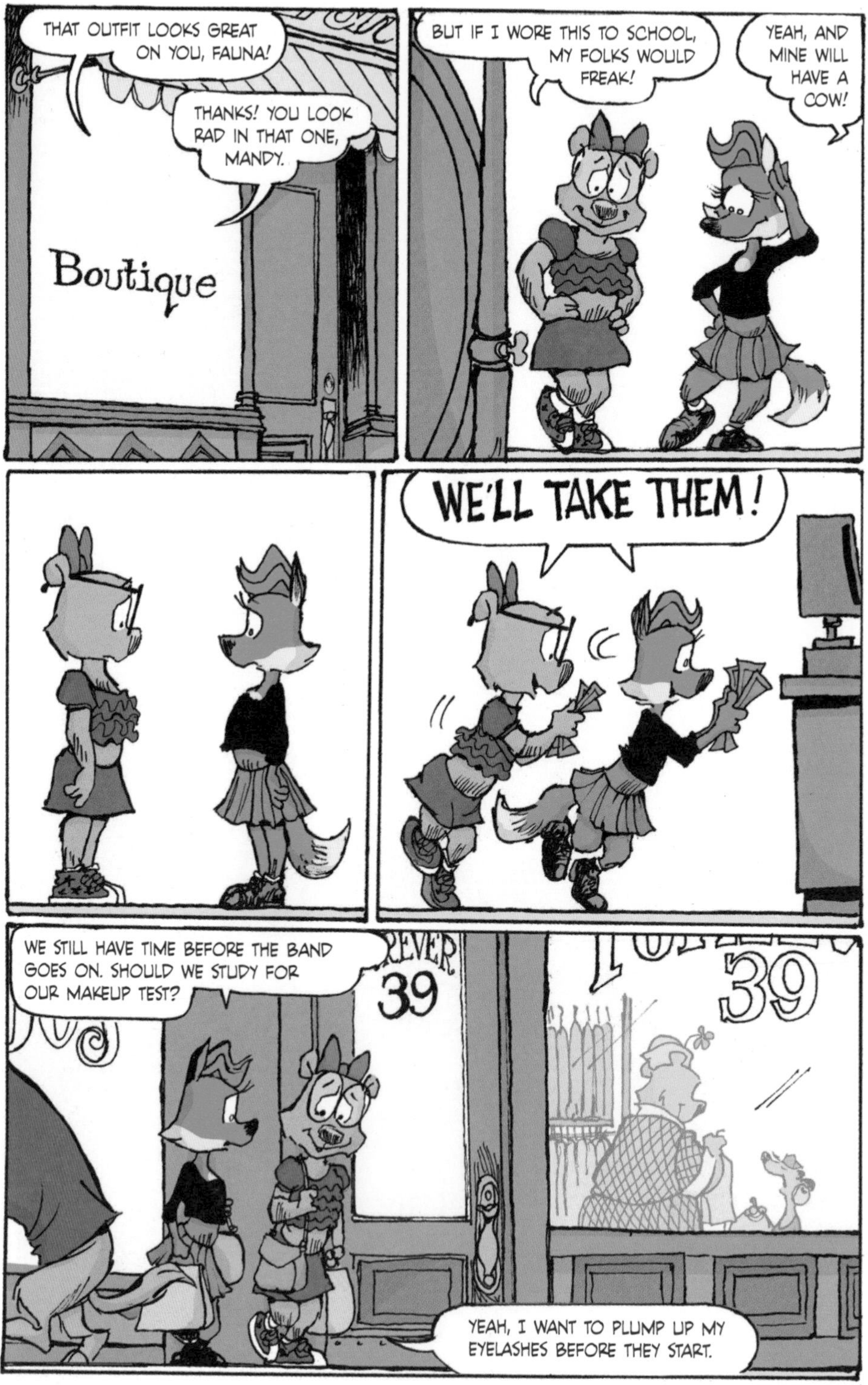
THAT OUTFIT LOOKS GREAT ON YOU, FAUNA!
THANKS! YOU LOOK RAD IN THAT ONE, MANDY.
Boutique
BUT IF I WORE THIS TO SCHOOL, MY FOLKS WOULD FREAK!
YEAH, AND MINE WILL HAVE A COW!
WE'LL TAKE THEM!
WE STILL HAVE TIME BEFORE THE BAND GOES ON. SHOULD WE STUDY FOR OUR MAKEUP TEST?
39
39
YEAH, I WANT TO PLUMP UP MY EYELASHES BEFORE THEY START.

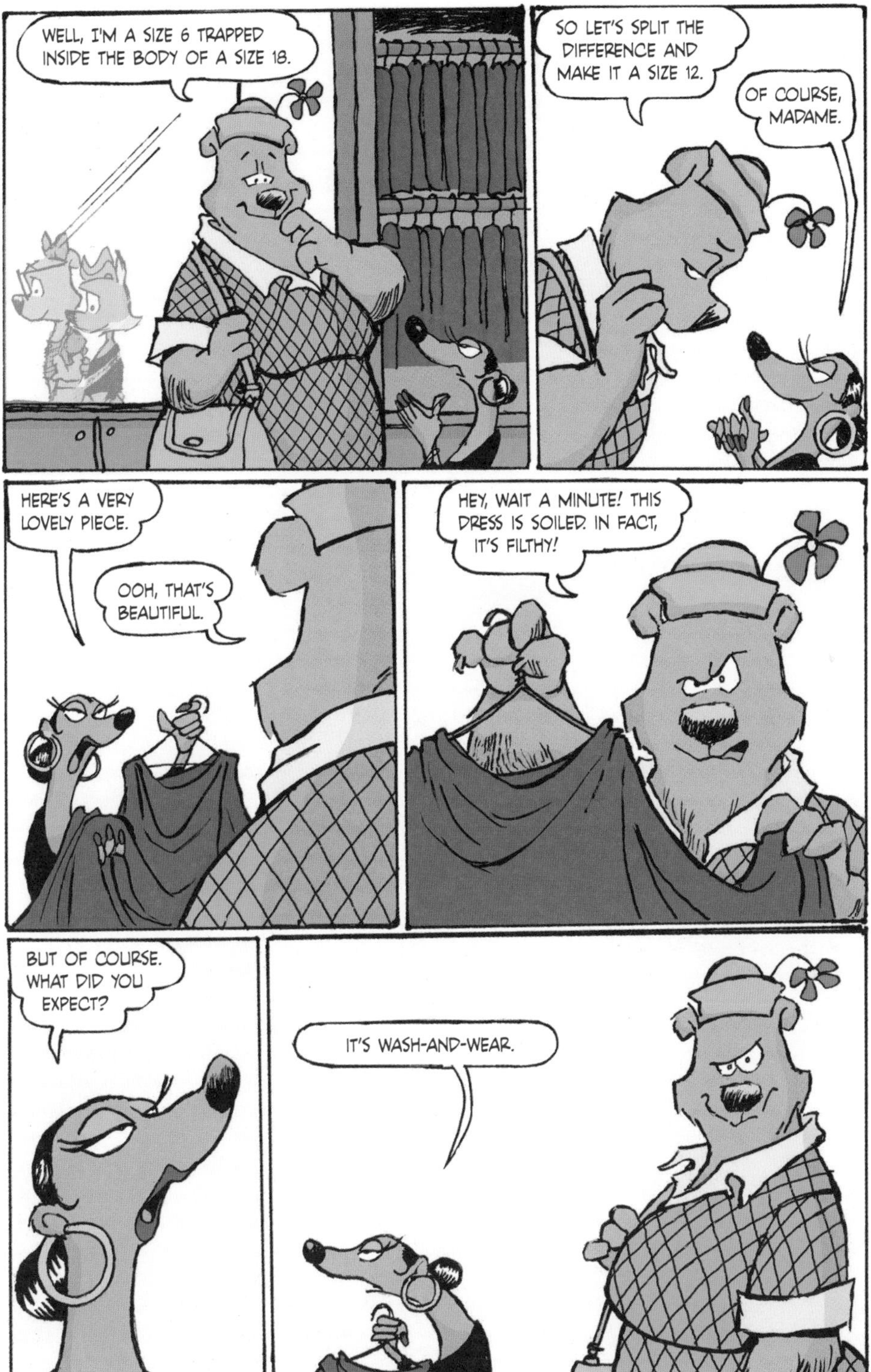
WELL, I'M A SIZE 6 TRAPPED INSIDE THE BODY OF A SIZE 18.
SO LET'S SPLIT THE DIFFERENCE AND MAKE IT A SIZE 12.
OF COURSE, MADAME.
HERE'S A VERY LOVELY PIECE.
OOH, THAT'S BEAUTIFUL.
HEY, WAIT A MINUTE! THIS DRESS IS SOILED. IN FACT, IT'S FILTHY!
BUT OF COURSE. WHAT DID YOU EXPECT?
IT'S WASH-AND-WEAR.

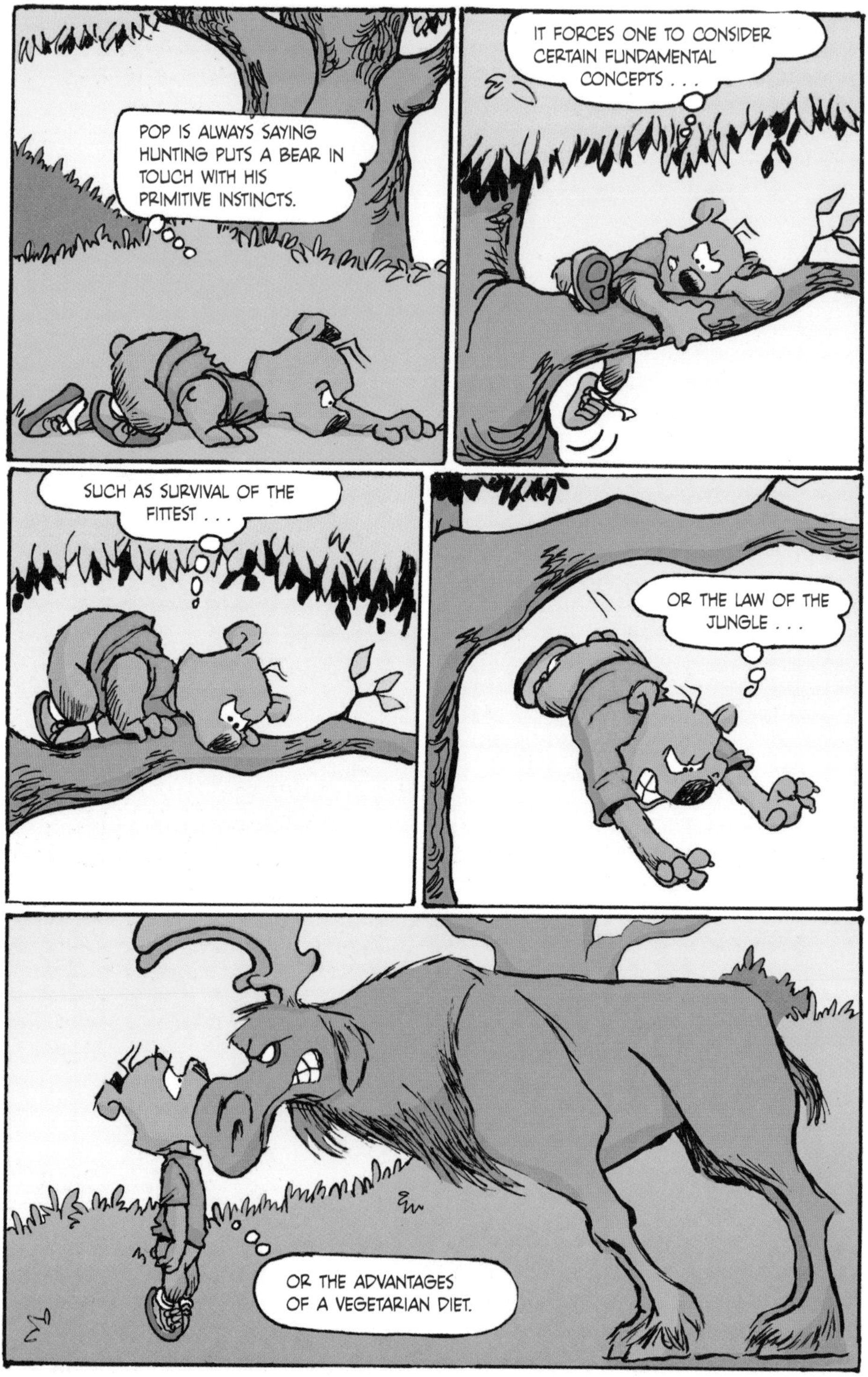
POP IS ALWAYS SAYING HUNTING PUTS A BEAR IN TOUCH WITH HIS PRIMITIVE INSTINCTS.
IT FORCES ONE TO CONSIDER CERTAIN FUNDAMENTAL CONCEPTS . . .
SUCH AS SURVIVAL OF THE FITTEST . . .
OR THE LAW OF THE JUNGLE . . .
OR THE ADVANTAGES OF A VEGETARIAN DIET.

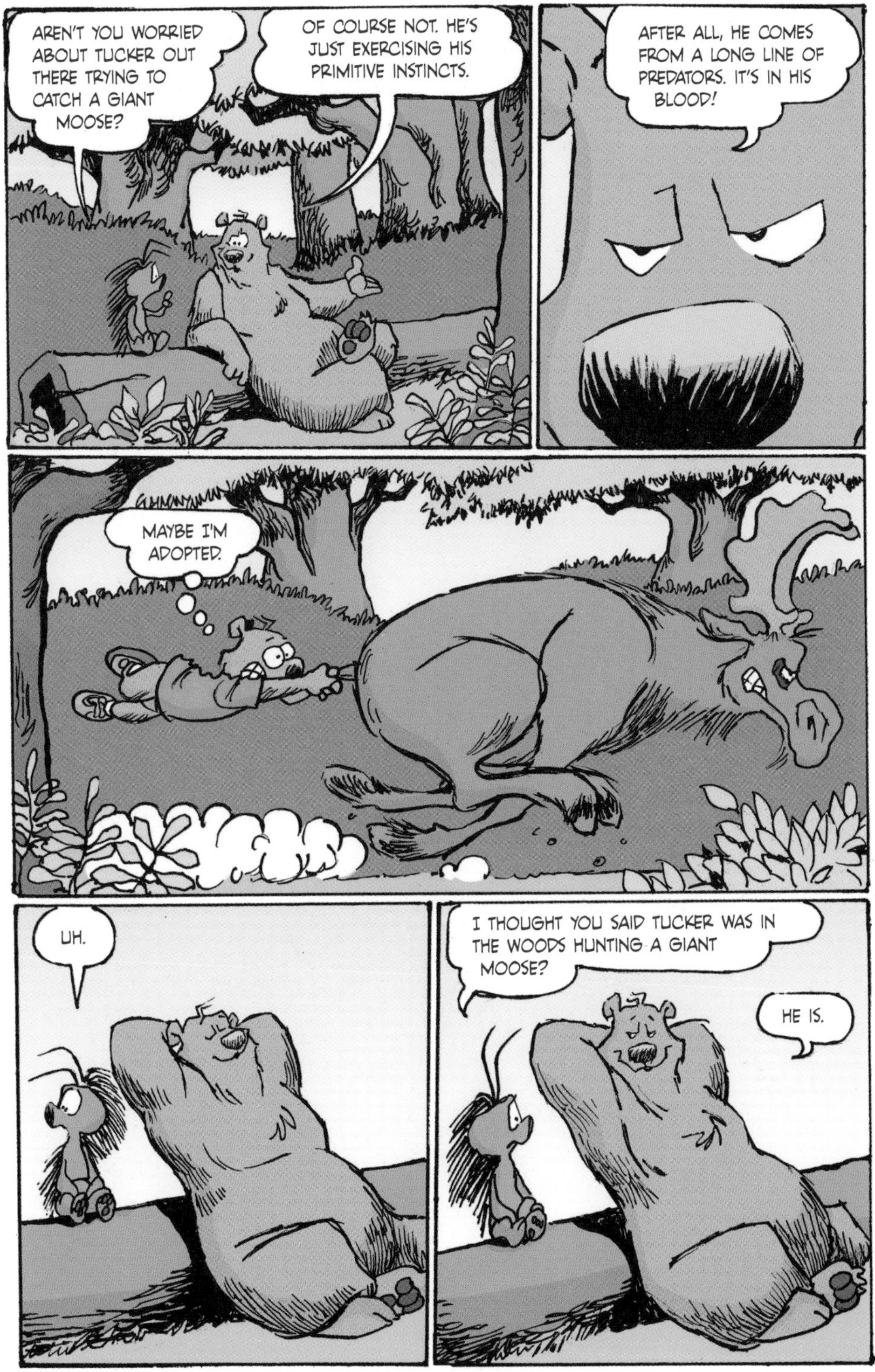
AREN'T YOU WORRIED ABOUT TUCKER OUT THERE TRYING TO CATCH A GIANT MOOSE?
OF COURSE NOT. HE'S JUST EXERCISING HIS PRIMITIVE INSTINCTS.
AFTER ALL, HE COMES FROM A LONG LINE OF PREDATORS. IT'S IN HIS BLOOD!
MAYBE I'M ADOPTED.
UH.
I THOUGHT YOU SAID TUCKER WAS IN THE WOODS HUNTING A GIANT MOOSE?
HE IS.

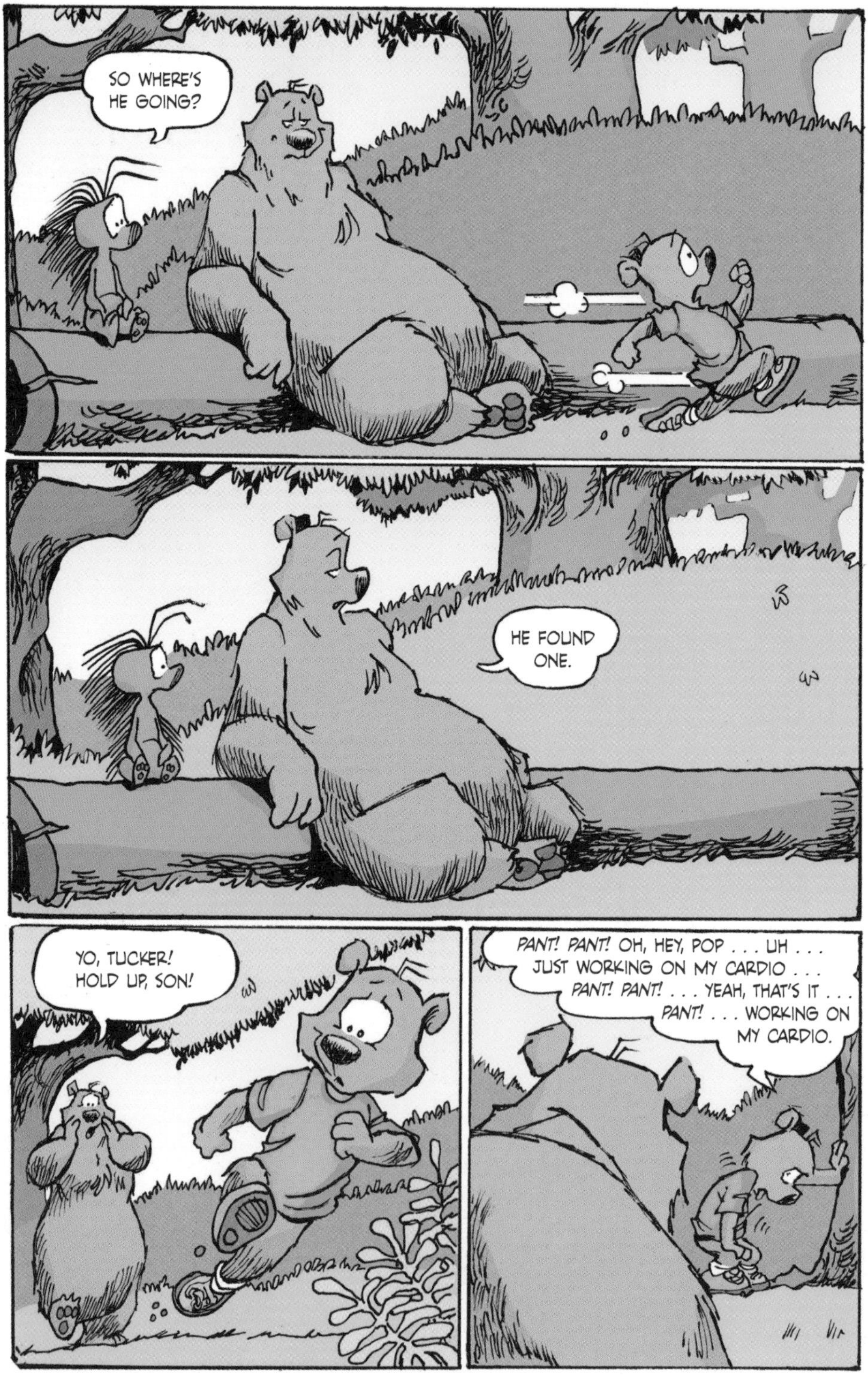
SO WHERE'S HE GOING?
HE FOUND ONE.
YO, TUCKER! HOLD UP, SON!
PANT! PANT! OH, HEY, POP . . . UH . . . JUST WORKING ON MY CARDIO . . . PANT! PANT! . . . YEAH, THAT'S IT . . . PANT! . . . WORKING ON MY CARDIO.

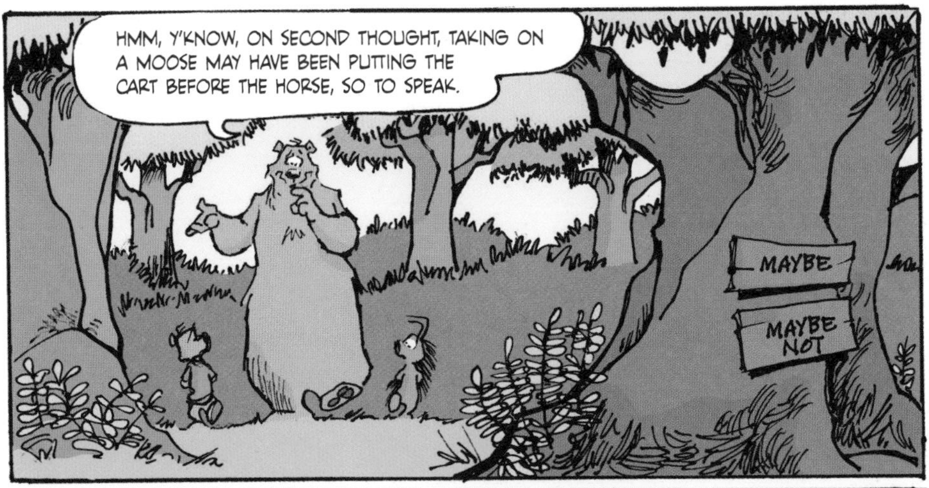
HMM, Y'KNOW, ON SECOND THOUGHT, TAKING ON A MOOSE MAY HAVE BEEN PUTTING THE CART BEFORE THE HORSE, SO TO SPEAK.
MAYBE
MAYBE NOT

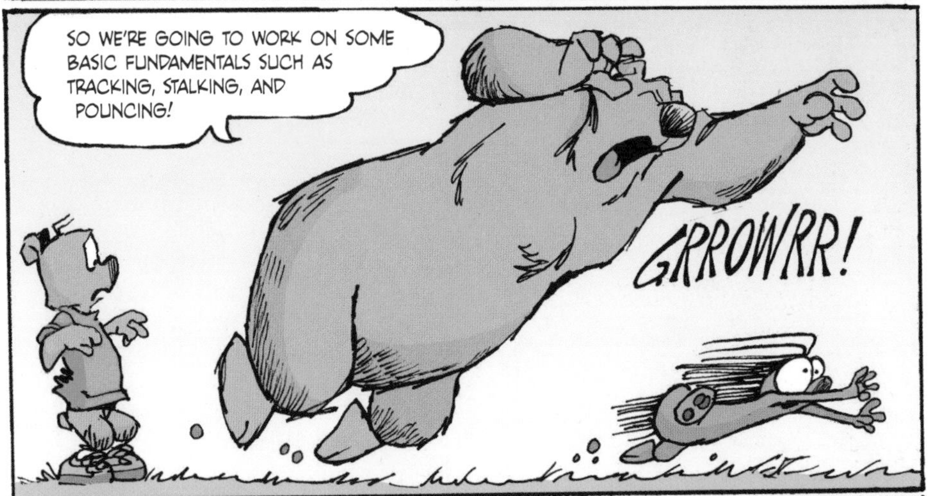
SO WE'RE GOING TO WORK ON SOME BASIC FUNDAMENTALS SUCH AS TRACKING, STALKING, AND POUNCING!
GRROWRR!

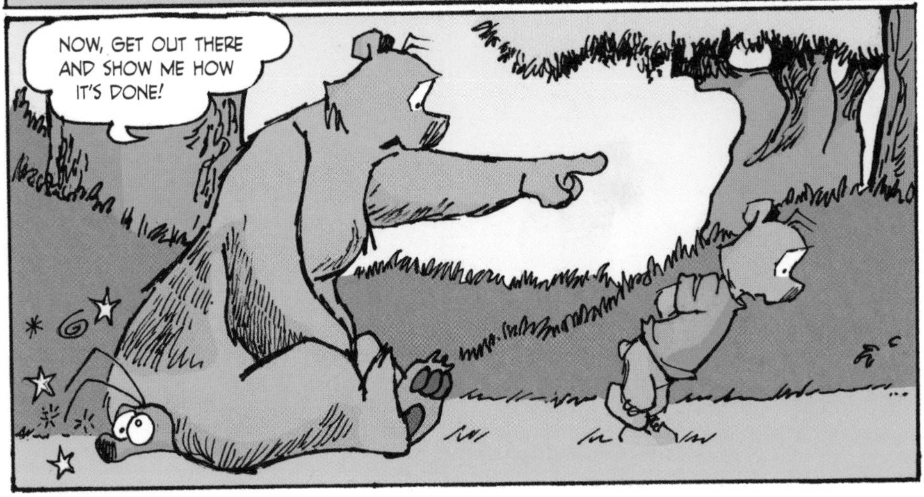
NOW, GET OUT THERE AND SHOW ME HOW IT'S DONE!

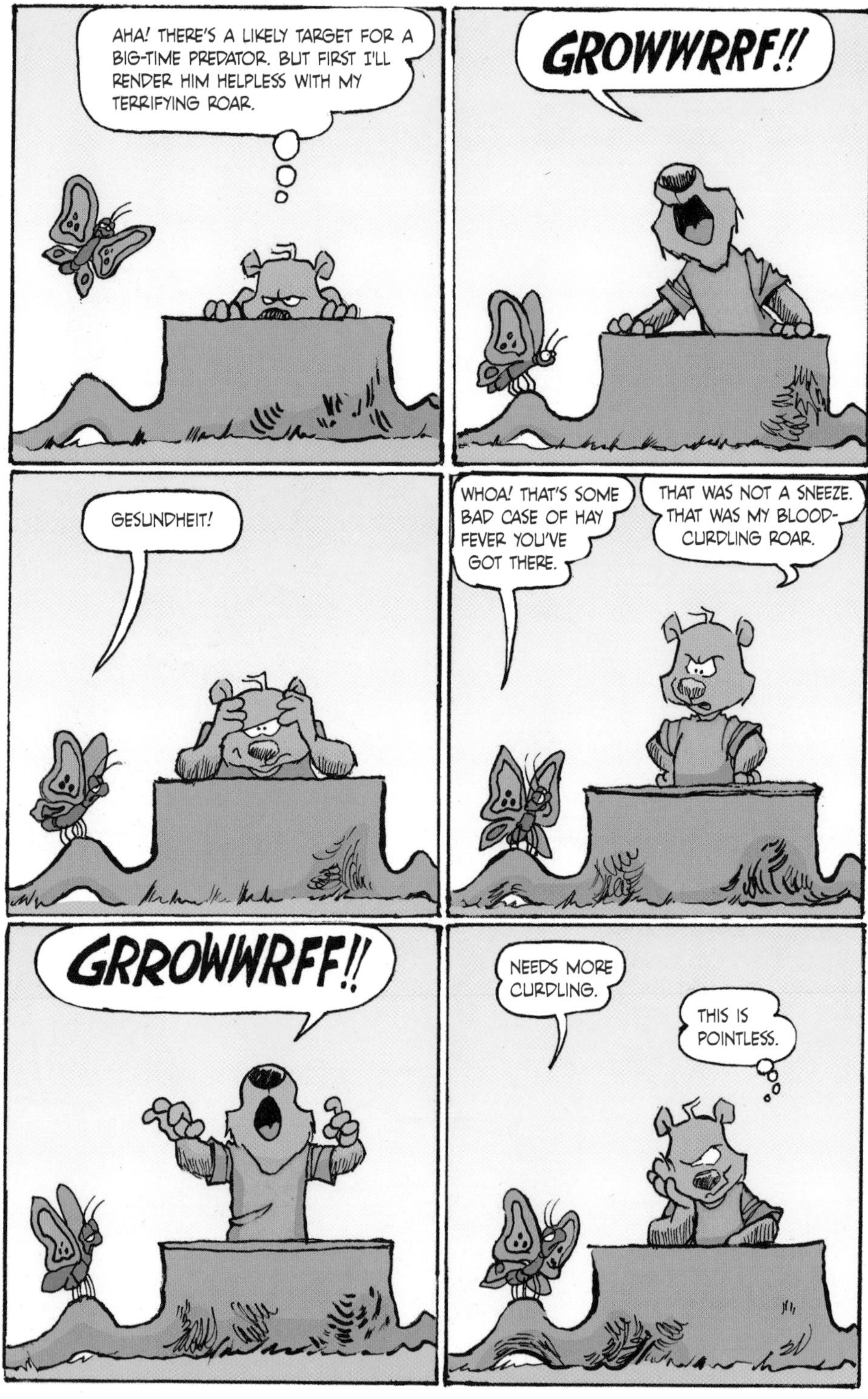
AHA! THERE'S A LIKELY TARGET FOR A BIG-TIME PREDATOR. BUT FIRST I'LL RENDER HIM HELPLESS WITH MY TERRIFYING ROAR.
GROWWRRF!!
GESUNDHEIT!
WHOA! THAT'S SOME BAD CASE OF HAY FEVER YOU'VE GOT THERE.
THAT WAS NOT A SNEEZE. THAT WAS MY BLOOD-CURDLING ROAR.
GRROWWRFF!!
NEEDS MORE CURDLING.
THIS IS POINTLESS.

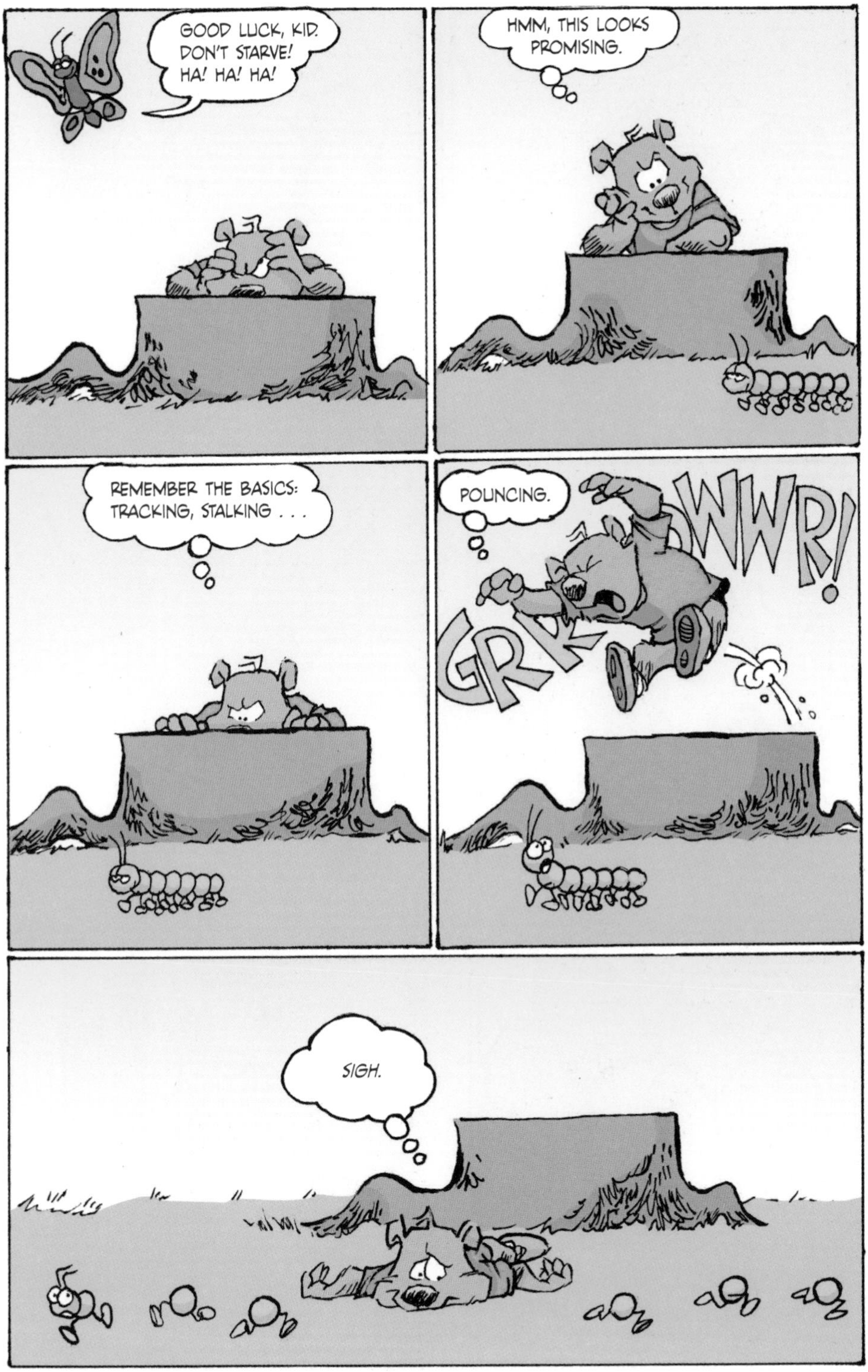
GOOD LUCK, KID. DON'T STARVE! HA! HA! HA!
HMM, THIS LOOKS PROMISING.
REMEMBER THE BASICS: TRACKING, STALKING . . .
POUNCING.
GRRWWR!
SIGH.

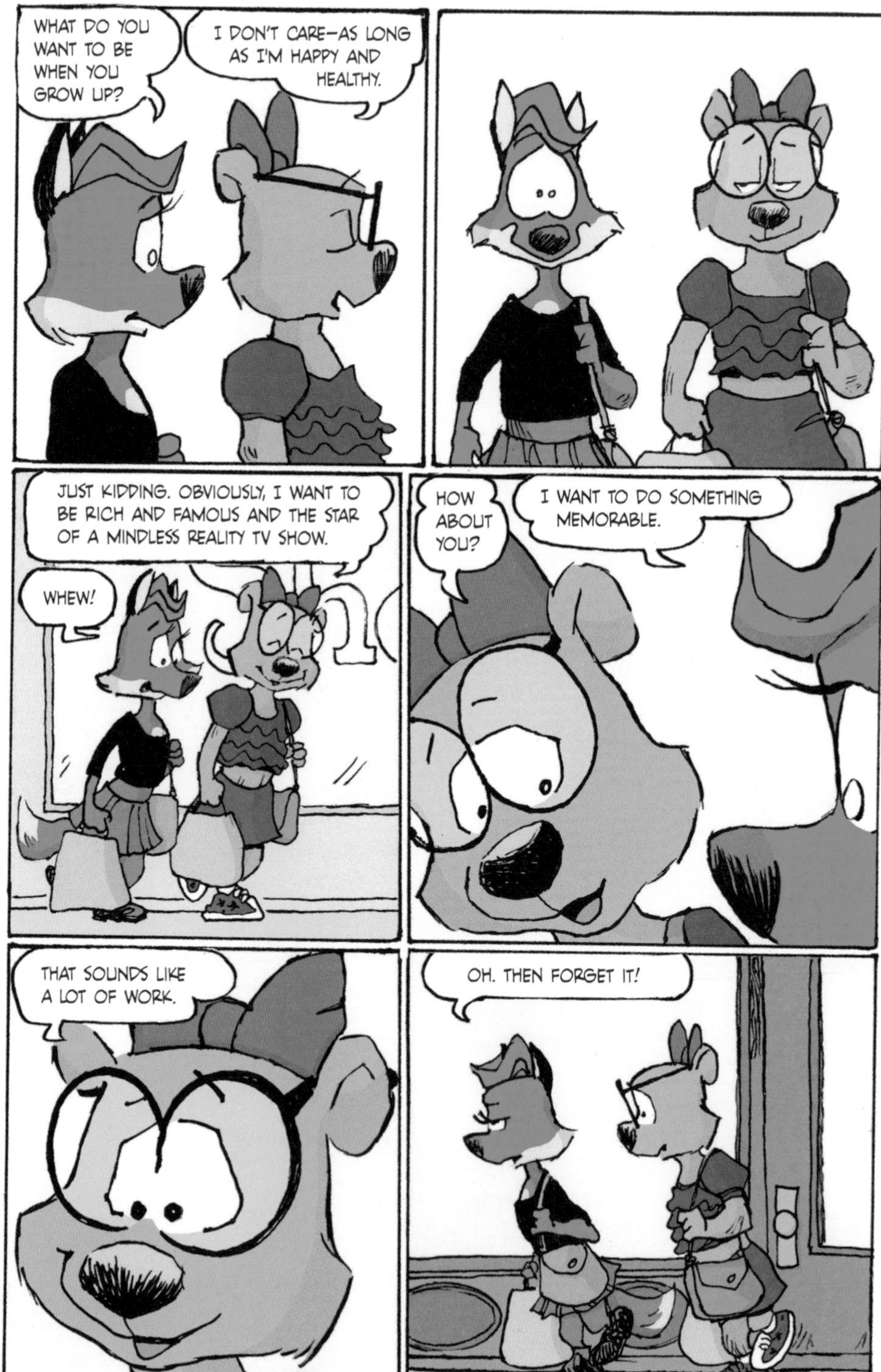
WHAT DO YOU WANT TO BE WHEN YOU GROW UP?
I DON'T CARE—AS LONG AS I'M HAPPY AND HEALTHY.
JUST KIDDING. OBVIOUSLY, I WANT TO BE RICH AND FAMOUS AND THE STAR OF A MINDLESS REALITY TV SHOW.
WHEW!
HOW ABOUT YOU?
I WANT TO DO SOMETHING MEMORABLE.
THAT SOUNDS LIKE A LOT OF WORK.
OH. THEN FORGET IT!

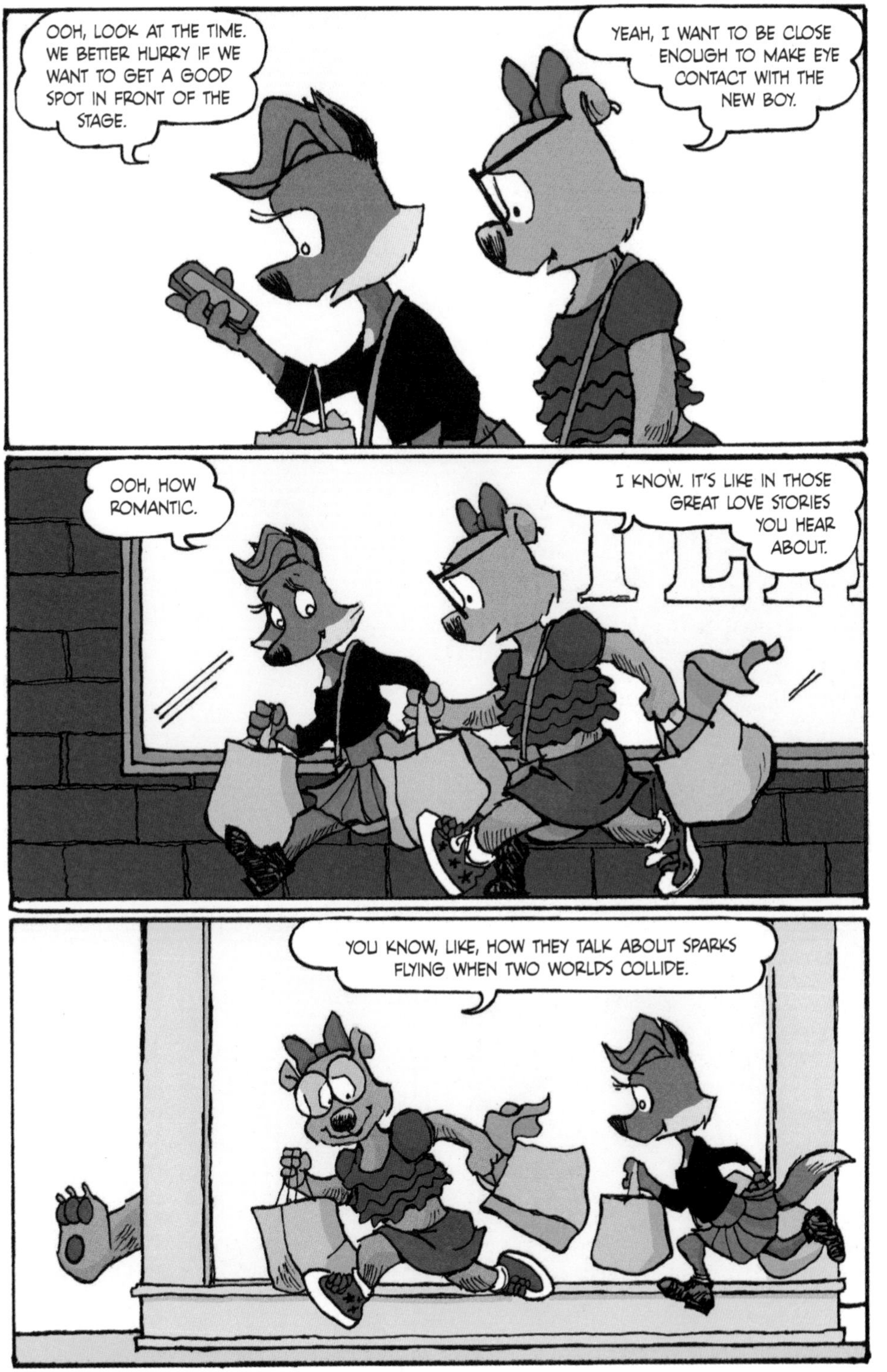
OOH, LOOK AT THE TIME. WE BETTER HURRY IF WE WANT TO GET A GOOD SPOT IN FRONT OF THE STAGE.
YEAH, I WANT TO BE CLOSE ENOUGH TO MAKE EYE CONTACT WITH THE NEW BOY.
OOH, HOW ROMANTIC.
I KNOW. IT'S LIKE IN THOSE GREAT LOVE STORIES YOU HEAR ABOUT.
YOU KNOW, LIKE, HOW THEY TALK ABOUT SPARKS FLYING WHEN TWO WORLDS COLLIDE.

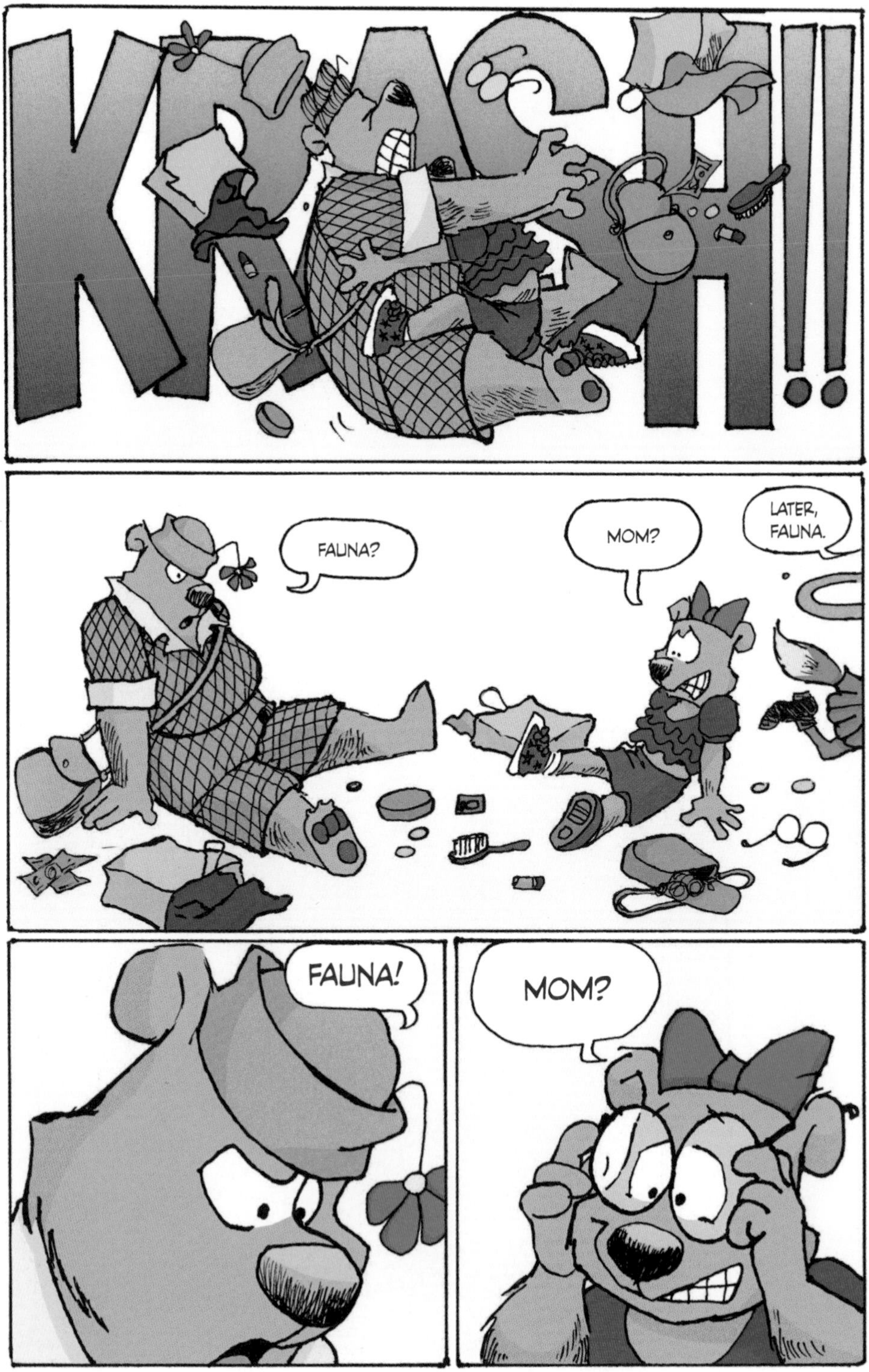
KRASH!!
FAUNA?
MOM?
LATER, FAUNA.
FAUNA!
MOM?

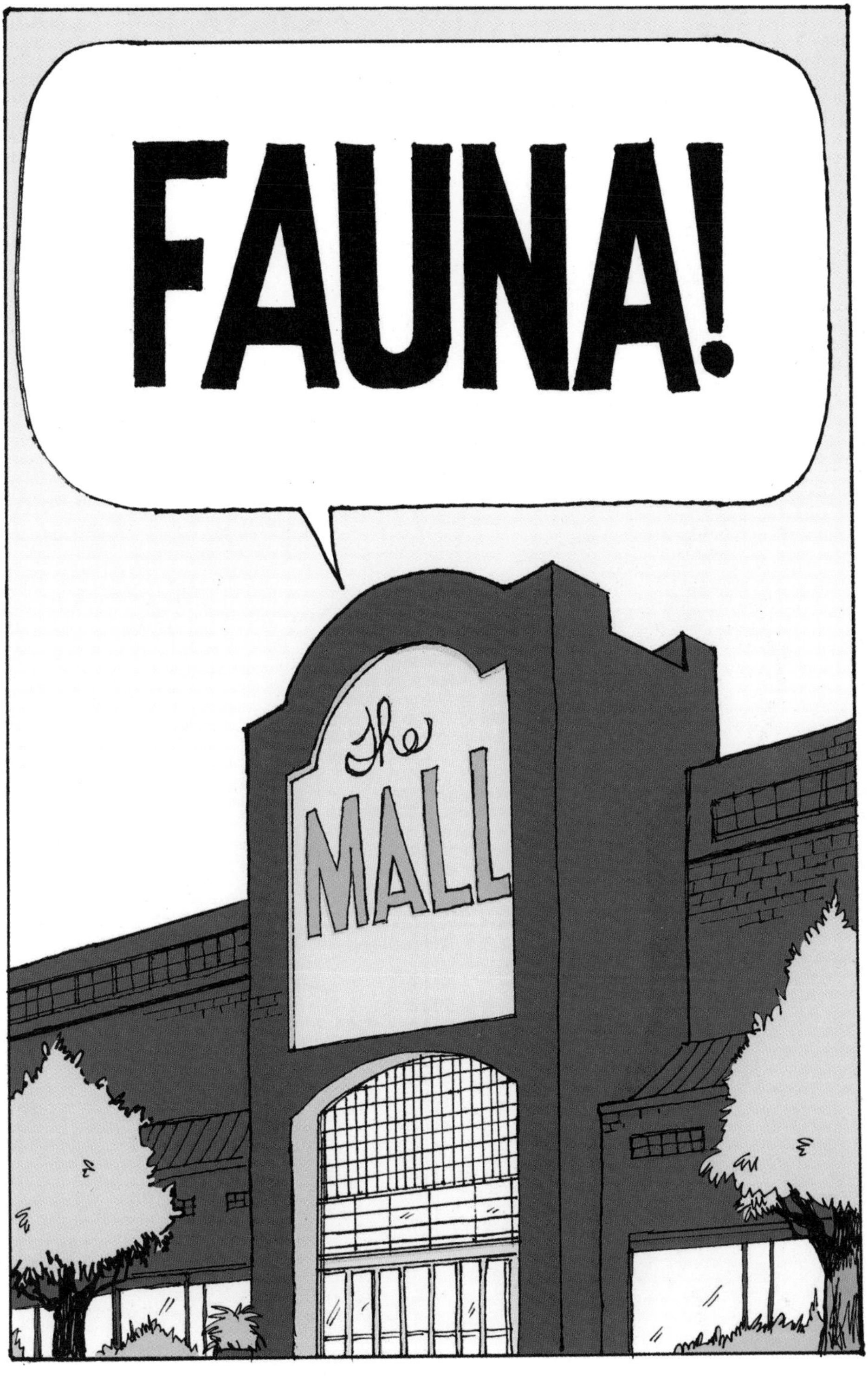
FAUNA!
The MALL

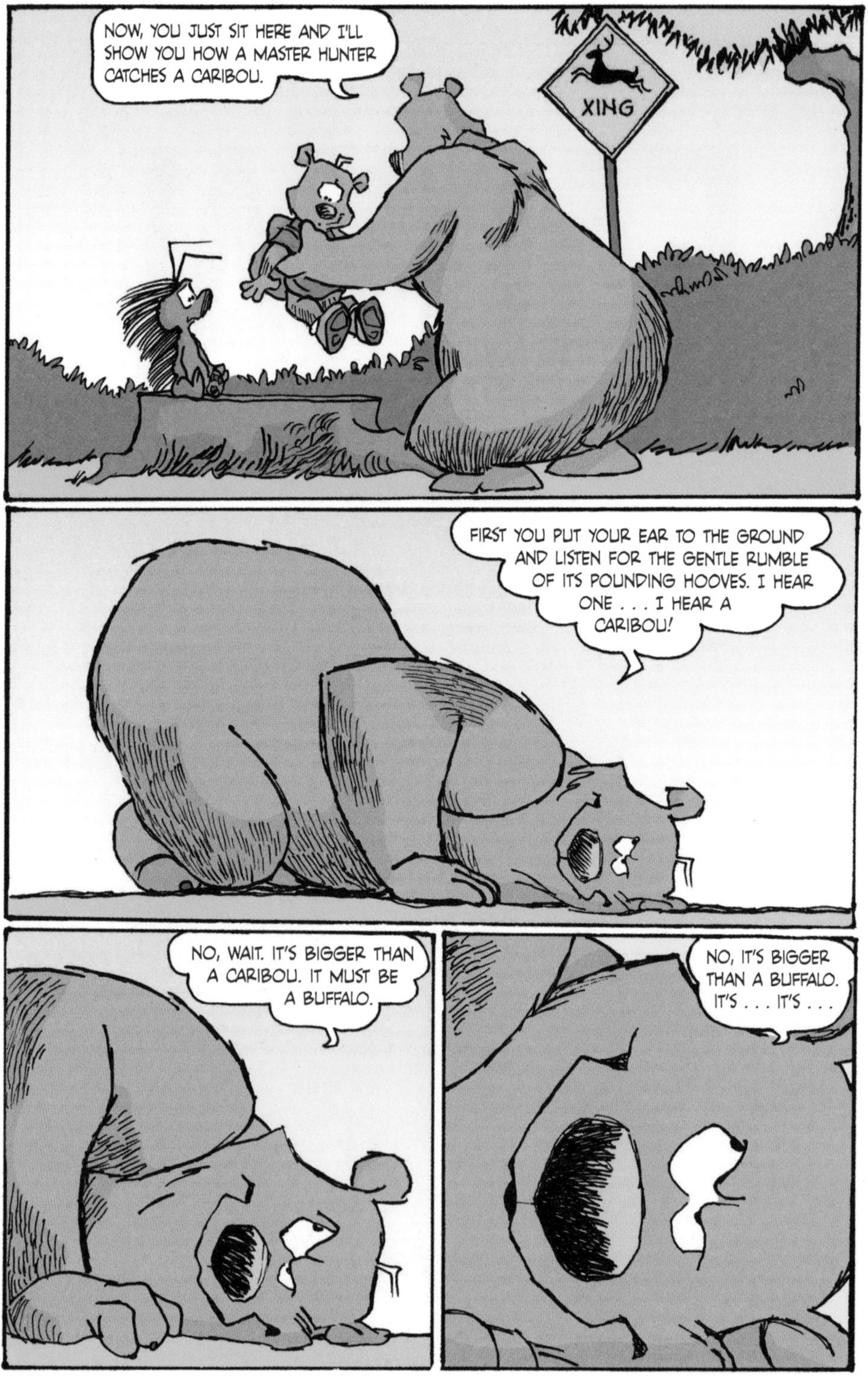
NOW, YOU JUST SIT HERE AND I'LL SHOW YOU HOW A MASTER HUNTER CATCHES A CARIBOU.
XING
FIRST YOU PUT YOUR EAR TO THE GROUND AND LISTEN FOR THE GENTLE RUMBLE OF ITS POUNDING HOOVES. I HEAR ONE . . . I HEAR A CARIBOU!
NO, WAIT. IT'S BIGGER THAN A CARIBOU. IT MUST BE A BUFFALO.
NO, IT'S BIGGER THAN A BUFFALO. IT'S . . . IT'S . . .

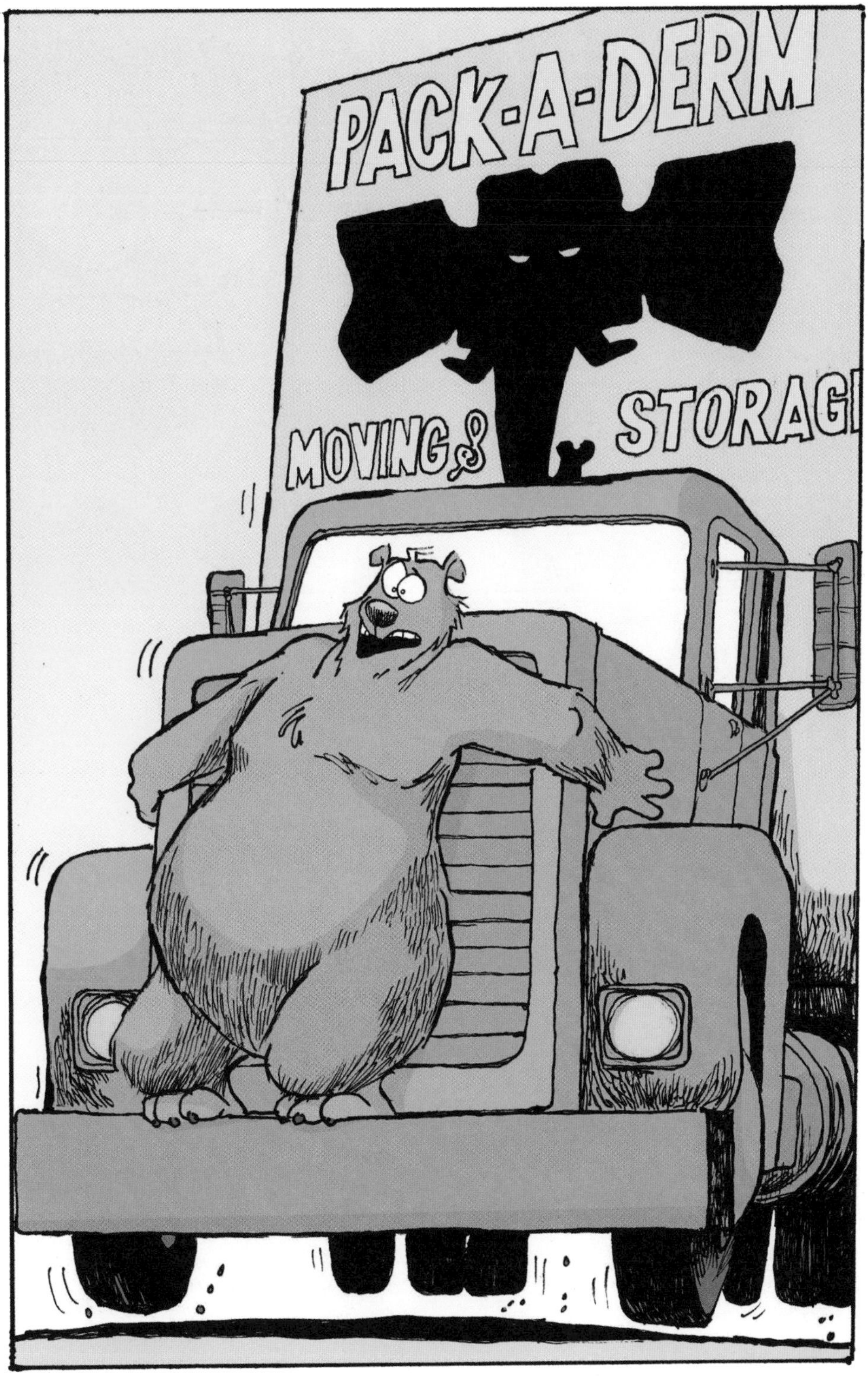
PACK-A-DERM
MOVING &
STORAG

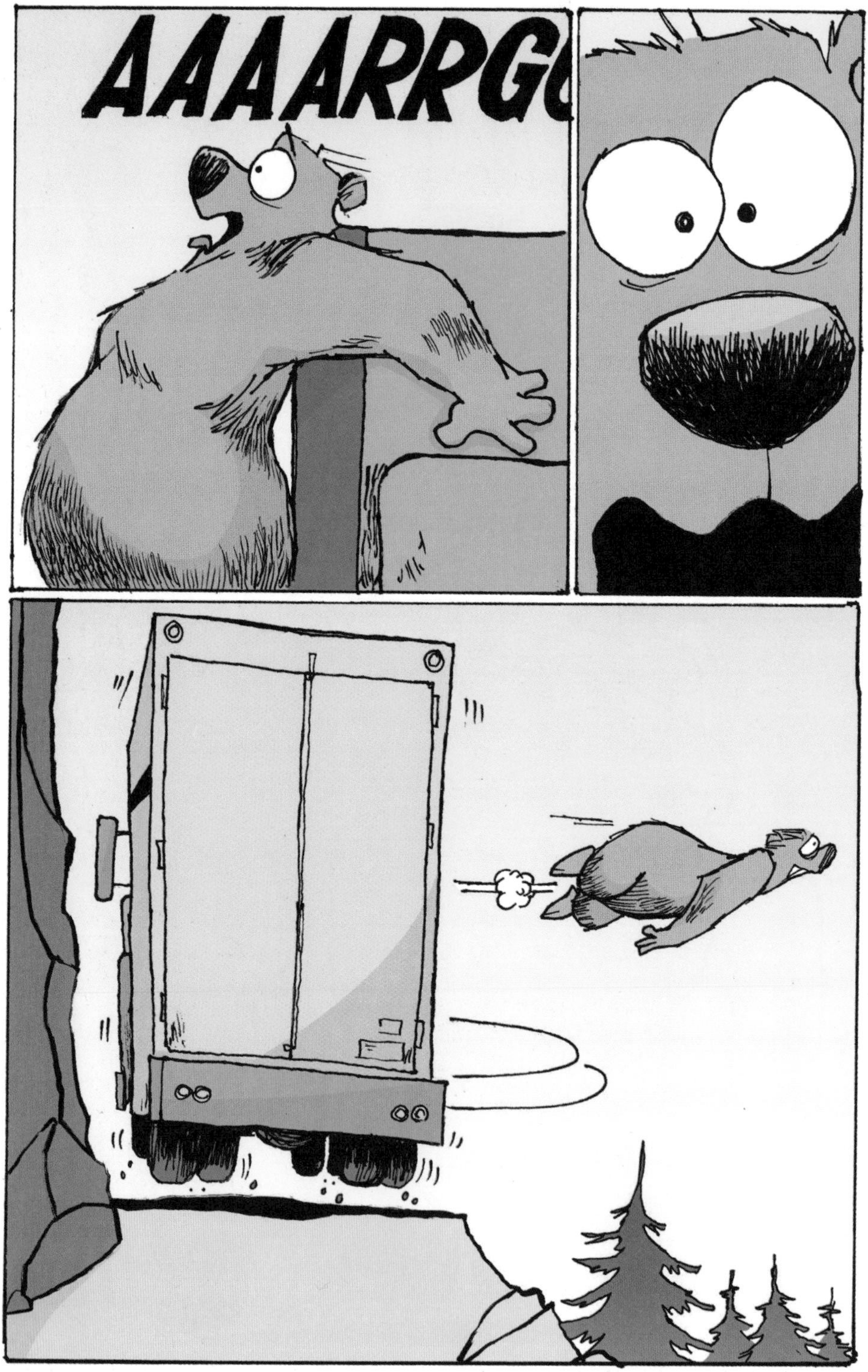
AAAARRGG

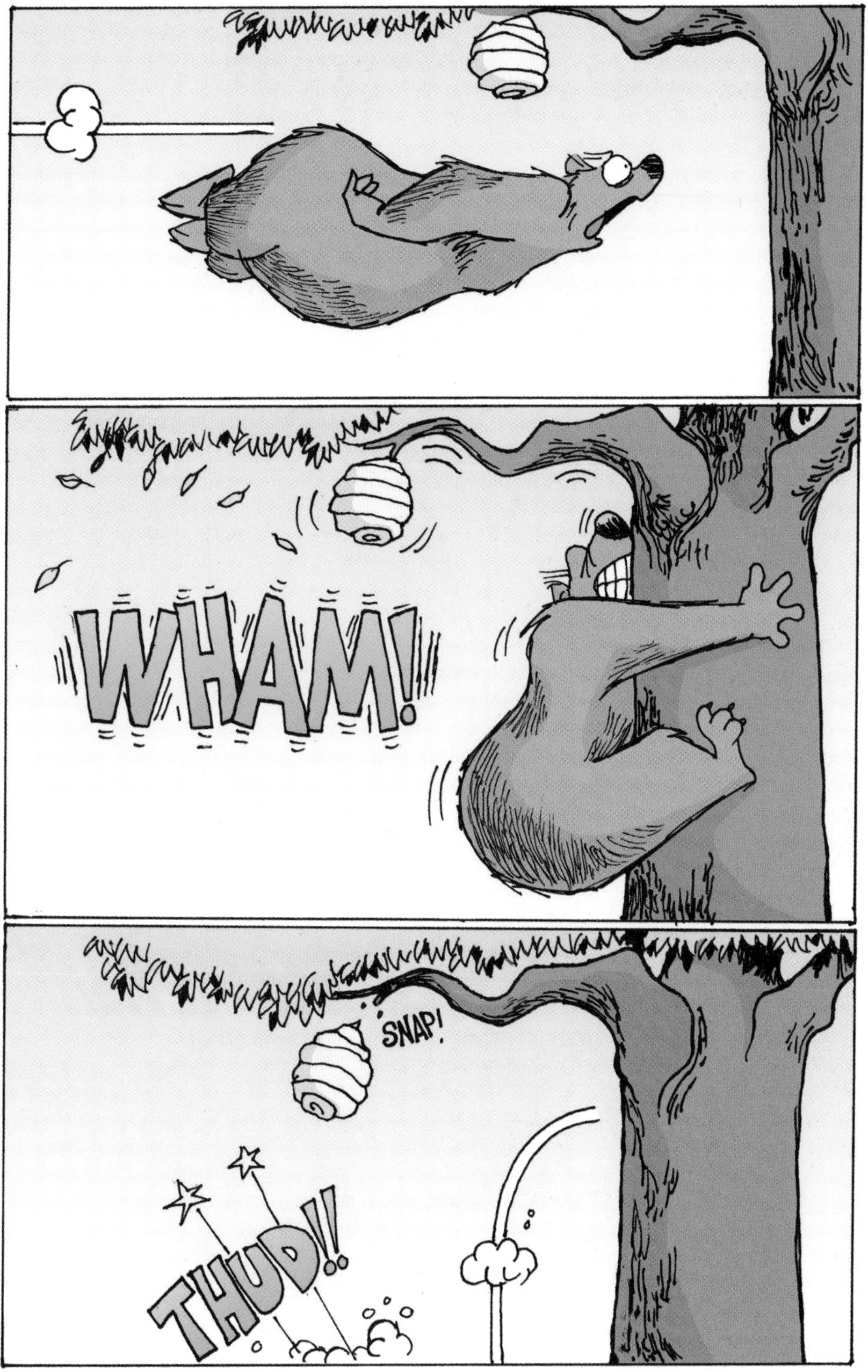
WHAM!
SNAP!
THUD!!

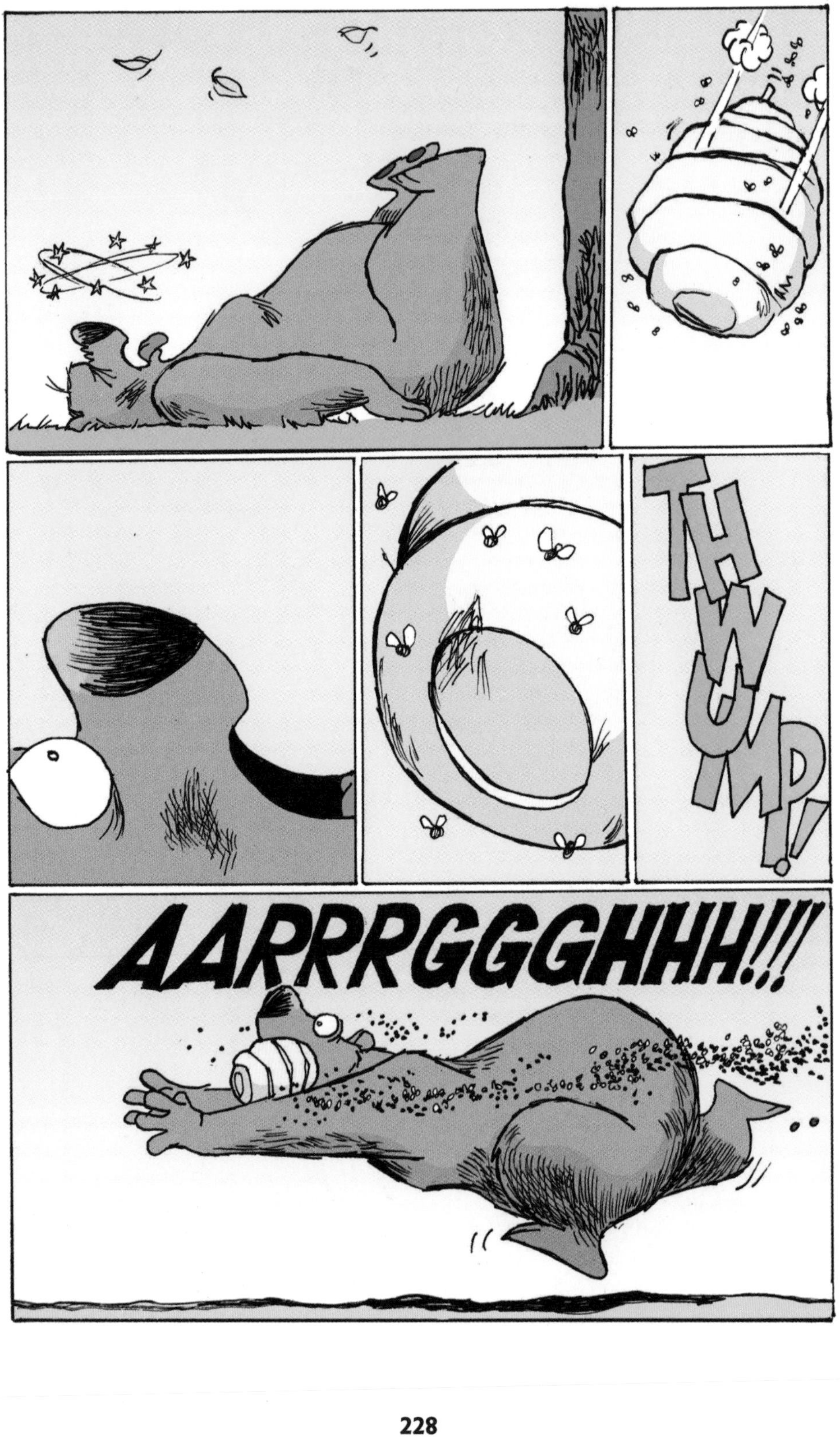
THWUMP!!
AARRRGGGHHH!!!

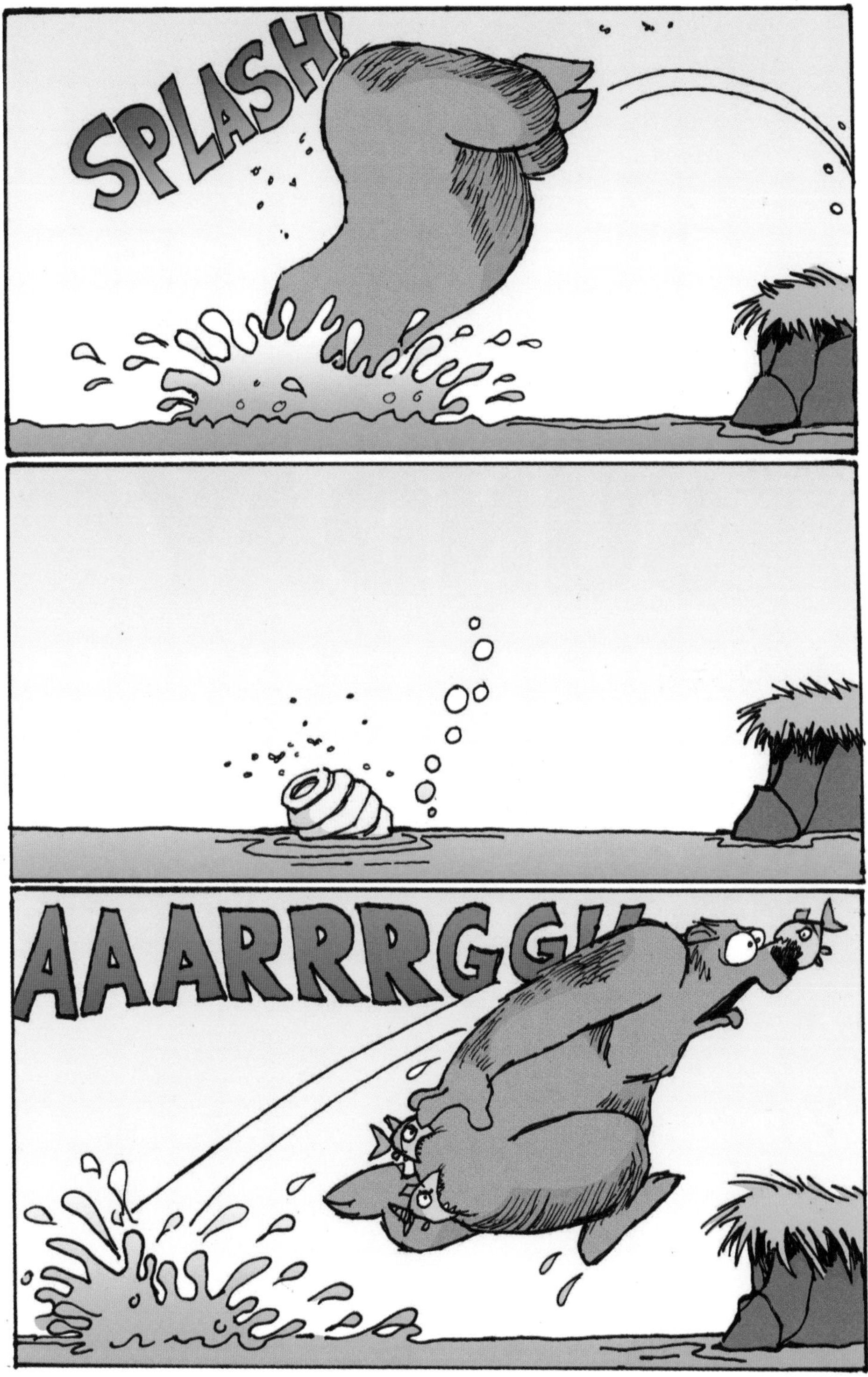
SPLASH!
AARRRGG

SUNDAY

AFTER THE TRUCK, THE BEES, AND THE PIRANHAS (THE PARKS DEPARTMENT SHOULD REALLY LOOK INTO WHERE THEY CAME FROM), POP DECIDED WE SHOULD SKIP THE SUNDAY PORTION OF JAWS AND CLAWS WEEKEND, WHICH WAS FINE BY ME.

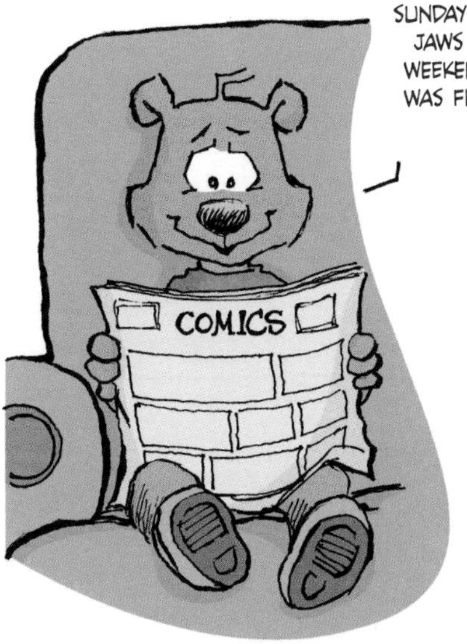
COMICS

BUT I HAVE TO ADMIT, I LEARNED SOME PRETTY COOL STUFF. POP SAID HE LEARNED SOMETHING TOO.

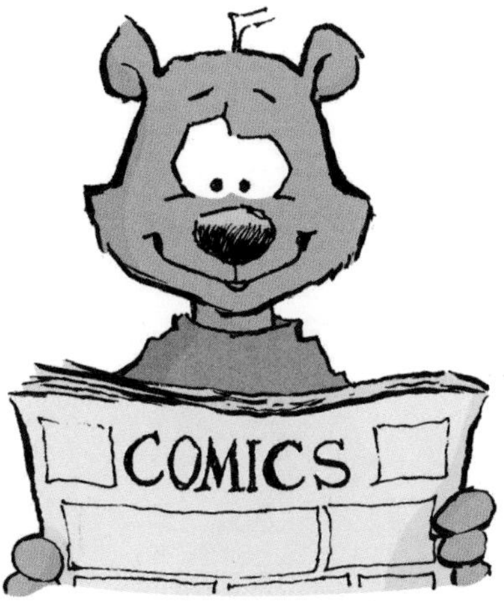
COMICS

HE SAID HE LEARNED THAT SOMETIMES THE BEST THING A PARENT CAN TEACH A CHILD IS HOW TO BE HIS OR HER OWN PERSON—ER, BEAR.

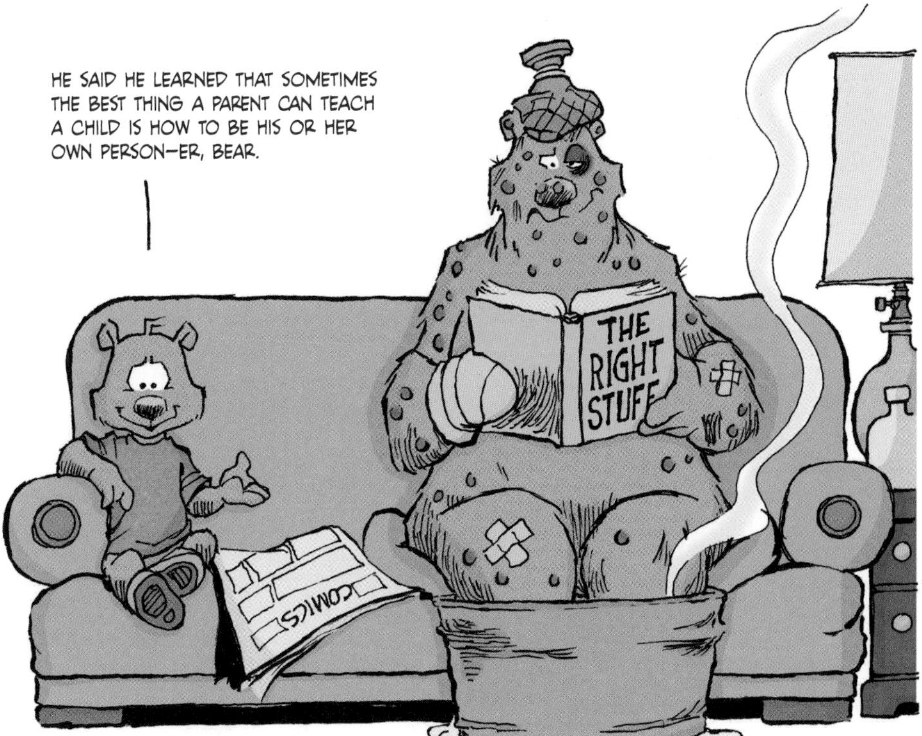
THE RIGHT STUFF
COMICS

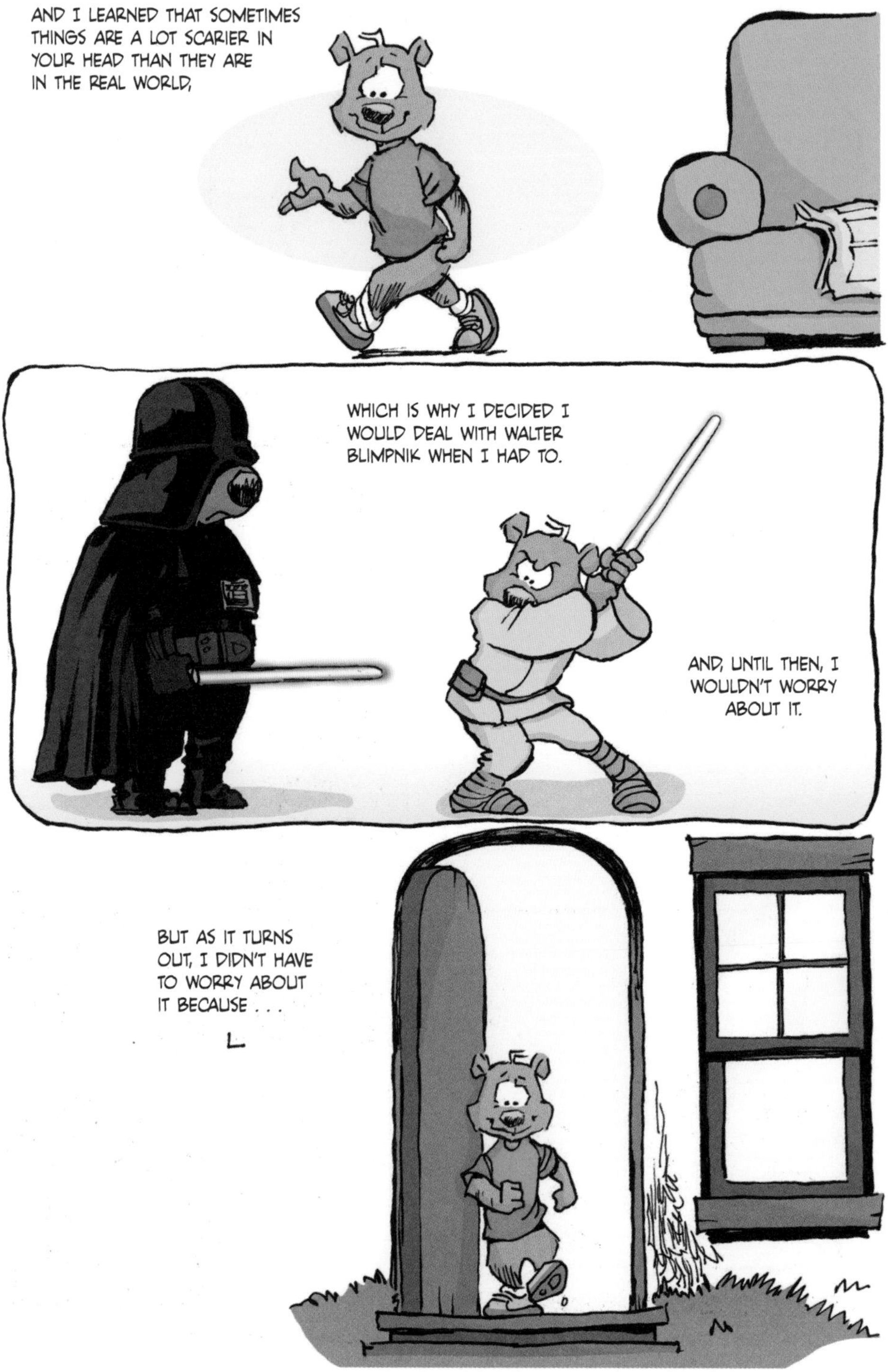
AND I LEARNED THAT SOMETIMES THINGS ARE A LOT SCARIER IN YOUR HEAD THAN THEY ARE IN THE REAL WORLD,
WHICH IS WHY I DECIDED I WOULD DEAL WITH WALTER BLIMPNIK WHEN I HAD TO.
AND, UNTIL THEN, I WOULDN'T WORRY ABOUT IT.
BUT AS IT TURNS OUT, I DIDN'T HAVE TO WORRY ABOUT IT BECAUSE . . .

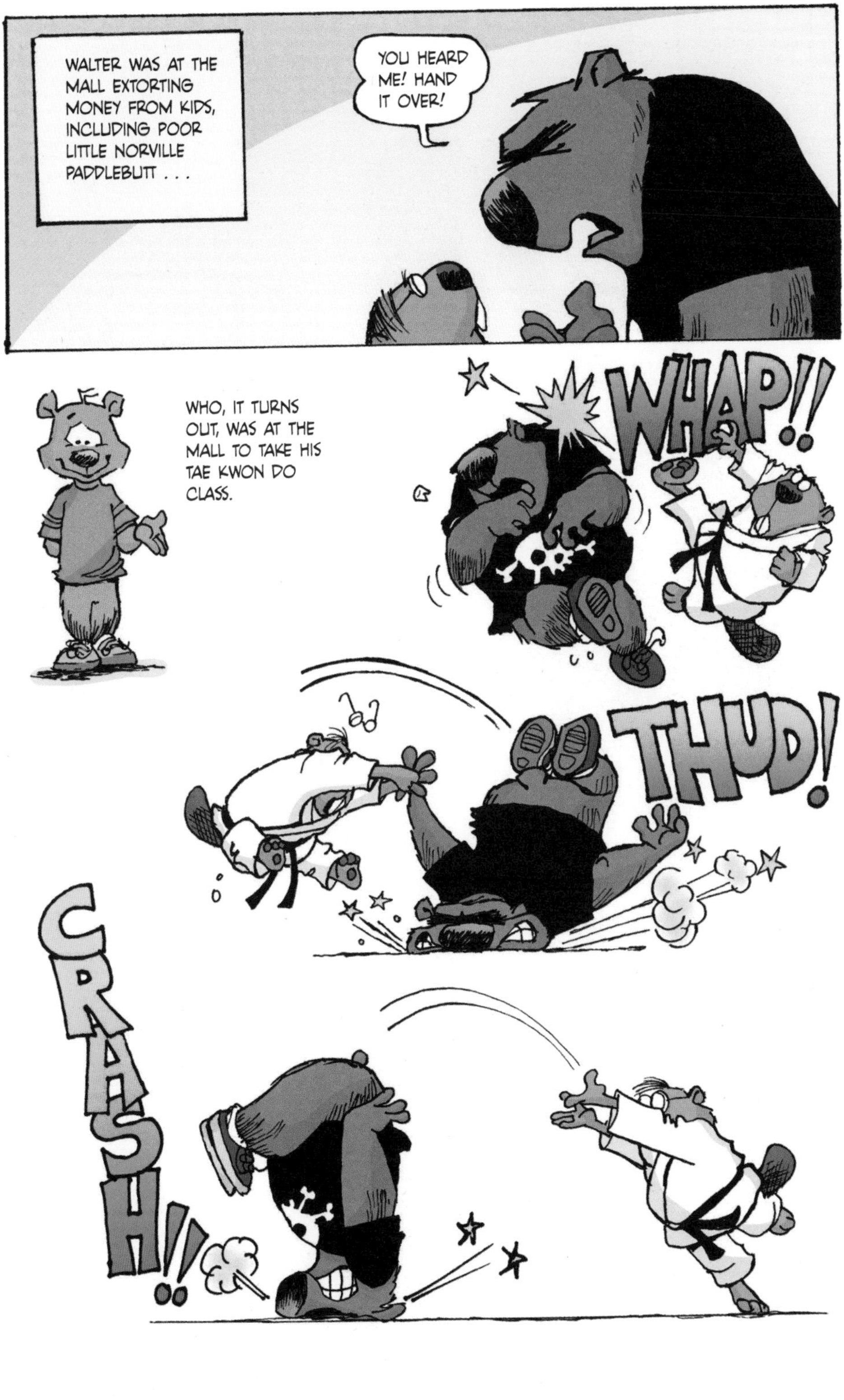
WALTER WAS AT THE MALL EXTORTING MONEY FROM KIDS, INCLUDING POOR LITTLE NORVILLE PADDLEBUTT . . .
YOU HEARD ME! HAND IT OVER!
WHO, IT TURNS OUT, WAS AT THE MALL TO TAKE HIS TAE KWON DO CLASS.
WHAP!!
THUD!
CRASH!!

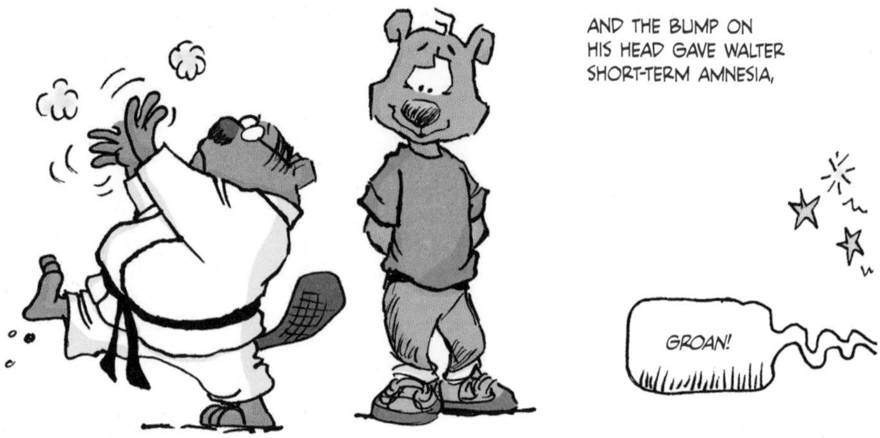
AND THE BUMP ON HIS HEAD GAVE WALTER SHORT-TERM AMNESIA,
GROAN!

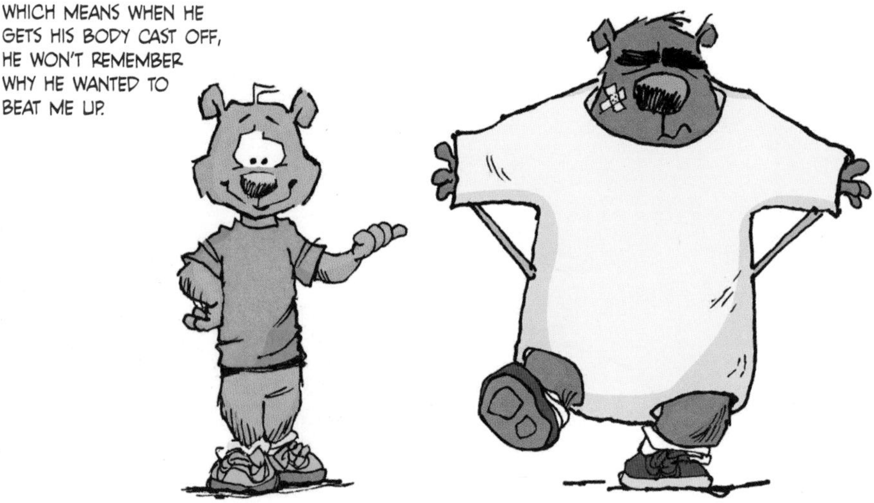
WHICH MEANS WHEN HE GETS HIS BODY CAST OFF, HE WON'T REMEMBER WHY HE WANTED TO BEAT ME UP.

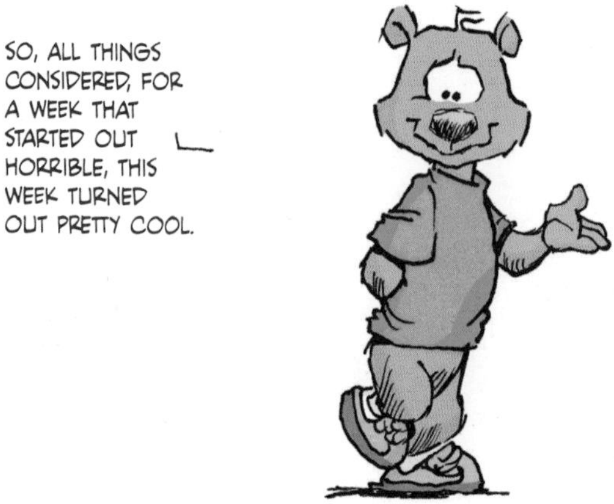
SO, ALL THINGS CONSIDERED, FOR A WEEK THAT STARTED OUT HORRIBLE, THIS WEEK TURNED OUT PRETTY COOL.

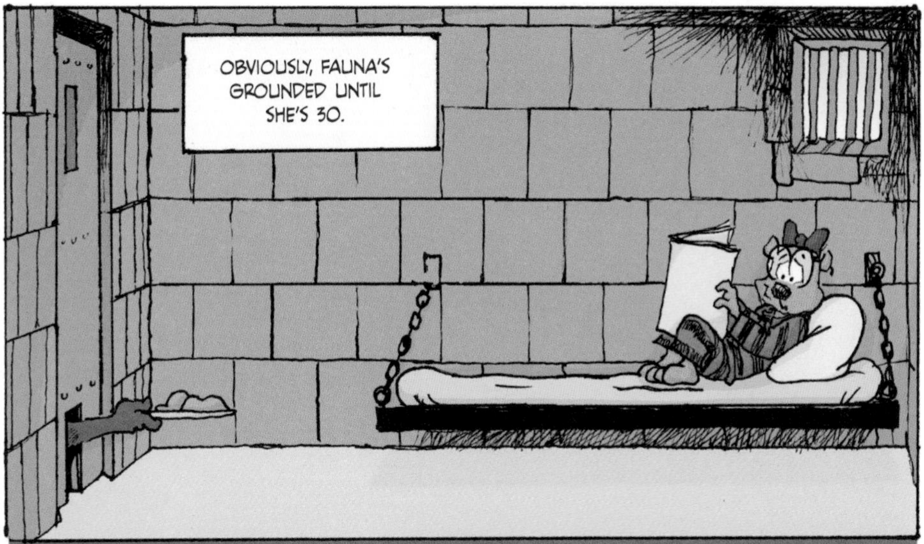
OBVIOUSLY, FAUNA'S GROUNDED UNTIL SHE'S 30.

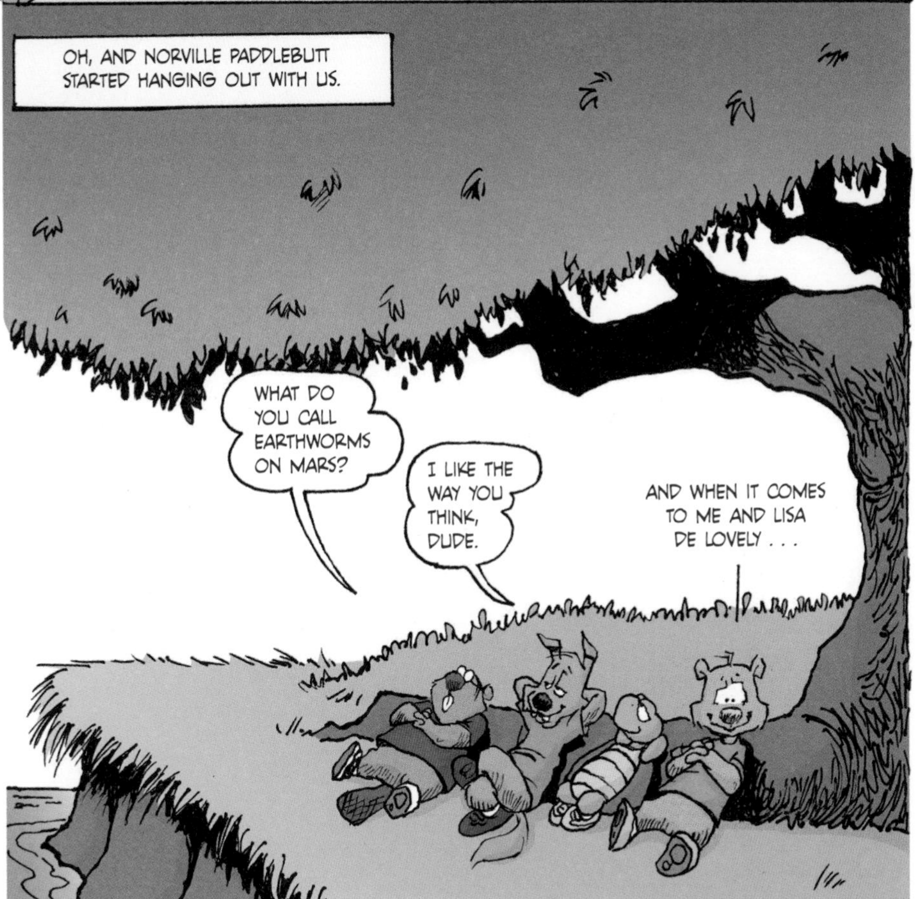
OH, AND NORVILLE PADDLEBUTT STARTED HANGING OUT WITH US.
WHAT DO YOU CALL EARTHWORMS ON MARS?
I LIKE THE WAY YOU THINK, DUDE.
AND WHEN IT COMES TO ME AND LISA DE LOVELY . . .

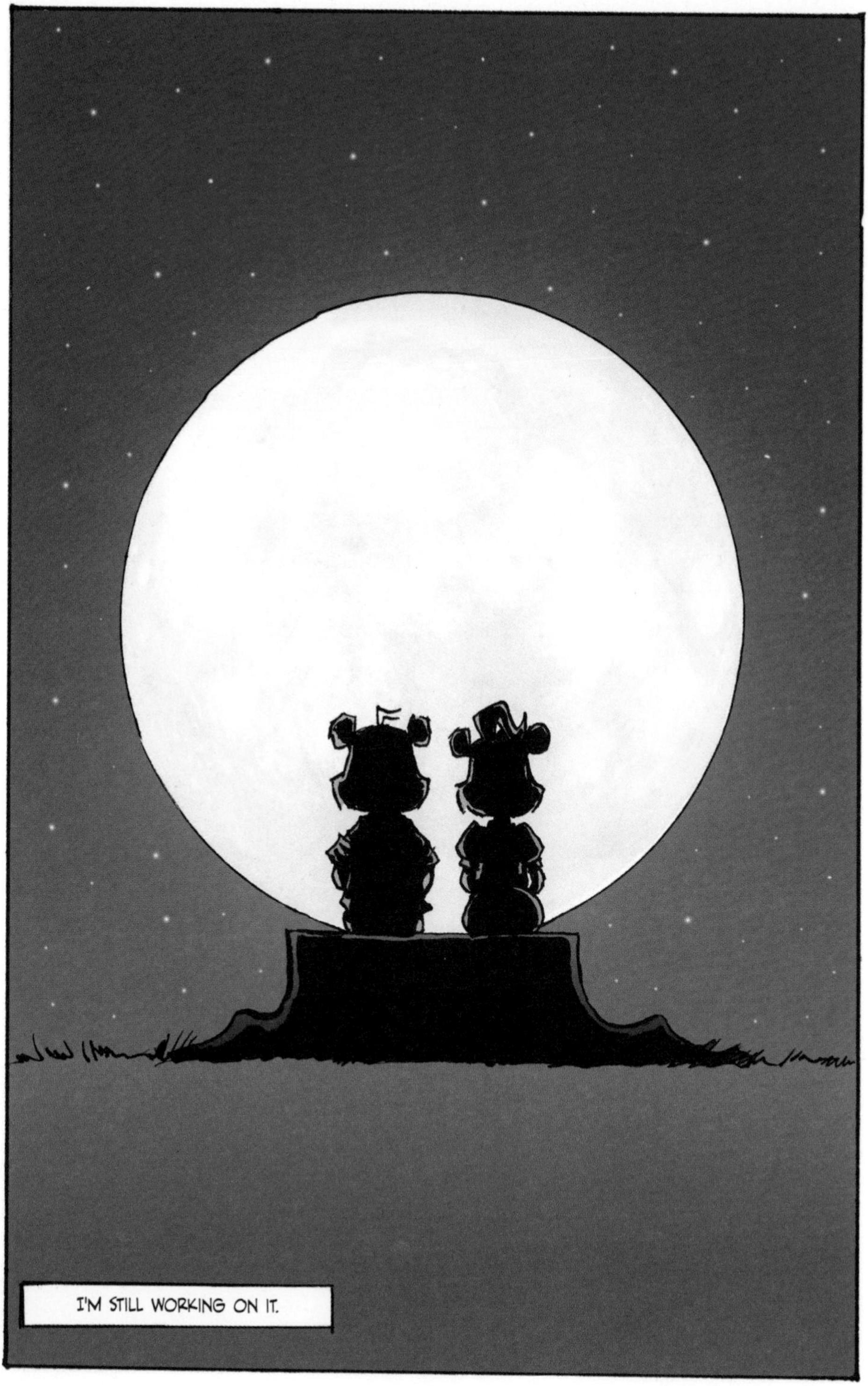
I'M STILL WORKING ON IT.

MORE
TO EXPLORE!
A special section
on bear facts!

THE BEAR FACTS

IF IT LOOKS LIKE A BEAR . . .

- Most bears are born without fur.

- Bears have nonretractable claws just like dogs.

- A bear's senses are essential to its survival. They have amazing eyesight, hearing, and sense of smell in order to find food as well as to detect danger.

- Like many mammals, bears can see in full color, rather than black and white.

IF IT ACTS LIKE A BEAR...

- Bears are fleet of foot (fast). They can run at speeds of 30 miles per hour.

- Bear cubs have enormous energy and enjoy burning much of it off by play-fighting with siblings. This exercise also teaches them essential self-defense skills. However, if they get too aggressive, the mother bear may swipe them with her massive paws to calm them down.

AND IF IT EATS LIKE A BEAR . . .

- Bears are very smart and have been known to even roll rocks into bear traps to release the trap, so they can take the bait safely.
- Bears are the only large predators that eat both meat and plants. Because of this, they have different teeth specifically for this purpose (both flat and pointed).
- Bears have been known to eat unusual things like snowmobile seats or rubber boots. However, still not as gross as grub worms, though.

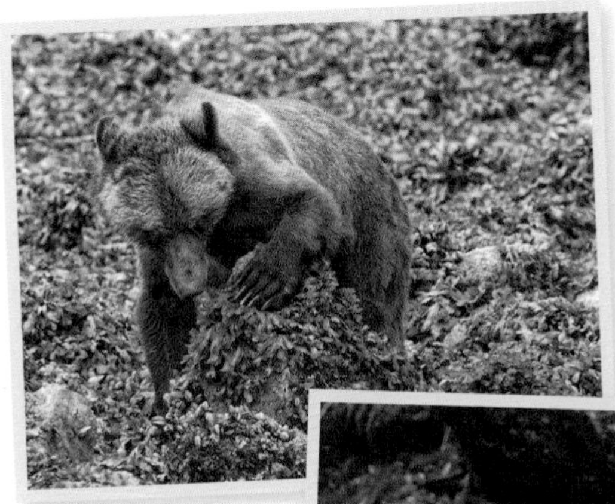

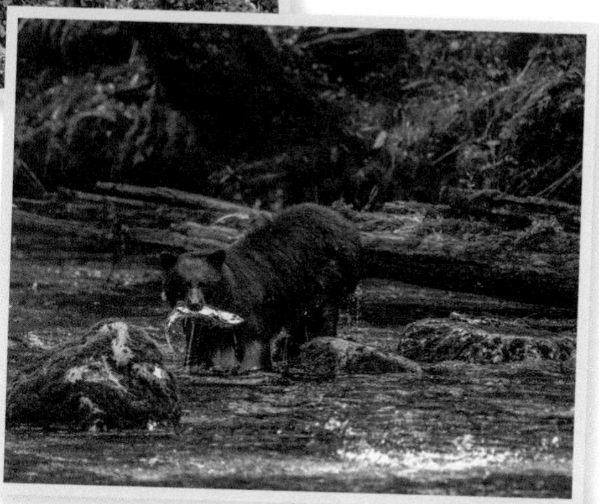

... IT'S PROBABLY A BEAR.

- A group of bears is called a sloth of bears. Makes you wonder what a group of sloths are called, doesn't it?

- There are eight species of bears, and many have sub-species.

- The eight species are: The brown bear, American black bear, Asiatic bear, polar bear, sloth bear, sun bear, spectacled bear, and last but not least, the panda bear.

- Grizzly bears are actually a subspecies of the brown bear and almost 98% of the grizzly bear population lives in Alaska.

BROWN BEARS . . .

- Like Tucker's family, brown bears are one of the largest and most powerful bears.
- They are most often solitary, though occasionally they enjoy gathering in groups at salmon-rich fishing spots.
- They inhabit North America, Europe, and Asia.

About the Authors

Bill Schorr began his career as an editorial cartoonist for the *Kansas City Star*. He then spent several years with the *Los Angeles Herald Examiner* before returning again to the *Star*. He was a staff editorial cartoonist at the *New York Daily News* from 1997 to 2001. Born in New York City, Schorr grew up in Albuquerque, New Mexico, and Riverside, California.

Ralph Smith began his career as staff artist at the *Sarasota Hearld-Tribune* following graduation from the Ringling College of Art and Design in Sarasota, Florida. While on assignment, he interviewed Dik Browne (creator of *Hägar the Horrible*) and eventually became Dik's assistant on *Hägar* for six years. Ralph has produced two syndicated strips of his own, *Captain Vincible* and *Through Thick and Thin*, both of which also ran for six years. Happily, he has written for Bill's strip, *The Grizzwells*, since the late '90s, surpassing his six-year jinx. He still resides in Sarasota.

Andrews McMeel Publishing
a division of Andrews McMeel Universal
1130 Walnut Street, Kansas City, Missouri 64106

www.andrewsmcmeel.com

17 18 19 20 21 SDB 10 9 8 7 6 5 4 3 2 1

ISBN: 978-1-4494-6910-8

Library of Congress Control Number: 2015960040

Editor: Jean Z. Lucas
Designer: Spencer Williams
Art Director: Tim Lynch
Production Manager: Chuck Harper
Production Editor: Grace Bornhoft

Made by:
Shenzhen Donnelley Printing Company Ltd.
Address and location of manufacturer:
No. 47, Wuhe Nan Road, Bantian Ind. Zone,
Shenzhen China, 518129
1st Printing—1/9/17

ATTENTION: SCHOOLS AND BUSINESSES

Andrews McMeel books are available at quantity discounts with bulk purchase for educational, business, or sales promotional use. For information, please e-mail the Andrews McMeel Publishing Special Sales Department: specialsales@amuniversal.com.

Check out these and other books at ampkids.com

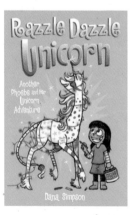

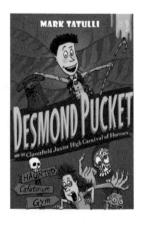